HONOUR AMONG THIEVES & KANE & ABEL

[illegible] *Penny More, Not a Penny Less*, his first novel, achieved instant success. Next came the tense [illegible] thriller *Shall We Tell the President?*, followed by his international bestseller *Kane and Abel*. His first collection of short stories, *A Quiver Full of Arrows*, came next, and then *The Prodigal Daughter*, the eagerly awaited sequel to *Kane and Abel*. This was followed by [illegible], complemented by [illegible] the first [illegible] about parliament since [illegible] thrilling [illegible] story *A Matter of Honour*, his second collection of stories *A Twist in the Tale*, and the novels *As the Crow Flies* and *Honour Among Thieves*. *Twelve Red Herrings*, his third collection of stories, was followed by the novels *The Fourth Estate* and *The Eleventh Commandment*. A collected edition of his short stories was published in 1997, followed by another [illegible] 2000.

[illegible] was born in 1940 and was educated at [illegible] and Brasenose College, Oxford. He represented Great Britain in the 100 metres in the early sixties and entered the House of Commons when he won the by-election at Louth in 1969. He wrote his first novel, *Not a Penny More, Not a Penny Less*, in 1974. From September 1985 to October 1986 he was Deputy Chairman of the Conservative Party, and he was created a Life Peer in the Queen's Birthday Honours of 1992. He is married with two children.

Jeffrey Archer is a master storyteller, the author of eleven novels which have all been worldwide bestsellers. *Not a Penny More, Not a Penny Less* was his first book, and it achieved instant success. Next came the tense and terrifying thriller *Shall We Tell the President?*, followed by his triumphant bestseller *Kane and Abel.* His first collection of short stories, *A Quiver Full of Arrows*, came next, and then *The Prodigal Daughter*, the superb sequel to *Kane & Abel.* This was followed by *First Among Equals*, considered by the *Scotsman* to be the finest novel about parliament since Trollope, the thrilling chase story *A Matter of Honour*, his second collection of stories, *A Twist in the Tale*, and the novels *As the Crow Flies* and *Honour Among Thieves. Twelve Red Herrings*, his third collection of stories, was followed by the novels *The Fourth Estate* and *The Eleventh Commandment.* A collected edition of his short stories was published in 1997, followed by another collection, *To Cut a Long Story Short.* His latest novel, *Sons of Fortune*, was published by Macmillan in 2002.

Jeffrey Archer was born in 1940 and educated at Wellington School, Somerset, and Brasenose College, Oxford. He represented Great Britain in the 100 metres in the early sixties, and entered the House of Commons when he won the by-election at Louth in 1969. He wrote his first novel, *Not a Penny More, Not a Penny Less*, in 1974. From September 1985 to October 1986 he was Deputy Chairman of the Conservative Party, and he was created a Life Peer in the Queen's Birthday Honours of 1992. He is married with two children.

ALSO BY JEFFREY ARCHER

NOVELS

Not a Penny More, Not a Penny Less
Shall We Tell the President?
The Prodigal Daughter
First Among Equals
A Matter of Honour
As the Crow Flies
The Fourth Estate
The Eleventh Commandment
Sons of Fortune

SHORT STORIES

A Quiver Full of Arrows
A Twist in the Tale
Twelve Red Herrings
The Collected Short Stories
To Cut a Long Story Short

PLAYS

Beyond Reasonable Doubt
Exclusive
The Accused

PRISON DIARIES

Volume One – Belmarsh: Hell
Volume Two – Wayland: Purgatory
Volume Three – North Sea Camp: Heaven

JEFFREY ARCHER

HONOUR AMONG THIEVES & KANE & ABEL

PAN BOOKS

Honour Among Thieves first published 1993 by HarperCollins.
First published by Pan Books 2003
Kane & Abel first published 1979 by Hodder and Stoughton.
First published by Pan Books 2003

This omnibus edition published 2005 by Pan Books
an imprint of Pan Macmillan Ltd
Pan Macmillan, 20 New Wharf Road, London N1 9RR
Basingstoke and Oxford
Associated companies throughout the world
www.panmacmillan.com

ISBN 0 330 44089 6

1 3 5 7 9 8 6 4 2

A CIP catalogue record for this book is available from the British Library.

Printed and bound in Great Britain by
Mackays of Chatham plc, Chatham, Kent

HONOUR AMONG THIEVES

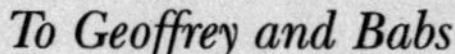

To Geoffrey and Babs

PART ONE

'*When in the Course of*
human events. . .'

1

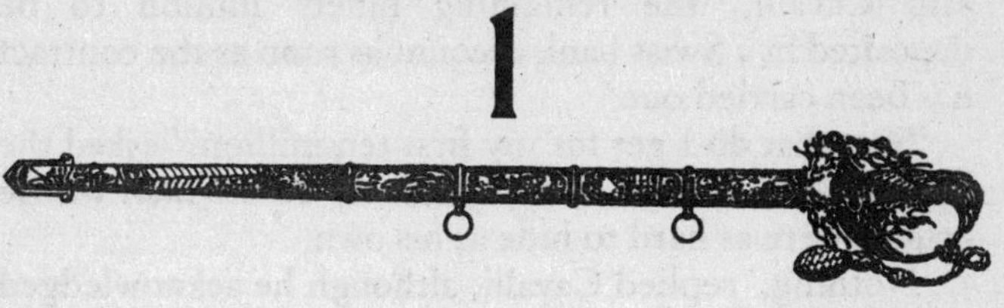

NEW YORK,
February 15th 1993

ANTONIO CAVALLI stared intently at the Arab, who he considered looked far too young to be a Deputy Ambassador.

'One hundred million dollars,' Cavalli said, pronouncing each word slowly and deliberately, giving them almost reverential respect.

Hamid Al Obaydi flicked a worry bead across the top of his well-manicured thumb, making a click that was beginning to irritate Cavalli.

'One hundred million is quite acceptable,' the Deputy Ambassador replied in a clipped English accent.

Cavalli nodded. The only thing that worried him about the deal was that Al Obaydi had made no attempt to bargain, especially as the figure the American had proposed was double that which he had expected to get. Cavalli had learned from painful experience not to trust anyone who didn't bargain. It inevitably meant that they had no intention of paying in the first place.

'If the figure is agreed,' he said, 'all that is left to discuss is how and when the payments will be made.'

The Deputy Ambassador flicked another worry bead before he nodded.

'Ten million dollars to be paid in cash immediately,' said Cavalli, 'the remaining ninety million to be deposited in a Swiss bank account as soon as the contract has been carried out.'

'But what do I get for my first ten million?' asked the Deputy Ambassador, looking fixedly at the man whose origins were as hard to hide as his own.

'Nothing,' replied Cavalli, although he acknowledged that the Arab had every right to ask. After all, if Cavalli didn't honour his side of the bargain, the Deputy Ambassador had far more to lose than just his government's money.

Al Obaydi moved another worry bead, aware that he had little choice – it had taken him two years just to get an interview with Antonio Cavalli. Meanwhile, President Clinton had settled into the White House, while his own leader was growing more and more impatient for revenge. If he didn't accept Cavalli's terms, Al Obaydi knew that the chances of finding anyone else capable of carrying out the task before July the fourth were about as promising as zero coming up on a roulette wheel with only one spin left.

Cavalli looked up at the vast portrait that dominated the wall behind the Deputy Ambassador's desk. His first contact with Al Obaydi had been only days after the war had been concluded. At the time the American had refused to deal with the Arab, as few people were convinced that the Deputy Ambassador's leader would still be alive by the time a preliminary meeting could be arranged.

As the months passed, however, it began to look to Cavalli as if his potential client might survive longer than President Bush. So an exploratory meeting was agreed.

The venue selected was the Deputy Ambassador's office in New York, on East 79th Street. Despite being a little too public for Cavalli's taste, it had the virtue of proving the credentials of the party claiming to be willing to invest one hundred million dollars in such a daring enterprise.

'How would you expect the first ten million to be paid?' enquired Al Obaydi, as if he were asking a real estate agent about a down-payment on a small house on the wrong side of the Brooklyn Bridge.

'The entire amount must be handed over in used, unmarked hundred-dollar bills and deposited with our bankers in Newark, New Jersey,' said the American, his eyes narrowing. 'And Mr Obaydi,' Cavalli added, 'I don't have to remind you that we have machines that can verify . . .'

'You need have no anxiety about us keeping to our side of the bargain,' interrupted Al Obaydi. 'The money is, as your Western cliché suggests, a mere drop in the ocean. The only concern I have is whether you are capable of delivering your part of the agreement.'

'You wouldn't have pressed so hard for this meeting if you doubted we were the right people for the job,' retorted Cavalli. 'But can I be as confident about you putting together such a large amount of cash at such short notice?'

'It may interest you to know, Mr Cavalli,' replied the Deputy Ambassador, 'that the money is already lodged in a safe in the basement of the United Nations building. After all, no one would expect to find such a vast sum deposited in the vaults of a bankrupt body.'

The smile that remained on Al Obaydi's face indicated that the Arab was pleased with his little witticism, despite the fact that Cavalli's lips hadn't moved.

'The ten million will be delivered to your bank by midday tomorrow,' continued Al Obaydi as he rose from the table to indicate that, as far he was concerned, the meeting was concluded. The Deputy Ambassador stretched out his hand and his visitor reluctantly shook it.

Cavalli glanced up once again at the portrait of Saddam Hussein, turned, and quickly left.

When Scott Bradley entered the room there was a hush of expectancy.

He placed his notes on the table in front of him, allowing his eyes to sweep around the lecture hall. The room was packed with eager young students holding pens and pencils poised above yellow legal pads.

'My name is Scott Bradley,' said the youngest Professor in the Law School, 'and this is to be the first of fourteen lectures on Constitutional Law.' Seventy-four faces stared down at the tall, somewhat dishevelled man who obviously hadn't noticed that the top button of his shirt was missing and who couldn't have made up his mind which side to part his hair that morning.

'I'd like to begin this first lecture with a personal statement,' he announced. Some of the pens and pencils were laid to rest. 'There are many reasons to practise law in this country,' he began, 'but only one which is worthy of you, and certainly only one that interests me. It applies to every facet of the law that you might be interested in pursuing, and it has never been better expressed than in the engrossed parchment of The Unanimous Declaration of the Thirteen United States of America.

' "We hold these truths to be self-evident, that all men are created equal, that they are endowed by their Creator with certain inalienable Rights, that among these are Life, Liberty and the pursuit of Happiness." That one sentence is what distinguishes America from every other country on earth.

'In some aspects, our nation has progressed mightily

since 1776,' continued the Professor, still not having referred to his notes as he walked up and down tugging the lapels of his well-worn Harris tweed jacket, 'while in others we have moved rapidly backwards. Each of you in this hall can be part of the next generation of law makers or law breakers –' he paused, surveying the silent gathering, '– and you have been granted the greatest gift of all with which to help make that choice, a first-class mind. When my colleagues and I have finished with you, you can if you wish go out into the real world and ignore the Declaration of Independence as if it were worth no more than the parchment it was written on, outdated and irrelevant in this modern age. Or,' he continued, 'you may choose to benefit society by upholding the law. That is the course great lawyers take. Bad lawyers, and I do not mean stupid ones, are those who begin to bend the law, which, I submit, is only a step away from breaking it. To those of you in this class who wish to pursue such a course I must advise that I have nothing to teach you, because you are beyond learning. You are still free to attend my lectures, but "attending" is all you will be doing.'

The room was so silent that Scott looked up to check they hadn't all crept out. 'Not my words,' he continued as he stared at the intent faces, 'but those of Dean Thomas W. Swan, who lectured in this theatre for the first twenty-seven years of this century. I see no reason not to repeat his philosophy whenever I address an incoming class of the Yale Law School.'

The Professor opened the file in front of him for the first time. 'Logic,' he began, 'is the science and art of reasoning correctly. No more than common sense, I hear you say. And nothing so uncommon, Voltaire reminds us. But those who cry "common sense" are often the same people who are too lazy to train their minds.

'Oliver Wendell Holmes once wrote: "The life of the law has not been logic, it has been experience." ' The pens and pencils began to scratch furiously across the yellow pages, and continued to do so for the next fifty minutes.

When Scott Bradley had come to the end of his lecture, he closed his file, picked up his notes and marched quickly out of the room. He did not care to indulge himself by remaining for the sustained applause that had followed his opening lecture for the past ten years.

Hannah Kopec had been considered an outsider as well as a loner from the start, although the latter was often thought by those in authority to be an advantage.

Hannah had been told that her chances of qualifying were slim, but she had now come through the toughest part, the twelve-month physical, and although, despite her background, she had never killed anyone – six of the last eight applicants had – those in authority were now convinced she was capable of doing so. Hannah knew she could.

As the plane lifted off from Tel Aviv's Ben Gurion airport for Heathrow, Hannah pondered once again what had caused a twenty-five-year-old woman at the height of her career as a model to want to apply to join the Institute for Intelligence and Special Tasks – better known as Mossad – when she could have had her pick of a score of rich husbands in a dozen capitals.

Thirty-nine Scuds had landed on Tel Aviv and Haifa during the Gulf War. Thirteen people had been killed. Despite much wailing and beating of breasts, no revenge had been sought by the Israeli Government because of some tough political bargaining by James

Baker, who had assured them that the Coalition forces would finish the job. The American Secretary of State had failed to fulfil his promise. But then, as Hannah often reflected, Baker had not lost his entire family in one night.

The day she was discharged from hospital, Hannah had immediately applied to join Mossad. They had been dismissive of her request, assuming she would, in time, find that the wound healed. Hannah visited the Mossad headquarters every day for the next two weeks, by which time even they acknowledged that the wound remained open and, more importantly, was still festering.

In the third week they reluctantly allowed her to join a course for trainees, confident that she couldn't hope to survive for more than a few days, and would then return to her career as a model. They were wrong a second time. Revenge for Hannah Kopec was a far more potent drug than ambition. For the next twelve months she worked hours that began before the sun rose and ended long after it had set. She ate food that would have been rejected by a tramp and forgot what it was like to sleep on a mattress. They tried everything to break her, and they failed. To begin with the instructors had treated her gently, fooled by her graceful body and captivating looks, until one of them ended up with a broken leg. He simply didn't believe Hannah could move that fast. In the classroom the sharpness of her mind was less of a surprise to her instructors, though once again she gave them little time to rest.

But now they'd come onto her own ground.

Hannah had always, from a young age, taken it for granted that she could speak several languages. She had been born in Leningrad in 1968, and when fourteen years later her father died, her mother immediately applied for an emigration permit to Israel. The new liberal wind that was blowing across the Baltics made it possible for her request to be granted.

Hannah's family did not remain in a kibbutz for long: her mother, still an attractive, sparkling woman, received several proposals of marriage, one of which came from a wealthy widower. She accepted.

When Hannah, her sister Ruth and brother David took up their new residence in the fashionable district of Haifa, their whole world changed. Their new step-father doted on Hannah's mother and lavished gifts on the family he had never had.

After Hannah had completed her schooling she applied to universities in America and England to study languages. Mama didn't approve, and had often suggested that with such a figure, glorious long black hair and looks that turned the heads of men from seventeen to seventy, she should consider a career in modelling. Hannah laughed and explained that she had better things to do with her life.

A few weeks later, after Hannah had returned from an interview at Vasser, she joined her family in Paris for their summer holiday. She also planned to visit Rome and London, but she received so many invitations from attentive Parisians that when the three weeks were over she found she hadn't once left the French capital. It was on the last Thursday of their holiday that the Mode Rivoli Agency offered her a contract that no amount of university degrees could have obtained for her. She handed her return ticket to Tel Aviv back to her mother and remained in Paris for her first job. While she settled down in Paris her sister Ruth was sent to finishing school in Zurich, and her brother David took up a place at the London School of Economics.

In January 1991, the children all returned to Israel to celebrate their mother's fiftieth birthday. Ruth was now a student at the Slade School of Art; David was completing his studies for a PhD; and Hannah was appearing once again on the cover of *Elle*.

At the same time the Americans were massing on the Kuwaiti border, and many Israelis were becoming anxious about a war, but Hannah's stepfather assured them that Israel would not get involved. In any case, their home was on the north side of the city and therefore immune to any attack.

A week later, on the night of their mother's fiftieth birthday, they all ate and drank a little too much, and then slept a little too soundly. When Hannah eventually woke, she found herself strapped down in a hospital bed. It was to be days before they told her that her mother, brother and sister had been killed instantly by a stray Scud, and only her stepfather had survived.

For weeks Hannah lay in that hospital bed planning her revenge. When she was eventually discharged her stepfather told her that he hoped she would return to modelling, but that he would support her in whatever she wanted to do.

Hannah informed him that she was going to join Mossad.

It was ironic that she now found herself on a plane to London that, under different circumstances, her brother might have been taking to complete his studies at the LSE. She was one of eight trainee agents being despatched to the British capital for an advanced course in Arabic. Hannah had already completed a year of night classes in Tel Aviv. Another six months and the Iraqis would believe she'd been born in Baghdad. She could now think in Arabic, even if she didn't always think like an Arab.

Once the 757 had broken through the clouds, Hannah stared down at the winding River Thames through the little porthole window. When she had lived in Paris she had often flown over to spend her mornings working in Bond Street or Chelsea, her afternoons at Ascot or Wimbledon, her evenings at Covent Garden or the Barbican. But on this occasion she felt no joy at returning to a city she had come to know so well.

Now, she was only interested in an obscure sub-faculty of London University and a terraced house in a place called Chalk Farm.

2

ON THE JOURNEY BACK to his office on Wall Street, Antonio Cavalli began to think more seriously about Al Obaydi and how they had come to meet. The file on his new client supplied by their London office, and updated by his secretary Debbie, revealed that although the Deputy Ambassador had been born in Baghdad, he had been educated in England.

When Cavalli leaned back, closed his eyes and recalled the clipped accent and staccato delivery, he felt he might have been in the presence of a British Army officer. The explanation could be found in Al Obaydi's file under Education: The King's School, Wimbledon, followed by three years at London University reading law. Al Obaydi had also eaten his dinners at Lincoln's Inn, whatever that meant.

On returning to Baghdad, Al Obaydi had been recruited by the Ministry of Foreign Affairs. He had risen rapidly, despite the self-appointment of Saddam Hussein as President and the regular placement of Ba'ath Party apparatchiks in posts they were patently unqualified to fill.

As Cavalli turned another page of the file, it became obvious that Al Obaydi was a man well capable of adapting himself to unusual circumstances. To be fair, that was something Cavalli also prided himself on. Like Al Obaydi he had studied law, but in his case at Columbia University in New York. When that time of the year came round for graduates to fill out their applications to join leading law firms, Cavalli was always shortlisted when the partners saw his grades, but once they realised who his father was, he was never interviewed.

After working fourteen hours a day for five years in one of Manhattan's less prestigious legal establishments, the young Cavalli began to realise that it would be at least another ten years before he could hope to see his name embossed on the firm's masthead, despite having married one of the senior partners' daughters. Tony Cavalli didn't have ten years to waste, so he decided to set up his own law practice and divorce his wife.

In January 1982 Cavalli and Co. was incorporated, and ten years later, on April 15th 1992, the company declared a profit of $157,000, paying its tax demand in full. What the company books did not reveal was that a subsidiary had also been formed in 1982, but not incorporated. A firm that showed no tax returns, and despite its profits mounting year on year, could not be checked up on by phoning Dun & Bradstreet and requesting a complete VIP business report. This subsidiary was known to a small group of insiders as 'Skills' – a company that specialised in solving problems that could not be taken care of by thumbing through the Yellow Pages.

With his father's contacts, and Cavalli's driving ambition, the unlisted company soon made a reputation for handling problems that their unnamed clients had previously considered insoluble. Among Cavalli's latest assignments had been the recovery of taped conversations between Sinatra and Nancy Reagan that were due to be published in *Rolling Stone* and the theft of a Vermeer from Ireland for an eccentric South American collector. These coups were discreetly referred to in the company of potential clients.

The clients themselves were vetted as carefully as if they were applying to be members of the New York Yacht Club because, as Tony's father had often pointed out, it would only take one mistake to ensure that he would spend the rest of his life in less pleasing surroundings than 23 East 75th Street, or their villa in Lyford Cay.

Over the past decade, Tony had built up a small network of representatives across the globe who supplied him with clients requiring a little help with a more 'imaginative' proposition. It was his Lebanese contact who had been responsible for introducing the man from Baghdad, whose proposal unquestionably fell into this category.

When Tony's father was first briefed on the outline of Operation 'Desert Calm' he recommended that his son demand a fee of one hundred million dollars to compensate for the fact that the whole of Washington would be at liberty to observe him going about his business.

'One mistake,' the old man warned him, licking his lips, 'and you'll make more front pages than the second coming of Elvis.'

Once he had left the lecture theatre, Scott Bradley hurried across Grove Street Cemetery, hoping that he might reach his apartment in St Ronan Street before being accosted by a pursuing student. He loved them all – well, almost all – and he was sure that in time he would allow the more serious among them to stroll back to his rooms in the evenings for a drink and to talk long into the night. But not until they were well into their second year.

Scott managed to reach the staircase before a single would-be lawyer had caught up with him. But then, few of them knew that he had once covered four hundred metres in 48.1 seconds when he'd anchored the Georgetown varsity relay team. Confident he had escaped, Scott leapt up the staircase, not stopping until he reached his apartment on the third floor.

He pushed open the unlocked door. It was always unlocked. There was nothing in his apartment worth stealing – even the television didn't work. The one file that would have revealed that the law was not the only field in which he was an expert had been carefully secreted on his bookshelf between Tax and Torts. He failed to notice the books that were piled up everywhere or the fact that he could have written his name in the dust on the sideboard.

Scott closed the door behind him and glanced, as he always did, at the picture of his mother on the sideboard. He dumped the pile of notes he was carrying by her side and retrieved the mail poking out from under the door. Scott walked across the room and sank into an old leather chair, wondering how many of those bright, attentive faces would still be attending his lectures in two years' time. Forty per cent would be good – thirty per cent more likely. Those would be the ones for whom fourteen hours' work a day became the norm, and not just for the last month before exams. And of them, how many would live up to the standards of the late Dean Thomas W. Swan? Five per cent, if he was lucky.

The Professor of Constitutional Law turned his attention to the bundle of mail he held in his lap. One from American Express – a bill with the inevitable hundred free offers which would cost him even more money if he took any of them up; an invitation from Brown to give the Charles Evans Hughes Lecture on the Constitution; a letter from Carol reminding him she hadn't seen him for some time; a circular from a firm of stockbrokers who didn't promise to double his money but . . .; and finally a plain buff envelope postmarked Virginia, with a typeface he recognised immediately.

He tore open the buff envelope and extracted the single sheet of paper which gave him his latest instructions.

Al Obaydi strolled onto the floor of the General Assembly and slipped into a chair directly behind his Head of Mission. The Ambassador had his earphones on and was pretending to be deeply interested in a speech being delivered by the Head of the Brazilian Mission. Al Obaydi's boss always preferred to have confidential talks on the floor of the General Assembly: he suspected it was the only room in the United Nations building that wasn't bugged by the CIA.

Al Obaydi waited patiently until the older man flicked one of the earpieces aside and leaned slightly back.

'They've agreed to our terms,' murmured Al Obaydi, as if it was he who had suggested the figure. The Ambassador's upper lip protruded over his lower lip, the recognised sign among his colleagues that he required more details.

'One hundred million,' Al Obaydi whispered. 'Ten million to be paid immediately. The final ninety on delivery.'

'"Immediately"?' said the Ambassador. 'What does "immediately" mean?'

'By midday tomorrow,' whispered Al Obaydi.

'At least Sayedi anticipated that eventuality,' said the Ambassador thoughtfully.

Al Obaydi admired the way his superior could always make the term 'my master' sound both deferential and insolent at the same time.

'I must send a message to Baghdad to acquaint the Foreign Minister with the details of your triumph,' added the Ambassador with a smile.

Al Obaydi would also have smiled, but he realised the

Ambassador would not admit to any personal involvement with the project while it was still in its formative stage. As long as he distanced himself from his younger colleague for the time being, the Ambassador could continue his undisturbed existence in New York until his retirement fell due in three years' time. By following such a course he had survived almost fourteen years of Saddam Hussein's reign while many of his colleagues had conspicuously failed to become eligible for their state pension. To his knowledge one had been shot in front of his family, two hanged and several others posted as 'missing', whatever that meant.

The Iraqi Ambassador smiled as his British counterpart walked past him, but he received no response for his trouble.

'Stuck-up snob,' the Arab muttered under his breath.

The Ambassador pulled the earpiece back over his ear to indicate that he had heard quite enough from his number two. He continued to listen to the problems of trying to preserve the rainforests of Brazil, coupled with a request for a further grant from the UN of a hundred million dollars.

Not something he felt Sayedi would be interested in.

Hannah would have knocked on the front door of the little terraced house, but it was opened even before she had closed the broken gate at the end of the pathway. A dark-haired, slightly overweight lady, heavily made-up and with a beaming smile came bustling out to greet her. Hannah supposed she would have been about the same age as her mother, had Mama still been alive.

'Welcome to England, my dear. I'm Ethel Rubin,' she announced in gushing tones. 'I'm sorry my husband's not here to meet you, but I don't expect him back from his chambers for another hour.' Hannah was about to speak when Ethel added, 'But first let me show you your room, and then you can tell me all your plans.' She picked up one of Hannah's bags and led her inside. 'It must be such fun seeing London for the first time,' she said as they climbed the stairs, 'and there will be so many exciting things for you to do during the next six months.'

As each sentence poured out Hannah became aware that Ethel Rubin had no idea why she was in London.

After she had unpacked and taken a shower Hannah joined her hostess in the sitting room. Mrs Rubin chatted on, barely listening to Hannah's intermittent replies.

'Do you know where the nearest gym is?' Hannah had asked.

'My husband should be back at any moment,' Mrs Rubin replied. But before she could get the next sentence out, the front door swung open and a man of about five foot three with dark, wiry hair and even darker eyes almost ran into the room. Once Peter Rubin had introduced himself and asked how her flight had been he didn't waste any words suggesting that Hannah might have come to London to enjoy the social life of the metropolis. Hannah quickly learned that Peter Rubin didn't ask any questions he realised she couldn't answer truthfully. Although Hannah felt sure Mr Rubin knew no details of her mission, he was obviously aware that she hadn't come to London on a package holiday.

Mrs Rubin, however, didn't allow Hannah to get to bed until well after midnight, by which time she was exhausted. Once her head had touched the pillow she slept soundly, unaware of Peter Rubin explaining to his wife in the kitchen that in future their guest must be left in peace.

3

THE DEPUTY AMBASSADOR'S chauffeur slipped out of the UN's private garage and headed west through the Lincoln Tunnel under the Hudson in the direction of New Jersey. Neither Al Obaydi nor he spoke for several minutes while the driver continually checked his rear-view mirror. Once they were on the New Jersey Turnpike he confirmed that no one was following them.

'Good,' was all Al Obaydi offered. He began to relax for the first time that day, and started to fantasise about what he might do if the ten million dollars were suddenly his. When they had passed a branch of the Midlantic National Bank earlier, he had asked himself for the thousandth time why he didn't just stop the car and deposit the money in a false name. He could be halfway across the globe by the following morning. That would certainly make his Ambassador sweat. And, with an ounce of luck, Saddam would be dead long before they caught up with him. And then who would care?

After all, Al Obaydi didn't believe, not even for one moment, that the great leader's outrageous plan was feasible. He had been hoping to report back to Baghdad after a reasonable period of time that no one reliable or efficient enough could be found to carry out such a bold coup. And then the Lebanese gentleman had flown into New York.

There were two reasons why Al Obaydi knew he could not touch one dollar of the money stuffed into the golf bag that rested on the seat beside him. First, there were his mother and younger sister, who resided in Baghdad in relative comfort and who, if the money suddenly disappeared, would be arrested, raped, tortured and hanged – the only explanation being that they had collaborated with a traitor. Not that Saddam ever needed an excuse to kill anyone, especially someone he suspected might have betrayed him.

Secondly, Al Obaydi – who fell on his knees five times daily, faced east and prayed that Saddam would eventually die a traitor's death – could not help observing that Gorbachev, Thatcher and Bush had found it considerably more difficult than the great Sayedi to cling on to power.

Al Obaydi had accepted from the moment he had been handed this assignment by the Ambassador that Saddam would undoubtedly die peacefully in his bed while his own chances of survival – the Ambassador's favourite word – were slim. And once the money had been paid over, if Antonio Cavalli failed to carry out his side of the bargain, it would be Al Obaydi who was called back to Baghdad on some diplomatic pretext, arrested, summarily tried and found guilty. Then all those fine words his law professor at London University had uttered would turn out to be so much sand in the desert.

The driver swung off the turnpike and headed for the centre of Newark as Al Obaydi's thoughts returned to what the money was being used for. The idea had all the hallmarks of his President. It was original, required daring, raw courage, nerve and a fair degree of luck. Al Obaydi still gave the plan no more than a one per cent chance of even reaching the starting blocks, let alone the finishing tape. But then, some people in the State Department had only given Saddam a one per cent chance of surviving Operation Desert Storm. And if the great Sayedi could pull this off, the United States would become a laughing stock and Saddam would have guaranteed himself a place in Arab history alongside Saladin.

Although Al Obaydi had already checked the exact location of the building, he instructed the driver to stop two blocks west of his final destination. An Iraqi getting out of a large black limousine right in front of the bank would be enough of an excuse for Cavalli to pocket the money and cancel the deal. Once the car had stopped, Al Obaydi climbed over the golf bag and out onto the pavement on the kerb side. Although he only had to cover a couple of hundred yards to the bank, this was the one part of the journey that he considered was a calculated risk. He checked up and down the street. Satisfied, he dragged the golf bag out onto the pavement and humped it up onto his shoulder.

The Deputy Ambassador felt he must have looked an incongruous sight as he marched down Martin Luther King Drive in a Saks Fifth Avenue suit with a golf bag slung over his shoulder.

Although it took less than two minutes to cover the short distance to the bank, Al Obaydi was sweating profusely by the time he reached the front entrance. He climbed up the well-worn steps and walked through the revolving door. He was met by two armed men who looked more like sumo wrestlers than bank clerks. The Deputy Ambassador was quickly guided to a waiting lift that closed the moment he stepped inside. The door slid open only when he reached the basement. As Al Obaydi stepped out he came face to face with another man, bigger, if anything, than the two who had originally greeted him. The giant nodded and led him towards a door at the end of a carpeted corridor. As he approached, the door swung open and Al Obaydi entered a room to find twelve men waiting expectantly round a large table. Although conservatively dressed and silent, none of them looked like bank tellers. The door closed behind him and he heard a lock turning. The man at the head of the table stood up and greeted him.

'Good morning, Mr Al Obaydi. I believe you have something to deposit for one of our customers.'

The Deputy Ambassador nodded and handed over the golf bag without a word. The man showed no surprise. He had seen valuables transported in everything from a crocodile to a condom.

He was, however, surprised by the weight of the bag as he humped it up onto the table, spilled out the contents and divided the spoils among the other eleven men. The tellers began counting furiously, making up neat piles of ten thousands. No one offered Al Obaydi a seat, so he remained standing for the next forty minutes, with nothing to do but watch them go about their task.

When the counting had been completed, the chief teller double-checked the number of piles. One thousand exactly. He smiled, a smile that was not directed at Al Obaydi but at the money, then looked up in the direction of the Arab and gave him a curt nod, acknowledging that the man from Baghdad had made the down-payment.

The golf bag was then handed back to the Deputy Ambassador, as it had not been part of the deal. Al Obaydi felt slightly stupid as he slung it over his shoulder. The chief teller touched a buzzer under the table and the door behind him was unlocked.

One of the men who had first met Al Obaydi when he had entered the bank was standing waiting to escort him back to the ground floor. By the time the Deputy Ambassador stepped out onto the street, his guide had already disappeared.

With an enormous sigh of relief, Al Obaydi began to

stroll the two blocks back to his waiting car. He allowed himself a small smile of satisfaction at the professional way he had carried out the whole exercise. He felt sure the Ambassador would be pleased to learn that there had been no mishaps. He would undoubtedly take most of the praise when the message was relayed back to Baghdad that 'Operation Desert Calm' had begun.

Al Obaydi collapsed on the sidewalk before he realised what had hit him: the golf bag had been wrenched from his shoulder before he could react. He looked up to see two youths moving swiftly down the street, one of them clutching their prize.

The Deputy Ambassador had been wondering how he was going to dispose of it.

Tony Cavalli joined his father for breakfast a few minutes after seven the following morning. He had moved back into their brownstone on 75th and Park soon after his divorce. Since his retirement, Tony's father spent most of his time pursuing his lifelong hobby of collecting rare books, manuscripts and historical documents. He had also spent many hours passing on to his son everything he'd learned as a lawyer, concentrating on how to avoid wasting too many years in one of the state's penitentiaries.

Coffee and toast were served by the butler as the two men went about their business.

'Nine million dollars has been placed in forty-seven banks across the country,' Tony told his father. 'Another million has been deposited in a numbered account with Franchard et cie in Geneva, in the name of Hamid Al Obaydi,' he added, buttering a piece of toast.

The father smiled at the thought of his son using an old ploy he had taught him so many years before.

'But what will you tell Al Obaydi when he asks how

his ten million is being spent?' the unofficial chairman of Skills enquired.

For the next hour, Tony took his father through Operation Desert Calm in great detail, interrupted only by the occasional question or suggestion from the older man.

'Can the actor be trusted?' he asked before taking another sip of coffee.

'Lloyd Adams still owes us a little over thirty thousand dollars,' Tony replied. 'He hasn't been offered many scripts lately – a few commercials . . .'

'Good,' said Cavalli's father. 'But what about Rex Butterworth?'

'Sitting in the White House waiting for his instructions.'

His father nodded. 'But why Columbus, Ohio?' he asked.

'The surgical facilities there are exactly what we require, and the Dean of the Medical School has the ideal qualifications. We've had his office and home bugged from top to bottom.'

'And his daughter?'

'We've got her under twenty-four-hour surveillance.'

The chairman licked his lips. 'So when do you press the button?'

'Next Tuesday, when the Dean is due to make a keynote speech at his daughter's school.'

The butler entered the room and began to clear the table.

'And how about Dollar Bill?' asked Cavalli's father.

'Angelo is on his way to San Francisco to try and convince him. If we're going to pull this off we'll need Dollar Bill. He's the best. In fact no one else comes close,' added Cavalli.

'As long as he's sober,' was all the chairman said.

4

THE TALL, ATHLETIC MAN stepped off the plane into the US Air terminal at Washington National Airport. He carried only hand luggage, so he didn't have to wait at the baggage carousel where someone might recognise him. He needed just one person to recognise him – the driver who was picking him up. At six foot one, his fair hair tousled and with almost chiselled fine features, and dressed in light blue jeans, cream shirt and a dark blue blazer, he made many women rather hope that he would recognise them.

The back door of an anonymous black Ford was opened as soon as he came through the automatic doors into the bright morning sunlight.

He climbed into the back of the car without a word and made no conversation during the twenty-five-minute journey that took him in the opposite direction to the capital. The forty-minute flight always gave him a chance to compose his thoughts and prepare his new persona. Twelve times a year he made the same journey.

It had all begun when Scott was a child back in his home town of Denver, and he had discovered his father was not a respectable lawyer but a criminal in a Brooks Brothers suit, a man who, if the price was right, could always find a way round the law. His mother had spent years protecting her only child from the truth, but when her husband was arrested, indicted and finally sentenced to seven years, the old excuse 'there must have been some misunderstanding' no longer carried any conviction.

His father survived three years in prison before dying of what was described in the coroner's report as a heart attack, without any explanation being given for the marks around his throat. A few weeks later, his mother did die of a heart attack, while he was coming to the end of his third year at Georgetown studying law. Once the body had been lowered into the grave and the sods of earth hurled on top of the coffin, he left the cemetery and never spoke of his family again.

When the final rankings were announced, Scott Bradley was placed first in the graduating class, and several universities and leading law firms contacted him to ask about his plans for the future. To the surprise of his contemporaries, Scott applied for an obscure professorship at Beirut University. He didn't explain to anyone why he needed a clean break with the past.

Appalled by the low standard of the students at the university and bored by the social life, Scott began to fill his hours by attending courses on everything from the Islamic religions to the history of the Middle East. When three years later the university offered him the Chair of American Law, he knew it was time to return to the United States.

A letter from the Dean of the Law Faculty at Georgetown suggested he should apply for a vacant professorship at Yale. He wrote the following day and packed his bags when he received their reply.

Once he had taken up his new post, whenever he was asked the casual question, 'What do your parents do?' he would simply reply, 'They're both dead and I'm an only child.' There was a certain type of girl who delighted in this knowledge – they assumed he would need mothering. Several of them entered his bed, but none of them became part of his life.

But he hid nothing from the people he was summoned to see twelve times a year. They couldn't tolerate deception of any kind, and were highly suspicious of his real motives when they learned of his father's criminal record. He told them simply that he wished to make amends for his father's disgrace, and refused to discuss the subject any further.

At first they didn't believe him. After a time they took him on his own terms, but it was still to be years before they trusted him with any classified information. It was when he started coming up with solutions for problems in the Middle East that the computer couldn't handle that they began to stop doubting his motives. When the Clinton Administration was sworn in, the new team welcomed Scott's particular expertise.

Twice recently he had penetrated the State Department itself to advise Warren Christopher. He had been amused to see Mr Christopher suggest on the early-evening news a solution to the problem of sanctions-busting by Saddam that he had put to him earlier that afternoon.

The car turned off Route 123 and drew to a halt outside a pair of massive steel gates. A guard came out to check on the passenger. Although the two men had seen each other regularly over the past nine years, the guard still asked to see his credentials.

'Welcome back, Professor,' the uniformed man finally offered before saluting.

The driver proceeded down the road and stopped outside an anonymous office block. The passenger climbed out of the car and entered the building through a turnstile. His papers were checked once again, followed by another salute. He walked down a long corridor with cream walls until he reached an unmarked oak door. He gave a gentle knock and entered before waiting for a reply.

A secretary was sitting behind a desk on the far side of the room. She looked up and smiled. 'Go right in, Professor Bradley, the Deputy Director is expecting you.'

Columbus School for Girls, Columbus, Ohio, is one of those establishments that prides itself on discipline and scholarship, in that order. The headmistress would often explain to parents that it was impossible to have the second without the first.

Breaking school rules could, in the headmistress's opinion, only be considered in rare circumstances. The request that she had just received fell into such a category.

That night, the graduating class of '93 was to be addressed by one of Columbus's favourite sons, T. Hamilton McKenzie, Dean of the Medical School at Ohio State University. His Nobel Prize for Medicine had been awarded for the advances he had made in the field of plastic and reconstructive surgery. T. Hamilton McKenzie's work on war veterans from Vietnam and the Gulf had been chronicled from coast to coast, and there were men in every city who, thanks to his genius, had been able to return to normal lives. Some lesser mortals who had trained under the Nobel Laureate used their skills to help women of a certain age appear more beautiful than their maker had originally intended. The headmistress of Columbus felt confident that the girls would only be interested in the work T. Hamilton McKenzie had done for 'our gallant war heroes', as she referred to them.

The school rule that the headmistress had allowed to be waived on this occasion was one of dress. She had agreed that Sally McKenzie, head of student government and captain of lacrosse, could go home one hour early from afternoon class and change into clothes of a casual but suitable nature to accompany her father when he addressed the class later that evening. After all, the headmistress had learned the previous week that Sally had won an endowed national scholarship to Oberlin College to study medicine.

A car service had been called with instructions to pick Sally up at four o'clock. She would miss one hour of school, but the driver had confirmed that he would deliver father and daughter back by six.

As four chimed on the chapel clock, Sally looked up from her desk. A teacher nodded and the student gathered up her books. She placed them in her bag, and left the building to walk down the long drive in search of the car. When Sally reached the old iron gates at the entrance to the drive, she was surprised to find the only car in sight was a Lincoln Continental stretch limousine. A chauffeur wearing a grey uniform and a peaked cap stood by the driver's door. Such extravagance, she knew only too well, was not the style of her father, and certainly not that of the headmistress.

The man touched the peak of his hat with his right hand and enquired, 'Miss McKenzie?'

'Yes,' Sally replied, disappointed that the long winding drive prevented her classmates from observing the whole scene.

The back door was opened for her. Sally climbed in and sank into the luxurious leather upholstery.

The driver jumped into the front, pressed a button and the window that divided the passenger from the driver slid silently up. Sally heard the safety lock click into place.

She allowed her mind to drift as she glanced out of the misty windows, imagining for a moment that this was the sort of lifestyle she might expect once she left Columbus.

It was some time before the seventeen-year-old girl realised the car wasn't actually heading in the direction of her home.

Had the problem been posed in textbook form, T. Hamilton McKenzie would have known the exact course of action to be taken. After all, he lived 'by the book', as he so often told his students. But when it happened in real life, he behaved completely out of character.

Had he consulted one of the senior psychiatrists at the university, they would have explained that many of the anxieties he'd kept suppressed over a long period of time had, in his new circumstances, been forced to the surface.

The fact that he adored his only child, Sally, was clear for all to see. So was the fact that for many years he had become bored with, almost completely uninterested in, his wife Joni. But the discovery that he was not good under pressure once he was outside the operating theatre – his own little empire – was something he could never have accepted.

T. Hamilton McKenzie became at first irritated, then exasperated, and finally downright angry when his daughter failed to return home that Tuesday evening. Sally was never late, or at least not for him. The journey by car from Columbus should have taken no more than thirty minutes, even in the rush-hour traffic. Joni would have picked Sally up if she hadn't fixed her hair appointment so late. 'It's the only time Julian could fit me in,' she explained. She always left everything to the last minute. At 4.50 T. Hamilton McKenzie phoned Columbus School for Girls to check there had been no late change of plan.

Columbus doesn't change its plans, the headmistress would have liked to tell the Nobel Laureate, but satisfied herself with assuring him that Sally had left school at four o'clock, and that the limousine company had phoned an hour before to confirm that they would be waiting for her at the end of the drive by the main school gates.

Joni kept repeating in that Southern accent he had once found so attractive, 'She'll be here at any minute, jus' you wait. You can always rely on our Sally.'

Another man, who was sitting in a hotel room on the other side of town and listening to every word they exchanged, poured himself a beer.

By five o'clock, T. Hamilton McKenzie had taken to looking out of the bedroom window every few moments, but the path to their front door lay obstinately unbeaten.

He had hoped to leave at 5.20 p.m., allowing himself enough time to arrive at the school with ten or fifteen minutes to spare. If his daughter did not appear soon, he would have to go without her. He warned his wife that nothing would stop him leaving at 5.20 p.m.

At 5.20 p.m. T. Hamilton McKenzie placed the notes for his speech on the hall table and began pacing up and down the front path as he waited for his wife and daughter to come from opposite directions. By 5.25 p.m., neither of them was at his side and his famous 'cool' was beginning to show distinct signs of steaming.

Joni had taken some considerable time to select an appropriate outfit for the occasion, and was disappointed when she appeared in the hall that her husband didn't even seem to notice.

'We'll have to go without her,' was all he said. 'If Sally hopes to be a doctor one day, she'll have to learn that people have a tendency to die when you keep them waiting.'

'Shouldn't we give her just a li'l longer, honey?' asked Joni.

'No,' he barked, and without even looking back set off for the garage. Joni spotted her husband's notes on the hall table and stuffed them into her handbag before she pulled the front door closed and double-locked it. By the time she reached the road, her husband was already waiting behind the wheel of his car, drumming his fingers on the gear lever.

They drove in silence towards Columbus School for Girls. T. Hamilton McKenzie checked every car heading towards Upper Arlington to see if his daughter was in the back seat.

A small reception party, led by the headmistress, was waiting for them at the foot of the stone steps at the school's main entrance. The headmistress walked forward to shake hands with the distinguished surgeon as he stepped out of the car, followed by Joni McKenzie. Her eyes searched beyond them for Sally. She raised an eyebrow.

'Sally never came home,' Dr McKenzie explained.

'She'll probably join us in a few minutes, if she's not already here,' suggested his wife. The headmistress knew Sally was not on the school premises, but did not consider it courteous to correct the guest of honour's wife, especially as she had just received a call from the car service that required an explanation.

At fourteen minutes to six they walked into the headmistress's study, where a young lady of Sally's age offered the guests a choice of dry sherry or orange juice. McKenzie suddenly remembered that in the anxiety of waiting for his daughter he had left his notes on the hall table. He checked his watch and realised that there wasn't enough time to send his wife back for them. In any case, he was unwilling to admit such an oversight in front of this particular gathering. Damn it, he thought. Teenagers are never an easy audience, and girls are always the worst. He tried to marshal his thoughts into some sort of order.

At three minutes to six, despite there still being no sign of Sally, the headmistress suggested they should all make their way to the Great Hall.

'Can't keep the girls waiting,' she explained. 'It would set a bad example.'

Just as they were leaving the room, Joni took her husband's notes out of her handbag and passed them over to him. He looked relieved for the first time since 4.50.

At one minute to six, the headmistress led the guest of honour onto the stage. He watched the four hundred girls rise and applaud him in what the headmistress would have described as a 'ladylike' manner.

When the applause had faded away, the headmistress raised and lowered her hands to indicate that the girls should be seated again, which they did with the minimum of noise. She then walked over to the lectern and gave an unscripted eulogy on T. Hamilton McKenzie that would have surely impressed the Nobel Committee. She talked of Edward Zeir, the founder of modern plastic surgery, of J.R. Wolte and Wilhelm Krause, and reminded her pupils that T. Hamilton McKenzie had followed in their great tradition by advancing the still-burgeoning science. She said nothing about Sally and her many achievements while at the school, although it had been in her original script. It was still possible to be punished for breaking school rules even if you had just won an endowed national scholarship.

When the headmistress returned to her place in the centre of the stage, T. Hamilton McKenzie made his way to the lectern. He looked down at his notes, coughed, and then began his dissertation.

'Most of you in the audience, I should imagine, think plastic surgery is about straightening noses, removing double chins and getting rid of bags from under your eyes. That, I can assure you, is not plastic but cosmetic surgery. Plastic surgery,' he continued – to the disappointment, his wife suspected, of most of those seated in front of him – 'is something else.' He then lectured for forty minutes on z-plasty, homograting, congenital malformation and third-degree burns without once raising his head.

When he finally sat down, the applause was not quite as loud as it had been when he had entered the room. T. Hamilton McKenzie assumed that was because showing their true feelings would have been considered 'unladylike'.

On returning to the headmistress's study, Joni asked the secretary if there had been any news of Sally.

'Not that I am aware of,' replied the secretary, 'but she might have been seated in the hall.'

During the lecture, versions of which Joni had heard a hundred times before, she had scanned every face in the room, and knew that her daughter was not among them.

More sherry was poured, and after a decent interval T. Hamilton McKenzie announced that they ought to be getting back. The headmistress nodded her agreement and accompanied her guests to their car. She thanked the surgeon for a lecture of great insight, and waited at the bottom of the steps until the car had disappeared from view.

'I have never known such behaviour in all my days,' she declared to her secretary. 'Tell Miss McKenzie to report to me before chapel tomorrow. The first thing I want to know is why she cancelled the car I arranged for her.'

* * *

Scott Bradley also gave a lecture that evening, but in his case only sixteen students attended, and none of them was under the age of thirty-five. Each was a senior CIA field officer, and as fit as any quarterback in America. When they talked of logic, it had a more practical application than the one suggested when Scott lectured his younger students at Yale.

These men were all operating in the front line, stationed right across the globe. Often Professor Bradley pressed them to go over, detail by detail, decisions they had made under pressure, and whether those decisions had achieved the result they'd originally hoped for.

They were quick to admit their mistakes. There was no room for personal pride – only pride in the service was considered acceptable. When Scott had first heard this sentiment he thought they were being corny, but after nine years of working with them in the classroom and in the gym, he'd learned otherwise.

For over an hour Bradley threw test cases at them, at the same time suggesting ways of how to think logically, always weighing known facts with subjective judgement before reaching any firm conclusion.

Over the past nine years, Scott had learned as much from them as they had from him, but he still enjoyed helping them put his knowledge to practical use. Scott had often felt he too would like to be tested in the field, and not simply in the lecture theatre.

When the session was over, Scott joined them in the gym for another workout. He climbed ropes, pumped iron and practised karate exercises, and they never once treated him as anything other than a full member of the team. Anyone who patronised the visiting professor from Yale often ended up with more than their egos bruised.

Over dinner that night – no alcohol, just Quibel –

Scott asked the Deputy Director if he was ever going to be allowed to gain some field experience.

'It's not a vacation job, you know,' came back Dexter Hutchins' reply as he lit up a cigar. 'Give up Yale and join us full time and then perhaps we'll consider the merits of allowing you out of the classroom.'

'I'm due for a sabbatical next year,' Bradley reminded his superior.

'Then take that trip to Italy you've always been promising yourself. After dining with you for the last seven years, I think I know as much about Bellini as ballistics.'

'I'm not going to give up trying for a field job – you realise that, Dexter, don't you?'

'You'll have to when you're fifty, because that's when we'll retire you.'

'But I'm only thirty-six . . .'

'You rise too easily to make a good field officer,' said the Deputy Director, puffing away at his cigar.

When T. Hamilton McKenzie opened the front door of his house, he ignored the ringing phone as he shouted, 'Sally? Sally?' at the top of his voice, but he received no response.

He finally snatched the phone, assuming it would be his daughter. 'Sally?' he repeated.

'Dr McKenzie?' asked a calmer voice.

'Yes, it is,' he said.

'If you're wondering where your daughter is, I can assure you that she's safe and well.'

'Who is this?' demanded McKenzie.

'I'll call later this evening, Dr McKenzie, when you've had time to calm down,' said the quiet voice. 'Meanwhile, do not, under any circumstances, contact the police or any private agency. If you do, we'll know immediately, and will be left with no choice but to return your lovely daughter –' he paused '– in a coffin.' The phone went dead.

T. Hamilton McKenzie turned white, and in seconds was covered in sweat.

'What's the matter, honey?' asked Joni, as she watched her husband collapse onto the sofa.

'Sally's been kidnapped,' he said, aghast. 'They said not to contact the police. They're going to call again later this evening.' He stared at the phone.

'Sally's been kidnapped?' repeated Joni in disbelief.

'Yes,' snapped her husband.

'Then we ought to tell the police right away,' Joni said, jumping up. 'After all, honey, that's what they're paid for.'

'No, we mustn't. They said they'd know immediately if we did, and would send her back in a coffin.'

'A coffin? Are you sure that's what they said?' Joni asked quietly.

'Damn it, of course I'm sure, but they told me she'll be just fine as long as we don't talk to the police. I don't understand it. I'm not a rich man.'

'I still think we ought to call the police. After all, Chief Dixon's a personal friend.'

'No, no!' shouted McKenzie. 'Don't you understand? If we do that they'll kill her.'

'All I understand,' replied his wife, 'is that you're out of your depth and our daughter is in great danger.' She paused. 'You should call Chief Dixon right now.'

'No!' repeated her husband at the top of his voice. 'You just don't begin to understand.'

'I understand only too well,' said Joni, her voice remarkably calm. 'You intend to play Chief of Police for Columbus as well as Dean of the Medical School, despite the fact that you're quite unqualified to do so. How would you react if a State Trooper marched into your operating theatre, leaned over one of your patients and demanded a scalpel?'

T. Hamilton McKenzie stared coldly at his wife, and assumed it was the strain that had caused her to react so irrationally.

The two men listening to the conversation on the other side of town glanced at each other. The man with earphones said, 'I'm glad it's him and not her we're going to have to deal with.'

When the phone rang again an hour later both T. Hamilton McKenzie and his wife jumped as if they had been touched by an electric wire.

McKenzie waited for several rings as he tried to compose himself. Then he picked up the phone. 'McKenzie,' he said.

'Listen to me carefully,' said the quiet voice, 'and don't interrupt. Answer only when instructed to do so. Understood?'

'Yes,' said McKenzie.

'You did well not to contact the police as your wife suggested,' continued the quiet voice. 'Your judgement is better than hers.'

'I want to talk to my daughter,' interjected McKenzie.

'You've been watching too many late-night movies, Dr McKenzie. There are no heroines in real life – or heroes, for that matter. So get that into your head. Do I make myself clear?'

'Yes,' said McKenzie.

'You've wasted too much of my time already,' said the quiet voice. The line went dead.

It was over an hour before the phone rang again, during which time Joni tried once more to convince her husband that they should contact the police. This time T. Hamilton McKenzie picked up the receiver without waiting. 'Hello? Hello?'

'Calm down, Dr McKenzie,' said the quiet voice. 'And this time, listen. Tomorrow morning at 8.30 you'll leave home and drive to the hospital as usual. On the way you'll stop at the Olentangy Inn and take any table in the corner of the coffee shop that is not already occupied. Make sure it can only seat two. Once we're confident that no one has followed you, you'll be joined by one of my colleagues and given your instructions. Understood?'

'Yes.'

'One false move, Doctor, and you will never see your daughter again. Try to remember, it's you who are in the business of extending life. We're in the business of ending it.'

The phone went dead.

5

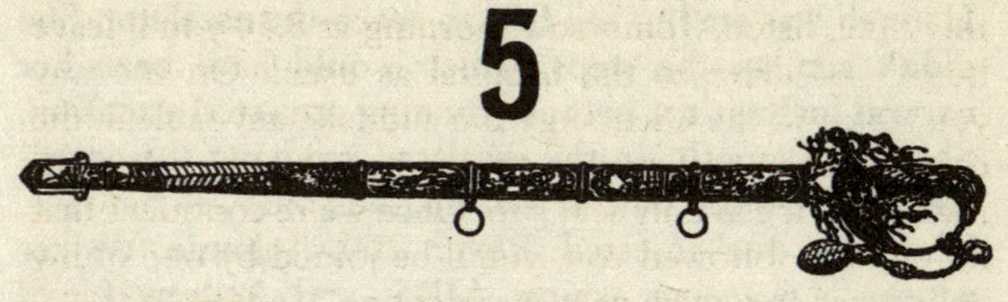

HANNAH WAS SURE that she could carry it off. After all, if she couldn't deceive them in London, what hope was there that she could do so in Baghdad?

She chose a Tuesday morning for the experiment, having spent several hours reconnoitring the area the previous day. She decided not to discuss her plan with anyone, fearing that one of the Mossad team might become suspicious if she were to ask one question too many.

She checked herself in the hall mirror. A clean white T-shirt and baggy sweater, well-worn jeans, sneakers, tennis socks and her hair looking just a little untidy.

She packed her small, battered suitcase – the one family possession they'd allowed her to keep – and left the little terraced house a few minutes after ten o'clock. Mrs Rubin had gone earlier to do what she called her 'big shop', an attempt to stock up at Sainsbury's for a fortnight.

Hannah walked slowly down the road, knowing that if she were caught they'd put her on the next flight home. She disappeared into the tube station, showed her travelcard to the ticket collector, went down in the lift and walked to the far end of the brightly-lit platform as the train rumbled into the station.

At Leicester Square she changed to the Piccadilly line,

and when the train pulled in to South Kensington, Hannah was among the first to reach the escalator. She didn't run up the steps, which would have been her natural inclination, because running attracted attention. She stood quietly on the escalator, studying the advertisements on the wall so that no one could see her face. The new fuel-injected Rover 200, Johnnie Walker whisky, a warning against AIDS, and Andrew Lloyd Webber's *Sunset Boulevard* at the Adelphi glared back at her. Once she'd emerged into the sunlight, Hannah quickly checked left and right before she crossed Harrington Road and walked towards the Norfolk Hotel, an inconspicuous medium-sized hostelry that she had carefully selected. She had checked it out the day before, and could walk straight to the ladies' rest room without having to ask for directions.

Hannah pushed the door open, and after quickly checking to confirm she was alone, chose the end cubicle, locked the door, and flicked open the catch of the battered suitcase. She began the slow process of changing identity.

Two sets of footsteps entered and left while she was undressing. During that time, Hannah sat hunched up on the lavatory seat, continuing only when she was confident she was alone.

The exercise took her nearly twenty minutes. When she emerged, she checked herself in the mirror and made a few minor adjustments.

And then she prayed, but not to their God.

Hannah left the ladies' room and made her way slowly up the stairs and back into the lobby of the hotel. She handed over her little case to the hall porter, telling him she'd collect it again in a couple of hours. She pushed a pound coin across the counter, and in return she received a little red ticket. She followed a tour party through the revolving doors and seconds later was back on the pavement.

She knew exactly where she was going and how long it would take to reach the front door, as she'd carried out a dry-run the previous day. She only hoped her Mossad instructor was right about the internal layout of the building. After all, no other agent had ever been inside before.

Hannah walked slowly along the pavement towards the Brompton Road.

She knew she couldn't afford to hesitate once she reached the front door. With twenty yards to go, she nearly decided to walk straight past the building. But once she reached the steps she found herself climbing them and then boldly knocking on the door. A few moments later, the door was opened by a bull of a man who towered a full six inches over her. Hannah marched in, and to her relief the guard stepped to one side, looked up and down the road and then slammed the door closed.

She walked down the corridor towards the dimly lit staircase without ever looking back. Once she reached the end of the fading carpet, she slowly climbed the wooden staircase. They'd assured her that it was the second door on the left on the first floor, and when she reached the landing she saw a door to the left of her, with peeling brown paint and a brass handle that looked as if it hadn't been polished for months. She turned the handle slowly and pushed the door open. As she entered, she was greeted by a babble of noise that suddenly ceased. The occupants of the room all turned to stare at her.

How could they know that Hannah had never been there before, when all they could see were her eyes?

Then one of them began talking again, and Hannah quietly took a seat in the circle. She listened carefully, and found that even when three or four of them were speaking at once she could understand almost every word. But the tougher test came when she decided to join in the conversation herself. She volunteered that her name was Sheka and that her husband had just arrived in London, but had only been allowed to bring one wife. They nodded their understanding and expressed their disbelief at British Immigration's inability to accept polygamy.

For the next hour, she listened to and discussed with them their problems. How dirty the English were, how decadent, all dying of AIDS. They couldn't wait to go home and eat proper food, drink proper water. And would it ever stop raining? Without warning, one of the black-clad women rose and bade her friends farewell. When a second got up to join her, Hannah realised this was her chance to leave. She followed the two women silently down the stairs, remaining a few paces behind. The massive man who guarded the entrance opened the door to let the three of them out. Two of them climbed into the back of a large black Mercedes and were whisked away, while Hannah turned west and began to retrace her steps to the Norfolk Hotel.

T. Hamilton McKenzie spent most of the night trying to work out what the man with the quiet voice could possibly want. He had checked his bank statements. He only had about $230,000 in cash and securities, and the house was probably worth another quarter of a million once the mortgage had been paid off – and this certainly wasn't a sellers' market, so that might take months to realise. All together, he could just about scrape up half a million. He doubted if the bank would advance him another cent beyond that.

Why had they selected him? There were countless

fathers at Columbus School who were worth ten or twenty times what he was – Joe Ruggiero, who never stopped reminding everybody that he owned the biggest liquor chain in Columbus, must have been a millionaire several times over. For a moment, McKenzie wondered if he was dealing with a gang that had simply picked the wrong man, amateurs even. But he dismissed that idea when he considered the way they'd carried out the kidnap and the follow-up. No, he had to accept that he was dealing with professionals who knew exactly what they wanted.

He slipped out of bed at a few minutes past six and, staring out of the window, discovered there was no sign of the morning sun. He tried to be as quiet as he could, although he knew that his motionless wife must surely be awake – she probably hadn't slept a wink all night. He took a warm shower, shaved, and for reasons he couldn't explain to himself, put on a brand new shirt, the suit he only wore when he went to church, and a flowered Liberty tie Sally had given him two Christmases before and which he had never had the courage to wear.

He then went down to the kitchen and made coffee for his wife for the first time in fifteen years. He took the tray back to the bedroom where he found Joni sitting upright in her pink nightgown rubbing her tired eyes.

McKenzie sat on the end of the bed and they drank black coffee together in silence. During the previous eleven hours they had exhausted everything there was to say.

He cleared the tray away and returned downstairs, taking as long as he could to wash and tidy up in the kitchen. The next sound he heard was the thud of the paper landing on the porch outside the front door.

He dropped the dishcloth, rushed out to get his copy of the *Dispatch* and quickly checked the front page, wondering if the press could have somehow got hold of the story. Clinton dominated the headlines, with trouble in Iraq flaring up again. The President was promising to send in more troops to guard the Kuwaiti border if it proved necessary.

'They should have finished off the job in the first place,' McKenzie muttered as he closed the front door. 'Saddam is not a man who works by the book.'

He tried to take in the details of the story but couldn't concentrate on the words. He gathered from the editorial that the *Dispatch* thought Clinton was facing his first real crisis. The President doesn't begin to know what a crisis is, thought T. Hamilton McKenzie. After all, his daughter had slept safely in the White House the previous night.

He almost cheered when the clock in the hall eventually struck eight. Joni appeared at the bottom of the stairs, fully dressed. She checked his collar and brushed some dandruff off his shoulder, as if he were about to leave for a normal day's work at the university. She didn't comment on his choice of tie.

'Come straight home,' she added, as she always did.

'Of course I will,' he said, kissing his wife on the cheek and leaving without another word.

As soon as the garage door swung up, he saw the flickering headlights and swore out loud. He must have forgotten to turn them off the previous night when he had been so cross with his daughter. This time he directed his anger at himself, and swore again.

He climbed in behind the wheel, put the key in the ignition and prayed. He switched the lights off and, after a short pause, turned the key. First quickly, then slowly, he tried to coax the engine into action, but it barely clicked as he pumped the accelerator pedal up and down.

'Not today!' he screamed, banging the steering wheel

with the palms of his hands. He tried a couple more times and then jumped out and ran back to the house. He didn't take his thumb off the bell until Joni opened the door with a questioning look on her face.

'My battery's flat. I need your car, quickly, quickly!'

'It's being serviced. You've been telling me for weeks to have it attended to.' T. Hamilton McKenzie didn't wait to offer an opinion. He turned his back on his wife, ran down the drive into the road and began searching the tree-lined avenue for the familiar yellow colour with a sign reading 444 4444 attached to the roof. But he realised there was a hundred to one chance of finding a cab driving around looking for a fare that early in the morning. All he could see was a bus heading towards him. He knew the stop was a hundred yards away, so he began running in the same direction as the bus. Although he was still a good twenty or thirty yards short of the stop when it passed him, the bus pulled in and waited.

McKenzie climbed up the steps, panting. 'Thank you,' he said. 'Does this bus go to Olentangy River Road?'

'Gets real close, man.'

'Then let's get going,' said T. Hamilton McKenzie. He checked his watch. It was 8.17 a.m. With a bit of luck he might still make the meeting on time. He began to look for a seat.

'That'll be a dollar,' said the driver, staring at his retreating back.

T. Hamilton McKenzie rummaged in his Sunday suit.

'Oh, my God,' he said. 'I've left . . .'

'Don't try that one, man,' said the driver. 'No cash, no dash.'

McKenzie turned to face him once again. 'You don't understand, I have an important appointment. A matter of life and death.'

'So is keeping my job, man. I gotta stick by the book. If

you can't pay, you've gotta debus 'cause that's what the regulations say.'

'But –' spluttered McKenzie.

'I'll give you a dollar for that watch,' said a young man seated in the second row who'd been enjoying the confrontation.

T. Hamilton McKenzie looked at the gold Rolex that had been presented to him for twenty-five years' service to the Ohio State University Hospital. He whipped it off his wrist and handed it over to the young man.

'It *must* be a matter of life and death,' said the young man as he exchanged the prize for a dollar. He slipped the watch onto his wrist. T. Hamilton McKenzie handed the dollar on to the driver.

'You didn't strike a good bargain there, man,' he said, shaking his head. 'You could have had a week in a stretch limo for a Rolex.'

'Come on, let's get going!' shouted McKenzie.

'It's not me who's been holding us up, man,' said the driver as he moved slowly away from the kerb.

T. Hamilton McKenzie sat in the front seat wishing it were he who was driving. He looked at his watch. It wasn't there. He turned round and asked the youth, 'What's the time?' The young man looked proudly at his new acquisition, which he hadn't taken his eyes off for one moment.

'Twenty-six minutes after eight and twenty seconds.'

McKenzie stared out of the window, willing the bus to go faster. It stopped seven times to drop and pick up passengers before they finally reached the corner of Independence, by which time the driver feared the watchless man was about to have a heart attack. As T. Hamilton McKenzie jumped off the steps of the bus, he heard the clock on the town hall strike 8.45 a.m.

'Oh God, let them still be there,' he said as he ran

towards the Olentangy Inn, hoping no one would recognise him. He stopped running only when he had reached the path that led up to reception. He tried to compose himself, aware that he was badly out of breath and sweating from head to toe.

He pushed through the swing door of the coffee shop and peered around the room, having no idea who or what he was looking for. He imagined that everyone was staring back at him.

The coffee shop had about sixty café tables in twos and fours, and he would have guessed it was about half full. Two of the corner tables were already taken, so McKenzie headed to the one that gave him the best view of the door.

He sat and waited, praying that they hadn't given up on him.

It was when Hannah arrived back at the crossing on the corner of Thurloe Place that she first had the feeling someone was following her. By the time she had reached the pavement on the South Kensington side, she was convinced of it.

A tall man, young, evidently not very experienced at shadowing, bobbed rather obviously in and out of doorways. Perhaps he thought she wasn't the type who would ever be suspicious. Hannah had about a quarter of a mile in which to plan her next move. By the time the Norfolk came in sight, she knew exactly what needed to be done. If she could get into the building well ahead of him, she estimated she only needed about thirty, perhaps forty-five, seconds at most, unless the porters were both fully occupied. She paused at the front window of a chemist's shop and stared at the array of beauty products that filled the shelves. She turned to look towards the lipsticks in the corner and saw his reflection in the brightly polished window. He was standing by a newspaper stand at the entrance to South Kensington tube station. He picked up a copy of the *Daily Mail* – amateur, she thought – which gave her the chance to cross the road before he could collect his change. She had reached the front door of the hotel by the time he had passed the chemist. Hannah didn't run up the steps, as it would have acknowledged his existence, but mistakenly pushed the revolving door so sharply that she sent an unsuspecting old lady tumbling onto the pavement much sooner than she'd intended.

The two porters were chatting as she shot across the lobby. The red ticket and another pound were already in her hand before she reached the porters' desk. Hannah slammed the coin down on the counter, which immediately attracted the older man's attention. When he spotted the pound, he quickly took the ticket, retrieved Hannah's little case and returned it to her just as her pursuer was coming through the revolving doors. She headed in the direction of the staircase at the end of the corridor, clutching the little case close to her stomach so the man following her would be unaware that she was carrying anything. When she reached the second step of the staircase she did run, as there was no one else in sight. Once down the staircase she bolted across the corridor and into the comparative safety of the ladies' room.

This time she was not alone. A middle-aged woman was leaning over a washbasin to check her lipstick. She didn't give Hannah so much as a glance when she disappeared into one of the cubicles. Hannah sat on the top of the lavatory, her knees tucked under her chin as she waited for the woman to finish her handiwork. It was two or three minutes before she finally left. Once Hannah heard the door close, she lowered her feet onto the cold marble floor, opened the battered suitcase to check everything was there and, satisfied that it was, changed back into her T-shirt, baggy sweater and jeans as quickly as she could.

She'd just managed to get her sneakers on when the door opened again, and she watched the lower part of two stockinged legs cross the floor and enter the cubicle next to hers. Hannah shot out, and buttoned up her jeans, before checking herself quickly in the mirror. She ruffled her hair a little and then began checking round the room. There was a large receptacle in the corner for depositing dirty towels. Hannah removed the plastic lid, took out all the towels that were there and forced her little case to the bottom, then quickly covered it with the towels and put the lid back in place. She tried to forget she had carried the bag from Leningrad to Tel Aviv to London – halfway across the world. She cursed in her native tongue before checking her hair in the mirror again. Then she strolled out of the ladies' room, attempting to appear calm, even casual.

The first thing Hannah saw when she stepped into the corridor was the young man sitting at the far end reading the *Daily Mail*. With luck, he wouldn't even give her a second thought. She had reached the bottom of the stairs when he glanced up. Rather good-looking, she thought, staring back at him for a second too long. She turned and began to climb the staircase. She was away; she'd made it.

'Excuse me, miss,' said a voice from behind her. Don't panic, don't run, act normally. She turned and smiled. He smiled back, almost flirting with her, and then blushed.

'Did you by any chance see an Arab lady when you were in the rest room?'

'Yes, I did,' replied Hannah. 'But why do you ask?' she demanded. Always put the enemy on the defensive whenever possible was the standard rule.

'Oh, it's not important. Sorry to have bothered you,' he said, and disappeared back around the corner.

Hannah climbed the stairs, returned to the lobby and headed straight for the revolving doors.

Pity, she thought once she was back on the pavement. He looked rather sexy. She wondered how long he would sit there, who he was working for, and to whom he would eventually be reporting.

Hannah began to retrace her steps home, regretting that she couldn't drop into Dino's for a quick spaghetti bolognese and then take in Frank Marshall's latest film, which was showing at the Cannon. There were still times when she yearned to be just a young woman in London. And then she thought of her mother, her brother, her sister, and once again told herself all of that would have to wait.

She sat alone for the first part of the tube journey, and was beginning to believe that if they sent her to Baghdad – as long as no one wanted to go to bed with her – she could surely now pass herself off as an Iraqi.

When the train pulled in to Green Park two youths hopped on. Hannah ignored them. But as the doors clamped shut she became aware that there was no one else in the carriage.

After a few moments, one of them sauntered over towards her and grinned vacantly. He was dressed in a black bomber jacket with the collar covered in studs, and his jeans were so tight they made him look like a ballet dancer. His spiky black hair stood up so straight that it looked as if he had just received convulsive shock therapy. Hannah thought he was probably in his early twenties. She glanced down at his feet to see that he was wearing heavy-duty army boots. Although he was a little overweight, she suspected from his movements that he was quite fit. His friend stood a few paces away, leaning against the railing by the door.

'So what do you say to my mate's suggestion of a quick strip?' he asked, removing a flick-knife from his pocket.

'Get lost,' Hannah replied evenly.

'Oh, a member of the upper classes, eh?' he said, offering the same vacant grin. 'Fancy a gang bang, do we?'

'Fancy a thick lip, do you?' she countered.

'Don't get clever with me, lady,' he said as the train pulled in to Piccadilly Circus.

His friend stood in the doorway so that anyone who might have considered entering the end carriage thought better of it.

Never seek attention, never cause a scene: the accepted rule if you work for any branch of the secret service, especially when you're stationed abroad. Only break the rules in extreme circumstances.

'My friend Marv fancies you. Did you know that, Sloane?'

Hannah smiled at him as she began planning the route she would have to take out of the carriage once the train pulled in to the next station.

'Quite like you myself,' he said. 'But I prefer black birds. It's their big bums, you know. They turn me on.'

'Then you'll like your friend,' said Hannah, regretting her words the moment she had said them. Never provoke.

She heard the click as a long thin blade shot out and flashed in the brightly lit carriage.

'Now there are two ways we can go about this, Sloane – quietly or noisily. It's your choice. But if you don't feel like co-operating, I might have to make a few etchings in that pretty face of yours.' The youth by the door began laughing. Hannah rose and faced her tormentor. She paused before slowly undoing the top button of her jeans.

'She's all yours, Marv,' said the young man as he turned to face his friend. He never saw the foot fly through the air as Hannah swivelled 180 degrees. The knife went flying out of his hand and shot across the floor to the far end of the carriage. A flat arm came down across his neck and he slumped to the ground in a heap, looking like a sack of potatoes. She stepped over his body and headed towards Marv.

'No, no, miss. Not me. Owen's always been the trouble-maker. I wouldn't have done nothin', not me, nothin'.'

'Take off your jeans, Marvin.'

'What?'

She straightened the fingers of her right hand.

'Anything you say, miss.' Marvin quickly undid his zip and pulled off his jeans to reveal a grubby pair of navy Y-fronts and a tattoo on his thigh that read 'Mum'.

'I do hope your mother doesn't have to see you like that too often, Marvin,' Hannah said as she picked up his jeans. 'Now the pants.'

'What?'

'You heard me, Marvin.'

Marvin slowly pulled off his Y-fronts.

'How disappointing,' said Hannah as the train pulled in to Leicester Square.

As the doors squelched closed behind her Hannah thought she heard, 'You filthy bitch, I'll . . .'

As she walked down the passage to the Northern line, Hannah couldn't find a litter bin in which to dispose of Marvin's grubby clothing. They had all been removed some time before after a sudden outbreak of IRA bombs in the London Underground. She had to carry the jeans and pants all the way to Chalk Farm, where she finally deposited them in a skip on the corner of Adelaide Road, then strolled quietly back home.

As she opened the front door, a cheery voice called

from the kitchen, 'Lunch is on the table, my dear.' Mrs Rubin walked through to join Hannah and declared, 'I've had the most fascinating morning. You wouldn't believe what happened to me at Sainsbury's.'

'What will it be, honey?' asked a waitress who wore a red skirt and a black apron and held a pad in her hand.

'Just black coffee, please,' said T. Hamilton McKenzie.

'Coming right up,' she said cheerfully.

He was about to check the time when he was reminded once again that his watch was on the wrist of a young man who was now probably miles away. McKenzie looked up at the clock above the counter. Eight fifty-six. He began to check everyone as they came through the door.

A tall, well-dressed man was the first to walk in, and as he scanned the room McKenzie became quite hopeful and willed him to look in his direction. But the man walked towards the counter and took a seat on a stool, with his back to the restaurant. The waitress returned and poured the nervous doctor a steaming black coffee.

Next to enter the room was a young woman, carrying a shopping bag with a long rope handle. She was followed a moment later by another smartly-dressed man who also searched the room with his eyes. Once again, T. Hamilton McKenzie's hopes were raised, only to be dashed when a smile of recognition flickered across the man's face. He too headed for the counter and took the stool next to the man who had come in a few moments earlier.

The girl with the shopping bag slipped into the place opposite him. 'That seat's taken,' said T. Hamilton McKenzie, his voice rising with every word.

'I know, Dr McKenzie,' said the girl. 'It's been taken by me.'

T. Hamilton McKenzie began to perspire.

'Coffee, honey?' asked the waitress who appeared by their side.

'Yes, black,' was all she said, not glancing up.

McKenzie looked at the young woman more carefully. She must have been around thirty – still at an age when she didn't require his professional services. From her accent, she was undoubtedly a native of New York, though with her dark hair, dark eyes and olive skin her family must surely have emigrated from southern Europe. She was slight, almost frail, and her neatly-patterned Laura Ashley dress of autumn browns, which could have been purchased in any one of a thousand stores across the country, made certain she would be forgettable in any crowd. She didn't touch the coffee that was placed in front of her.

McKenzie decided to go on the attack. 'I want to know how Sally is.'

'She's fine, just fine,' said the woman calmly. She reached down and with a gloved hand removed a single sheet of paper from her bag. She passed it over to him. He unfolded the anonymous-looking sheet:

Dear Daddy

They are treating me well but please agree to whatever they want.

Love Sal.

It was her writing, no question of that, but she would never have signed herself 'Sal'. The coded message only made him more anxious.

The woman leaned across and snatched the letter back.

'You bastards. You won't get away with it,' he said, staring across at her.

'Calm down, Dr McKenzie. No amount of threats or rhetoric is going to influence us. It's not the first time we've carried out this sort of operation. So, if you hope to see your daughter again . . .'

'What do you expect me to do?'

The waitress returned to the table with a fresh pot of coffee, but when she saw that neither party had taken a sip she said, 'Coffee's getting cold, folks,' and moved on.

'I've only got about $200,000 to my name. You must have made some mistake.'

'It's not your money we're after, Dr McKenzie.'

'Then what *do* you want? I'll do anything to get my daughter back safely.'

'The company I represent specialises in gathering skills, and one of our clients is in need of your particular expertise.'

'But you could have called and made an appointment like anyone else,' he said in disbelief.

'Not for what we have in mind, I suspect. And, in any case, we have a time problem, and we felt Sally might help us get to the front of the queue.'

'I don't understand.'

'That's why I'm here,' said the woman. Twenty minutes later, when both cups of coffee were stone cold, T. Hamilton McKenzie understood exactly what was expected of him. He was silent for some time before he said, 'I'm not sure if I can do it. To begin with, it's professionally unethical. And do you realise just how hard –'

The woman leaned down and removed something else from her bag. She tossed a small gold earring over to his side of the table. 'Perhaps this will make it a little easier for you.' T. Hamilton McKenzie picked up his daughter's earring. 'Tomorrow you get the other earring,' the woman continued. 'On Friday the first ear. On Saturday the other ear. If you keep on worrying about your ethics, Dr McKenzie, there won't be much of your daughter left by this time next week.'

'You wouldn't . . .'

'Ask John Paul Getty III if we wouldn't.'

T. Hamilton McKenzie rose from the table and leaned across.

'We can speed the whole process up if that's the way you want it,' she added, displaying not the slightest sign of fear.

McKenzie slumped back into his seat and tried to compose himself.

'Good,' she said. 'That's better. At least we now seem to understand each other.'

'So what happens next?' he asked.

'We'll be back in touch with you sometime later today. So make sure you're in. Because I feel confident that by then you'll have come to terms with your professional ethics.'

McKenzie was about to protest when the woman stood up, took a five-dollar bill out of her bag and placed it on the table.

'Can't have Columbus's leading surgeon washing up the dishes, can we?' She turned to leave and had reached the door before it struck McKenzie that they even knew he had left the house without his wallet.

T. Hamilton McKenzie began to consider her proposition, not certain if he had been left with any alternative.

But he was certain of one thing. If he carried out their demands, then President Clinton was going to end up with an even bigger problem.

A QUIET MAN sat on a stool at the end of the bar emptying the final drops in his glass. The glass had been almost empty of Guinness for some time, but the Irishman always hoped that the movement would arouse some sympathy in the barman, and he might just be kind enough to pour a drop more into the empty glass. But not this particular barman.

'Bastard,' he said under his breath. It was always the young ones who had no heart.

The barman didn't know the customer's real name. For that matter, few people did except the FBI and the San Francisco Police Department.

The file at the SFPD gave William Sean O'Reilly's age as fifty-two. A casual onlooker might have judged him to be nearer sixty-five, not just because of his well-worn clothes, but from the pronounced lines on his forehead, the wrinkled bags under his eyes and the extra inches around his waist. O'Reilly blamed it on three alimonies, four jail sentences and going too many rounds in his youth as an amateur boxer. He never blamed it on the Guinness.

The problem had begun at school when O'Reilly discovered by sheer chance that he could copy his classmates' signatures when they signed chits to withdraw pocket money from the school bank. By the time he had completed his first year at Trinity College, Dublin, he could forge the signatures of the provost and the bursar so well that even they believed that they had awarded him a bursary.

While at St Patrick's Institution for Offenders, Bill was introduced to the banknote by Liam the Counterfeiter. When they opened the gates to let him out, the young apprentice had nothing left to learn from the master. Bill discovered that his mother was unwilling to allow him to return to the bosom of the family, so he forged the signature of the American Consul in Dublin and departed for the brave new world.

By the age of thirty, he had etched his first dollar plate. The work was so good that, during the trial that followed its discovery, the FBI acknowledged that the counterfeit was a masterpiece which would never have been detected without the help of an informer. O'Reilly was sentenced to six years and the crime desk of the *San Francisco Chronicle* dubbed him 'Dollar Bill'.

When Dollar Bill was released from jail, he moved on to tens, twenties and later fifties, and his sentences increased in direct proportion. In between sentences he managed three wives and three divorces. Something else his mother wouldn't have approved of.

His third wife did her best to keep him on the straight and narrow, and Bill responded by producing documents only when he couldn't get any other work – the odd passport, the occasional driver's licence or social security claim – nothing really criminal, he assured the judge. The judge didn't agree and sent him back down for another five years.

When Dollar Bill was released this time, nobody would touch him, so he had to resort to doing tattoos at fairgrounds and, in desperation, pavement paintings which, when it didn't rain, just about kept him in Guinness.

Bill lifted the empty glass and stared once again at the barman, who returned a look of stony indifference. He failed to notice the smartly-dressed young man who took a seat on the other side of him.

'What can I get you to drink, Mr O'Reilly?' said a voice he didn't recognise. Bill looked round suspiciously. 'I'm retired,' he declared, fearing that it was another of those young plain-clothes detectives from the San Francisco Police Department who hadn't made his quota of arrests for the month.

'Then you won't mind having a drink with an old con, will you?' said the younger man, revealing a slight Bronx accent.

Bill hesitated, but the thirst won.

'A pint of draught Guinness,' he said hopefully.

The young man raised his hand and this time the barman responded immediately.

'So what do you want?' asked Bill, once he'd taken a swig and was sure the barman was out of earshot.

'Your skill.'

'But I'm retired. I already told you.'

'And I heard you the first time. But what I require isn't criminal.'

'So what are you hoping I'll knock up for you? A copy of the *Mona Lisa*, or is it to be the Magna Carta?'

'Nearer home than that,' said the young man.

'Buy me another,' said Bill, staring at the empty glass that stood on the counter in front of him, 'and I'll listen to your proposition. But I warn you, I'm still retired.'

After the barman had filled Bill's glass a second time, the young man introduced himself as Angelo Santini, and began to explain to Dollar Bill exactly what he had in mind. Angelo was grateful that at four in the afternoon there was no one else around to overhear them.

'But there are already thousands of those in circulation,' said Dollar Bill when Angelo had finished. 'You could buy a good reproduction from any decent tourist shop.'

'Maybe, but not a perfect copy,' insisted the young man.

Dollar Bill put down his drink and thought about the statement.

'Who wants one?'

'It's for a client who's a collector of rare manuscripts,' Angelo said. 'And he'll pay a good price.'

Not a bad lie, as lies go, thought Bill. He took another sip of Guinness. 'But it would take me weeks,' he said, almost under his breath. 'In any case, I'd have to move to Washington.'

'We've already found a suitable place for you in Georgetown, and I'm sure we can lay our hands on all the materials you'd need.'

Dollar Bill considered this claim for a moment, before taking another gulp and declaring, 'Forget it – it sounds too much like hard work. As I explained, it would take me weeks and, worse, I'd have to stop drinking,' he added, placing his empty glass back on the counter. 'You must understand, I'm a perfectionist.'

'That's exactly why I've travelled from one side of the country to the other to find you,' said Angelo quietly. Dollar Bill hesitated and looked at the young man more carefully.

'I'd want \$25,000 down and \$25,000 on completion, with all expenses paid,' said the Irishman.

The young man couldn't believe his luck. Cavalli had authorised him to spend up to \$100,000 if he could guarantee the finished article. But then he remembered that his boss never trusted anyone who didn't bargain.

'\$10,000 when we reach Washington and another \$20,000 on completion.'

Dollar Bill toyed with his empty glass.

'$30,000 on completion if you can't tell the difference between mine and the original.'

'But we'll need to tell the difference,' said Angelo. 'You'll get your $30,000 if no one else can.'

Scott heard the phone ringing when he was at the foot of the stairs. His mind was still going over the morning lecture he had just given, but he leaped up the stairs three at a time, pushed open the door of his apartment and grabbed the phone, knocking his mother to the floor.

'Scott Bradley,' he said as he picked up the photograph and replaced it on the sideboard.

'I need you in Washington tomorrow. My office, nine o'clock sharp.'

Scott was always impressed by the way Dexter Hutchins never introduced himself, and assumed that the work he did for the CIA was more important than his commitment to Yale.

It took Scott most of the afternoon to rearrange his teaching schedule with two understanding colleagues. He couldn't use the excuse of not feeling well, as everyone on campus knew he hadn't missed a day's work through illness in nine years. So he fell back on 'woman trouble', which always elicited sympathy from the older professors, but didn't lead them to ask too many questions.

Dexter Hutchins never gave any details over the phone as to why Scott was needed, but as all the morning papers had carried pictures of Yitzhak Rabin arriving in Washington for his first meeting with President Clinton, he made the obvious assumption.

Scott removed the file that was lodged between Tax and Torts and extracted everything he had about the new

Israeli Prime Minister. His policy towards America didn't seem to differ greatly from that of his predecessor. He was better educated than Shamir, more conciliatory and gentler in his approach, but Scott suspected that if it came to a knife fight in a downtown bar, Rabin was the one who would come out unmarked.

He leaned back and started thinking about a blonde named Susan Anderson who had been present at the last briefing he had been asked to attend with the new Secretary of State. If she was at the meeting, the trip to Washington might prove worthwhile.

The following morning a black limousine with smoked windows pulled up outside Ohio State University Hospital. The chauffeur parked in the space reserved for T. Hamilton McKenzie, as he had been instructed to do.

His only other orders were to pick up a patient at ten o'clock and drive him to the University of Cincinnati and Homes Hospital.

At 10.10, two white-coated orderlies wheeled a tall, well-built man in a chair out through the swing doors and, seeing the car parked in the Dean's space, guided him towards it. The driver jumped out and quickly opened the back door. Poor man, he thought, his head all covered in bandages and only a small crack left for his lips and nostrils. He wondered if it had been burns.

The stockily-built man clambered from the wheelchair into the back, sank into the luxurious upholstery and stretched out his legs. The driver told him, 'I'm going to put on your seatbelt,' and received a curt nod in response.

He returned to his seat in the front and lowered his window to say goodbye to the two orderlies and an older, rather distinguished-looking man who stood behind them. The driver had never seen such a drained face.

The limousine moved off at a sedate pace. The chauffeur had been warned not, under any circumstances, to break the speed limit.

T. Hamilton McKenzie was overcome with relief as he watched the car disappear down the hospital drive. He hoped the nightmare was at last coming to an end. The operation had taken him seven hours, and the previous night had been the first time he had slept soundly for the past week. The last order he had received was to go home and wait for Sally's release.

When the demand had been put to him by the woman who left five dollars on the table at the Olentangy Inn, he had considered it impossible. Not, as he had suggested, on ethical grounds, but because he had thought he could never achieve a true likeness. He had wanted to explain to her about autografting, the external epithelium and the deeper corium, and how unlikely it was that . . . But when he saw the unnamed man in his private office, he immediately realised why they had chosen him. He was almost the right height, perhaps a shade short – an inch, no more – and he might have been five to ten pounds too light. But shoe lifts and a few Big Macs would sort out both of those problems.

The skull and features were remarkable and bore a stunning resemblance to the original. In fact in the end it had only proved necessary to perform rhinoplasty and a partial thickness graft. The results were good, very good. The surgeon assumed that the man's red hair was irrelevant because they could shave his head and use a wig. With a new set of teeth and good make-up, only his immediate family would be able to tell the difference.

McKenzie had had several different teams working with him during the seven hours in the operating theatre. He'd told them he needed fresh help whenever he began to tire. No one ever questioned T. Hamilton McKenzie inside the hospital, and only he had seen the final result. He had kept his side of the bargain.

She parked the Ford Taurus – America's most popular car – a hundred yards from the house, but not before she'd swung it round to face the direction in which she would be leaving.

She changed her shoes in the car. The only time she had nearly been caught was when some mud had stuck to the soles of her shoes and the FBI had traced it to within yards of a spot she had visited a few days before.

She swung her bag over her shoulder and stepped out onto the road. She began to walk slowly towards the house.

They had chosen the location well. The farmhouse was several miles from the nearest building – and that was an empty barn – at the end of a track that even desperate lovers would have thought twice about.

There was no sign of anyone being in the house, but she knew they were there, waiting, watching her every move. She opened the door without knocking and immediately saw one of them in the hall.

'Upstairs,' he said, pointing. She did not reply as she walked past him and began to climb the stairs.

She went straight into the bedroom and found the young girl sitting on the end of the bed reading. Sally turned and smiled at the slim woman in the green Laura Ashley dress, hoping that she had brought another book with her.

The woman placed a hand in her bag and smiled shyly, before pulling out a paperback and passing it over to the young girl.

'Thank you,' said Sally, who took the book, checked the cover and then quickly turned it over to study the plot summary.

While Sally became engrossed by the promised story, the woman unclipped the long plaited rope that was attached to the two sides of her shopping bag.

Sally opened the book at the first chapter, having already decided she would have to read every page very slowly. After all, she couldn't be sure when the next offering might come.

The movement was so fast that she didn't even feel the rope go round her neck. Sally's head jerked back and with one flick her vertebra was broken. Her chin slumped onto her chest.

Blood began to trickle out of her mouth, down her chin and onto the cover of *A Time to Love and a Time to . . .*

The driver of the limousine was surprised to be flagged down by a traffic cop just as he was about to take the exit ramp onto the freeway. He felt sure he hadn't broken the speed limit. Then he spotted the ambulance in his rear-view mirror, and wondered if they simply wanted to pass him. He looked to the front again to see the motorcycle cop was firmly waving him onto the hard shoulder.

He immediately obeyed the order and brought the car to a standstill, puzzled as to what was going on. The ambulance drew in and stopped behind him. The cop dismounted from his motorcycle, walked up to the driver's door and tapped on the window. The chauffeur touched a button in the armrest and the window slid silently down.

'Is there a problem, officer?'

'Yes, sir, we have an emergency on our hands,' the

policeman said without raising his visor. 'Your patient has to return to the Ohio State University Hospital immediately. There have been unforeseen complications. You're to transfer him to the ambulance and I will escort them back into the city.'

The wide-eyed driver agreed with a series of consenting nods. 'Should I go back to the hospital as well?' he asked.

'No, sir, you're to continue to Cincinnati and report to your office.'

The driver turned his head to see two paramedics dressed in white overalls standing by the side of the car. The policeman nodded and one of them opened the back door while the other released the seatbelt so that he could help the patient out.

The driver glanced in the rear-view mirror and watched the paramedics guide the well-built man towards the ambulance. The siren on the motorcycle brought his attention back to the policeman who was now directing the ambulance up the exit ramp so that it could cross the bridge over the highway and begin its journey back into the city.

The whole changeover had taken less than five minutes, leaving the driver in the limousine feeling somewhat dazed. He then did what he felt he should have done the moment he saw the policeman, and telephoned his headquarters in Cincinnati.

'We were just about to call you,' said the girl on the switchboard. 'They don't need the car any longer, so you may as well come straight back.'

'Suits me,' said the driver. 'I just hope the client pays the bill.'

'They paid cash in advance last Thursday,' she replied. The driver clicked the phone back on its cradle and began his journey to Cincinnati. But something was nagging in the back of his mind. Why had the policeman stood so close to the door that he couldn't get out, and why hadn't he raised his visor? He dismissed such thoughts. As long as the company had been paid, it wasn't his problem.

He drove up onto the freeway, and didn't see the ambulance ignore the signpost to the city centre and join the stream of traffic going in the opposite direction. The man behind the wheel was also contacting his headquarters.

'It went as planned, boss,' was all he replied to the first question.

'Good,' said Cavalli. 'And the chauffeur?'

'On his way back to Cincinnati, none the wiser.'

'Good,' Cavalli repeated. 'And the patient?'

'Fine, as far as I can tell,' said the driver, glancing in the rear-view mirror.

'And the police escort?'

'Mario took a detour down a side road so he could get changed into his Federal Express uniform. He should catch up with us within the hour.'

'How long before the next switch?'

The driver checked the milometer. 'Must be about another ninety miles, just after we cross the state line.'

'And then?'

'Four more changes between there and the Big Apple. Fresh drivers and a different car each time. The patient should be with you around midnight tomorrow, though he may have to stop off at a rest room or two along the way.'

'No rest rooms,' said Cavalli. 'Just take him off the highway and hide him behind a tree.'

7

DOLLAR BILL'S NEW HOME turned out to be the basement of a house in Georgetown, formerly an artist's studio. The room where he worked was well lit without glare and, at his request, the temperature was kept at sixty-six degrees with a constant humidity.

Bill attempted several 'dry runs' as he called them, but he couldn't get started on the final document until he had all the materials he needed. 'Nothing but perfection will do,' he kept reminding Angelo. He would not have his name associated with anything that might later be denounced as a forgery. After all, he had his reputation to consider.

For days they searched in vain for the right pen nibs. Dollar Bill rejected them all until he was shown a picture of some in a small museum in Virginia. He nodded his approval and they were in his hands the following afternoon.

The curator of the museum told a reporter from the *Richmond Times Dispatch* that she was puzzled by the theft. The pens were not of any historic importance or particularly valuable. There were far more irreplaceable objects in the next display case.

'Depends who needs them,' said Dollar Bill when he was shown the press cutting.

The ink was a little easier once Bill had found the right

shade of black. When it was on the paper he knew exactly how to control the viscosity by temperature and evaporation to give the impression of old age. Several pots were tested until he had more than enough to carry out the job.

While others were searching for the materials he needed, Dollar Bill read several books from the Library of Congress and spent a few minutes every day in the National Archives until he discovered the one mistake he could afford to make.

But the toughest requirement proved to be the parchment itself, because Dollar Bill wouldn't consider anything that was less than two hundred years old. He tried to explain to Angelo about carbon dating.

Samples were flown in from Paris, Amsterdam, Vienna, Montreal and Athens, but the forger rejected them all. It was only when a package arrived from Bremen with a selection dated 1781 that Dollar Bill gave a smile which only Guinness normally brought to his lips.

He touched, caressed and fondled the parchment as a young man might a new lover but, unlike a lover, he pressed, rolled and flattened the object of his attentions until he was confident it was ready to receive the baptism of ink. He then prepared ten sheets of exactly the same size, knowing that only one would eventually be used.

Bill studied the ten parchments for several hours. Two were dismissed within a moment, and four more by the end of the day. Using one of the four remaining sheets, the craftsman worked on a rough copy that Angelo, when he first saw it, considered perfect.

'Perfect to the amateur eye, possibly,' Bill said, 'but a professional would spot the seventeen mistakes I've made within moments. Destroy it.'

During the next week three copies of the text were

executed in the basement of Dollar Bill's new home in Georgetown. No one was allowed to enter the room while he was working, and the door remained locked whenever he took a break. He worked in two-hour shifts and then rested for two hours. Light meals were brought to him twice a day and he drank nothing but water, even in the evening. At night, exhausted, he would often sleep for eight hours without stirring.

Once he had completed the three copies of the forty-six-line text, Dollar Bill declared himself satisfied with two of them. The third was destroyed.

Angelo reported back to Cavalli, who seemed pleased with Dollar Bill's progress, although neither of them had been allowed to see the two final copies.

'Now comes the hard part,' Bill told Angelo. 'Fifty-six signatures, every one requiring a different nib, a different pressure, a different shade of ink, and every one a work of art in itself.'

Angelo accepted this analysis, but was less happy to learn that Dollar Bill insisted on a day off before he began to work on the names because he needed to get paralytically drunk.

Professor Bradley flew into Washington on Tuesday evening and booked himself into the Ritz Carlton – the one luxury the CIA allowed the schizophrenic agent/professor. After a light dinner in the Jockey Club, accompanied only by a book, Scott retired to his room on the fifth floor. He flicked channels from one bad movie to another before falling asleep thinking about Susan Anderson.

He woke at six-thirty the next morning, rose, and read the *Washington Post* from cover to cover, concentrating on the articles dealing with Rabin's visit. He got dressed watching a CNN report on the Israeli Prime Minister's speech at a White House dinner that had taken place the previous evening. Rabin assured the new President he wanted the same warm relationship with America that his predecessor had enjoyed.

After a light breakfast, Scott strolled out of the hotel to find a company car waiting for him.

'Good morning, sir,' were the only words his driver spoke on the entire journey. It was a pleasant trip out of the city that Wednesday morning, but Scott smiled wryly as he watched commuters blocking all three lanes going in the opposite direction.

When he arrived at Dexter Hutchins' office ten minutes before his appointment, Tess, the Deputy Director's secretary, waved him straight through.

Dexter greeted Scott with a firm handshake and a cursory attempt at an apology.

'Sorry to pull you in at such short notice,' he said, removing the butt of a cigar from his mouth, 'but the Secretary of State wants you to be present for his working meeting with the Israeli Prime Minister. They're having one of the usual official lunches, rack of lamb and irrelevant small talk, and they expect to start the working session around three.'

'But why would Christopher want me there?' asked Scott.

'Our man in Tel Aviv says Rabin is going to come up with something that isn't officially on the agenda. That's all he could find out. No details. You know as much about the Middle East as anyone in the department, so Christopher wants you around. I've had Tess put the latest data together so that you'll be right up to date by the time we get to this afternoon's meeting.' Dexter Hutchins picked up a pile of files from the corner of his desk and handed them to Scott. The inevitable 'Top

Secret' was stamped on each of them, despite the fact that a lot of the information they contained could be found strewn across the Foreign Desk of the *Washington Post*.

'The first file is on the man himself and Labour Party policy; the others are on the PLO, Lebanon, Iran, Iraq, Syria, Saudi Arabia and Jordan, all in reference to our current defence policy. If Rabin's hoping to get more money out of us, he can think again, especially after Clinton's speech last week on domestic policy. There's a copy in the bottom file.'

'Marked "Top Secret", no doubt,' said Scott.

Dexter Hutchins raised his eyebrows as Scott bundled up the files and left without another word. Tess unlocked a door that led to a small empty office next to her own. 'I'll make sure you're not disturbed, Professor,' she promised.

Scott turned the pages of the first file, and began to study a report on the secret talks that had been taking place in Norway between the Israelis and the PLO. When he came to the file on the Iraq–Iran conflict there was a whole section he'd written himself only two weeks before, recommending a surprise bombing mission on the Mukhbarat headquarters in Baghdad if the UN inspection team continued to be frustrated in their efforts to check Iraqi defence installations.

At twelve o'clock, Tess brought in a plate of sandwiches and a glass of milk as he began to read the reports on no-fly zones beyond the 36th and 32nd parallels in Iraq. When he had finished reading the President's speech, Scott spent another hour trying to puzzle out what change of course or surprise the new Prime Minister of Israel might have in mind. He was still deep in thought when Dexter Hutchins stuck his head round the door and said, 'Five minutes.'

In the car on the way to the State Department, Dexter asked Scott if he had any theories about what the Israeli leader might be going to surprise them with.

'Several, but I need to observe the man in action before I try to second guess. After all, I've only seen him once before, and on that occasion he still thought Bush might win the election.'

When they arrived at the C Street entrance it took almost as long for the two men from the CIA to reach the seventh floor as it always did for Scott to penetrate the inner sanctum of Langley.

At 2.53 they were ushered into an empty conference room. Scott selected a chair against the wall, just behind where Warren Christopher would be seated but slightly to his left so he would have a clear view of Prime Minister Rabin across the table. Dexter sat on Scott's right.

At one minute to three, five senior staffers entered the room, and Scott was pleased to see that Susan Anderson was among them. Her fine fair hair was done up in a coil, making her look rather austere, and she wore a tailored blue suit that accentuated her slim figure. The spotted white blouse with the little bow at the neck would have frightened off most men; it appealed to Scott.

'Good afternoon, Professor Bradley,' she said when Scott stood up. But she took a seat on the other side of Dexter Hutchins, and informed him that the Secretary of State would be joining them in a few moments.

'So how are the Orioles doing?' Scott asked, leaning forward and looking straight across at Susan, trying not to stare at her slim shapely legs. Susan blushed. From some file, Scott had recalled that she was a baseball fan, and when she wasn't accompanying the Secretary of State abroad, she never missed a game. Scott knew only too well that they had lost their last three matches.

'Doing about as well as Georgetown did in the NCAAs,' came back her immediate reply.

Scott could think of no suitable reply. Georgetown had failed to make the national tournament for the first time in years.

'Fifteen all,' said Dexter, who was obviously enjoying sitting on the high stool between them.

The door suddenly swung open and Warren Christopher entered the room accompanied by the Prime Minister of Israel, and followed by officials from both countries. They split down each side of the long table, taking their places according to seniority.

When the Secretary of State reached his seat at the centre of the table, in front of the American flag, he spotted Scott for the first time, and nodded an acknowledgement of his presence.

Once everyone was settled, the Secretary of State opened the meeting with a predictably banal speech of welcome, most of which could have been used for anyone from Yeltsin to Mitterrand. The Prime Minister of Israel responded in kind.

For the next hour they discussed a report on the meeting in Norway between representatives of the Israeli government and the PLO.

Rabin expressed his conviction that an agreement was progressing satisfactorily, but it remained vital that any further exchanges should continue in the utmost secrecy, as he feared that if his political opponents in Jerusalem got to hear of it, they could still scupper the whole plan before he was ready to make a public announcement.

Christopher nodded his agreement, and said it would be appreciated by the State Department if any such announcement could be made in Washington. Rabin smiled, but made no concession. The game of poker had begun. If he was to deliver the Americans such a public relations coup, he would expect something major in return. Only one more hand remained to be dealt before the home team discovered what that 'something' was.

It was during 'any other business' that Rabin raised the subject no one had anticipated. The Prime Minister circled around the problem for a few minutes, but Scott could see exactly where he was heading. Christopher was obviously being given the opportunity, if he wanted it, to kill any discussion stone dead before Rabin raised it officially.

Scott scribbled a note on a piece of paper and passed it over to Susan. She read his words, nodded, leaned across and placed the note on the blotting pad in front of the Secretary of State. He unfolded the single sheet, glanced at the contents but showed no sign of surprise. Scott assumed that Christopher had also worked out the size of the bombshell that was about to be dropped.

The Prime Minister had switched the discussion to the role of Israel in relation to Iraq, and reminded the Secretary of State three times that they had gone along with the Allied policy on Operation Desert Storm, when it was Tel Aviv and Haifa that were being hit by Scuds, not New York or Little Rock. It amused Scott that at the last meeting Rabin had said 'New York or Kennebunkport'.

He went on to say he had every reason to believe that Saddam was, once again, developing a nuclear weapon, and Tel Aviv and Haifa still had to be the first candidates for any warhead.

'Try not to forget, Mr Secretary, that we've already had to take out their nuclear reactors once in the past decade,' the Prime Minister said. 'And if necessary, we'll do so again.'

Christopher nodded, but made no comment.

'And were the Iraqis to succeed in developing a nuclear weapon,' continued Rabin, 'no amount of compensation or sympathy would help us this time. And I'm not willing to risk the consequences of that happening to the Israeli people while I'm Prime Minister.'

Christopher still offered no opinion.

'For over two years since the Gulf War ended, we have waited for the downfall of Saddam Hussein, either at the hands of his own people or, at least, by some outside influence encouraged by you. As each month goes by, the Israeli people are increasingly wondering if Operation Desert Storm was ever a victory in the first place.'

Christopher still didn't interrupt the Israeli Prime Minister's flow.

'The Israeli Government feels it has waited long enough for others to finish the job. We have therefore prepared a plan to assassinate Saddam Hussein.' He paused to allow the implications of his statement to sink in. 'We have at last found a way of breaching Saddam's security, and possibly of being invited into his bunker. Even so, this will still be a more difficult operation than those which led to the capture of Eichmann and the rescue of the hostages at Entebbe.'

The Secretary of State looked up. 'And are you willing to share this knowledge with us?' he asked quietly.

Scott knew what the reply would be even before the Prime Minister spoke, and so, he suspected, did Christopher.

'No, sir, I am not,' replied Rabin, looking down at the page in front of him. 'The only purpose of my statement is to ensure we do not clash with your colleagues from the CIA, as we have information which suggests that they are currently considering such a plan themselves.'

Dexter Hutchins thumped his knee with a clenched

fist. Scott hastily wrote a two-word note and passed it across to Susan. She removed her glasses, read the message and looked back at him. Scott nodded firmly, so she once again leaned forward and placed the note in front of the Secretary of State. He glanced at Scott's words, and this time he reacted immediately.

'We have no such plan,' said Christopher. 'I can assure you, Prime Minister, that your information is not correct.' Rabin looked surprised. 'And may I add that we naturally hope you will not consider any such action yourselves without keeping President Clinton fully informed.'

It was the first time the President's name had been brought into play, and Scott admired the way the Secretary of State had applied pressure without any suggestion of a threat.

'I hear your request,' replied the Prime Minister, 'but I must tell you, sir, that if Saddam is allowed to continue developing his nuclear arsenal, I cannot expect my people to sit by and watch.'

Christopher had reached the compromise he needed, and perhaps even gained a little time. For the next twenty minutes the Secretary of State tried to steer the conversation onto more friendly territory, but everyone in that room knew that once their guests had departed only one subject would come under discussion.

When the meeting was concluded the Secretary instructed his own staff to wait in the conference room while he accompanied the Prime Minister to his limousine. He returned a few minutes later with only one question for Scott.

'How can you be so sure Rabin was bluffing when he suggested we were also preparing a plan to eliminate Saddam? I watched his eyes and he gave away nothing,' said Christopher.

'I agree, sir,' replied Scott. 'But it was the one sentence he delivered in two hours that he read word for word. I don't even think he had written it himself. Some adviser had prepared the statement. And, more important, Rabin didn't believe it.'

'Do you believe the Israelis have a plan to assassinate Saddam Hussein?'

'Yes, I do,' said Scott. 'And what's more, despite what Rabin says about restraining his people, I suspect it was his idea in the first place. I think he knows every detail, including the likely date and place.'

'Do you have any theories on how they might go about it?'

'No, sir, I don't,' replied Scott.

Christopher turned to Susan. 'I want to meet with Ed Djerijian and his senior Middle Eastern people in my office in one hour, and I must see the President before he departs for Houston.'

Christopher turned to leave, but before he reached the door, he glanced back. 'Thank you, Scott. I'm glad you were able to get away from Yale. It looks as if we're going to be seeing a lot more of you over the next few weeks.' The Secretary of State disappeared out of the room.

'May I add my thanks, too,' said Susan as she gathered up her papers and scurried after her master.

'My pleasure,' said Scott, before adding, 'Care to join me for dinner tonight? Jockey Club, eight o'clock?'

Susan stopped in her tracks. 'You must do your research more thoroughly, Professor Bradley. I've been living with the same man for the past six years and . . .'

'. . . and I heard it wasn't going that well lately,' interjected Scott. 'In any case, he's away at a conference in Seattle, isn't he?'

She scribbled a note and passed it over to Dexter Hutchins. Dexter read the two words and laughed before passing it on to Scott: 'He's bluffing.'

When the two of them had been left alone, Dexter Hutchins also had one question that he needed answering.

'How could you be so sure that we aren't planning to take Saddam out?'

'I'm not,' admitted Scott. 'But I am certain that the Israelis don't have any information to suggest we are.'

Dexter smiled and said, 'Thanks for coming down from Connecticut, Scott. I'll be in touch. I've got a hunch the plane to Washington is going to feel like a shuttle for you over the next few months.' Scott nodded, relieved that the term was just about to end and no one would expect to see him around for several weeks.

Scott took a cab back to the Ritz Carlton, returned to his room and began to pack his overnight case. During the past year he'd considered a hundred ways that the Israelis might plan to assassinate Saddam Hussein, but all of them had flaws because of the massive protection that always surrounded the Iraqi President wherever he went. Scott felt certain also that Prime Minister Rabin would never sanction such an operation unless there was a good chance that his operatives would get home alive. Israel didn't need that sort of humiliation on top of all its other problems.

Scott flicked on the evening news. The President was heading to Houston to carry out a fund-raiser for Senator Bob Krueger, who was defending Lloyd Bentsen's seat in the special May elections. His plane had been late taking off from Andrews. There was no explanation as to why he was behind schedule – the new President was quickly gaining a reputation for working by Clinton Standard Time. All the White House correspondent was willing to say was that he had been locked in talks with the Secretary of State. Scott switched off the news and checked his watch. It was a little after seven, and his flight wasn't scheduled until 9.40. Just enough time to grab a bite before he left for the airport. He had only been offered sandwiches and a glass of milk all day, and considered that the CIA at least owed him a decent meal.

Scott went downstairs to the Jockey Club and was taken to a seat in the corner. A noisy congressman was telling a blonde half his age that the President had been locked in a meeting with Warren Christopher because 'they were discussing my amendment to the defence budget'. The blonde looked suitably impressed, even if the maître d' didn't.

Scott ordered the smoked salmon, a sirloin steak and a half bottle of Mouton Cadet before once again going over everything the Israeli Prime Minister had said at the meeting. But he concluded that the shrewd politician had given no clues as to how or when – or even whether – the Israelis would carry out their threat.

On the recommendation of the maître d', he agreed to try the house special, a chocolate soufflé. He convinced himself that he wasn't going to be fed like this again for some time and, in any case, he could work it off in the gym the next day. When he had finished the last mouthful, Scott checked his watch: three minutes past eight – just enough time for a coffee before grabbing a taxi to the airport.

Scott decided against a second cup, raised his hand and scribbled in the air to indicate that he'd like the check. When the maître d' returned, he had his MasterCard ready.

'Your guest has just arrived,' said the maître d', without indicating the slightest surprise.

'My guest . . .?' began Scott.

'Hello, Scott. I'm sorry I'm a little late, but the

President just went on and on asking questions.'

Scott stood up and slipped his MasterCard back into his pocket before kissing Susan on the cheek.

'You did say eight o'clock, didn't you?' she asked.

'Yes, I did,' said Scott, as if he had simply been waiting for her.

The maître d' reappeared with two large menus and handed them to her customers.

'I can recommend the smoked salmon and the steak,' she said without even a flicker of a smile.

'No, that sounds a bit too much for me,' said Susan. 'But don't let me stop you, Scott.'

'No, President Clinton's not the only one dieting,' said Scott. 'The consommé and the house salad will suit me just fine.' Scott looked at Susan as she studied the menu, her glasses propped on the end of her nose. She had changed from her well-cut dark blue suit into a calf-length pink dress that emphasised her slim figure even more. Her blonde hair now fell loosely on to her shoulders and for the first time in his memory she was wearing lipstick. She looked up and smiled.

'I'll have the crab cakes,' she told the maître d'.

'What did the President have to say?' asked Scott, as if they were still in a State Department briefing.

'Not a lot,' she said, lowering her voice. 'Except that if Saddam were to be assassinated he feels that he would become the Iraqis' number-one target.'

'A human enough response,' suggested Scott.

'Let's not talk politics,' said Susan. 'Let's talk about more interesting things. Why do you feel Ciseri is underrated and Bellini overrated?' she enquired. Scott realised Susan must have also read his internal file from cover to cover.

'So that's why you came. You're an art freak.'

For the next hour they discussed Bellini, Ciseri,

Caravaggio, Florence and Venice, which kept them fully occupied until the maître d' reappeared by their side.

She recommended the chocolate soufflé, and seemed disappointed that they both rejected the suggestion.

Over coffee, Scott told his guest about his life at Yale, and Susan admitted that she sometimes regretted she had not taken up an offer to teach at Stanford.

'One of the five universities you've honoured with your scholarship.'

'But never Yale, Professor Bradley,' she said before folding her napkin. Scott smiled. 'Thank you for a lovely evening,' she added as the maître d' returned with the check.

Scott signed it quickly, hoping she couldn't see, and that the CIA accounts department wouldn't query why it was a bill for three people.

When Susan went to the ladies' room Scott checked his watch. Ten twenty-five. The last plane had taken off nearly an hour before. He walked down to the front desk and asked if they could book him in for another night. The receptionist pressed a few keys on the computer, studied the result and said, 'Yes, that will be fine, Professor Bradley. Continental breakfast at seven and the *Washington Post* as usual?'

'Thank you,' he said as Susan reappeared by his side.

She linked her arm in his as they walked towards the taxis parked in the cobblestone driveway. The doorman opened the back door of the first taxi as Scott once again kissed Susan on the cheek.

'See you soon, I hope.'

'That will depend on the Secretary of State,' said Susan with a grin as she stepped into the back of the taxi. The doorman closed the door behind her and Scott waved as the car disappeared down Massachusetts Avenue.

Scott took a deep breath of Washington air and felt that after two meals a walk round the block wouldn't do him any harm. His mind switched constantly between Saddam and Susan, neither of whom he felt he had the full measure of.

He strolled back into the Ritz Carlton about twenty minutes later, but before going up to his room he returned to the restaurant and handed the maître d' a twenty-dollar bill.

'Thank you, sir,' she said. 'I hope you enjoyed both meals.'

'If you ever need a day job,' Scott said, 'I know an outfit in Virginia that could make good use of your particular talents.' The maître d' bowed. Scott left the restaurant, took the lift to the fifth floor and strolled down the corridor to room 505.

When he removed his key from the lock and pushed the door open he was surprised to find he'd left a light on. He took his jacket off and walked down the short passageway into the bedroom. He stopped and stared at the sight that met him. Susan was sitting up in bed in a rather sheer negligé, reading his notes on the afternoon's meeting, her glasses propped on the end of her nose. She looked up and gave Scott a disarming smile.

'The Secretary of State told me that I was to find out as much as I possibly could about you before our next meeting.'

'When's your next meeting?'

'Tomorrow morning, nine sharp.'

8

BUTTON GWINNETT WAS PROVING to be a problem. The writing was spidery and small, and the *G* sloped forward. It was several hours before Dollar Bill was willing to transfer the signature onto the two remaining parchments. In the days that followed, he used fifty-six different shades of ink and subtle changes of pressure on the dozen nibs he tried out before he felt happy with Lewis Morris, Abraham Clark, Richard Stockton and Caesar Rodney. But he felt his masterpiece was undoubtedly John Hancock, in size, accuracy, shade and pressure.

The Irishman completed two copies of the Declaration of Independence forty-eight days after he had accepted a drink from Angelo Santini at a downtown bar in San Francisco.

'One is a perfect copy,' he told Angelo, 'while the other has a tiny flaw.'

Angelo stood looking at the two documents in amazement, unable to think of the words that would adequately express his admiration.

'When William J. Stone was asked to make a copy back in 1820, it took him nearly three years,' said Dollar Bill. 'And, more important, he had the blessing of Congress.'

'Are you going to tell me the one difference between the final copy you've chosen and the original?'

'No, but I will tell you it was William J. Stone who pointed me in the right direction.'

'So what's next?' asked Angelo.

'Patience,' said the craftsman, 'because our little soufflé needs time to rise.'

Angelo watched as Dollar Bill transferred the two parchments carefully onto a table in the centre of the room where he had rigged up a water-cooled Xenon lamp. 'This gives out a light similar to daylight, but of much greater intensity,' he explained. He flicked the switch on and the room lit up like a television studio. 'If I've got my calculations right,' said Bill, 'that should achieve in thirty hours what nature took over two hundred years to do for the original.' He smiled. 'Certainly enough time to get drunk.'

'Not yet,' said Angelo, hesitating. 'Mr Cavalli has one more request.'

'And what might that be?' asked Dollar Bill in his warm Irish brogue.

He listened to Mr Cavalli's latest whim with interest. 'I feel I ought to be paid double in the circumstances,' was the forger's only response.

'Mr Cavalli has agreed to pay you another ten thousand,' said Angelo.

Dollar Bill looked down at the two copies, shrugged his shoulders and nodded.

Thirty-six hours later, the chairman and the chief executive of Skills boarded a shuttle for Washington.

They had two assessments to make before flying back to New York. If both came out positively, they could then arrange a meeting of the executive team they hoped would carry out the contract.

If, however, they came away unconvinced, Cavalli

would return to Wall Street and make two phone calls. One to Mr Al Obaydi, explaining why it would be impossible to fulfil his request, and the second to their contact in the Lebanon to tell him that they could not deal with a man who had demanded that ten per cent of the money be lodged in a Swiss bank account in his name. Cavalli would even supply the number of the account they had opened in Al Obaydi's name in Geneva, and thus the blame for failure would be shifted from the Cavallis to the Deputy Ambassador from Iraq.

When the two men stepped out of the main terminal, a car was waiting to ferry them into Washington. Crossing the 14th Street bridge they proceeded east on Constitution Avenue where they were dropped outside the National Gallery, a building that neither of them had ever visited before.

Once inside the East Wing, they took a seat on a little bench against the wall just below the vast Calder mobile and waited.

It was the clapping that first attracted their attention. When they looked up to see what was causing the commotion, they watched as flocks of tourists quickly stood to one side, trying to make a clearing.

When they saw him for the first time, the Cavallis automatically stood. A group of bodyguards, two of whom Antonio recognised, was leading the man through a human passage while he shook hands with as many people as possible.

The chairman and the chief executive took a few paces forward to get a better view of what was taking place. It was remarkable: the broad smile, the gait and walk, even the same turn of the head. When he stopped in front of them and bent down to speak to a little boy for a moment they might, if they hadn't known the truth, have believed it themselves.

When the man reached the front of the building, the bodyguards led him towards the third limousine in a line of six. In moments he had been whisked away, the sound of sirens fading into the distance.

'That two-minute exercise cost us one hundred thousand dollars,' said Tony as they made their way back towards the entrance. As he pushed through the revolving door a little boy rushed past him shouting at the top of his voice, 'I've just seen the President! I've just seen the President!'

'Worth every penny,' said Tony's father. 'Now all we need to know is whether Dollar Bill also lives up to his reputation.'

Hannah received an urgent call asking her to attend a meeting at the embassy when there was still another four months of her course to complete. She assumed the worst.

In the exams which were conducted every other Friday, Hannah had consistently scored higher marks than the other five trainee agents who were still in London. She was damned if she was going to be told at this late stage that she wasn't up to it.

The unscheduled appointment with the Councillor for Cultural Affairs, a euphemistic title for Colonel Kratz, Mossad's top man in London, was for six that evening.

At her morning tutorial, Hannah failed to concentrate on the works of the Prophet Mohammed, and during the afternoon she had an even tougher time with The British Occupation and Mandate in Iraq, 1917–32. She was glad to escape at five o'clock without being set any extra work.

The Israeli Embassy had, for the past two months, been forbidden territory for all the trainee agents unless specifically invited. If you were summoned you knew it was simply to collect your return ticket home: we no longer have any use for you. 'Goodbye,' and, if you were lucky, 'Thank you.' Two of the trainees had already taken that route during the past month.

Hannah had only seen the embassy once, when she was driven quickly past it on her first day back in the capital. She wasn't even sure of its exact location. After consulting an A–Z map of London, she discovered it was in Palace Green, Kensington, slightly back from the road.

Hannah stepped out of the High Street Kensington underground station a few minutes before six. She strolled up the wide pavement into Palace Green and on as far as the Philippine Embassy before turning back to reach the Israeli Mission just before the appointed hour. She smiled at the policeman as she climbed the steps up to the front door.

Hannah announced her name to the receptionist, and explained she had an appointment with the Councillor for Cultural Affairs. 'First floor. Once you reach the top of the stairs, it's the green door straight in front of you.'

Hannah climbed the wide staircase slowly, trying to gather her thoughts. She felt a rush of apprehension as she knocked on the door. It was immediately opened with a flourish.

'A pleasure to meet you, Hannah,' said a young man she had never seen before. 'My name is Kratz. Sorry to call you in at such short notice, but we have a problem. Please take a seat,' he added, pointing to a comfortable chair on the other side of a large desk. Not a man given to small talk, was Hannah's first conclusion.

Hannah sat bolt upright in the chair and stared at the man opposite her, who looked far too young to be the Councillor for Cultural Affairs. But then she recalled the real reason for the Colonel's posting to London. Kratz had a warm, open face, and if he hadn't been going prematurely bald at the front, he might even have been described as handsome.

His massive hands rested on the desk in front of him as he looked across at Hannah. His eyes never left her and she began to feel unnerved by such concentration.

Hannah clenched her fists. If she was to be sent home she would at least state her case, which she had already prepared and rehearsed.

The Councillor hesitated as if he were deciding how to express what needed to be said. Hannah wished he would get on with it. It was worse than waiting for the result of an exam you knew you had failed.

'How are you settling in with the Rubins?' Kratz enquired.

'Very well, thank you,' said Hannah, without offering any details. She was determined not to hold him up from the real purpose of their meeting.

'And how's the course working out?'

Hannah nodded and shrugged her shoulders.

'And are you looking forward to going back to Israel?' asked Kratz.

'Only if I've got a worthwhile job to go back to,' Hannah replied, annoyed that she had lowered her guard. She wished Kratz would look away for just a moment.

'Well, it's possible you may not be going back to Israel,' said Kratz.

Hannah shifted her position in the chair.

'At least, not immediately,' added Kratz. 'Perhaps I ought to explain. Although you have four more months of your course to complete' – he opened a file that lay on the desk in front of him – 'your tutor has informed us that you are likely to perform better in the final exams than any of the other five remaining agents, as I'm sure you know.'

It was the first time she had ever been described as an agent.

'We have already decided you'll be part of the final team,' Kratz said, as if anticipating her question. 'But, as so often happens in our business, an opportunity has arisen which we feel you are the best-qualified person to exploit at short notice.'

Hannah leaned forward in her chair. 'But I thought I was being trained to go to Baghdad.'

'You are, and in good time you will go to Baghdad, but right now we want to drop you into a different enemy territory. No better way of finding out how you'll handle yourself under pressure.'

'Where do you have in mind?' asked Hannah, unable to disguise her delight.

'Paris.'

'Paris?' repeated Hannah in disbelief.

'Yes. We have picked up information that the head of the Iraqi Interest Section has asked his government to supply him with a second secretary. The girl has been selected and will leave Baghdad for Paris in ten days' time. If you are willing to take her place, she will never reach Charles de Gaulle airport.'

'But they'd know I was the wrong person within minutes.'

'Unlikely,' said Kratz, taking out a thicker file from a drawer of his desk and turning a few pages. 'The girl in question was educated at Putney High School and then went on to Durham University to study English, both on Iraqi government grants. She wanted to remain in England but was forced to return to Baghdad when student visas were rescinded just over two years ago.'

'But her family . . .'

'Father was killed in the war with Iran and the mother has gone to live with her sister, just outside Karbala.'

'Brothers and sisters?'

'A brother in the Republican Guard, no sisters. It's all in the file. You'll be given a few days to study the background before you have to make up your mind. Tel Aviv is convinced we've a good chance of dropping you in her place. Your detailed knowledge of Paris is an obvious bonus. We would only leave you there for three to six months at the most.'

'And then?'

'Back to Israel in final preparation for Baghdad. By the way, if you decide to take on this assignment, our primary purpose is not to use you as a spy. We already have an agent in Paris. We simply want you to assimilate everything around you and get used to living with Arabs and thinking like them. You must not keep any records, or even make notes. Commit everything to memory. You will be debriefed when we take you out. Never forget that your final assignment is far more important to the state of Israel than this could ever be.' He smiled for the first time. 'Perhaps you'd like a few days to think it over.'

'No, thank you,' said Hannah. This time it was Kratz who looked anxious. 'I'm happy to take on the job, but I have a problem.'

'What's that?' asked Kratz.

'I can't type, and certainly not in Arabic.'

The young man laughed. 'Then we'll have to lay on a crash course for you. You'd better leave the Rubins' immediately and get yourself moved into the embassy by tomorrow night. They won't ask you for an explanation, and don't offer any. Meanwhile, study this.' He passed over a manila folder with the name 'Karima Saib' written across the top in bold letters. 'Within ten days you must know its contents by heart. The knowledge you retain may save your life.'

Kratz rose from his side of the desk and walked round to accompany Hannah to the door. 'Just one more thing,' he said as he opened the door for her. 'I believe this is yours.'

The Councillor for Cultural Affairs handed Hannah a small, battered suitcase.

In a car on the way to Georgetown, Cavalli explained to his father that within a hundred yards of the gallery the sirens would have been turned off and the limousines would peel away one after another as they reached the next six intersections, losing themselves in the normal morning traffic.

'And the actor?'

'With his wig removed and wearing dark glasses, no one would give Lloyd Adams a second look. He'll be taking the Metroliner back to New York this afternoon.'

'Clever.'

'Once their licence plates have been switched, the six limos will return to the city in a couple of days with their original New York plates.'

'You've done a highly professional job,' said his father.

'Yes, but that was only the dress rehearsal of a single scene. What we're planning in four weeks' time is to put on a three-act opera with the whole of Washington as our invited audience.'

'Try not to forget that we're being paid one hundred million for our troubles,' the old man reminded him.

'If we deliver, it will be good value for money,' said Cavalli as the car drove past the Four Seasons Hotel. The chauffeur turned left down a side street and came to a halt outside a quaint old wooden house. Angelo was waiting by a little iron gate at the top of a small flight of stone steps. The chairman and chief executive got out of the car and followed Angelo down the steps at a brisk pace, without speaking.

The door at the bottom was already open. Once they were inside, Angelo introduced them to Bill O'Reilly. Bill led them down the corridor to his room. When he reached the locked door he turned the key as if they were about to enter Aladdin's cave. He opened the door and paused for just a moment before switching on the lights, then led his little party to the centre of the room, where the two manuscripts awaited their inspection. He explained to his visitors that only one was a perfect copy of the original.

Bill passed both men a magnifying glass, then took a pace backwards to await their judgement. Tony and his father were not quite sure where to start, and began studying both documents for several minutes without uttering a word. Tony took his time as he went over the opening paragraph, 'When in the course of human events . . .', while his father became fascinated by the signatures of Francis Lightfoot Lee and Carter Braxton, whose colleagues from Virginia had left them so little room at the foot of the parchment to affix their names.

After some time, Tony's father stood up to his full height, turned towards the little Irishman and handed back the magnifying glass, and said, 'Maestro, all I can say is that William J. Stone would have been proud to know you.'

Dollar Bill bowed, acknowledging the ultimate forger's compliment.

'But which one is the perfect copy and which one has the mistake?' asked Cavalli.

'Ah,' said the forger. 'It was also William J. Stone who

pointed me in the right direction for solving that little conundrum.'

The Cavallis waited patiently for Dollar Bill to continue his explanation. 'You see, when Timothy Matlock engrossed the original in 1776, he made three mistakes. Two he was able to correct by simple insertions.' Dollar Bill pointed to the word 'represtative', where the letters *e* and *n* were missing, and then to the word 'only', which had been omitted a few lines further down. Both of the corrections had been inserted with a /\.

'But,' continued Dollar Bill, 'Mr Matlock also made one spelling mistake which he did not correct. On one of the copies, you will find, I *have*.'

9

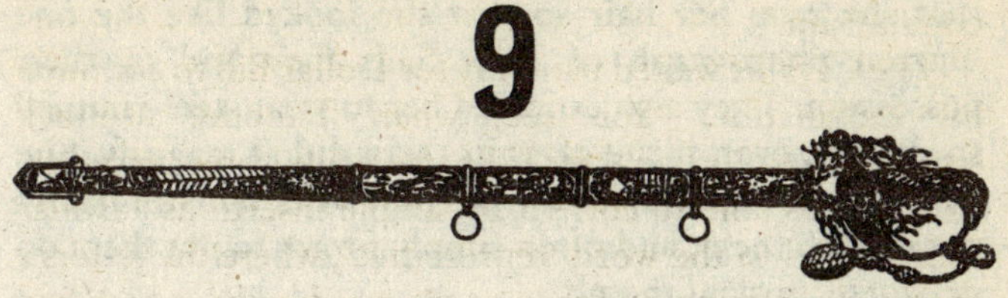

HANNAH LANDED AT Beirut airport the night before she was due to fly to Paris. No one from Mossad accompanied the new agent, to avoid the risk of compromising her. Any Israeli found in the Lebanon is automatically arrested on sight.

Hannah had taken over an hour to be cleared by customs, but she finally emerged carrying a British passport, hand luggage and a few Lebanese pounds. Twenty minutes later she booked herself into the airport Hilton. She explained to the receptionist that she would only be staying one night and paid her bill in advance with the Lebanese pounds. She went straight to her room on the ninth floor and did not venture out again that evening.

She received just one phone call, at 7.20. To Kratz's question she simply replied 'Yes,' and the line went dead.

She climbed into bed at 10.40, but couldn't sleep for more than an hour at a time. She occasionally flicked on the television to watch spaghetti Westerns dubbed into Arabic. In between she managed to catch moments of restless sleep. She rose at ten to seven the following morning, ate a slab of chocolate she found in the tiny fridge, cleaned her teeth and took a cold shower.

She dressed in clothes taken from her hand luggage of a type which the file had indicated Karima favoured, and sat on the corner of the bed staring at herself in the mirror. She didn't like what she saw. Kratz had insisted that she crop her hair so that she looked like the one blurred photograph of Miss Saib they had in their possession. They also expected her to wear steel-rimmed spectacles, even if the glass in them didn't magnify. She had worn the spectacles for the past week but still hadn't got used to them, and often simply forgot to put them on or, worse, mislaid them.

At 8.19 a.m. she received a second phone call to let her know the plane had taken off from Amman with the 'cargo' on board.

When Hannah heard the morning cleaners chatting in the corridor a few moments later, she opened the door and quickly switched the sign on the knob outside to 'Do Not Disturb'. She waited impatiently in her room for a call saying either 'Your baggage has been mislaid,' which meant she was to return to London because they had failed to kidnap the girl, or 'Your baggage has been retrieved,' the code to show they had succeeded. If it was the second message she was to leave the room immediately, take the hotel minibus to the airport and go to the bookshop on the ground floor, where she was to browse until she was contacted.

A courier would then arrive at Hannah's side and leave a small package containing Saib's passport with the photograph changed, the airline ticket in Saib's name and any baggage tickets and personal items that had been found on her.

Hannah was then to board the flight to Paris as quickly as possible with only the one piece of hand luggage she had brought with her from London. Once she had landed at Charles de Gaulle she was to pick up Karima Saib's luggage from the carousel and get herself to the VIP carpark. She would be met by the Iraqi Ambassador's chauffeur, who would take her to the

Jordanian Embassy, where the Iraqi Interest Section was currently located, the Iraqi Embassy in Paris being officially closed. From that moment, Hannah would be on her own, and at all times she was to obey the instructions given by the embassy staff, particularly remembering that in direct contrast to Jewish women, Arab women were subservient to men. She must never contact the Israeli Embassy or attempt to find out who the Mossad agent in Paris was. If it ever became necessary, he would contact her.

'What do I do about clothes if Saib's don't fit?' she had asked Kratz. 'We know I'm taller than she is.'

'You must carry enough in your overnight bag to last for the first few days,' he had told her, 'and then purchase what you will need for six months in Paris.' Two thousand French francs had been supplied for this purpose.

'It must be some time since you've been shopping in Paris,' she had told him. 'That's just about enough for a pair of jeans and a couple of T-shirts.' Kratz had reluctantly handed over another five thousand francs.

At 9.27 the phone rang.

When Tony Cavalli and his father entered the boardroom, they took the remaining chairs at each end of the table, as the chairman and chief executive of any distinguished company might. Cavalli always used the oak-panelled room in the basement of his father's house on 75th Street for such meetings, but no one present believed they were there to conduct a normal board meeting. They knew there would be no agenda and no minutes.

In front of each of the six places where the board members were seated was a notepad, pencil and a glass of water, as there would have been at a thousand such meetings across America that morning. But at this particular gathering, in front of every place were also two long envelopes, one thin and one bulky, neither giving any clue as to its contents.

Tony's eyes swept the faces of the men seated round the table. All of them had two things in common: they had reached the top of their professions, and they were willing to break the law. Two of them had served jail sentences, albeit some years before, while three of the others would have done so had they not been able to afford the finest lawyers available. The sixth was himself a lawyer.

'Gentlemen,' Cavalli began, 'I've invited you to join me this evening to discuss a business proposition that might be described as a little unusual.' He paused before continuing, 'We have been requested by an interested party to steal the Declaration of Independence from the National Archives.'

Tony paused for a moment as uproar broke out immediately and the guests tried to outdo each other with one-liners.

'Just roll it up and take it away.'

'I suppose we could bribe *every* member of the staff.'

'Set the White House on fire. That would at least cause a diversion.'

'Write in and tell them that you won it on a game show.'

Tony was content to wait for his colleagues to run out of wisecracks before he spoke again.

'Exactly my reaction when we were first approached,' he admitted. 'But after several weeks of research and preparation, I hope you will at least grant me an opportunity to present my case.'

They quickly came to order and began concentrating on Tony's every word, though 'scepticism' would have best described the expression on their faces.

'During the past weeks, my father and I have been working on a draft plan to steal the Declaration of Independence. We are now ready to share that knowledge with you, because I must admit that we have reached a point where we cannot advance further on this project without the professional abilities of everyone seated around this table. Let me assure you, gentlemen, that your selection has not been a random exercise.

'But first I would like you all to see the Declaration of Independence for yourself.' Tony pressed a button underneath the table and the doors behind him swung open. The butler entered the room carrying two thin sheets of glass, a parchment held between them. He placed the glass frame on the centre of the table. The six sceptics leaned forward to study the masterpiece. It was several moments before anyone offered an opinion.

'Bill O'Reilly's work, would be my guess,' said Frank Piemonte, the lawyer, as he leaned over to admire the fine detail of the signatures below the text. 'He once offered to pay me in forged bills, and I would have accepted if I'd got him off.'

Tony nodded, and after they had all spent a little more time studying the parchment, he said, 'So, allow me to reword my earlier statement. We are not so much planning to steal the Declaration of Independence as to replace the original with this copy.' A smile settled on the lips of two of the previously sceptical guests.

'You will now be aware,' said Tony, 'of the amount of preparation that has gone into this exercise so far, and, indeed, the expense my father and I have been put to. But the reason we have continued is because we feel the rewards if we are successful far outweigh the risk of being caught. If you will open the thin envelopes in front of you, I believe the contents will make my point more clearly. Inside each envelope you will find a piece of paper on which is written the sum of money you will receive if you decide to become a member of the executive team.'

While the six men tore open the thinner of their two envelopes, Tony continued, 'If you feel, on discovering the amount involved, that the reward does *not* warrant the risk, now is the time to leave. I trust that those of us who remain may have confidence in your discretion because, as you will be only too aware, our lives will be in your hands.'

'And theirs in ours,' said the chairman, speaking for the first time.

A ripple of nervous laughter broke out around the table as each of the six men eyed the unsigned cheque in front of him.

'That figure,' said Tony, 'is the payment you will receive should we fail. If we succeed, the amount will be tripled.'

'So will the jail sentence if we get caught,' said Bruno Morelli, speaking for the first time.

'Summing up, gentlemen,' said Cavalli, ignoring the comment, 'if you decide to join the executive team, you will receive ten per cent of that payment in advance when you leave tonight, and the remaining sum within seven days of the contract being completed. This would be paid into any bank of your choice in any country of your choosing.

'Before you make your decision, there's one further thing I'd like you all to see.' Once again Tony pressed a button under the table, and this time the doors opened at the far end of the room. The sight that greeted them caused two of the guests to immediately stand, one to gasp and the remaining three to simply stare in disbelief.

'Gentlemen, I am happy that you were able to join me

today. I wanted to assure you all of my commitment to this project, and I hope you'll feel able to be part of the executive team. I'll have to leave you now, gentlemen,' said the man standing next to the chairman in the Ozark accent that had become so familiar to the American people during the past few months, 'so that you can study Mr Cavalli's proposition in greater detail. You can be confident that I'll do everything I can to help make the change this country needs. But for now, I have one or two pressing engagements. I feel sure you'll understand.' The actor smiled, and shook hands warmly with everyone around the table before strolling out of the boardroom.

Spontaneous applause broke out after the door had closed behind him. Tony allowed himself a smile of satisfaction.

'Gentlemen, my father and I will now leave you for a few minutes to consider your decision.'

The chairman and chief executive rose without another word and left the room.

'What do you think?' asked Tony as he poured his father a whisky and water from the cabinet in his study.

'A lot of water,' he replied. 'I have a feeling we may be in for a long night.'

'But did they buy it?'

'Can't be certain,' replied the old man. 'I was watching their faces while you were giving the presentation, and sure as hell, they didn't doubt the work you've put in. They were all impressed by the parchment and Lloyd Adams' performance, but other than Bruno and Frank they didn't give much away.'

'Let's start with Frank,' said Tony.

'First in then out, as Frank always is, but he likes money far too much to walk away from an offer as good as this.'

'You're that confident?' said Tony.

'It's not just the money,' replied his father. 'Frank's not going to have to be there on the day, is he? So he'll get his share whatever happens. I've never yet met a lawyer who would make a good field commander. They're too used to being paid whether they win or lose.'

'If you're right, Al Calabrese may turn out to be a problem. He's got the most to lose.'

'As our trade union leader, he'll certainly have to be out there on centre stage most of the day, but I suspect he won't be able to resist the challenge.'

'And what about Bruno? If –' began the chief executive, but he was cut short as the doors swung open and Al Calabrese walked into the room. 'We were just talking about you, Al.'

'Not too politely, I hope.'

'Well, that depends on . . .' said Tony.

'On whether I'm in?'

'Or out,' said the chairman.

'I'm in up to my neck is the answer,' said Al, smiling. 'So you'd better have a foolproof plan to present to us.' He turned to face Tony. 'Because I don't want to spend the rest of my life on top of America's most wanted list.'

'And the others?' asked the chairman, as Bruno Morelli brushed past them without even saying goodnight.

10

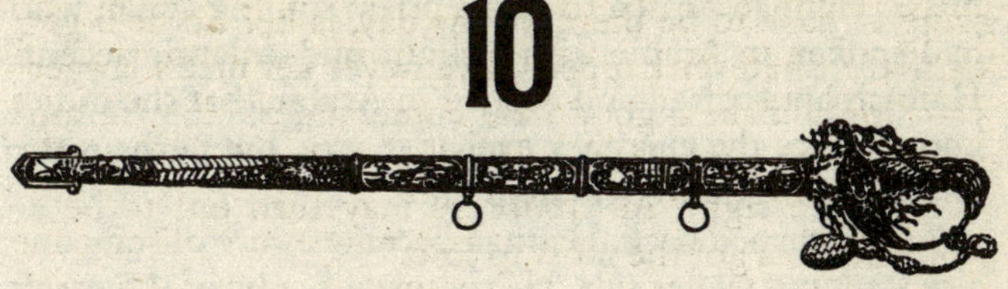

HANNAH NERVOUSLY GRABBED the ringing phone. 'This is Reception, madam. We were just wondering if you'll be checking out before midday, or do you require the room for an extra night?'

'No, thank you,' said Hannah. 'I'll have left by twelve, one way or the other.'

Two minutes later, the phone rang again. It was Colonel Kratz. 'Who were you speaking to a moment ago?'

'Reception were asking me when I would be checking out.'

'I see,' said Kratz. 'Your baggage has been retrieved,' was all he added.

Hannah replaced the phone and stood up. She felt a shot of adrenalin go through her body as she prepared for her first real test. She picked up her overnight bag and left the room, switching the sign on the door to 'Clean Me Please'.

Once she had reached the foyer, she had to wait only a few minutes before the hotel minibus returned from the airport on its circular journey. She sat alone in the back for the short trip to the departure area, then headed straight for the bookshop as instructed. She began to browse among the hardbacks, struck by how many American and British authors were obviously read by the Lebanese.

'Do you know where I can get some money changed, miss?' Hannah turned to find a priest smiling at her, who had spoken in Arabic with a slight mid-Atlantic accent. Hannah apologised and replied in Arabic that she didn't know where the currency exchange was, but perhaps the girl at the counter could help him.

As she turned back, Hannah became aware of someone else standing by her side. He removed a copy of *A Suitable Boy* from the shelf and replaced it with a small package. 'Good luck,' he whispered, and was gone even before she had seen his face. Hannah removed the package from the shelf and strolled slowly out of the bookshop. She began to search for the check-in counter for Paris. It turned out to be the one with the longest queue.

When she reached the front, Hannah requested a non-smoking seat.

The girl behind the counter checked her ticket and then began tapping away on her computer terminal. She looked puzzled. 'Were you unhappy with the seat previously allocated to you, Miss Saib?'

'No, it's just fine,' said Hannah, cursing herself for having made such a simple mistake. 'Sorry to have bothered you.'

'The flight will be boarding at Gate 17 in about fifteen minutes,' the girl added with a smile.

A man pretending to read the Vikram Seth novel he had just purchased watched as the plane took off. Satisfied he had carried out his instructions, he went to the nearest phone booth and rang first Paris and then Colonel Kratz to confirm that 'The bird has flown.'

The man in the priest's collar also watched Miss Saib board her plane, and he too made a phone call. Not to Paris or London, but to Dexter Hutchins in Langley, Virginia.

* * *

Cavalli and his father walked back into the room and once again resumed their places at each end of the table. One seat was empty.

'Too bad about Bruno,' said the chairman, licking his lips. 'We'll just have to find someone else to make the sword.'

Cavalli opened one of the six files in front of him. It was marked 'Transport'. He passed a copy to Al Calabrese.

'Let's start with the Presidential motorcade, Al. I'm going to need at least four limos, six motorcycle cops, two or three staff cars, two vans with surveillance cameras and a counter-assault team in a black Chevy Suburban – all of them able to pass the most eagle eye. I'll also want an additional van that would normally carry the White House media pool – the death-watch. Don't forget, the motorcade will be under far more scrutiny than last week, when we only had to turn on the sirens at the last moment, and then for just a few seconds. There's bound to be someone in the crowd who either works in government or is a White House junkie. It's often children who spot the most elementary mistakes and then tell their parents.'

Al Calabrese opened his file to find dozens of photographs of the President's motorcade leaving the White House on its way to the Hill. The photographs were accompanied by as many pages of notes.

'How long will it take you to have everything in place?' asked Cavalli.

'Three weeks, maybe four. I've got a couple of big ones in stock that would pass muster, and a bulletproof limo that the government often hires when minor heads of state are visiting the capital. I think the last crest we had to paint on the door was Uruguay, and the poor guy never even got to see the President – he ended up just getting twenty-five minutes with Warren Christopher.'

'But now for the hard part, Al. I need six outriders, riding police motorcycles, and all wearing the correct uniform.'

Al paused. 'That could take longer.'

'We haven't got any longer, Al. A month's going to be the outside for all of us.'

'It's not that easy, Tony. I can't exactly put an ad in the *Washington Post* asking for police –'

'Yes you can, Al. In a moment you'll all see why. Most of you round this table must be wondering why we've been honoured by the presence of Johnny Scasiatore, a man nominated for an Oscar for his direction of *The Honest Lawyer*.' What Cavalli didn't add was that since the police had found Johnny in bed with a twelve-year-old girl, the studios hadn't been in touch quite as frequently as in the past.

'I was beginning to wonder myself,' admitted Johnny.

The chief executive smiled. 'The truth is, you're the reason we'll be able to pull this whole plan off. Because you're going to direct the entire operation.'

'You're going to steal the Declaration of Independence and make a movie of it at the same time?' asked Johnny in disbelief. Cavalli waited for the laughter that broke out around the table to die down.

'Not exactly. But everyone in Washington on that day is going to believe that you are making a movie, not of us stealing the Declaration of Independence, but of the President visiting Congress. The fact that he drops into the National Archives on the way to the Capitol is something they won't ever need to know.'

'I'm lost already,' said Frank Piemonte, the team's lawyer. 'Can you take it a little slower?'

'Sure, Frank, because this is where you come in. I need a city permit to close down the route between the White

House and Congress for one hour on any day I choose in the last week in May. Deal direct with the city's motion picture and television office.'

'What reason do I give?' asked Piemonte.

'That Johnny Scasiatore, the distinguished director, wants to film the President of the United States on his way to the Senate to address a joint session of Congress.' Piemonte looked doubtful. 'Clint Eastwood managed it last year, so there's no reason why you shouldn't.'

'Then you'd better put $250,000 into the Fraternal Order of Police, Lodge No. 1,' suggested Piemonte. 'And the Mayor will probably expect the same amount for her re-election fund.'

'You can bribe any city official you know,' continued Tony, 'and I also want every member of the City Police Force on our books squared for the day – all they have to believe is that we're making a movie about the new President.'

'Do you have any idea what mounting an operation like this is likely to cost?' asked Johnny Scasiatore.

'Looking at the budget of your last film, and the return we made on our investment, I'd say yes,' replied Tony. 'And by the way, Al,' he added, turning his attention back to the old Teamster Union boss, 'sixty cops are due for retirement from the DCPD in April. You can employ as many of them as you need. Tell them it's a crowd scene and pay them double.' Al Calabrese added a note to his file.

'Now, the key to the operation's success,' continued Tony, 'is the half-block from the intersection of 7th Street and Pennsylvania Avenue to the delivery entrance of the National Archives.' He unfolded a large map of Washington and placed it in the centre of the table, then ran his finger along Constitution Avenue. 'Once they leave you, Johnny, it's for real.'

'But how do we get in and out of the Archives?'

'That's not your problem, Johnny. Your contribution ends when the six motorcycles and the Presidential motorcade turn right onto 7th Street. From then on, it's up to Gino.'

Until that moment, Gino Sartori, an ex-Marine who ran the best protection racket on the West Side, had not spoken. His lawyer had told him many times: 'Don't speak unless I tell you to.' His lawyer wasn't present, so he hadn't opened his mouth.

'Gino, you're going to supply me with the heavy brigade. I need eight Secret Service agents to act as the counter-assault team, preferably government-trained and well-educated. I only plan to be in the building for about twenty minutes, but we're going to have to be thinking on our feet for every second of that time. Debbie will continue to act as a secretary and Angelo will be dressed in naval uniform and carrying a small black case. I'll be there as the President's assistant, along with Dollar Bill as the President's physician.'

His father looked up, frowning. 'You're going to be inside the National Archives building when the document is switched?'

'Yes,' replied Tony firmly. 'I'll be the only person who knows every part of the plan, and I'm sure not watching this one from the sidewalk.'

'A question,' said Gino. 'If, and I only say if, I am able to supply the twenty or so people you need, tell me this: when we reach the National Archives, are they just going to open the doors, invite us in, and then hand over the Declaration of Independence?'

'Something like that,' replied Cavalli. 'My father taught me that the successful conclusion of any enterprise is always in the preparation. I still have one more surprise for you.' Once again he had their undivided attention. 'We have our own Special Assistant to the President in the White House. His name is Rex Butterworth, and he's on temporary assignment from the Department of Commerce for six months. He returns to his old job when the Clinton nominee has completed his contract in Little Rock and joins the President's staff. That's another reason why we have to go in May.'

'Convenient,' said Frank.

'Not particularly,' said Cavalli. 'It turns out that the President has forty-six Special Assistants at any one time, and when Clinton made his interest in commerce clear, Butterworth volunteered for the job. He's fixed a few overseas contracts for us in the past, but this will be the biggest thing he's done for us yet. For obvious reasons, it will also have to be his last assignment.'

'Can he be trusted?' asked Frank.

'He's been on the payroll for fifteen years, and his third wife is proving rather expensive.'

'Show me one who isn't,' said Al.

'Butterworth's looking for a big payday to get himself out of trouble, and this is it. And that brings me on to you, Mr Vicente, and your particular expertise as one of the biggest tour operators in Manhattan.'

'That's the legit side of my business,' replied the elderly man who sat on the right of the chairman, as befitted his oldest friend.

'Not for what I have in mind,' promised Tony. 'Once we have the Declaration in our possession, we'll need it kept out of sight for a few days and then smuggled abroad.'

'As long as no one realises it's been removed and I'm told well in advance where you want it delivered, that should be simple.'

'You'll get a week,' said Cavalli.

'I'd prefer two,' said Vicente, raising an eyebrow.

'No, Nick, you get a week,' the chief executive repeated.

'Can you give me a clue what distance it will have to travel?' Vicente asked, turning the pages of the file Tony had passed across to him.

'Several thousand miles. And as far as you're concerned it's COD, because if you fail to deliver, none of us gets paid.'

'That figures. But I'll still need to know how it has to be transported. For starters, will I have to keep the Declaration between two sheets of glass the whole time?'

'I don't know myself yet,' replied Cavalli, 'but I'm hoping you'll be able to roll it up and deposit it in a cylindrical tube of some kind. I'm having one specially made.'

'Does that explain why I've got several sheets of blank paper in my file?' asked Nick.

'Yes,' said Tony. 'Except those sheets aren't paper but parchment, each one of them 29¾ inches by 24¼ inches, the exact size of the Declaration of Independence.'

'So now all I've got to hope is that every customs agent and coastguard patrol won't be looking for it.'

'I want you to assume the whole world will be looking for it,' replied Cavalli. 'You aren't being paid this sort of money for doing a job I could handle with one call to Federal Express.'

'I thought you might say something like that,' said Nick. 'Still, I had the same problem when you wanted the Vermeer of Russborough stolen, and Irish Customs still haven't worked out how I got the painting out of the country.'

Cavalli smiled. 'So now we all know what's expected of us. And I think in future we should meet at least twice a week to start with, every Sunday at three o'clock and every Thursday at six, to make sure none of us falls behind schedule. One person out of synch and nobody else will be able to move.' Tony looked up and was greeted by nods of agreement.

It always fascinated Cavalli that organised crime needed to be as efficiently run as any public company if it hoped to show a dividend. 'So we'll meet again next Thursday at six?'

All five men nodded and made notes in their diaries.

'Gentlemen, you may now open the second of your two envelopes.' Once again, the five men ripped open their envelopes, and each pulled out a thick wad of thousand-dollar bills.

The lawyer began to count each note.

'Your down-payment,' Tony explained. 'Expenses will be met at the end of every week, receipts whenever possible. And, Johnny,' said Tony, turning to the director, 'this is not *Heaven's Gate* we're financing.' Scasiatore managed a smile.

'Thank you, gentlemen,' said Tony, rising. 'I look forward to seeing you all next Thursday at six o'clock.'

The five men rose and made their way to the door, each stopping to shake hands with Tony's father before he left. Tony accompanied them to their cars. When the last one had been driven away, he returned to find his father had moved to the study and was toying with a whisky while staring at the perfect copy of the Declaration that Dollar Bill had intended to destroy.

11

'CALDER MARSHALL, PLEASE.'

'The Archivist can't be interrupted right now. He's in a meeting. May I ask who's calling?'

'It's Rex Butterworth, Special Assistant to the President. Perhaps the Archivist would be kind enough to call me back when he's free. He'll find me at the White House.'

Rex Butterworth put the phone down without waiting to hear what usually happened once it was known the call had come from the White House: 'Oh, I feel sure I can interrupt him, Mr Butterworth, can you hold on for a moment?'

But that wasn't what Butterworth wanted. No, the Special Assistant needed Calder Marshall to phone back himself, because once he had gone through the White House switchboard, Marshall would be hooked. Butterworth also realised that, as one of forty-six Special Assistants to the President, and in his case only on temporary assignment, the switchboard might not even recognise his name. A quick visit to the little room that housed the White House telephone operators had dealt with that problem.

He drummed his fingers on the desk and gazed down with satisfaction at the file in front of him. One of the

President's two schedulers had been able to supply him with the information he needed. The file revealed that the Archivist had invited each of the last three Presidents – Bush, Reagan and Carter – to visit the National Archives, but due to 'pressing commitments' none of them had been able to find the time.

Butterworth was well aware that the President received, on average, 1,700 requests every week to attend some function or other. The latest letter from Mr Marshall, dated January 22nd 1993, had evoked the reply that although it was not possible for the President to accept his kind invitation at the present time, Mr Clinton hoped to have the opportunity to do so at some date in the future – the standard reply that about 1,699 requests in the weekly postbag were likely to receive.

But on this occasion, Mr Marshall's wish was about to be granted. Butterworth continued to drum his fingers on the desk as he wondered how long it would take Marshall to return his call. Less than two minutes would have been his guess. He allowed his mind to wander back over the events of the past week.

When Cavalli had first put the idea to him, he had laughed more loudly than any of the six men who had gathered round the table at 75th Street. But after studying the parchment for over an hour and still not being able to identify the mistake, and then later meeting with Lloyd Adams, he began to believe, like the other sceptics, that switching the Declaration might just be possible.

Over the years, Butterworth had served the Cavalli family well. Meetings had been arranged with politicians at a moment's notice, words were dropped in the ears of trade officials from someone thought to be well placed in Washington, and the odd piece of inside information had been passed on, ensuring that Butterworth's income was commensurate with his own high opinion of his true worth.

As he lay awake that night thinking about the proposition, he also came to the conclusion that Cavalli couldn't take the next step without him, and more important, his role in the deception would probably be obvious within minutes of the theft being discovered, in which case he could end up spending the rest of his life in Leavenworth. Against that possibility he had to weigh the fact that he was fifty-seven years old, had only three years to go before retirement, and a third wife who was suing him for a divorce he couldn't afford. Butterworth no longer dreamed of promotion. He was now simply trying to come to terms with the fact that he was probably going to have to spend the rest of his life alone, eking out some sort of existence on a meagre government pension.

Cavalli was also aware of these facts, and the offer of a million dollars – a hundred thousand the day he signed up, a further nine hundred thousand on the day the exchange took place – and a first-class ticket to any country on earth, almost convinced Butterworth that he should agree to Cavalli's proposition.

But it was Maria who tilted the balance in Cavalli's favour.

At a trade conference in Brazil the previous year, Butterworth had met a local girl who answered most of his questions during the day and the rest of them at night. He'd phoned her the morning after Cavalli's first approach. Maria seemed pleased to hear from him, a pleasure which became more vocal when she learned that he'd be leaving the service and, having come into 'a reasonable inheritance', was thinking of settling down somewhere abroad.

The President's Special Assistant joined the team the following day.

He had spent most of the hundred thousand dollars by the end of the week, clearing his debts and getting up to date with his first two wives' alimony. With only a few thousand left, there was now nothing to do but commit himself wholeheartedly to the plan. He didn't give a moment's thought to changing his mind, because he knew he could never hope to repay the money. He hadn't forgotten that the man he had replaced on Cavalli's payroll *had* once neglected to repay a far smaller sum after making certain promises. Once had been enough: Cavalli's father had had him buried under the World Trade Center when he'd failed to secure the promised contract for the building. A similar departure did not appeal to Butterworth.

The phone rang on Butterworth's desk, as he had predicted, in under two minutes, but he allowed it to continue ringing for some time before he picked it up. His temporary secretary announced that there was a Mr Marshall on the line and asked if he wanted to take the call.

'Yes, thank you, Miss Daniels.'

'Mr Butterworth?' enquired a voice.

'Speaking.'

'This is Calder Marshall over at the National Archives. I understand you phoned while I was in a meeting. Sorry I wasn't available.'

'No problem, Mr Marshall. It's just that I wondered if it would be possible for you to drop by to the White House. There's a private matter I'd like to discuss with you.'

'Of course, Mr Butterworth. What time would be convenient?'

'I'm up to my eyes the rest of this week,' Butterworth

said, looking down at the blank pages in his diary, 'but the President's away at the beginning of next week, so perhaps we could schedule something for then?'

There was a pause which Butterworth assumed meant Marshall was checking his diary. 'Would Tuesday, 10 a.m. suit you?' the Archivist eventually asked.

'Let me check my other diary,' said Butterworth, staring into space. 'Yes, that looks fine. I have another appointment at 10.30, but I'm confident we'll have covered everything I need to go over with you by then. Perhaps you would be kind enough to come to the Pennsylvania Avenue entrance of the Old Executive Office building. There'll be someone there to meet you and after you've cleared security they'll bring you up to my office.'

'The Pennsylvania Avenue entrance,' said Marshall. 'Of course.'

'Thank you, Mr Marshall. I look forward to seeing you next Tuesday at ten o'clock,' said Butterworth before replacing the receiver.

The President's Special Assistant smiled as he dialled Cavalli's private number.

Scott promised Dexter Hutchins he would be around when Dexter's son came to Yale for his admission interview.

'He's allowing me to tag along,' said Dexter, 'which will give me a chance to bring you up to date on our little problem with the Israelis. And I may even have found something to tempt you.'

'Dexter, if you're hoping that I'll get your son into Yale in exchange for a field job, I think I ought to let you know I have absolutely no influence with the Admissions Office.' Dexter's laugh crackled down the phone. 'But I'll still be happy to show you both over the place and give the boy any help I can.'

Dexter Jr could not have turned out to be more like his father: five foot ten, heavily built, a perpetual five o'clock shadow and the same habit of calling everything that moved 'sir'. When, after an hour strolling round the grounds, he left his father for his interview with the head of the Admissions Office, the Professor of Constitutional Law took the Deputy Director of the CIA back to his rooms.

Even before the door was closed, Dexter had lit up a cigar. After a few puffs he said, 'Have you been able to make any sense of the coded message sent by our operative in Beirut?'

'Only that everyone who joins the intelligence community has some strange personal reason for wanting to do so. In my case, it's because of my father and a Boy Scout determination to balance the books morally. In the case of Hannah Kopec, Saddam Hussein wipes out her family, so she immediately offers her talents to Mossad. With that powerful a motive, I wouldn't want to cross her path.'

'But that's exactly what I'm hoping you will do,' said Dexter. 'You're always saying you want to be tested in the field. Well, this could be your opportunity.'

'Am I hearing you properly?'

'Yale's spring term is about to end, right?'

'Yes. But that doesn't mean I don't have a lot of work to do.'

'Oh, I see. A happy amateur, twelve times a year when it suits you, but the moment you might have to get your hands dirty . . .'

'I didn't say that.'

'Well then, hear me out. First, we know Hannah Kopec was one of eight girls selected from a hundred to go to London for six months to study Arabic. This followed a year's intensive physical course at Herzliyah, where they covered the usual self-defence, fieldcraft and surveillance work. The reports on her were excellent. Second, a chat with her host's wife at Sainsbury's in Camden Town, wherever the hell that is, and we discover that she left suddenly, despite the fact that she was almost certainly meant to return to Israel as part of the team that was working on the assassination of Saddam. That's when we lose sight of her. Then we get one of those breaks that only come from good detective work. One of our agents who works at Heathrow spots her in duty free, when she's buying some cheap perfume.

'After she boards a plane for the Lebanon he phones our man in Beirut, who shadows her from the moment she arrives. Not that easy, I might add. We lost her for several hours. Then, out of nowhere, up she pops again, but this time as Karima Saib, who Baghdad are under the impression is on her way to Paris as second secretary to the Ambassador. Meanwhile, the real Miss Saib is abducted at Beirut airport and is now being held at a safe house somewhere across the border on the outskirts of Tel Aviv.'

'Where's all this leading, Dexter?'

'Patience, Professor,' he said, relighting the stub of his cigar, which hadn't been glowing for several minutes. 'Not all of us are born with your academic acuity.'

'Get on with it,' said Scott with a smile, 'because my academic acuity hasn't been stretched yet.'

'Now I come to a bit you're going to enjoy. Hannah Kopec has not been placed in the Iraqi Interest Section of the Jordanian Embassy in Paris to spy.'

'Then why bother to put her there in the first place? In any case, how can you be certain?' asked Scott.

'Because the Mossad agent in Paris – how shall I put

it? – does a little work for us on the side, and he hasn't even been informed of her existence.'

Scott scowled. 'So why *has* the girl been placed in the embassy?'

'We don't know, but we sure as hell would like to find out. We think Rabin can't give the go-ahead to strike Saddam while Kopec is still in France, so the least we need to know is when she's expected back in Israel. And that's where you come in.'

'But we must have a man in Paris already.'

'Several, actually, but every one of them is known by Mossad at a hundred paces, and, I suspect, even by the Iraqis at ten. So, if Hannah Kopec is in Paris without the Mossad sleeper knowing, I'd like you to be in Paris without our people knowing. That is, if you feel you can spare the time away from Susan Anderson.'

'She broke away from me the day her boyfriend returned from his conference. I don't know what it is I do to women. She called me last week to tell me they're getting married next month.'

'All the more reason for you to go to Paris.'

'On a wild goose chase.'

'This goose may just be about to lay us a golden egg, and in any case, I don't want to read about another brilliant Israeli coup on the front page of the *New York Times* and then have to explain to the President why the CIA knew nothing about it.'

'But where would I even start?'

'In your own time, you try to make contact with her. Tell her you're the Mossad agent in Paris.'

'But she would never believe –'

'Why not? She doesn't know who the agent is, only that there is one. Scott, I need to know –'

The door swung open and Dexter Jr came in.

'How did it go?' asked his father. The young man

walked across the room and slumped into an armchair, but did not utter a word.

'That bad, eh son?'

'Mr Marshall, how nice to meet you,' said Butterworth, thrusting out his hand to greet the Archivist of the United States.

'It's nice to meet you, too, Mr Butterworth,' Calder Marshall replied nervously.

'Good of you to find the time to come over,' said Butterworth. 'Do have a seat.'

Butterworth had booked the Roosevelt Room in the West Wing for their meeting. It had taken a lot of persuading of a particularly officious secretary who knew Mr Butterworth's station in life only too well. She reluctantly agreed to release the room for thirty minutes, and then only because he was seeing the Archivist of the United States. She also agreed to his second request, as the President would be out of town that day. The Special Assistant had placed himself at the top of a table that usually seated twenty-four, and beckoned Mr Marshall to be seated on his right, facing Tade Stykal's portrait of *Theodore Roosevelt on Horseback*.

The Archivist must have been a shade over six foot, and as thin as most women half his age would have liked to be. He was almost bald except for a semicircle of grey tufts around the base of his skull. He wore an ill-fitting suit that looked as if it normally experienced outings only on a Sunday morning. From his file, Butterworth knew the Archivist was younger than himself, but he vainly felt that if they had been seen together, no one would have believed it.

He must have been born middle-aged, thought Butterworth, but the Special Assistant had no such disparaging thoughts about the quality of the man's mind. After a *magna cum laude* at Duke University, Marshall had written a book on the history of the Bill of Rights that was now considered to be the standard text for every undergraduate studying American history. It had made him a small fortune – not that one could have guessed it by the way he dressed, thought Butterworth.

On the table in front of him was a file stamped 'Confidential', and above that the name 'Calder Marshall' in bold letters. Despite the fact that the Archivist was wearing horn-rimmed glasses with thick lenses, Butterworth felt he could hardly have missed it.

Butterworth paused before he began a speech he'd prepared every bit as assiduously as the President had his inauguration address. Marshall sat, fingers intertwined, nervously waiting for Butterworth to proceed.

'You have, over the past sixteen years,' began the Special Assistant, 'made several requests for the President to visit the National Archives.' Butterworth was pleased to observe that Marshall was looking hopeful. 'And, indeed, this particular President wishes to accept your invitation.' Mr Marshall's smile broadened. 'To that end, in our weekly meeting, President Clinton asked me to convey a private message to you, which he hoped you would understand must be in the strictest confidence.'

'In the strictest confidence. Of course.'

'The President felt sure he could rely on your discretion, Mr Marshall. So, I feel I can let you know that we're trying to clear some time during the last week of this month for him to visit the Archives, but nothing, as yet, has been scheduled.'

'Nothing, as yet, has been scheduled. Of course.'

'President Clinton has also requested that it be a

strictly private visit, which would not be open to the public or the press.'

'Not be open to the press. Of course.'

'After the explosion at the World Trade Center, one can't be too careful.'

'Can't be too careful. Of course.'

'And I would be obliged if you did not discuss any aspect of the visit with your staff, however senior, until we are able to confirm a definite date. These things have a habit of getting out and then, for security reasons, the visit might have to be cancelled.'

'Have to be cancelled. Of course. But if it's to be a private visit,' said the Archivist, 'is there anything the President particularly wants to see, or will it just be the standard tour of the building?'

'I'm glad you asked that question,' said Mr Butterworth, opening the file in front of him. 'The President has made one particular request, apart from which he will be in your hands.'

'In my hands. Of course.'

'He wants to see the Declaration of Independence.'

'The Declaration of Independence. That's easy enough.'

'That is not the request,' said Butterworth.

'Not the request?'

'No. The President wishes to see the Declaration, but not as he saw it when he was a freshman at Georgetown, under a thick pane of glass. He wishes the frame to be removed so he can study the parchment itself. He hopes you will grant this request, if only for a few moments.'

This time the Archivist did not immediately say 'Of course.' Instead he said, 'Most unusual,' and added, 'Hopes I would grant him this request, if only for a few moments.' There was a long pause before he said, 'I'm sure that will be possible, of course.'

'Thank you,' said Mr Butterworth, trying not to sound too relieved. 'I know the President will be most appreciative. And, if I could impress on you again, not a word until we've been able to confirm the date.'

Butterworth rose and glanced at the long-case clock at the far end of the room. The meeting had taken twenty-two minutes. He would still be able to escape from the conference room before he was thrown out by the officious woman from Scheduling.

The Special Assistant to the President guided his guest towards the door.

'The President wondered if you would like to see the Oval Office while you're here?'

'The Oval Office. Of course, of course.'

12

HAMID AL OBAYDI was left alone in the centre of the room. After two of the four guards had stripped him naked, the other two had expertly checked every stitch of his clothing for anything that might endanger the life of their President.

On a nod from the man who appeared to be the chief guard, a side door opened and a doctor entered the room, followed by an orderly who carried a chair in one hand and a rubber glove in the other. The chair was placed behind Al Obaydi, and he was invited to sit. He did so. The doctor first checked his nails and ears before instructing him to open his mouth wide while he tapped every tooth with a spatula. He then placed a clamp in his jaw so that it opened even wider, which allowed him to look into every crevice. Satisfied, he removed the clamp. He then asked Al Obaydi to stand up, turn round, place his legs straight and wide while bending over until his hands touched the seat of the chair. Al Obaydi heard the rubber glove being placed on the doctor's hand and felt a sudden burst of pain as two fingers were thrust up his rectum. He cried out and the guards facing him began to laugh. The fingers were extracted just as abruptly, repeating the jab of pain a second time.

'Thank you, Deputy Ambassador,' said the doctor, as if he had just checked Al Obaydi's temperature for a mild dose of 'flu. 'You can get dressed now.' Al Obaydi knelt down and picked up his pants as the doctor and the orderly left the room.

As he dressed, Al Obaydi couldn't help wondering if each member of the Security Council went through the same humiliation every time Saddam called a meeting of the Revolutionary Command Council.

The order to return to Baghdad to give Sayedi an update on the latest position, as the Ambassador to the UN had described the summons, filled Al Obaydi with considerable apprehension, despite the fact that following his most recent meeting with Cavalli he felt he had the answers to any questions the President might put to him.

Once Al Obaydi had reached Baghdad after a seemingly endless journey through Jordan – direct flights having been suspended as part of the UN sanctions – he hadn't been allowed to rest or even given the chance to change his clothes. He'd been driven direct to Ba'ath headquarters in a black Mercedes.

When Al Obaydi had finished dressing, he checked himself in a small mirror on the wall. His apparel was, on this occasion, modest compared with the outfits he'd left in his apartment in New York: Saks Fifth Avenue suits, Valentino sweaters, Church's shoes and a solid gold Cartier watch. All this had been rejected in favour of the one set of cheap Arab clothing he retained in the bottom drawer of his wardrobe in Manhattan.

When Al Obaydi turned away from the mirror, one of the guards beckoned him to follow as the door at the end of the room opened for the first time. The contrast to the bare, almost barrack-room surroundings of the examination room took him by surprise. A thickly carpeted, ornately painted corridor was well lit by chandeliers that hung every few paces.

The Deputy Ambassador followed the guard down the corridor, becoming more aware with each step of the massive gold-painted door that loomed up ahead of him. But when he was only a few paces away, the guard opened a side door and ushered him into an ante-room that echoed the opulence of the corridor.

Al Obaydi was left alone in the room, but no sooner had he taken a seat on the large sofa than the door opened again. Al Obaydi jumped to his feet only to see a girl enter carrying a tray, in the centre of which was a small cup of Turkish coffee.

She placed the coffee on a table beside the sofa, bowed and left as silently as she had come. Al Obaydi toyed with the cup, aware that he had fallen into the Western habit of preferring cappuccino. He drank the muddy black liquid simply out of a nervous desire to be doing something.

An hour passed slowly: he became increasingly nervous, with nothing in the room to read and only a massive portrait of Saddam Hussein to stare at. Al Obaydi spent the time going over every detail of what Cavalli had told him, wishing he could refer to the file in his small attaché case, which the guards had whisked away long before he'd reached the examination room.

During the second hour, his confidence began to drain away. During the third, he started to wonder if he would ever get out of the building alive.

Then suddenly the door swung open and Al Obaydi recognised the red-and-yellow flash on the uniform of one of Saddam's Presidential Guards: the Hemaya.

'The President will see you now,' was all the young officer said, and Al Obaydi rose and followed him quickly down the corridor towards the gold-painted door.

The officer knocked, opened the massive door and stood on one side to allow the Deputy Ambassador to join a full meeting of the Revolutionary Command Council.

Al Obaydi stood and waited, like a prisoner in the dock hoping to be told by the judge that he might at least be allowed to sit. He remained standing, well aware that no one ever shook hands with the President unless invited to do so. He stared round at the twelve-man council, noticing that only two, the Prime Minister, Tariq Aziz, and the State Prosecutor, Nakir Farrar, were wearing suits. The other ten members were dressed in full military uniform but did not wear sidearms. The only hand gun, other than those worn by General Hamil, the Commander of the Presidential Guard, and the two armed soldiers directly behind Saddam, was on the table in front of the President, placed where other heads of state would have had a memo pad.

Al Obaydi became painfully aware that the President's eyes had never left him from the moment he had entered the room. Saddam waved his Cohiba cigar at the Deputy Ambassador to indicate that he should take the vacant seat at the opposite end of the table.

The Foreign Minister looked towards the President, who nodded. He then turned his attention to the man who sat nervously in the far chair.

'This, Mr President, as you know, is Hamid Al Obaydi, our Deputy Ambassador at the United Nations, whom you honoured with the responsibility of carrying out your orders to steal the Declaration of Independence from the American infidels. On your instructions, he has returned to Baghdad to inform you, in person, of what progress he has made. I have not had an opportunity to speak to him, Mr President, so you will forgive me if I appear, like yourself, to be a seeker after information.'

Saddam waved his cigar again to let the Foreign Minister know that he should get on with it.

'Perhaps I could start, Deputy Ambassador' – Al Obaydi was surprised by such a formal address, as their two families had known each other for generations, but he accepted that to show friendship of any kind in front of Saddam was tantamount to an admission of conspiracy – 'by asking you to bring us all up to date on the President's imaginative scheme.'

'Thank you, Foreign Minister,' replied Al Obaydi, as if he had never met the man before. He turned back to face Saddam, whose black eyes remained fixed on him.

'May I begin, Mr President, by saying what an honour it has been to be entrusted with this task, especially remembering the idea had emanated from Your Excellency personally.' Every member of the Council was now concentrating his attention on the Deputy Ambassador, but Al Obaydi noticed that from time to time each of them would glance in Saddam's direction to see how he was reacting.

'I am happy to be able to report that the team led by Mr Antonio Cavalli . . .'

Saddam raised a hand and looked towards the State Prosecutor, who opened a thick file in front of him.

Nakir Farrar, the State Prosecutor, was feared second only to Saddam in the Iraqi regime. Everyone knew of his reputation. A first-class honours degree in jurisprudence at Oxford, President of the Union, and a bencher at Lincoln's Inn. That was where Al Obaydi had first come across him. Not that Farrar had ever acknowledged his existence. He had been tipped to be the first QC Iraq had ever produced. But then came the invasion of the Nineteenth Province and the British expelled the high-flyer, despite several appeals from people in high places. Farrar returned to a city he had deserted at the age of eleven, and immediately offered his remarkable talent for Saddam Hussein's personal use. Within a year

Saddam had appointed him State Prosecutor. A title, it was rumoured, he had selected himself.

'Cavalli is a New York criminal, Mr President, who, because he has a law degree and heads a private legal practice, creates a legitimate front for such an operation.' Saddam nodded and turned his attention back to Al Obaydi.

'Mr Cavalli has completed the preparation stage and his team is now ready to carry out the President's orders.'

'Do we have a date yet?' asked Farrar.

'Yes, State Prosecutor. May 25th. Clinton has a full day's schedule at the White House, with his speechwriters in the morning, and his wife's health-policy task unit in the afternoon, and he' – the Iraqi Ambassador to the UN had warned Al Obaydi never to refer to Clinton as 'the President' – 'will therefore not be involved in any public engagements that day, which would have made our task impossible.'

'And tell me, Deputy Ambassador,' said the State Prosecutor, 'did Mr Cavalli's lawyer succeed in getting a permit to close down the road between the White House and the National Archives during the time when Clinton will be involved in these internal meetings?'

'No, State Prosecutor, he did not,' came back Al Obaydi's reply. 'The Mayor's Office did, however, grant a permit for filming to take place on Pennsylvania Avenue from 13th Street east. But the road can only be closed for forty-five minutes. It seems this Mayor was not as easy to convince as her predecessor.'

A few members of the Council looked puzzled. 'Not as easy to convince?' asked the Foreign Minister.

'Perhaps "persuade" would be a better word.'

'And what form did this persuasion take?' asked General Hamil, who sat on the right of the President and knew only one form of persuasion.

'A $250,000 contribution to her re-election fund.'

Saddam began to laugh, so the others round the table followed suit.

'And the Archivist, is he still convinced it's Clinton who will be visiting him?' asked the State Prosecutor.

'Yes, he is,' said Al Obaydi. 'Just before I flew out Cavalli had taken eight of his own men over the building posing as a Secret Service preliminary reconnaissance team, carrying out a site survey. The Archivist could not have been more co-operative, and Cavalli was given enough time to check out everything. That exercise should make the switching of the Declaration on May 25th far easier for him.'

'But if, and I only say if, they succeed in getting the original out, have they made arrangements for passing the document over to you?' asked the State Prosecutor.

'Yes,' replied Al Obaydi confidently. 'I understand that the President wants the document to be delivered to Barazan Al-Tikriti, our venerated Ambassador to the United Nations in Geneva. When he has received the parchment, and not before, I will authorise the final payment.'

The President nodded his approval. After all, the venerated Ambassador in Geneva was his half-brother. The State Prosecutor continued his questioning.

'But how can we be sure that what is handed to us will be the original, and not just a first-class copy?' he demanded. 'What's to prevent them from making a show of walking in and out of the National Archives, but not actually switching the documents?'

A smile appeared on Al Obaydi's lips for the first time. 'I took the precaution, State Prosecutor, of demanding such proof,' he replied. 'When the fake replaces the original, it will continue to be displayed for the general public to view. You can be assured that I shall be among the general public.'

'But you have not answered my question,' said the State Prosecutor sharply. 'How will you know ours is the original?'

'Because on the original document penned by Timothy Matlock, there is a simple spelling mistake, which has been corrected on the copy executed by Bill O'Reilly.'

The State Prosecutor reluctantly sat back in his chair when his master raised a hand.

'Another criminal, Excellency,' explained the Foreign Minister. 'This time a forger, who has been responsible for making the copy of the document.'

'So,' said the State Prosecutor, leaning forward once again, 'if the incorrect spelling is still on the document displayed in the National Archives on May 25th, you will know we have a fake and will not pay out another cent. Is that right?'

'Yes, State Prosecutor,' said Al Obaydi.

'Which word on the original has been incorrectly spelt?' demanded the State Prosecutor.

When the Deputy Ambassador told him, all Nakir Farrar said was, 'How appropriate,' and then closed the file in front of him.

'However, it will still be necessary for me to have the final payment to hand,' continued Al Obaydi, 'should I be satisfied that they have carried out their part of the bargain, and that we are in possession of the original parchment.'

The Foreign Minister looked towards Saddam who, again, nodded.

'It will be in place by May 25th,' said the Foreign Minister. 'I would like the opportunity to go over some of the details with you before your return to New York.

As long as that meets with the President's approval?'

Saddam waved a hand to indicate that such a request was not important to him. His eyes remained fixed on Al Obaydi. The Deputy Ambassador wasn't sure if he was meant to leave or await further questioning. He favoured caution, and remained seated and silent. It was some time before anyone spoke.

'You must be curious, Hamid, about why I place such importance on this scrap of useless paper.' As the Deputy Ambassador had never met the President before, he was surprised to be called by his first name.

'It is not for me to question Your Excellency's reasoning,' replied Al Obaydi.

'Nevertheless,' continued Saddam, 'you would be less than human not to wonder why I am willing to spend one hundred million dollars and at the same time risk international embarrassment should you fail.'

Al Obaydi noted the word 'you' with some discomfort.

'I would be fascinated to know, Sayedi, if you felt able to confide in such an unworthy soul.'

Twelve members of the Council looked towards the President to gauge his reaction to the Deputy Ambassador's comment. Al Obaydi felt immediately that he had gone too far. He sat, terrified, during what felt like the longest silence in his life.

'Then I shall let you share my secret, Hamid,' said Saddam, his black eyes boring into the Deputy Ambassador. 'When I captured the Nineteenth Province for my beloved people, I found myself at war not with the traitors we had invaded, but the combined strength of the Western world – and that despite an agreement previously reached with the American Ambassador. "Why?" I had to ask, when everyone knew that Kuwait was run by a few corrupt families who had little interest in the welfare of their own people. I'll tell you why. In one word, oil. Had it been coffee beans that the Nineteenth Province was exporting, you would never have seen as much as an American rowing boat armed with a catapult enter the Gulf.'

The Foreign Minister smiled and nodded.

'And who were the leaders who ganged up against me? Thatcher, Gorbachev and Bush. That was less than three years ago. And what has happened to them since? Thatcher was removed by a coup carried out by her own supporters; Gorbachev was deposed by a man he himself had sacked only a year before and whose own position now looks unstable; Bush suffered a humiliating defeat at the hands of the American people. While I remain the Supreme Leader and President of my country.'

There followed a burst of applause which died instantly when Saddam began speaking again.

'That, of course, would be ample reward for most people. But not me, Hamid. Because Bush's place has been taken by this man Clinton, who has learned nothing from his predecessor's mistakes, and who now also wishes to challenge my supremacy. But this time it is my intention to humiliate him along with the American infidels long before they are given the opportunity to do so. And I shall go about this in such a way that will make it impossible for Clinton to recover any credibility in his lifetime. I intend to make Clinton and the American people the laughing stock of the world.'

The heads continued nodding.

'You have already witnessed my ability to turn the greed of their own people into a willingness to steal the most cherished document in their nation's history. And you, Hamid, are the chosen vessel to ensure that my genius will be acknowledged.' Al Obaydi lowered his head.

'Once I am in possession of the Declaration I shall

wait patiently until the fourth of July, when the whole of America will be spending a peaceful Sunday celebrating Independence Day.' No one in the room uttered a word while the President paused.

'I shall also celebrate Independence Day, not in Washington or New York, but in Tahrir Square, surrounded by my beloved people. When I, Saddam Hussein, President of Iraq, will in front of the entire world's media burn to a cinder the American Declaration of Independence.'

Hannah lay awake in her barrack-room bed, feeling not unlike the child she had been some thirteen years before when she had spent her first night at boarding school.

She had collected Karima Saib's cases from the carousel at Charles de Gaulle airport, dreading what she might find inside them.

A driver had picked her up as promised, but as he had been unwilling to make any attempt at conversation she had no idea what to expect when they pulled up outside the Jordanian Embassy. Hannah was surprised by its size.

The beautiful old house which was set back from the boulevard Maurice Barrès was formerly the home of the late Aga Khan. The Iraqi annexe had been allocated two complete floors, tangible proof that the Jordanians did not wish to get on the wrong side of Saddam.

On entering the annexe to the embassy, the first person she met was Abdul Kanuk, the Chief Administrator. He certainly didn't look like a diplomat, and when he opened his mouth she realised he wasn't. Kanuk informed her that the Ambassador and his senior secretary Muna Ahmed were tied up in meetings and that she was to unpack and then wait in her room until called for.

The cramped accommodation was just about large enough for a bed and two suitcases, and might, she thought, have been a store room before the Iraqi delegation moved in. When she eventually forced open Karima Saib's suitcase she quickly discovered that the only things that fitted from her wardrobe were her shoes. Hannah didn't know whether to be relieved, because of Saib's taste, or anxious about how little of her own she had to wear.

Muna Ahmed, the senior secretary, joined her in the kitchen for supper later that evening. It seemed that secretaries in the embassy were treated on the same level as servants. Hannah managed to convince Muna that it was better than she had expected, especially since they were only able to use the annexe to the Jordanian Embassy. Muna explained that as far as the Corps Diplomatique of France was concerned, the Iraqi Ambassador was to be treated only as a Head of Interest Section, although they were to address him at all times as 'Your Excellency' or 'Ambassador'.

During the first few days in her new job, Hannah sat in the room next to the Ambassador's on the other side of Muna's desk. She spent most of her time twiddling her fingers. Hannah quickly discovered that no one took much interest in her as long as she completed any work the Ambassador had left for her on his dictating machine. In fact that soon became Hannah's biggest problem, as she had to slow down in order to make Muna look more efficient. The only thing Hannah ever forgot was to keep wearing her see-through glasses.

In the evenings, over supper in the kitchen, Hannah learned from Muna everything that was expected of an Iraqi woman abroad, including how to avoid the advances of Abdul Kanuk, the Chief Administrator. By the second week, her learning curve had already slowed down, and increasingly Hannah found the Ambassador was relying on her skills. She tried not to show too much initiative.

Once they had finished their work, Hannah and Muna were expected to remain indoors, and were not allowed to leave the building at night unless accompanied by the Chief Administrator, a prospect that didn't tempt either of them. As Muna had no interest in music, the theatre or even going to cafés, she was happy to pass the time in her room reading the speeches of Saddam Hussein.

As the days slowly passed Hannah began to hope that the Mossad agent in Paris would contact her so that she could be pulled out and sent back to Israel to prepare for her mission – not that she had any clue who the Mossad agent was. She wondered if they had one in the embassy. Alone in her room, she often speculated. The driver? Too slow. The gardener? Too dumb. The cook? Certainly possible – the food was bad enough to believe it was her second job. Abdul Kanuk, the Chief Administrator? Hardly, since, as he pointed out at least three times a day, he was a cousin of Barazan Al-Tikriti, Saddam Hussein's half-brother and the UN Ambassador in Geneva. Kanuk was also the biggest gossip in the embassy, and supplied Hannah with more information about Saddam Hussein and his entourage in one night than the Ambassador managed in a week. In truth, the Ambassador rarely spoke of Sayedi in her presence, and when he did he was always guarded and respectful.

It was during the second week that Hannah was introduced to the Ambassador's wife. Hannah quickly discovered that she was fiercely independent, partly because she was half Turkish, and didn't consider that it was necessarily her duty always to stay inside the embassy compound. She did things that were thought extreme by Iraqi standards, like accompanying her husband to cocktail parties, and she had even been known to pour herself a drink without waiting to be asked. She also went – which was more important for Hannah – twice a week to swim at the nearby public baths in the boulevard Lannes. The Ambassador agreed, after a little persuasion, that it would be acceptable for the new secretary to accompany his wife.

Scott arrived in Paris on a Sunday. He had been given a key to a small flat on the avenue de Messine, and they had opened an account for him at the Société Générale on boulevard Haussmann in the name of Simon Rosenthal.

He was to telephone or fax Langley only after he had located the Mossad agent. No other operative had been informed of his existence, and he had been told not to make contact with any field agent he had worked with in the past who was now stationed in Europe.

Scott spent the first two days discovering the nine places from which he could observe the front door of the Jordanian Embassy without being seen by anyone in the building.

By the end of a week he had begun to realise for the first time what agents really meant by the expression 'hours of solitude'. He even started to miss some of his students.

He developed a routine. Every morning before breakfast he would run for five miles in the Parc Monceau, before he began the morning shift. Every evening he would spend two hours in a gym on rue de Berne before cooking supper, which he ate alone in his flat.

Scott began to despair of the Mossad agent ever leaving the embassy compound, and to wonder if Miss Kopec was even in there. The Ambassador's wife seemed to be the only woman to come and go as she pleased.

And then without warning, on the Tuesday of his second week, someone else left the building accompanying the Ambassador's wife. Was it Hannah Kopec? He only caught a fleeting glimpse as the car sped away.

He followed the chauffeur-driven Mercedes, always remaining at an angle that would make it difficult for the Ambassador's driver to spot him in his rear-view mirror. The two women were dropped outside the swimming pool on the boulevard Lannes. He watched them get out of the car. In the photographs he had been shown at Langley, Hannah Kopec had had long black hair. The hair was now cropped, but it was unquestionably her.

Scott drove a hundred yards further down the road, turned right and parked the car. He walked back, entered the building and purchased a spectator's ticket at a cost of two francs. He strolled up to the balcony which overlooked the pool. By the time he had selected an obscure seat in the gallery the Mossad agent was already swimming up and down. It only took moments for Scott to realise how fit she was, even if the Iraqi version of a swimsuit wasn't all that alluring. Her pace slowed when the Ambassador's wife appeared at the edge of the pool, after which she ventured only an occasional dog-paddle from one side to the other.

Some forty minutes later, when the Ambassador's wife left the pool, Kopec immediately quickened her pace, covering each length in under a minute. When she had swum ten lengths she pulled herself out of the water and disappeared towards the changing room.

Scott returned to his car, and when the two women reappeared he allowed the Mercedes to overtake him before following them back to the embassy.

Later that night he faxed Dexter Hutchins at Langley

to let him know he had seen her, and would now try to make contact.

The following morning, he bought a pair of swimming trunks.

It was on the Thursday that Hannah first noticed him. He was doing the crawl at a steady rate, completing each length in about forty seconds, and looked as if he might once have been a useful athlete. She tried to keep up with his pace but could only manage five lengths before he stretched away. She watched him pull himself out of the water after another dozen lengths and head off in the direction of the men's changing room.

On Monday morning the following week, the Ambassador's wife informed Hannah that she wouldn't be able to go for their usual swim the next day as she would be accompanying the Ambassador on his visit to Saddam Hussein's half-brother in Geneva. Hannah had already been told about the trip by the Chief Administrator, who seemed to know even the finest details.

'I can't think why you haven't been invited to join the Ambassador as well,' said the cook that evening. The Chief Administrator was silenced for about two minutes until Muna left the kitchen to go to her room. Then he revealed a piece of information that disturbed Hannah.

The following day Hannah was given permission to go swimming by herself. She was glad to have an excuse to get out of the building, especially as Kanuk was in charge of the delegation in the Ambassador's absence. He had taken the Mercedes for himself, so she made her own way to the boulevard Lannes by Métro. She was disappointed to find that the man who swam so well was nowhere to be seen when she started off on her thirty lengths. Once she had completed her exercise she clung onto the side, tired and slightly out of breath. Suddenly, she was aware that he was swimming towards her in the outside lane. When he touched the end he turned smoothly and said distinctly, 'Don't move, Hannah, I'll be back.'

Hannah assumed he must be someone who remembered her from her days as a model, and her immediate reaction was to make a run for it. But she continued to tread water as she waited for him to return, thinking he might perhaps be the Mossad agent Kratz had referred to.

She watched him swimming towards her, and became more apprehensive with each stroke. When he touched the edge he came to a sudden halt and asked, 'Are you alone?'

'Yes,' she replied.

'I thought I couldn't see the Ambassador's wife. She usually displaces a great deal of water without much forward motion. By the way, I'm Simon Rosenthal. Colonel Kratz instructed me to make contact. I have a message for you.'

Hannah felt stupid shaking hands with the man while they were both clinging onto the edge of the pool.

'Do you know the avenue Bugeaud?'

'Yes,' she replied.

'Good. See you at the Bar de la Porte Dauphine in fifteen minutes.'

He pulled himself out of the pool in one movement and disappeared in the direction of the men's changing room before she had a chance to reply.

A little over fifteen minutes later Hannah walked into the Bar de la Porte Dauphine. She searched around the room and almost missed him perched behind one of the high-backed wooden chairs directly below a large, colourful mural.

He rose to greet her and then ordered another coffee.

He warned her that they must spend only a few minutes together, because she ought to return to the embassy without delay. As she sipped the first real coffee she had tasted in weeks, Hannah took a closer look at him, and began to recall what it was like just to enjoy a drink with someone interesting. His next sentence snapped her back into the real world.

'Kratz plans to pull you out of Paris in the near future.'

'Any particular reason?' she asked.

'The date of the Baghdad operation has been settled.'

'Thank God,' said Hannah.

'Why do you say that?' asked Scott, risking his first question.

'The Ambassador expects to be called back to Baghdad to take up a new post. He intends to ask me to go with him,' replied Hannah. 'Or that's what the Chief Administrator is telling everyone, except Muna.'

'I'll warn Kratz.'

'By the way, Simon, I've picked up two or three scraps of information that Kratz might find useful.'

He nodded and listened as Hannah began to give him details of the internal organisation of the embassy, and of the comings and goings of diplomats and businessmen who publicly spoke out against Saddam while at the same time trying to close deals with him. After a few minutes he stopped her and said, 'You'd better leave now. They might begin to miss you. I'll try and arrange another meeting whenever it's possible,' he found himself adding.

She smiled, rose from the table and left, without looking back.

Later that evening, Scott sent a coded message to Dexter Hutchins in Virginia to let him know that he had made contact with Hannah Kopec.

A fax came back an hour later with only one instruction.

13

ON MAY 25TH 1993, the sun rose over the Capitol a few minutes after five. Its rays crept along the White House lawn and minutes later seeped unnoticed into the Oval Office. A few hundred yards away, Cavalli was slapping his hands behind his back.

Cavalli had spent the previous day in Washington, checking the finer details for what felt like the hundredth time. He had to assume that something must go wrong and, whatever it turned out to be, it would automatically become his responsibility.

Johnny Scasiatore walked over and handed Cavalli a steaming mug of coffee.

'I had no idea it could be this cold in Washington,' Cavalli said to Johnny, who was wearing a sheepskin jacket.

'It's cold at this time of the morning almost everywhere in the world,' replied Johnny. 'Ask any film director.'

'And do you really need six hours to get ready for three minutes of filming?' Cavalli asked incredulously.

'Two hours' preparation for a minute's work is the standard rule. And don't forget, we'll have to run through this particular scene twice, in somewhat unusual circumstances.'

Cavalli stood on the corner of 13th Street and

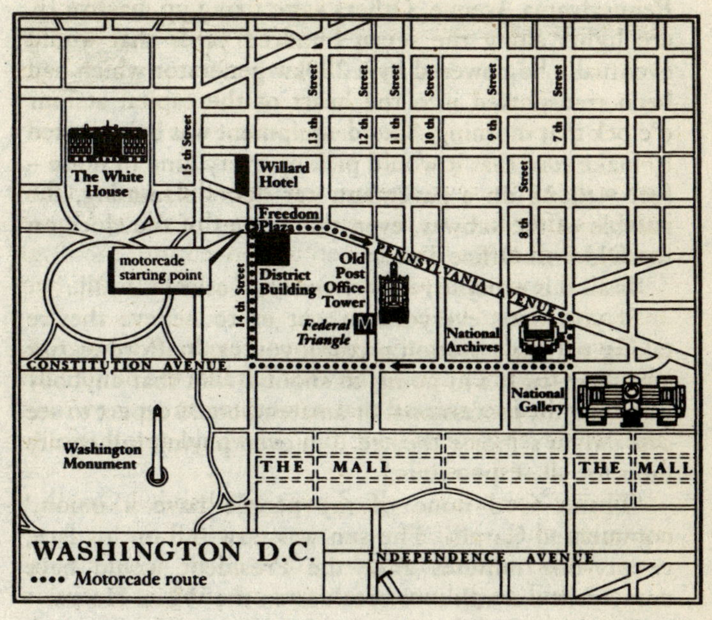

15 th Street
13 th Street
12 th Street
11 th Street
10 th Street
9 th Street
7 th Street
8 th Street
14 th Street
The White House
Willard Hotel
Freedom Plaza
motorcade starting point
District Building
Old Post Office Tower
Federal Triangle
M
PENNSYLVANIA AVENUE
National Archives
CONSTITUTION AVENUE
National Gallery
Washington Monument
THE MALL
THE MALL
INDEPENDENCE AVENUE
WASHINGTON D.C.
•••• Motorcade route

Pennsylvania Avenue and eyed the fifty or so people who came under Johnny's direction. Some were preparing a track along the pavement that would allow a camera to follow the six cars as they travelled slowly down Pennsylvania Avenue. Others were fixing up massive IK arc lights along the seven hundred yards that would eventually be powered by a 200kw generator which had been transported into the heart of the capital at four o'clock that morning. Sound equipment was being tested to make sure that it would pick up every kind of noise – feet walking on a pavement, car doors slamming, the rumble of the subway, even the chimes of the clock on the Old Post Office Tower.

'Is all this expense really necessary?' asked Cavalli.

'If you want everyone except us to believe they're taking part in a motion picture, you can't afford to risk any short-cuts. I'm going to shoot a film that anybody watching us, professional or amateur, could expect to see one day in a movie theatre. I'm even paying full equity rates for all of the extras.'

'Thank God none of my people have a union,' commented Cavalli. The sun was now full on his face, twenty-one minutes after the President would have enjoyed its warmth over breakfast in the White House.

Cavalli looked down at the checklist on his clipboard. Al Calabrese already had all his twelve vehicles in place on the kerbside, and the drivers were standing around in a huddle drinking coffee, sheltered from the wind by one of the walls of Freedom Plaza. The six limousines glistened in the morning sun as passers-by, cleaners and janitors leaving offices and early-morning commuters coming up from the Federal Triangle Metro slowed to admire the spectacle. A painter was just touching up the Presidential Seal on the third car while a girl was unfurling a flag on the right-hand fender.

Cavalli turned to see a police truck, tailboard down, parked in front of the District Building. Barriers were being lifted off and carried onto the pavement to make sure innocent passers-by did not stray onto the set during those crucial three minutes when the filming would be taking place.

Lloyd Adams had spent the previous day going over his lines one last time and dipping into yet another book on the history of the Declaration of Independence. That night he had sat in bed replaying again and again a video of Bill Clinton on his Georgia Avenue walk, noting the tilt of the head, the Razorback accent, the way he subconsciously bit his lower lip. The Monday before, Adams had purchased a suit that was identical to the one the President had worn to welcome the British Prime Minister in February – straight off the rack from Dillard's Department Store. He chose a red, white and blue tie, a rip-off of the one Clinton wore on the cover of the March issue of *Vanity Fair*. A Timex Ironman had been the final addition to his wardrobe. During the past week a second wig had been made, this time a little greyer, which Adams felt more comfortable with. The director and Cavalli had taken him through a dress rehearsal the previous evening: word perfect – though Johnny had commented that his collapse at the end of the scene was a bad case of overacting. Cavalli felt the Archivist would be far too overwhelmed to notice.

Cavalli asked Al Calabrese to go over the breakdown of his staff yet again. Al tried not to sound exasperated, as he had gone over it in great detail during their last three board meetings: 'Twelve drivers, six outriders,' he rattled off. 'Four of them are ex-cops or military police and all of them have worked with me before. But as none of them are going into the National Archives, they've simply been told they're involved in a movie. Only those working directly under Gino Sartori know what we're really up to.'

'But are they fully briefed on what's expected of them once they reach the Archives?'

'You'd better believe it,' replied Al. 'We went over it at least half a dozen times yesterday, first on a map in my office, and then we came down here in the afternoon and walked the route. They drive down Pennsylvania Avenue at ten miles an hour while they're being filmed and continue east until they reach 7th Street. Then they take a sharp right, when they'll be out of sight of everyone involved in the filming, not to mention the police. Then they turn right again at the delivery entrance of the National Archives, where they'll come to a halt in front of the loading dock. Angelo, Dollar Bill, Debbie, you and the counter-assault team leave their vehicles and accompany the actor into the building, where they'll be met by Calder Marshall.

'Once your party has entered the building the cars will go back up the ramp and take a right on 7th Street, another right on Constitution Avenue and then right on 14th Street before returning to the location where the filming began. By then, Johnny will be ready for a second take. On the signal from you that the Declaration of Independence has been exchanged for a fake, the second take will begin immediately, except this time we'll be picking up the thirteen operatives we dropped outside the National Archives.'

'And, if all goes to plan, the Declaration of Independence as well,' said Cavalli. 'Then what happens?' he asked, wanting to be sure that nothing had changed since their final board meeting in New York.

'The limos leave Washington by six separate routes,' continued Al. 'Three of them return to the capital during the afternoon, but not until they've changed their licence plates; two others go on to New York, and one drives to a destination known only to you; that will be the vehicle carrying the Declaration.'

'If it all runs as smoothly as that, Al, you'll have earned your money. But it won't, and that's when we'll really find out how good you are.' He nodded as Al left to grab a mug of coffee and rejoin his men.

Cavalli checked his watch: 7.22. When he looked up he saw Johnny heading towards him, red in the face. Thank God I don't have to work in Hollywood, thought Cavalli.

'I'm having trouble with a cop who says I can't put my lighting equipment on the sidewalk until 9.30 a.m. That means I won't be able to begin filming until after ten, and if I've only got forty-five minutes to start with –'

'Calm down, Johnny,' said Cavalli, and checked his list of personnel. He looked up and began to search the crowd of workers that was flowing off Freedom Plaza onto the pavement. He spotted the man he needed. 'You see the tall guy with grey hair practising his charm on Debbie?' he said, pointing.

'Yeah,' said Johnny.

'That's Tom Newbolt, ex-Deputy Chief of the DCPD, now a security consultant. We've hired him for the day. So go and tell him what your problem is, and then we'll find out if he's worth the five thousand dollars his company is charging me.'

Cavalli smiled as Johnny stormed off in Newbolt's direction.

Angelo stood over the slumbering body. He leaned across, grabbed Dollar Bill's shoulders, and began to shake him furiously.

The little Irishman was belching out a snore that

sounded more like an old tractor than a human being. Angelo leaned closer, only to find Dollar Bill smelt as if he had spent a night in the local brewery.

Angelo realised that he should never have left Bill the previous evening, even for a moment. If he didn't get the bastard to the Archives on time, Cavalli would kill them both. He even knew who'd carry out the job, and the method she would use. He went on shaking, but Dollar Bill's eyes remained determinedly closed.

At eight o'clock a klaxon sounded and the film crew took a break for breakfast.

'Thirty minutes. Union regulations,' explained Johnny when Cavalli looked exasperated. The crew surrounded a parked trailer – another expensive import – on the pavement, where they were served eggs, ham and hash browns. Cavalli had to admit that the crowds gathered behind the police barriers and the passers-by lingering on the pavement never seemed to doubt for a moment that this was a film crew getting ready for a shoot.

Cavalli decided to use the thirty-minute break to check for himself that, once the cars had turned right on 7th Street, they could not be seen by anyone involved in the filming back on Pennsylvania Avenue.

He strode briskly away from the commotion, and when he reached the corner of 7th Street he turned right. It was as if he'd entered a different world. He joined a group of people who were quite unaware of what was taking place less than half a mile away. It was just like Washington on a normal Tuesday morning. He was pleased to spot Andy Borzello sitting on the bench in the bus shelter near the loading dock entrance to the National Archives, reading the *Washington Post*.

By the time Cavalli had returned, the film crew were beginning to move back and start their final checks; no one wanted to be the person responsible for a retake.

The crowds at the barriers were growing thicker by the minute, and the police spent a considerable amount of their time explaining that a film was going to be shot, but not for at least another couple of hours. Several people looked disappointed at this information and moved on, only to allow others to take up the places they had vacated.

Cavalli's cellular phone began ringing. He pressed the talk button and was greeted by the sound of his father's Brooklyn vowels. The chairman was cautious over the phone, and simply asked if there were any problems.

'Several,' admitted Tony. 'But none so far that we hadn't anticipated or can't overcome.'

'Don't forget, cancel the entire operation if you're not satisfied with the response to your nine o'clock phone call. Either way, he mustn't be allowed to return to the White House.' The line went dead. Cavalli knew that his father was right on both counts.

Cavalli checked his watch again: 8.43. He strolled over to Johnny.

'I'm going across to the Willard. I don't expect to be too long, so just keep things rolling. By the way, I see you got all your equipment on the sidewalk.'

'Sure thing,' said Johnny. 'Once Newbolt talked to that cop, he even helped us carry the damn stuff.'

Cavalli smiled and began walking towards the National Theater on the way to the Willard Hotel. Gino Sartori was coming in the opposite direction.

'Gino,' Cavalli said, stopping to face the ex-Marine. 'Are all your men ready?'

'Every one of the bastards.'

'And can you guarantee their silence?'

'Like the grave. That is, if they don't want to end up digging their own.'

'So where are they now?'

'Coming from eight different directions. All of them are due to report to me by nine-thirty. Smart dark suits, sober ties, and holsters that aren't too obvious.'

'Let me know the moment they're all signed in.'

'Will do,' said Gino.

Cavalli continued his journey to the Willard Hotel, and after checking his watch again began to lengthen his stride.

He strolled into the lobby, and found Rex Butterworth marching nervously up and down the centre of the hall as if his sole aim in life was to wear out the blue-and-gold carpet. He looked relieved when he saw Cavalli, and joined him as he strode towards the elevator.

'I told you to sit in the corner and wait, not parade up and down in front of every freelance journalist looking for a story.'

Butterworth mumbled an apology as they stepped into the elevator and Cavalli pressed button eleven. Neither of them spoke again until they were safely inside 1137, the room in which Cavalli had spent the previous night.

Cavalli looked more carefully at Rex Butterworth now they were alone. He was sweating as if he had just finished a five-mile jog, not travelled up eleven floors in an elevator.

'Calm down,' said Cavalli. 'You've played your part well so far. Only one more phone call and you're through. You'll be on your flight to Rio before the first outrider even reaches the National Archives. Now, are you clear about what you have to say to Marshall?'

Butterworth took out some handwritten notes, mouthed a few words and said, 'Yes, I'm clear and I'm ready.' He was shaking like a jelly.

Cavalli dialled the private number of the Archivist's office half a mile away, and when he heard the first ring, passed the receiver over to Butterworth. They both listened to the continuing ringing. Eventually Cavalli put his hand out to take back the receiver. They would have to try again in a few minutes' time. Suddenly there was a click and a voice said, 'Calder Marshall speaking.'

Cavalli went into the bathroom and picked up the extension. 'Good morning, Mr Marshall. It's Rex Butterworth at the White House, just checking everything's all set up and ready your end.'

'It certainly is, Mr Butterworth. Every member of my staff has been instructed to be at their desks by nine o'clock sharp. In fact, I've seen most of them already, but only my deputy and the Senior Conservator know the real reason I've asked them all not to be late this morning.'

'Well done,' said Butterworth. 'The President is running on time and we anticipate he will be with you around ten, but I'm afraid he still has to be back at the White House by eleven.'

'By eleven, of course,' said the Archivist. 'I only hope we can get him round the whole building in fifty minutes, because I expect there are many of my staff who would like to meet him.'

'We'll just have to hope that fifty minutes is enough time to fit them all in,' said Butterworth. 'Can I assume that there are still no problems with the President's personal request?'

'None that I'm aware of,' said Marshall. 'The Conservator is quite happy to remove the glass so that the President can study the parchment in its original form. We'll keep the Declaration in the vault until the President has left the building. I hope to have the document back on view to the general public a few minutes after he departs.'

'It sounds to me as if you have everything under control, Mr Marshall,' said Butterworth, the sweat pouring off his forehead. 'I'm just off to see the President, so I'm afraid I'll be out of contact for the rest of the morning, but let's talk again this afternoon and you can tell me how it all went.'

Cavalli placed the phone on the side of the bath and bolted back into the bedroom, coming to a halt in front of the President's Special Assistant. Butterworth looked terrified. Cavalli shook his head frantically from side to side.

'Actually, now that I look at my schedule, Mr Marshall, I see you won't be able to reach me again today because I promised my wife I'd leave the office a little earlier than usual to prepare for our annual vacation which begins tomorrow.'

'Oh. Where are you going?' asked Marshall, innocently.

'Off to see my mother in Charleston. But I feel confident that the President's visit to the Archives will be a great success. Why don't we get together as soon as I'm back?'

'I would enjoy that,' said Marshall. 'And I do hope you have a pleasant break in South Carolina; the azaleas should still be blooming.'

'Yes, I suppose they will,' said Butterworth as he watched Cavalli pulling a finger across his throat. 'My other line is ringing,' he added, and without another word put the phone down.

'You said too much, you fool. We don't ever want him trying to contact you again.'

Butterworth looked apprehensive.

'How long will it be before the White House wonders where you are?' asked Cavalli.

'At least a week,' replied Butterworth. 'I really am due for my annual leave, and even my boss thinks I'm going to Charleston.'

'Well, that's something you did right,' said Cavalli, as he handed Butterworth a one-way ticket to Rio de Janeiro and a letter of confirmation that the sum of nine hundred thousand dollars had been deposited in the Banco do Brazil.

'I have to get back to the set,' said Cavalli. 'You stay put for ten minutes and then take a taxi to Dulles airport. And when you get to Brazil, don't spend all the money on a girl. And Rex, don't even think about coming back. If you do, it won't just be the Feds who are waiting for you at the airport.'

Angelo had somehow managed to get Dollar Bill dressed, but he still stank of Guinness, and he certainly didn't look like the President's personal physician – or anybody else's physician for that matter.

'Sorry, lad. Sorry, lad,' Dollar Bill kept repeating. 'I hope this won't get you into any trouble.'

'It will if you don't sober up in time to play your part and see that the parchment is transferred into the special cylinder. Because if Cavalli ever finds out I wasn't with you last night, you're dead, and more important, so am I.'

'Settle down, lad, and just make me a Bloody Mary. Two parts tomato juice and one part vodka. I'll be as right as rain in no time, you'll see.' Angelo looked doubtful as the little man's head fell back on the pillow.

As Cavalli closed the door of room 1137, a woman pushing a large laundry basket passed him in the corridor.

He took the lift to the ground floor and walked

straight out of the hotel. The first thing he saw as he left the Willard and crossed the plaza that divided the hotel from Pennsylvania Avenue was that the morning traffic was backed up for half a mile down 15th Street.

Al and Johnny came running towards him from different directions. 'What's going on?' were Cavalli's first words.

'Normal morning traffic coming in from Virginia, the police assure us, except we're blocking a lane and a half with our twelve vehicles and six outriders.'

'Damn, my mistake,' said Cavalli. 'I should have anticipated it. So what do you suggest, Al?'

'I send my boys over to Atlantic Garage on 13th and F until the police get the traffic on the move again, and then bring them back nearer the starting time.'

'It's a hell of a risk,' said Johnny. 'That permit only allows me to film for forty-five minutes, and they aren't going to stretch it by a second.'

'But if my cars stay put you might never get started at all,' said Al.

'OK, Al, you get moving, but make sure you're back on the grid by 9.50.' Cavalli checked his watch. 'That's twenty-seven minutes.' Al began running towards the parked cars.

Cavalli turned his attention to the director. 'What time are you bringing the actor out?'

'Nine-fifty-five, or the moment the last car is back in place. He's being made up in that trailer over there,' said Johnny.

Cavalli watched as the sixth limousine pulled away, and was relieved to see the traffic start to flow again.

'And Gino's Secret Service agents, what will happen to them now that the cars have gone?'

'Most of them are hanging around with the extras, but they aren't looking too convincing.'

Cavalli's cellular phone began to ring. 'I have to get back or you won't have a film, real or otherwise,' said Johnny. Cavalli nodded and said 'Yes,' into the mouthpiece as the director rushed away. Something caught Cavalli's eye as he tried to concentrate on the voice on the other end of the line.

'The helicopter is all set to take off at ten o'clock sharp, boss; but it loses its slot at seven minutes past. The traffic cops won't let it go up after that, however much you gave to the Fraternal Order of Police.'

'We're still running to schedule, despite some problems,' said Cavalli, 'so take her up at ten and just hover over the route. Marshall and his staff must be able to see and hear you when we arrive at the Archives. That's all I care about.'

'OK, boss. Understood.'

Cavalli checked his watch again. It was 9.36 and the traffic was now flowing smoothly. He walked over to the officer co-ordinating the shoot for the city's motion picture and television office.

'Don't worry,' said the Lieutenant even before Cavalli had opened his mouth. 'The traffic will be stopped and the detour signs in place by 9.59. We'll have you moving on time, I promise.'

'Thank you, officer,' said Cavalli, and quickly dialled Al Calabrese.

'I think you'd better start getting your boys back . . .'

'Number one has already left with two outriders. Number two's just about to go; after that, they leave at twenty-second intervals.'

'You should have been an army general,' said Cavalli.

'You can blame the government for that. I just didn't get the right education.'

Suddenly, Pennsylvania Avenue was ablaze with lights. Cavalli, like everyone else, shielded his eyes and then, just as suddenly, the lights were switched off, making the morning sun appear like a dim lightbulb.

'Good sparks,' Cavalli heard the director shout. 'I could only spot one that didn't function. The seventh on the right.'

Cavalli stood on the pavement and looked towards the corner of 13th Street, where he could see the first of Al's limousines with two outriders edging its way back through the traffic. The sight of the shining black limo made him feel nervous for the first time.

A tall, well-built, bald man wearing dark glasses, a dark blue suit, white shirt and a red, white and blue striped tie was walking towards him. He stopped by Cavalli's side as the first of the two outriders and the leading police car drew in to the kerb.

'How are you feeling?' asked Cavalli.

'Like all first nights,' said Lloyd Adams. 'I'll be just fine once the curtain goes up.'

'Well, you sure knew your lines word perfect last night.'

'My lines aren't the problem,' said Adams. 'It's Marshall's I'm worried about.'

'What do you mean?' asked Cavalli.

'He's not been able to attend any of our rehearsals, has he?' replied the actor. 'So he doesn't know his cues.'

The second car drew into line, accompanied by two more outriders, as Al Calabrese came running across the pavement and Lloyd Adams strode off in the direction of the trailer.

'Can you still do it in eleven minutes?' asked Cavalli, looking at his watch.

'As long as Chief Thomas's finest don't foul things up like they do every other morning,' said Al. He headed on towards the cars and immediately began to organise the unfurling of the Presidential flag on the front of the third car before checking on any specks of dirt that might have appeared on the bodywork after one trip round the block.

The staff van drew up in line. Scasiatore immediately swung round on his high stool and, through a megaphone, told the actor, the secretary, the Lieutenant and the physician to be ready to climb into the third and fourth cars.

When the director asked for the Lieutenant and the physician, Cavalli suddenly realised that he hadn't seen Dollar Bill or Angelo all morning. Perhaps they'd been waiting in the trailer.

The fourth limousine drew up as Cavalli's eyes swept the horizon, searching for Angelo.

The klaxon sounded again for several seconds, this time to warn the film crew that they had ten minutes left before shooting. The noise almost prevented Cavalli from hearing his phone ringing.

'It's Andy reporting in, boss. I'm still outside the National Archives. Just to let you know it's no busier than when you checked up an hour ago.'

'At least someone's awake,' said Cavalli.

'There can't be more than twenty or thirty people around at the moment.'

'Glad to hear it. But don't call me again unless something goes wrong.' Cavalli flicked off the phone and tried to remember what it was that had been worrying him before it rang. Eleven vehicles and six outriders were now in place. One vehicle was still missing. But something else was nagging at the back of Cavalli's mind. He became distracted when an officer standing in the middle of Pennsylvania Avenue began shouting at the top of his voice that he was ready to stop the traffic whenever the director gave the word. Johnny stood up on his chair and pointed frantically to the twelfth car, which remained obstinately stuck in traffic a couple of hundred yards away.

'If you divert the traffic now,' shouted Johnny, 'that one's never going to end up in the motorcade.'

The officer remained in the middle of the road and waved the traffic through as fast as he could in the hope of getting the limousine there quicker, but it didn't make a lot of difference.

'Extras on the street!' shouted Johnny, and several people who Cavalli had supposed were members of the public strolled onto the pavement and began walking up and down professionally.

Johnny stood up on his chair again and this time turned to face the crowd huddled behind the barriers. An aide handed him a megaphone so that he could address them.

'Ladies and gentlemen,' he began. 'This is a short cut for a movie about the President going to the Hill to address a joint session of Congress. I'd be grateful if you could wave, clap and cheer as if it were the real President. Thank you.' Spontaneous applause broke out, which made Cavalli laugh for the first time that morning. He hadn't noticed that the former Deputy Police Chief had crept up behind him during the director's address. He whispered in his ear, 'This is going to cost you a whole lot of money if you don't pull it off first time.'

Cavalli turned to face the ex-policeman and tried not to show how anxious he felt.

'The hold-up, I mean. If you don't get the shoot done this morning, the authorities aren't going to let you go through this charade again for one hell of a time.'

'I don't need to be reminded of that,' snapped Cavalli. He turned his attention back to Johnny, who had climbed down from his chair and was walking over to take his seat on the tracking dolly, ready to move as soon as the twelfth vehicle was in place. Once again, the aide passed Johnny the megaphone. 'This is a final check. Check your positions, please. This is a final check. Everyone ready in car one?' There was a sharp honk in reply. 'Car two?' Another honk. 'Car three?' Another sharp honk from the driver of Lloyd Adams' car. Cavalli stared in through the window as the bald actor removed the top of his wig box. 'Car four?' Not a sound came from car four.

'Is everyone in car four who should be in car four?' barked the director.

It was then that Cavalli remembered what had been nagging at him: he still hadn't seen Angelo or Dollar Bill all morning. He should have checked earlier. He hurried towards the director as a naval Lieutenant jumped out of a car which he'd left stranded in the middle of the road. He was six foot tall, with short-cropped hair, wearing a white uniform with a sword swinging by his side and medals for service in Panama and the Gulf on his chest. In his right hand he carried a black box. A policeman began chasing after him while Dollar Bill, carrying a small leather bag, followed a few yards behind at a slower pace. When Cavalli saw what had happened he changed direction and walked calmly out into the middle of the road, and the naval officer came to a halt by his side.

'What the hell do you think you're playing at?' barked Cavalli.

'We got held up in the traffic,' said Angelo lamely.

'If this whole operation fails because of you . . .'

Angelo turned the colour of his uniform as he thought about what had happened to Bruno Morelli.

'And the sword?' snapped Cavalli.

'A perfect fit.'

'And our physician. Is *he* fit?'

'He'll be able to do his job, I promise you,' Angelo said, looking over his shoulder.

'Which car are you both in?'

'Number four. Directly behind the President.'

'Then get in, and right now.'

'Sorry, sorry,' Dollar Bill said, as he arrived panting. 'My fault, not Angelo's. Sorry, sorry,' he repeated as the back door of car four was held open for him by the Lieutenant, who was gripping his sword. Once Dollar Bill was safely in, Angelo joined the would-be physician and slammed the door behind him.

The policeman who'd been chasing Angelo took his notebook out as Cavalli turned round looking for Tom Newbolt. Tom was already running across the road.

'Leave him to me,' was all he said.

The second van with surveillance cameras on board screeched to a halt to complete the line. The front window purred down. 'Sorry, boss,' said the driver. 'Some jerk just dumped his car right in front of me.' The clock on the Old Post Office Tower struck ten. At that moment, on a signal from the co-ordinating officer, several policemen walked out into the road. Some held up the traffic coming down Pennsylvania Avenue while others placed diversion signs to direct the cars away from where the filming was taking place.

Cavalli turned his attention to the other end of Pennsylvania Avenue, a mere seven hundred yards away. It was still bumper to bumper with slow-moving traffic.

'Come on, come on!' he shouted out loud as he checked his watch and waited impatiently for the all clear.

'Any moment now,' shouted back the officer, who was standing in the middle of the road.

Cavalli looked up to see the blue-and-white police helicopter hovering noisily overhead.

Neither he nor the officer spoke again until a couple of minutes later when they heard a sharp whistle blow three times from the far end of Pennsylvania Avenue. Cavalli checked his watch. They'd lost six precious minutes.

'I'll kill Angelo,' he said. 'If –'

'All clear!' shouted the co-ordinating officer. He turned to face Cavalli, who gave the director a thumbs-up sign.

'You've still got thirty-nine minutes,' bellowed the officer. 'That should easily be enough time to complete the shoot twice.' But Cavalli didn't hear the last few words as he ran to the second car, pulled open the door and jumped into the seat next to the driver.

And then a nagging thought hit him. Looking out of the side window, Cavalli began to scan the crowd once again.

'Lights!' screamed the director, and Pennsylvania Avenue lit up like Christmas Eve at Macy's.

'OK, everybody, we're going to shoot in sixty seconds.'

The limousines and motorcycles switched on their engines and began revving up. The extras strolled up and down while the police continued to divert commuters away from the scene. The director leaned back over his chair to check the lights and see if the seventh in line was working.

'Thirty seconds.' Johnny looked at the driver of the first car and said through the megaphone, 'Don't forget to take it easy. My tracking dolly can only manage ten miles an hour going backwards. And walkers,' – the director checked up and down the pavement – 'please look as if you're walking, not auditioning for *Hamlet*.'

The director turned his attention to the crowd. 'Now, don't let me down behind the barriers. Clap, cheer and wave, and please remember we're going to do the whole exercise again in about twenty minutes, so stick around if you possibly can.

'Fifteen seconds,' said the director as he swung back to face the first car in line. 'Good luck, everybody.'

Tony stared at Scasiatore, willing him to get on with it. They were now eight minutes late – which with this particular President, he had to admit, added an air of authenticity.

'Ten seconds. Rolling. Nine, eight, seven, six, five, four, three, two, one – action!'

The woman pushing the laundry basket down the corridor ignored the 'Do Not Disturb' sign on Room 1137 and walked straight in.

A rather overweight man, sweating profusely, was seated on the edge of the bed. He was jabbing out some numbers on the phone when he looked round and saw her.

'Get out, you dumb bitch,' he said, and turned back to concentrate on redialling the numbers.

In three silent paces she was behind him. He turned a second time just as she leaned over, took the phone cord in both hands and pulled it round his neck. He raised an arm to protest as she flicked her wrists in one sharp movement. He slumped forward and fell off the bed onto the carpet, just as the voice on the phone said, 'Thank you for using AT & T.'

She realised that she shouldn't have used the phone cord. Most unprofessional – but nobody called her a dumb bitch.

She replaced the phone on the hook and bent down, deftly hoisting the Special Assistant to the President onto her shoulder. She dropped him into the laundry basket. No one would have believed such a frail woman could have lifted such a heavy weight. In truth the only use she had ever made of a degree in physics was to apply the principles of fulcrums, pivots and levers to her chosen profession.

She opened the door and checked the passageway. At this hour it was unlikely there'd be many people around. She wheeled the basket down the corridor until she reached the housekeepers' elevator, faced the wall and waited patiently. When the lift arrived she pressed the button that would take her to the garage.

When the lift came to a halt on the lower ground floor she wheeled the basket out and over to the back of a Honda Accord, the second-most popular car in America.

Shielded by a pillar, she quickly transferred the Special Assistant from the basket into the boot of the car. She then wheeled the basket back to the lift, took off her baggy black uniform, dropped it into the laundry basket, removed her carrier bag with the long cord handle and despatched the laundry basket to the twenty-fifth floor.

She straightened up her Laura Ashley dress before climbing into the car and placing her carrier bag under the front seat. She drove out of the car park onto F Street, and had only travelled a short distance before she was stopped by a traffic cop.

She wound the window down.

'Follow the diversion sign,' he said, without even looking at her.

She glanced at the clock on her dashboard. It was 10.07.

AS THE LEAD POLICE CAR moved slowly away from the kerb, the director's tracking dolly began running backwards at the same pace along its rails. The crowds behind the barriers started to cheer and wave. If they had been making a real film the director would have called 'Cut' after twenty seconds because that fool of a co-ordinating officer was still standing in the middle of the road, hands on hips, oblivious to the fact that he wasn't the star of the movie.

Cavalli didn't notice the officer as he concentrated on the road ahead of him. He phoned through to Andy, who he knew would still be seated on the bench on 7th Street reading the *Washington Post*.

'Not much action this end, boss. A little activity at the bottom of the ramp, but no one on the street is showing any real interest. Is everything all right your end? You're running late.'

'Yes, I know, but we should be with you in about sixty seconds,' said Cavalli, as the director reached the end of his private railroad track and put one thumb in the air to indicate that the cars could now accelerate to twenty-five miles per hour. Johnny Scasiatore jumped off the dolly and walked slowly back down Pennsylvania Avenue so he could prepare himself for the second take.

Cavalli flicked the phone off and took a deep intake of

breath as the motorcade passed 9th Street; he stared at the FDR Monument that was set back on a grass plot in front of the main entrance of the Archives. The first car turned right on 7th Street; a mere half-block remained before they would reach the driveway into the loading dock. The lead motorcycles speeded up and when they were opposite Andy standing on the pavement, they swung right and drove down the ramp.

The rest of the motorcade formed a line directly opposite the delivery entrance, while the third limousine drove down the ramp to the loading dock.

The counter-assault team were the first onto the street, and eight of them quickly formed a circle facing outwards around the third car.

After the eight men had stared in every direction for a few seconds, Cavalli jumped out of the second car, ran across to join them and opened the back door of the third car so that Lloyd Adams could get out.

Calder Marshall was waiting on the loading dock, and walked forward to greet the President.

'Nice to meet you, Mr Marshall,' said the actor, thrusting out his hand. 'I've been looking forward to this occasion for some time.'

'As, indeed, have we, Mr President. May I on behalf of my staff welcome you to the National Archives of the United States. Will you please follow me.'

Lloyd Adams and his entourage dutifully followed Marshall straight into the spartan freight elevator. As one of the Secret Service agents kept his finger on the 'open' button, Cavalli gave the order for the motorcade to return to its starting point. Six motorcycles and the twelve vehicles moved off and began the journey back to rejoin the director and prepare for the second shoot.

The whole exercise of getting the actor into the building and the motorcade started on its return journey had taken less than two minutes, but Cavalli was dismayed to see that a small crowd had already gathered on the far side of the road by the Federal Trade Commission, obviously sensing something important was taking place. He only hoped Andy could deal with the problem.

Cavalli quickly slipped into the elevator, wedging himself behind Adams. Marshall had begun a short history of how the Declaration of Independence had ended up in the National Archives.

'Most people know that John Adams and Thomas Jefferson drafted the Declaration that was approved by Congress on July 4th 1776. Few, however, know that the second and third Presidents died on the same day, July 4th 1826 – fifty years to the day after the official signing.' The elevator doors opened on the ground floor and Marshall stepped out into a marble corridor and led them in the direction of his office.

'The Declaration had a long and turbulent journey, Mr President, before it ended up safely in this building.'

When they reached the fifth door on the left, Marshall guided the President and his staff into his office, where coffee awaited them. Two of the Secret Service agents stepped inside while the other six remained in the corridor.

Lloyd Adams sipped his coffee as Marshall ignored his in favour of continuing the history lesson. 'After the signing ceremony, on August 2nd 1776, the Declaration was filed in Philadelphia, but because of the danger of the document being captured by the British, the engrossed parchment was taken to Baltimore in a covered wagon.'

'Fascinating,' said Adams in a soft drawl. 'But had it been captured by the British infantry, copies would still have been in existence, no doubt?'

'Oh certainly, Mr President. Indeed, we have a good

example of one in this building executed by William J. Stone. However, the original remained in Baltimore until 1777, when it was returned to the relative safety of Philadelphia.'

'In another wagon?' asked the President.

'Indeed,' said Marshall, not realising his guest was joking. 'We even know the name of the man who drove it, a Mr Samuel Smith. Then, in 1800, by direction of President Adams, the Declaration was moved to Washington, where it first found a home in the Treasury Department, but between 1800 and 1814 it was moved all over the city, eventually ending up in the old War Office building on 17th Street.'

'And, of course, we were still at war with Britain at that time,' said the actor.

Cavalli admired the way Adams had not only learned his lines, but done his research so thoroughly.

'That is correct, Mr President,' said the Archivist. 'And when the British fleet appeared in Chesapeake Bay, the Secretary of State, James Monroe, ordered that the document be moved once again. Because, as I am sure you know, Mr President, it is the Secretary of State who is responsible for the safety of the parchment, not the President.'

Lloyd Adams did know, but wasn't sure if the President would have, so he decided to play safe. 'Is that right, Mr Marshall? Then perhaps it should be Warren Christopher who is here today to view the Declaration, and not me.'

'The Secretary of State was kind enough to visit us soon after he took office,' Marshall replied.

'But he didn't want the document moved again,' said the actor. Marshall, Cavalli, the Lieutenant and the physician dutifully laughed before the Archivist continued.

'Monroe, having spotted the British advancing on Washington, despatched the Declaration on a journey up the Potomac to Leesburg, Virginia.'

'August 24th,' said Adams, 'when they razed the White House to the ground.'

'Precisely,' said Marshall. 'You are well informed, sir.'

'To be fair,' said the actor, 'I've been well briefed by my Special Assistant, Rex Butterworth.'

Marshall showed his recognition of the name, but Cavalli wondered if the actor was being just a little too clever.

'That night,' continued Marshall, 'while the White House was ablaze, thanks to Monroe's foresight the Declaration was stored safely in Leesburg.'

'So when did they bring the parchment back to Washington?' asked Adams, who could have told the Archivist the exact date.

'Not for several weeks, sir. On September 17th 1814, to be precise. With the exception of a trip to Philadelphia for the centennial celebrations and its time in Fort Knox during World War II, the Declaration has remained in the capital ever since.'

'But not in this building,' said Adams.

'No, Mr President, you are right again. It has had several other homes before ending up here, the worst being the Patent Office, where it hung opposite a window and was for years exposed to sunlight, causing the parchment irreparable damage.'

Bill O'Reilly stood in the corner, thinking how many hours of work he had had to do and how many copies he had had to destroy during the preparation stage because of that particular piece of stupidity. He cursed all those who had ever worked in the Patent Office.

'How long did it hang there?' asked Adams.

'For thirty-five years,' said Marshall, with a sigh that

showed he was every bit as annoyed as Dollar Bill that his predecessors had been so irresponsible. 'In 1877 the Declaration was moved to the State Department library. Not only was smoking common at the time, but there was also an open fireplace in the room. And, I might add, the building was damaged by fire only months after the parchment had been moved.'

'That was a close one,' said Adams.

'After the war was over,' continued Marshall, 'the Declaration was taken from Fort Knox and brought back to Washington in a Pullman carriage before it was housed in the Library of Congress.'

'I hope it wasn't exposed to the light once again,' said Adams as Cavalli's phone rang.

Cavalli slipped into the corner and listened to the director tell him, 'We're back on the starting line, ready to go whenever you are.'

'I'll call when I need you,' was all Cavalli said. He switched his phone off and returned to listen to the Archivist's disquisition.

'. . . in a Thermapane case equipped with a filter to screen out damaging ultra-violet light.'

'Fascinating. But when did the document finally reach this building?' asked Adams.

'On December 13th 1952. It was transported from the Library of Congress to the National Archives in a tank under the armed escort of the US Marine Corps.'

'First a covered wagon, and finally a tank,' said the actor, who noticed that Cavalli kept glancing at his watch. 'Perhaps the time has come for me to see the Declaration in its full glory.'

'Of course, Mr President,' said the Archivist.

Marshall led the way back into the corridor, followed by the actor and his entourage.

'The Declaration can normally be seen by the public

in the rotunda on the ground floor, but we shall view it in the vault where it is stored at night.' When they reached the end of the corridor the Archivist led the President down a flight of stairs while Cavalli kept checking over the route that would allow them the swiftest exit if any trouble arose. He was delighted to find that the Archivist had followed his instructions and kept the corridors clear of any staff.

At the bottom of the steps, they came to a halt outside a vast steel door at which an elderly man in a long white coat stood waiting. His eyes lit up when he saw the actor.

'This is Mr Mendelssohn,' said Marshall. 'Mr Mendelssohn is the Senior Conservator and, I confess, the real expert on anything to do with the parchment. He will be your guide for the next few minutes before we visit the rest of the building.'

The actor stepped forward, and once again thrust out his hand. 'Good to meet you, Mr Mendelssohn.'

The elderly man bowed, shook the actor's hand, and pushed the steel door open.

'Please follow me, Mr President,' he said in a mid-European accent. Once inside the tiny vault, Cavalli watched his men spread out in a small circle, their eyes checking everything except the President. Bill O'Reilly, Angelo and Debbie also took their places as they had rehearsed the previous evening.

Cavalli quickly glanced at Dollar Bill, who looked as if it was he who might be in need of a physician.

Mendelssohn guided the actor towards a massive block of concrete that took up a large area of the far wall.

He patted the slab of concrete and explained that the protective shell had been built at a time when the nation's greatest fear had been a nuclear attack.

'The Declaration is covered in five tons of interlocking leaves of metal, embedded in the fifty-five-ton concrete and steel vault you see before you. I can assure you, Mr President,' Mendelssohn added, 'if Washington was razed to the ground, the Declaration of Independence would still be in one piece.'

'Impressive,' said Adams, 'most impressive.'

Cavalli checked his watch; it was 10.24, and they'd already been inside the building for seventeen minutes. Although the limousines were waiting, he had no choice but to allow the Conservator to carry on at his own pace. After all, their hosts were aware of the limitations on the President's time if they were still hoping to show him round the rest of the building.

'The entire system, Mr President,' continued the Conservator enthusiastically, 'is worked electronically. At the press of a button, the Declaration, which is always exhibited and stored in an upright position, travels up from this level through interlocking doors which open before the document finally comes to rest in a case of solid bronze, protected by ballistically tested glass and plastic laminate. Ultra-violet filters in the laminate give the inner layer a slightly greenish hue.' The actor looked lost, but Mr Mendelssohn continued, quite unconcerned. 'We are presently standing some twenty-two feet below the exhibit hall, and as the mechanics can be worked manually, I am able to stop the machinery at any time. With your permission, Mr Marshall.'

The Archivist nodded, and the Conservator touched a button that neither the actor nor Cavalli had spotted until that moment. The five-ton leaves began to slide apart above their heads, and a sudden whirling and clanking sounded as the massive brass frame that housed the parchment began its daily journey towards the ceiling. When the frame had reached desk height, Mr Mendelssohn pressed a second button, and the whirling sound instantly ceased. He then raised an open palm in the direction of the casing.

Lloyd Adams took a pace forward and stared across at the nation's most important historic document.

'Now, remembering your personal wish, Mr President, we in turn have a small request of you.'

The actor seemed uncertain what his lines were meant to be, and glanced towards Cavalli in the wings.

'And what might that request be?' prompted Cavalli, apprehensive of any change of plan at this late stage.

'Simply,' said Mr Mendelssohn, 'that while the Archivist and I are removing the outer casing of the Declaration, your men will be kind enough to turn and face the wall.'

Cavalli hesitated, aware that the Secret Service would never allow a situation to arise where they could not see the President at all times.

'Let me make it easier for you, Mr Mendelssohn,' said Adams. 'I'll be the first to comply with your request.' The actor turned away from the document, and the rest of the team followed suit.

In the brief space of time that the team were unable to see what was going on behind them, Cavalli heard twelve distinct clicks and the exaggerated sighs of two men not used to moving heavy weights.

'Thank you, Mr President,' said Calder Marshall. 'I hope that didn't put you to too much inconvenience.'

The thirteen intruders turned round to face the massive frame. The bronze casing had been lifted over to leave the impression of an open book.

Lloyd Adams, with Cavalli and Dollar Bill a pace behind, stepped forward to admire the original while Marshall and the Conservator continued to stare at the old parchment. Suddenly, without warning, the actor reeled back, clutching his throat, and collapsed to the ground. Four of the Secret Service agents immediately surrounded Adams while the other four bundled the Archivist and the Conservator out of the vault and into the corridor before they could utter a word. Tony had to admit Johnny was right – it had been a bad case of over-acting.

Once the door was closed, Cavalli turned to see Dollar Bill already staring at the parchment, his eyes alight with excitement, the Lieutenant by his side.

'Time for us to get to work, Angelo,' said the Irishman. He stretched his fingers out straight. The Lieutenant removed a pair of thin rubber gloves from the doctor's bag and pulled them over his hands. Dollar Bill wiggled his fingers like a concert pianist about to begin a recital. Once the gloves were in place, Angelo bent down again and lifted a long, thin knife out of the bag, placing the handle firmly in Dollar Bill's right hand.

While these preparations were being carried out, Dollar Bill's eyes had never once left the document. Those who remained in the room were so silent that it felt like a tomb as the forger leaned over towards the parchment and placed the blade of the knife gently under the top right-hand corner. It peeled slowly back, and he transferred the knife to the left-hand corner, and that too came cleanly away. Dollar Bill passed the knife back to Angelo before he began rolling the parchment up slowly and as tightly as he could without harming it.

At the same time, Angelo flicked back the handle of his dress sword and held the long shaft out in front of him. Cavalli took a pace forward and slowly pulled out Dollar Bill's counterfeit copy from the specially constructed chamber where the sword's blade would normally have lodged.

Cavalli and Dollar Bill exchanged their prizes and reversed the process. While Cavalli slid the original

Declaration inch by inch down the scabbard of the dress sword, Dollar Bill began to unroll his fake carefully onto the backplate of the laminated glass, the moist chemical mixture helping the document to remain in place. The counterfeiter sniffed loudly. The strong smell suggested thymol to his sensitive nose. Dollar Bill gave his copy one more long look, checked the spelling correction and then took a pace backward, reluctantly leaving his masterpiece to the tender care of the National Archives and its concrete prison.

Once he had completed his task Dollar Bill walked quickly over to the side of Lloyd Adams. Debbie had already undone his collar, loosened his tie and applied a little pale foundation to his face. The forger bent down on one knee, took off the rubber gloves and dropped them into a physician's bag full of make-up as Cavalli dialled a number on his cellphone.

It was answered even before he heard a ring, but Cavalli could only just make out a faint voice.

'Take two,' said Cavalli firmly, and rang off before pointing at the door. One of the Secret Service agents swung the steel grid wide open and Cavalli watched carefully as Mr Mendelssohn came charging through the gap and headed straight to the brass encasement, while Marshall, who was pale and quivering, went immediately to the side of the President.

Cavalli was relieved to see a smile come across the lips of the Conservator as he leaned over the fake Declaration. With the help of Angelo, he pulled the brass casing across and gave the manuscript a loving stare before fixing the lid back into place, then quickly tightened the twelve locks around the outside of the casing. He pressed one of the buttons and the whirling and clanking noise began again as the massive brass frame slowly disappeared back into the ground.

Cavalli turned his attention to the actor and watched as two of the Secret Service agents helped him to his feet, while Dollar Bill fastened his physician's bag.

'What chemical is it that protects the parchment?' asked Dollar Bill.

'Thymol,' replied the Archivist.

'Of course, I should have guessed. With the President's allergy problem, I might have expected this reaction. Don't panic. As long as we get him out in the fresh air as quickly as possible, he'll be back to normal in no time.'

'Thank God for that,' said Marshall, who hadn't stopped shaking.

'Amen,' said the little Irishman as the actor was helped towards the door.

Marshall quickly rushed to the front and led them back up the stairs, with the Secret Service agents following as close behind as possible.

Cavalli left Lloyd Adams stumbling behind him while he caught up with the Archivist. 'No one, I repeat, no one, must hear about this incident,' he said, running by Marshall's side. 'Nothing could be more damaging to the President when he has only been in office for such a short time, especially remembering what Mr Bush went through after his trip to Japan.'

'After his trip to Japan. Of course, of course.'

'If any of your staff should ask why the President didn't complete his tour of the building, stick to the line that he was called back to the White House on urgent business.'

'Called back on urgent business. Of course,' said Marshall, who was now whiter than the actor.

Cavalli was relieved to find his earlier orders about no staff being allowed in the lower corridor while the President was in the building still remained in force.

Once they had reached the freight elevator, and all the group were inside, they descended to the level of the loading dock. Cavalli sprinted out ahead of them and up the ramp onto 7th Street.

He was annoyed to find that there was still a small crowd on the far pavement, and no sign of the motorcade. He looked anxiously to his right, where Andy was now standing on the bench, pointing towards Pennsylvania Avenue. Cavalli turned to look in the same direction and saw the first motorcycle escort turning right into 7th Street.

He ran back down the ramp to find Lloyd Adams next to a Federal Express pick-up box, being propped up by two Secret Service agents.

'Let's make it snappy,' said Cavalli. 'There's a small crowd out there and they're beginning to wonder what's going on.' He turned to face the Archivist, who was standing next to the Conservator on the loading dock.

'Please remember, the President was called back to the White House on urgent business.' They both nodded vigorously. Four of the Secret Service agents rushed forward just as the third car, engine running, pulled up to the loading dock at the bottom of the ramp.

Cavalli opened the door of the third limousine and frantically waved the actor in. The lead riders on the motorcycles held up the traffic as the final car came to a halt at the mouth of the delivery entrance. As Lloyd Adams was assisted into the limousine, the small crowd on the other side of the road began pointing and clapping.

One of the Secret Service agents nodded back in the direction of the building. Angelo jumped into the second car, still clinging onto the sword, while Dollar Bill and the secretary piled into the fourth. By the time Cavalli had joined Angelo in the back of the second car and given the signal to move, the motorcycle escort was already in the middle of 7th Street holding up the traffic to allow the motorcade to proceed towards Constitution Avenue.

As the sirens blared and the limousines began their journey down 7th Street, Cavalli looked back and was relieved to see there was no longer any sign of Marshall or Mendelssohn.

He quickly switched his attention to the east side of 7th Street, where Andy was explaining to the crowd that it had not been the President but simply a rehearsal for a movie, nothing more. Most of the onlookers showed their obvious disappointment and quickly began to disperse.

Then he thought he saw him again.

As Cavalli's car sped down Constitution Avenue, the lead police car was already turning right into 14th Street, accompanied by two of the outriders. The sirens had been turned off, and the rest of the motorcade peeled off one by one as they reached their allotted intersections.

The first car swung right on 9th Street and right again back onto Pennsylvania Avenue before heading away in the direction of the Capitol. The third continued on down Constitution Avenue, keeping to the centre lane, while the fourth turned left onto 12th Street and the sixth right at 13th.

The fifth turned left on 23rd Street, crossing Memorial Bridge and following the signs to Old Town, while the second car turned left at 14th Street and headed towards the Jefferson Memorial and onto the George Washington Parkway.

Cavalli, who was seated in the back of the second car, dialled the director. When Johnny answered the phone, the only words he heard were, 'It's a wrap.'

15

SCOTT PRAYED THAT the Ambassador's wife would be unable to get away on Thursday, or might still be in Geneva. He remembered Dexter Hutchins saying, 'Patience is not a virtue when you work for the CIA, it's nine-tenths of the job.'

When he stopped at the end of the pool Hannah told him that the Ambassador's wife hadn't returned from Switzerland. They didn't bother to swim another length, but agreed to meet later at the amusement park in the bois de Vincennes.

The moment he saw her walking across the road he wanted to touch her. There were no instructions in any of the CIA handbooks on how to deal with such a situation, and no agent had ever raised the problem with him during the past nine years.

Hannah briefed him on everything that was happening at the embassy, including 'something big' taking place in Geneva that she didn't yet know the details of. Scott told her in reply to her question that he had reported back to Kratz, and that it wouldn't be long before she was taken out. She seemed pleased.

Once they began to talk of other things, Scott's training warned him that he ought to insist she return to the embassy. But this time he left Hannah to make the decision as to when she should leave. She seemed to relax for the first time, and even laughed at Scott's stories about the macho Parisians he met up with in the gym every evening.

As they strolled around the amusement park, Scott discovered it was Hannah who won the teddy bears at the shooting gallery and didn't feel sick on the big dipper.

'Why are you buying cotton candy?' he asked.

'Because then no one will think we're agents,' she replied. 'They'll assume we're lovers.'

When they parted two hours later he kissed her on the cheek. Two professionals behaving like amateurs. He apologised. She laughed and disappeared.

Shortly after ten o'clock, Hamid Al Obaydi joined a small crowd that had formed on the pavement opposite a side entrance of the National Archives. He had to wait some twenty minutes before the door opened again and Cavalli came running up the ramp just as the motorcade reappeared on the corner of 7th Street. Cavalli gave a signal and they all came rushing out to the waiting cars. Al Obaydi couldn't believe his eyes. The deception completely fooled the small crowd, who began waving and cheering.

As the first car disappeared around the corner, a man who had been there all the time explained that it was not the President but simply the rehearsal for a film.

Al Obaydi smiled at this double deception while the disappointed crowd drifted away. He crossed 7th Street and joined a long line of tourists, schoolchildren and the simply curious who had formed a queue to see the Declaration of Independence.

The thirty-nine steps of the National Archives took as many minutes to ascend, and by the time the Deputy Ambassador entered the rotunda the river of people had thinned to a tributary which flowed on across the marble hall to a single line up a further nine steps, ending in a trickle under the gaze of Thomas Jefferson and John Hancock. Before him stood the massive brass frame that housed the Declaration of Independence.

Al Obaydi noted that when a person reached the parchment, they were only able to spend a few moments gazing at the historic document. As his foot touched the first of the steps his heart started beating faster, but for a different reason from everyone else waiting in the queue. He removed from his inside pocket a pair of spectacles whose glass could magnify the smallest writing by a degree of four.

The Deputy Ambassador walked across to the centre of the top step and stared at the Declaration of Independence. His immediate reaction was one of horror. The document was so perfect it must surely be the original. Cavalli had fooled him. Worse, he had succeeded in stealing ten million dollars by a clever deception. Al Obaydi checked that the guards on each side of the encasement were showing no particular interest in him before putting on the spectacles.

He leaned over so that his nose was only an inch from the glass as he searched for the one word that had to be spelt correctly if they expected to be paid another cent.

His eyes widened in disbelief when he came to the sentence: 'Nor have We been wanting in attentions to our British brethren.'

The Ambassador's wife returned from Geneva with her husband the following Friday. Hannah and Scott had managed to steal a few hours together that morning.

It had been less than three weeks since he had first seen her in the public baths in the boulevard Lannes.

Little more than a fortnight since that first hastily arranged meeting at the café on the avenue Bugeaud. That was when the lies had begun; small ones to start with, that grew larger until they had spun themselves into an intricate web of deceit. Now Scott longed to tell her the truth, but as each day passed it became more and more impossible.

Langley had been delighted with the coded messages, and Dexter had congratulated him on doing such a first-class job. 'As good a junior field officer as I can remember,' Dexter admitted. But Scott had discovered no code to let the Deputy Director know he was falling in love.

He had read Hannah's file from cover to cover, but it gave no clue as to her real character. The way she laughed – a smile that could make you smile however sad or angry you were. A mind that was always fascinating and fascinated by what was happening around her. But most of all a warmth and gentleness that made their time apart seem like an eternity.

And whenever he was with her, he was suddenly no more mature than his students. Their clandestine meetings had rarely been for more than an hour, perhaps two, but it made each occasion all the more intense.

She continued to tell him everything about herself with a frankness and honesty that belied his deceit, while he told her nothing but a string of lies about being a Mossad agent whose front, while he was stationed in Paris, was writing a book, a travel book, which would never be published. That was the trouble with lies – each one created the next in a never-ending spiral. And that was the trouble with trust; she believed his every word.

When he returned home that evening, he made a decision he knew Langley would not approve of.

* * *

As the car edged its way into the outside lane of the George Washington Memorial Parkway bound for the airport the driver checked the rear-view mirror and confirmed no one was following them. Cavalli breathed a deep sigh of relief, though he had two alternative plans worked out if they were caught with the Declaration. He'd realised early on that it would be necessary to get as far away from the scene of the crime as quickly as possible. It had always been a crucial part of the plan that he would hand over the document to Nick Vicente within two hours of its leaving the National Archives.

'So let's get on with it,' said Cavalli, turning his attention to Angelo, who was seated opposite him. Angelo unbuckled the sword that hung from the belt around his waist. The two men then faced each other like Japanese sumo wrestlers, each waiting for the other to make the first move. Angelo placed the sword firmly between his legs, the handle pointing towards his boss. Cavalli leaned over and snapped the top back. Then, with the nail of his right thumb and forefinger, he extracted the thin black plastic cylinder from its casing. Angelo pressed the handle back in place and hitched the sword onto his belt.

Cavalli held the twenty-six-inch-long slim plastic cylinder in his hands.

'It must be tempting to have a look,' said Angelo.

'There are more important things to do at the moment,' said Cavalli, placing the cylinder on the seat next to him. He picked up the carphone, pressed a single digit followed by 'Send', and waited for a response.

'Yes?' said a recognisable voice.

'I'm on my way, and I'll have something to export when I arrive.' There was a long silence, and Cavalli wondered if he had lost the connection.

'You've done well,' came back the eventual reply. 'But are you running to schedule?'

Cavalli looked out of the window. The exit sign for Route 395 South flashed past. 'I'd say we're about a couple of minutes from the airport. As long as we make our allocated time slot, I still hope to be with you around one o'clock.'

'Good, then I'll have Nick join us so that the contract can be picked up and sent on to our client. We'll expect you around one.'

Cavalli replaced the phone and was amused to find Angelo was dressed only in a vest and underpants. He smiled and was about to comment when the phone rang. Cavalli picked it up.

'Yes,' he said.

'It's Andy. I thought you'd like to know it's back on display to the general public and the queues are as long as ever. By the way, an Arab stood around in the crowd the whole time you were in the building, and then joined the line to see the Declaration.'

'Well done, Andy. Get yourself back to New York. You can fill me in on the details tomorrow.'

Cavalli put the phone down and considered Andy's new piece of information as Angelo was completing a Windsor knot on a tie no lieutenant would have been seen dead in. He still didn't have his trousers on.

The smoked glass between the driver and the passengers slid down.

'We're just coming up to the terminal, sir. No one has followed us at any point.'

'Good,' said Cavalli as Angelo hurriedly pulled on his trousers. 'Once you've changed your licence plates, drive back to New York.'

The driver nodded as the limousine came to a halt outside Signature Flight Support.

Cavalli grabbed the plastic tube, jumped out of the car, ran through the terminal and out onto the tarmac. His eyes searched for the white Learjet. When he spotted it, a door opened and the steps were lowered to the ground. Cavalli ran towards them as Angelo followed, trying to pull on his jacket in the high wind.

The Captain was waiting for them on the top step. 'You've just made it in time for us to keep our slot,' he told them. Cavalli smiled, and once they had both clicked on their seatbelts, the Captain pressed a button to allow the steps to swing back into place.

The plane lifted off seventeen minutes later, banking over the Kennedy Center, but not before the steward had served them each a glass of champagne. Cavalli rejected the offer of a second glass as he concentrated on what still needed to be done before he could consider his role in the operation was finished. His thoughts turned once again to Al Obaydi, and he began to wonder if he'd underestimated him.

When the Learjet landed at La Guardia fifty-seven minutes later, Cavalli's driver was waiting by his car, ready to whisk them into the city.

As the driver continually switched lanes and changed direction on the highway that would eventually take them west over the Triborough Bridge, Cavalli checked his watch. They were now lost in a sea of traffic heading into Manhattan, only eighty-seven minutes after leaving Calder Marshall outside the delivery entrance of the National Archives. Roughly the time it would take a Wall Street banker to have lunch, Cavalli thought.

Cavalli was dropped outside his father's 75th Street brownstone just before one, leaving Angelo to go on to the Wall Street office and monitor the checking-in calls as each member of the team filed his report.

The butler held open the front door of No. 23 as Tony stepped out of the car.

'Can I take that for you, sir?' he asked, eyeing the plastic tube.

'No, thank you, Martin,' said Tony. 'I'll hold onto it for the moment. Where's my father?'

'He's in the boardroom with Mr Vicente, who arrived a few minutes ago.'

Tony jogged down the staircase that led to the basement and continued across the corridor. He strode into the boardroom to find his father sitting at the head of the table, deep in conversation with Nick Vicente. The chairman stood up to greet his son, and Tony passed him the plastic tube.

'Hail, conquering hero,' were his father's first words. 'If you'd pulled off the same trick for George III, he would have made you a knight. "Arise, Sir Antonio." But as it is, you'll have to be satisfied with a hundred million dollars' compensation. Is it permissible for an old man to see the original before Nick whisks it away?'

Cavalli laughed and removed the cap from the top of the cylinder before slowly extracting the parchment and placing it gently on the boardroom table. He then unrolled two hundred years of history. The three men stared down at the Declaration of Independence and quickly checked the spelling of 'Brittish'.

'Magnificent,' was all Tony's father said as he began licking his lips.

'Interesting how the names on the bottom were left with so little space for their signatures,' observed Nick Vicente after he had studied the document for several minutes.

'If they'd all signed their names the same size as John Hancock, we would have needed a Declaration of twice the length,' added the chairman as the phone on the boardroom table started to ring.

The chairman flicked a button on his intercom. 'Yes, Martin?'

'There's a Mr Al Obaydi on the private line, says he would like to have a word with Mr Tony.'

'Thank you, Martin,' said the chairman, as Tony leaned over to pick up the call. 'Why don't you take it in my office, then I can listen in on the extension.'

Tony nodded and left the room to go next door, where he picked up the receiver on his father's desk. 'Antonio Cavalli,' he said.

'Hamid Al Obaydi here. Your father suggested I call back around this time.'

'We are in possession of the document you require,' was all Cavalli said.

'I congratulate you, Mr Cavalli.'

'Are you ready to complete the payment as agreed?'

'All in good time, but not until you have delivered the document to the place of our choosing, Mr Cavalli, as I'm sure you will recall was also part of the bargain.'

'And where might that be?' asked Cavalli.

'I shall come to your office at twelve o'clock tomorrow, when you will receive your instructions.' He paused. 'Among other things.' The line went dead.

Cavalli put the phone down and tried to think what Al Obaydi could possibly mean by 'Among other things.' He walked slowly back to the boardroom to find his father and Nick poring over the Declaration. Tony noticed that the parchment had been turned round.

'What do you think he meant by "Among other things"?' Tony asked.

'I've no idea,' replied his father as he gave the parchment one last look and then began slowly to roll it up.

'No doubt I'll find out tomorrow,' said Tony as the

chairman handed the document to his son, who carefully slipped it back into its plastic container.

'So where's its final destination to be?' asked Nick.

'I'll be given the details at twelve o'clock tomorrow,' said Tony, a little surprised that his father hadn't reported his phone conversation with Al Obaydi to his oldest friend.

16

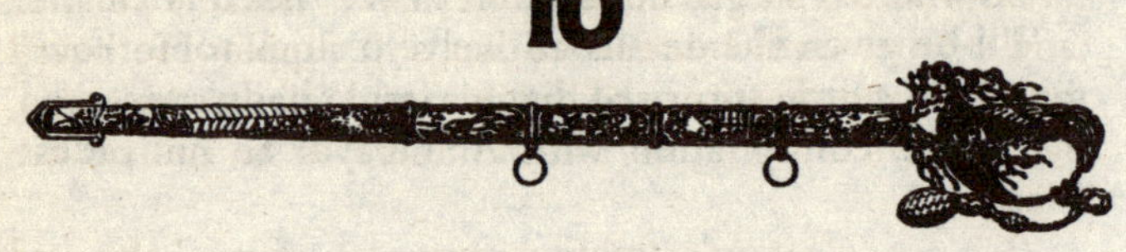

HE LAY WATCHING HER, his head propped up in the palm of his hand, as the first sunlight of the morning crept into the room. She stirred but didn't wake as Scott began to run a solitary finger down her spine. He couldn't wait for her to open her eyes and revive his memories of the previous night.

When Scott had, in those early days, watched Hannah walking from the Jordanian Embassy, dressed in those drab clothes so obviously selected with Karima Saib's tastes in mind, he thought she still looked stunning. Some packages, when you remove the brightly-coloured wrapping, fail to live up to expectation. When Hannah had first taken off the dowdy little two-piece suit she had been wearing that day, he had stood there in disbelief that anyone could be so beautiful.

He pulled back the single sheet that covered her and admired the sight that had taken his breath away the night before. Her short-cropped hair; he wondered how the long flowing strands would look when they fell on her shoulders as she wanted them to. The nape of her neck, the smooth olive skin of her back, and the long, shapely legs.

His hands were like a child's that had opened a stocking full of presents and wanted to touch everything at once. He ran his fingers down her shoulders to the arch of her back, hoping she would turn over. He moved a little closer, leaned across and began to circle her firm breasts with a single finger. The circles became smaller and smaller until he reached her soft nipple. He heard her sigh, and this time she did turn and fall into his arms, her fingers clinging to his shoulders as he pulled her closer.

'It's not fair, you're taking advantage of me,' she said drowsily as his hand moved up the inside of her thigh.

'I'm sorry,' he said, removing his hand and kissing her cheek.

'Don't be sorry. For heaven's sake, Simon, I want you to take advantage of me,' she said, pulling his body closer to her. He continued to stroke her skin, all the time discovering new treasures.

When he entered her, she sighed a different sigh, the sigh of morning love, calmer and more gentle than the demands of the night, but every bit as enjoyable.

For Scott it had been a new experience. Although he had made love many more times than he cared to remember, it had never been with the same excitement.

When they finished making love, she rested her head on his shoulder and he brushed a hair from her cheek, praying the next hour would go slowly. He hated the thought of her returning to the embassy that morning as he knew she eventually must. He didn't want to share her with anybody.

The room was now bathed in the morning sun, which only made him wonder when he would next be allowed to spend a whole night with her.

The Head of Interest Section had been called straight back to Geneva on urgent business, and had taken only one secretary with him, leaving Hannah in Paris on her own for the weekend. She only wished she could tell

Simon what it was all about, so he could pass the information on to Kratz.

She had double-locked her room and left the embassy compound by the fire escape. Hannah told him that she had felt like a schoolgirl creeping out of her dormitory to join a midnight feast.

'Better than any feast I can remember,' were his last words before they fell asleep in each other's arms.

The day had begun when they had gone shopping together in the boulevard Saint-Michel and bought clothes she couldn't wear and a tie he would never have considered before he met her. They'd had lunch at a corner café and taken two hours to eat a salad and drink a bottle of wine. They had strolled down the Champs-Élysées, hand in hand as lovers should, before joining the queue to see the Clodion exhibition at the Louvre. A chance to teach her something he thought he knew about, only to find it was he who did the learning. He bought her a floppy tourist hat in the little shop at the base of the Eiffel Tower and was reminded that she always looked stunning whatever she wore.

They had dinner at Maxim's but only ate one course, as they both knew by then that all they really wanted to do was return to his little flat on the Left Bank.

He remembered how he had stood there mesmerised as Hannah removed each garment until she became so embarrassed that she began to take off his clothes. It was almost as if he didn't want to make love to her, because he hoped the anticipation might go on forever.

Of all the women, including the occasional promiscuous student, with whom he had had one-night stands, casual affairs, even sometimes what he had imagined was love, he had never known anything like this. And afterwards, he discovered something else he had never experienced before: the sheer joy of just lying in her arms was every bit as exhilarating as making love.

His finger ran down the nape of her neck. 'What time do you have to be back?' he asked, almost in a whisper.

'One minute before the Ambassador.'

'And when's he expected?'

'His flight's due in from Geneva at 11.20. So I'd better be at my desk before twelve.'

'Then we still have time to make love once more,' he said as he placed a finger on her lips.

She bit the finger gently.

'Ow,' he said mockingly.

'Only once?' she replied.

Debbie brought the Deputy Ambassador through to Cavalli's office at twenty past twelve. Neither man commented on the fact that Al Obaydi was late. Tony indicated the chair on the other side of his desk, and waited for his visitor to be seated. For the first time, he felt strangely uneasy about the Arab.

'As I mentioned yesterday,' Cavalli began, 'we are now in possession of the document you require. We are therefore ready to exchange it for the sum agreed.'

'Ah, yes, ninety million dollars,' said the Iraqi, placing the tips of his fingers together just below his chin while he considered his next statement. 'Cash on delivery, if I remember correctly.'

'You do,' said Cavalli. 'So now all we need to know is where and when.'

'We require the document to be delivered to Geneva by twelve o'clock next Tuesday. The recipient will be a Monsieur Pierre Dummond of the bankers Dummond et cie.'

'But that only gives me six days to find a safe route out of the country and . . .'

'Your God created the world in that time, if I remember correctly,' said Al Obaydi.

'The Declaration will be in Geneva by Tuesday midday,' said Cavalli.

'Good,' said Al Obaydi. 'And if Monsieur Dummond is satisfied that the document is authentic, he has been given instructions to release the sum of ninety million dollars by wire transfer to any bank of your choice in the world. If, on the other hand, you fail to deliver, or the document proves to be a fake, we will have lost ten million dollars, with nothing to show for it but a three-minute film made by a world-famous director. In that eventuality, a package similar to this one will be posted to the Director of the FBI and the Commissioner of the IRS.'

Al Obaydi removed a thick envelope from his inside pocket and tossed it across the table. Cavalli's expression did not change as the Deputy Ambassador rose, bowed and walked out of the room without another word.

Cavalli felt sure he was about to discover what 'Among other things' meant.

He ripped open the bulky yellow envelope and allowed the contents to spill out onto his desk. Photographs, dozens of them, and documents with banknote serial numbers attached to them. He glanced at the photographs of himself in deep conversation with Al Calabrese on the pavement in front of the National Café, another of himself with Gino Sartori in the centre of Freedom Plaza, and yet another with the director sitting on the dolly as they talked to the former Chief of the DC Police Department. Al Obaydi had even taken a photograph of Rex Butterworth entering the Willard Hotel and of the actor, bald-headed, sitting in the third car, and later getting into the limo outside the Archives' loading dock.

Cavalli began drumming his fingers on the table. It was then that he remembered the nagging doubt at the back of his mind. It was Al Obaydi he had seen in the crowd the previous day. He had underestimated the Iraqi. Perhaps the time had come to call their man in the Lebanon and inform him of the Swiss bank account he had opened in the Deputy Ambassador's name.

No. That would have to wait until the ninety million had been paid in full.

'What do I do, Simon, if he offers me the job?'

Scott hesitated. He had no idea what Mossad would expect her to do. He knew exactly what *he* wanted her to do. It was no use putting the question to Dexter Hutchins in Virginia, because they wouldn't have hesitated to tell him to continue using Hannah for their own purposes.

Hannah turned towards what Scott laughingly described as the kitchen. 'Perhaps you could ask Colonel Kratz what I should do,' she suggested when he didn't reply. 'Explain to him that the Ambassador wants me to take Muna's place, but that another problem has arisen.'

'What's that?' asked Scott anxiously.

'The Ambassador's term of office comes to an end early next month. He may well be asked to stay in Paris, but the Chief Administrator is telling everyone that he's going to be called back to Baghdad and promoted to Deputy Foreign Minister.'

Scott still didn't offer an opinion.

'What's the matter, Simon? Are you incapable of making a decision at this time in the morning?' Scott still said nothing. 'You're just as pathetic on your feet as you are in bed,' she teased.

Scott decided the time had come to tell her everything. He wasn't going to wait another minute. He walked out of the kitchen, took her in his arms and stroked her hair. 'Hannah, I need to –' he had begun, when the phone rang. He broke away to answer it.

He listened for a few moments before saying to Dexter Hutchins, 'Yes, sure. I'll call you back as soon as I've had time to think about it.' What was the man doing up in the middle of the night, wondered Scott as he replaced the receiver.

'Another lover, lover?' Hannah asked with a smile.

'My publishers wanting to know when my manuscript will be finished. It's already overdue.'

'And what will your answer be?'

'I'm currently distracted.'

'Only currently?' she said, pressing her finger on his nose.

'Well, perhaps permanently,' he admitted.

She kissed him gently on the cheek and whispered, 'I must get back to the embassy, Simon. Don't come down with me, it's too risky.'

He held her in his arms and wanted to protest but settled for 'When will I see you again?'

'Whenever the Ambassador's wife feels in need of a swim,' Hannah said. She broke away. 'But I'll keep on reminding her how good it is for her figure, and that perhaps she ought to be taking even more exercise.' She laughed and left without another word.

Scott stood by the window, waiting for her to reappear. He hated the fact that he couldn't just phone, write or make contact with her whenever he felt like it. He longed to send her flowers, letters, cards and notes to let her know how much he loved her.

Hannah ran out onto the pavement, a smile on her face. She looked up and blew Scott a kiss before she vanished around the corner.

Another man, who was cold and tired from hours of waiting, also watched her, not from a window in a warm room but from a doorway on the opposite side of the road.

The moment Scott disappeared from sight, the man stepped out of the shadows and followed the Ambassador's second secretary back to the embassy compound.

17

'I DON'T BELIEVE YOU,' she said.

'I fear that the truth of the matter is you don't want to believe me,' said Kratz, who had flown in from London that morning.

'But he can't be working for any enemy of Israel.'

'If that's the case, perhaps you can explain why he passed himself off as a Mossad agent?'

For the last two hours Hannah had tried to think of a logical reason why Simon would have deceived her, but had to admit that she had been unable to come up with a convincing answer.

'Have you told us everything you passed on to him?' Kratz demanded.

'Yes,' she said, suddenly feeling ashamed. 'But have you checked with all the friendly agencies?'

'Of course we have,' said Kratz. 'No one in Paris has ever heard of the man. Not the French, not the British, and certainly not the CIA. Their Head of Station told me personally that they have never had anyone on their books called Simon Rosenthal.'

'So what will happen to me now?' asked Hannah.

'Do you wish to continue working for your country?'

'You know I do,' she said, glaring back at him.

'And are you still hoping to be included in the team for Baghdad?'

'Yes, of course I am. Why would I have put myself through all this in the first place if I didn't want to be part of the final operation?'

'Then you will also want to abide by the oath you swore in the presence of your colleagues in Herzliyah.'

'Nothing would make me break that oath. You know that. Just tell me what you expect me to do.'

'I expect you to kill Rosenthal.'

Scott was delighted when Hannah confirmed on Thursday afternoon that she would be able to slip away for dinner on Friday evening, and might even find it possible to stay overnight. It seemed that the Ambassador had been called away to Geneva again. Something big was happening, but she still didn't know exactly what.

Scott had already decided that three things were going to take place when they next met. First, he would cook the meal himself, despite Hannah's comments about his inadequate kitchen. Second, he was going to tell her the truth about himself, whatever interruptions occurred. And third . . .

Scott felt more relaxed than he had in weeks once he had decided to 'come clean', as his mother had described it whenever he'd tried to get away with something. He knew that he would be recalled to the States once he had informed Dexter of what had happened, and that a few weeks later he would be quietly discharged. But that was no longer of any significance, because third, and most important of all, he was going to ask Hannah to come back to America with him, as his wife.

Scott spent the afternoon shopping in the market for freshly baked bread, the finest wild mushrooms, succulent lamb chops and tiny ripe oranges. He returned home to prepare a feast he hoped she would never forget. He had also prepared a speech he believed she would, in time, find it possible to forgive.

During the evening, Scott found himself looking up at the kitchen clock every few moments. He felt robbed if she was ever more than a few minutes late. She had failed to turn up for their previous meeting, though he accepted that she had no way of letting him know when something unexpected came up. He was relieved to see her walk through the door soon after the clock had struck eight.

Scott smiled when Hannah removed her coat, and he saw she was wearing the dress he had chosen for her when they'd gone shopping together for the first time. A long blue dress that hung loosely off the shoulders, and made her appear both elegant and sexy.

He immediately took her in his arms, and was surprised by her response. She seemed distant, almost cold. Or was he being over-sensitive? Hannah broke away and stared at the table laid for two with its red-and-white check tablecloth and two sets of unmatching cutlery.

Scott poured her a glass of the white wine he had selected to go with the first course before he disappeared into the kitchen to put the final touches to his culinary efforts, aware that he and Hannah always had so little time together.

'What are you cooking?' she asked, in a dull, flat voice.

'Wait and see,' he replied. 'But I can tell you the starter is something I learned when –' He stopped himself. 'Many years ago,' he added rather lamely.

He didn't see her grimace at his failure to finish the original sentence.

Scott returned to join her a few moments later, carrying two plates of piping-hot wild mushrooms, with a small slice of garlic bread. 'But not too much garlic,' he promised her, 'for obvious reasons.' No witty or sharp response came flying back, and he wondered if she was unable to stay overnight. He might have questioned her more closely had he not been concentrating on the dinner as well as wanting to get his speech over with.

'I wish we could get out of Paris and see Versailles, like normal people,' said Scott as he dug his fork into a mushroom.

'That would be nice,' she said.

'And even better . . .' She looked up and stared at him.

'A weekend at the Colmendor. I promised myself long ago when I first read the life of Matisse at . . .' He hesitated once again, and she lowered her head. 'And that's only France,' he said, trying to recover. 'We could take a lifetime over Italy. They have a hundred Colmendors.'

He looked hopefully towards her but her eyes remained staring at the half-empty plate.

What had he done? Or was *she* fearful of telling *him* something? He dreaded the thought of learning that she was going to Baghdad when all he wanted to do was take her to Venice, Florence and Rome. If it was Baghdad that was making her anxious, he would do everything in his power to change her mind.

Scott cleared away the plates to return a few moments later with the succulent lamb Provençal. 'Madam's favourite, if I remember correctly.' But he was rewarded only with a weak smile.

'What is it, Hannah?' he asked as he took the seat opposite her. He leaned across to touch her hand, but she removed it quickly from the table.

'I'm just a little tired,' she replied unconvincingly. 'It's been a long week.'

Scott tried to discuss her work, the theatre, the Clodion exhibition at the Louvre and even Clinton's attempts to bring the three living Beatles together, but with each new effort he received the same bland response. They continued to eat in silence until his plate was empty.

'And now, we shall end on my *pièce de résistance*.' He expected to be playfully chastised about his efforts as a chef; instead he received only the flicker of a smile and a distant, sad look from those dark, beautiful eyes. He disappeared into the kitchen and returned immediately, carrying a bowl of freshly sliced oranges with a touch of Cointreau. He placed the delicate morsels in front of her, hoping they would change her mood. But while Scott continued with his monologue Hannah remained an unreceptive audience.

He removed the bowls, his empty, hers hardly touched, and returned moments later with coffee, hers made exactly as she liked it: black, with a touch of cream floating across the top, and no sugar. His black, steaming, with too much sugar.

Just as he sat down opposite her, determined this was the moment to tell her the truth, she asked for some sugar. Scott jumped up, somewhat surprised, returned to the kitchen, tipped some sugar into a bowl, grabbed a teaspoon and came back to see her snapping closed her tiny evening bag.

After he had sat down and placed the sugar on the table he smiled at her. He had never seen such sadness in those eyes before. He poured them both a brandy, whirled his round the balloon, took a sip of his coffee and then faced her. She had not touched her coffee or brandy, and the sugar she had asked for remained in the centre of the table, its little mound undented.

'Hannah,' Scott began softly, 'I have something important to tell you, and I wish I had told you a long time ago.' He looked up, to find her on the verge of tears.

He would have asked her why, but feared that if he allowed her to change the subject he might never tell her the truth.

'My name is not Simon Rosenthal,' he said quietly. Hannah looked surprised, but not in the way he had expected – more anxious than curious. He took another sip of coffee and then continued. 'I have lied to you from the day we met, and the more deeply I fell in love with you, the more I lied.'

She didn't speak, for which he was grateful, because on this occasion, like his lectures, he needed to proceed without interruption. His throat began to feel a little dry, so he sipped his coffee again.

'My name is Scott Bradley. I am an American, but not from Chicago as I told you when we first met. I'm from Denver.' A puzzled look came into Hannah's eyes, but she still didn't interrupt him. Scott ploughed on.

'I am not Mossad's agent in Paris writing a travel book. Far from it, though I confess the truth is much stranger than the fiction.' He held her hand and this time she didn't try to remove it. 'Please, let me explain, and then perhaps you'll find it in your heart to forgive me.' His throat suddenly felt drier. He finished his coffee and quickly poured himself another cup, taking an extra teaspoonful of sugar. She still hadn't touched hers. 'I was born in Denver, where I went to school. My father was a local lawyer who ended up in jail for fraud. I was so ashamed that when my mother died, I took a post at Beirut University because I could no longer face anyone I knew.' Hannah looked up and her eyes began to show sympathy. It gave Scott the confidence to go on.

'I do not work for Mossad in any capacity, nor have I ever done so.' Her lips formed a straight line. 'My real job is nowhere near as romantic as that. After Beirut I returned to America to become a university professor.'

She looked mystified, and then her expression suddenly changed to one of anxiety.

'Oh, yes,' he said, his words beginning to sound slightly slurred, 'this time I'm telling the truth. I teach Constitutional Law at Yale. Let's face it, no one would make up a story like that,' he added, trying to laugh.

He drank more coffee. It tasted less bitter than the first cup.

'But I am also what they call in the trade a part-time spy, and as it's turned out, not a very good one. Despite many years of training and lecturing other people on how it should be done.' He paused. 'But that was only in the classroom.'

She looked more anxious.

'You need have no fears,' he said, trying to reassure her. 'I work for the good side, though I suppose even that depends on where you're looking from. I'm currently a temporary Field Officer with the CIA.'

'The CIA?' she stammered in disbelief. 'But they told me . . .'

'What did they tell you?' he asked quickly.

'Nothing,' she said, and lowered her head again.

Had she already known about his background, or perhaps guessed his original story didn't add up? He didn't care. All he wanted to do was tell the woman he loved everything about himself. No more lies. No more deceit. No more secrets. 'Well, as I'm confessing, I mustn't exaggerate,' he continued. 'I go to Virginia twelve times a year to discuss with agents the problems they've faced while working in the field. I was full of bright ideas to assist them in the peace and comfort of Langley, but I'll treat them with more respect now I've experienced some of the problems they come up against, especially having made such a mess of things myself.'

'It can't be true,' she said suddenly. 'Tell me you're making it up, Simon.'

'I'm afraid not, Hannah. This time it's all true,' he said. 'You must believe me. I only ended up in Paris after years of demanding to be tested in the field, because, with all my theoretical knowledge, I assumed I'd be a whizz if they just gave me the chance to prove myself. Scott Bradley, Professor of Constitutional Law. Infallible in the eyes of his adoring students at Yale and the senior CIA operatives at Langley. There'll be no standing ovation after this performance, of that we can both be sure.'

Hannah stood and stared down at him. 'Tell me it's not true, Simon,' she said. 'It mustn't be true. Why did you choose me? Why me?'

He stood and took her in his arms. 'I didn't choose you, I fell in love with you. They chose me. My people . . . my people needed to find out why Mossad had put you . . . put you in the Jordanian Embassy attached to the Iraqi Interest Section.' He was finding it difficult to remain coherent, and couldn't understand why he felt so sleepy.

'But why you?' she asked, clinging on to him for the first time that evening. 'Why not a regular CIA agent?'

'Because . . . because they wanted to put someone in . . . someone who wouldn't be recognised by any of the professionals.'

'Oh, my God, who am I meant to believe?' she said, breaking away. She stared helplessly at him.

'You can believe me, because I'll prove . . . prove all I've said is true.' Scott began to move away from the table. He felt unsteady as he walked slowly over to the sideboard, bent down to pull open the bottom drawer, and after some rummaging around removed a small leather case with the initials S.B. printed in gold on the top right-hand corner. He smiled a triumphant smile and turned back. He attempted to steady himself by resting one hand on the sideboard. He looked towards the blurred figure of the woman he loved, but could no longer see the desperate look on her face. He tried to remember how much he had already told her and how much she still needed to know.

'Oh, my darling, what have I done?' she said, her eyes now pleading.

'Nothing, it's all been my fault,' said Scott. 'But we'll have the rest of our lives to laugh about it. That, by the way, was a proposal. Feeble, I agree, but I couldn't love you any more than I do. You must surely realise that,' he added as he tried to take a pace towards her. She stood staring at him helplessly as he lurched forward before attempting to take a second step. Then he tried again, but this time he stumbled and collapsed across the table, finally landing with a thud on the floor at her feet.

'I can't blame you if you don't feel the same way as . . .' were his final words, as the leather case burst open, disgorging its contents all around a body that was suddenly still.

Hannah fell on her knees and took his head in her hands. She began to sob uncontrollably. 'I love you, of course I love you, Simon. But why didn't you trust me enough to tell me the truth?'

Her eyes rested on a small photo lodged between his fingers. She snatched it from his grasp. Written on the back were the words 'Katherine Bradley – Summer '66'. It must have been his mother. She grabbed the passport that lay by the side of his head and quickly turned the pages, trying to read through her tears. Male. Date of birth: 11.7.56. Profession: University Professor. She turned another page and a photo from *Paris Match* fell out. She stared at herself modelling an Ungaro suit from the spring collection of 1990.

'No, no. Don't let it be true,' Hannah said as she lifted him back into her arms. 'Let it be just more lies.'

And then her eyes settled on the envelope simply addressed 'Hannah'. She lowered his body gently to the ground, picked up the envelope and ripped it open.

My dearest Hannah,

I have tried to think of a hundred ways to begin this letter. There's one simple way. I love you. And, as important, I have never loved before, and now I know I can never love anyone like this again.

'No!' she screamed, 'No!' almost unable to read his words through her tears.

You are not only my lover but my closest friend. I'll never want or need anyone else ever again. I rejoice at the thought of spending the rest of my life with you, and wonder how I deserve to be so lucky.

'Please, God, no,' she wept as her head fell on his chest. 'I love you, too, Simon. I love you so much.'

I want three daughters and two sons and I must warn you that I won't settle for less. We'll discuss grandchildren later. I fear I'll be irascible and tiresome in old age, but I'll never stop loving you. Don't let's wait

'No, no, no . . .' Hannah cried as she bent down to kiss him. She suddenly leaped up and rushed over to the phone. She dialled 17 and screamed, 'Please God, let one pill not be enough. Answer, answer, answer!' she shrieked at the phone as the door of Scott's apartment flew open. Hannah turned to see Kratz and another man whom she didn't recognise come bursting in.

She dropped the phone on the floor and ran towards them, throwing herself at Kratz and knocking him to the ground.

'You bastard, you bastard!' she screamed. 'You made me kill the only person I ever really loved! I hope you rot in hell!' she said as her fists pumped down into his face.

The unknown man moved quickly across and threw Hannah to one side, before the two of them picked up Scott's limp body and carried him out of the room.

Hannah lay in the corner, weeping.

An hour passed, maybe two, before she crawled slowly back to the table, opened her bag and removed the second pill.

18

'WHITE HOUSE.'

'Mr Butterworth, please.'

There was a long silence. 'I don't show anyone by that name, sir. Just a moment and I'll put you through to Personnel.'

The Archivist waited patiently, made aware as each second passed that the new telephone system ordered by the Clinton administration was clearly overdue.

'Personnel office,' said a female voice. 'How can I help you?'

'I'm trying to locate Mr Rex Butterworth, Special Assistant to the President.'

'Who's calling?'

'Marshall, Calder Marshall, Archivist.'

'Of – ?'

'Of the United States of America.'

There was another long silence.

'The name Butterworth rings no bells with me, sir, but I'm sure you realise there are more than forty Special and Deputy Assistants to the President.'

'No, I didn't realise,' admitted Marshall. There followed another long silence.

'According to our records,' said the female voice, 'he seems to have returned to the Department of Commerce. He was a Schedule A – just here on temporary assignment.'

'Would you have a number where I might reach him?'

'No, I don't. But if you call the department locator at the Commerce Department, I'm sure they will find him for you.'

'Thank you for your help.'

'Glad to have been of assistance, sir.'

Hannah could never recall how long she had lain huddled up in the corner of Simon's room. She couldn't think of him as Scott, she would always think of him as Simon. An hour, possibly two. Time no longer had any relevance for her. She could remember crawling back to the centre of the room, avoiding overturned chairs and tables that would have looked more appropriate in a nightclub that had just experienced a drunken brawl.

She removed the pill from her bag and flushed it down the lavatory, the automatic action of any well-drilled agent. She then began to search among the debris for any photographs she could find and, of course, the letter addressed simply to 'Hannah'. She stuffed these few mementoes into her bag and tried, with the help of a fallen chair, to get back on her feet.

Later that night she lay in her bed at the embassy, staring up at the blank white ceiling, unable to recall her journey back, the route she had taken or even if she had climbed the fire escape or entered by the front door. She wondered how many nights it would be before she managed to sleep for more than a few minutes at a time. How much time would have to pass before he wasn't her every other thought?

She knew Mossad would want to take her out, hide her, protect her – as they saw it – until the French police had completed their investigation. Governments would have their diplomatic arms twisted up their diplomatic backs. The Americans would expect a lot in return for killing one of their agents, but eventually a bargain would be struck. Hannah Kopec, Simon Rosenthal and Professor Scott Bradley would become closed files. For all three of them were numbers: interchangeable, dispensable and, of course, replaceable.

She wondered what they would do with his body, the body of the man she loved. An honourable but anonymous grave, she suspected. They would argue that it must be in the interest of the greater good. Wherever they buried him, she knew they would never allow her to find his grave.

She wouldn't have dropped the pill in the coffee in the first place if Kratz hadn't talked again and again of the thirty-nine Scuds that had landed on the people of Israel, and in particular of the one which had killed her mother, her brother and her sister.

She might even have drawn back at the last moment if they hadn't threatened to carry out the job themselves, should she refuse. They promised her that if that was the case, it would be a far more unpleasant death.

Just as Hannah was about to take the first pill out of her bag, she had asked Simon for some sugar, one last lifeline. Why hadn't he grabbed at it? Why didn't he question her, tease her about her weight, do anything that would have made her have second thoughts? But then why, why had he waited so long to tell her the truth?

If he had only realised that she had things to tell him, too. The Ambassador had been called back to Iraq – a promotion, he explained. He was, as Kanuk had been telling everyone, to become Deputy Foreign Minister, which meant that in the absence of Muhammad Saeed Al-Zahiaf, he would be working directly with Saddam Hussein.

His place at the embassy was to be taken by a Hamid

Al Obaydi, the number two at the United Nations, who had recently rendered some great service for Iraq, of which she would eventually learn. The Ambassador had offered her the choice of remaining in Paris to serve under Al Obaydi, or returning to Iraq and continuing to work with him. Only days before, Mossad would have considered such an offer an irresistible opportunity.

Hannah so wanted to tell Simon that she no longer cared about Saddam, that he had made it possible for her to overcome her hatred of the Scuds, even made the death of her family a wound that might in time be healed. She knew that she was no longer capable of killing anyone, as long as she had someone to live for.

But now that Simon was dead, her desire for revenge was even stronger than before.

'Department of Commerce.'

'Rex Butterworth, please.'

'What agency?'

'I'm not sure I understand,' said the Archivist.

'What agency is Mr Butterworth with?' asked the operator, pronouncing each word slowly, as if she were addressing a four-year-old.

'I have no idea,' admitted the Archivist.

'We don't show anyone by that name.'

'But the White House told me –'

'I don't care what the White House told you. If you don't know which agency –'

'May I have the Personnel Office?'

'Just a minute.' It turned out to be far longer than a minute.

'Office of Personnel.'

'This is Calder Marshall, Archivist of the United States. May I speak to the director?'

'I'm sorry, but he's not available. Would you like to speak to his executive assistant, Alex Wagner?'

'Yes. That would be just fine,' said Marshall.

'She's not in today. Could you call again tomorrow?'

'Yes,' said Marshall with a sigh.

'Glad to have been of assistance, sir.'

When Kratz's car screeched to a halt outside the Centre Cardio-vasculaire on bois Gilbert there were three doctors, two orderlies and a nurse waiting for them on the hospital steps. The embassy must have pulled out every stop.

The two orderlies ran forward and lifted the body gently but firmly out of the back seat of the car, carrying Scott quickly up the steps before placing him on a waiting trolley.

Even as the trolley was being wheeled down the corridor the three doctors and the nurse surrounded the body and began their examination. The nurse quickly removed Scott's shirt and trousers while the first doctor opened his mouth to check his breathing. The second, a consultant, lowered his ear onto Scott's chest and tried to listen for a heartbeat, while the third checked his blood pressure; none of them looked hopeful.

The consultant turned to the Mossad leader and said firmly, 'Don't waste any time with lies. How did it happen?'

'We poisoned him, but he turned out not to be –'

'I'm not interested,' he said. 'What poison did you administer?'

'Ergot alkaloid,' said Kratz.

The consultant switched his attention to one of his assistants. 'Ring the Hospital Widal and get me details of its action and the correct antidote, fast,' he said as the orderlies crashed through the rubber doors and into a private operating theatre.

The first doctor had managed to keep Scott's mouth open during the short journey and create an airway. He had already pressed down the tongue to leave a clear passageway to the larynx. Once the trolley had come to a stop in the theatre he inserted a clear angled plastic tube of about five inches in length to ensure the tongue could not be swallowed.

The nurse then placed a mask over Scott's nose and mouth that was connected to an oxygen supply on the wall. Attached to the side of the mask was a rubber bag, which she began pumping regularly every three or four seconds with her left hand as she held his head steady with her right. Scott's lungs were immediately filled with oxygen.

The consultant placed an ear over Scott's heart again. He could still hear nothing. He raised his head and nodded to an orderly who began rubbing paste on different parts of Scott's chest. Another nurse followed him, placing small electronic discs on the paste marks. The wires from the discs were connected to a heart monitor machine that stood on a table by the side of the trolley.

The fine line that ran across the machine and registered the strength of the heartbeat produced a weak signal.

The consultant smiled below his mask, as the nurse continued to pump oxygen into the patient's mouth and nose.

Suddenly, without warning, the heart machine gave out a piercing sound. Everyone in the operating theatre turned to face the monitor, which was now showing a thin, flat line running from one side of the screen to the other.

'Cardiac arrest!' shouted the consultant. He jumped

forward and placed the heel of his hand over Scott's sternum, and with both arms firmly locked he began to rock backwards and forwards as he tried to push a volume of blood from the heart to resuscitate his patient. Like a proficient weightlifter, he was able to pump away with his arms at a rate of forty to fifty times a minute.

A houseman wheeled forward the defibrillator. The consultant placed two large electric clamps onto the front and side of Scott's chest.

'Two hundred joules,' said the consultant. 'Stand clear.' They all took a pace back as a shock was transferred from the electric discharge machine and ran through Scott's body.

They stared at the monitor as the consultant jumped forward again and continued to pump Scott's chest with the palms of his hands, but the thin green line did not respond. 'Two hundred joules, stand clear,' he repeated firmly, and they all stood back again to watch the effect of the electric shock. But the line remained obstinately flat. The consultant quickly returned to pumping Scott's chest with his hands.

'Three hundred and sixty joules, stand clear,' said the consultant in desperation, but the nurse who raised the number on the dial knew the patient was already dead.

The consultant pressed a button, and they all watched the highest shock allowed pass through Scott's body, assuming that must be the end. They turned their attention to the monitor.

'We've lost him,' was on the consultant's lips, when to their astonishment they saw the line begin to show a faint flicker. He leaped forward and began pumping away with the palms of his hands as the flicker continued to show irregular fibrillation. 'Three hundred and sixty joules, stand clear,' he said once again. The button was pressed and their attention returned to the monitor. Fibrillation returned to a normal rhythm. The youngest doctor cheered.

The consultant quickly located a vein in Scott's left arm and jabbed a needle directly into it, leaving a cannula sticking out to which a saline drip was quickly attached.

Another doctor rushed into the theatre and, facing his superior, said, 'The antidote is GTN.'

A nurse went straight over to the poisons cabinet and extracted a phial of glyceryl trinitrate, which she passed to the consultant, who had a syringe ready. He extracted the blue liquid from the phial, shot a little into the air to be sure it was flowing freely, then pumped the antidote into a side valve of the intravenous drip. He turned to watch the monitor. The flicker maintained a constant rhythm.

The consultant turned to the senior nurse and said, 'Do you believe in miracles?'

'No,' she replied. 'I'm a Jew. Miracles are only for Christians.'

Hannah began to form a plan, a plan that would brook no interference from Kratz. She had made the decision to accept the job as senior secretary to the Ambassador, and to accompany him back to Iraq.

As the hours passed, her plan began to take shape. She was aware there would be problems. Not from the Iraqi side, but from her own people. Hannah knew that she would have to circumvent Mossad's attempts to take her out, which meant that she could never leave the embassy, even for one moment, until the time came for the Ambassador to return to Iraq. She would use all the techniques they had taught her over the past two years to defeat them.

When she was in Iraq, Hannah would make herself

indispensable to the Ambassador, bide her time and, once she had achieved her objective, happily die a martyr's death.

She had been left with only one purpose in life now that Simon was dead. To assassinate Saddam Hussein.

'Department of Commerce.'

'Alex Wagner, please,' said the Archivist.

'Who?'

'Alex Wagner. Office of Personnel.'

'Just a minute.' Another stretched minute.

'Personnel.'

'This is Calder Marshall, Archivist of the United States. I called yesterday for Ms Wagner and you told me to try again today.'

'I wasn't here yesterday, sir.'

'Well, it must have been one of your colleagues. Is Ms Wagner available?'

'Just a minute.'

This time the Archivist waited several minutes.

'Alex Wagner,' said a brisk female voice.

'Ms Wagner, my name is Calder Marshall. I'm the Archivist of the United States, and it's extremely important that I contact Mr Rex Butterworth, who was recently detailed to the White House by the Commerce Department.'

'Are you a former employer of Mr Butterworth's?' asked the brisk voice.

'No, I am not,' replied Marshall.

'Are you a relative?'

'No.'

'Then I'm afraid I cannot help you, Mr Marshall.'

'Why's that?' asked the Archivist.

'Because the Privacy Act prohibits us from giving

out any personal information about government employees.'

'Can you tell me the name of the Commerce Director, or is that covered by the Privacy Act too?' the Archivist asked.

'Dick Fielding,' said the voice abruptly.

'Thank you for your assistance,' said the Archivist.

The phone went dead.

When Scott woke, his first memory was of Hannah. And then he slept.

When he woke a second time, all he could make out were blurred figures who appeared to be bending over him. And then he slept.

When he woke again, the blurs began to take some shape. Most of them seemed to be dressed in white. And then he slept.

When he woke the next time it was dark and he was alone. He felt so weak, so limp, as he tried to remember what had happened. And then he slept.

When he woke, for the first time he could hear their voices, soothing, gentle, but he could not make out the words, however hard he tried. And then he slept.

When he woke again, they had propped him up in bed. They were trying to feed him a warm, tasteless liquid through a plastic straw. And then he slept.

When he woke, a man in a long white coat, with a stethoscope and a warm smile, was asking in a pronounced accent, 'Can you hear me?' He tried to nod, but fell asleep.

When he woke, another doctor – this time he could see him clearly – was listening attentively as Scott attempted his first words. 'Hannah. Hannah,' was all he said. And then he slept.

He woke again, and an attractive woman with short dark hair and a caring smile was leaning over him. He returned her smile and asked the time. It must have sounded strange to her, but he wanted to know.

'It's a few minutes after three in the morning,' the nurse told him.

'How long have I been here?' he managed.

'Just over a week, but you were so close to death. I think in English you have the expression "touch and go". If your friends had been a moment –' And then he slept.

When he woke, the doctor told Scott that when he'd first arrived they thought it was too late, and twice he'd been pronounced technically dead. 'Antidotes and electrostimulation of the heart, combined with a rare determination to live and one nurse's theory that you might be a Gentile, defied the technical pronouncement,' he declared with a smile.

Scott asked if someone called Hannah had been to see him. The doctor checked the board at the end of his bed. There had been only two visitors that he was aware of, both of them men. They came every day. And then Scott slept.

When he woke, the two men the doctor had mentioned were standing one on each side of his bed. Scott smiled at Dexter Hutchins, who was trying not to cry. Grown men don't cry, he wanted to say, especially when they work for the CIA. He turned to the other man. He had never seen a face so full of shame, so ridden with guilt, or eyes so red from not sleeping. Scott tried to ask what had caused him such unhappiness. And then he slept.

When he woke, both men were still there, now resting on uncomfortable chairs, half asleep.

'Dexter,' he whispered, and they both woke immediately. 'Where's Hannah?'

The other man, who Scott noticed was recovering from a black eye and a broken nose, took some time answering his question. And then Scott slept, never wanting to wake again.

19

'DEPARTMENT OF COMMERCE.'

'The Director, please.'

'Who's calling?'

'Marshall, Calder Marshall.'

'Is he expecting your call?'

'No, he is not.'

'Mr Fielding only takes calls from people who have previously booked to speak to him.'

'What about his secretary?' asked Marshall.

'She never takes calls.'

'So how do I get a booking with Mr Fielding?'

'You have to speak to Miss Zelumski in reservations.'

'Can I be put through to Miss Zelumski, or do I have to make a reservation to speak to her as well?'

'There is no need to be sarcastic, sir. I'm only doing my job.'

'I'm sorry. Perhaps you'd put me through to Miss Zelumski.'

Marshall waited patiently.

'Miss Zelumski speaking.'

'I'd like to reserve a call to speak to Mr Fielding.'

'Is it domestic, most-favoured status or foreign?' asked a bored-sounding voice.

'It's personal.'

'Does he know you?'

'No, he doesn't.'

'Then I can't help. I only deal with domestic, most-favoured status or foreign.'

The Archivist hung up before Miss Zelumski was given the chance to say 'Glad to have been of assistance, sir.'

Marshall tapped his fingers on the desk. The time had come to play by new rules.

Cavalli had checked into the Hôtel de la Paix in Geneva the previous evening. He had booked a modest suite overlooking the lake. Neither expensive nor conspicuous. After he had undressed, he climbed into bed and tuned in to CNN. He watched for a few moments, but found that the news of Bill Clinton having his hair cut on board Air Force One while it was parked on a runway at Los Angeles airport was getting more coverage than the Americans shooting down a plane in the no-fly zone over Iraq. It seemed the new President was determined to prove to Saddam that he was every bit as tough as Bush.

When Cavalli woke in the morning, he jumped out of bed, strolled across to the window, opened the curtains and admired the fountain in the centre of the lake whose water spouted like a gushing well high into the air. He turned to see that an envelope had been pushed under the door. He tore it open to discover a note confirming his appointment to 'take tea' with his banker, Monsieur Franchard, at eleven o'clock that morning. Cavalli was about to drop the card into the waste-paper basket when he noticed some words scribbled on the bottom:

I do hope you find the brand appropriate.
Have a good party. *N.V.*

After a light breakfast in his room, Cavalli packed his suitcase and hanging bag before going downstairs. The doorman answered his questions in perfect English, and confirmed the directions to Franchard et cie. In Switzerland hall porters know the location of banks, just as their London counterparts can direct you to theatres and football grounds.

As Cavalli left the hotel and started the short walk to the bank, he couldn't help feeling something wasn't quite right. And then he realised that the streets were clean, the people he passed were well-dressed, sober and silent. A contrast in every way to New York.

Once he reached the front door of the bank, Cavalli pressed the discreet bell under the equally discreet brass plate announcing 'Franchard et cie'.

A doorman responded to the call. Cavalli walked into a marble-pillared hall of perfect proportions.

'Perhaps you would like to go straight to the tenth floor, Mr Cavalli? I believe Monsieur Franchard is expecting you.'

Cavalli had only entered the building twice before in his life. How did they manage it? And the porter turned out to be as good as his word, because when Cavalli stepped out of the lift, the chairman of the bank was waiting there to greet him.

'Good morning, Mr Cavalli,' he said. 'Shall we go to my office?'

The chairman's office was a modest, tastefully decorated room, Swiss bankers not wishing to frighten away their customers with a show of conspicuous wealth.

Cavalli was surprised to see a large brown parcel placed in the centre of the boardroom table, giving no clue as to its contents.

'This arrived for you this morning,' the banker

explained. 'I thought it might have something to do with our proposed meeting.'

Cavalli smiled, leaned over and pulled the parcel towards him. He quickly ripped off the brown-paper covering to find a packing case with the words 'TEA: BOSTON' stamped across it.

With the help of a heavy silver letter-opener which he picked up from a side table, Cavalli prised the wooden lid slowly open. He didn't notice the slight grimace that came over the chairman's face.

Cavalli stared inside. The top of the box was filled with styrofoam packing material, which he cupped out with his hands and scattered all over the boardroom table.

The chairman quickly placed a waste-paper basket by his side, which Cavalli ignored as he continued to dig into the box until he finally came to some objects wrapped in tissue-paper.

He removed a piece of the tissue-paper to reveal a teacup in the Confederate colours of the First Congress.

It took Cavalli several minutes to unwrap an entire tea set, which he laid out on the table in front of the puzzled banker. Once it was unpacked, Cavalli also appeared a little mystified. He dug into the box again, and retrieved an envelope. He tore it open and began reading the contents out loud.

> This is a copy of the famous tea set made in 1777 by Pearson and Son to commemorate the Boston Tea Party. Each set is accompanied by an authentic copy of the Declaration of Independence. Your set is number 20917, and has been recorded in our books under the name of J. Hancock.

The letter had been signed and verified by the present chairman, H. William Pearson VI.

Cavalli burst out laughing as he dug deeper into the wooden box, removing yet more packing material until he came across a thin plastic cylinder. He had to admire the way Nick Vicente had fooled the US Customs into allowing him to export the original. The banker's expression remained one of bafflement. Cavalli placed the cylinder in the centre of the table, before going over in considerable detail how he wanted the meeting at twelve to be conducted.

The banker nodded from time to time, and made the occasional note on the pad in front of him.

'I would also like the plastic tube placed in a strongbox for the time being. The key to the box should be handed over to Mr Al Obaydi when, and only when, you have received the full payment by wire transfer. The money should then be deposited in my No. 3 account in your Zurich branch.'

'And are you able to tell me the exact sum you anticipate receiving from Mr Al Obaydi?' asked the banker.

'Ninety million dollars,' said Cavalli.

The banker didn't raise an eyebrow.

The Archivist looked up the name of the Commerce Secretary in his government directory, then picked up his phone and pressed one button. 482 2000 was now programmed into his speed dial.

'Department of Commerce.'

'Dick Fielding, please.'

'Just a moment.'

'Office of the Director.'

'This is Secretary Brown.'

The Archivist had to wait only a few seconds before the call was put through.

'Good morning, Mr Secretary,' said an alert voice.

'Good morning, Mr Fielding. This is Calder Marshall, Archivist of the United States of America.'

'I thought . . .'

'You thought . . .?'

'I guess I must have picked up the wrong phone. How may I help you, Mr Marshall?'

'I'm trying to trace a former employee of yours. Rex Butterworth.'

'I can't help you on that one.'

'Why? Are you bound by the Privacy Act as well?'

Fielding laughed. 'I only wish I was.'

'I don't understand,' said the Archivist.

'Last week we sent Butterworth a merit bonus, and it was returned, "No forwarding address".'

'But he has a wife.'

'She got the same response to her last letter.'

'And his mother in South Carolina?'

'She's been dead for years.'

'Thank you,' said Calder Marshall, and put the phone down. He knew exactly who he had to call next.

Dummond et cie is one of Geneva's more modern banking establishments, having been founded as late as 1781. Since then the bank has spent over two hundred years handling other people's money, without religious or racial prejudice. Dummond et cie had always been willing to deal with Arab sheik or Jewish businessman, Nazi Gauleiter or British aristocrat, in fact anyone who required their services. It was a policy that had reaped dividends in every trading currency throughout the world.

The bank occupied twelve floors of a building just off the place de la Fusterie. The meeting that had been arranged that Tuesday at noon was scheduled to take place in the boardroom on the eleventh floor, the floor below the chairman's office.

The chairman of the bank, Pierre Dummond, had held his present position for the past nineteen years, but even he had rarely experienced a more unlikely coupling than that between an educated Arab from Iraq and the son of a former Mafia lawyer from New York.

The boardroom table could seat sixteen, but on this occasion it was only occupied by four. Pierre Dummond sat in the centre of one of the long sides under a portrait of his uncle, the former chairman, François Dummond. The present chairman wore a dark suit of elegant cut and style that would not have looked out of place had it been worn by any of the chairmen of the forty-eight banks located within a square mile of the building. His shirt was of a shade of blue that was not influenced by Milan fashions, and his tie was so discreet that, moments after leaving the room, only a remarkably observant client would have been able to recall its colour or pattern.

On Monsieur Dummond's right sat his client, Mr Al Obaydi, whose dress, although slightly more fashionable, was nonetheless equally conservative.

Opposite Monsieur Dummond sat the chairman of Franchard et cie, who, any observer would have noticed, must have shared the same tailor as Monsieur Dummond. On Franchard's left sat Antonio Cavalli, wearing a double-breasted Armani suit, who looked as if he had dropped in on the wrong meeting.

The little carriage clock that sat on the Louis-Philippe mantelpiece behind Monsieur Dummond completed twelve strokes. The chairman cleared his throat and began the proceedings.

'Gentlemen, the purpose of this meeting, which was called at our instigation but with your agreement, is to exchange a rare document for an agreed sum of money.' Monsieur Dummond pushed his half-moon spectacles further up his nose. 'Naturally, I must begin, Mr Cavalli, by asking if you are in possession of that document?'

'No, he is not, sir,' interjected Monsieur Franchard, as prearranged with Cavalli, 'because he has entrusted the document's safekeeping to our bank. But I can confirm that, as soon as the sum has been transferred, I have been given power of attorney to release the document immediately.'

'But that is not what we agreed,' interrupted Dummond, who leaned forward, feigning shock, before adding, 'My client's government has no intention of paying another cent without full scrutiny of the document. You agreed to deliver it here by midday, and in any case we still have to be convinced of its authenticity.'

'That is understood by my client,' said Monsieur Franchard. 'Indeed, you are most welcome to attend my office at any time convenient to you in order to carry out such an inspection. Following that inspection, the moment you have transferred the agreed amount the document will be released.'

'This is all very well,' countered Monsieur Dummond, pushing his half-moon spectacles back up his nose, 'but your client has failed to keep to his original agreement, which in my view allows my client's government' – he emphasised the word 'government' – 'to reconsider its position.'

'My client felt it prudent, in the circumstances, to protect his interest by depositing the document in his own bank for safekeeping,' came back the immediate reply from Monsieur Franchard.

Anyone watching the two bankers sparring with each other might have been surprised to learn that they played chess together every Saturday night, which Monsieur

Franchard invariably won, and tennis after lunch on Sunday, which he regularly lost.

'I cannot accept this new arrangement,' said Al Obaydi, speaking for the first time. 'My government has charged me to pay only a further forty million dollars if the original agreement is breached in any way.'

'But this is ridiculous!' said Cavalli, his voice rising with every word. 'We are quibbling over a matter of a few hours at the most and a building less than half a mile away. And as you well know, the figure agreed on was ninety million.'

'But you have since broken our agreement,' said Al Obaydi, 'so the original terms can no longer be considered valid by my government.'

'No ninety million, no document!' said Cavalli, banging his fist on the table.

'Let us be realistic, Mr Cavalli,' said Al Obaydi. 'The document is no longer of any use to you, and I have a feeling you would have settled for fifty million in the first place.'

'That is not the –'

Monsieur Franchard touched Cavalli's arm. 'I would like a few minutes alone with my client, and, if I may, the use of a telephone.'

'Of course,' said Monsieur Dummond, rising from his place. 'We will leave you. Please press the button under the table the moment you wish us to return.'

Monsieur Dummond and his client left the room without another word.

'He's bluffing,' said Cavalli. 'He'll pay. I know it.'

'I don't think so,' said Franchard.

'What makes you say that?'

'The use of the words "my government".'

'What does that tell us that we didn't already know?'

'The expression was repeated four times,' said

Franchard, 'which suggests to me that the financial decision has been taken out of the hands of Mr Al Obaydi, and only forty million has been deposited by his government with Dummond et cie.'

Cavalli began pacing round the room, but stopped by the phone which rested on a small side table.

'I presume that's bugged,' said Cavalli, pointing at the phone.

'No, Mr Cavalli, it is not.'

'How can you be so sure?' asked his client.

'Monsieur Dummond and I are currently involved in several transactions, and he would never allow our relationship to suffer for the sake of one deal. And in any case, he sits on the opposite side of the table from you today but, like every Swiss banker, that won't stop him from thinking of you as a potential customer.'

Cavalli checked his watch. It was 6.20 a.m. in New York. His father would have been up for at least an hour. He jabbed out the fourteen numbers and waited.

His father answered the phone, sounding wide awake, and after preliminary exchanges listened carefully to his son's account of what had taken place in the bank's boardroom. Cavalli also repeated Monsieur Franchard's view of the situation. The chairman of Skills didn't take long considering what advice he should give his son, advice which took Cavalli by surprise.

He replaced the phone and informed Monsieur Franchard of his father's opinion.

Monsieur Franchard nodded as if to show he agreed with the older man's judgement.

'Then let's get on with it,' said Cavalli reluctantly. Monsieur Franchard pressed the button under the boardroom table.

Monsieur Dummond and his client entered the room a few moments later and returned to the seats they had previously occupied. The old banker pushed his half-moon spectacles up his nose once again and stared over the top of them as he waited for Monsieur Franchard to speak.

'If the transaction is completed within one hour, we will settle for forty million dollars. If not, the deal is off and the document will be returned to the United States.'

Dummond removed his spectacles and turned to glance at his client. He was pleased that Franchard had picked up the significance of 'my government', a phrase he had recommended Mr Al Obaydi should use as often as possible.

'White House?'

'Yes, sir.'

'May I speak to the President's scheduler, please?'

'Can I ask who's calling?'

'Marshall, Calder Marshall, Archivist of the United States. And before you ask, yes, I do know her, and yes, she is expecting my call.'

The line went dead. Marshall wondered if he had been cut off.

'Patty Watson speaking.'

'Patty, this is Calder Marshall. I'm the –'

'Archivist of the United States.'

'I don't believe it.'

'Oh, yes, I'm a great fan of yours, Mr Marshall. I've even read your book on the history of the Constitution, the Bill of Rights and the Declaration. How can I help you? – Are you still there, Mr Marshall?'

'Yes, Patty, I am. I only wanted to check on the President's schedule on the morning of May 25th this year.'

'Certainly, sir. I'll just be a moment.'

The Archivist did not have long to wait.

'Ah yes, May 25th. The President spent the morning in the Oval Office with his speech writers, David Kusnet and Carolyn Curiel. He was preparing the text for his address on the GATT at the Chicago Council on Foreign Relations. He took a break to have lunch with Senator Mitchell, the Majority Leader. At three, the President –'

'Did President Clinton remain in the White House the whole morning?'

'Yes, sir. He didn't leave the White House all day. He spent the afternoon with Mrs Clinton in discussions with her health-policy task unit.'

'Could he have slipped out of the building without even you knowing, Patty?'

The scheduling secretary laughed. 'That's not possible, sir. If he had done that, the Secret Service would have informed me immediately.'

'Thank you, Patty.'

'Glad to have been of assistance, sir.'

Once the meeting at Dummond et cie had broken up, Cavalli returned to his hotel room to wait for Franchard to call and confirm that the sum of forty million dollars had been deposited in his No. 3 account in Zurich.

As long as the transaction was closed within the hour, he would still have easily enough time to catch the 4.45 out of Geneva for Heathrow and make the early-evening connection to New York.

Cavalli began to get a little anxious after thirty minutes passed and there had been no call, and even more so after forty. After fifty, he found himself pacing around the room, staring out at the fountain, and checking his watch every few moments.

When the phone eventually rang, he grabbed it.

'Mr Cavalli?' enquired a voice.

'Speaking.'

'Franchard here. The document has been verified and taken away. It might interest you to know that Mr Al Obaydi studied one word on the parchment for some time before he agreed to transfer the money. The agreed sum has been credited to your No. 3 account in Zurich as you specified.'

'Thank you, Monsieur Franchard,' said Cavalli without further comment.

'My pleasure, as always, Mr Cavalli. And is there anything else we can do for you while you're here?'

'Yes,' replied Cavalli. 'I need to transfer a quarter of a million dollars to a bank in the Cayman Islands.'

'The same name and account as the last three transactions?' asked the banker.

'Yes,' replied Cavalli. 'And the Zurich account, presently registered in the name of Mr Al Obaydi: I want to withdraw one hundred thousand dollars from it and . . .'

Monsieur Franchard listened carefully to his client's further instructions.

'State Department.'

'Can I speak to the Secretary of State?'

'Just a moment.'

'Office of the Secretary.'

'This is Calder Marshall. I'm the Archivist of the United States. It's vitally important that I speak with Secretary Christopher.'

'I'll put you through to his executive assistant, sir.'

'Thank you,' said Marshall, and waited for a very short time.

'This is Jack Leigh. I'm executive assistant to the Secretary. How may I help you, sir?'

'To start with, Mr Leigh, how many executive assistants does the Secretary of State have?'

'Five, sir, but there is only one senior to me.'

'Then I need to speak to the Secretary of State urgently.'

'Right now he's out of the office. Perhaps the Deputy Secretary can help?'

'No, Mr Leigh, he cannot help.'

'Well, I'll certainly let Secretary Christopher know you called, sir.'

'Thank you, Mr Leigh. And perhaps you'd be kind enough to pass a message on to him?'

'Of course, sir.'

'Would you let him know that my resignation will be on his desk tomorrow morning by nine a.m. This call is simply to apologise for the harm it will undoubtedly do to the President, particularly given the short period of time he has been in office.'

'You haven't spoken to anyone from the media about this, have you, sir?' asked the executive assistant, sounding anxious for the first time.

'No, I have not, Mr Leigh, and I shall not do so until noon tomorrow, which should give the Secretary ample time in which to prepare answers to any questions that he and the President will undoubtedly be asked by the press when they learn my reason for resigning.'

'I'll have the Secretary get back to you as quickly as I can, sir.'

'Thank you, Mr Leigh.'

'Glad to have been of assistance, sir.'

* * *

She flew into the Cayman Islands that morning and took a taxi to Barclays Bank in Georgetown. She checked her account to find it had been credited with three payments of two hundred and fifty thousand dollars. One on March 9th, another on April 27th, and a further one on May 30th.

There was one still to come. But, to be fair, Cavalli might not learn of the death of T. Hamilton McKenzie until he had returned from Geneva.

'And we have another package for you, Miss Webster,' said the smiling West Indian behind the counter.

Far too familiar, she thought. Once again the time had come for her to move her account to another bank in another country, in another name. She dropped the package into her carrier bag, threw it over her shoulder and left without a word.

She didn't attempt to open the thick brown envelope until she had called for coffee at the end of an unhurried meal at a hotel she would never book into. She then carefully slit open the top of the bulky package with her bread knife, allowing the contents to spill out onto the table.

The usual photos, from every angle, plus addresses past and present, and the daily habits and haunts of the intended victim. Cavalli never left any room for mistakes.

She studied the photos of a little fat man sitting on a bar stool. He looked harmless enough. The contract was always the same. To be carried out within fourteen days. Payment two hundred and fifty thousand dollars to account specified.

It wasn't Columbus or Washington this time, but San Francisco. She hadn't been to the West Coast in years, and she tried to remember if they had a Laura Ashley store.

* * *

'National Archives.'

'Mr Marshall, please.'

'Who's calling?'

'Christopher. Warren Christopher.'

'And you're with which agency?'

'I have a feeling he'll know.'

'I'll put you through, sir.' The Secretary waited patiently.

'Calder Marshall speaking.'

'Calder, it's Warren Christopher.'

'Good morning, Mr Secretary.'

'Good morning, Calder. I've just received your letter of resignation.'

'Yes, sir. I thought it was the only course of action I could take in the circumstances.'

'Very commendable, I feel sure, but have you let anyone else into your confidence?'

'No, sir. I intended to brief my staff at eleven and hold a press conference at twelve, as stated in my letter. I hope that doesn't inconvenience you, sir.'

'Well, I wondered if before you did that, you might find the time to have a meeting with the President and myself?'

Marshall hesitated only because the request had taken him by surprise.

'Of course, sir. What time would suit you?'

'Shall we say ten o'clock?'

'Yes, sir. Where would you like me to come?'

'The North Entrance of the White House.'

'The North Entrance, of course.'

'Jack Leigh, my executive assistant, will meet you in the West Wing reception area and accompany you to the Oval Office.'

'The Oval Office.'

'And Calder . . .'

'Yes, Mr Secretary?'

'Please do not mention your resignation to anyone until you've seen the President.'

'Until I've seen the President. Of course.'

'Thank you, Calder.'

'Glad to have been of assistance, sir.'

20

'I'D LIKE TO BEGIN by thanking you all for attending this meeting at such short notice,' said the Secretary of State. 'And, in particular, Scott Bradley, who has only recently recovered from . . .' Christopher hesitated for a moment, '. . . a near-tragic accident. I know we are all delighted by the speed of his recovery. I should also like to welcome Colonel Kratz, who is representing the Israeli Government, and Dexter Hutchins, the Deputy Director of the CIA.

'Only two of my staff are with me today: Jack Leigh, my executive assistant, and Susan Anderson, one of my senior Middle East advisers. The reason for numbers being limited on this occasion will become all too obvious to you. The issue we are about to discuss is so sensitive that the fewer people who are aware of it, the better. To suggest in this instance that silence is golden would be to underestimate the value of gold.

'Perhaps, at this juncture, I could ask the Deputy Director of the CIA to bring us up to date on the latest situation. Dexter.'

Dexter Hutchins unlocked his briefcase and removed a file marked 'For the Director's Eyes Only'. He placed the file on the table in front of him and turned its cover.

'Two days ago, Mr Marshall, the Archivist of the United States, reported to the Secretary of State that the Declaration of Independence had been stolen from the National Archives; or, to be more accurate, had been switched for a quite brilliant copy that had not only passed the scrutiny of Mr Marshall, but also that of the Senior Conservator, Mr Mendelssohn.

'It was only when Mr Marshall attempted to re-contact a Mr Rex Butterworth, who had been temporarily assigned to the White House as a Special Assistant to the President, that he became worried.'

'If I could just interject, Mr Hutchins,' said Jack Leigh, 'and point out that though Mr Butterworth was a former employee of the Commerce Department, should the press ever get hold of this you can be certain they would only refer to him as a "Special Assistant to the President".' Warren Christopher nodded his agreement.

'When Calder Marshall discovered that Butterworth hadn't returned after his vacation,' continued Dexter Hutchins, 'and that he had also left without giving a forwarding address, he naturally became suspicious. Under the circumstances, he considered it prudent to ask Mr Mendelssohn to check and see if the Declaration had in any way been tampered with. After putting the parchment through several preliminary tests – a separate memorandum has been sent to all of you on this – he came to the conclusion that they were still in possession of the original document.

'But Mr Marshall, a cautious man, remained sceptical, and contacted the President's scheduler, Miss Patty Watson – details also enclosed. Following that conversation, he asked the Conservator to carry out a more rigorous scrutiny.

'Mr Mendelssohn spent several hours alone that evening going over the parchment word by word with a magnifying glass. It was when he came to the sentence, "Nor have We been wanting in attentions to our British brethren", that the Conservator realised that the word "British" had been spelt correctly, and not with two *t*s as in the original Declaration executed by Timothy Matlock. When this piece of news was imparted to Mr Marshall, he immediately offered his resignation to the Secretary of State, a copy of which you all have.'

'If I could come in here, Dexter,' said Secretary Christopher. 'Just for the record, the President and I saw Mr Marshall in the Oval Office yesterday. He could not have been more co-operative. He assured us that he and his colleague, Mr Mendelssohn, will say and do nothing in the immediate future. He did add, however, his feeling of disgust at continuing to display a counterfeit copy of the Declaration to the general public. He made us both, that is to say the President and myself, agree that should we fail to recover the original document before its disappearance becomes common knowledge, we would confirm that his resignation had been dated May 25th 1993 and accepted by myself as custodian of the Declaration. He wished it to be confirmed in writing that he had in no way connived to deceive his staff or the nation he served. "I am not in the habit of being deceitful," were his final words before leaving the Oval Office.

'If it is possible,' continued Christopher, 'for a public servant to make the President and the Secretary of State feel morally inferior, Mr Marshall achieved it with considerable dignity. However, that does not change the fact that if we don't get the original parchment back before its theft becomes public knowledge, the media are going to roast the President and myself slowly over a spit. One thing's also for sure: the Republicans, led by Dole, will happily wash their collective hands in public. Carry on, Dexter.'

'Under the Secretary of State's instructions, we immediately formed a small task force at Langley to profile every aspect of the problem we are facing. But we quickly discovered that we were working under some severe restrictions. To begin with, because of the sensitivity of the subject and the people involved, we could not do what we automatically would have done in normal circumstances, namely consult the FBI and liaise with the DC Police Department. That, we felt, would have guaranteed us the front page of the *Washington Post*, and probably the following morning. We mustn't forget that the FBI is still smarting over the Waco siege, and they'd like nothing better than for the CIA to replace them on the front pages.

'The next problem we faced was having to tiptoe round people we'd usually bring in for questioning, for fear that they too might discover our real purpose. However, we have been able to come up with several leads without talking to any members of the public. Following a routine check of permit records at the DCPD, we discovered that a movie was being made in Washington on the same day as the document was stolen. The director of that movie was Johnny Scasiatore, who is currently on bail facing an indecency charge. Three others involved in the enterprise turn out to have criminal records. And some of those people fit the descriptions Mr Marshall and Mr Mendelssohn have given us of the group who arrived at the National Archives posing as the Presidential party. They include a certain Bill O'Reilly, a well-known forger who has spent several years in more than one of our state penitentiaries, and an actor who played the President so convincingly that both Mr Marshall and Mr Mendelssohn accepted it was him without question.'

'Surely we can discover who that was,' said Christopher.

'We already have. His name is Lloyd Adams. But we daren't bring him in.'

'How did you find him?' asked Leigh. 'After all, there are quite a few actors who can manage a passable resemblance to Clinton.'

'Agreed,' said the Deputy Director, 'but only one who's been operated on by America's leading plastic surgeon within the past few months. We have reason to believe that the ringleaders killed the surgeon and his daughter, which is why his wife reported everything she knew to the local Chief of Police.

'However, the whole operation would never have got off the ground without the inside help of Mr Rex Butterworth, who was last seen on the morning of May 25th and has since disappeared off the face of the earth. He booked a flight to Brazil, but he never showed. We have agents across the globe searching for him.'

'None of this is of any importance if we are no nearer to finding out where the original Declaration is at this moment, and who took it,' said Christopher.

'That's the bad news,' replied Dexter. 'Our agents spend hours on routine investigations that many American citizens consider a waste of taxpayers' money. But just now and then, it pays off.'

'We're all listening,' said Christopher.

'The CIA keeps under surveillance several foreign diplomats who work at the United Nations. Naturally, they would be outraged if any of them could prove what we were up to, and if we ever think they're onto us we back off immediately. In the case of Iraqis at the UN, we have people shadowing them round the clock. Our problem is that we can't operate within the UN complex itself, because if we were caught inside that building it would cause an international outcry. So, occasionally, their representatives are bound to slip our net.

'But we believe it was not a coincidence that Iraq's Deputy Ambassador to the United Nations, a Mr Hamid

Al Obaydi, was in Washington on the day the Declaration was switched, and took several photographs of the bogus filming that was taking place. The agent who was tracking Al Obaydi at the time also reported that, at 10.37, after the Declaration had gone back on display in the National Archives, Al Obaydi joined the public queue, waiting over an hour to view the parchment. But here's the clincher. He studied the document once, and then he looked at it a second time, with glasses.'

'Perhaps he's near-sighted,' said Susan.

'Our agent reports that he's never before or since seen him wearing glasses of any kind,' replied Dexter Hutchins. 'Now for the *really* bad news,' he continued.

'That wasn't it?' said Christopher.

'No, sir. Al Obaydi flew on to Geneva a week later and was spotted by our local station officer leaving a bank.' Dexter referred to his notes. 'Franchard et cie. He was carrying a plastic cylinder, and I quote, "a little over two feet in length and about two inches in diameter".'

'Who's going to tell the President?' said Christopher, putting his hands over his eyes.

'He took this cylinder by car straight to the Palais des Nations, and it hasn't been seen since.'

'And Barazan Al-Tikriti, Saddam's half-brother, is the Iraqi Ambassador to the United Nations in Geneva,' said Susan.

'Don't remind me,' said Christopher. 'But what I want to know is, why the hell didn't your man jump Al Obaydi when it was obvious what he was carrying? I would have found a way of keeping the Swiss in line.'

'We would have done so if we'd known what he was carrying, but at that stage we weren't even aware the Declaration had been stolen, and our surveillance was just routine.'

'So what you're telling us, Mr Hutchins, is that the Declaration could well be in Baghdad by now,' said Leigh. 'Because if it was sent through the diplomatic pouch, the Swiss wouldn't have let us get anywhere near it.'

No one spoke for several moments.

'Let's work on the worst-case scenario,' said the Secretary of State finally. 'The Declaration is already in Saddam's possession. So what's his next move likely to be? Scott, you're our man of logic. Can you second-guess what he might get up to?'

'No, sir, Saddam's not a man you can second-guess. Especially after his failed attempt to assassinate George Bush on his visit to Kuwait in April. Although the whole world accused him of being behind the plot, how did he react? Not with the usual bellicose shouting and screaming about the lies of the American imperialists, but with a reasoned, coherent statement from his Ambassador at the UN denying any personal involvement. Why? The press tells us it's because Saddam is hoping Clinton will be more reasonable in the long term than Bush. I don't believe it. I suspect Saddam realises that Clinton's position doesn't differ greatly from that of his predecessor. I don't think that's his reasoning at all. No, I suspect he believes that with the Declaration in his possession, he has a weapon so powerful that he can humiliate the United States, and in particular the new President, as and when he pleases.'

'When and how, Scott? If we knew that . . .'

'I have two theories on that, sir,' replied Scott.

'Let's hear them both.'

'Neither is going to make you feel any happier, Mr Secretary.'

'Nevertheless . . .'

'First he sets up a press conference, inviting the

world's media to attend. He selects some public place in Baghdad where he is safely surrounded by his own people, and then he tears up, burns, destroys, does whatever he likes to the Declaration. I have a feeling it would make prime-time television.'

'But we'd bomb Baghdad to the ground if he tried that,' said Dexter Hutchins.

'I doubt it,' said Scott. 'How would our allies, the British, the French, not to mention the other friendly Arab nations, react to our bombing innocent civilians because Saddam had stolen the Declaration of Independence from right under our eyes?'

'You're right, Scott,' said Warren Christopher. 'The President would be vilified as a barbarian if he retaliated by bombing innocent Iraqis after what a lot of the world would consider nothing more than a public relations coup, though I must tell you, in the strictest confidence, that we *do* have plans to bomb Baghdad if Saddam continues to undermine the UN inspection teams' attempts to examine Iraqi nuclear installations.'

'Has a date been decided on?' asked Scott.

Christopher hesitated. 'Sunday June 27th,' he said.

'The timing might well turn out to be unfortunate for us,' said Scott.

'Why? When do you think Saddam is likely to move?' asked Christopher.

'That's not so easy to answer, sir,' replied Scott, 'because you have to think the way he thinks. What makes that almost impossible is that he's capable of changing his mind from hour to hour. But if he thinks the problem through logically, my guess is he'll be considering two alternatives. Either on some symbolic date, maybe an anniversary associated with the Gulf War, or . . .'

'Or . . .?' said Christopher.

'Or he intends to hold on to it as a bargaining chip to allow him to retake the oilfields in Kuwait. After all, he's always claimed he had an agreement with us on that in the first place.'

'Either scenario is too horrific to contemplate,' said the Secretary of State. Turning to the Deputy Director, he asked, 'Have you begun to form any plan for getting the document back?'

'Not at the moment, sir,' replied Dexter Hutchins, 'as I suspect the parchment will be every bit as well protected as Saddam himself, and frankly we only learned of its likely destination last night.'

'Colonel Kratz,' said Christopher, turning his attention to the Mossad man, who had not uttered a word. 'Your Prime Minister informed us a few weeks ago that he was considering a plan to take out Saddam at some time in the near future.'

'Yes, sir, but he recognises your present dilemma, and all our activities have been shelved until the problem over the Declaration has been resolved, one way or the other.'

'I have already informed Mr Rabin how much I appreciate his support, especially as he can't even tell his own cabinet the true reason for his change of heart.'

'But we have our own problem, sir,' said the Israeli.

'Make my day, Colonel.'

The burst of laughter that followed helped to ease the tension for a moment – but only for a moment.

'We have been training an agent who was going to be part of the team for the final operation to eliminate Saddam, a Hannah Kopec.'

'The girl who . . .' said Christopher, half-glancing towards Scott.

'Yes, sir. She was totally blameless. But that is not the problem. After she returned to the Iraqi Embassy that evening, we were unable to get anywhere near Miss Kopec to let her know what had happened, because during the next few days she never once left the building, night or day. She and the Iraqi Ambassador have since returned to Baghdad under heavy guard. However, Agent Kopec remains under the misapprehension that she has killed Scott Bradley, and we suspect her only interest now is to eliminate Saddam.'

'She'll never get anywhere near him,' said Leigh.

'I wish I believed that,' said Scott quietly.

'She is a bold, imaginative and resourceful young woman,' said Kratz. 'And, worse, she has the assassin's greatest weapon.'

'Namely?' said Christopher.

'She no longer cares about her own survival.'

'Can this get any worse?' asked Christopher.

'Yes, sir. She knows nothing about the disappearance of the Declaration, and we have no way of contacting her to let her know.'

The Secretary of State paused for a moment, as if he was coming to a decision. 'Colonel Kratz, I want to put something to you which is likely to stretch your personal loyalty.'

'Yes, Mr Secretary,' said Kratz.

'This plan to assassinate Saddam. How long have you been working on it?'

'Nine months to a year,' replied Kratz.

'And it obviously entailed you getting a person or persons into Saddam's palace or bunker?'

Kratz hesitated.

'Yes or no will suffice,' said Christopher.

'Yes, sir.'

'My question is extremely simple, Colonel. May we therefore take advantage of the year's preparation you've already carried out and – dare I suggest – steal your plan?'

'I would have to take advice from my government before I could consider . . .'

Christopher took an envelope from his pocket. 'I will be happy to let you see Mr Rabin's letter to me on this subject, but first allow me to read it to you.'

The Secretary opened the envelope and extracted the letter. He placed his glasses on the end of his nose and unfolded the single sheet.

From the Prime Minister

Dear Mr Secretary,
You are correct in thinking that the Prime Minister of the State of Israel is Chief Minister and Minister of Defence while at the same time having overall responsibility for Mossad.

However, I confess that when it comes to any ideas we may be considering for future relations with Saddam, I have only been kept in touch with the outline proposals. I have not yet been fully briefed on the finer details.

If you believe on balance that such information as we possess may make the difference between success or failure with your present difficulties, I will instruct Colonel Kratz to brief you fully and without reservation.

Yours
Yitzhak Rabin

Christopher turned the letter around and pushed it across the table.

'Colonel Kratz, let me assure you on behalf of the United States Government that I believe such information as you have in your possession may make the difference between success and failure.'

PART TWO

'Nor have We been wanting
in attentions to
our Brittish brethren.'

21

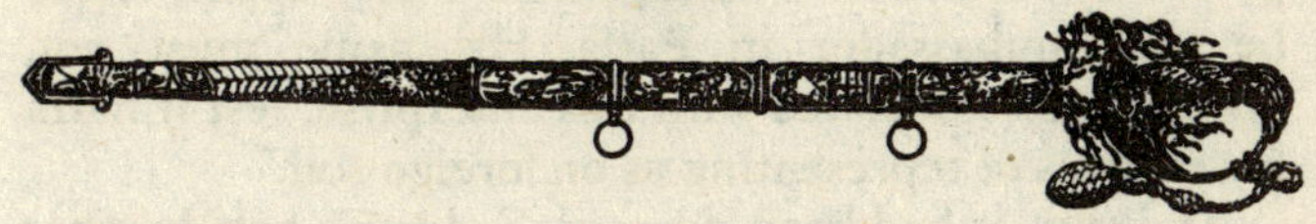

THE DECLARATION OF INDEPENDENCE was nailed to the wall behind him.

Saddam continued puffing at his cigar as he lounged back in his chair. All of them seated around the table waited for him to speak. He glanced to his right.

'My brother, we are proud of you. You have served our country and the Ba'ath Party with distinction, and when the moment comes for my people to be informed of your heroic deeds, your name will be written in the history of our nation as one of its great heroes.'

Al Obaydi sat at the other end of the table, listening to the words of his leader. His fists, hidden under the table, were clenched to stop himself shaking. Several times on the journey back to Baghdad he had been aware that he was being shadowed. They had searched his luggage at almost every stop, but they had found nothing, because there was nothing to find. Saddam's half-brother had seen to that. Once the Declaration had reached the safety of their mission in Geneva he hadn't even been allowed to pass it over to the Ambassador in person. Its guaranteed route in the diplomatic pouch made it impossible to intercept even with the combined efforts of the Americans and the Israelis.

Saddam's half-brother now sat on the President's right-hand side, basking in his leader's eulogy.

Saddam swung himself slowly back round and stared down at the other end of the table.

'And I also acknowledge,' he continued, 'the role played by Hamid Al Obaydi, whom I have appointed to be our Ambassador in Paris. His name must not, however, be associated with this enterprise, lest it harm his chances of representing us on foreign soil.'

And thus it had been decreed. Saddam's half-brother was to be acknowledged as the architect of this triumph, while Al Obaydi was to be a footnote on a page, quickly turned. Had Al Obaydi failed, Saddam's half-brother would have been ignorant of even the original idea, and Al Obaydi's bones would even now be rotting in an unmarked grave. Since Saddam had spoken no one round that table, except for the State Prosecutor, had given Al Obaydi a second look. All other eyes, and smiles, rested on Saddam's half-brother.

It was at that moment, in the midst of the meeting of the Revolutionary Command Council, that Al Obaydi came to his decision.

Dollar Bill sat slouched on a stool, leaning on the bar in unhappy hour, happily sipping his favourite liquid. He was the establishment's only customer, unless you counted the slip of a woman in a Laura Ashley dress who sat silently in the corner. The barman assumed she was drunk, as she hadn't moved a muscle for the past hour.

Dollar Bill wasn't at first aware of the man who stumbled through the swing doors, and wouldn't have given him a second look had he not sat himself on the stool next to his. The intruder ordered a gin and tonic. Dollar Bill had a natural aversion to any man who drank gin and tonic, especially if they occupied the seat next to his when the rest of the bar was empty. He considered moving but decided on balance that he didn't need the exercise.

'So how are you, old timer?' the voice next to him asked. Dollar Bill didn't care to think of himself as an 'old timer', and refused to grace the intruder with a reply.

'What's the matter, not got a tongue in your head?' the man asked, slurring his words. The barman turned to face them when he heard the raised voice, and then returned to drying the glasses left over from the lunchtime rush.

'I have, sir, and it's a civil one,' replied Dollar Bill, still not so much as glancing at his interrogator.

'Irish. I should have known it all along. A nation of stupid, ignorant drunks.'

'Let me remind you, sir,' said Dollar Bill, 'that Ireland is the land of Yeats, Shaw, Wilde, O'Casey and Joyce.' He raised his glass in their memory.

'I've never heard of any of them. Drinking partners of yours, I suppose?' This time the young barman put his cloth down and began to pay closer attention.

'I never had that honour,' replied Dollar Bill, 'but, my friend, the fact that you have not heard of them, let alone read their works, is your loss, not mine.'

'Are you accusing me of being ignorant?' said the intruder, placing a rough hand on Dollar Bill's shoulder.

Dollar Bill turned to face him, but even at that close range he couldn't focus clearly through the haze of alcohol he had consumed during the past two weeks. He did, however, observe that, although he appeared to be part of the same alcoholic haze, the intruder was somewhat larger than himself. Such a consideration had never worried Dollar Bill in the past.

'No, sir, it was not necessary to accuse you of ignorance. For you have been condemned by your own utterances.'

'I won't take that from anyone, you Irish drunk,' said

the intruder. Keeping his hand on Dollar Bill's shoulder, he swung at him and landed a blow on the side of his jaw. Dollar Bill staggered back off his high stool, falling to the floor in a heap.

The intruder waited some time for Bill to rise to his feet before he aimed a second blow to the stomach. Once again, Dollar Bill ended up on the floor.

The young man behind the bar had already begun dialling the number his boss had instructed he should call if ever such a situation arose. He only hoped they would come quickly as he watched the Irishman somehow get back on his feet. This time it was his turn to aim a punch at the intruder's nose, a punch which ended up flying through the air over his assailant's right shoulder. A further blow landed on the side of Dollar Bill's throat. Down he went a third time, which in his days as an amateur boxer would have been considered a technical knock-out; but as there seemed to be no referee present to officiate, he rose once again.

The young barman was relieved to hear a siren in the distance, and was praying they weren't on their way to another call when suddenly four policemen came bursting through the swing doors.

The first one caught Dollar Bill just before he hit the ground for a fourth time, while two of the others grabbed the intruder, thrust his arms behind his back and forced a pair of handcuffs on him. Both men were bundled out of the bar and thrown into the back of a waiting police van. The siren continued its piercing sound as the two drunks were driven away.

The barman was grateful for the speed with which the San Francisco Police Department had come to his aid. It was only later that night that he remembered he hadn't given them an address.

* * *

As Hannah sat alone at the back of the plane bound for Amman, she began to consider the task she had set herself.

Once the Ambassador's party had left Paris, she had returned to the traditional role of an Arab woman. She was dressed from head to toe in a black abayah, and apart from her eyes, her face was covered by a small mask. She spoke only when asked a question directly, and never posed a question herself. She felt her Jewish mother would not have survived such a regime for more than a few hours.

Hannah's one break had come when the Ambassador's wife had enquired where she intended to stay once they had returned to Baghdad. Hannah explained that she had made no immediate plans as her mother and sister were living in Karbala, and she could not stay with them if she hoped to hold on to her job with the Ambassador.

Hannah had hardly finished the second sentence before the Ambassador's wife insisted that she come and live with them. 'Our house is far too large,' she explained, 'even with a dozen servants.'

When the plane touched down at Queen Alia airport, Hannah looked out of the tiny window to watch a large black limousine that would have looked more in place in New York than Amman driving towards them. It drew up by the side of the aircraft and a driver in a smart blue suit and dark glasses jumped out.

Hannah joined the Ambassador and his wife in the back of the car and they sped away from the airport in the direction of the border with Iraq.

When the car reached the customs barrier, they were waved straight through with bows and salutes, as if the border didn't exist. They travelled a further mile and passed a second customs post on the Iraqi side, where they were treated in much the same manner as the first, before joining the six-lane highway to Baghdad.

On the long journey to the capital, the speedometer rarely fell below seventy miles per hour. Hannah soon became bored with the beating sun and the sight of miles and miles of flat sand that stretched to the horizon and beyond, with only the occasional cluster of palm trees to break the monotony. Her thoughts returned to Simon and what might have been . . .

Hannah dozed off as the air-conditioned limousine sped quietly along the highway. Her mind drifted from Simon to her mother, to Saddam, and then back to Simon.

She woke with a start to find they were entering the outskirts of Baghdad.

It had been many years since Dollar Bill had seen the inside of a jail, but not so long that he had forgotten how much he detested having to associate with drug peddlers, pimps and muggers.

Still, the last time he had been foolish enough to get himself involved in a bar-room brawl, he had started it. But even then he only ended up with a fifty-dollar fine. Dollar Bill felt confident that the jails were far too overcrowded for any judge to consider the thirty-day mandatory sentence for such cases.

In fact he had tried to slip one of the policemen in the van fifty dollars. They normally happily accepted the money, opened the back door of the van and kicked you out. He couldn't imagine what the San Francisco police were coming to. Surely with all the muggers and drug addicts around they had more important things to deal with than mid-afternoon middle-aged bar-room drunks.

As Dollar Bill began to sober up, the stench got to him, and he hoped that he'd be among the first to be put up in front of the night court. But as the hours passed, and he became more sober and the stench became greater, he began to wonder if they might end up keeping him overnight.

'William O'Reilly,' shouted the police Sergeant as he looked down the list of names on his clipboard.

'That's me,' said Bill, raising his hand.

'Follow me, O'Reilly,' the policeman barked as the cell door clanked open and the Irishman was gripped firmly by the elbow.

He was marched along a corridor that led into the back of a courtroom. He watched the little line of derelicts and petty criminals who were waiting for their moment in front of the judge. He didn't notice a woman a few paces away from him, tightly gripping the rope handle of a holdall.

'Guilty. Fifty dollars.'

'Can't pay.'

'Three days in jail. Next.'

After three or four cases were dispensed with in this cursory manner within as many minutes, Dollar Bill watched the man who had shown no respect for the canon of Irish literature take his place in front of the judge.

'Drunk and disorderly, disturbing the peace. How do you plead?'

'Guilty, Your Honour.'

'Any previous known record?'

'None,' said the Sergeant.

'Fifty dollars,' said the judge.

It interested Dollar Bill that his adversary had no previous convictions, and was also able to pay his fine immediately.

When it came to Dollar Bill's own turn to plead, he couldn't help thinking, as he looked up at the judge, that he appeared to be awfully young for the job. Perhaps he really was now an 'old timer'.

'William O'Reilly, Your Honour,' said the Sergeant, looking down at the charge sheet. 'Drunk and disorderly, disturbing the peace.'

'How do you plead?'

'Guilty, Your Honour,' said Dollar Bill, fingering a small wad of bills in his pocket as he tried to remember the location of the nearest bar that served Guinness.

'Thirty days,' said the judge, without raising his head. 'Next.'

Two people in the courtroom were stunned by the judge's decision. One of them reluctantly loosened her grip on the rope handle of her holdall, while the other stammered out, 'Bail, Your Honour?'

'Denied.'

22

THE TWO MEN REMAINED SILENT until David Kratz had come to the end of his outline plan.

Dexter was the first to speak. 'I must admit, Colonel, I'm impressed. It just might work.'

Scott nodded his agreement, and then turned to the Mossad man who only a few weeks before had given Hannah the order that he should be killed. Some of the guilt had been lifted since they had been working so closely with each other, but the lines on the forehead and the prematurely grey hair of the Israeli leader remained a perpetual reminder of what he had been through. During their time together Scott had come to admire the sheer professional skill of the man who had been put in charge of the operation.

'I still need some queries answered,' said Scott, 'and a few other things explained.'

The Israeli Councillor for Cultural Affairs to the Court of St James nodded.

'Are you certain that they plan to put the safe in the Ba'ath Party headquarters?'

'Certain, no. Confident, yes,' said Kratz. 'A Dutch company completed some building work in the basement of the headquarters nearly three years ago, and among their final drawings was a brick construction, the dimensions of which would house the safe perfectly.'

'And is this safe still in Kalmar?'

'It was three weeks ago,' replied Kratz, 'when one of my agents carried out a routine check.'

'And does it belong to the Iraqi Government?' asked Dexter Hutchins.

'Yes, it has been fully paid for, and is now legally the property of the Iraqis.'

'Legally that may be the position, but since the Gulf War the UN has imposed a new category of sanctions,' Scott reminded him.

'How can a safe be considered a piece of military equipment?' asked Dexter.

'Exactly the Iraqis' argument,' replied Kratz. 'But, unfortunately for them, when they placed the original order with the Swedes, among the explicit specifications was the requirement that the safe "must be able to withstand a nuclear attack". The word "nuclear" was all that was needed to start the bells ringing at the UN.'

'So how do you plan to get round that problem?' asked Scott.

'Whenever the Iraqi Government submits a new list of items that they consider do not break UN Security Council Resolution 661, the safe is always included. If the Americans, the British and the French didn't raise any objection, it could slip through.'

'And the Israeli Government?'

'We would protest vociferously in front of the Iraqi delegation, but not behind closed doors to our friends.'

'So let us imagine for one moment that we're in possession of a giant safe that can withstand a nuclear attack. What good does that do us?' asked Scott.

'Someone has to be responsible for getting that safe from Sweden to Baghdad. Someone has to install it when they get there, and someone has to explain to Saddam's people how to operate it,' said Kratz.

'And you have someone who is six feet tall, a karate expert, and speaks fluent Arabic?'

'We did have, but she was only five feet ten.' The two men stared at each other. Scott remained silent.

'And how were you proposing to assassinate Saddam?' asked Dexter quickly. 'Lock him up in the safe and hope he would suffocate?'

Kratz realised the comment had been made to take Scott's mind off Hannah, so he responded in kind. 'No, we discovered that was the CIA's plan, and dismissed it. We had something more subtle in mind.'

'Namely?' asked Scott.

'A tiny nuclear device was to be planted inside the safe.'

'And the safe would be in the passage next to where the Revolutionary Command Council meet. Not bad,' said Dexter.

'And the device was to be set off by a five-foot-ten, Arabic-speaking Jewish girl?' asked Scott.

Kratz nodded.

'Thirty days? What did I do to deserve thirty days, that's what I want to know.' But no one was listening as Dollar Bill was hustled out of the courtroom, along the corridor and then out through a door at the rear of the building, before being pushed into the back seat of an unmarked car. Three men with military-style haircuts, Ray-Bans, and small earplugs connected to wires running down the backs of their collars, accompanied him.

'Why wasn't I given bail? And what about my appeal? I have the right to a lawyer, damn it. And by the way, where are you taking me?' However many questions he asked, Dollar Bill received no answers.

Although he was unable to see anything out of the

smoked-glass side windows, Dollar Bill could tell by looking over the driver's shoulder when they reached the Golden Gate Bridge. As they proceeded along Route 101, the speedometer touched fifty-five for the first time, but the driver never once exceeded the speed limit.

When twenty minutes later the car swung off the highway at the Belvedere exit, Dollar Bill had no idea where he was. The driver continued up a small, winding road, until the car slowed down as a massive set of wrought-iron gates loomed up in front of them.

The driver flashed his lights twice and the gates swung open to allow the car to continue its journey down a long, straight gravel drive. It was another three or four minutes before they came to a halt in front of a large country house which reminded Dollar Bill of his youth in County Kerry, when his mother had been a scullery maid up at the manor house.

One of Dollar Bill's escorts leaped out of the car and opened the door for him. Another ran ahead of them up the steps and pressed a bell, as the car sped away across the gravel.

The massive oak door opened to reveal a butler in a long black coat and a white bow tie.

'Good evening, Mr O'Reilly,' he declared in a pronounced English accent even before Dollar Bill had reached the top step. 'My name is Charles. Your room is already prepared. Perhaps you'd be kind enough to accompany me, sir.' Dollar Bill followed him into the house and up the wide staircase without uttering a word. He would have tried some of his questions on Charles, but as he was English, Dollar Bill knew he couldn't expect an honest reply. The butler guided him into a small, well-furnished bedroom on the first floor.

'I do hope you will find that the clothes are the correct fitting, sir,' said Charles, 'and that everything else is to your liking. Dinner will be served in half an hour.'

Dollar Bill bowed and spent the next few minutes looking round the suite. He checked the bathroom. French soap, safety razors and fluffy white towels; even a toothbrush and his favourite toothpaste. He returned to the bedroom and tested the double bed. He couldn't remember when he had last slept on anything so comfortable. He then checked the wardrobe and found three pairs of trousers and three jackets, not unlike the ones he had purchased a few days after returning from Washington. How did they know?

He looked in the drawers: six shirts, six pairs of pants and six pairs of socks. They had thought of everything, even if he didn't care that much for their choice of ties.

Dollar Bill decided to join in the game. He took a bath, shaved and changed into the clothes provided. They were, as Charles had promised, the correct fitting.

He heard a gong sound downstairs, which he took as a clear signal that he had been summoned. He opened the door, stepped into the corridor and proceeded down the wide staircase to find the butler standing in the hall.

'Mr Hutchins is expecting you. You'll find him in the drawing room, sir.'

'Yes, of course I will,' said Dollar Bill, and followed Charles into a large room where a tall, burly man was standing by the fireplace, the stub of a cigar in the corner of his mouth.

'Good evening, Mr O'Reilly,' he said. 'My name is Dexter Hutchins. We've never met before, but I've long been an admirer of your work.'

'That's kind of you, Mr Hutchins, but I don't have the same advantage of knowing what you do to pass the unrelenting hour.'

'I do apologise. I am the Deputy Director of the CIA.'

'After all these years, I get to have dinner in a large

country house with the Deputy Director of the CIA simply because I was involved in a bar-room brawl. I'm tempted to ask, what do you lay on for mass murderers?'

'I must confess, Mr O'Reilly, that it was one of my men who threw the first punch. But before we go any further, what would you like to drink?'

'I don't think Charles will have my favourite brew,' said Dollar Bill, turning to face the butler.

'I fear the Guinness is canned and not on tap, sir. If I had been given a little more notice . . .' Dollar Bill bowed again and the butler disappeared.

'Don't you think I'm entitled to know what this is all about, Mr Hutchins? After all . . .'

'You are indeed, Mr O'Reilly. The truth is, the government is in need of your services, not to mention your expertise.'

'I didn't realise that Clintonomics had resorted to forgery to help balance the budget deficit,' said Dollar Bill as the butler returned with a large glass of Guinness.

'Not quite as drastic as that, but every bit as demanding,' said Hutchins. 'But perhaps we should have a little dinner before I go into any details. I fear it's been a long day for you.' Dollar Bill nodded and followed the Deputy Director through to a small dining room, where the table had been set for two. The butler held a chair back for Dollar Bill, and when he was comfortably seated asked, 'How do you like your steak done, sir?'

'Is it sirloin or entrecôte?' asked Dollar Bill.

'Sirloin.'

'If the meat is good enough, tell the chef to put a candle under it – but only for a few moments.'

'Excellent, sir. Yours, Mr Hutchins, will I presume be well done?'

Dexter Hutchins nodded, feeling the first round had definitely gone to Dollar Bill.

'I'm enjoying this charade enormously,' said Dollar Bill, taking a gulp of Guinness. 'But I'd like to know what the prize is, should I be fortunate enough to win.'

'You might equally well be interested to know what the forfeit will be if you are unfortunate enough to lose.'

'I should have realised this had to be too good to last.'

'First, allow me to fill you in with a little background,' said Dexter Hutchins as a lightly grilled steak was placed in front of his guest. 'On May 25th this year, a well-organised group of criminals descended on Washington and carried out one of the most ingenious crimes in the history of this country.'

'Excellent steak,' said Dollar Bill. 'You must give my compliments to the chef.'

'I certainly will, sir,' said Charles, who was hovering behind his chair.

'This crime consisted of stealing from the National Archives, in broad daylight, the Declaration of Independence, and replacing it with a brilliant copy.'

Dollar Bill looked suitably impressed, but felt it would be unwise to comment at this stage.

'We have the names of several people involved in that crime, but we cannot make any arrests for fear of making those who are now in possession of the Declaration aware that we might be after them.'

'And what's this got to do with me?' asked Dollar Bill, as he devoured another succulent piece of meat.

'We thought you might be interested to know who had financed the entire operation, and is now in possession of the Declaration of Independence.'

Until that moment, Dollar Bill had learned nothing new, but he had long wanted to know where the document had ended up. He had never believed Angelo's tale of 'in private hands, an eccentric collector'. He put his knife and fork down and stared across the table at the

Deputy Director of the CIA, who had at last captured his attention.

'We have reason to believe that the Declaration of Independence is currently in Baghdad, in the personal possession of Saddam Hussein.'

Dollar Bill's mouth opened wide, although he remained silent for some considerable time. 'Is there no longer honour among thieves?' he finally said.

'There still could be,' said Hutchins, 'because our only hope of returning the parchment to its rightful home rests in the hands of a small group who are willing to risk their lives by switching the document, in much the same way as the criminals did originally.'

'If I had known . . .' Dollar Bill paused. 'How can I help?' he asked quietly.

'At this moment, we are in urgent need of a perfect copy of the original. And we believe you are the only person who is capable of producing one.'

Dollar Bill knew exactly where there was a perfect copy, hanging on a wall in New York, but couldn't admit as much without bringing on himself even greater wrath than Mr Hutchins was capable of.

'You made mention of a prize,' said Dollar Bill.

'And a forfeit,' said Dexter Hutchins. 'The prize is that you remain here at our West Coast safe house, in what I think you will agree are pleasant surroundings. While you are with us, you will produce a counterfeit of the Declaration that would pass an expert's eye. If you achieve that, you will go free, with no charges preferred against you.'

'And the forfeit?'

'After coffee has been served you will be released and allowed to leave whenever you wish.'

'Released,' repeated Dollar Bill in disbelief, 'and allowed to leave whenever I wish?'

'Yes,' said the Deputy Director.

'Then why shouldn't I just enjoy the rest of this excellent meal, return to my humble establishment in Fairmont, and forget we ever met?'

The Deputy Director removed an envelope from an inside pocket. He extracted four photographs and pushed them across the table. Dollar Bill studied them. The first was of a girl aged about seventeen lying on a slab in a morgue. The second was of a middle-aged man huddled foetus-like in the boot of a car. The third was of a heavily-built man dumped by the side of a road. And the fourth was of an older, distinguished-looking man. A broken neck was all the four of them had in common. Dollar Bill pushed the photos back across the table.

'Four corpses. So what?'

'Sally McKenzie, Rex Butterworth, Bruno Morelli, and Dr T. Hamilton McKenzie. And we have every reason to believe someone out there is planning the same happy ending for you.'

Dollar Bill speared the last pea left on his plate and downed the final drop of Guinness. He paused for a moment as if searching for inspiration.

'I'll need paper from Bremen, pens from a museum in Richmond, Virginia, and nine shades of black ink that can be made up for me by a firm in Cannon Street, London EC4.'

'Anything else?' asked Dexter Hutchins once he had finished writing down Dollar Bill's shopping list on the back of the envelope.

'I wonder if Charles would be kind enough to bring me another large Guinness. I have a feeling it may be my last for some considerable time.'

23

BERTIL PEDERSSON, the chief engineer of Svenhalte AC, was at the factory gate in Kalmar to greet Mr Riffat and Mr Bernstrom when the two men arrived that morning. He had received a fax from the United Nations the previous day confirming their flight times to Stockholm, and had checked with the arrivals desk at the airport to be informed that their plane had touched down only a few minutes late.

As they stepped out of their car, Mr Pedersson came forward, shook hands with both men and introduced himself.

'We are pleased to meet you at last, Mr Pedersson,' said the shorter of the two men, 'and grateful to you for making the time to see us at such short notice.'

'Well, to be frank with you, Mr Riffat, it came as quite a surprise to us when the United Nations lifted the restrictions on Madame Bertha.'

' "Madame Bertha"?'

'Yes, that is how we at the factory refer to the safe. I promise you, gentlemen, that despite your neglect, she has been a good girl. Many people have come to admire her, but nobody touches,' Mr Pedersson laughed. 'But I feel sure that after such a long journey you will want to see her for yourself, Mr Riffat.'

The short, dark-haired man nodded, and they both

accompanied Pedersson as he led them across the yard.

'You responded most quickly to the UN's sudden change of heart, Mr Riffat.'

'Yes, our leader had given orders that the safe should be delivered to Baghdad the moment the embargo was lifted.'

Pedersson laughed again. 'I fear that may not be so easy,' he said once they reached the other side of the yard. 'Madame Bertha was not built for speed, as you are about to discover.'

The three men continued to walk towards a large, apparently derelict building, and Pedersson strode through an opening where there must once have been a door. It was so dark inside that the two foreigners were unable to see more than a few feet in front of them. Pedersson switched on a single light, which was followed by what sounded like the sigh of an unrequited lover.

'Mr Riffat, Mr Bernstrom, allow me to introduce you to Madame Bertha.' The two men stared at the massive structure that stood majestically in the middle of the old warehouse floor.

'Before I make a formal introduction,' Pedersson continued, 'first let me tell you Madame Bertha's vital statistics. She is nine feet tall, seven feet wide and eight feet deep. She is also thicker skinned than any politician, about six inches of solid steel to be precise, and she weighs over five tons. She was built by a specialist designer, three craftsmen and eight engineers. Her gestation from conception to delivery was eighteen months. But then,' he whispered, 'to be fair, she is almost the size of an elephant. I lower my voice only because she can hear every word I say, and I have no wish to offend her.'

Mr Pedersson did not see the puzzled looks that came over the faces of his two visitors. 'But, gentlemen, you have only seen her exterior, and I can promise you that what she has to offer is more than skin deep.

'First, I must tell you that Madame Bertha will not allow anyone to enter her without a personal introduction. She is, gentlemen, not a promiscuous lady, despite what you may have been told about the Swedes. She requires to know three things about you before she will consider revealing her innermost parts.'

Although the two guests remained puzzled as to what he meant, they did not interrupt Mr Pedersson's steady flow.

'And so, gentlemen, to begin with you must study Bertha's chest. You will observe three red lights above three small dials. By knowing the six-number code on all three dials, you will be able to turn one of the lights from red to green. Allow me to demonstrate. First number to the right, second to the left, third to the right, fourth to the left, fifth to the right, sixth to the left. The first number for the first dial is 2, the second is 8, the third zero, the fourth 4, the fifth 3 and the sixth 7. 2-8-0-4-3-7.'

'The date of Sayedi's birthday,' said the tall, fair-haired visitor.

'Yes, I worked that one out, Mr Bernstrom,' said Pedersson. 'The second,' he said, turning his attention to the middle dial, 'is 1-6-0-7-7-9.' He turned the final number to the left.

'The day Sayedi became President.'

'We also managed that one, Mr Riffat. But I confess the third sequence fooled me completely. No doubt you will know what our client has planned for that particular day.' Mr Pedersson began twirling the third dial: 0-4-0-7-9-3.

Pedersson looked hopefully towards Mr Bernstrom, who shrugged his shoulders. 'I've no idea,' he lied.

'You will now note, gentlemen, that after entering the correct figures on all three dials, only one of Madame Bertha's lights has turned green, while two still remain obstinately red. But now that you have discovered her three codes, she will consider a more personal relationship. You will observe that below the three dials there is painted a small white square about the size of your hand. Watch carefully.' Pedersson took a pace forward and placed his right hand firmly on the white square. He left it there for several seconds, until the second light turned green.

'Even when she knows your palm print, she still won't open her heart. Not until I have spoken to her. If you look even more closely, gentlemen, you will see that the white square conceals a thin wire mesh, which houses a voice activator.' Both men stepped forward to look.

'At the present time, Bertha is programmed to react only to my vocal cords. It doesn't matter what I say, because as soon as she recognises the voice, the third light will turn green. But she will not even consider listening to me unless the first two lights are already green.'

Pedersson stepped forward and placed his lips opposite the wire mesh. 'Two gentlemen have come from America to see you, and desire to know what you look like inside.'

Even before he had finished the sentence, the third red light had flicked to green, and a noisy unclamping sound could be heard.

'Now, gentlemen, we come to the part of the demonstration of which my company is particularly proud. The door, which weighs over a ton, is nevertheless capable of being opened by a small child. Our company has developed a system of phosphor-bronze bearings that are a decade ahead of their time. Please, Mr Riffat, why don't you try for yourself?'

The shorter man stepped forward, gripped the handle of the safe firmly, and pulled. All three lights immediately turned red, and a noisy clamping sound began again.

Pedersson chuckled. 'You see, Mr Riffat, unless Madame Bertha knows you personally, she clams up and sends you back to the red-light district.' He laughed at a joke his guests suspected he had told many times before. 'The hand that opens the safe,' he continued, 'must be the same one that passed the palm-print test. A good safety device, I think you'll agree.' Both men nodded in admiration as Pedersson quickly fiddled with the three dials, placed his hand on the square and then spoke to Madame Bertha. One by one the three lights dutifully turned from red to green.

'She is now prepared to let me, and me alone, open her up. So watch carefully. Although, as I said, the door weighs a ton, it can be opened with the gentlest persuasion, thus.'

Pedersson pulled back the ton of massive steel with no more exertion than he would have used to open the front door of his home. He jumped inside the safe and began walking around, first with his arms outstretched to show that he could not touch the sides while standing in the centre, and then with his hands above his head, showing he was unable to reach the roof. 'Do please enter, gentlemen,' he cried from inside.

The two men stepped up gingerly to join him.

'In this case, three is not a crowd,' said Pedersson, laughing again. 'And you will be happy to discover that it is impossible for me to get myself locked in.' He gripped the handle on the inside of the safe and pulled the great door shut.

Two of the occupants did not find this part of the experiment quite so appealing.

'You see, gentlemen,' continued Pedersson, who could not hide the satisfaction in his voice, 'Bertha cannot lock herself again unless it is my hand on the outside handle.' With one small push, the door swung open and Pedersson stepped out, closely followed by his two customers.

'I once had to spend an evening inside her before the system was perfected – a sort of one-night stand, you might call it,' said Pedersson. He laughed even louder as he pushed the door back in place. The three lights immediately flashed to red and the clamps noisily closed in place.

He turned to face them. 'So, gentlemen, you have been introduced to Madame Bertha. Now, if you would be kind enough to accompany me back to my office, I will present you with a delivery note and, more important, Bertha's bible.'

As they returned across the yard, Pedersson explained to his two visitors that the book of instructions had been treated by the company as top secret. They had produced one in Swedish, which the company retained in its own safe, and another in Arabic, which Pedersson said he would be happy to hand over to them.

'The bible itself is 108 pages in length, but simple enough to understand if you are an engineer with a first-class honours degree.' He laughed again. 'We Swedish are a thorough race.'

Neither of the men felt able to disagree with him.

'Will you require anyone to accompany Madame Bertha on her journey?' Pedersson asked, his eyes expressing hope.

'No, thank you,' came back the immediate reply. 'I think we can handle the problem of transport.'

'Then I have only one more question for you,' Pedersson said, as he entered his office. 'When do you plan to take her away?'

'We hoped to collect the safe this afternoon. We understood from the fax you sent to the United Nations that your company has a crane that can lift the safe, and a trolley on which it can be moved from place to place.'

'You are right in thinking we have a suitable crane, and a trolley that has been specially designed to carry Madame Bertha on short journeys. I am also confident I can have everything ready for you by this afternoon. But that doesn't cover the problem of transport.'

'We already have our own vehicle standing by in Stockholm.'

'Excellent, then it is settled,' said Mr Pedersson. 'All I need to do in your absence is to programme out my hand and voice so that she can accept whoever you select to take my place.' Pedersson looked forlorn for a second time. 'I look forward to seeing you again this afternoon, gentlemen.'

'I'll be coming back on my own,' said Riffat. 'Mr Bernstrom will be returning to America.'

Pedersson nodded and watched the two men climb into their car before he walked slowly back to his office. The phone on his desk was ringing.

He picked it up, said, 'Bertil Pedersson speaking,' and listened to the caller's request. He placed the receiver on his desk and ran to the window, but the car was already out of sight. He returned to the phone. 'I am so sorry, Mr Al Obaydi,' said Pedersson, 'the two gentlemen who came to see the safe have just this moment left, but Mr Riffat will be returning this afternoon to take her away. Shall I let him know you called?'

Al Obaydi put the phone down in Baghdad, and began to consider the implications of what had started out as a routine call.

As Deputy Ambassador to the UN, it was his responsibility to keep the sanctions list up to date. He had hoped to pass on the file within a week to his as-yet-unappointed successor.

In the past two days, despite phones that didn't connect and civil servants who were never at their desks – and even when they were, were too terrified to answer the most basic questions – he was almost in a position to complete the first draft of his report.

The problem areas had been: agricultural machinery, half of which the UN Sanctions Committee took for granted was military equipment under another name; hospital supplies, including pharmaceuticals, on which the UN accepted most of their requests; and food, which they were allowed to purchase – although most of the produce that came across the border seemed to disappear on the black market long before it reached the Baghdad housewife.

A fourth list was headed 'miscellaneous items', and included among these was a massive safe which, when Al Obaydi checked its measurements, turned out to be almost the size of the room he was presently working in. The safe, an internal report confirmed, had been ordered before the planned liberation of the Nineteenth Province, and was now sitting in a warehouse in Kalmar, waiting to be collected. Al Obaydi's boss at the UN had confessed privately that he was surprised that the Sanctions Committee had lifted the embargo on the safe, but this did not deter him from assuring the Foreign Minister that they had only done so as a result of his painstaking negotiating skills.

Al Obaydi sat at his laden desk for some time, considering what his next move should be. He wrote a short list of headings on the notepad in front of him:

1 M.o.I.
2 State Security
3 Deputy Foreign Minister
4 Kalmar

Al Obaydi glanced at the first heading, M.o.I. He had remained in contact with a fellow student from London University days who had risen to Permanent Secretary status at the Ministry of Industry. Al Obaydi felt his old friend would be able to supply the information he required without suspecting his real motive.

He dialled the Permanent Secretary's private number, and was delighted to find that someone was at his desk.

'Nadhim, it's Hamid Al Obaydi.'

'Hamid, I heard you were back from New York. The rumour is that you've got what remains of our embassy in Paris. But one can never be sure about rumours in this city.'

'For once, they're accurate,' Al Obaydi told his friend.

'Congratulations. So, what can I do for you, Your Excellency?'

Al Obaydi was amused that Nadhim was the first person to address him by his new title, even if he was being sarcastic.

'UN sanctions.'

'And you claim you're my friend?'

'No, it's just a routine check. I've got to tie up any loose ends for my successor. Everything's in order as far as I can tell, except I'm unable to find out much about a gigantic safe that was made for us in Sweden. I know we've paid for it, but I can't discover what is happening about its delivery.'

'Not this department, Hamid. The responsibility was taken out of our hands about a year ago after the file was marked "High Command", which usually means for the President's personal use.'

'But someone must be responsible for a movement order from Kalmar to Baghdad,' said Al Obaydi.

'All I know is that I was instructed to pass the file on to our UN office in Geneva, as we don't have an embassy in Oslo. I'm surprised you didn't know that, Hamid. More your department than mine, I would have thought.'

'Then I'll have to get in touch with Geneva and find out what they're doing about it,' said Al Obaydi, not adding that New York and Geneva rarely informed each other of anything they were up to. 'Thanks for your help, Nadhim.'

'Any time. Good luck in Paris, Hamid. I'm told the women are fabulous, and despite what you hear, they like Arabs.'

Al Obaydi put the phone down and stared at the list on his pad. He took even longer deciding if he should make the second call.

The correct course of action with the information he now possessed would be to contact Geneva, alert the Ambassador of his suspicions and let Saddam's half-brother once again take the praise for something he himself had done the work on. He checked his watch. It was midday in Switzerland. He asked his secretary to get Barazan Al-Tikriti on the phone, knowing she would log every call. He waited for several minutes before a voice came on the line.

'Can I speak to the Ambassador?' he asked politely.

'He's in a meeting, sir,' came back the inevitable reply. 'Shall I disturb him?'

'No, no, don't bother. But would you let him know that Hamid Al Obaydi called from Baghdad, and ask him if he would be kind enough to return my call.'

'Yes, sir,' said the voice, and Al Obaydi replaced the phone. He had carried out the correct procedure.

He opened the sanctions file on his desk and scribbled on the bottom of his report: 'The Ministry of Industry have sent the file concerning this item direct to Geneva. I phoned our Ambassador there, but was unable to make contact with him. Therefore, I cannot make any progress from this end until he returns my call. Hamid Al Obaydi.'

Al Obaydi considered his next move extremely carefully. If he decided to do anything, his actions must once again appear on the surface to be routine, and well within his accepted brief. Any slight deviation from the norm in a city that fed on rumour and paranoia, and it would be him who would end up dangling from a rope, not Saddam's half-brother.

Al Obaydi looked down at the second heading on his notepad. He buzzed his secretary and asked her to get General Saba'awi Al-Hassan, Head of State Security, on the line. The post was one that had been held by three different people in the last seven months. The General was available immediately, there being more Generals than Ambassadors in the Iraqi regime.

'Ambassador, good morning. I've been meaning to call you. We ought to have a talk before you take up your new appointment in Paris.'

'My thoughts exactly,' said Al Obaydi. 'I have no idea who we still have representing us in Europe. It's been a long time since I served in that part of the world.'

'We're a bit thin on the ground, to be honest. Most of our best people have been expelled, including the so-called students whom we've always been able to rely on in the past. Still, not a subject to be discussed over the phone. When would you like me to come and see you?'

'Are you free between four and five this afternoon?'

There was a pause before the General said, 'I could be with you around four, but would have to be back in my office by five. Do you think that will give us enough time?'

'I feel sure you'll be able to brief me fully in that period, General.' Al Obaydi put the phone down on another routine call.

He stared at the third name on the list, one he feared might prove a little harder to bluff.

He spent the next few minutes rehearsing his questions before dialling an internal number. A Miss Saib answered the phone.

'Is there a particular subject you wish to raise with the Deputy Foreign Minister?' she asked.

'No,' replied Al Obaydi, 'I'm phoning at his specific request. I'm due for a little leave at the end of the week, and the Deputy Foreign Minister made it clear he wished to brief me before I take up my new post in Paris.'

'I'll come back to you with a time as soon as I've had a chance to discuss your request with the Minister,' Miss Saib promised.

Al Obaydi replaced the phone. Nothing to raise any suspicions there. He looked back at his pad and added a question mark, two arrows and another word to his list.

Kalmar ← ? → Geneva

Some time in the next forty-eight hours, he was going to have to decide which direction he should take.

The first question Kratz put to Scott on the journey from Kalmar to Stockholm was the significance of the numbers 0-4-0-7-9-3. Scott snapped out of a daydream where he was rescuing Hannah on a white charger, and returned to the real world, which looked a lot less promising.

'The fourth of July,' he responded. 'What better day could Saddam select to humiliate the American people, not to mention a new President.'

'So now at least we know when our deadline is,' said Kratz.

'Yes, but we've only been left with eleven days,' replied Scott. 'One way or the other.'

'Still, we've got Madame Bertha,' said Kratz, trying to lighten the mood.

'True,' said Scott. 'And where do you intend to take her on her first date?'

'All the way,' said Kratz. 'That is to say, Jordan, which is where I'm expecting you to join up with us again. In fact, my full team is already in Stockholm waiting to pick her up before they begin the journey to Baghdad. All the paperwork has been sorted out for us by Langley, so there should be no hold-ups on the way. Our first problem will be crossing the Jordanian border, but as we have all the requisite documents demanded by the UN, a few extra dollars supplied to the right customs official should ensure that his stamping hand lands firmly on the correct page of all our passports.'

'How much time have you allocated for the journey to Jordan?' Scott asked, remembering his own tight schedule.

'Six or seven days, eight at the outside. I've got a six-man team, all with considerable field experience. None of them will have to drive for more than four hours at a time without then getting sixteen hours' rest. That way there will be no need to stop at any point, other than to fill up with petrol.' They passed a sign indicating ten kilometres to Stockholm.

'So I've got a week,' said Scott.

'Yes, and we must hope that that's enough time for Bill O'Reilly to complete a perfect new copy of the Declaration,' said Kratz.

'It ought to be a lot easier for him a second time,' said Scott. 'Especially as every one of his requests was dealt with within hours of his asking. They even flew over nine shades of black ink from London on Concorde the next morning.'

'I wish we could put Madame Bertha on Concorde.'

Scott laughed. 'Tell me more about your back-up team.'

'The best I've ever had,' said Kratz. 'All of them have had front-line experience in several official and unofficial wars. Five Israelis and one Kurd.'

Scott raised an eyebrow.

'Few people realise,' continued Kratz, 'that Mossad has an Arab section, not large in numbers, but once we've trained them, only the Gurkhas make better killers. The test will be if you can spot which one he is.'

'How many are coming over the border with us?'

'Only two. We can't afford to make it look like an army. One engineer and a driver. At least, that's how they'll be described on the manifest, but they only have one job description as far as I'm concerned, and that's to get you into Baghdad and back out with the Declaration in the shortest possible time.'

Scott looked straight ahead of him. 'And Hannah?' he said simply.

'That would be a bonus if we got lucky, but it's not part of my brief. I consider the chances of your even seeing her are remote,' he said as they passed a 'Welcome to Stockholm' sign.

Scott began thumping Bertha's bible up and down on his knees. 'Careful with that,' said Kratz. 'It still needs to be translated, otherwise you won't know how to go about a proper introduction to the lady. After all, it will only be your palm and your voice she'll be opening her heart to.'

Scott glanced down at the 108-page book and wondered how long it would take him to master its secrets, even after it had been translated into English.

Kratz suddenly swung right without warning and drove down a deserted street that ran parallel to a disused railway line. All Scott could see ahead of him was a tunnel that looked as if it led nowhere.

When he was a hundred yards from the entrance, Kratz checked in his rear-view mirror to see if anyone was following them. Satisfied they were alone, he flashed his headlights three times. A second later, from what appeared to be the other end of a black hole, he received the same response. He slowed down and drove into the tunnel without his lights on. All Scott could now see was a torch indicating where they should pull up.

Kratz followed the light and came to a halt in front of what appeared to be an old army truck. It was stationed just inside the far end of the tunnel.

He jumped out of the car and Scott quickly followed, trying to accustom himself to the half-light. Then he saw three men standing on each side of the vehicle. The man nearest them came to attention and saluted. 'Good morning, Colonel,' he said.

'Put your men at ease, Feldman, and come and meet Professor Bradley,' said Kratz. Scott almost laughed at the use of his academic title among these men, but there were no smiles on the faces of the six soldiers who came forward to meet him.

After Scott had shaken hands with each of them he took a walk round the truck. 'Do you really believe this old heap is capable of carrying Madame Bertha to Baghdad?' he asked Kratz in disbelief.

'Sergeant Cohen.'

'Sir,' said a voice in the dark.

'You're the trained mechanic. Why don't you brief Professor Bradley?'

'Yes, sir.' Another figure appeared out of the gloom. Scott couldn't see his features clearly, as he was covered in grease, but from his accent he would have guessed he had spent most of his life in London. 'The Heavy Expanded Mobile Tactical Truck, or HEMTT, was built in Wisconsin. She has five gears, four forward, one reverse. She can be used on all terrains in most weather conditions in virtually any country. She weighs twenty tons and can carry up to ten tons, but with that weight on board you cannot risk driving over thirty miles per hour. Any higher than that and she would be impossible to stop, even though if pushed she can top 120 miles per hour.'

'Thank you, Cohen. A useful piece of kit, I think you'll agree,' said Kratz, looking back at Scott. 'We've wanted one of these for years, and then suddenly you arrive on the scene and Uncle Sam offers us the prototype model overnight. But then, at a cost of nearly a million dollars of taxpayers' money, you'd expect the Americans to be choosy about who they loan one out to.'

'Would you care to join us for lunch, Professor?' asked the man who had been introduced as Feldman.

'Don't tell me the HEMTT cooks as well,' said Scott.

'No, sir, we have to rely on the Kurd for that. Aziz's speciality is hamburger and French fries. If you've never had the experience before, it can be quite tasty.'

The eight of them sat cross-legged on the ground, using the reverse side of a backgammon board as a table. Scott couldn't remember enjoying a burnt hamburger more. He was also glad of the chance to chat to the men he would be working with on the operation. Kratz began to talk through the different contingency plans they would have to consider once they had reached the Jordan–Iraq border. It didn't take more than a few minutes for Scott to realise how professional these men were, or to see their desire to be part of the final team. He grew confident that the operation was in good hands, and that Kratz's team had not been chosen at random.

After a third hamburger he was sorry when the Mossad Colonel reminded him he had a flight to catch. He rose and thanked the cook for a memorable meal.

'See you in Jordan, sir,' said Sergeant Cohen.

'See you in Jordan,' said Scott.

As Scott was being driven to the airport, he asked Kratz, 'How are you going to select the final two?'

'They'll decide for themselves. Nothing to do with me, I'm only their commanding officer.'

'What do you mean?'

'They're going to play round-robin backgammon on the way to Jordan. The two winners get a day trip to Baghdad, all expenses paid.'

'And the losers?'

'Get a postcard saying "Wish you were here".'

24

HANNAH GATHERED UP all the files that the Deputy Foreign Minister would require for his meeting with the Revolutionary Command Council.

By working hours that no one else knew existed, and completing tasks the Minister had never thought would get done, Hannah had quickly made herself indispensable. Whenever the Minister needed something, it was there on his desk: she could anticipate his every need, and never sought praise for doing so. But, despite all this, she rarely left the office during the day or the house at night, and certainly seemed to be no nearer to coming into contact with Saddam. The Ambassador's wife tried valiantly to help on the social side, and on one occasion she even invited a young soldier round to dinner. He was good looking, Hannah thought, and seemed to be pleasant enough, although he hardly opened his mouth all evening and left suddenly without a word. Perhaps she was unable to hide the fact that she no longer had any interest in men.

Hannah had sat in on several meetings with individual Ministers, even members of the Command Council, including Saddam's half-brother, the Iraqi Ambassador to the UN in Geneva, but she felt no nearer to Saddam himself than she had been when she lived in a cul-de-sac in Chalk Farm. She was becoming despondent, and began to fear that her frustration might become obvious for all to see. As an antidote she channelled her energies into generating reports on interdepartmental spending, and set up a filing system that would have been the envy of the mandarins in Whitehall. But one of the many things Mossad had taught her during her arduous days of training was always to be patient, and ready, because in time an opening would appear.

It was early on a Thursday morning, when most of the Minister's staff had begun their weekends, that the first opening presented itself. Hannah was typing up her notes from a meeting the Deputy Minister had had the previous day with the newly-appointed Head of Interest Section in Paris, a Mr Al Obaydi, when the call came through. Muhammad Saeed Al-Zahiaf, the Foreign Minister, wished to speak to his deputy.

A few moments later, the Deputy Minister came rushing out of his office, barking at Hannah to follow him. Hannah grabbed a notepad and chased after the Minister down the long passageway.

Although the Foreign Minister's office was only at the other end of the corridor, Hannah had never been inside it before. When she followed her Minister into the room, she was surprised to find how modern and dull it was, with only the panoramic view over the Tigris as compensation.

The Foreign Minister did not bother to rise, but hastily motioned his subordinate into a chair on the opposite side of the desk, explaining that the President had requested a full report on the subject they had discussed at the Revolutionary Council the previous evening. He went on to explain that his own secretary had gone home for the weekend, so Miss Saib should take down a record of their meeting.

Hannah could not believe the discussion that followed. Had she not been aware that she was listening to two Ministers who were loyal members of the Revolutionary Command Council, she would have dismissed their conversation as an outrageous piece of propaganda. The President's half-brother had apparently succeeded in stealing the Declaration of Independence from the National Archives in Washington, and the document was now nailed to a wall of the room in which the Council met.

The discussion concentrated on how the news of this triumph should be released to an astonished world, and the date that had been selected to guarantee the greatest media coverage. Details were also discussed as to which square in the capital the President should deliver his speech from before he publicly burned the document, and whether Peter Arnett or Bernard Shaw of CNN should be granted special access to film the President standing next to the parchment the night before the burning ceremony took place.

After two hours the meeting broke up and Hannah returned with the Deputy Minister to his office. Without so much as a glance in her direction, he ordered her to make a fair copy of the decisions that had been taken that morning.

It took Hannah the rest of the morning to produce a first draft, which the Minister read through immediately. After making a few changes and emendations, he told her to produce a final copy to be delivered to the Foreign Minister with a recommendation that it should, if it met with his approval, be sent on to the President.

As she walked home through the streets of Baghdad that evening, Hannah felt helpless. She wondered what she could possibly do to warn the Americans. Surely they were planning some counter-measures in order to try to recapture the Declaration, or would at least be preparing some form of retaliation once they knew the day that had been selected for the public burning.

Did they even know where it was at that moment? Had Kratz been informed? Had Mossad been called in to advise the Americans on the operation they had themselves been planning for the past year? Were they now trying to get in touch with her? What would Simon have expected her to do?

She stopped at a cigarette kiosk and purchased three postcards of Saddam Hussein addressing the Revolutionary Command Council.

Later, in the safety of her bedroom, she wrote the same message to Ethel Rubin, David Kratz and the Professor of Arabic Studies at London University. She hoped one of them would work out the significance of the date in the top right-hand corner and the little biro'd square full of stars she had drawn on the wall by the side of Saddam's head.

'What time is the flight for Stockholm expected to depart?' he asked.

'It shouldn't be long now,' said the girl behind the SAS desk at Charles de Gaulle. 'I'm afraid it's only just landed on its inward journey, so it's difficult for me to be more precise.'

Another opportunity to turn back, thought Al Obaydi. But following his meeting with the Head of State Security and, the next morning, with the Deputy Foreign Minister, he felt confident that they had both considered what he had told them no more than routine. Al Obaydi had dropped into the conversation the fact that he was due for some leave before taking up his new appointment in Paris.

After Al Obaydi had collected his luggage from the carousel, he deposited all the large cases in storage, retaining only one bulky briefcase. He then took a seat in the corner of the departure lounge and thought about his actions during the past few days.

The Head of State Security hadn't had a lot to offer. The truth – not that he was going to admit it – was that he had enough problems at home without worrying about what was going on abroad. He had supplied Al Obaydi with an out-of-date instruction book on what precautions any Iraqi citizen should take when in Europe, including not to shop at Marks and Spencers or to mix socially with foreigners, and an out-of-date collection of photographs of known Mossad and CIA agents active on the Continent. After looking through the photographs, Al Obaydi wouldn't have been surprised to find that most of them had long retired, and that some had even died peacefully in their beds.

The following day, the Deputy Foreign Minister had been courteous without being friendly. He had given him some useful tips about how to conduct himself in Paris, including which embassies would be happy to deal with him despite their official position, and which would not. When it came to the Jordanian Embassy itself and the Iraqi annexe, he gave Al Obaydi a quick briefing on the resident staff. He had left Miss Ahmed there to guarantee some sort of continuity. He described her as willing and conscientious, the cook as awful but friendly, and the driver as stupid but brave. His only guarded warning was to be wary of Abdul Kanuk, the Chief Administrator, a wonderful title which did not describe his true position, his only qualification being that he was a distant cousin of the President. The Deputy Foreign Minister was careful not to voice a personal opinion, but his eyes told Al Obaydi everything he needed to know. As he left, the

Minister's secretary, Miss Saib, had presented him with another file. This one turned out to be full of useful information about how to get by in Paris without many friends. Places where he would be made welcome and others he should avoid.

Perhaps Miss Saib should have listed Sweden as somewhere to avoid.

Al Obaydi felt little apprehension about the trip, as he had no intention of remaining in Sweden for more than a few hours. He had already contacted the chief engineer of Svenhalte AC, who assured him he had made no mention of his earlier call to Mr Riffat when he returned that afternoon. He was also able to confirm that Madame Bertha, as he kept calling the safe, was definitely on her way to Baghdad.

'Would passengers travelling to Stockholm . . .' Al Obaydi made his way through the departure lounge to the exit gate and, after his boarding card had been checked, was shown to a window seat in economy. This section of the journey would not be presented as a claim against expenses.

On the flight across northern Europe, Al Obaydi's mind drifted from his work in Baghdad back to the weekend, which he had spent with his mother and sister. It was they who had helped him make the final decision. His mother had no interest in leaving their comfortable little home on the outskirts of Baghdad, and even less in moving to Paris. So now Al Obaydi accepted that he could never hope to escape: his only future rested in trying to secure a position of power within the Foreign Ministry. He was in no doubt that he could now perform a service for the President that would make him indispensable in Saddam's eyes; it might even present him with the chance of becoming the next Foreign Minister. After all, the Deputy was due for retirement in a couple of years, and sudden promotion never surprised anyone in Baghdad.

When the plane landed at Stockholm, Al Obaydi disembarked, using the diplomatic channel to escape quickly.

The journey to Kalmar by taxi took just over three hours, and the newly-appointed Ambassador spent most of the time gazing aimlessly out of the grubby window, pondering the unfamiliar sight of green hills and grey skies. When the taxi finally came to a halt outside the works entrance of Svenhalte AC, Al Obaydi was greeted by the sight of a man in a long brown coat who looked as if he had been standing there for some time.

Al Obaydi noticed that the man had a worried expression on his face. But it turned to a smile the moment the Ambassador stepped out of the car.

'How agreeable to meet you, Mr Al Obaydi,' said the chief engineer in English, the tongue he felt they would both feel most comfortable in. 'My name is Pedersson. Won't you please come to my office?'

After Pedersson had ordered coffee – how nice to taste cappuccino again, Al Obaydi thought – his first question proved just how anxious he was.

'I hope we did not do wrong?'

'No, no,' said Al Obaydi, who had himself been put at ease by the chief engineer's gushing words and obvious anxiety. 'I assure you this is only a routine check.'

'Mr Riffat was in possession of all the correct documents, both from the UN and from your government.'

Al Obaydi was becoming painfully aware that he was dealing with a group of highly-trained professionals.

'You say they left here on Wednesday afternoon?' Al Obaydi asked, trying to sound casual.

'Yes, that is correct.'

'How long do you imagine it will take them to reach Baghdad?'

'At least a week, perhaps ten days in that old truck, if they make it at all.'

Al Obaydi looked puzzled. 'An old truck?'

'Yes, they came to pick up Madame Bertha in an old army truck. Though, I must confess, the engine had a good sound to it. I took some pictures for my album. Would you like to see them?'

'Pictures of the truck?' said Al Obaydi.

'Yes, from my window, with Mr Riffat standing by the safe. They didn't notice.'

Pedersson opened the drawer of his desk and took out several pictures. He pushed them across his desk with the same pride that another man might have displayed when showing a stranger snapshots of his family.

Al Obaydi studied the photographs carefully. Several of them showed Madame Bertha being lowered onto the truck.

'There is a problem?' asked Pedersson.

'No, no,' said Al Obaydi, and added, 'Would it be possible to have copies of these photographs?'

'Oh yes, please keep them, I have many,' said the chief engineer, pointing to the open drawer.

Al Obaydi picked up his briefcase, opened it and placed the pictures in a flap at the front before removing some photographs of his own.

'While I'm here, perhaps you could help me with one more small matter.'

'Anything,' said Pedersson.

'I have some photographs of former employees of the state, and it would be helpful if you were able to remember if any of them were among those who came to collect Madame Bertha.'

Once again, Pedersson looked unsure, but he took the photographs and studied each one at length. He repeated, 'No, no, no,' several times, until he came to one which he took longer over. Al Obaydi leaned forward.

'Yes,' said Pedersson eventually. 'Although it must have been taken some years ago. This is Mr Riffat. He has not put on any weight, but he has aged and his hair has turned grey. A very thorough man,' Pedersson added.

'Yes,' said Al Obaydi, 'Mr Riffat is a very thorough man,' he repeated as he glanced at the details in Arabic printed on the back of the photograph. 'It will be a great relief for my government to know that Mr Riffat is in charge of this particular operation.'

Pedersson smiled for the first time as Al Obaydi downed the last drop of his coffee. 'You have been most helpful,' the Ambassador said. He rose before adding, 'I feel sure my government will be in need of your services again in the future, but I would be obliged if you made no mention of this meeting to anyone.'

'Just as you wish,' said Pedersson as they walked back down to the yard. The smile remained on his face as he watched the taxi drive out of the factory gate, carrying off his distinguished customer.

But Pedersson's thoughts did not match his expression. 'All is not well,' he muttered to himself. 'I do not believe that gentleman feels Madame Bertha is in safe hands, and I am certain he is no friend of Mr Riffat.'

It surprised Scott to find that he liked Dollar Bill the moment he met him. It didn't surprise him that once he had seen an example of his work, he also respected him.

Scott landed in San Francisco seventeen hours after he had taken off from Stockholm. The CIA had a car waiting for him at the airport. He was driven quickly up into Marin County and deposited outside the safe house within the hour.

After snatching some sleep, Scott rose for lunch, hoping to meet Dollar Bill straight away, but to his disappointment the forger was nowhere to be seen.

'Mr O'Reilly takes breakfast at seven and doesn't appear again before dinner, sir,' explained the butler.

'And what does he do for sustenance in between?' asked Scott.

'At twelve, I take him a bar of chocolate and half a pint of water, and at six, half a pint of Guinness.'

After lunch, Scott read an update on what had been going on at the State Department during his absence, and then spent the rest of the afternoon in the basement gym. He staggered out of the session around five, nursing several aches and pains from excessive exercise and one or two bruises administered by the judo instructor.

'Not bad for thirty-six,' he was told condescendingly by the instructor, who looked as if he might have been only a shade younger himself.

Scott sat in a warm bath trying to ease the pain as he turned the pages of Madame Bertha's bible. The document had already been translated by six Arabic scholars from six universities within fifty miles of where he was soaking. They had been given two non-consecutive chapters each. Dexter Hutchins had not been idle since his return.

When Scott came down for dinner, still feeling a little stiff, he found Dollar Bill standing with his back to the fire in the drawing room, sipping a glass of water.

'What would you like to drink, Professor?' asked the butler.

'A very weak shandy,' Scott replied before introducing himself to Dollar Bill.

'Are you here, Professor, out of choice, or were you simply arrested for drunk driving?' was Dollar Bill's first question. He had obviously decided to give Scott just as hard a time as the judo instructor.

'Choice, I fear,' replied Scott with a smile.

'From such a reply,' said Dollar Bill, 'I can only deduce you teach a dead subject or one that is no use to living mortals.'

'I teach Constitutional Law,' Scott replied, 'but I specialise in Logic.'

'Then you manage to achieve both at once,' said Dollar Bill as Dexter Hutchins entered the room.

'I'd like a gin and tonic, Charles,' said Dexter as he shook Scott's hand warmly. 'I'm sorry I didn't catch up with you earlier, but those guys in Foggy Bottom haven't been off the phone all afternoon.'

'There are many reasons to be wary of your fellow creatures,' Dollar Bill observed, 'and by asking for a gin and tonic, Mr Hutchins has just demonstrated two of them.'

Charles returned a moment later carrying a shandy and a gin and tonic on a silver tray, which he offered to Scott and the Deputy Director.

'In my university days, logic didn't exist,' said Dollar Bill after Dexter Hutchins had suggested they go through to dinner. 'Trinity College, Dublin would have no truck with the subject. I can't think of a single occasion in Irish history when any of my countrymen have ever relied on logic.'

'So what did you study?' asked Scott.

'A lot of Fleming, a little of Joyce, with a few rare moments devoted to Plato and Aristotle, but I fear not enough to engage the attention of any member of the board of examiners.'

'And how is the Declaration coming on?' asked Dexter, as if he hadn't been following the conversation.

'A stickler for the work ethic is our Mr Hutchins,

Professor,' said Dollar Bill as a bowl of soup was placed in front of him. 'Mind you, he *is* a man who would rely on logic to see him through. However, as there is no such thing in life as a free meal, I will attempt to answer my jailer's question. Today, I completed the text as originally written by Timothy Matlock, Assistant to the Secretary of Congress. It took him seventeen hours you know. I fear it has taken me rather longer.'

'And how long do you think it will take you to finish the names?' pressed Dexter.

'You are worse than Pope Julius II, forever demanding of Michelangelo how long it would take him to finish the ceiling of the Sistine Chapel,' said Dollar Bill as the butler removed the soup bowls.

'The names,' demanded Dexter. 'The names.'

'Oh, impatient and unsubtle man.'

'Shaw,' said Scott.

'I grow to like you more by the minute,' said Dollar Bill.

'The names,' repeated Dexter as Charles placed an Irish stew on the table. Dollar Bill immediately helped himself.

'Now I see why you are the *Deputy* Director,' said Dollar Bill. 'Do you not realise, man, that there are fifty-six names on the original document, each one of them a work of art in itself? Let me demonstrate to you, if I may. Paper, please, Charles. I require paper.'

The butler took a pad that lay next to the telephone and placed it by O'Reilly's side. Dollar Bill removed a pen from his inside pocket and began to scribble.

He showed his two dinner companions what he had written: 'Mr O'Reilly may have the unrestricted use of the company helicopter whenever he wishes.'

'What does that prove?' asked Dexter.

'Patience, Mr Hutchins, patience,' said Dollar Bill, as

he retrieved the piece of paper and signed it first with the signature of Dexter Hutchins, and then, changing his pen, wrote 'Scott Bradley'.

Once again he allowed them to study his efforts.

'But how . . .?' said Scott.

'In your case, Professor, it was easy. All I needed was the visitors' book.'

'But *I* didn't sign the visitors' book,' said Dexter.

'I confess it would be a strange thing for you to do when you are the Deputy Director,' said Dollar Bill, 'but, in your case nothing would surprise me. However, Mr Hutchins, you do have the infuriating habit of signing and dating the inside cover of any book you have purchased recently. I suspect in the case of first editions it will be the nearest you get to posterity.' He paused. 'But enough of this idle banter. You can both see for yourself the task I face.' Without warning, Dollar Bill folded his napkin, rose from the table leaving his half-finished stew, and walked out of the room. His companions jumped up and quickly followed him across to the west wing without another word being spoken. After they had climbed a small flight of stone steps they entered Dollar Bill's makeshift study.

On an architect's drafting board below a bright light rested the parchment. Both men walked across the room, stood over the board and studied the completed script. It had been inscribed above a large empty space covered in tiny pencil crosses that awaited the fifty-six signatures.

Scott stared in admiration at the work.

'But why didn't you . . .'

'Take up a proper occupation?' asked Dollar Bill, anticipating the question. 'And have ended up as a schoolmaster in Wexford, or perhaps have climbed to the dizzy heights of being a councillor in Dublin? No, sir, I would prefer the odd stint in jail rather than be considered by my fellow men as mediocre.'

'How many days before you have to leave us, young man?' Dexter Hutchins asked Scott.

'Kratz phoned this afternoon,' Scott replied, turning to face the Deputy Director. 'He says they caught the Trelleborg–Sassnitz ferry last night. They're now heading south, hoping to cross the Bosphorus by Monday morning.'

'Which means they should be at the border with Iraq by next Wednesday.'

'The perfect time of year to be sailing the Bosphorus,' said Dollar Bill. 'Especially if you hope to meet a rather remarkable girl when you reach the other side,' he added, looking up at Scott. 'So, I'd better have the Declaration finished by Monday, hadn't I, Professor?'

'At the latest,' said Hutchins as Scott stared down at the little Irishman.

25

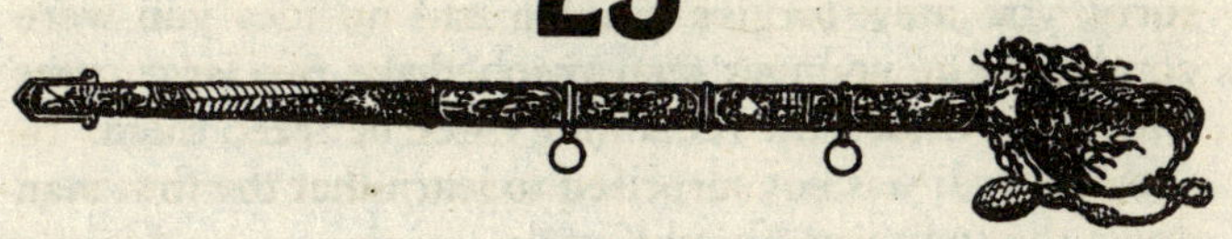

WHEN AL OBAYDI ARRIVED back in Paris he collected his bags from the twenty-four-hour storage depot, then joined the queue for a taxi.

He gave the driver an address, without saying it was the Iraqi annexe to the Jordanian Embassy – one of the tips in Miss Saib's 'do's and don'ts' in Paris. He hadn't warned the staff at the embassy that he would be arriving that day. He wasn't officially due to take up his appointment for another fortnight, and he would have gone straight on to Jordan that evening if there had been a connecting flight. Once he had realised who Mr Riffat was, he knew he would have to get back to Baghdad as quickly as possible. By reporting direct to the Foreign Minister, he would have gone through the correct channels. This would protect his position, while at the same time guaranteeing that the President knew exactly who was responsible for alerting him to a possible attempt on his life, and which Ambassador, however closely related, had left several stones unturned.

The taxi dropped Al Obaydi outside the annexe to the embassy in Neuilly. He pulled his cases out of the back without any help from the driver, who remained seated obstinately behind the wheel of his car.

The embassy front door opened just an inch, and was then flung wide, and a man of about forty came running down the steps towards him, followed by two girls and a younger man.

'Excellency, Excellency,' the first man exclaimed. 'I am sorry, you must forgive me, we had no idea you were coming.' The younger man grabbed the two large cases and the girls took the remaining three between them.

Al Obaydi was not surprised to learn that the first man down the steps was Abdul Kanuk.

'We were told you would be arriving in two weeks' time, Excellency. We thought you were still in Baghdad. I hope you will not feel we have been discourteous.'

Al Obaydi made no attempt to interrupt the non-stop flow of sycophancy that came pouring out, feeling the man must eventually run out of steam. In any case, Kanuk was not a man to get on the wrong side of on his first day.

'Would Your Excellency like a quick tour of our quarters while the maid unpacks your bags?'

As there were questions Al Obaydi felt only this man could answer, he took advantage of the offer. Not only did he get the guided tour from the Chief Administrator, but he was also subjected to a stream of uninterrupted gossip. He stopped listening after only a few minutes; he had far more important things on his mind. He soon longed to be shown to his own room and left alone to be given a chance to think. The first flight to Jordan was not until the next morning, and he needed to prepare in his mind how he would present his findings to the Foreign Minister.

It was while he was being shown round what would shortly be his office looking out over a Paris that was turning from the half-light of dusk to the artificial light of night, that the Administrator said something Al Obaydi didn't quite catch. He felt he should have been paying closer attention.

'I'm sorry to say that your secretary is on holiday, Excellency. Like the rest of us, Miss Ahmed wasn't expecting you for another fortnight. I know she had planned to be back in Paris a week ahead of you, so that she would have everything ready by the time you arrived.'

'It's not a problem,' said Al Obaydi.

'Of course, you'll know Miss Saib, the Deputy Foreign Minister's secretary?'

'I came across Miss Saib when I was in Baghdad,' replied Al Obaydi.

The Chief Administrator nodded, and seemed to hesitate for a moment.

'I think I'll have a rest before dinner,' the Ambassador said, taking advantage of the temporary halt in an otherwise unending flow.

'I'll have something sent up to your room, Excellency. Would eight suit you?'

'Thank you,' said Al Obaydi, in an attempt to put an end to the conversation.

'Shall I place your passport and tickets in the safe, as I always did for the previous Ambassador?'

'A good idea,' said Al Obaydi, delighted to have at last found a way of getting rid of the Chief Administrator.

Scott put the phone down and turned to face Dexter Hutchins, who was leaning back in the large leather chair at his desk, his hands clasped behind his head and a questioning look on his face.

'So where are they?' asked Dexter.

'Kratz wouldn't give me the exact location, for obvious reasons, but at his current rate of progress he feels confident they'll reach the Jordanian border within the next three days.'

'Then let's pray that the Iraqi Ministry of Industry is as inefficient as our experts keep telling us it is. If so, the advantage should be with us for at least a few more days. After all, we did move the moment sanctions were lifted, and until you showed up in Kalmar, Pedersson hadn't heard a peep out of anyone for the past two years.'

'I agree. But I worry that Pedersson might be the one weak link in Kratz's chain.'

'If you're going to take these sorts of risks, no plan can ever be absolutely watertight,' said Dexter.

Scott nodded.

'And if Kratz is less than three days from the border, you'll have to catch a flight for Amman on Monday night, assuming Mr O'Reilly has finished his signatures by then.'

'I don't think that's a problem any longer,' said Scott.

'Why? He still had a lot of names to copy when I last looked at the parchment.'

'It can't be that many,' said Scott, 'because Mr Mendelssohn flew in from Washington this morning in order to pass his judgement, and that seems to be the only opinion Bill is interested in.'

'Then let's go and see for ourselves,' said Dexter as he swung himself up out of his chair.

As they left the office and made their way down the corridor, Dexter asked, 'And how's Bertha's bible coming along? I turned a few pages of the introduction this morning and couldn't begin to get a grasp of why the bulbs turn from red to green.'

'Only one man knows Madame Bertha more intimately than I do, and at this moment he's pining away in Scandinavia,' said Scott as they climbed the stone steps to Dollar Bill's private room.

'I also hear that Charles has designed a special pair of trousers for you,' Dexter said.

'And they're a perfect fit,' replied Scott with a smile.

As they reached the top of the steps, Dexter was about to barge in when Scott put an arm on his shoulder.

'Perhaps we should knock? He might be . . .'

'Next you'll be wanting me to call him "sir".'

Scott grinned as Dexter knocked quietly, and when there was no reply, eased the door open. He crept in to see Mendelssohn stooping over the parchment, magnifying glass in hand.

'Benjamin Franklin, John Morton and George Clymer,' muttered the Conservator.

'I had a lot of trouble with Clymer,' said Dollar Bill, who was looking out of the window over the bay. 'It was the damn man's squiggles, which I had to complete in one flow. You'll find a couple of hundred of them in the waste-paper basket.'

'May we approach the bench?' asked Dexter. Dollar Bill turned and waved them in.

'Good afternoon, Mr Mendelssohn. I'm Dexter Hutchins, Deputy Director of the CIA.'

'Could you possibly be anything else?' asked Dollar Bill.

Dexter ignored the comment and asked Mendelssohn, 'What's your judgement, sir?'

Dollar Bill continued to stare out of the window.

'It's every bit as good as the copy we currently have on display at the National Archives.'

'You are most generous, sir,' said Dollar Bill, who turned round to face them.

'But I don't understand why you have spelt the word "British" correctly, and not with two *t*s as it was on the original,' said Mendelssohn, returning his attention to the document.

'There are two reasons for that,' said Dollar Bill as six suspicious eyes stared back at him. 'First, if the exchange is carried out successfully, Saddam will not be able to claim he still has his hands on the original.'

'Clever,' said Scott.

'And second?' asked Dexter, who remained suspicious of the little Irishman's motives.

'It will stop the Professor from bringing back this copy and trying to pass it off as the original.'

Scott laughed. 'You always think like a criminal,' he said.

'And you'd better be thinking like one yourself over the next few days, if you're going to get the better of Saddam Hussein,' said Dollar Bill as Charles entered the room, carrying a pint of Guinness on a silver tray.

Dollar Bill thanked Charles, removed his reward from the tray and walked to the far side of the room before taking the first sip.

'May I ask . . .?' began Scott.

'I once spilt the blessed nectar all over a hundred-dollar etching that I had spent some three months preparing.'

'So what did you do then?' asked Scott.

'I fear that I settled for second best, which caused me to end up in the slammer for another five years.' Even Dexter joined in the laughter. 'However, on this occasion I raise my glass to Matthew Thornton, the final signatory on the document. I wish him good health wherever he is, despite the damn man's *ts*.'

'So, am I able to take the masterpiece away now?' asked Scott.

'Not yet, young man,' said Dollar Bill. 'I fear you must suffer another evening of my company,' he added before placing his drink on the window ledge and returning to the document. 'You see, the one problem I have been fighting is time. In Mr Mendelssohn's judgement, the parchment has an 1830s feel about it. Am I right, sir?'

The Conservator nodded, and raised his arms as if

apologising for daring to mention such a slight blemish.

'So what can be done about that?' asked Dexter Hutchins.

Dollar Bill flicked on a switch and the Xenon lamps above his desk shone down on the parchment and filled the room with light, making it appear like a film set.

'By nine o'clock tomorrow morning the parchment will be nearer 1776. Even if, because you have failed to give me enough time, I miss perfection by a few years, I remain confident that there'll be no one in Iraq who'll be able to tell the difference, unless they are in possession of a Carbon 14 dating machine, and know how to use it.'

'Then we can only hope that the original hasn't already been destroyed,' said Dexter Hutchins.

'Not a chance,' said Scott.

'How can you be so confident?' asked Dexter.

'The day Saddam destroys that parchment, he will want the whole world to witness it. Of that I'm sure.'

'Then, I'm thinking a toast might be in order,' said the Irishman. 'That is, with my gracious host's permission.'

'A toast, Bill?' said the Deputy Director, sounding surprised. 'Who do you have in mind?' he asked suspiciously.

'To Hannah,' said the little Irishman, 'wherever she may be.'

'How did you know?' asked Scott. 'I've never mentioned her name.'

'No need to, when you write it on everything from the backs of envelopes to steaming windows. She must be a very special lady, Professor.' He raised his glass and repeated the words, 'To Hannah.'

The Chief Administrator sat and waited patiently until the maid had removed the Ambassador's dinner tray. He then closed his door at the other end of the corridor.

He waited for another two hours, until he felt certain all the embassy staff had gone to bed. Confident he would be the only one left awake, he crept back down to his office and looked up a telephone number in Geneva. He dialled the code slowly and deliberately. It rang for a long time before it was eventually answered.

'I need to speak to the Ambassador,' he whispered.

'His Excellency retired to bed some time ago,' said a voice. 'You'll have to call back in the morning.'

'Wake him. Tell him it's Abdul Kanuk in Paris.'

'If you insist.'

'I do insist.'

The Chief Administrator waited for some time before a sleepy voice eventually came on the line.

'This had better be good, Abdul.'

'Al Obaydi has arrived in Paris unannounced, and two weeks before he was expected.'

'You woke me in the middle of the night to tell me this?'

'But he didn't come direct from Baghdad, Excellency. He made a slight detour.'

'How can you be so sure?' said the voice, sounding a little more awake.

'Because I am in possession of his passport.'

'But he's on holiday, you fool.'

'I know. But why spend the day in a city not known for attracting tourists?'

'You're talking in riddles. If you've got something to tell me, tell me.'

'Earlier today, Ambassador Al Obaydi paid a visit to Stockholm, according to the stamp on his passport, but he returned to Paris the same evening. Not my idea of a holiday.'

'Stockholm . . . Stockholm . . . Stockholm . . .' repeated

the voice on the other end of the line, as if trying to register its significance. A pause, and then, 'The safe. Of course. He must have gone on to Kalmar to check on Sayedi's safe. What has he found out that he thought worth hiding from me, and does Baghdad know what he's up to?'

'I have no idea, Excellency,' said the Administrator. 'But I do know he's flying back to Baghdad tomorrow.'

'But if he's on holiday, why would he return to Baghdad so quickly?'

'Perhaps being the Head of Interest Section in Paris is not reward enough for him, Excellency. Could he have his eyes on some greater prize?'

There was a long pause before the voice in Geneva said, 'You did well, Abdul. You were right to wake me. I shall have to phone Kalmar first thing in the morning. First thing,' he repeated.

'You did promise, Excellency, should I once again manage to bring to your attention . . .'

Tony Cavalli waited until Martin had poured them both a drink.

'Arrested in a bar-room brawl,' said his father after he had listened to his son's report.

'Yes,' said Cavalli, placing a file on the table by his side, 'and what's more, he was sentenced to thirty days.'

'Thirty days?' said his father in disbelief. The old man paused before he added, 'What instructions have you given Laura?'

'I've put her on hold until July 15th, when Dollar Bill will be released,' Tony replied.

'So where have they locked him up this time? The county jail?'

'No. According to the records at the district court in

Fairmont, they've thrown him back into the state pen.'

'For being involved in a bar-room brawl,' said the older man. 'It doesn't make sense.' He stared up at the Declaration of Independence on the wall behind his desk and didn't speak again for some moments.

'Who have we got on the inside?'

Cavalli opened the file on the table by his side and extracted a single sheet of paper. 'One senior officer and six inmates,' he said, passing his research across, pleased to have anticipated his father's question.

The old man studied the list of names for some time before he began licking his lips. 'Eduardo Bellatti must be our best bet,' he said, looking up at his son. 'If I remember correctly, he was sentenced to ninety-nine years for blowing away a judge who once got in our way.'

'Correct, and what's more, he's always been happy to kill anyone for a packet of cigarettes,' said Tony. 'So, if he takes care of Dollar Bill before July 15th, it would also save us a quarter of a million dollars.'

'Something isn't quite right,' said his father as he toyed with a whisky, which he hadn't touched. 'Perhaps it's time to dig a little deeper,' he added, almost as if he was talking to himself. He checked down the list of names once again.

Al Obaydi woke early the following morning, restless to be on his way to Baghdad so that he could brief the Foreign Minister on everything he'd learned. Once he was back on Iraqi soil he would prepare a full, written report. He went over the outline again and again in his mind.

He would first explain to the Foreign Minister that, while he was carrying out a routine sanctions check, he had learned that the safe that had been ordered by the President was already on its way to Baghdad. On discovering this, he had become suspicious that an enemy of the state might be involved in an assassination attempt on the life of the President. Not being certain who could be trusted, he had used his initiative, and even his own time and money, to discover who was behind the plot. Within moments of his reporting the details to the Foreign Minister, Saddam was sure to find out whose responsibility the safe was and, more important, who had failed to take care of the President's well-being.

A tap on the door interrupted his thoughts. 'Come in,' he called, and a maid entered carrying a breakfast tray of two pieces of burnt toast and a cup of thick Turkish coffee. Once she had closed the door behind her, Al Obaydi rose, had a cold shower – not by choice – and dressed quickly. He then poured the coffee down the washbasin and ignored the toast.

The Ambassador left his room and walked down one flight of stairs to his office, where he found the Chief Administrator standing behind his desk. Had he been sitting in his chair a moment before?

'Good morning, Excellency,' he said. 'I hope you had a comfortable night.'

Al Obaydi was about to lose his temper, but Kanuk's next question took him by surprise.

'Have you been briefed on the bombings in Baghdad, Excellency?'

'What bombings?' asked Al Obaydi, not pleased to be wrong-footed.

'It seems that at two o'clock this morning the Americans launched several Tomahawk Missiles at Mukhbarat headquarters in the centre of the city.'

'And what was the result?' Al Obaydi asked anxiously.

'A few civilians were killed,' replied the Chief Administrator matter-of-factly, 'but you'll be glad to know that our beloved leader was not in the city at the time.'

'That is indeed good news,' said Al Obaydi. 'But it makes it even more imperative that I return to Baghdad immediately.'

'I have already confirmed your flight reservations, Excellency.'

'Thank you,' said Al Obaydi, staring out of the window at the Seine.

Kanuk bowed low. 'I will see that you are met at the airport when you return, Excellency, and that this time everything is fully prepared for your arrival. Meanwhile, I'll go and fetch your passport. If you'll excuse me.'

Al Obaydi sat down behind his desk. He wondered how long he would be merely Head of Interest Section in Paris once Saddam learned who had saved his life.

Tony dialled the number on his private line.

The phone was picked up by the Deputy Warden, who confirmed in answer to Cavalli's first question that he *was* alone. He listened to Cavalli's second question carefully before he replied.

'If Dollar Bill's anywhere to be found in this jailhouse, then he's better hidden than Leona Helmsley's tax returns.'

'But the county court files show him as being registered with you on the night of June 16th.'

'He may have been registered with us, but he sure never showed up,' said the voice on the other end of the line. 'And it doesn't take eight days to get from San Francisco County Court to here, unless they've gone back to chaining cons up and making them walk the whole way. Perhaps that wouldn't be such a bad idea,' he added with a nervous laugh.

Cavalli didn't laugh. 'Just be sure you keep your mouth shut and your ears open, and let me know the moment you hear anything,' was all he said before putting the phone back down.

Cavalli remained at his desk for an hour after his secretary had left, working out what needed to be done next.

26

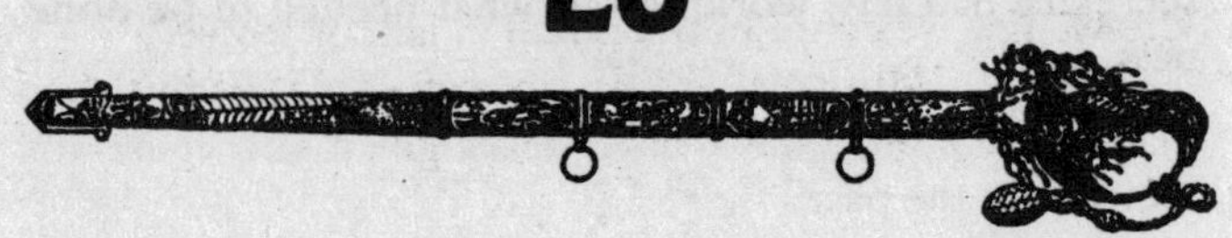

THE SECOND EMERGENCY meeting between the Foreign Minister and his deputy took place on the Tuesday morning, again at short notice. This time it was an unexpected direct call from the President that had both Ministers rushing off to the palace.

All Hannah had been able to piece together from the several phone calls that had gone back and forth that morning was that at some point Saddam's half-brother had called from Geneva, and from that moment the Deputy Foreign Minister appeared to forget the report he was preparing on the American bombing of Mukhbarat headquarters. He fled from the room in a panic, leaving secret papers strewn all over his desk.

Hannah remained at her desk in the hope that she might pick up some more information as the day progressed. While both Ministers were at the palace, she continued to check through old files, aware that she now had enough material to fill several cabinets at Mossad headquarters, but no one to pass her findings on to.

The two Ministers returned from the palace in the late afternoon, and the Deputy Foreign Minister seemed relieved to find Miss Saib was still at her desk.

'I need to make a written report on what was agreed at the meeting this morning with the President,' he said, 'and I cannot overstress the importance of confidentiality in this matter. It would not be an exaggeration to suggest that if anything I am about to tell you became public knowledge, we could both end up in jail, or worse.'

'I hope, Minister,' said Hannah as she put her glasses back on, 'that I have never given you cause for concern in the past.'

The Minister stared across at her, and then began dictating at a rapid pace.

'The President invited the Foreign Minister and myself to a confidential meeting at the palace this morning – date this memo today. Barazan Al-Tikriti, our trusted Ambassador in Geneva, contacted the President during the night to warn him that, after weeks of diligent surveillance, he has uncovered a plot by a group of Zionists to steal a safe from Sweden and use it as a means of illegally entering Iraq. The safe was due for delivery to Baghdad following the lifting of an embargo under UN Security Council Resolution 661. The President has ordered that General Hamil be given the responsibility for dealing with the terrorists' – Hannah thought she saw the Deputy Foreign Minister shudder – 'while the Foreign Ministry has been asked to look into the role played in this particular conspiracy by one of its own staff, Hamid Al Obaydi.

'Our Ambassador in Geneva has discovered that Al Obaydi visited the engineering firm of Svenhalte AC in Kalmar, Sweden, on Monday June 28th, without being directed to do so by any of his superiors. During that visit he was informed of the theft of the safe and the fact that it was being transported to Baghdad. Following his trip to Kalmar, Al Obaydi stayed overnight at our Interest Section in Paris, when he would have had every opportunity to inform Geneva or Baghdad of the Zionist plot, but he made no attempt to do so.

'Al Obaydi left Paris the following morning and, although we know he boarded a flight to Jordan, he has not yet shown up at the border. The President has ordered that if Al Obaydi crosses any of our national frontiers, he should be arrested and taken directly to General Hamil at the headquarters of the Revolutionary Command Council.'

Hannah's pencil flew across the pages of her shorthand notebook as she tried to keep up with the Minister.

'The safe,' continued the Deputy Foreign Minister, 'is currently being transported aboard an old army truck, and is expected to arrive at the border with Jordan some time during the next forty-eight hours.

'All customs officers have received a directive to the effect that the safe is the personal property of the President, and therefore when it reaches the border it must be given priority to continue its journey on to Baghdad.

'Our Ambassador in Geneva, having had a long conversation with a Mr –' the Minister checked his notes '– Pedersson, is convinced that the group accompanying the safe are agents of the CIA, Mossad, or possibly even the British SAS. Like the President, the Ambassador feels the infiltrators' sole interest is in recovering the Declaration of Independence. The President has given orders that the document should not be moved from its place on the wall of the Council Chamber, as this could alert any internal agent to warn the terrorist group not to enter the country.

'Twenty of the President's special guards are already on their way to the border with Jordan,' continued the Minister. 'They will be responsible for monitoring the progress of the safe, and will report directly to General Hamil.

'Once the agents of the West have been apprehended

and thrown in jail, the world's press will be informed that their purpose was to assassinate the President. The President will immediately appear in public and on television, and will make a speech denouncing the American and Zionist warmongers. Sayedi believes that neither the Americans nor the Israelis will ever admit to the real purpose of their raid, but that they will be unable to deny the President's claim. Sayedi feels this whole episode can be turned into a public relations triumph, because if the assassination attempt is announced on the same day that the President publicly burns the Declaration of Independence, it will make it even harder for the Americans to retaliate.

'Starting tomorrow, the President requires a situation update every morning at nine and every evening at six. Both the Foreign Minister and myself are to report to him direct. If Al Obaydi is picked up, the President is to be informed immediately, whatever the time, night or day.'

Hannah's pencil hadn't stopped scribbling across her note pad for nearly twenty minutes. When the Deputy Minister finally came to an end, she tried to take in the full significance of the information she now possessed.

'I need one copy of this report drafted as quickly as possible, no further copies to be made, nothing put on tape, and all your shorthand notes must be shredded once the memo has been handed to me.' Hannah nodded as the Deputy Foreign Minister picked up the phone and dialled the internal number of his superior.

Hannah returned to her room and began typing up the dictation slowly, at the same time trying to commit the salient points to memory. Forty-five minutes later she placed a single copy of the report on the Minister's desk.

He read the script carefully, adding the occasional note in his own hand. When he was satisfied that the memo fully covered the meeting that had taken place that morning, he set off down the corridor to rejoin the Foreign Minister.

Hannah returned to her desk, aware that the team bringing the safe from Sweden were moving inexorably towards Saddam's trap. And if they had received her postcard . . .

When Al Obaydi landed in Jordan, he could not help feeling a sense of triumph.

Once he had passed through customs at Queen Alia airport and was out on the road, he selected the most modern taxi he could find. The old seventies Chevy had no air conditioning and showed 187,000 miles on the clock. He asked the driver to take him to the Iraqi border as quickly as possible.

The car never left the slow lane on its six-hour journey to the border, and because of the state of the roads Al Obaydi was unable to sleep for more than a few minutes at a time. When the driver eventually reached the highway, he still couldn't go much faster because of the oil that had been spilt from lorries carrying loads they had illegally picked up in Basra, to sell at four times the price in Amman. Loads that Al Obaydi had assured the United Nations Assembly time and again were a figment of the Western world's imagination. He also became aware of trucks travelling in the opposite direction that were full of food that he knew would be sold to black-marketeers, long before any of it reached Baghdad.

Al Obaydi checked his watch. If the driver kept going at this speed he wouldn't reach the border before the customs post closed at midnight.

* * *

When Scott landed at Queen Alia airport later that day and stepped on to the tarmac, the first thing that hit him was a temperature of ninety-five degrees. Even dressed in an open-neck shirt, jeans and sneakers, he felt roasted before he had reached the airport terminal. Once he'd entered the building, he was relieved to find it was air conditioned, and his one bag came up on the carousel just as quickly as it would have done in the States. He checked his watch and changed it to Central Eastern time.

The immigration officer hadn't seen many Swedish passports before, but as his father had been an engineer, he wished Mr Bernstrom a successful trip.

As Scott strolled through the green channel, he was stopped by a customs official who was chewing something. He instructed the foreigner to open his bulky canvas bag. After rummaging around inside, the only thing the officer showed any interest in was a long, thin cardboard tube that had been wedged along the bottom of the bag. Scott removed the cap on the end of the tube, pulled out the contents and unrolled a large poster, which was greeted by the official with such puzzled amazement that he even stopped chewing for a moment. He waved Scott through.

Once Scott had reached the main concourse, he walked out onto the road in search of a taxi. He studied the motley selection of cars that were parked by the side of the pavement. They made New York Yellow Cabs look like luxury limousines.

He instructed the driver parked at the front of the queue to take him to the Roman theatre in the centre of the city. The eleven-mile journey into Amman took forty minutes, and when Scott was dropped outside the third-century theatre he handed the driver two ten-dinar notes – enough, the experts at Langley had told him, to cover the cost of the trip. The driver pocketed the notes but did not smile.

Scott checked his watch. He was still well in time for the planned reunion. He walked straight past the ancient monument that was, according to his guidebook, well worth a visit. As instructed by Kratz, he then proceeded west for three blocks, occasionally having to step off the pavement into the road to avoid the bustling crowds. When he reached a Shell petrol station he turned right, leaving the noisy shoppers behind. He then took the second turning on the left, and after that another to the right. The roads became less crowded with locals and more full of potholes with each stride he took. Another left, followed by another right, and he found himself entering the promised cul-de-sac. At the end of the road, when he could go no further, he came to a halt outside a scrapyard. He smiled at the sight that greeted him.

By the time Al Obaydi reached the border, it was already pitch dark. All three lanes leading to the customs post were bumper to bumper with waiting lorries, covered with tarpaulins for the night. The taxi driver came to a halt at the barrier and explained to his passenger that he would have to hire an Iraqi cab once he was on the other side. Al Obaydi thanked the driver and gave him a handsome tip before going to the front of the queue outside the customs shed. A tired official gave him a languid look and told him the border was closed for the night. Al Obaydi presented his diplomatic passport and the official quickly stamped his visa and ushered him through, aware that there would be no little red notes accompanying such a document. Al Obaydi felt exhilarated as he strolled the mile between the two customs posts. He walked to the front of another queue, produced his passport once again, and received another smile from the customs officer.

'There is a car waiting for you, Ambassador,' was all the official said, pointing to a large limousine that was parked near the highway. A smiling chauffeur stood waiting. He touched the peak of his cap and opened the back door.

Al Obaydi smiled. The Chief Administrator must have warned them that he would be coming over the border late that night. He thanked the customs official, walked over to the highway and slipped into the back of the limousine. Someone else was already there, who also appeared to be waiting for him. Al Obaydi began to smile again, when suddenly an arm shot across his throat and threw him to the floor. His hands were pinned behind his back, and a pair of handcuffs clicked into place.

'How dare you?' shouted Al Obaydi. 'I am an Ambassador!' he screamed as he was hurled back up onto the seat. 'Don't you realise who I am?'

'Yes, I do,' came back the reply. 'And you're under arrest for treason.'

Scott had to admit that the HEMTT carrying Madame Bertha looked quite at home among the colourful collection of old American cars and lorries piled high on three sides of the scrapyard. He ran across to the truck and jumped up into the cab on the passenger side. He shook hands with Kratz, who seemed relieved to see him. When Scott saw who was seated behind the wheel, he said, 'Good to see you again, Sergeant Cohen. Am I to assume you play a mean game of backgammon?'

'Two doubles inside the board clinched it for me in the final game, Professor, though God knows how the Kurd even reached the semi-final,' Cohen said as he switched on the engine. 'And because he's a mate of mine, the others are all claiming I fixed the dice.'

'So where's Aziz now?' asked Scott.

'On the back with Madame Bertha,' said the Sergeant. 'Best place for him. Mind you, he knows the back streets of Baghdad like I know the pubs in Brixton, so he may turn out to be useful.'

'And the rest of the team?' asked Scott.

'Feldman and the others slipped over the border during the night,' said Kratz. 'They're probably in Baghdad waiting for us by now.'

'Then they'd better keep well out of sight,' said Scott, 'because after the bombing last Sunday, I suspect death might prove the least of their problems.'

Kratz offered no opinion as Sergeant Cohen eased the massive vehicle slowly out of the yard and onto the street; this time the roads became wider with each turning he took.

'Are we keeping to the plan that was agreed in Stockholm?' asked Scott.

'With two refinements,' said Kratz. 'I spent yesterday morning phoning Baghdad. After seven attempts, I got through to someone at the Ministry of Industry who knew about the safe, but it's the age-old problem with the Arabs: if they don't see the damn thing in front of their eyes, they don't believe it exists.'

'So our first stop will have to be the Ministry?' said Scott.

'Looks like it,' replied Kratz. 'But at least we know we've got something they want. Which reminds me, have you brought the one thing they don't want?'

Scott unzipped his bag and pulled out the cardboard tube.

'Doesn't look a lot to be risking your life for,' said Kratz as Scott slipped it back into his bag.

'And the second refinement?' asked Scott.

Kratz removed a postcard from his inside pocket and passed it over to Scott. A picture of Saddam Hussein addressing the Revolutionary Command Council stared back at him. A little biro'd square full of stars had been drawn in by the side of his head. Scott turned the card over and studied her unmistakable handwriting: 'Wish you were here.'

Scott didn't speak for several moments.

'Notice the date, did you?'

Scott looked at the top right-hand corner: 4.7.93.

'So, now we know where it is, and she's also confirmed exactly when Saddam intends to let the rest of the world into his secret.'

'Who's Ethel Rubin?' asked Scott. 'And how did you get your hands on the card?'

'The lady Hannah was billeted with in London. Her husband is Mossad's legal representative in England. He took the card straight to the embassy the moment it arrived and they sent it overnight in the diplomatic pouch. It reached our embassy in Amman this morning.'

Once they had reached the outskirts of the town, Scott began to study the barren terrain as the lorry continued its progress along the oil-covered, potholed roads.

'Sorry to be going so slowly, Professor,' said Cohen, 'but if I throw my brakes on with the road in this condition, Madame Bertha might travel another hundred yards before the wheels even have a chance to lock.'

Kratz went over every contingency he could think of as Cohen drove silently towards the border. The Mossad leader ended up by describing the layout of the Ba'ath headquarters once again.

'And the alarm system?' asked Scott when he had come to an end.

'All you have to remember is that the red buttons by

the light switches activate the alarm, but at the same time close all the exits.'

Scott nodded, but it was some time before he asked his next question. 'And Hannah?'

'Nothing's changed. My first task is to get you in and then back out with the original document. She still remains an unlikely bonus, although she obviously knows what's going on.'

Neither of them spoke again until Sergeant Cohen pulled off the highway into a large gravel layby packed with lorries. He parked the vehicle at an angle so that only the most inquisitive could observe what they were up to, then jumped out of the cab, pulled himself over the tailboard and grinned at the Kurd who was lounging against the safe. Between them they removed the tarpaulin that covered the massive structure as Scott and Kratz climbed up to join them in the back of the truck.

'What do you think, Professor?' asked Aziz.

'She hasn't lost any weight, that's for sure,' said Scott, as he tried to remember the nightly homework he had done in preparation for this single exam.

He stretched his fingers and smiled. All three bulbs above the white square were red. He first turned all three dials to a code that only he and a man in Sweden were aware of. He then placed his right hand on the white square, and left it there for several seconds. He leaned forward, put his lips up against the square and spoke softly. 'My name is Andreas Bernstrom. When you hear this voice, and only this voice, you will unlock the door.' Scott waited as the other three looked on in bemused silence. He then swivelled the dials. All three bulbs remained red.

'Now we discover if I understood the instructions,' said Scott. He bit his lip and advanced again. Once more he twiddled the dials, but this time to the numbers selected by Saddam, ending with 0-4-0-7-9-3. The first light went from red to green. Aziz smiled. Scott placed the palm of his hand in the white square and left it there for several seconds. The second light switched to green.

Scott heard Kratz sigh audibly as he stepped forward again. He put his lips to the white square so they just touched the thin wire mesh. 'My name is Andreas Bernstrom. It's now time for the safe to –' The third light turned green even before he had completed the sentence. Cohen offered up a suppressed cheer.

Scott grasped the handle and pulled. The ton of steel eased open.

'Not bad,' said Cohen. 'What do you do for an encore?'

'Use you as a guinea-pig,' said Scott. 'Why don't you try and close the safe, Sergeant?'

Cohen took a step forward and with both hands shoved the door closed. The three bulbs immediately began flashing red.

'Easy, once you get the hang of it,' he said.

Scott smiled and pulled the door back open with his little finger. Cohen stared open-mouthed as the lights returned to green.

'The lights might flash red,' said Scott, 'but Bertha can only handle one man at a time. No one else can open or close the safe now except me.'

'And I was hoping it was because he was a Jew,' said Aziz.

Scott smiled as he pushed the door of the safe closed, swivelled the dials and waited until all three bulbs turned red.

'Let's go,' said Kratz, who Scott felt sounded a little irritated – or was it just the first sign of tension? Aziz threw the tarpaulin back over Madame Bertha while his colleagues jumped over the side and returned to the cab.

No one spoke as they continued their journey to the border until Cohen let out a string of expletives when he spotted the queue of lorries ahead of them. 'We're going to be here all night,' he said.

'And most of tomorrow morning, I expect,' said Kratz. 'So we'd better get used to it.' They came to a halt behind the last lorry in the queue.

'Why don't I just drive on up front and try to bluff my way through?' said Cohen. 'A few extra dollars ought to . . .'

'No,' said Kratz. 'We don't want to attract undue attention at any time between now and when we cross back over that border.'

During the next hour, while the truck moved forward only a couple of hundred yards, Kratz went over his plans yet again, covering any situation he thought might arise once they reached Baghdad.

Another hour passed, and Scott was thankful for the evening breeze that helped him doze off, although he realised that he would soon have to wind the window up if he wished to avoid freezing. He began to drift into a light sleep, his mind switching between Hannah and the Declaration, and which, given the choice, he would rather bring home. He realised that Kratz was in no doubt why he had volunteered to join the team when the chances of survival were so slim.

'What's this joker up to then?' said Cohen in a stage whisper. Scott snapped awake and quickly focused on a uniformed official talking to the driver of the lorry in front of them.

'It's a customs official,' said Kratz. 'He's only checking to see that drivers have the right papers to cross the border.'

'Most of this lot will only have two little bits of red paper about five inches by three,' said Cohen.

'Here he comes,' said Kratz. 'Try and look as bored as he does.'

The officer strolled up to the cab and didn't even give Cohen a first look as he thrust a hand through the open window.

Cohen passed over the papers that the experts at Langley had provided. The official studied them and then walked slowly round the lorry. When he returned to the driver's side, he barked an order at Cohen that none of them understood.

Cohen looked towards Kratz, but a voice from behind rescued them.

'He says we're to go to the front of the queue.'

'Why?' asked Kratz suspiciously. Aziz repeated the question to the official.

'We're being given priority because of the letter signed by Saddam.'

'And who do we thank for that?' asked Kratz, still not fully convinced.

'Bill O'Reilly,' said Scott, 'who was only too sorry he couldn't join us on the trip. But he's been given to understand that it's quite impossible to get draught Guinness anywhere in Iraq.'

Kratz nodded, and Sergeant Cohen obeyed the official's instructions, allowing himself to be directed into the lane of oncoming traffic as he began an unsteady two-mile journey to the front of the queue. Vehicles legally progressing towards Amman on the other side of the road found they had to swerve onto the loose rubble of the hard shoulder if they didn't want a head-on collision with Madame Bertha.

As Cohen completed the last few yards to the border post, an angry official came running out of the customs shed waving a fist. Once again it was Aziz who came to their rescue, by recommending that Kratz show him the letter.

After one look at the signature, the fist was quickly exchanged for a salute.

'Passport,' was the only other word he uttered.

Kratz passed over three Swedish and one Iraqi passport with two red notes attached to the first page of each document. 'Never pay above the expected tariff,' he had warned his team. 'It only makes them suspicious.'

The four passports were taken to a little cubicle, studied, stamped and returned by the official, who even offered them the suggestion of a smile. The barrier on the Jordanian side was raised, and the lorry began its mile-long journey towards the Iraqi checkpoint.

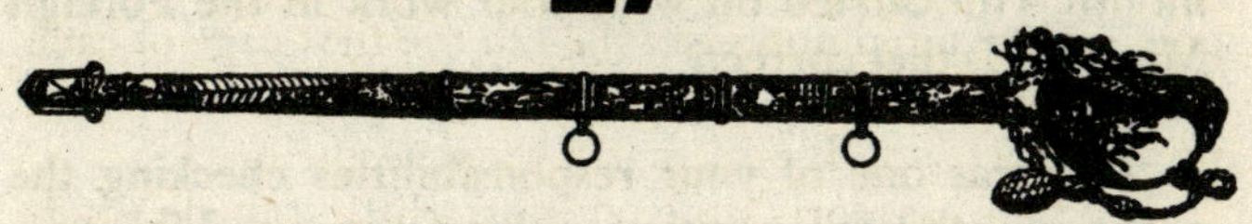

HAMID AL OBAYDI was dragged into the Council Chamber by two of the Presidential Guards and then dumped in a chair several yards away from the long table.

He raised his head and looked around at the twelve men who made up the Revolutionary Command Council. None of their eyes came into contact with his, with the exception of the State Prosecutor.

What had he done that these people had decided to arrest him at the border, handcuff him, throw him in jail, leave him to sleep on the stone floor and not even offer him the chance to use a lavatory?

Still dressed in the suit he had crossed the border in, he was now sitting in his own excrement.

Saddam raised a hand, and the State Prosecutor smiled.

But Al Obaydi did not fear Nakir Farrar. Not only was he innocent of any trumped-up charge, but he also had information they needed. The State Prosecutor rose slowly from his place.

'Your name is Hamid Al Obaydi?'

'Yes,' replied Al Obaydi, looking directly at the State Prosecutor.

'You are charged with treason and the theft of state property. How do you plead?'

'I am innocent, and Allah will be my witness.'

'If Allah is to be your witness, I'm sure he won't

mind me asking you some simple questions.'

'I will be most happy to answer anything.'

'When you returned from New York earlier this month, you carried on with your work in the Foreign Ministry. Is that correct?'

'It is.'

'And was one of your responsibilities checking the government's latest position with reference to UN sanctions?'

'Yes. That was part of my job as Deputy Ambassador to the UN.'

'Quite so. And when you carried out these checks, you came across certain items on which embargoes had been lifted. Am I right?'

'Yes, you are,' said Al Obaydi confidently.

'Was one of those items a safe?'

'It was,' said Al Obaydi.

'When you realised this, what did you do about it?'

'I telephoned the Swedish company who had built the safe to ascertain what the latest position was, so that I could enter the facts in my report.'

'And what did you discover?'

Al Obaydi hesitated, not sure how much the Prosecutor knew.

'What did you discover?' insisted Farrar.

'That the safe had been collected that day by a Mr Riffat.'

'Did you know this Mr Riffat?'

'No, I did not.'

'So what did you do next?'

'I rang the Ministry of Industry, as I was under the impression that they were responsible for the safe.'

'And what did they tell you?'

'That the responsibility had been taken out of their hands.'

'Did they also tell you into whose hands the responsibility had been entrusted?' asked the Prosecutor.

'I don't remember exactly.'

'Well, let me try and refresh your memory – or shall I call the Permanent Secretary to whom you spoke on the phone that morning?'

'I think he may have said that it was no longer in their hands,' said Al Obaydi.

'Did he tell you whose hands it was in?' repeated the Prosecutor.

'I think he said something about the file being sent to Geneva.'

'It may interest you to know that the official has submitted written evidence to confirm just that.'

Al Obaydi lowered his head.

'So, once you knew that the file had been passed on to Geneva, what did you do next?'

'I phoned Geneva and was told the Ambassador was not available. I left a message to say that I had called,' said Al Obaydi confidently, 'and asked if he would call back.'

'Did you really expect him to call back?'

'I assumed he would.'

'You assumed he would. So what did you write in your report, in the sanctions file?'

'The file?' asked Al Obaydi.

'Yes. You were making a report for your successor. What information did you pass on to him?'

'I don't remember,' said Al Obaydi.

'Then allow me to remind you once again,' said the Prosecutor, lifting a slim brown file from the table. ' "The Ministry of Industry have sent the file concerning this item direct to Geneva. I phoned our Ambassador there, but was unable to make contact with him. Therefore, I cannot make any progress from this end until he returns my call. Hamid Al Obaydi." Did you write that?'

'I can't remember.'

'You can't remember what the Permanent Secretary said to you; you can't remember what you wrote in your own report when property of the state might have been stolen, or worse . . . But I shall come to that later. Perhaps you would like to check your own handwriting?' said the Prosecutor as he walked from the table and thrust the relevant sheet in front of Al Obaydi's face. 'Is that your writing?'

'Yes, it is. But I can explain.'

'And is that your signature at the bottom of the page?'

Al Obaydi leaned forward, studied the signature and nodded.

'Yes or no?' barked the Prosecutor.

'Yes,' said Al Obaydi quietly.

'Did you, that same afternoon, visit General Al-Hassan, the Head of State Security?'

'No. He visited me.'

'Ah, I have made a mistake. It was he who visited you.'

'Yes,' said Al Obaydi.

'Did you alert him to the fact that an enemy agent might be heading towards Iraq, having found a way of crossing the border with the intention of perhaps assassinating our leader?'

'I couldn't have known that.'

'But you must have suspected something unusual was going on?'

'I wasn't certain at that time.'

'Did you let General Al-Hassan know of your uncertainty?'

'No. I did not.'

'Was it because you didn't trust him?'

'I didn't know him. It was the first time we had met.

The previous . . .' Al Obaydi regretted the words the moment he had said them.

'You were about to say?' said the Prosecutor.

'Nothing.'

'I see. So, let us move on to the following day, when you paid a visit – because I feel confident that he didn't visit you – to the Deputy Foreign Minister.' This induced some smiles around the table, but Al Obaydi did not see them.

'Yes, a routine call to discuss my appointment to Paris. He was, after all, the former Ambassador.'

'Quite. But is he not also your immediate superior?'

'Yes, he is,' said Al Obaydi.

'So, did you tell *him* of your suspicions?'

'I wasn't sure there was anything to tell him.'

'Did you tell him of your suspicions?' asked the Prosecutor, raising his voice.

'No, I did not.'

'Was he not to be trusted either? Or didn't you know him well enough?'

'I wasn't sure. I wanted more proof.'

'I see. You wanted more proof. So what did you do next?'

'I travelled to Paris,' said Al Obaydi.

'On the next day?' asked the State Prosecutor.

'No,' said Al Obaydi, hesitating.

'On the day after, perhaps? Or the day after that?'

'Perhaps.'

'Meanwhile, the safe was on its way to Baghdad. Is that right?'

'Yes, but –'

'And you *still* hadn't informed anyone? Is that also correct?'

Al Obaydi didn't reply.

'Is that also correct?' shouted Farrar.

'Yes, but there was still enough time –'

'Enough time for what?' asked the State Prosecutor.

Al Obaydi's head sank again.

'For you to reach the safety of our embassy in Paris?'

'No,' said Al Obaydi. 'I travelled on to –'

'Yes?' said Farrar. 'You travelled on to where?'

Al Obaydi realised he had fallen into the trap.

'To Sweden, perhaps?'

'Yes,' said Al Obaydi. 'But only because –'

'You wanted to check the safe was well on its way? Or was it, as you told the Foreign Minister, that you were simply going on holiday?'

'No, but . . .'

' "Yes but, no but." Were you on holiday in Sweden? Or were you representing the state?'

'I was representing the state.'

'Then why did you travel economy, and not charge the state for the expense that was incurred?'

Al Obaydi made no reply.

The Prosecutor leaned forward. 'Was it because you didn't want anyone to know you were in Sweden, when your superiors thought you were in Paris?'

'Yes, but in time . . .'

'After it was too late, perhaps. Is that what you're trying to tell us?'

'No. I did not say that.'

'Then why did you not pick up a phone and ring our Ambassador in Geneva? He could have saved you all the expense and the trouble. Was it because you didn't trust him either? Or perhaps he didn't trust you?'

'Neither!' shouted Al Obaydi, leaping to his feet, but the guards grabbed him by the shoulders and threw him back onto the chair.

'Now that you've got that little outburst out of the way,' said the Prosecutor calmly, 'perhaps we can continue. You travelled to Sweden, to Kalmar to be exact, to keep an appointment with a Mr Pedersson, whom you did seem willing to phone.' The Prosecutor checked his notes again. 'And what was the purpose of this visit, now that you have confirmed it was not a holiday?'

'To try and find out who it was who had stolen the safe.'

'Or was it to make sure the safe was on the route you had already planned for it?'

'Certainly not,' said Al Obaydi, his voice rising. 'After all, it was I who discovered that Riffat was the Mossad agent Kratz.'

'You *knew* that Riffat was a Mossad agent?' queried the Prosecutor in mock disbelief.

'Yes, I found out when I was in Kalmar,' said Al Obaydi.

'But you told Mr Pedersson that Mr Riffat was a thorough man, a man who could be trusted,' said the State Prosecutor, checking his notes. 'Am I right? So now at last we've found someone you can trust.'

'It was quite simply that I didn't want Pedersson to know what I'd discovered.'

'I don't think you wanted *anyone* to know what you had discovered, as I shall go on to show. What did you do next?'

'I flew back to Paris.'

'And did you spend the night at the embassy?'

'Yes, I did, but I was only stopping overnight on my way to Jordan.'

'I'll come to your trip to Jordan in a moment, if I may. But what I should like to know now is why, when you were back at our embassy in Paris, you didn't immediately call our Ambassador in Geneva to inform him of what you had discovered? Not only was the Ambassador in residence, but he took a call from another member of the embassy staff after you had gone to bed.'

Al Obaydi suddenly realised how Farrar knew everything. He tried to collect his thoughts.

'My only interest was getting back to Baghdad to let the Foreign Minister know the danger our leader might be facing.'

'Like the imminent dropping of American bombs on Mukhbarat headquarters?' suggested the State Prosecutor.

'I could not have known what the Americans were planning,' shouted Al Obaydi.

'I see,' said Farrar. 'It was no more than a happy coincidence that you were safely tucked up in bed in Paris while Tomahawk missiles were showering down on Baghdad.'

'But I returned to Baghdad immediately I learned of the bombing,' insisted Al Obaydi.

'Perhaps you wouldn't have been in quite such a hurry to return if the Americans had succeeded in assassinating our leader.'

'But my report would have proved . . .'

'And where is that report?'

'I intended to write it on the journey from Jordan to Baghdad.'

'How convenient. And did you advise your trustworthy friend Mr Riffat to ring the Minister of Industry to find out if he was expected?'

'No, I did not,' said Al Obaydi. 'If any of this were true,' he added, 'why would I have worked so hard to see that our great leader secured the Declaration?'

'I'm glad you mentioned the Declaration,' said the State Prosecutor softly, 'because I'm also puzzled by the role you played in that particular exercise. But first, let me ask you, did you trust our Ambassador in Geneva to see that the Declaration was delivered to Baghdad?'

'Yes, I did.'

'And did it reach Baghdad safely?' asked the Prosecutor, glancing at the battered parchment, still nailed to the wall behind Saddam.

'Yes, it did.'

'Then why not entrust the knowledge you had acquired about the safe to the same man, remembering that it was his responsibility?'

'This was different.'

'It certainly was, and I shall show the Council just how different. How was the Declaration paid for?'

'I don't understand,' said Al Obaydi.

'Then let me make it easier for you. How was each payment dealt with?'

'Ten million dollars was to be paid once the contract had been agreed, and a further forty million when the Declaration was handed over.'

'And how much of that money – the state's money – did you keep for yourself?'

'Not one cent.'

'Well, let us see if that is totally accurate, shall we? Where did the meetings take place for the exchange of these vast sums of money?'

'The first payment was made to a bank in New Jersey, and the second to Dummond et cie, one of our banks in Switzerland.'

'And the first payment of ten million dollars, if I understand you correctly, you insisted should be in cash?'

'That is not correct,' said Al Obaydi. 'The other side insisted that it should be in cash.'

'How convenient. But then, once again, we only have your word for that, because our Ambassador in New York has stated it was you who insisted the first payment had to be in cash. Perhaps he misunderstood you as well. But let us move on to the second payment, and do correct me if I have misunderstood you.' He paused. 'That was paid direct into Franchard et cie?'

'That is correct,' said Al Obaydi.

'And did you receive, I think the word is a "kickback", after either of these payments?'

'Certainly not.'

'Well, what *is* certain is that, as the first payment was made in cash, it would be hard for anyone to prove otherwise. But as for the second payment . . .' The Prosecutor paused to let the significance of his words sink in.

'I don't know what you're talking about,' snapped Al Obaydi.

'Then you must be having another lapse of memory, because during your absence, when you were rushing back from Paris to warn the President of the imminent danger to his life, you received a communication from Franchard et cie which, because the letter was addressed to our Ambassador in Paris, ended up on the desk of the Deputy Foreign Minister.'

'I've had no communication with Franchard et cie.'

'I'm not suggesting you did,' said the Prosecutor, as he strode forward to within a foot of Al Obaydi. 'I'm suggesting *they* communicated with *you*. Because they sent you your latest bank statement in the name of Hamid Al Obaydi, dated June 25th 1993, showing that your account was credited with one million dollars on February 18th 1993.'

'It's not possible,' said Al Obaydi defiantly.

'It's not possible?' said the Prosecutor, thrusting a copy of the statement in front of Al Obaydi.

'This is easy to explain. The Cavalli family is trying to get revenge because we didn't pay the full amount of one hundred million as originally promised.'

'Revenge, you claim. The money isn't real? It doesn't

exist? This is just a piece of paper? A figment of our imagination?'

'Yes,' said Al Obaydi. 'That is the truth.'

'So perhaps you can explain why one hundred thousand dollars was withdrawn from this account on the day after you had visited Franchard et cie?'

'That's not possible.'

'Another impossibility? Another figment of the imagination? Then you have not seen this withdrawal order for one hundred thousand dollars, sent to you by the bank a few days later? The signature on which bears a remarkable resemblance to the one on the sanctions report which you accepted earlier was authentic.'

The Prosecutor held both documents in front of Al Obaydi so they touched the tip of his nose. He looked at the two signatures and realised what Cavalli must have done. The Prosecutor proceeded to sign his death warrant, even before Al Obaydi had been given the chance to explain.

'And now you are no doubt going to ask the Council to believe that it was Cavalli who also had your signature forged?'

A little laughter trickled round the table, and Al Obaydi suspected that the Prosecutor knew that he had only spoken the truth.

'I have had enough of this,' said the one person in the room who would have dared to interrupt the State Prosecutor.

Al Obaydi looked up in a last attempt to catch the attention of the President, but with the exception of the State Prosecutor the Council were looking towards the top of the table and nodding their agreement.

'There are more pressing matters for the Council to consider.' He waved a hand as if he were swatting an irritating fly.

Two soldiers stepped forward and removed Al Obaydi from his sight.

'That was a whole lot easier than I expected,' said Cohen, once they had passed through the Iraqi checkpoint.

'A little too easy, perhaps,' said Kratz.

'It's good to know that we've got one optimist and one pessimist on this trip,' said Scott.

Once Cohen was on the highway he remained cautious of pushing the vehicle beyond fifty miles per hour. The lorries that passed in the opposite direction on their way to Jordan rarely had more than two of their four headlights working, which sometimes made them appear like motorcycles in the distance, so overtaking became hazardous. But his eyes needed to be at their most alert for those lorries in front of him: for them, one red taillight was a luxury.

Kratz had always thought the three-hundred-mile journey from the border to Baghdad would be too long to consider covering in one stretch, so he had decided they should have a rest about forty miles outside the Iraqi capital. Scott asked Cohen what time he thought they might reach their rest point.

'Assuming I don't drive straight into a parked lorry that's been abandoned in the middle of the road or disappear down a pothole, I'd imagine we'll get there around four, five at the latest.'

'I don't like the sight of all these army vehicles on the road. What do you think they're up to?' asked Kratz, who hadn't slept a wink since they crossed the border.

'A battalion on the move, I'd say, sir. Doesn't look that unusual to me, and I don't think we'd need to worry about them unless they were going in the same direction as us.'

'Perhaps you're right,' said Kratz.

'You wouldn't give them a second thought if you'd crossed the border legally,' said Scott.

'Possibly. But Sergeant,' Kratz said, turning his attention back to Cohen, 'let me know the moment you spot anything you consider unusual.'

'You mean, like a woman worth a second glance?'

Kratz made no comment. He turned to ask Scott a question, only to find he had dozed off again. He envied Scott's ability to sleep anywhere at any time, especially under such pressure.

Sergeant Cohen drove on through the night, not always in a straight line, as he circumvented the occasional burned-out tank or large crater left over from the war. On and on they travelled, through small towns and seemingly uninhabited sleeping villages, until a few minutes past four, when Cohen swung off the highway and up a track that could have only considered one-way traffic. He drove for another twenty minutes, finally coming to a halt when the road ended at an overhanging ledge.

'Even a vulture wouldn't find us here,' said Cohen as he turned off the engine. 'Permission to have a smoke and a bit of shut-eye, Colonel?'

Kratz nodded and watched Cohen jump out of the cab and offer Aziz a cigarette before disappearing behind a palm tree. He checked the surrounding countryside carefully, and decided Cohen was right. When he returned to the truck, he found Aziz and the Sergeant were already asleep, while Scott was sitting on the ledge watching the sun come up over Baghdad.

'What a peaceful sight,' he said as Kratz sat down beside him, almost as though he had been talking to someone else. 'Only God could make a sunrise as beautiful as that.'

'Something isn't right,' muttered Kratz under his breath.

28

SADDAM NODDED TO THE PROSECUTOR. 'Now we have dealt with the traitor, let us move on to the terrorists. What is the latest position, General?'

General Hamil, known as the Barber of Baghdad, opened the file in front of him – he kept a file on everybody, including those sitting around the table. Hamil had been educated at Sandhurst and returned to Iraq to receive the King's Commission, only to find there was no King to serve. So he switched his loyalty to the new President, Abdul Karim Qasim. Then a young Captain changed sides in the 1963 coup and the Ba'ath Party took power. Once again Hamil switched his loyalty, and was rewarded with an appointment to the personal staff of the new Vice-President, Saddam Hussein. Since that day he had risen rapidly through the ranks. He was now Saddam's favourite General, and Commander of the Presidential Guard. He had the distinction of being the only man, with the exception of the President's bodyguards, allowed to wear a side-arm in Saddam's presence. He was Saddam's executioner. His favourite hobby was to shave his victims' heads before they were hanged, with a blunt cut-throat razor that he never bothered to sharpen. Some of them disappointed him by dying before he could get the rope around their necks.

Hamil studied his file for a few moments before offering an opinion. 'The terrorists,' he began, 'crossed the border at 21.26 last night. Four passports were presented to the immigration officer for stamping. Three were of Swedish origin, and one was from Iraq.'

'I'll skin that one personally,' said Saddam.

'The four men are travelling in a truck that appears to be quite old, but as we are unable to risk taking too close a look, I cannot be sure if we are dealing with a Trojan horse or not. The safe that you ordered, Mr President, is undoubtedly on the back of the truck.

'The truck has driven non-stop through the night at a steady pace of around forty miles per hour in the direction of Baghdad, but at 4.09 this morning it turned off into the desert, and we ceased to monitor its movements, as that particular path leads nowhere. We believe they have simply come off the road to rest before travelling on to the capital later this morning.'

'How many miles are they from Baghdad at this moment?' asked the Minister of the Interior.

'Forty, perhaps fifty – an hour to an hour and a half at the most.'

'So, if we now have them trapped in the desert, General, why don't we just send troops in and cut them off?'

'While they are still bringing the safe to Baghdad?' interrupted Saddam. 'No. That way lies our only danger.'

'I'm not sure I understand, Sayedi,' said the Minister of the Interior, turning to face his leader.

'Then I will explain, *Minister*,' Saddam said, exaggerating the final word cruelly. 'If we arrest them in the desert, who will believe us when we tell the world they are terrorists? The Western press will even claim that we planted their passports on them. No, I want them arrested right here in the Council Chamber, when it will be impossible for Mossad to deny their involvement and, more important, we will have exposed their plot and made fools of them in the eyes of the Zionist people.'

'Now I understand your profound wisdom, Sayedi.'

Saddam waved a hand and turned his attention to the Minister of Industry.

'Have my orders been carried out?'

'To the letter, Excellency. When the terrorists arrive at the Ministry, they will be made to wait, and will be treated curtly, until they produce the documentation that claims to come from your office.'

'They presented such a letter at the border,' interrupted General Hamil, still looking down at his file.

'The moment such a letter is presented to my office,' continued the Minister for Industry, 'a crane will be supplied so that the safe can be transferred into this building. I fear that we will have to remove the doors on the front of the building, but only –'

'I am not interested in the doors,' said Saddam. 'When do you anticipate that the safe will arrive outside the building?'

'Around midday,' said General Hamil. 'I shall personally take over the entire operation once the safe is inside the building, Mr President.'

'Good. And make sure the terrorists see the Declaration before they are arrested.'

'What if they were to try to destroy the document, Excellency?' asked the Interior Minister, attempting to recover some lost ground.

'Never,' said Saddam. 'They have come to Baghdad to steal the document, not to destroy their pathetic piece of history.' Two or three people round the table nodded their agreement. 'None of you except General Hamil and his immediate staff will come anywhere near this building for the next twenty-four hours. The fewer people who know what's really happening, the better. Don't even brief the officer of the day. I want the security to appear lax. That way they will fall right into our trap.'

General Hamil nodded.

'Prosecutor,' said Saddam, turning his attention to the other end of the table, 'what will the international community say when they learn I have arrested the Zionist pigs?'

'They are terrorists, Excellency, and for terrorists, there can be only one sentence. Especially after the Americans launched their missiles on innocent civilians only days ago.'

Saddam nodded. 'Any other questions?'

'Just one, Your Excellency,' said the Deputy Foreign Minister. 'What do you want to do about the girl?'

'Ah, yes,' said Saddam, smiling for the first time. 'Now that she has served her purpose, I must think of a suitable way to end her life. Where is she at the moment?'

As the truck began its slow journey back along the tiny desert path, with Aziz taking his turn behind the wheel and Cohen in the back with Madame Bertha, Scott felt the atmosphere inside the cab had changed. When they pulled off the highway to rest, he still believed they were in no real danger. But the grim silence of morning made him suddenly aware of the task they had set themselves.

They had Kratz to thank for the original idea, and mixed with his particular cocktail of imagination, discipline, courage, and the assumption that no one knew what they were up to, Scott felt they had a better than even chance of getting away with it, especially now they knew exactly where the Declaration was situated.

When they reached the main road, Aziz jokingly asked, 'Right or left?'

Scott said 'Left,' but Aziz turned dutifully right.

As they travelled along the highway towards Baghdad the sun shone from a cloudless sky that would have delighted any tourist board, although the burned-out tanks and the craters in the road might not have been considered obvious attractions. No one spoke as the miles sped by: there was no need for them to go over the plans another time. That would be like an Olympian training on the morning of a race – either too late, or no longer of any value.

For the last ten miles, they joined an expressway that was equal to anything they might have found in Germany. As they crossed a newly reconstructed bridge over the Euphrates, Scott began to wonder how close he was to Hannah, and whether he could get himself into the Foreign Ministry without alerting Kratz, let alone the Iraqis.

When they reached the outskirts of Baghdad, with its glistening skyscrapers and modern buildings, they could have been entering any major city in the world – until they saw the people. There were lines of cars at petrol pumps in a land where the main asset was oil, but their length was dwarfed only by the queues for food. All four of them could see that sanctions were biting, however much Saddam denied it.

They drove nearer to the city centre, along the road that passed under the Al-Naser, the massive archway of two crossed swords gripped by casts of Saddam's hand. There was no need to direct Aziz to the Ministry of Industry. He wished he still lived in Baghdad, but he hadn't entered the city since his father had been executed for his part in the failed coup of 1987. Looking out of the window at his countrymen, he could still smell their fear in his nostrils.

As they passed the bombed-out remains of the Mukhbarat headquarters, Scott noticed an unmanned ambulance parked outside the Iraqi intelligence centre. It was strategically placed for the CNN television cameras rather than for any practical purpose, he suspected.

When Aziz saw the Ministry of Industry building looming up ahead of him, he pointed it out to Scott, who remembered the façade from the mass of photographs supplied by Kratz. But Scott's eyes had moved up to the gun turrets on top of the Foreign Ministry, a mere stone's throw away.

Aziz brought the lorry to a halt a hundred yards beyond the entrance to the Ministry. Scott said, 'I'll be as quick as I can,' as he jumped out of the cab and headed back towards the building.

As he climbed the steps to the Ministry, he did not see a man in a window of the building opposite who was speaking on the telephone to General Hamil.

'The truck has stopped about a hundred metres beyond the Ministry. A tall, fair-haired man who was in the front of the vehicle is now entering the building, but the other three, including Kratz, have remained with the safe.'

Scott pushed through the swing doors and strolled past two guards who looked as if they didn't move more than a few feet every day. He walked over to the information desk and joined the shortest of three queues. The one-handed clock above the desk indicated that it was approximately 9.30.

It took another fifteen minutes before Scott reached the counter. He explained to the girl that his name was Bernstrom and that he needed to see Mr Kajami.

'Do you have an appointment?' she asked.

'No,' said Scott. 'We called from Jordan to warn him that a safe the government had ordered was on its way to Baghdad. He asked us to inform him the moment it arrived.'

'I will see if he's in,' said the receptionist. Scott waited, staring up at a massive portrait of Saddam Hussein in uniform holding a Kalashnikov. It dominated the otherwise blank grey walls of the reception area.

The girl listened carefully to whoever it was on the other end of the line before saying, 'Someone will be down to see you in a few minutes.' She turned her attention to the next person in the queue.

Scott hung around for another thirty minutes before a tall, thin man wearing a smart Western suit stepped out of the lift and walked over to him.

'Mr Bernstrom?'

'Yes?' said Scott, as he swung round to face the man.

'Good morning,' he said confidently in English. 'I am Mr Ibrahim, Mr Kajami's personal assistant. How can I help you?'

'I have brought a safe from Sweden,' said Scott. 'It was ordered by the Ministry some years ago, but, due to the UN sanctions, could not be delivered any earlier. We were told that when we reached Baghdad we should report to Mr Kajami.'

'Do you have any papers to verify your claim?'

Scott removed a file from his bag and showed Mr Ibrahim its contents.

The man read through each document slowly until he came to the letter signed by the President. He read no further. Looking up, he asked, 'May I see this safe, Mr Bernstrom?'

'Certainly,' said Scott. 'Please follow me.' He led the official out onto the street and took him over to the truck.

Cohen stared down at them. When Kratz gave the order, he whipped the tarpaulin off the safe so that the civil servant could inspect Madame Bertha for himself.

Scott was fascinated by the fact that those passing in

the street didn't give the safe a second look. If anything, they quickened their pace. Fear manifested itself among these people by their lack of curiosity.

'Please come with me, Mr Bernstrom,' said Ibrahim. Scott accompanied him back to the reception area, where he returned upstairs without another word.

Scott was left waiting for another thirty minutes before Ibraham came back.

'You are to take the safe to Victory Square, where you will see a barrier with a tank in front of a large white building. They are expecting you.'

Scott was about to ask where Victory Square was when Ibrahim turned and walked away. He went back to the truck, and joined Kratz and Aziz in the front before passing on the news. Aziz didn't need to be told the way.

'No special treatment there, I'm glad to see,' said Kratz.

Scott nodded his agreement as Aziz eased the truck back into the road. The traffic was much heavier now. Lorries and cars were honking their horns, managing to move only a few inches at a time.

'It must be an accident,' said Scott, until they turned the corner and saw the three bodies hanging from a makeshift gallows: a man wearing an expensive designer suit, a woman perhaps a little younger, and another much older woman. It was hard to be certain, with their heads shaven.

Mr Kajami sat at his desk, dialled the number that had been passed to him, and waited.

'Deputy Foreign Minister's Office, Miss Saib speaking.'

'This is the Minister of Industry calling. Could you put me through to the Deputy Foreign Minister.'

'I'm afraid he's out of the office at the moment, Mr Kajami. Shall I ask him to return your call, or would you like to leave a message?'

'I will leave a message, but perhaps he could also call me when he gets back.'

'Certainly, Minister.'

'Could you let him know that the safe has arrived from Sweden and can therefore be crossed off the sanctions list.' There was a long pause. 'Are you still there, Miss Saib?'

'Yes. I was just writing down what you said, sir.'

'If he needs to see the relevant forms we still have them at the Ministry, but if it's the safe he wants to check on, it's already on its way to the Ba'ath headquarters.'

'I understand, sir. I'll see he gets the message just as soon as he comes in.'

'Thank you, Miss Saib.'

Kajami replaced the phone on the hook, glanced across his desk at the Deputy Foreign Minister and smiled.

29

AZIZ BROUGHT THE TRUCK to a halt in front of a tank. A few soldiers were moving around, but there didn't appear to be a great deal of activity.

'I was expecting a bigger show of force than this,' said Kratz. 'It's the Ba'ath Party headquarters, after all.'

'Saddam's probably at the palace, or even out of Baghdad,' suggested Aziz as two soldiers advanced towards the truck. The first one shouted 'Out!' and they obeyed slowly. Once all four of them were on the ground, the soldier ordered them to stand a few yards away from the truck while a couple of other soldiers jumped up on the back and removed the tarpaulin.

'This one's a Major,' whispered Aziz as a portly man covered in battle ribbons and carrying a mobile phone advanced towards them. He stopped and looked up at the safe suspiciously before turning to Kratz and introducing himself as Major Saeed.

'Open,' was all he added.

Kratz pointed to Scott, who climbed up onto the back of the lorry while several more soldiers surrounded it to watch him perform the opening ceremony. Once Scott had pulled the great door open, the Major joined him on the back of the truck, but not until one of the soldiers had given him a hand-up. He stood a pace back and ordered two of his men to go inside. They appeared apprehensive at first, but once they had entered the safe they began touching the sides and even jumping up to try to reach the roof. A few moments later, Saeed joined them, and banged the walls with his swagger stick. He then stepped back out, jumped heavily off the truck and turned towards Scott.

'Now we wait for a crane,' he said, sounding a little more friendly. He dialled a number on the phone.

Cohen climbed into the cab and sat behind the wheel, the keys still in the ignition, while Aziz remained on the back with the safe. Scott and Kratz leaned against a wall, trying to appear bored, while having a conversation on the alternatives they now faced.

'We must find some way of getting into the building ahead of the safe,' said Kratz. Scott nodded his agreement.

The clock in Victory Square had struck 12.30 before Aziz spotted the tall, thin structure progressing slowly round the massive statue of Saddam. The four of them watched as soldiers ran out into the street to hold up the flow of traffic and allow the vast crane to continue its progress uninterrupted.

Scott explained to the Major that the truck now needed to be moved to a position opposite the front door. He agreed without a phone call. When the truck was parked exactly where Scott wanted it, Major Saeed finally conceded that the doors would have to come off their hinges if they were ever going to get the safe and its trolley inside the building.

This time he did make a phone call, and to Scott's question, 'How long?' he simply shrugged his shoulders and replied, 'Must wait.'

Scott was determined to use the 'must wait' period, and explained to Major Saeed that he needed to walk the route that the safe would travel once they had entered the building.

The Major hesitated, made a further phone call, held on for some time before he received an answer, and then, pointing to Scott, said, 'You, only.'

Scott left Kratz to organise the crane as it prepared to lift the safe off the lorry, and followed the Major into the building.

The first thing that Scott noticed as he walked down the carpeted corridor was its width and solid feel. Every few paces there were soldiers lounging against the wall who sprang to attention the moment they saw Major Saeed.

At the end of the corridor was an elevator. The Major produced a key and turned it in a lock on the wall. The doors of the elevator opened slowly. It struck Scott that the size of the safe must have been determined by the width of the lift. He doubted if there would be much more than an inch to spare all round once they had succeeded in getting Madame Bertha on board.

The Major pressed a button marked '– 6', which, Scott noted, was as far down as they could go. The lift dropped slowly. When the doors opened Scott followed Major Saeed into a long corridor. This time he had the feeling that the passageway had been built to survive an earthquake. They came to a halt outside a pair of heavy, reinforced doors, guarded by two soldiers carrying rifles.

Saeed asked a question, and both guards shook their heads. 'The Chamber is empty, so we can go straight through,' he explained, then proceeded to unlock the door. Scott followed him into the Council Chamber.

His eyes searched quickly round the room. The first thing he saw on the far wall was another massive portrait of Saddam, this time in a dark double-breasted suit. Then he spotted one of the red alarm buttons next to a light switch that Kratz had warned him about. The

Major hurried on through the Chamber, giving the impression of a man who hadn't the right to be there, while Scott went as slowly as he felt he could get away with. And then he saw it, just for a moment, and his heart sank: the Declaration of Independence was nailed to the wall, a corner torn and some of the signatures looking distinctly blurred.

The Major unlocked the far door and Scott reluctantly followed him through into the adjoining corridor. They continued for only a few more paces before coming to a halt in front of a massive recess of inlaid brick that Scott didn't need to measure to realise had been purpose-built in anticipation of the arrival of the safe.

Scott took some time measuring the space, as he tried to think of how he could get a longer look at the Declaration. After a few minutes, Major Saeed tapped him on the shoulder with his swagger stick and indicated that it was time for them to return to the courtyard. Scott reluctantly followed him back down the short corridor and into the Council Chamber, which the Major scurried through while Scott lingered to measure the doors. He was pleased to discover that they would have to be taken off their hinges. He stood a pace back as if considering the problem. The Major returned and slapped the side of his leg with his swagger stick, muttering something under his breath that Scott suspected wasn't altogether flattering.

Scott stole a glance to the right, and confirmed his worst fears: even if he were able to exchange the two documents, it would take an even greater genius than Dollar Bill to repair the damage that Saddam had already inflicted.

'Come. Come. We must go,' said the Major.

'And so must these doors,' said Scott, and turning, added, 'and those two as well,' pointing to the pair at the other end of the Chamber. But Major Saeed was already striding off down the long corridor towards the open lift.

Hannah put the phone down and tried to stop herself trembling. They had warned her many times at Herzliyah that however tough you think you are, and however well trained you've been, you will still tremble.

She checked her watch. Her lunch break was due in twenty minutes, and although she rarely left the building during the day except on official business, she knew she could no longer sit in that office and just wait for events to happen all around her.

The Deputy Foreign Minister had left for the palace at eight that morning, and had told her not to expect him back until five at the earliest. A muscle in her cheek twitched as she began to type out the Minister of Industry's message.

For fifteen minutes, she sat at her desk and planned how the hour could be best spent. As soon as she was clear in her mind what needed to be done, she picked up her phone and asked a girl on the switchboard to cover her calls during the lunch break.

Hannah put on her glasses, left the room and walked quickly down the corridor, remaining close to the wall with her head bowed, so that those passing didn't give her a second look.

She took the stairs rather than the lift, slipped across the hall past reception, through the swing doors and out onto the steps of the Foreign Ministry.

'Saib's just left the building,' said a voice from the other side of the road into a mobile phone. 'She's going in the direction of Victory Square.'

Hannah continued walking towards the square. The crowds were so large and noisy that she feared another public hanging must have taken place. When she reached the end of the road and turned the corner, she averted her eyes as she made a path between those who were standing, staring, some even laughing at the spectacle.

'Quite a high-up official,' someone joked. Another more serious voice said that he had heard he was a diplomat recently back from America who had been caught with his fingers in the till. A third, an elderly woman, wept when someone suggested that the other two were the man's innocent mother and sister.

Once Hannah could see the barrier she slowed her pace. She stopped and stared across the road at the Ba'ath Party headquarters. She was pleased to be hidden in such a large crowd, even if it did occasionally obscure her view.

'She's facing the Ba'ath Party headquarters. Everyone else is looking in the opposite direction.'

Hannah's eyes settled on the truck that was surrounded by soldiers, and then she saw the massive safe that was perched on the back of the vehicle and the two young men who were attaching large coils of steel to its base. One was Middle Eastern in appearance, the other vaguely European. And then she saw Kratz – or was it Kratz? Whoever it was disappeared behind the far side of the truck. She waited for the man to reappear. When he did, a few moments later, she was left in no doubt that it was the Mossad leader.

She realised that she could not wait around in such a public place for much longer, and decided to return to her office and consider what needed to be done next. She gave Kratz one last look as a group of cleaners came out of the building, walked across the tarmac and passed by the barrier without any of the soldiers paying them the slightest attention.

Hannah began to walk away from Victory Square, just

as Major Saeed and Scott emerged from the building into the courtyard.

'She's on the move again, but she doesn't seem to be returning to the Ministry.' The man on the mobile phone listened for a moment and then replied, 'I don't know, but I'll follow her and report back.'

When Scott stepped back into the courtyard he was pleased to see that Kratz had already got the crane into position to lift the safe off the truck. Aziz and Cohen were fastening long steel coils around the body of Madame Bertha while the specially constructed trolley, of which Mr Pedersson was so proud, had been placed on the ground between the front door and the side of the truck.

Scott looked up at the crane that was taller than the building itself and back down at the operator, sitting in his wide cab near the base. Once Cohen and Aziz had jumped off the truck Kratz gave the operator the thumbs-up.

Scott pointed at the safe and beckoned to Kratz, who walked over, looking puzzled. He thought the operation was going rather well.

'What's the problem?' he asked. Scott continued pointing at the safe, and with exaggerated movements indicated how he thought it would have to be moved, while whispering to Kratz: 'I've seen the Declaration.' He moved to the other side of the safe. Kratz followed, now also pretending to take a close interest in the safe.

'Great news,' said Kratz. 'So where is it?'

'The news is not so great,' said Scott.

'What do you mean?' asked Kratz anxiously.

'It's in the Council Chamber, exactly where Hannah said it would be. But it's nailed to the wall,' replied Scott.

'Nailed to the wall?' said Kratz under his breath.

'Yes, and it looks as if it's beyond repair,' said Scott, as he heard the crunch of a gear shifting into place. He watched as the steel cords tightened, followed by a raucous revving of the engine. But Madame Bertha refused to budge an inch. The revving noise became even louder a second time, but she still remained unmoved by their solicitations.

The operator pushed the long gear lever forward another notch, and tried a third time. Finally Bertha rose an inch off the back of the lorry, swaying gently from side to side. Some of the soldiers started to cheer, but they stopped immediately when the Major turned to stare in their direction.

Kratz nodded and Cohen ran across the tarmac and lowered the tailboard, before getting into the cab and jumping behind the wheel of the truck. He switched on the engine, pushed the gear lever into first and moved the vehicle slowly forward until the safe was left dangling in mid-air. Aziz and Kratz then pushed the trolley a few yards across the tarmac so that it was directly below the dangling safe, Kratz gave the thumbs-up a second time, and the crane operator slowly began lowering the five tons of steel, inch by inch, until it came to rest on the trolley, causing the large rubber wheels to compress abruptly.

The safe now rested in front of the double doors, waiting for the carpenter to arrive before it could progress on its inward journey. The Major shrugged his shoulders even before Kratz had mouthed the question.

As Cohen backed the lorry into a parking space designated by the Major, an Iraqi, dressed in a dishdash and a red-and-white keffiyeh and carrying a tool bag appeared at the barrier.

Once the guards had thoroughly checked the tool bag,

tipping all its contents out onto the ground, they allowed him through. The carpenter gathered up his tools, took one look at the safe, another at the double doors, and understood immediately why his boss had described the problem as urgent. Scott stood back and watched the craftsman as he began to unscrew the hinges on one of the doors.

'So where's Dollar Bill's counterfeit at the moment?' asked Kratz.

'Still in my bag,' said Scott. 'I'm going to have to do some work on it, or they'll spot the difference the moment I've exchanged it for the original.'

'Agreed,' said Kratz. 'You'd better get on with it while the carpenter's working on the door. I'll try and keep the Major occupied.'

Kratz sauntered over to the carpenter and started chatting to him while Scott disappeared into the front of the truck carrying his bag. Once the Major saw what Kratz was doing he ran across to join them.

Scott stared through the cab window as he extracted Dollar Bill's copy from the cylinder and tried to recall where the main damage was on the original. First he made a tear in the top right-hand corner, then he spat on the names of John Adams and Robert Treat Paine. After he had studied his handiwork he decided he hadn't gone far enough and, placing the copy on the floor, he rubbed the soles of his shoes gently over the surface. He glanced up to see the Major ordering Kratz to let the carpenter get on with his job. Kratz shrugged his shoulders as Scott rolled up the copy of the Declaration and returned it to the cylinder, before sliding it down the specially-sewn long thin pocket on the inside of his trouser leg. A perfect fit.

A few moments later the carpenter got off his knees and smiled to show he had completed his task. At the

Major's command four soldiers stepped forward and removed the doors. They carried them a few paces away and leaned them up against an outside wall.

The Major ordered several more soldiers to push the trolley as Scott guided Madame Bertha through the doorway. Kratz and Aziz tried to follow, but the Major waved an arm firmly to indicate that only Scott could enter the building. It was Scott's turn to shrug his shoulders.

Inch by inch, they eased the trolley down the long corridor. The lift doors had been left open, but it still took forty hands to lever the five tons of metal safely inside. Scott knew from his research that this part of the building had been built to survive a nuclear attack, but he wondered if the lift would ever recover from having to carry the five-ton safe down six floors. He was only thankful that Madame Bertha was going down, not up.

The lift doors slowly closed and the Major quickly led Scott through a side door and down the back stairs, followed by a dozen soldiers. When they reached the basement, the doors of the lift were already open and Madame Bertha stood there, majestically waiting. The Major pointed to the floor with his swagger stick: ten of the soldiers fell to their knees and began pulling the trolley inch by inch until they finally managed to coax it into the corridor. The lift was then sent up to – 5, and six of the soldiers ran back up the stairs, jumped into the empty lift and returned to the basement so they could push the safe from the other side.

The carpenter had already removed the first set of doors they would encounter when the safe entered the Council Chamber, but was still working on the second set when the trolley reached the entrance. The delay gave Scott an opportunity to supervise the moving of the large table up against the side wall and the placing of the chairs on the table so that the safe would have a clear passage into the far corridor.

As he went back and forth Scott had several opportunities to stare at the Declaration, even study the spelling of the word 'Brittish'. He quickly realised that the parchment was in an even worse condition than he had thought.

Once the doors were finally removed, the soldiers began pushing the safe across the Chamber and out into the short corridor on the last few yards of its journey. When they had reached the end of the corridor opposite the specially prepared recess, Scott supervised the last few inches of its move until they could push the five tons of steel no further. Madame Bertha had finally come to her resting place against the far wall.

Scott smiled, and Major Saeed made another phone call.

The old woman explained to Hannah that the next shift was to be at three o'clock that afternoon, and they would be expected to have the Council Chamber ready for the meeting that was to take place at six the following day. They hadn't been able to do a proper job on the first shift that morning because of that safe.

Hannah had followed the cleaners, watching as they peeled off one by one and went their separate ways. She selected an old woman carrying the heaviest bags, and offered to help her across the road. They quickly got into conversation, and Hannah continued to carry the bags all the way to her front door, explaining that she only lived a few streets away.

'Come inside, my dear,' the old lady said.

'Thank you,' replied Hannah, feeling more like the wolf than Little Red Riding Hood.

Slipping a small whisky into the old woman's coffee had proved harmless enough, and it certainly loosened her tongue. Two Valium dropped in the cleaner's second coffee ensured that it would be several hours before she woke. Mossad had taught Hannah five different ways of breaking into a car, a hotel room, a briefcase, even a small safe, so a drugged old woman's handbag was no great challenge. She removed the special pass and slipped out of the house.

'She's now heading back in the direction of the Ministry,' said the voice into the mobile phone. 'We've checked the old woman. She passed out and probably won't come round until this time tomorrow. The only thing that's been taken is her security pass.'

When Hannah arrived back at her desk there was no sign that the Deputy Foreign Minister had returned, so she checked with the switchboard. There had only been three calls: two said they would call back tomorrow, and the third didn't leave a message.

Hannah replaced the handset and typed out a note explaining that she had gone home as she wasn't certain whether the Deputy Foreign Minister would be returning that day. As long as he didn't check his messages until after five o'clock, there would be no reason for him to become suspicious.

In the privacy of her little room, Hannah exchanged her office clothes for the traditional black abaya with a pushi covering her face. She checked herself in the mirror before once again leaving the building, silently and anonymously.

'I'm almost sure it's her coming out of the Ministry,' said the voice into the mobile phone, 'but she's changed into traditional dress and is no longer wearing glasses. She's heading towards Victory Square again. I'll keep you briefed.'

Hannah was back in Victory Square a few minutes before the first cleaner was expected to arrive for work. Although the crowd was now smaller, she was still able to remain inconspicuous. She looked across the road towards the courtyard. The safe was no longer to be seen, and the crane too had disappeared. The truck was now backed up against the wall. Hannah strained to see if Kratz was one of the figures sitting in the front of the truck, but she couldn't penetrate the haze of smoke.

Hannah turned her attention to a building she had never entered but felt she knew so well. A full-scale plan of each floor was attached to a board in the operations room of Mossad's headquarters in Herzliyah, and you couldn't take the second paper of any exam on Iraq without being able to draw every floor of the building in detail. Information was added all the time, from the strangest sources: escaped refugees, former diplomats, ex-Cabinet Ministers who were Kurds or Shi'ites, even the former British Prime Minister Edward Heath.

The first cleaner arrived a few minutes before three, presented her pass and then hurried across the tarmac before disappearing into a side door of the building. The second appeared a few moments later, and followed the same procedure. When Hannah spotted the third making her way along the far side of the pavement, she slipped across the road and filed in behind her as she walked towards the barrier.

'She's crossed the road, reached the barrier, and the guard is now checking her pass,' said the voice into the mobile phone. 'As instructed, they've let her through. She's now walking across the tarmac and following another woman through the side door. She's in, the door's closed. We've got her.'

* * *

'Now you open the safe,' said Major Saeed.

Scott swivelled the dials to their coded numbers, and the first bulb turned green. The Major was impressed. Scott then placed the palm of his hand on the white square, and a few seconds later the middle bulb turned green. The Major was mesmerised. Scott leaned forward and spoke into the voice box, and the third light turned green. The Major was speechless.

Scott pulled the handle and the door swung open. He jumped inside and immediately extracted the cardboard tube from the inside of his trouser leg.

The Major spotted it at once, and flew into a rage. Scott quickly flicked off the cap, took out the poster of Saddam Hussein and unpeeled it, letting the backing paper fall to the ground before he strolled to the far side of the safe and fixed the portrait of Saddam to the wall. A smile returned to the Major's face as Scott bent down, rolled up the backing paper and slid it into the tube.

'Now I teach you,' said Scott.

'No, no, not me,' said Major Saeed. He held his phone up in the air and said, 'We must go back upstairs.'

Scott felt like swearing as he stepped out of the safe, dropping the tube and allowing it to roll across the floor to the darkest corner. The plan he had so carefully prepared with Kratz would no longer be possible. He reluctantly left the open safe and joined the Major as he marched quickly towards the Council Chamber, this time not allowing Scott any opportunity to hold him up.

Hannah joined the other cleaners inside the building, and told them that her mother had been taken ill and that she had been sent to cover for her. She tried to assure them that it was not the first time she had done so, and was surprised when they asked no questions. She assumed that they were fearful of being involved with a stranger.

Hannah picked up a box of cleaning equipment and made her way down the back stairs. The plan displayed on the walls at Herzliyah was proving impressively accurate, even if nobody had managed the exact number of steps to the basement.

When she reached the door that led into the bottom corridor she could hear voices coming from the direction of the Council Chamber. Whoever it was must be heading for the lift. Hannah backed up against the wall so she could just see them through the thick pane of wire-mesh glass in the centre of the door.

The two men passed. Hannah didn't recognise the Major, but when she saw who was with him, her legs gave way and she almost collapsed onto the ground.

Once they were back in the courtyard, the Major dialled a number. Scott strolled over to Kratz, who was standing behind the truck.

'Did you manage to switch the Declaration?' were Kratz's first words.

'No, I didn't have time. It's still on the wall of the Chamber.'

'Damn. And the copy?'

'I left it in the tube on the floor of the safe. I couldn't risk bringing it out.'

'So how are you going to get back into the building?' asked Kratz, looking towards the Major. 'You were meant to use the time –'

'I know. But it turns out he's not the one who'll be in charge of the safe. He's getting in touch with whoever it is I'll have to instruct.'

'Not what we needed. I suspect that with the Major

our first plan would have been a lot easier,' said Kratz. 'I'd better brief the others so we can work on an alternative if things go wrong again.'

Scott nodded his agreement, and he and the Mossad leader strolled over to the truck where Aziz and Cohen were sitting in the cab smoking. As the Colonel climbed into the front, two cigarettes were quickly stubbed out. Kratz explained why they were still waiting, and warned them that this could be the Professor's last chance to get back into the Council Chamber. 'So when he comes out next time,' he explained, 'we must be ready to go. With a little luck, we might still make the border by midnight.'

How could he possibly be alive? Hannah thought. Hadn't she killed him? She had seen his dead body carried out of the room. She tried to organise her thoughts, which ranged from absolute joy to utter fear. She recalled her senior instructor telling her, 'When you're in the front line, never be surprised by anything.' She felt she now had the right to contradict him, if she was ever given the chance.

Hannah pushed open the door and crept into the corridor, which was deserted except for a pair of soldiers chatting by the entrance to the Chamber. She realised she couldn't hope to get past them without being questioned.

With a pace to go, she was told to stop, and came to a halt between them. After they had checked the cleaning box thoroughly, the one with two stripes on his arm said, 'You know it's our duty to search you as well?' Hannah made no comment while he bent down, lifted her long black robe and placed his hands on her ankles. The second one let out a raucous laugh as he put his fingers round the front of her neck, and began moving his hands down over her shoulders and across her breasts, while his colleague moved his hands up her legs and onto her thighs. As the first soldier reached the top of her legs, his colleague pinched her nipples. Hannah pushed them both away and stepped into the Chamber. They made no attempt to follow, although their laughter increased in volume.

The table had been returned to the centre of the room and the chairs casually rearranged around it. She began by straightening the table before placing the chairs at an equal distance from each other. She was still trying to take in the fact that Simon was alive. But why would the CIA send him to Baghdad? Unless . . . she stared up at the massive portrait of Saddam Hussein as she straightened his chair at the head of the table. Then her eyes came to rest on the document that was nailed next to his picture.

The American Declaration of Independence was fixed to the wall in exactly the place the Deputy Foreign Minister had claimed it was.

30

TWO CARS SWEPT UP TO the barrier and were ushered quickly through without the suggestion of a check. Scott watched carefully as a large group of soldiers surrounded the vehicles.

When a tall, heavily-built man stepped out of the second car, Aziz said under his breath, 'General Hamil, the Barber of Baghdad. He carries a cut-throat razor on his keyring.'

Kratz nodded. 'I know his complete life history,' he said. 'Even the name of the young Lieutenant he's currently living with.'

Major Saeed was now standing to attention, saluting the General, and Scott didn't need to be told that this man was of a different rank and calibre to the one he had been dealing with until then. He studied the face of the man dressed in an immaculate tailored uniform with several more rows of battle ribbons than the Major, wearing black leather gloves and carrying a swagger stick. It was a cruel face. The troops who stood around him were unable to disguise their fear.

The Major pointed to Scott and said, 'You, come.'

'I've got a feeling he means you,' said Kratz.

Scott nodded and strolled across to join them.

'Mr Bernstrom,' the General said, removing the glove from his right hand, 'I am General Hamil.' Scott shook his hand. 'I am sorry to have kept you waiting. But don't let me hold you up any longer. Please show me your safe, which Major Saeed seems so impressed by.'

Without another word the General turned and began walking towards the building, leaving Scott with little choice but to follow. For the first time in his life, Scott was terrified.

Hannah picked up a duster and some polish and began to rub in small circles on the table while taking a more careful look at the Declaration of Independence. The parchment was in such terrible condition that she doubted if it could be repaired even if Simon were able to get it back to Washington.

She peered round the door into the short corridor, and spotted the safe she had seen on the truck earlier that day. It was open, but was guarded by two more thugs, chatting as much as the other two who were stationed at the door of the Council Chamber.

Hannah made her way slowly down the corridor, dusting and polishing the ledge of the wooden skirting until she was opposite the safe and had a clear view inside. She took a pace forward and peered in as if she had never seen anything like it in her life before. One of the soldiers kicked her and she fell into the safe. The inevitable raucous laughter followed. She was about to turn round and retaliate when she saw the long cardboard cylinder in one corner, almost hidden in the shadow. She leaned across and rolled it quickly towards her until it was safely under her long skirt. She wondered if she could use it to get a message to Simon. Hannah left her duster and polish on the floor of the safe, stepped out backwards and bolted down the corridor, as if to escape the guards.

Once she was back in the Chamber she removed

another rag from the cleaning box and began polishing the table until she was in a position where no one could see her from either passageway. She then lowered herself slowly onto her knees until she was below the table, and let the cardboard tube fall to the floor in front of her. She quickly flicked off the cap, to find the cylinder wasn't empty. She pulled out the parchment, unrolled it and studied it in disbelief: a magnificent copy of the Declaration of Independence, obviously made by a craftsman, even if someone had tried to deface it. She realised immediately that Simon must have been hoping to find some way of switching the copy for the original.

Kratz watched Scott follow General Hamil into the building, then walked slowly across to the truck and climbed into the cab. He stared through the front window. No one was taking any particular interest in what they were up to.

'This is too easy,' he said. 'Far too easy.' Cohen and Aziz looked straight ahead, but didn't offer an opinion. 'If Hamil is involved, they must suspect something. The time has come for us to find out who knows what.'

'What do you have in mind, sir?' asked Cohen.

'I have a feeling that our switchboard Major isn't fully aware of what's going on. Either they haven't briefed him, or they think he's not up to the job.'

'Or both,' suggested Aziz.

Kratz nodded. 'Or both. So let's find out. Aziz, I want you and Cohen to take a stroll down to the barrier. Tell the guards that you're going for something to eat, and that you'll be back in a few minutes. If they refuse to let you through, we've got a real problem, because that will mean they know what we're up to. In which case, come back to the cab and I'll start working on what we have to do next.'

'And if they let us through?' asked Cohen.

'Get out of sight,' said Kratz, 'but keep in visual contact with the truck. That shouldn't be too hard, with these gawking crowds. If Professor Bradley comes out with his cardboard tube and I rest my arm on the window ledge as I'm doing now, get back here fast, because we won't want to be hanging about. And by the way, Cohen: if I'm not around for any reason, and the Professor should suggest a detour to the Foreign Ministry, overrule him.' Cohen nodded, without a clue what the Colonel was talking about. 'But if you spot that we're in trouble, keep well out of the way for one hour, and then pray that the whopper works.'

'Understood, sir,' said Cohen.

'Take the keys with you,' said Kratz. 'Now get going.'

Kratz stepped back down onto the tarmac, strolled over to where Major Saeed was listening to one of his interminable phone calls, and placed himself a few feet to his left as if wanting to attract his attention. At the same time he looked over his shoulder to watch Aziz and Cohen walking towards the barrier.

Kratz continued to try and attract the Major's attention as Aziz came to a halt at the barrier and started joking with one of the guards.

A few moments later Kratz saw both of his men step under the barrier. Within seconds they were lost in the crowd.

Major Saeed came off the phone. 'What is the problem this time?' he asked. Kratz took out a cigarette and asked the Major for a light.

'Don't smoke,' he said, and waved him away.

Kratz walked slowly back to the cab and took his place behind the steering wheel, his eyes never leaving the open doorway of the Ba'ath Party headquarters.

* * *

Hannah stared at the Declaration hanging on the wall. It was only a few paces away from her. She waited until she heard another roar of laughter from the soldiers before walking over to the document and quickly trying to remove the nails. Three came out with the minimum of effort, but the one at the top right-hand corner refused to budge, and the Declaration continued to dangle from it. After a few more seconds, she felt she was left with no choice but to ease the document over the head of the nail. Once the parchment was in her hand she went back to the table, placed the original on the floor and returned quickly to attach the copy to the wall.

She hardly glanced at her handiwork before she turned back to the table, knelt on the ground, and rapidly rolled up the original, replacing it in the cylinder. Once again she tucked it under her skirt. It had been the longest two minutes of her life. She remained on her knees, trying to think. She knew she couldn't risk trying to get the tube out of the building, as the guards might decide to 'search' her again. There was no alternative. She walked quickly back down the short corridor and was in the safe even before the two soldiers had stopped talking. She let the cylinder fall to the floor, then pushed it back into the darkest corner, exactly where she had first seen it. Then she picked up the duster and polish she had left behind, stepped back out of the safe and showed them to the soldiers, and ran back down the corridor towards the Chamber.

Hannah knew she must get out of the building as quickly as possible, and somehow pass a message to Simon.

And then she heard the voices.

The lift doors slid apart at the basement floor. The General stepped out into the corridor and headed towards the Council Chamber.

'And just how large is this safe?' he asked Scott.

'Nine feet in height, seven feet in width and eight feet in depth,' responded Scott immediately. 'You could hold a private meeting in there if you wished to, General.'

'Is that so?' said Hamil. 'But I am informed the safe can only be operated by one person. Is that true?'

'That is correct, General. We followed the exact specifications your government requested.'

'I am also told that the safe can withstand a nuclear attack. Is that the case?'

'Yes,' replied Scott. 'The safe has a six-inch skin and would be unaffected by any explosion other than a direct hit. In any other circumstances, everything in the safe would be preserved, even if the building it was standing in was completely demolished.'

'Impressive,' said the General as the guards sprang to attention and he touched the rim of his beret with his swagger stick. He marched into the Chamber and Scott followed, annoyed to find there was a woman polishing the table. He certainly didn't need her hanging around when he came back out. The General didn't even look at Hannah as he strode through the Chamber.

Scott glanced across at the parchment before he followed the General out of the room.

'Ah,' Hannah heard the General say when he was still several yards from the end of the corridor. 'Pure statistics don't do your safe justice, Mr Bernstrom.' The two soldiers remained rigidly at attention as the General studied the safe for some time, before stepping inside. When he saw the cardboard tube on the floor he bent down and picked it up.

'Just to protect the picture,' explained Scott as he stepped in to join him. He pointed to the portrait of Saddam Hussein.

'You are a thorough man, Mr Bernstrom,' said Hamil.

'You would have made an excellent colonel in one of my regiments.' He laughed and passed the cardboard tube over to Scott.

Hannah listened intently to every word, and concluded that she must get out of the building as quickly as possible and alert Kratz to what she had done.

'Would you like me to show you how to programme the safe?' she heard Scott ask as she reached the entrance of the Chamber.

'No, no, not me,' said General Hamil. 'The President will be the only one who will be allowed to operate the safe.' Those were the last words Hannah heard as she walked out of the Chamber, past the guards, and continued purposefully down the long corridor.

When she reached the doors that led to the staircase she turned back to see the General striding into the Chamber and, some way behind him, Scott following. He was holding the tube.

Hannah wanted to scream with delight.

Scott realised he would never be given a chance to carry out the switch once Saddam was in the building. When he reached the Chamber he allowed the General to get a few paces ahead of him. His eyes swept the room, and he was relieved to find the cleaner was no longer anywhere to be seen. The guards sprang to attention as the General strode out of the Council Chamber into the far corridor.

Scott stared at the alarm button on the wall ahead of him. 'Don't look round,' he begged under his breath as he kept his eyes on the retreating back of the General. With a yard to go before he reached the door, Scott lunged forward and jabbed his thumb on the red button. The doors immediately slammed closed and clamped with a deafening noise.

Hannah was just about to push open the door that led to the back stairs when the alarm gave out a piercing sound and all the exits were immediately bolted. She turned to discover she was alone in the corridor with General Hamil and four of his republican guards.

The General smiled at her. 'Miss Kopec, I believe. I'm delighted to make your acquaintance. I fear it will be a couple of minutes before Professor Bradley is able to join us.'

The guards surrounded Hannah as the General looked up at a television screen above the door. He watched as Scott, inside the Chamber, pressed a button on the side of his watch. Scott then ran over to the wall, quickly extracted the copy of the document from the tube, and checked it against the original. He felt he had done a fair job back in the cab of the truck, but he spat on Lewis Morris and John Witherspoon for good measure, then spent a few seconds rubbing the parchment on the stone floor before comparing it once again to the one on the wall. He looked at his watch: forty-five seconds. He began to pull the nails out of the wall, but was unable to get the top right-hand one to budge, so he eased the Declaration over its head. Sixty seconds.

Hannah stared up at the television screen in horror, watching Simon undo all her work, while the General made a phone call.

Once Scott had removed the document from the wall he placed it on the table. He then fastened the copy that he had taken out of the cardboard cylinder back on the wall, easing the parchment over the nail in the top right-hand corner, which still stubbornly refused to budge. Ninety seconds. He picked up Dollar Bill's copy from the table, rolled it up and dropped it into the cylinder. One hundred and ten seconds. He walked over to the door that led to the lifts and stood inhaling deeply for a moment before the alarm stopped and the doors swung open.

Scott knew that it would take them a few minutes

before the source of the alarm could be checked, so when he saw the General, he shrugged his shoulders and smiled.

Kratz sat on the front seat of the truck, keeping a wary eye on Major Saeed. There was a ringing sound: Saeed pressed a button and placed his phone to his ear. Suddenly, without warning, he turned, whipped out his pistol and looked anxiously towards the cab. He barked out an order, and within seconds every soldier in sight surrounded the truck, their rifles pointing directly at Kratz.

The Major rushed up. 'Where are the other two?' he demanded. Kratz shrugged his shoulders. Saeed turned on his heels and ran into the building, shouting another order as he went.

Kratz placed his right hand over his left wrist and slowly began to unpeel the plaster, a second skin, secreted beneath his watch. He delicately removed the tiny green pill stuck to the plaster and transferred it to the palm of his hand. Sixty or seventy eyes were staring at him. He began coughing, and slowly put his hand up to his mouth, lowered his head and swallowed the pill.

Saeed came rushing back out of the building and began barking new orders. Within seconds, a car pulled up beside the truck.

'Out!' the Major screamed at Kratz, who stepped down onto the tarmac and allowed a dozen fixed bayonets to guide him towards the back door of the car. He was pushed onto the seat, and two men in dark suits took a place on each side of him. One quickly turned him and tied his hands behind his back, while the other blindfolded him.

Cohen and Aziz watched from the other side of the square as the car sped away from them.

31

THE GENERAL RETURNED Scott's smile.

'I won't introduce you to Miss Saib,' he said, 'as I believe you've already met.'

Scott looked blank as he stared at the woman dressed in a black abaya and a pushi that covered her face. She was surrounded by four soldiers, their bayonets drawn.

'We have a lot to thank Miss Saib for, because of course it was she who led us to you in the first place, not to mention her postcard to Mrs Rubin that helped you find the Declaration so quickly. We did try to make it as easy as possible for you.'

'I don't know Miss Saib,' said Scott.

'Oh, come, Professor – or should I call you Agent Bradley? I admire your gallantry, but while you may claim not to know Miss Saib, you certainly know Hannah Kopec,' the General said as he ripped off Hannah's pushi.

Scott stared at Hannah, but still said nothing.

'Ah, I see you do remember her. But then, it would be hard to forget someone who tried to kill you, wouldn't it?'

Hannah's eyes pleaded with Scott.

'How touching, my dear, he's forgiven you. But I fear I don't share his forgiving nature.' The General turned to see Major Saeed running towards him. He listened carefully to what the Major whispered to him, then began banging his swagger stick rapidly against his long leather boots.

'You're a fool!' he shouted at the top of his voice, and suddenly struck the Major across the face with his swagger stick.

He turned back to face Scott. 'It seems,' he said, 'that the reunion I had planned for you and your friends will have to wait a little longer, because although we have Colonel Kratz safely locked up, the Jew and the Kurdish traitor have escaped. But it can only be a matter of time before we catch them.'

'How long have you known?' asked Hannah quietly.

'You made the mistake so many of our enemies make, Miss Kopec, of underestimating our great President,' replied the General. 'He dominates the affairs of the Middle East to a far greater extent than Gorbachev did the Russians, Thatcher the British, or Bush the American people. I ask myself, how many citizens in the West any longer believe the Allies won the Gulf War? But then, you were also stupid enough to underrate his cousin, Abdul Kanuk, our newly appointed Ambassador to Paris. Perhaps he wasn't quite that stupid when he followed you all the way to your lover's flat and stood in a doorway the rest of the night before following you back to the embassy. It was he who informed our Ambassador in Geneva what "Miss Saib" was up to.

'Of course, we needed to be sure, not least because our Deputy Foreign Minister found it so hard to accept such a tale about one of his most loyal members of staff. Such a naïve man. So, when you came to Baghdad, the Ambassador's wife invited Miss Saib's brother to dinner. But, sadly, he didn't recognise you. Your cover, as the more vulgar American papers would describe it, was blown. Those same papers keep asking pathetically, "Why doesn't Mossad assassinate President Saddam?" If only they knew how many times Mossad has tried and failed. What Colonel Kratz didn't tell you at your training school in Herzliyah, Miss Kopec, was that you are the seventeenth Mossad agent who has attempted to infiltrate our ranks during the past five years, and all of them have experienced the same tragic end as your Colonel is about to. And the real beauty of the whole exercise is that we don't have to admit we killed any of you in the first place. You see, the Jewish people are unwilling to accept, after Entebbe and Eichmann, that such a thing could possibly happen. I feel sure you will appreciate the logic of that, Professor.'

'I'll make a bargain with you,' said Scott.

'I'm touched, Professor, by your Western ethics, but I fear you have nothing to bargain with.'

'We'll trade Miss Saib if you release Hannah.'

The General burst out laughing. 'Professor, you have a keen sense of the ridiculous, but I won't insult you by suggesting that you don't understand the Arab mind. Do allow me to explain. You will be killed, and no one will comment because, as I have already explained, the West is too proud to admit that you even exist. Whereas we in the East will throw our hands in the air and ask why Mossad has kidnapped a gentle, blameless secretary on her way to Paris, and is now holding her in Tel Aviv against her will. We even know the house where she is captive. We have already arranged for sentimental pictures of her to be released to every paper in the Western world, and a distraught mother and son have been coached for weeks by one of your own public relations companies to face the Western press. We'll even have Amnesty International protesting outside Israeli embassies across the world on her behalf.'

Scott stared at the General.

'Poor Miss Saib will be released within days. Both of

you, on the other hand, will die an unannounced, unheralded and unmourned death. To think that all you sacrificed your lives for was a scrap of paper. And while we are on that subject, Professor, I will relieve you of the Declaration.'

The four soldiers stepped forward and thrust their bayonets at Scott's throat as the General snatched the cardboard tube from his grasp.

'You did well to switch the documents in two minutes, Professor,' said the General, glancing up at the television screen above him. 'But you can be assured that it remains our intention to burn the original very publicly on the fourth of July, and I feel confident that we will destroy President Clinton's flimsy reputation along with it.' The General laughed. 'You know, Professor, I have for many years enjoyed killing people, but I shall gain a particular pleasure from your deaths, because of the appropriate way you will be departing this world.'

The soldiers surrounded Hannah and Scott and forced them back into the Chamber and on towards the short corridor. The General followed them down the passage. They all came to a halt in front of the open safe.

'Allow me,' said General Hamil, 'to inform you of one statistic you failed to mention, Professor, when you briefed me on this amazing feat of engineering. Perhaps you simply didn't know, although I am bound to admit that you have done your homework thoroughly. But did you realise that one person locked in a safe of this size, with a capacity of 504 cubic feet, can only hope to survive for six hours? I do not yet know the exact length of time two people can hope to survive while sharing the same amount of oxygen. But I will very shortly.' He removed a stopwatch from his pocket, waved his swagger stick, and the soldiers hurled first Hannah and then Scott into the safe. The smile remained on the General's face as two of the soldiers pushed the massive door closed. The lights all began flashing red.

The General clicked his stopwatch.

When the car came to a halt, Kratz reckoned that the distance they had travelled was under a mile. He heard the door open and felt a shove on his arm to indicate he should get out of the car. He was pushed up three stone steps before entering a building and walking into a long corridor. His footsteps echoed on the wooden floor. Then he was guided into a room on his left, where he was pushed down onto a chair, tied and gagged. His shoes and socks were removed. When he heard the door close, he sensed he was alone.

It was a long time – he couldn't be sure just how long – before the door opened again. The first voice he heard was General Hamil's. 'Remove the gag,' was all he said.

Kratz could hear him pacing round the chair, but at first the General said nothing. Kratz began to concentrate. He knew the pill was good for two hours, no more, and he suspected that it was already forty or fifty minutes since they had driven him away from Ba'ath headquarters.

'Colonel Kratz, I have waited some time for the privilege of making your acquaintance. I have long admired your work. You are a perfectionist.'

'Cut the crap,' said Kratz, 'because I don't admire you or your work.'

He waited for the first slap of gloves across his face or for a fist to come crashing into his jaw, but the General simply continued to circle the chair.

'You mustn't be too disappointed,' said the General. 'I feel sure, after all you've heard about us, that you must have expected at least some electric shocks by now, perhaps the Chinese water torture, even the rack, but I fear – unlike Mossad, Colonel – that when dealing with people of your seniority we long ago dispensed with such primitive methods. We have found them to be outmoded, a thing of the past. Worse, they just don't get results. You Zionists are tough and well trained. Few of you talk, very few. So we've had to resort to more scientific methods to gain the information we need.'

If it was still within the hour, thought Kratz, he had judged it well.

'A simple injection of PPX will ensure that we learn everything we want to know,' continued the General, 'and once we have the information we require, we'll simply kill you. So much more efficient than in the past, and with all the environmental complaints one gets nowadays, so much more tidy. Though, I must confess, I miss the old methods. So you'll appreciate why I couldn't resist locking Miss Kopec and Professor Bradley in their safe, especially as they hadn't seen each other for so long.'

Kratz's hand was pressed back and held against the arm of the chair. He felt fingers searching for a vein, and when the needle went in, he flinched. He began counting: one, two, three, four, five, six . . .

He was about to find out if one of Europe's leading chemists had, as she claimed, found the antidote for the Iraqis' latest truth drug. Mossad had tracked down the supplier in Austria. Strange how many people think there are no Jews left in Austria.

. . . thirty-seven, thirty-eight, thirty-nine . . .

The drug was still in its testing stage, and needed to be proved under non-laboratory conditions. If a person could remain fully in control of his senses while appearing to be under hypnosis, then they would know their antidote was a success.

. . . one minute, one minute one, one minute two, one minute three . . .

The test would come when they stuck the second needle in, and that might be anywhere. Then the trick was to show no reaction whatsoever, or the General would immediately realise that the original injection had failed to have the required effect. The training programme for this particular 'realistic experience' was not universally popular among agents, and although Kratz had experienced 'the prick', as it was affectionately known, once a month for the past nine months, you only had a single chance in 'non-laboratory conditions' to discover if you could pass the test.

. . . one minute thirty-seven, one minute thirty-eight, one minute thirty-nine . . .

The injection was meant to take effect after two minutes, and every agent had been taught to expect the second needle at some time between two and three minutes, thus the counting.

. . . one minute fifty-six, one minute fifty-seven . . .

Relax, it must come at any moment. Relax.

Suddenly the needle was jabbed in and out of the big toe on his left foot. Kratz stopped gritting his teeth; even his breathing remained regular. He had won the Israeli Pincushion Award, First Class. Mossad made jokes about everything.

32

'. . . AND ALL THAT TIME I really thought you were dead.'

'We had no way of letting you know,' said Scott.

'Still, it's no longer of any importance, Simon,' said Hannah. 'Sorry. "Scott" will take a bit of getting used to. I may not be able to manage it in the time we've got left.'

'We may have more time left than you think,' said Scott.

'How can you say that?'

'One of the contingency plans that Kratz and I worked on was that if any of us were caught and tortured while someone else was still free, we'd hold out for one hour before telling them the whopper.'

Hannah knew exactly what Mossad meant by the whopper, even if on this occasion she didn't know the details.

'Although I have to admit this is one scenario we never considered,' said Scott. 'In fact, the exact opposite. We thought that if we were able to convince them we had another purpose for bringing the safe to Baghdad, they'd immediately evacuate the building and clear the surrounding area.'

'And what would that have achieved?'

'We hoped that with the building empty, even if we'd been captured, the other agents who came over the border a day ahead of us might have a clear hour to get into the Council Chamber and remove the Declaration.'

'But wouldn't the Iraqis have taken the document away with them?'

'Not necessarily. Our plan was that we would tell them exactly what would happen to their beloved leader if the safe was closed by anyone other than me. We felt that would cause panic, and they'd probably leave everything behind.'

'So Kratz drew the short straw.'

'Yes,' said Scott quietly. 'Not that his original plan is relevant any longer, after I was stupid enough to hand over the Declaration to Hamil. So now we'll have to use the time to get out, not in.'

'But you didn't hand it over,' said Hannah. 'The Declaration is still on the wall of the Chamber.'

'I'm afraid not,' said Scott. 'Hamil was right. I switched the copies after I set the alarm off. So I ended up giving Hamil back the original.'

'No, you didn't,' said Hannah. 'It's because you believed you switched the original that you fooled Hamil as well as yourself.'

'What are you talking about?' said Scott.

'I'm the one responsible,' said Hannah. 'I found the cardboard tube in the safe and switched the two documents, thinking I could get out of the building and then pass on a message to let Kratz know what I'd done. The trouble was, you and General Hamil arrived just as I was about to leave. So, when you locked yourself in the Chamber, you put the original back on the wall, and then you handed over the copy to Hamil.'

Scott took her in his arms again. 'You're a genius,' he said.

'No I'm not,' said Hannah. 'So you'd better let me in on the secret of what you've planned for this particular scenario. To start with, how do we get out of a locked safe?'

'That's the beauty of it,' said Scott. 'It isn't locked. It's programmed so that it can only be opened and closed by me.'

'Who dreamed that one up?'

'A Swede who would happily take our place, but he's stuck in Kalmar. The first thing I have to do is discover which wall is the door.'

'That's easy,' said Hannah. 'It has to be exactly opposite me because I'm sitting below the picture of Saddam, remember?'

Scott and Hannah began the short crawl on their hands and knees to the other side of the safe. 'Now we go to the right-hand corner,' he said, 'so that when we push, the leverage will be easier.'

Hannah nodded, and then remembered they couldn't see each other. 'Yes,' she said.

Scott checked the luminous dial of his watch. 'But not quite yet,' he added. 'We'll have to give Kratz a little more time.'

'Enough time to tell me what the whopper is?' asked Hannah.

'Good,' said the General, when Kratz didn't react to the needle being jabbed into his big toe. 'Now we can find out all we need to know. But to begin with, some simple questions. Your Mossad rank?'

'Colonel,' said Kratz. The secret was to tell them only facts you felt confident they already knew.

'Your initiation number?'

'78216,' he said. If in doubt, assume they know, otherwise you could be caught out.

'And your official position?'

'Councillor for Cultural Affairs to the Court of St James in London.' You are allowed three testing lies and one whopper, but no more.

'What are the names of your three colleagues who accompanied you on this mission?'

'Professor Scott Bradley, an expert on ancient manuscripts,' – the first testing lie – 'Ben Cohen, and Aziz Zeebari.' The truth.

'And the girl, Hannah Kopec, what is her rank in Mossad?'

'She is still a trainee.'

'How long has she been with Mossad?'

'Just over two years.'

'And her role?'

'To be placed in Baghdad to discover where the Declaration of Independence was located.' The second lie.

'You are doing well, Colonel,' said the General, looking at the long, thin cardboard tube he held in his right hand.

'And was this your overall responsibility as her commanding officer?'

'No. I was simply to accompany the safe from Kalmar.' The third lie.

'But surely that was nothing more than an excuse to locate the Declaration of Independence?'

Kratz hesitated. Experts had been able to show that even under the influence of a truth drug a highly trained agent would still hesitate when asked a secret he had never revealed in the past.

'What was the true purpose of your bringing the safe to Baghdad, Colonel?'

Kratz still remained silent.

'Colonel Kratz,' said the General, his voice rising with every word, 'what was the real reason you brought the safe to Baghdad?'

Kratz counted to three before he spoke.

'To blow up the Ba'ath Party headquarters with a tiny nuclear device secreted in the safe, in the hope of killing the President along with all the members of the Revolutionary Command Council.' The whopper.

How Kratz wished he could see the General's face. It was Hamil who was hesitating now.

'How was the bomb to be activated?'

Again Kratz did not reply.

'I will ask you once again, Colonel. How was the bomb to be activated?'

Still Kratz said nothing.

'When will it go off?' shouted the General.

'Two hours after the safe has been closed by anyone other than the Professor.'

The General checked his watch, rushed to the only phone in the room and shouted to be put through to the President immediately. He waited until he heard Saddam's voice. He didn't notice that Kratz had fainted and fallen from his chair to the floor.

Scott eased himself into the corner before once again checking the little sulphur dots on his watch. It was 5.19. He and Hannah had been in the safe for an hour and seventeen minutes.

'I'm going to push now. If you hear anything, shove as hard as you can. If there's anyone still out there our only hope will be to take them by surprise.'

Scott began to exert the minimum amount of pressure on the corner of the door with the tips of his fingers, and it eased open an inch. He stopped and listened, but could hear nothing. He took a look through the tiny crack, and could see no one. He pushed another inch. Still no sound. Both of them now had a clear view of the corridor.

Scott looked at Hannah and nodded, and together they shoved as hard as they could. The ton of steel shot open. They both leaped into the corridor, but there was no one to be seen. There was an eerie silence.

Scott and Hannah walked slowly down the short corridor, keeping to the sides until they reached the Chamber. Still no sound. Scott put a foot into the Chamber and glanced to his left. The Declaration of Independence was still hanging on the wall next to the portrait of Saddam.

Hannah moved silently to the far end of the Chamber and looked into the long corridor. She then turned back to Scott and nodded. Scott checked the spelling of 'Brittish' before saying a silent hallelujah. He pulled out three of the nails, then eased the Declaration over the remaining nail in the top right-hand corner, trying to forget that he had spat on a national treasure and rubbed it in the dust. He gave Saddam one last look before rolling up the parchment and joining Hannah in the corridor.

Hannah slid along the wall, then pointed to the lift. She pulled a finger across her throat to show Scott she wanted to avoid using it in favour of the back stairs. He nodded his agreement and followed her out of the side door.

They moved quickly but silently up the six flights of stairs until they reached the ground floor. Hannah beckoned Scott into the side room where the cleaners had collected their boxes. She had reached the window on the far side of the room and was on her knees even before Scott had closed the door. He joined her and they stared out on a deserted Victory Square. There was no one to be seen in any direction.

'God bless Kratz,' said Scott.

Hannah nodded and beckoned him to follow her again. She led him back into the corridor and guided him quickly to the side door. Scott opened the door tentatively and slipped out ahead of her. A moment later she joined him on the tarmac.

He pointed to a group of palm trees halfway across the courtyard, and she nodded once again. They covered the twenty yards to its relative safety in under three seconds. Scott turned to look back at the building and saw the truck standing up against the wall. He assumed that, in the panic, it was just something else that had been left behind.

He tapped Hannah on the shoulder and indicated that he wanted to return to the building. They covered the ground at the same pace as before, ducking back inside the door. Scott led Hannah to the main corridor, where they found the front door was swinging on its hinges. He looked through the gap and pointed to the truck, mimed to which side he would go and touched her shoulder. Again they sprinted across the tarmac as if reacting to a starting pistol.

Scott jumped behind the wheel as Hannah leaped in the other side.

'Where the hell –' was Scott's first reaction when he discovered the ignition key wasn't in place. They began frantically to search the glove compartment, under the seats, on the dashboard. 'The bastards must have taken the key with them.'

'Simon, look out!' screamed Hannah. Scott turned to see a figure leaping up onto the footplate.

Hannah moved quickly into position to attack the intruder, but Scott blocked her.

'Good afternoon, miss,' said the stranger. 'Sorry we haven't been properly introduced,' he added before turning to Scott. 'Move over, Professor,' he said as he put the key back in the ignition. 'If you recall, it was agreed that I'd do the driving.'

'What in heaven's name are you doing here, Sergeant?' asked Scott.

'Now that's what I call a real American welcome,' replied Cohen. 'But, to answer your question, I was just obeying orders. I was told if you came out of that door carrying a cardboard tube, I was to get myself back here and move the hell out of it, but not under any circumstances to allow you to make a detour to the Foreign Ministry. By the way, where's the tube?'

'Look out!' shouted Hannah again, as she turned and saw an Arab charging towards them from the other side.

'That one won't do you any harm,' said Cohen, 'he's bloody useless. Doesn't even know the difference between a Diet Coke and a Pepsi.' Aziz leaped onto the running board and said to Scott, 'I think we've got about another twenty minutes, Professor, before they work out that there's no bomb in the safe.'

'Then let's get out of here,' said Scott.

'But where to?' asked Hannah.

'Aziz and I have already done a recce, sir. As soon as the sirens sounded we knew that Kratz must have sold them the whopper, because they couldn't move fast enough to get themselves below. Soldiers and police first seems to be the rule out here. Aziz and I have had the run of the city centre for the last hour. In fact the only person we bumped into was one of our own agents, Dave Feldman. He'd already sussed out the best route to give us a chance of avoiding any military.'

'Not bad, Cohen,' said Scott.

Cohen turned suddenly and stared at the Professor.

'I didn't do it for you, sir, I did it for Colonel Kratz. He got me out of jail once, and he's the only officer that's ever treated me like a human being. So whatever it is that you're holding in your hands, Professor, it had bloody well better be worth his life.'

'Thousands have given their lives for it over the years,' said Scott quietly. 'It's the American Declaration of Independence.'

'Good God,' said Cohen. 'How did the bastards get their hands on that?' He paused briefly. 'Am I meant to believe you?'

Scott nodded and unrolled the parchment. Cohen and Aziz stared in disbelief for several seconds.

'Right then, we'd better get you home, Professor, hadn't we?' said Cohen. 'Aziz will take over while we're in his neck of the woods.' He jumped out of the cab and the Kurd came running round to take his place behind the wheel. Once Cohen had clambered over the tail-board, he banged the roof of the truck and Aziz switched the engine on.

They accelerated round the courtyard, drove straight through the barrier and out onto Victory Square. The only other vehicles to be seen had long since been abandoned, and there was no sign of anyone on the streets.

'The area has been cleared for three miles in every direction, so it will be a little time before we come across anything,' Aziz said as he turned left into Kindi Street. He quickly moved the lorry up to sixty miles per hour, a speed only Saddam had ever experienced before on that particular road.

'I'm going to take the old Baquba Road out of the city, travelling through the areas where we're least likely to see any sign of the military,' explained Aziz as he passed the fountain made famous by Ali Baba. 'I'm still hoping to reach the highway out of Baghdad within the magic two hours.'

Aziz took a sudden right, switching gears but hardly losing any speed as he continued through what gave every impression of being a ghost town. Scott looked up at the sun as they crossed a bridge over the Tigris; in an hour or so it would have disappeared behind the highest buildings, and their chances of remaining undetected would greatly improve.

Aziz swung past Karmel Junblat University and into Jamila Street. There were still no people on the roads or pavements, and Scott felt that if anyone did see them now they would assume they were part of an army unit on patrol.

It was Hannah who spotted the first person: an old man, bent double, sitting on the edge of the pavement as if nothing in particular had taken place. They drove past him at sixty miles per hour, but he didn't even look up.

Aziz swung into the next road and found himself facing a group of young looters carrying off televisions and electronic equipment. They scattered when they saw the truck. Around the next corner there were more looters, but still no sign of police or soldiers.

When Aziz spotted the first dark-green uniforms he swerved quickly right, down a side street that on any other Wednesday would have been packed with shoppers and where a vehicle would have been lucky to average more than five miles per hour. But today Aziz managed to keep the speedometer above fifty. He turned right again, and they saw some of the first of the locals who had ventured back onto the streets. Once they had reached the end of the road, Aziz was able to join the main thoroughfare out of Baghdad. The traffic was still light.

Aziz eased the truck across into the outside lane, checking his rear-view mirror every few seconds and complying with the speed limit of fifty miles per hour. 'Never get stopped for the wrong reasons,' Kratz had warned him a thousand times.

When Aziz switched his sidelights on, Scott's hopes began to rise. Although the two hours had to be up, he doubted that anybody would be out searching for them yet, and it was well understood that with every mile out of Baghdad the citizens became less and less loyal to Saddam.

Once Aziz had left the Baghdad boundary sign behind him he pushed the speedometer up to sixty. 'Give me twenty minutes, Allah,' he said. 'Give me twenty minutes and I'll get them to Castle Post.'

'Castle Post?' said Scott. 'We're not on a Red Indian scouting mission.'

Aziz laughed. 'No, Professor, it's the site of a First World War British Army post, where we can hide for the night. If I can get there before –' All three of them spotted the first army lorry coming towards them. Aziz swung off to the left, skidded into a side road, and was immediately forced to drop his speed.

'So now where are we heading?' asked Scott.

'Khan Beni Saad,' said Aziz, 'the village where I was born. It will only be possible for us to stay for one night, but no one will think of looking for us there. Tomorrow, Professor, you will have to decide which of the six borders we're going to cross.'

General Hamil had been pacing around his office for the past hour. The two hours had long passed, and he was starting to wonder if Kratz might have got the better of him. But he couldn't work out how.

He was even beginning to regret that he had killed the man. If Kratz had still been alive, at least he could have fallen back on the tried and trusted method of torture. Now he would never know how he would have responded to his particular shaving technique.

Hamil had already ordered a reluctant lieutenant and his platoon back to the basement of the Ba'ath headquarters. The lieutenant had returned swiftly to report that the safe door was wide open and the truck had disappeared, as had the document that had been hanging on the wall. The General smiled. He remained confident that he was in possession of the original Declaration, but he extracted the parchment from the cylinder and laid it on his desk to double-check. When he came to the word 'British', he turned first white, and then, by several degrees, deeper and deeper shades of red.

He immediately gave an order to cancel all military leave, and then commanded five divisions of the elite guard to mount a search for the terrorists. But he had no way of knowing how much start they had on him, how far they might have already travelled, and in which direction.

However, he did know that they couldn't remain on the main roads in that truck for long, without being spotted. Once it was dark, they would probably retreat into the desert to rest overnight. But they would have to come out the following morning, when they must surely try to cross one of the six borders. The General had already given an order that if even one of the terrorists managed to cross any border, guards from every customs post would be arrested and jailed, whether they were on duty or not. The two soldiers who were supposed to have closed the safe door had already been shot for not carrying out his orders, and the Major detailed to supervise the moving of the safe had been immediately arrested. At least Major Saeed's decision to take his own life had saved Hamil the trouble of a court martial: within an hour the Major had been found hanging in his cell. Obviously leaving a coil of rope in the middle of the floor below a hook in the ceiling had proved to be a compelling enough hint. And as for the two young medical students who'd been responsible for the injections, and who had witnessed his conversation with Kratz, they were already on their way to the southern borders, to serve with a less than elite regiment. They were such nice-looking boys, the General thought; he gave them a week at the most.

Hamil picked up the phone and dialled a private number that would connect him to the palace. He needed to be certain that he was the first person to explain to the President what had taken place that afternoon.

33

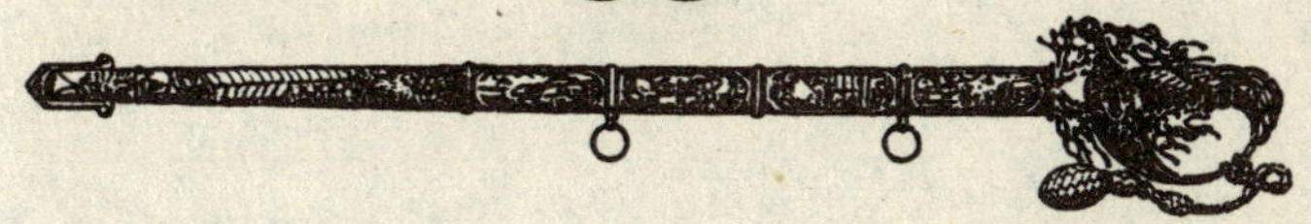

SCOTT HAD ALWAYS CONSIDERED his own countrymen to be an hospitable race, but he had never experienced such a welcome as Aziz's family gave to the three strangers.

Khan Beni Saad, the village in which Aziz was born, had, he told them, just over 250 inhabitants at the last count, and barely survived on the income it derived from selling its small crop of oranges, tangerines and dates to the housewives of Kirkuk and Arbil.

The chief of the tribe, who turned out to be one of Aziz's uncles, immediately opened his little stone home to them so that they could make use of the one bath in the village. The women of the house – there seemed to be a lot of them – kept boiling water until all of the visitors were pronounced clean.

When Scott finally emerged from the chief's home, he found a table had been set up under a clump of citrus trees in the Huwaider fields. It was laden with strange fish, meat, fruit and vegetables. He feared they must have gathered something from every home in the village.

Under a clear starlit night, they devoured the fresh food and drank mountain water that, if bottled, a Californian would happily have paid a fortune for.

But Scott's thoughts kept returning to the fact that tomorrow they would have to leave these idyllic

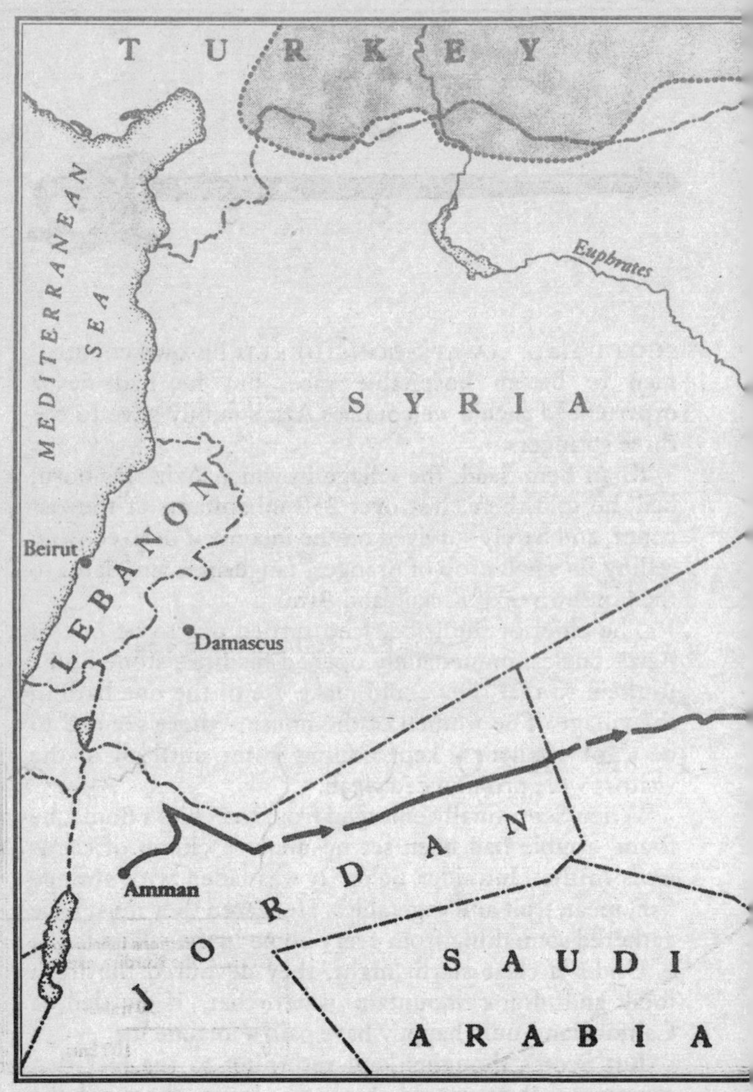
TURKEY
MEDITERRANEAN SEA
Euphrates
SYRIA
LEBANON
Beirut
Damascus
Amman
JORDAN
SAUDI ARABIA

Silope
KURDISTAN
Arbil
Tigris
Kirkuk
Tuz
Khurmatoo
IRAN
Baquba
BAGHDAD
Khan Beni
Saad
IRAQ
Regions inhabited by
the Kurdish nation
0
50 miles
0
100 kms

surroundings, and that he would somehow have to get them all across one of the six borders.

After coffee had been served in various different-sized cups and mugs, the chief rose from his place at the head of the table to make a speech of welcome, which Aziz translated. Scott made a short reply which was applauded even before Aziz had been given the chance to interpret what he had said.

'That's one thing they have in common with us,' said Hannah, taking Scott's hand. 'They admire brevity.'

The chief ended the evening with an offer for which Scott thanked him, but felt unable to accept. He wanted to order all of his family out of the little house so that his guests could sleep indoors.

Scott continued to protest until Aziz explained, 'You must agree, or you insult his home by suggesting it is not good enough for you to rest in. And by the way, it is an Arab tradition that the greatest compliment you can pay your host is to make your woman pregnant while she sleeps under his roof.' Aziz shrugged.

Scott lay awake most of the night, staring through the glassless window, while Hannah hardly stirred in his arms. Having attempted to pay the chief the greatest possible compliment, Scott's mind went back to the problem of getting his team over one of the borders and ensuring that the Declaration of Independence was returned safely to Washington.

When the first ray of light crept across the woven rug that covered their bed, Scott released Hannah and kissed her on the forehead. He slipped from under the sheets to find that the little tin bath was already full of warm water, and the women had begun boiling more urns over an open fire.

Once Scott was dressed, he spent an hour studying maps of the country, searching for possible routes across

Iraq's six borders. He quickly dismissed Syria and Iran as impossible, because the armies of both would be happy to slaughter them on sight. He also felt that to return over the Jordanian border would be far too great a risk. By the time Hannah had joined him he had also dismissed Saudi Arabia as too well guarded, and was now down to only five routes and two borders.

As his hosts began to prepare breakfast, Scott and Hannah wandered down into the village hand in hand, as any lovers might on a summer morning. The locals smiled, and some bowed. Although none could hold a conversation with them, they all spoke so eloquently with their eyes that they both understood.

Once they had reached the end of the village, they turned and strolled back up the path towards the chief's house. Cohen was frying eggs on an open fire, and Hannah stopped to watch how the women baked the thin, circular pieces of bread which, covered in honey, were a feast in themselves. The chief, once again sitting at the head of the table, beckoned Scott to the place beside him. Cohen had already taken a seat on a stool and was about to begin his breakfast when a goat walked up and tugged the eggs straight off the plate. Hannah laughed and cracked Cohen another egg before he had a chance to voice his opinion.

Scott spread some honey on a piece of warm bread, and a woman placed a mug of goat's milk in front of him.

'Worked out what we have to do next, have you, Professor?' asked Cohen as Hannah dropped a second fried egg on to his plate. In one sentence, he had brought them all back to reality.

A villager came up to the table, knelt by the side of the chief and whispered in his ear. The message was passed on to Aziz.

'Bad news,' Aziz told them. 'There are soldiers blocking all the roads that lead back to the main highway.'

'Then we'll have to go across the desert,' said Scott. He unfolded his map and spread it across the table. Alternative routes were highlighted by a dozen blue felt-tip lines. He pointed to a path leading to a road which would take them to the city of Khalis.

'That is not a path,' said Aziz. 'It was once a river, but it dried up many years ago. We could walk along it, but we would have to leave the truck behind.'

'It won't be enough to leave the truck,' said Scott. 'We'll have to destroy it. If it were ever found by Saddam's soldiers, they would raze the village to the ground and massacre your people.'

The chief looked perplexed as Aziz translated all Scott had said. The old man stroked the rough morning stubble on his chin and smiled as Scott and Hannah listened to his judgement, unable to understand a word.

'My uncle says you must have his car,' Aziz translated. 'It is old, but he hopes that it still runs well.'

'He is kind,' said Scott. 'But if we cannot drive a truck across the desert, how can we possibly go by car?'

'He understands your problem,' said Aziz. 'He says you must take the car to pieces bit by bit, and his people will carry it the twelve miles across the desert until you reach the road that leads to Khalis. Then you can put it together again.'

'We cannot accept such a gesture,' said Scott. 'He is too generous. We will walk and find some form of transport when we reach Huwaider.' He pointed to the first village along the road.

Aziz translated once again: his uncle looked sad and murmured a few words. 'He says it is not really his car, it was his brother's car. It now belongs to me.'

For the first time, Scott realised that Aziz's father had been the village chief, and how much his uncle was willing to risk to save them from being captured by Saddam's troops.

'But even if we could take the car to pieces and put it together again, what about army patrols once we reach that road?' he asked. 'By now thousands of Hamil's men are bound to be out there searching for us.'

'But not on those roads,' Aziz replied. 'The army will stick to the highway. They realise that's our only hope of getting across the border. No, our first problem will come when we reach the roadside check at Khalis.' He moved his finger a few inches across the map. 'There's bound to be at least a couple of soldiers on duty there.'

Scott studied the different routes again while Aziz listened to his uncle.

'And could we get as far as Tuz Khurmatoo without having to use the highway?' asked Scott, not looking up from the map.

'Yes, there's a longer route, through the hills, that the army would never consider, because they'd run the risk of being attacked by the Peshmerga guerrillas so near the border with Kurdistan. But once you've gone through Tuz Khurmatoo it's only a couple of miles to the main highway, though it's still another forty-five miles from there, with no other way of crossing the border.'

Scott held his head in his hands and didn't speak for some moments. 'So if we took that route we would be committed to crossing the border at Kirkuk,' he eventually said. 'Where both sides could prove to be unfriendly.'

The chief started tapping Kirkuk on the map with his finger while talking urgently to his nephew.

'My uncle says Kirkuk is our best chance. Most of the inhabitants are Kurdish and hate Saddam Hussein. Even the Iraqi soldiers have been known to defect and become Kurdish Peshmergas.'

'But how will they know which side we're on?' asked Scott.

'My uncle will get a message to the Peshmergas, so that when you reach the border they will do everything they can to help you to cross it. It's not an official border, but once you're in Kurdistan you'll be safe.'

'The Kurds sound our best bet,' said Hannah, who had been listening intently. 'Especially if they believe our original mission was to kill Saddam.'

'It might just work, sir,' said Cohen. 'That is, if the car's up to it.'

'You're the mechanic, Cohen, so only you can tell us if it's possible.'

Once Aziz had translated Scott's words the chief rose to his feet and led them to the back of his house. He came to a halt beside a large oblong object covered by a black sheet. He and Aziz lifted off the cover. Scott couldn't believe his eyes.

'A pink Caddy?' he said.

'A classic 1956 Sedan de Ville, to be exact, sir,' said Cohen, rubbing his hands with delight. He opened the long, heavy door and climbed behind the vast steering wheel. He pulled a lever under the dashboard and the bonnet flicked up. He got out, lifted the bonnet and studied the engine for some minutes.

'Not bad,' he said. 'If I can nick a few parts from the truck, I'll give you a racing car within a couple of hours.'

Scott checked his watch. 'I can only spare you an hour if we're hoping to cross the border tonight.'

Scott and Hannah returned to the house and once again pored over the map. The road Aziz had recommended was roughly twelve miles away, but across terrain that would be hard going even if they were carrying nothing.

'It could take hours,' Scott said.

'What's the alternative if we can't use the highway?' asked Hannah.

While she and Scott continued working on the route and Cohen on the car, Aziz rounded up thirty of the strongest men in the village. At a few minutes past the hour, Cohen reappeared in the house, his hands, arms, face and hair covered in oil.

'It's ready to be taken apart, Professor.'

'Well done. But we'll have to get rid of the truck first,' said Scott as he rose from the table.

'That won't be possible, sir,' said Cohen. 'Not now that I've removed one or two of the best parts of its engine. That Cadillac should be able to do over a hundred miles per hour,' he said, with some pride. 'In third gear.'

Scott laughed, and accompanied by Aziz went in search of the chief. Once again he explained the problem.

This time the chief's face showed no anxiety. Aziz translated his thoughts. ' "Do not fear, my friend," he says. "While you are marching across the desert we will strip the truck and bury each piece in a place Saddam's soldiers could never hope to discover in a thousand years." '

Scott looked apprehensive, but Aziz nodded his agreement. Without waiting for Scott's opinion the chief led his nephew to the back of the house, where they found Cohen supervising the stripping of the Cadillac and the distribution of its pieces among the chosen thirty.

Four men were to carry the engine on a makeshift stretcher, and another six would lift the chrome body onto their shoulders like pallbearers. Four more each carried a wheel with its white-rimmed tyre, while another four transported the chassis. Two held onto the red-and-white leather front seat, another two the back seat, and one the dashboard. Cohen continued to distribute the remaining pieces of the Cadillac until he came to the back of the line, where three children who looked no more than ten or eleven were given responsibility for two five-gallon cans of petrol and a tool bag. Only the roof was to be left behind.

Aziz's uncle led his people to the last house in the village so he could watch his guests begin their journey towards the horizon.

Scott shook hands with the chief, but could find no words adequate to thank him. 'Give me a call the next time you're passing through New Haven,' was what he would have said to a fellow American.

'I will return in better times,' he told the old man, and Aziz translated.

'My people wait for that day.'

Scott turned to watch Cohen, compass in hand, leading his improbable platoon on what appeared likely to be an endless journey. He took one of the five-gallon cans from the smallest of the children, and pointed back towards the village, but the little boy shook his head and quickly grabbed Scott's canvas bag.

Would history ever reveal this particular mode of transport for the Declaration of Independence, Scott wondered, as Cohen shouted 'Forward!'

General Hamil continued to pace round his office, as he waited for the phone to ring.

When Saddam had learned the news of Major Saeed's incompetence in allowing the terrorists to escape with the Declaration, he was only furious that he had not been able personally to end the man's life.

The only order he had given the General was that a message should be put out on state radio and television stations hourly, stating that there had been an attempt on his life which had failed, but that the Zionist terrorists were still at large. Full descriptions of the would-be assassins were given, and he asked his beloved countrymen to help him in his quest to hunt down the infidels.

Had the matter been less urgent, the General would have counselled against releasing such information, on the grounds that most of those who came across the terrorists might want to help them, or at best turn a blind eye. The only advice he did give his leader was to suggest that a large reward should be offered for their capture. Enlightened self-interest, he had found, could so often overcome almost any scruples.

The General came to a halt in front of a map pinned to the wall behind his desk, temporarily covering a portrait of Saddam. His eye passed down the many thin red lines that wriggled between Baghdad and Iraq's borders. There were a hundred villages on both sides of every one of the roads, and the General was painfully aware that most of them would be only too happy to harbour the fugitives.

And then he recollected one of the names Kratz had given him. Aziz Zeebari – a common enough name, yet it had been nagging at him the whole morning.

'Aziz Zeebari . . . Aziz Zeebari . . . Aziz Zeebari . . .' he repeated. And then he remembered. He had executed a man of that name who had been involved in an attempted coup about seven years before. Could it possibly have been the traitor's father?

The load-bearers halted every fifteen minutes to rest, change responsibilities and place the strain on yet-untested muscles. 'Pit stops', Cohen called them. They managed two miles in the first hour, and between them drank far more water than any car would have devoured.

When Scott checked his watch at midday, he estimated that they had only covered a little over two thirds of the distance to the road: it had been a long time since they had lost sight of the village but there was still no sign of life on the horizon. The sun beat down as they continued their journey, the pace slowing with each mile.

It was the eyes of a ten-year-old child that were the first to see movement. He ran to the front and pointed. Scott could see nothing as the little boy jogged ahead, and it was to be another forty minutes before they could all clearly see the dusty road. The sight made them quicken their pace.

Once they reached the side of the road, Aziz gave the order that the pieces of the car should be lowered gently to the ground, and a little girl, who Scott hadn't noticed before, handed out bread, goats' cheese and water while they rested.

Cohen was the first up and began walking around his platoon, checking on the various pieces. By the time he had returned to the chassis, they were all impatient to put the car together again.

Scott sat on the ground and watched as thirty untrained mechanics, under the direction of Sergeant Cohen, slowly bolted the old Cadillac together piece by piece. When the last wheel had been screwed on, Scott had to admit it *looked* like a car, but wondered if the old veteran would ever be able to start.

All the villagers surrounded the massive pink vehicle as Cohen sat in the driver's seat.

Aziz waited until the children had emptied their last drop of petrol into the tank. He then screwed on the big steel cap and shouted, 'Go for it!'

Cohen turned the key in the ignition.

The engine turned over slowly, but wouldn't catch. Cohen leaped out, lifted the bonnet and asked Aziz to take his place behind the wheel. He made a slight re-adjustment to the fan belt, checked the distributor and cleaned the spark plugs of the last few remaining grains of sand before screwing them in tightly. He stuck his head out from under the bonnet.

'Have a go, Kurd.'

Aziz turned the key and pressed the accelerator. The engine turned over a little more quickly but still didn't want to start. Sixty eyes stared beneath the bonnet, but offered no advice as Cohen spent several more minutes working on the distributor.

'Once again, and give it more throttle!' he shouted. Aziz switched on the ignition. The chug became a churn, and then suddenly a roar as Aziz pressed the accelerator – a noise only exceeded by the cheers of the villagers.

Cohen took Aziz's place in the front and lifted the gear lever on the steering column up into first. But the car refused to budge, as the wheels spun round and it bedded itself deeper and deeper into the sand. Cohen turned off the engine and jumped out. Sixty hands were flattened against the car as it was rocked backwards and forwards, and then, with one great shove, it was eased out of its deep trough. The villagers pushed it a further twenty yards and then waited for the Sergeant's next order.

Cohen pointed to the little girl who had distributed the food. She came shyly forward and he lifted her into the front of the car. With sign language, Cohen instructed her to kneel by the accelerator pedal and press down. Without getting into the car, Cohen leaned across, checked that the gears were in neutral, and switched on the engine. The little girl continued to push on the accelerator with both hands, and the engine revved into action. She immediately burst into tears, as the villagers cheered even louder. Cohen quickly lifted the little girl out onto the sand and then beckoned to Aziz.

'You're about half my weight, mate, so get in, put it into first gear and see if you can keep it going for about a hundred yards. If you can, we'll all jump in. If you can't, we'll have to push the bloody thing all the way to the border.'

Aziz stepped gingerly into the Cadillac. Sitting on the edge of the leather seat he gently lifted the lever into first gear and pressed down on the accelerator. The car inched forward and the villagers began to cheer again as Scott, Hannah and Cohen ran along beside it.

Hannah opened the passenger door, pushed the seat forward and jumped into the back as the car continued at its slow pace. Cohen leaped in after her and shouted, 'Second gear!'

Aziz pulled the lever down, across and up. The car lurched forward.

'That's third, you stupid Kurd!' shouted Cohen. He turned to see Scott running almost flat out. Cohen reached across to hold the door open as Scott threw his bag into the back. Scott leaped in and Cohen grabbed him round the shoulders. Scott's head landed in Aziz's lap, but although the Kurd swerved the car still kept going on the firmer sand. Aziz continued swinging the car from side to side to avoid the mounds of sand that had blown on to the road.

'I can see why there aren't likely to be any army patrols on this road,' was Cohen's only comment.

Scott turned back to see the villagers waving frantically. Returning their wave seemed inadequate after all they had done. He hadn't thanked them properly or even said goodbye.

The villagers didn't move until the car was out of sight.

* * *

General Hamil swung round, angry that anyone had dared to enter his office without knocking. His ADC came to a halt in front of his desk. He was shaking, only too aware of the mistake he had made. The General raised his swagger stick and was about to strike the young officer across the face when he bleated out, 'We've discovered the village that the traitor Aziz Zeebari comes from, General.'

Hamil lowered his arm slowly until the swagger stick came to rest on the officer's right shoulder. The tip pushed forward until it was about an inch away from the ball of his right eye.

'Where?'

'Khan Beni Saad,' said the young man in terror.

'Show me.'

The Lieutenant ran over to the map, studied it for a few moments and then placed a finger on a village about ten miles north-east of Baghdad.

General Hamil stared at the spot and smiled for the first time that day. He returned to his desk, picked up the phone and barked out an order.

Within an hour, hundreds of troops would be swarming all over the little village.

Even if Khan Beni Saad did only have a population of 250, the General felt confident someone would talk, however young.

Aziz was able to keep up a steady thirty miles per hour while Scott tried to work out where they were on the map. He couldn't pinpoint their exact location until they had been driving for nearly an hour, when they came across a crude handpainted signpost lying in the road that read 'Khalis 25km'.

'Keep going for now,' said Scott. 'But we'll have to

stop a couple of miles outside town so I can figure out how we get past the checkpoint.'

Scott's confidence in the old chief's judgement that there would be no army vehicles on that road was growing with every mile of flat desert road they covered. He continued to study the map carefully, now certain of the route that would have to be taken if they hoped to cross the border that day.

'So what *do* we do when we reach the checkpoint?' asked Cohen.

'Maybe it'll be easier than we think,' said Scott. 'Don't forget, they're looking for four people in a massive army truck.'

'But we *are* four people.'

'We won't be by the time we reach the checkpoint,' explained Scott, 'because by then you and I will be in the boot.'

Cohen scowled.

'Just be thankful it's a Caddy,' said Aziz, grinning as he tried to maintain the steady speed.

'Perhaps I should take over the wheel now,' said Cohen.

'Not here,' said Scott. 'While we're on these roads, Aziz stays put.'

It was Hannah who saw her first. 'What the hell does she think she's up to?' she said, pointing to a woman who had jumped out into the middle of the road and was waving her arms excitedly.

Scott gripped the side of the window ledge as Cohen leaned forward to get a clearer view.

'Don't stop,' said Scott. 'Swerve round her if you have to.' Suddenly Aziz began laughing.

'What's so funny, Kurd?' asked Cohen, keeping his eyes fixed on the woman, who remained determinedly in the middle of the road.

'It's only my cousin Jasmin.'

'Another cousin?' said Hannah.

'We are all cousins in my tribe,' Aziz explained as he brought the Cadillac to a halt in front of her. He leaped out of the car and threw his arms around the young woman, as the others joined them.

'Not bad,' said Cohen when he was finally introduced to cousin Jasmin, who hadn't stopped talking even when she shook hands with Scott and Hannah.

'So what's she jabbering on about, then?' demanded Cohen, before Aziz had been given the chance to translate his cousin's words.

'It seems the Professor was right. The soldiers have been warned to look out for an army truck being driven by four terrorists. But her uncle has already been in touch this morning to warn her we'd be in the Cadillac.'

'Then it must be a hell of a risk to try and get past them,' said Hannah.

'A risk,' agreed Aziz, 'but not a hell of a risk. Jasmin crosses this checkpoint twice a day, every day, to sell oranges, tangerines and dates from our village. So she's well known to them, and so is my uncle's car. My uncle says she must be in the Cadillac when we go through the checkpoint. That way they won't be suspicious.'

'But if they decide to search the boot?'

'Then they won't get their daily ration of cigarettes, or fruit for their families, will they? You see, they all take it for granted we must be smuggling something.'

Jasmin started chattering again and Aziz listened dutifully. 'She says you must all climb into the boot before someone passing spots us.'

'It's still a hell of a risk, Professor,' said Cohen.

'It's just as big a risk for Jasmin,' said Scott, 'and I don't see any other route.' He folded up the map, walked round to the back of the car, opened the boot and climbed in. Hannah and Cohen followed without another word.

'Not as comfortable as the safe,' remarked Hannah as she put her arms round Scott. Aziz wedged the bag between her and Cohen. Hannah laughed.

'One bang on the side of the door,' said Aziz, 'and I'll be stopping at the checkpoint.'

He slammed down the boot. Jasmin grabbed her bags from the side of the road and jumped in next to her cousin.

The three of them in the boot heard the engine splutter into action and begin its more stately progress over the last few miles towards Khalis.

Jasmin used the time to brief Aziz on her routine whenever she crossed the checkpoint.

34

THE CHIEF WAS HANGED FIRST. Then his brothers, one by one, in front of the rest of the village, but none of them uttered a word. Then they moved on to his cousins, until a twelve-year-old girl, who hoped to save her father's life, told them about the strangers who had stayed in the chief's house the previous night.

They promised the little girl that her father would be saved if she told them everything she knew. She pointed out into the desert to show them where they had buried the lorry. Twenty minutes of digging by the soldiers and they were able to confirm that she had been telling the truth.

They contacted General Hamil by field phone. He found it hard to believe that thirty of the Zeebari tribe had taken the chief's Cadillac to pieces and carried it bit by bit across the open desert.

'Oh, yes,' the little girl assured them. 'I know it's true because my brother carried one of the wheels all the way to the road on the other side of the desert,' she declared, pointing proudly towards the horizon.

General Hamil listened carefully to the information over the phone before ordering that the girl's father and brother should also be hanged.

He returned to the map on the wall and quickly pinpointed the only possible road they could have taken.

His eye moved along the path across a stretch of desert until it joined another winding road, and then he realised which town they would have to pass through.

He looked at the clock on his desk: 4.39. 'Get me the checkpoint at Khalis,' he instructed the young Lieutenant.

Aziz saw a stationary van in the distance being inspected by a soldier. Jasmin warned him it was the checkpoint and tipped out the contents of one of her bags onto the seat between them.

Aziz banged on the side of his door, relieved to see there were only two soldiers in sight, and that one of them was sleeping in a comfortable old chair on the other side of the road.

When the car came to a halt Scott could hear laughter coming from somewhere. Aziz passed a packet of Rothmans to the guard.

The soldier was just about to wave them through when the other guard stirred from his drowsy slumber like a cat who had been resting for hours on a radiator. He pushed himself up, moved slowly towards the car, and looked over it with admiration, as he had done many times before. He began to stroll around it. As he passed the boot he gave it a loving slap with the palm of his hand. It flicked open a few inches. Scott pulled it gently closed as Jasmin dropped a carton of two hundred Rothmans on the ground by her side of the car.

The border guard moved quickly for the first time that day. Jasmin gave him a smile as he retrieved the cigarettes, and whispered something in his ear. The soldier looked at Aziz and started laughing, as a large lorry stacked with crates of beer came to a halt behind them.

'Move on, move on,' shouted the first soldier, as the

sight of greater rewards caught his eye. Aziz quickly obeyed and lurched forward in second gear, nearly throwing Cohen and the holdall out of the back.

'What did you say to that soldier?' asked Aziz once they were out of earshot.

'I told him you were gay, but I would be returning on my own later.'

'Have you no family pride?' asked Aziz.

'Certainly,' said Jasmin. 'But he is also a cousin.'

On Jasmin's advice, Aziz took the longer southern route around the town. He was unable to avoid all the potholes, and from time to time he heard groans coming from the boot. Jasmin pointed to a junction ahead of them, and told Aziz that that was where he should stop. She gathered up her bags, leaving some fruit on the seat between them. Aziz came to a halt by a road that led back into the centre of the town. Jasmin jumped out, smiled and waved. Aziz waved back, and wondered when he would see his cousin again.

He drove on alone to the far side of the town, still unable to risk letting his colleagues out of the boot while the few locals around could observe what was going on.

Once Khalis was a couple of miles behind him, Aziz came to a halt at a crossroads which displayed two signposts. One read 'Tuz Khurmatoo 120km', and the other 'Tuz Khurmatoo 170km'. He checked in every direction before climbing out of the car, opening the boot and letting the three baggage passengers tumble out onto the road. While they stretched their limbs and took deep breaths of air, Aziz pointed to the signposts. Scott didn't need to look at the map to decide which road they would have to take.

'We must take the longer route,' he said, 'and hope that they still think we're in the truck.' Hannah slammed down the boot with feeling before they all four jumped back into the car.

Aziz averaged forty miles an hour on the winding road, his three passengers ducking out of sight whenever another vehicle appeared on the horizon.

The four of them devoured the fresh fruit Jasmin had left on the front seat.

When they passed a signpost indicating twenty kilometres to Tuz Khurmatoo Scott said to Aziz, 'I want you to stop a little way outside the village and go in alone before we decide if it's safe for us to drive straight through. Don't forget it's only another three miles beyond Tuz Khurmatoo to the highway, so the place could be swarming with soldiers.'

'And to the Kurdish border?' asked Hannah.

'About forty-five miles,' said Scott as he continued to study the map. Aziz drove for another twenty minutes before he came over the brow of a hill and could see the outline of a village nestling in the valley. A few moments later he pulled the car off the road and parked it under a row of citrus trees that sheltered them from the sun and the prying eyes of those in passing vehicles. Aziz listened carefully to Scott's instructions, got out of the car and jogged off in the direction of Tuz Khurmatoo.

General Hamil was too furious to speak when the young Lieutenant informed him that the Cadillac had passed through the Khalis checkpoint less than an hour before, and neither of the soldiers on duty had bothered to check the boot.

After a minimum of torture, one of them had confessed that the terrorists must have been helped by a young girl who regularly passed through the checkpoint.

'She will never pass through it again,' had been the General's sole observation.

The only other piece of information they were able to get out of the soldiers was that whoever had been driving the car was the girl's cousin, and a homosexual. Hamil wondered how they could possibly know that.

Once again, the General returned to the map on the wall behind his desk. He had already given orders for an army of helicopters, lorries, tanks and motorcycles to cover every inch of the road between Khalis and the border, but still no one had reported seeing a Cadillac on the highway. He was mystified, knowing they couldn't possibly have turned back or they would have run straight into his troops.

His eyes searched every route between the checkpoint and the border yet again. 'Ah,' he said finally, 'they must have taken the road through the hills.' The General ran his finger along a thin winding red line until it joined the main highway.

'So that's where you are,' he said, before bellowing out some new orders.

It was almost an hour before Cohen announced, 'One Kurd heading towards us, sir.'

As Aziz came running up the slope the grin remained on his face. He had been into Tuz Khurmatoo and he was able to reassure them that the village was going about its business as usual. But the government radio was blasting out a warning to be on the lookout for four terrorists who had attempted to assassinate the Great Leader, so all the main roads were now crawling with soldiers. 'They've got good descriptions of all four of us, but the radio bulletin an hour ago was still saying we were in the truck.'

'Right, Aziz,' said Scott, 'drive us through the village. Hannah, sit in the front with Aziz. The Sergeant and I will lie down in the back. Once we're on the other side of Tuz we'll keep out of sight and only continue on to the border after it's dark.'

Aziz took his place behind the wheel, and the Cadillac began its slow journey into Tuz.

The main road through the village must have been about three hundred yards long and just about wide enough to take two cars. Hannah looked at the little timber shops and the men who were growing old sitting on steps and leaning against walls. A dirty old Cadillac travelling slowly through the village, she thought, would probably be the highlight of their day, until she saw the vehicle at the other end of the road.

'There's a jeep coming towards us,' she said calmly. 'Four men, one of them sitting behind what looks like an anti-aircraft gun mounted on the back.'

'Just keep driving slowly, Aziz,' said Scott. 'And Hannah, keep talking us through it.'

'They're about a hundred yards away from us now and beginning to take an interest.' Cohen pointed to the tool bag and grabbed a wrench. Scott selected a spanner as they both turned over slowly and rested on their knees.

'The jeep has swung across in front of us,' said Hannah. 'We're going to be forced to stop in about five seconds.'

'Does it still look as if there are four of them?' asked Scott.

'Yes,' said Hannah. 'I can't see any more.'

The Cadillac came to a halt.

'The jeep has stopped only a few yards in front of us. One of the soldiers is getting out and another is following. Two are staying in the jeep. One is behind the mounted gun and the other is still at the wheel. We'll take the first two,' said Hannah. 'You'll have to deal with the two in the jeep.'

'Understood,' said Scott.

The first soldier reached the driver's side as the second passed the bumper on Hannah's right. Both Aziz and Hannah had their outside hands on the armrests, their doors already an inch open.

The instant Aziz saw the first soldier glance into the back and go for his gun, he swung his door open so fast that the crack of the soldier's knees sounded like a bullet as he collapsed to the ground. Aziz was out of the car and on top of him long before he had time to recover. The second soldier ran towards Hannah as Scott leaped out of the car. Hannah delivered one blow to his carotid artery and another to the base of his spine as he tried to pull out his gun. A bullet would not have killed him any quicker. The third soldier started firing from the back of the jeep. Cohen dived out into the road, and the fourth soldier jumped from behind the wheel and ran towards him, firing his pistol. Cohen hurled the wrench at him, causing him to step to one side and straight into the firing line of the mounted gun. The bullets stopped immediately, but Cohen was already at his throat. The soldier sank as if he had been hit by a ton of bricks, and his gun flew across the road. Cohen gave him one blow to the jugular vein and another to the back of the neck: he went into spasms and began wriggling on the ground. Cohen quickly turned his attention to the man seated behind the gun, who was lining him up in his sights. At ten yards' distance, Cohen had no hope of reaching him, so he dived for the side of the car as bullets sprayed into the open door, two of them ripping into his left leg. Scott was now running towards the jeep from the other side. As the soldier swung the gun round to face him, Scott propelled himself through the air and onto the top of the jeep.

Bullets flew everywhere as they tumbled clumsily off the back, Scott still clinging onto his spanner. They were both quickly on their feet, and Scott brought the spanner down across the gunner's neck – the soldier raised an arm to fend off the blow, but Scott's left knee jack-knifed into his crotch. The gunner sank to the ground as the second blow from the spanner found its mark and broke the soldier's neck cleanly. He lay splayed out on the road, looking like a breast-stroke swimmer halfway through a stroke. Scott stood over him, mesmerised, until Aziz dived at his legs and knocked him to the ground. Scott couldn't stop shaking.

'It's always hardest the first time,' was the Kurd's only comment.

The four of them were now facing outwards, covering every angle as they waited for the locals to react. Cohen climbed unsteadily up into the jeep, blood pouring from his leg, and took his place behind the mounted gun. 'Don't fire unless I say so,' shouted Scott as he checked up and down the road. There wasn't a person to be seen in either direction.

'On your left!' said Hannah, and Scott turned to see an old man dressed in a long white dishdash with a black-and-white spotted keffiyeh on his head, a thick belt hung loosely around his waist. He was walking slowly towards them, his hands held high in the air.

Scott's eyes never left the old man, who came to a halt a few yards away from the Cadillac.

'I have been sent by the village elders because I am the only one who speaks English,' he said. The man was trembling and the words came stumbling out. 'We believe you are the terrorists who came to kill Saddam.'

Scott said nothing.

'Please go. Leave our village and go quickly. Take the jeep and we will bury the soldiers. Then no one will ever know you were here. If you do not, Saddam will murder us all. Every one of us.'

'Tell your people we wish them no harm,' said Scott.

'I believe you,' said the old man, 'but please, go.'

Scott ran forward and stripped the tallest soldier of his uniform while Cohen kept his gun trained on the old man. Aziz stripped the other three while Hannah grabbed Scott's bag from the Cadillac before jumping into the back of the jeep.

Aziz threw the uniforms into the jeep and then leaped into the driving seat. The engine was still running. He put the vehicle into reverse and swung round in a semicircle as Scott took his place in the front. Aziz began to drive slowly out of Tuz Khurmatoo. Cohen turned the gun round in the direction of the village, at the same time thumping his left leg with his clenched fist.

Scott continued to look behind him as a few of the villagers moved tentatively out into the road and started to drag the soldiers unceremoniously away. Another climbed into the Cadillac and began to reverse it down a side road. A few moments later they had all disappeared from sight. Scott turned to face the road ahead of him.

'It's about another three miles to the highway,' said Aziz. 'What do you want me to do?'

'We've only got one chance of getting across that border,' said Scott, 'so for now pull over into that clump of trees. We can't risk going out onto the highway until it's pitch dark.' He checked the time. It was 7.35.

Hannah felt blood dripping onto her face. She looked up, and saw the deep wounds in Cohen's leg. She immediately tore off the corner of her yashmak and tried to stem the flow of blood.

'You all right, Cohen?' asked Scott anxiously.

'No worse than when I was bitten by a woman in Tangier,' he replied.

Aziz began laughing.

'How can you laugh?' said Hannah, continuing to clean the wound.

'Because he was the reason she bit me,' said Cohen.

After Hannah had completed the bandaging, the four of them changed into the Iraqi uniforms. For an hour they kept their eyes on the road, looking for any sign of more soldiers. A few villagers on donkeys, and more on foot, passed them in both directions, but the only vehicle they saw was an old tractor that chugged by on its way back to the village at the end of a day's service.

As the minutes slipped by, it became obvious that the villagers had kept to their promise and made no contact with any army patrols.

When Scott could no longer see the road in front of them, he went over his plan for the last time. All of them accepted that their options were limited.

The nearest border was forty-five miles away, but Scott now accepted the danger they could bring to any village simply by passing through it. He didn't feel his plan was foolproof, far from it, but they couldn't wait in the hills much longer. It would only be a short time before Iraqi soldiers were swarming all over the area.

Scott checked the uniforms. As long as they kept on the move, it would be hard for anyone to identify them in the dark as anything other than part of an army patrol. But once they reached the highway, he knew they couldn't afford to stay still for more than a few seconds. Everything depended on how close they could get to the border post without being spotted.

When Scott gave the order, Aziz swung the jeep onto the winding road to begin the three-mile journey to the highway. He covered the distance in five minutes, and during that time they didn't come across another vehicle. But once they hit the highway, they found the road was covered with lorries, jeeps, even tanks, travelling in both directions.

None of them saw the two motorcycles, the tank and three lorries that swung off the highway and headed at speed down the little road towards Tuz Khurmatoo.

Aziz went as fast as he could, while Cohen remained seated on the back behind the gun. Scott watched the road ahead of him, his beret pulled well down. Hannah sat below Cohen, motionless, a gun in her hand. The first road sign indicated that it was sixty kilometres to the border. For a moment Scott was distracted by an oil well that kept pumping away on the far side of the road. Nobody spoke as the distance to Kirkuk descended from fifty-five to forty-six, to thirty-two, but with each sign and each new oil well, the traffic became heavier and their speed began to drop rapidly. The only relief was that none of the passing patrols seemed to show any interest in the jeep.

Within minutes the little village was swarming with soldiers from Saddam's elite guard. Even in the dark, it took only ten bullets and as many minutes for them to find out where the Cadillac was, and another thirty bullets to discover the unfilled graves of the four dead soldiers.

General Hamil listened to the senior officer when he phoned in with the details. All he asked for was the radio frequency of the jeep that had been in Tuz Khurmatoo earlier that evening. The General slammed down the phone, checked his watch, and keyed in the frequency.

The single tone continued for some time.

* * *

'They must still be looking for a truck or a pink Cadillac,' Scott was saying when the radio phone began ringing. They all four froze.

'Answer it, Aziz,' said Scott. 'Listen carefully, and find out what you can.'

Aziz picked up the handset, listened to a short message, then said, 'Yes, sir,' in Arabic, and put the handset down.

'They've found the Cadillac, and are ordering all jeeps to report to their nearest army post,' he said.

'It can't be long before they realise it's not one of their men driving this jeep,' said Hannah. 'If they don't already know.'

'With luck we might still have twenty minutes,' said Scott. 'How far to the border?'

'Nine miles,' said Aziz.

The General knew it had to be Zeebari, or he would have responded with the elite guards' code number.

So now he knew what vehicle they were in, and which border they were heading for. He immediately picked up the phone and barked another order. Two officers accompanied him as he ran out of the room and into a large yard at the back of the building. The blades of his personal helicopter were already slowly rotating.

It was Aziz who first spotted the end of a long queue of oil tankers waiting to cross the unofficial border. Scott checked the inside track and asked Aziz if he could drive down such a narrow strip.

'Not possible, sir,' the young Kurd told him. 'We'd only end up in the ditch.'

'Then we've no alternative but to go straight down the middle.'

Aziz moved the jeep out into the centre of the road and tried desperately to maintain his speed. To begin with he was able to stay clear of the lorries and avoid the oncoming traffic. The first real trouble came four miles from the border, when an army truck heading towards them refused to move over.

'Shall I blast him off the road?' said Cohen.

'No,' said Scott. 'Aziz, keep going, but prepare to jump and take cover among the tankers, then we'll regroup.' Just as Scott was about to leap, the lorry swerved across the road and ended up in the ditch on the far side.

'Now they all know where we are,' said Scott. 'How many miles to the customs post, Aziz?'

'Three, three and a half at the most.'

'Then step on it,' said Scott, although he realised Aziz was already going as fast as he could. They had managed to cover the next mile in just over a minute when a helicopter swung above them, beaming down a searchlight that lit up the entire road. The radio phone began ringing again.

'Ignore it,' shouted Scott as Aziz tried to keep the jeep on the centre of the road and maintain his speed. They passed the two-mile mark as the helicopter swung back, confident it had spotted its prey, and began to focus its beam directly on them.

'We've got a jeep coming up our backside,' said Cohen, as he swung round to face it.

'Get rid of it,' said Scott.

Cohen obliged, sending the first few shots through the windscreen and the next into the tyres, thankful for the light from above. The pursuing jeep swung across the road, crashing into an oncoming lorry. Another quickly took its place. Hannah reloaded the gun with a magazine of bullets that was lying on the floor while Cohen concentrated on the road behind them.

'One and a half miles to go,' shouted Aziz, nearly crashing into lorries on both sides of the road. The helicopter hovered above them and began to fire indiscriminately, hitting vehicles going in both directions.

'Don't forget that most of them haven't a clue who's chasing what,' said Scott.

'Thanks for sharing that piece of logic with me, Professor,' said Cohen. 'But I've got a feeling that helicopter knows exactly who he's chasing.' Cohen began to pepper the next jeep with bullets the moment it came into range. This time it simply slowed to a halt, causing the car behind to run straight into it and creating a concertina effect as one after another the pursuing jeeps crashed into the back of the vehicle in front of them. The road behind was suddenly clear, as if Aziz had been the last car through a green light.

'One mile to go,' shouted Aziz as Cohen swung round to concentrate on what was going on in front of him and Hannah reloaded the automatic gun with the last magazine of bullets. Scott could see the lights of a bridge looming up in front of him: the Kirkuk fortress on the side of the hill that Aziz had told them signalled the customs post was only about half a mile away. As the helicopter swung back and once again sprayed the road with bullets, Aziz felt the front tyre on his side suddenly blow as he drove onto the bridge.

Scott could now see the Kurdish checkpoint ahead of him as the helicopter swung even lower on its final attempt to stop them. A flurry of bullets hit the jeep's bonnet, ricocheted off the bridge and into the windscreen. As the helicopter swung away, Scott looked up and for a second stared into the eyes of General Hamil.

Scott looked back down and punched a hole in the shattered windscreen, only to discover he was faced with two rows of soldiers lined up in front of him, their rifles aiming straight at the jeep.

Behind the row of soldiers were two small exits for those wishing to enter Kurdistan and two entrances on the other side of the road for those driving out of Kirkuk.

The two exits to Kurdistan were blocked with stationary vehicles, while the two entrances had been left clear – although no one at that moment was showing any desire to enter Saddam's Iraq.

Aziz decided that he would have to swing across the road and risk driving the jeep at an acute angle through one of the small entrances, where he might be faced with an oncoming vehicle – in which case they would be trapped. He was still losing speed, and could feel that the rim of the front left-hand wheel was now touching the ground.

Once they were within range, Cohen opened fire on the line of soldiers in front of him. Some fired back, but he managed to hit several before the rest scattered.

With a hundred yards to go and still losing speed, Aziz suddenly swung the jeep across the road and tried to steer it towards the second entrance. The jeep hit the right-hand wall, careered into the short, dark tunnel and bounced onto the left-hand wall before lurching out into no-man's land, between the two customs posts.

Suddenly there were dozens of soldiers pursuing them from the Iraqi side. 'Keep going, keep going!' shouted Scott as they emerged from the little tunnel.

Aziz was still losing speed as he steered the jeep back to the left and pointed it in the direction of the border with Kurdistan, a mere four hundred yards away. He pressed his foot flat down on the accelerator but the speedometer wouldn't rise above two miles per hour. Another row of soldiers, this time from the Kurdish border, was facing them, their rifles pointing at the jeep. But none of them was firing.

Cohen swung around as a stray bullet hit the back of the jeep and another flew past his shoulder. Once again he fired a volley towards the Iraqi border, and those who could quickly retreated behind their checkpoint. The jeep trundled on for a few more yards before it finally whimpered to a halt halfway between the two unofficial barriers that the UN refused to recognise.

Scott looked towards the Kurdish border. A hundred Peshmergas were lined up, their rifles now firing – but not in the direction of the jeep. Scott turned back to see another line of soldiers tentatively advancing from the Iraqi side. He and Hannah began firing their pistols as Cohen let forth another burst which came to a sudden stop. The Iraqi soldiers had started to retreat again, but sensed immediately that their enemy had finally run out of ammunition.

Cohen leaped down off the jeep and quickly took out his pistol. 'Come on, Aziz!' he shouted as he rushed forward and crouched beside the driver's door. 'We'll have to cover them so the Professor can get his bloody Declaration across the border.'

Aziz didn't reply. His body was slumped lifelessly over the wheel, the horn sounding intermittently. The unanswered radio phone was still ringing.

'The bastards have killed my Kurd!' shouted Cohen. Hannah grabbed the canvas bag as Scott lifted Aziz out of the front of the jeep. Together, they began to drag him the last few hundred yards towards the border with Kurdistan.

Another line of Iraqi soldiers started to advance towards the jeep as Scott and Hannah carried the dead body of Aziz nearer and nearer to his Kurdish homeland.

They heard more shots whistle past them, and turned to see Cohen running towards the Iraqis screaming, 'You killed my Kurd, you bastards! You killed my Kurd!' One of the Iraqis fell, another fell, one retreated. Another fell, another retreated, as Cohen went on advancing towards them. Suddenly, he fell to his knees, but somehow he kept crawling forward, until a final volley rang out. The Sergeant collapsed in a pool of blood a few yards from the Iraqi border.

While Scott and Hannah carried the dead Kurd into the land of his people, Saddam's soldiers dragged the body of the Jew back into Iraq.

'Why were my orders disobeyed?' Saddam shouted.

For several moments no one around the table spoke. They knew the chances of all of them returning to their beds alive that night had to be marginal.

General Hamil turned the cover of a thick file, and looked down at the handwritten note in front of him.

'Major Saeed was to blame, Mr President,' stated the General. 'It was he who allowed the infidels to escape with the Declaration, and that is why his body is now hanging in Tohrir Square for your people to witness.'

The General listened intently to the President's next question.

'Yes, Sayedi,' he assured his master. 'Two of the terrorists were killed by guards from my own regiment. They were by far the most important members of the team. They were the two who managed to escape from Major Saeed's custody before I arrived. The other two were an American professor and the girl.'

The President asked another question.

'No, Mr President. Kratz was the commanding officer,

and I personally arrested the infamous Zionist leader before questioning him at length. It was during that interrogation that I discovered that the original plan had been to assassinate you, Sayedi, and I made certain that he, like those who came before him, failed.'

The General had no well-rehearsed answer to the President's next question, and he was relieved when the State Prosecutor intervened.

'Perhaps we can turn this whole episode to our advantage, Sayedi.'

'How can that be possible,' shouted the President, 'when two of them have escaped with the Declaration and left us with a useless copy that anyone who can spell "British" will immediately realise is a fake? No, it is I who will be made the laughing stock of the world, not Clinton.'

Everyone's eyes were now fixed on the Prosecutor.

'That may not necessarily be the case, Mr President. I suspect that when the Americans see the state of their cherished treasure, they will not be in a hurry to put it back on display at the National Archives.'

The President did not interrupt this time, so the Prosecutor continued.

'We also know, Mr President, that because of your genius, the parchment currently on display in Washington to an unsuspecting American public is, to quote you, "a useless copy that anyone who can spell 'British' will immediately realise is a fake".'

The President's expression was now one of concentration.

'Perhaps the time has come, Sayedi, to inform the world's press of your triumph.'

'My triumph?' said the President in disbelief.

'Why, yes, Sayedi. Your triumph, not to mention your magnanimity. After all, it was you who gave the order to hand over the battered Declaration to Professor Bradley after the gangster Cavalli had attempted to sell it to you.'

The President's expression turned to one of deep thought.

'They have a saying in the West,' added the Prosecutor, 'about killing two birds with one stone.'

Another long silence followed, during which no one offered an opinion until the President smiled.

PART THREE

'. . .we mutually pledge to each other our Lives, our Fortunes and our sacred Honor.'

35

THE OFFICIAL STATEMENT issued by the Iraqi government on July 2nd was that there was no truth in the report that there had been a shooting incident on the border posts at Kirkuk in which several Iraqi soldiers had been killed and more wounded.

The Kurdish leaders were unable to offer any opinion on the subject, as the only two satellite phones in Iraqi Kurdistan had been permanently engaged with requests for assistance from the State Department in Washington.

When Charles Streator, the American Ambassador in Istanbul, was telephoned and asked by the Reuters Bureau Chief in the Middle East why a US Air Force jet had landed at the American base in Silope on the Turkish border, and then returned to Washington with two unknown passengers as its cargo, His Excellency told his old friend that he had absolutely no idea what he was talking about. The Bureau Chief considered the Ambassador to be an honest man, although he accepted that it was part of the job to lie for his country.

The Ambassador had in fact been up all night following a call from the Secretary of State requesting that one of their helicopters should be despatched to the outskirts of Kirkuk to pick up five passengers, one American, one

Arab and three Israelis, who were then to be flown back to the base at Silope.

The Ambassador had called Washington later that morning to inform Warren Christopher that unfortunately only two people had managed to cross the border alive: an American named Scott Bradley and an Israeli woman, Hannah Kopec. He had no information on the other three.

The American Ambassador was totally thrown by the Secretary of State's final question. Did Professor Bradley have a cardboard tube in his possession? The Ambassador was only disappointed that the Reuters correspondent hadn't asked him the same thing, because then he would have been telling him the truth when he said, 'I've absolutely no idea what you're talking about.'

Scott and Hannah slept for most of the flight back to America. When they stepped off the plane at the military air base they found Dexter Hutchins at the bottom of the steps waiting to greet them. Neither of them was surprised when customs showed little interest in Scott's canvas bag. A CIA car whisked them off in the direction of Washington.

On the journey into the capital, Dexter warned them that they would be going direct to the White House for a top-level meeting, and briefed them on who else would be present.

They were met at the West Wing reception entrance by the President's Chief of Staff, who conducted them to the Oval Office. Scott couldn't help feeling that, as it was his first meeting with the President, he would have preferred to have shaved at some time during the last forty-eight hours, and not to have been dressed in the same clothes that he'd worn for the past three days.

Warren Christopher was there to greet them at the door of the Oval Office, and he introduced Scott to the President as if they were old friends. Bill Clinton welcomed Scott home, and thanked Hannah for the part she had played in securing the safe return of the Declaration.

Scott was delighted to meet Calder Marshall for the first time, Mr Mendelssohn for the second time, and to be reunited with Dollar Bill.

Dollar Bill bowed to Hannah. 'Now I understand why the Professor was willing to cross the earth to bring you back,' was all the little Irishman had to say.

The moment the handshakes were over, none of them could hide their impatience to see the Declaration. Scott unzipped his bag and carefully took out a bath towel, from which he extracted the document before handing it over to its rightful custodian, the Secretary of State. Christopher slowly unrolled the parchment. No one in the room was able to hide their dismay at the state the Declaration was in.

The Secretary passed the document over to the Archivist who, accompanied by the Conservator and Dollar Bill, walked across to the large window overlooking the South Lawn. The first word they checked was 'Brittish', and the Archivist smiled.

But it was only a few moments more before Calder Marshall announced their combined judgement. 'It's a fake,' was all he said.

'How can you be so certain?' asked the President.

'*Mea culpa*,' said Dollar Bill, looking a little sheepish.

'So does that mean that Saddam is still in possession of the original?' asked the Secretary of State in disbelief.

'No, sir, he has the copy Scott took to Baghdad,' said Dollar Bill. 'So clearly he was already in possession of a fake before Scott did the exchange.'

'Then who has the original?' the other four asked in unison.

'Alfonso Mario Cavalli would be my guess,' said Dollar Bill.

'And who's he?' asked the President, no wiser.

'The gentleman who paid me to make the copy that is currently in the National Archives,' said Dollar Bill, 'and to whom I released the only other copy, which I am now holding in my hands.'

'But if the word "Brittish" is spelt with two *ts*, how can you be so certain it's a fake?' asked Dexter Hutchins.

'Because, of the fifty-six signatures on the original Declaration, six have the Christian name George. Five of them signed *Geo*, which was the custom of the time. Only George Wythe of Virginia appended his full name. On the copy I presented to Cavalli I made the mistake of also writing *Geo* for Congressman Wythe, and had to add the letters *rge* later. Although the lettering is perfect, I used a slightly lighter shade of ink. A simple mistake, and discernible only to an expert eye.'

'And even then, only if they knew what they were looking for,' added Mendelssohn.

'I never bothered to tell Cavalli,' continued Dollar Bill, 'because once he had checked the word "Brittish" he seemed quite satisfied.'

'So, at some time Cavalli must have switched his copy with the original, and then passed it on to Al Obaydi?' said Dexter Hutchins.

'Well done, Deputy Director,' said Dollar Bill.

'And Al Obaydi in turn handed the copy on to the Iraqi Ambassador in Geneva, who had it delivered to Saddam in Iraq. And, as Al Obaydi had seen Dollar Bill's copy on display at the National Archives with "British" spelt correctly, he was convinced he was in possession of the original,' said Dexter Hutchins.

'You've finally caught up with the rest of us,' said Dollar Bill. 'Though to be fair, sir, I should have known what Cavalli was capable of doing when I said to you a month ago: "Is there no longer honour among thieves?" '

'So, where is the original now?' demanded the President.

'I suspect it's hanging on a wall in a brownstone house in Manhattan,' said Dollar Bill, 'where it must have been for the past ten weeks.'

The light on the telephone console to the right of the President began flashing. The President's Chief of Staff picked up an extension and listened. The normally unflappable man turned white. He pushed the hold button.

'It's Bernie Shaw at CNN for me, Mr President. He says Saddam is claiming that the bombing of Baghdad last weekend was nothing more than a smokescreen set up to give a group of American terrorists the chance to retrieve the Declaration of Independence, which a Mafia gang had tried to sell him and which he personally returned to a man called Bradley. Saddam's apparently most apologetic about the state the Declaration is in, but he has television pictures of Bradley spitting and stamping on it and nailing it to a wall. If you don't believe him, Saddam says you can check the copy of the Declaration that's on display at the National Archives, because anyone who can spell "British" will realise it's a fake. Shaw's asking if you have any comment to make, as Saddam intends to hold a press conference tomorrow morning to let the whole world know the truth.'

The President pursed his lips.

'My bet is that Saddam has given CNN an exclusive on this story, but probably only until tomorrow,' the Chief of Staff added.

'Whatever you do,' said Hutchins, 'try to keep it off the air for tonight.'

The Chief of Staff hesitated for a moment until he saw the President nodding his agreement. He pressed the button to re-engage the call. 'If you want to go on the air with a story like that, Bernie, it's your reputation on the line, not mine.'

The Chief of Staff listened carefully to Shaw's reply while everyone else in the room waited in silence.

'Be my guest,' were the last words the Chief of Staff offered before putting the phone down.

He turned to the President and told him: 'Shaw says he will have a crew outside the National Archives the moment the doors open at ten tomorrow morning, and, I quote: if the word "British" is spelt correctly, he'll crucify you.'

The President glanced up at the carriage clock that stood on the mantelpiece below the portrait of Abraham Lincoln. It was a few minutes after seven. He swivelled his chair round to face the Deputy Director of the CIA.

'Mr Hutchins,' he said, 'you've got fifteen hours to stop me being crucified. Should you fail, I can assure you there won't be a second coming for me in three years, let alone three days.'

36

THE LEAK STARTED in the early morning of Sunday July 4th, in the basement of number 21, the home of the Prestons, who were on vacation in Malibu.

When their Mexican housekeeper answered the door a few minutes after midnight, she assumed the worst. An illegal immigrant with no Green Card lives in daily fear of a visit from any government official.

The housekeeper was relieved to discover that these particular officials were only from the gas company. Without much prompting, she agreed to accompany them down to the basement of the brownstone and show them where the gas meters were located.

Once they had gained entry it only took a few moments to carry out the job. The loosening of two gas valves ensured a tiny leak which gave off a smell that would have alarmed any layman. The explosives expert assured his boss that there was no real cause for concern, as long as the New York Fire Department arrived within twenty minutes.

The senior official calmly asked the housekeeper to phone the fire department and warn them they had a gas leak in number 21 which, if not dealt with quickly, could cause an explosion. He told her the correct code to give.

The housekeeper dialled 911, and when she was finally put through to the fire department, stammered out the problem, adding that it was 21 East 75th, between Park and Madison.

'Get everyone out of the building,' instructed the Fire Chief, 'and we'll be right over.'

'Yes, sir,' said the housekeeper, not pausing for a moment before fleeing onto the street. The expert quickly repaired the damage he had caused, but the smell still lingered.

To their credit, seven minutes later a New York Fire Department hook and ladder, sirens blasting, sped into 75th Street. Once the Fire Chief had carried out an inspection of the basement of number 21 he agreed with the official – whom he had never met before – that safety checks would also have to be carried out on numbers 17, 19, 23 and 25, especially as the gas pipe ran parallel to the city's sewerage system.

The Deputy Director of the CIA then retired to the far side of the road to watch the Fire Chief go about his work. As the sirens had woken almost everyone in the neighbourhood, it wasn't proving too hard to coax the residents out onto the street.

Dexter Hutchins lit a cigar and waited. As soon as he had left the White House, he had begun rounding up a select team of agents who rendezvoused in a New York hotel two hours later for a briefing, or, to be more accurate, half a briefing. Because once the Deputy Director had explained to them that this was a Level 7 inquiry, the old-timers realised they would be told only half the story, and not the better half.

It had taken another two hours before they got their first break, when one of the agents discovered that the Prestons in number 21 were on vacation. Dexter Hutchins and his explosives expert had arrived on the doorstep of number 21 just after midnight. The Mexican immigrant without a Green Card turned out to be a bonus.

The Deputy Director relit his cigar, his eyes fixed on one particular doorway. He breathed a sigh of relief when Tony Cavalli and his father emerged in their dressing gowns, accompanied by a butler. He decided it would be sensible to wait for another couple of minutes before he asked the Fire Chief's permission to inspect number 23.

The whole operation could have been underway a lot earlier if only Calder Marshall hadn't balked at the idea of removing the fake Declaration from the vault of the National Archives and placing it at Dexter Hutchins' disposal. The Archivist made two stipulations before he finally agreed to the Deputy Director's request: should the CIA fail to replace the copy with the original before ten o'clock the following morning, Marshall's resignation statement, dated May 25th, would be released an hour before the President or the Secretary of State made any statement of their own.

'And your second condition, Mr Marshall?' the President had asked.

'That Mr Mendelssohn be allowed to act as custodian of the copy remaining with the Deputy Director at all times, so that he will be present should they locate the original.'

Dexter Hutchins realised he had little choice but to go along with Marshall's conditions. The Deputy Director stared across at the Conservator, who was standing between Scott and the explosives expert, on the pavement opposite number 23. Dexter Hutchins had to admit that Mendelssohn looked more convincing as an official from the gas company than anyone else in his team.

As soon as Hutchins saw two of his agents emerging from number 19 he stubbed out his cigar and strolled across the road in the direction of the Fire Chief. His three colleagues followed a few paces behind.

'All right for us to check on number 23 now?' he asked casually.

'Fine by me,' said the Fire Chief. 'But the owners are insisting the butler sticks with you.'

Hutchins nodded his agreement. The butler led the four of them into the lobby, down to the basement and directly to the cupboard that housed the gas supply. He assured them that there had not been the slightest smell of gas before he went to bed, some time after his master had retired.

The explosives expert carried out his job deftly, and in moments the basement stank of gas. Hutchins recommended to the butler that for his own safety he should return to the street. With a handkerchief covering his nose and mouth Martin reluctantly agreed, leaving them to try and locate the leak.

While the expert repaired the damage, Scott and Dexter began checking every room in the basement. Scott was the first to enter Cavalli's study and discover the parchment hanging on the wall, exactly where Dollar Bill had promised it would be. Within seconds the other two had joined him. Mendelssohn stared lovingly at the document. He checked the word 'Brittish' before lifting the glass frame gently off the wall and placing it on the boardroom table. Scott unzipped the large tool bag one of the agents had put together earlier in the evening, containing screwdrivers of all sizes, knives of all lengths, chisels of several widths and even a small drill, in fact everything that would be required by a professional picture framer.

The Conservator checked the back of the frame and requested a medium-sized screwdriver. Scott selected one and passed it across to him.

Mendelssohn slowly and methodically removed all eight of the screws that held the two large steel clamps to the back of the frame. Then he turned the glass over on its front. Dexter Hutchins couldn't help thinking that he might have shown a little more sense of urgency.

The Conservator, oblivious to the Deputy Director's impatience, rummaged around in the bag until he had selected an appropriate chisel. He wedged it between the two pieces of laminated glass at the top right-hand corner of the frame. At the same time, Scott extracted from the cylinder supplied by Mendelssohn the copy of the Declaration they had taken from the National Archives earlier that evening.

When the Conservator lifted the top piece of the laminated glass and rested it on the boardroom table, Scott could tell from the smile on his face that he believed he was staring down at the original.

'Come on,' said Dexter, 'or they'll start getting suspicious.'

Mendelssohn didn't seem to hear the Deputy Director's urgings. He once again checked the spelling of 'Brittish' and, satisfied, turned his attention to the five 'Geo's and one 'George' before glancing, first quickly and then slowly, over the rest of the parchment. The smile never left his face.

Without a word, the Conservator slowly rolled up the original, and Scott replaced it with the copy from the National Archives. Once Scott had the sheets of glass back in position he screwed the two steel clamps firmly in place.

Mendelssohn deposited the cylinder in the work bag while Scott hung the copy on the wall.

They both heard Dexter Hutchins' deep sigh of relief.

'Now for Christ's sake let's get out of here,' said the Deputy Director as six cops, guns drawn, burst into the room and surrounded them.

'Freeze!' said one of them. Mendelssohn fainted.

37

ALL FOUR WERE ARRESTED, handcuffed and had their rights read out to them. They were then driven in separate police cars to the Nineteenth Precinct.

When they were questioned, three refused to speak without an attorney present. The fourth pointed out to the Desk Sergeant that if the bag which had been taken from him was opened at any time other than in the presence of his attorney, a writ would be issued and a separate action taken out against the NYPD.

The Desk Sergeant looked at the smartly-dressed, distinguished-looking man and decided not to take any risks. He labelled the bag with a red tag and threw it in the night safe.

The same man insisted on his legal right to make one phone call. The request was granted, but not until another form had been completed and signed. Dexter Hutchins put a collect call through to the Director of the CIA at 2.27 a.m.

The Director confessed to his subordinate that he hadn't been able to sleep. He listened intently to Hutchins' report and praised him for not revealing his name or giving the police any details of the covert assignment. 'We don't need anyone to know who you are,' he added. 'We must be sure at all times not to embarrass the President.' He paused for a moment. 'Or, more important, the CIA.'

When the Deputy Director put the phone down, he and his three colleagues were hustled away to separate cells.

The Director of the CIA put on his dressing gown and went down to his study. After he had written up a short summary of the conversation he had had with his deputy, he checked a number on his desk computer. He slowly dialled the 212 area code.

The Commissioner of the New York City Police Department uttered some choice words when he answered the phone, until he was sufficiently alert to take in who it was sounding so wide awake on the other end of the line. He then switched on the bedside light and began to make some notes on a pad. His wife turned over, but not before she had added a few choice words of her own.

The Director of the CIA ended his part of the conversation with the comment, 'I owe you one.'

'Two,' said the Commissioner. 'One for trying to sort out your problem.'

'And the second?' asked the Director.

'For waking up my wife at three o'clock in the morning.'

The Commissioner remained seated on the edge of the bed while he looked up the home number of the Captain in charge of that particular precinct.

The Captain recognised his chief's voice immediately he picked up the phone, and simply said, 'Good morning, Commissioner,' as if it were a routine mid-morning call.

The chief briefed the Captain without making any mention of a call from the Director of the CIA or giving any clues about who the four men languishing in his night cells were – not that he was absolutely certain himself. The Captain scribbled down the salient facts on the back of his wife's copy of *Good Housekeeping*. He didn't bother to shower or shave, and dressed quickly in the clothes he had worn the previous day. He left his apartment in Queens at 3.21 and drove himself into Manhattan, leaving his car outside the front of the precinct a few minutes before four.

Those officers who were fully awake at that time in the morning were surprised to see their boss running up the steps and into the front hall, especially as he looked dishevelled, unshaven, and was carrying a copy of *Good Housekeeping* under his arm.

He strode into the office of the Duty Lieutenant, who quickly removed his feet from the desk.

The Lieutenant looked mystified when asked about the four men who'd been arrested earlier, as he'd only just finished interrogating a drug pusher.

The Desk Sergeant was called for and joined the Captain in the Duty Lieutenant's office. The veteran policeman, who thought he had seen most things during a long career in the force, admitted to booking the four men, but remained puzzled by the whole incident, because he couldn't think of anything to charge them with – despite the fact that one of the householders, a Mr Antonio Cavalli, had called within the last few minutes to ask if the four men were still being held in custody, as a complication had arisen. None of the residents had reported anything stolen, so theft did not apply. There could be no charge of breaking and entering, as on each occasion they had been invited into the buildings. There was certainly no assault involved, and trespass couldn't be considered, as they had left the premises the moment they were asked to do so. The only charge the Sergeant could come up with was impersonating gas company officials.

The Captain didn't show any interest in whether or

not the Desk Sergeant could find something to charge them with. All he wanted to know was: 'Has the bag been opened?'

'No, Captain,' said the Sergeant, trying to think where he had put it.

'Then release them on bail, pending further charges,' instructed the Captain. 'I'll deal with the paperwork.'

The paperwork took the Captain some considerable time, and the four men were not released until a few minutes after six.

When they ran down the precinct steps together, the little one with the pebble glasses was clinging firmly on to the unopened bag.

Antonio Cavalli woke with a start. Had he dreamed that he'd been dragged out of bed and onto the street in the middle of the night?

He flicked on the bedside light and picked up his watch. It was 3.47. He began to recall what had taken place a few hours earlier.

Once they were out on the street, Martin had accompanied the four men back into the house. Too many for a simple gas leak, Cavalli had thought. And what gas company official would smoke cigars and could afford a Saks Fifth Avenue suit? After they had been inside for fifteen minutes, Cavalli had become even more suspicious. He asked the Fire Chief if the men were personally known to him. The Chief admitted that, although they had been able to give him the correct code over the phone, he had never come across them before. He decided Mr Cavalli was right when he suggested that perhaps the time had come to make some checks with Consolidated Edison. Their switchboard informed him that they had no engineers out on call that night on 75th

Street. The Fire Chief immediately passed this information on to the police. A few minutes later six police officers had entered number 23 and arrested all four men.

After they had been driven away to the station, his father and Martin had helped Tony check every room in the house, but as far as they could see nothing was missing. They had gone back to bed around 1.45.

Cavalli was now fully awake, though he thought he could hear a noise coming from the ground floor. Was it the same noise that had woken him? Tony checked his watch again. His father and Martin often rose early, but rarely between the hours of three and four.

Cavalli swung out of bed and placed his feet on the ground. He still felt sure he could hear voices.

He slipped on a dressing gown and walked over to the bedroom door. He opened it slowly, went out onto the landing and peered over the balustrade. He could see a light shining from under the door of his father's study.

Cavalli moved swiftly down the one flight of stairs and silently across the carpeted hallway until he came to a halt outside the study. He tried to remember where the nearest gun was.

He listened carefully, but could hear no movement coming from inside. Then, suddenly, a gravelly voice began cursing loudly. Tony flung open the door to find his father, also in his dressing gown, standing in front of the Declaration of Independence and holding a magnifying glass in his right hand. He was studying the word 'British'.

'Are you feeling all right?' Tony asked his father.

'You should have killed Dollar Bill when I told you to,' was his father's only comment.

'But why?' asked Tony.

'Because they've stolen the Declaration of Independence.'

'But you're standing in front of it,' said Tony.

'No I'm not,' said his father. 'Don't you understand what they've done?'

'No, I don't,' admitted Tony.

'They've exchanged the original for that worthless copy you put in the National Archives.'

'But the copy on the wall was the other one made by Dollar Bill,' said Tony. 'I saw him present it to you.'

'No,' said his father. 'Mine was the original, not a copy.'

'I don't understand,' said Tony, now completely baffled. The old man turned and faced his son for the first time.

'Nick Vicente and I switched them when you brought the Declaration back from Washington.' Tony stared at his father in disbelief. 'You didn't think I'd allow part of our national heritage to fall into the hands of Saddam Hussein?'

'But why didn't you tell me?' asked Tony.

'And let you go to Geneva knowing you were in possession of a fake, while the deal still hadn't been closed? No, it was always part of my plan that you would believe the original had been sent to Franchard et cie, because if you believed it, Al Obaydi would believe it.'

Tony said nothing.

'And you certainly wouldn't have put up such a fight over the loss of fifty million if you'd known all along that the document you had in Geneva was a counterfeit.'

'So where the hell is the original now?' asked Tony.

'Somewhere in the offices of the Nineteenth Precinct, would be my bet,' replied his father. 'That is, assuming they haven't already got clean away. And that's what I intend to find out right now,' he added as he walked over to his desk and picked up the phone book.

The chairman dialled seven digits and asked to speak to the duty officer. He checked his watch as he waited to be put through. It was 4.22.

When the Desk Sergeant came on the line, Cavalli explained who he was, and asked two questions. He listened carefully to the replies, then put the phone back on the hook.

Tony raised an eyebrow.

'They're still locked up in the cells, and the bag's been placed in a safe. Have we got anybody on the Nineteenth Precinct payroll?' asked his father.

'Yes, a lieutenant who's done very little for us lately.'

'Then the time has come for him to pay his dues,' said his father as he began walking towards the door.

Tony passed him, taking the stairs three at a time on the way back to his bedroom. He was dressed within minutes, and walked back down the staircase, expecting to have to wait some time for his father to reappear, but he was already standing in the hallway.

His father unlocked the front door and Tony followed him out onto the pavement, passing him to look up the street in search of a Yellow Cab. But none chose to turn right down 75th Street at that time in the morning.

'We'll have to take the car,' shouted his father, who had already begun to cross the road in the direction of the all-night garage. 'We can't afford to waste another minute.' Tony dashed back into the house and removed the car keys from the drawer of the hall table. He caught up with his father long before he reached their parking space.

As Tony fastened his seatbelt, he turned and asked his father, 'If we do manage to get the Declaration back, what the hell do you intend to do then?'

'To start with, I'm going to kill Dollar Bill myself, so I

can be certain that he never makes another copy. And then –' Tony turned the key in the ignition.

The explosion that followed woke the entire neighbourhood for the second time that morning.

The four men came running down the precinct steps. The smallest of them was clinging on to a bag. A car whose engine had been turning over for the past hour swung across the road and came to a halt by their side. One of the men walked off into the half-light of the morning, still not certain why his expertise had been required in the first place.

Dexter Hutchins joined the driver in the front, while Scott and the Conservator climbed quickly into the back.

'LaGuardia,' said Dexter and then thanked the agent for sitting up half the night. Scott looked between the two front seats as the digital clock changed from 6:11 to 6:12.

The agent swung on to the outside lane.

'Don't break the speed limit,' ordered Dexter. 'We don't need any more delays at this stage.' The agent edged back into the centre lane.

'What time's the next shuttle?' asked Scott.

'Delta, seven-thirty,' replied the driver. Dexter picked up the phone and punched in ten numbers. When a voice at the other end said, 'Yes,' the Deputy Director replied, 'We're on our way, sir. We should have everything back in place by ten.'

Dexter replaced the phone and turned round to assure himself that the silent Conservator was still with them. He was clutching the bag that was now resting on his legs.

'Better take everything out of the bag other than the cylinder,' said Dexter. 'Otherwise we'll never get past security.'

Mendelssohn unzipped the bag and allowed Scott to remove the screwdrivers, knives, chisels and finally the drill, which he placed on the floor between them. He zipped the bag back up.

At 6.43 the driver pulled off the highway and followed the signs for LaGuardia. No one spoke until the car came to a halt at the kerb opposite the Marine Air terminal entrance.

As Dexter stepped out of the car, three men in tan Burberrys jumped out of a car that had drawn in immediately behind them, and preceded the Deputy Director into the terminal. Another man in a smart charcoal-grey suit, with a raincoat over his arm, held out an envelope as Dexter passed him. The Deputy Director took the package like a good relay runner, without breaking his stride, as he continued towards the departure lounge, where three more agents were waiting for him.

Once he had checked in, Dexter Hutchins would have liked to pace up and down as he waited to board the aircraft. Instead, he stood restlessly one yard away from the Declaration of Independence, surrounded by a circle of agents.

'The shuttle to Washington is now boarding at Gate Number 4,' announced a voice over the intercom. Nine men waited until everyone else had boarded the aircraft. When the agent standing by the gate nodded, Dexter led his team past the ticket collector, down the boarding ramp, and onto the aircraft. They took their seats, 1A–F and 2A–F. 2E was occupied only by the bag, 2D and 2F by two men who weighed five hundred pounds between them.

The pilot welcomed them aboard and warned them there might be a slight delay. Dexter checked his watch: 7.27. He began drumming his fingers on the armrest that divided him from Scott. The flight attendant offered every one of the nine men in the first two rows a copy of *USA Today*. Only Mendelssohn took up her offer.

At 7.39 the aircraft taxied out onto the runway to prepare for take-off. When it stopped, Dexter asked the flight attendant what was holding them up.

'The usual early-morning traffic,' she replied. 'The Captain has just told me that we're seventh in the queue, so we should be airborne in about ten to fifteen minutes.'

Dexter continued drumming his fingers on the armrest, while Scott couldn't take his eyes off the bag. Mendelssohn turned another page of his *USA Today*.

The plane swung round onto the take-off runway at 7.51, its jets revving before it moved slowly forward, then gathered speed. The wheels left the ground at 7.53.

Within moments the flight attendant returned, offering them all breakfast. She didn't get a positive response until she reached row seven. When later she gave the three crew members on the flight deck their usual morning coffee, she asked the Captain why rows three to six were unoccupied, especially as it was Independence Day.

The Captain couldn't think of a reason, and simply said, 'Keep your eye on the passengers in rows one and two.' He became even more curious about the nine men at the front of the aircraft when he was cleared for landing as soon as he announced to air traffic control that he was seventy miles away from Washington.

He began his descent at 8.33, and was at the gate on schedule for the first time in months. When he had turned the engine off, three men immediately blocked the gangway and remained there until the Deputy Director and his party were well inside the terminal. When Dexter Hutchins emerged into the Delta gate area, one agent played John the Baptist, while three others fell in behind, acting as disciples. The Director had obviously taken seriously that fine line between protection and drawing attention. Dexter spotted four more agents as he passed through the terminal, and suspected there were at least another twenty hidden at strategic points on his route to the car.

As Dexter passed under the digital clock, its red numbers clicked to 9:01. The doors slid open and he marched out onto the pavement. Three black limousines were waiting in line with drivers by their doors.

As soon as they saw the Deputy Director, the drivers of the first and third cars jumped behind their wheels and turned on their engines, while the driver of the second car held open the back door to allow Scott and Mendelssohn to climb in. The Deputy Director joined the agent in the front.

The lead car headed out in the direction of the George Washington Parkway, and within minutes the convoy was crossing the 14th Street bridge. As the Jefferson Memorial came into sight Dexter checked his watch yet again. It was 9.12. 'Easily enough time,' he remarked. Less than a minute later, they were caught in a traffic jam.

'Damn!' said Dexter. 'I forgot the streets would be cordoned off for the Independence Day parade.'

When they had moved only another half a mile in the next three minutes, Dexter told his driver they were left with no choice. 'Hit the sirens,' he said.

The driver flashed his lights, turned on his siren at full blast, and watched as the lead car veered into the inside lane and managed a steady forty miles per hour until they came off the freeway.

Dexter was now checking his watch every thirty seconds as the three cars tried to manoeuvre themselves from lane to lane, but some of Washington's citizens, unmoved by sirens and flashing lights, weren't willing to let them through.

The lead car swerved between two police barriers and turned into Constitution Avenue at 9.37. When Dexter saw the floats lining up for the parade, he gave the order to turn the sirens off. The last thing he needed was inquisitive eyes when they finally came to a halt outside the National Archives.

It was Scott who saw them first. He tapped Dexter on the shoulder and pointed ahead of him. A television crew was standing at the head of a long queue outside the front door of the National Archives.

'We'll never get past them,' said Dexter. Turning to Mendelssohn, he asked, 'Are there any alternative routes into the building?'

'There's a delivery entrance on 7th Street,' replied Mendelssohn.

'How appropriate,' said Dexter Hutchins.

'Drive past the front door and then drop me off on the corner,' said the Conservator. 'I'll cross Constitution and go in by the delivery entrance.'

'Drop you off on the corner?' said Dexter in disbelief.

'If I'm surrounded by agents, everyone will . . .' began Mendelssohn.

'Yes, yes, yes,' said the Deputy Director, trying to think. He picked up the phone and instructed the two other cars to peel off.

'We're going to have to risk it,' said Scott.

'I know,' said Dexter. 'But at least you can go with him. After all, you've never looked like an agent.' Scott wasn't sure whether he should take the remark as a compliment or not.

As they drove slowly past the National Archives, Dexter looked away from the impatient camera crew.

'How many of them?' he asked.

'About six,' said Scott. 'And I think that must be Shaw with his back to us.'

'Show me exactly where you want the car to stop,' said the Deputy Director, turning to face Mendelssohn.

'Another fifty yards,' came back the reply.

'You take the bag, Scott.'

'But . . .' began Mendelssohn. When he saw the expression on Dexter Hutchins' face, he didn't bother with a second word.

The car drew into the kerb and stopped. Scott grabbed the bag, jumped out, and held the door open for Mendelssohn. Eight agents were walking up and down the pavement trying to appear innocent. None of them was looking towards the steps of the National Archives. The two unlikely looking companions quickly crossed Constitution Avenue and began running up 7th Street.

When they reached the delivery entrance, Scott came face to face with an anxious Calder Marshall, who had been pacing back and forth at the bottom of the ramp.

'Thank God,' was all the Archivist said when he saw Scott and the Conservator running down the ramp. He led them silently into the open freight elevator. They travelled up two floors and then ran along the corridor until they reached the staircase that led down to the vault. Marshall turned to check that the two men were still with him before he began running down the steps, something no member of staff had ever seen him do before. Scott chased after the Archivist, followed by Mendelssohn. None of them stopped until they reached a set of massive steel doors.

Marshall nodded, and a slightly breathless Conservator leaned forward and pressed a code into a little box beside the door. The steel grid opened slowly to allow the three of them to enter the vault. Once they were inside, the Conservator pressed another button, and the door slid back into place.

They paused in front of the great concrete block that

had been built to house the Declaration of Independence, just as a priest might in front of an altar. Scott checked his watch. It was 9.51.

Mendelssohn pressed the red button and the familiar clanking and whirling sound began as the concrete blocks parted and the massive empty frame came slowly into sight. He touched the button again when the glass casing had reached chest height.

The Archivist and the Conservator walked forward while Scott unzipped the bag. The Archivist took two keys from his jacket pocket and passed one over to his colleague. They immediately set about unlocking the twelve bolts that were evenly spaced around the thick brass rim. Once they had completed the task they leaned over and heaved across the heavy frame until it came to rest like an open book.

Scott removed the container and passed it over to the Archivist. Marshall eased the cap off the top of the cylinder, allowing Mendelssohn to carefully extract its contents.

Scott watched as the Archivist and the Conservator slowly unpeeled the Declaration of Independence, inch by inch, onto the waiting glass, until the original parchment was finally restored to its rightful place. Scott leaned over and took one last look at the misspelt word before the two men heaved the brass cover back into place.

'My God, the British still have a lot to answer for,' was all the Archivist said.

Calder Marshall and the Conservator quickly tightened up the twelve bolts surrounding the frame and took a pace back from the Declaration.

They paused for only a second while Scott checked his watch again. 9.57. He looked up to find Marshall and Mendelssohn hugging each other and jumping up and down like children who had been given an unexpected gift.

Scott coughed. 'It's 9.58, gentlemen.' The two men immediately reverted to character.

The Archivist walked back over to the concrete block. He paused for a moment and then pressed the red button. The massive frame rose, continuing its slow journey upwards to the gallery to be viewed by the waiting public.

Calder Marshall turned to face Scott. A flicker of a smile showed his relief. He bowed like a Japanese warrior to indicate that he felt honour had been satisfied. The Conservator shook hands with Scott and then walked over to the door, punched a code into the little box and watched the grid slide open.

Marshall accompanied Scott out into the corridor, up the staircase and back down in the freight elevator to the delivery entrance.

'Thank you, Professor,' he said as they shook hands on the loading dock. Scott loped up the ramp and turned to look back once he had reached the pavement. There was no sign of the Archivist.

He jogged across 7th Street and joined Dexter in the waiting car.

'Any problems, Professor?' asked the Deputy Director.

'No. Not unless you count two decent men who look as if they've aged ten years in the past two months.'

The tenth chime struck on the Old Post Office Tower clock. The doors of the National Archives swung open and a television crew charged in.

The Deputy Director's car moved out into the centre of Constitution Avenue, where it got caught up between the floats for Tennessee and Texas. A police officer ran across and ordered the driver to pull over into 7th Street.

When the car came to a halt, Dexter wound down his window, smiled at the officer and said, 'I'm the Deputy Director of the CIA.'

'Sure. And I'm Uncle Sam,' the officer replied as he began writing out a ticket.

38

THE DEPUTY DIRECTOR of the CIA phoned the Director at home to tell him that it was business as usual at the National Archives. He didn't mention the traffic ticket.

The Conservator phoned his wife and tried to explain why he hadn't come home the previous night.

A woman holding a carrier bag with a rope handle contacted the Iraqi Ambassador to the UN on her mobile phone and let him know that she had killed two birds with one stone. She gave the Ambassador an account number for a bank in the Bahamas.

The Director of the CIA rang the Secretary of State and assured him that the document was in place. He avoided saying '*back* in place'.

Susan Anderson rang Scott to congratulate him on the part he had played in restoring the document to its rightful home. She also mentioned in passing the sad news that she had decided to break off her engagement.

The Iraqi Ambassador to the UN instructed Monsieur Franchard to transfer the sum of nine hundred thousand dollars to the Royal Bank of Canada in the Bahamas and at the same time to close the Al Obaydi account.

The Secretary of State rang the President at the White House to inform him that the press conference scheduled for eleven o'clock that morning had been cancelled.

A reporter on the *New York Daily News* crime beat filed his first-edition copy from a phone booth in an underground garage on 75th Street. The headline read 'Mafia Slaying in Manhattan'.

Lloyd Adams' phone never stopped ringing, as he was continually being offered parts in everything from endorsements to a feature film.

The Archivist did not return a call from one of the President's Special Assistants at the White House, inviting him to lunch.

A CNN producer called in to the news desk to let them know that it must all have been a hoax. Yes, he had verified the spelling of 'Brittish', and only Dan Quayle could have thought it had two *t*s.

Scott phoned Hannah and told her how he wanted to spend Independence Day.

THE END

In CONGRESS, July 4, 1776.

The unanimous Declaration of the thirteen united States of America

When, in the course of human events, it becomes necessary for one people to dissolve the political bands which have connected them with another, and to assume among the powers of the earth, the separate and equal station to which the Laws of Nature and of Nature's God entitle them, a decent respect to the opinions of mankind requires that they should declare the causes which impel them to the separation. — We hold these truths to be self-evident, that all men are created equal, that they are endowed by their Creator with certain unalienable Rights, that among these are Life, Liberty and the Pursuit of Happiness. — That to secure these rights, Governments are instituted among Men, deriving their just powers from the consent of the governed, — That whenever any Form of Government becomes destructive of these ends, it is the Right of the People to alter or to abolish it, and to institute new Government, laying the foundation on such principles and organizing its powers in such form, as to them shall seem most likely to effect their Safety and Happiness. Prudence, indeed, will dictate that Governments long established should not be changed for light and transient causes; and accordingly all experience hath shewn, that mankind are more disposed to suffer, while evils are sufferable, than to right themselves by abolishing the forms to which they are accustomed. But when a long train of abuses and usurpations, pursuing invariably the same Object evinces a design to reduce *them under absolute Despotism, it is their right, it is their duty, to throw off such Government, and to provide new Guards for their future security. — Such has been the patient sufferance of these Colonies; and such is now the necessity which constrains them to alter their former Systems of Government. The history of the present King of Great Britain is a history of repeated injuries and usurpations, all having in direct object the establishment of an absolute Tyranny over these States. To prove this, let Facts be submitted to a candid world. — He has refused his Assent to Laws, the most wholesome and necessary for the public good. — He has forbidden his Governors to pass Laws of immediate and pressing importance, unless suspended in their operation till his Assent should be obtained; and when so suspended, he has utterly neglected to attend to them. —— —— He has refused to pass other Laws for the accommodation of large districts of people, unless those people would relinquish the right of Representation in the Legislature, a right inestimable to them and formidable to tyrants only. — He has called together legislative bodies at places unusual, uncomfortable, and distant from the depository of their Public Records, for the sole purpose of fatiguing them into compliance with his measures. — He has dissolved Repres/en\tative Houses repeatedly, for opposing with manly firmness his invasions on the rights of the people. — He has refused for a long time, after such dissolutions, to cause others to be elected; whereby the Legislative powers, incapable of Annihilation, have returned to the People at large for their exercise; the State remaining in the mean time exposed to all the dangers of invasion from without, and convulsions within. —— He has endeavoured to prevent the Population of these States; for that purpose obstructing the Laws for Naturalization of*

Foreigners; refusing to pass others to encourage their migrations hither, and raising the conditions of new Appropriations of Land. — He has obstructed the Administration of Justice, by refusing his Assent to Laws for establishing Judiciary Powers. — He has made Judges dependent on his Will alone, for the tenure of their offices, and the amount and payment of their salaries. ———— He has erected a multitude of New Offices, and sent hither swarms of Officers to harass our People, and eat out their substance. — He has combined us, in times of peace, Standing Armies without the Consent of our legislatures. — He has affected to unite the Military independent of and superior to the Civil power. — He has combined with others to subject us to a jurisdiction foreign to our constitution, and unacknowledged by our laws; giving his Assent to their Acts of pretended Legislation: — For quartering large bodies of armed troops among us: — For protecting them, by a mock Trial, from punishment for any Murders which they should commit on the Inhabitants of these States: — For cutting off our Trade with all parts of the world: — For imposing Taxes on us without our Consent: — For depriving us, in many cases, of the benefits of Trial by Jury: — For transporting us beyond Seas to be tried for pretended offences. — For abolishing the free System of English Laws in a neighbouring Province, establishing therein an Arbitrary government, and enlarging its Boundaries so as to render it at once an example and fit instrument for introducing the same absolute rule into these Colonies: — For taking away our Charters, abolishing our most valuable Laws, and altering fundamentally the Forms of our Governments: — For suspending our own Legislations, and declaring themselves invested with power to *legislate for us in all cases whatsoever. — He has abdicated his Government here, by declaring us out of his Protection and waging War against us. — He has plundered our seas, ravaged our Coasts, burnt our towns, and destroyed the lives of our people. — He is at this time transporting large Armies of foreign Mercenaries to compleat the works of death, desolation and tyranny, already begun with circumstances of Cruelty and Perfidy scarcely paralleled in the most barbarous ages, and totally unworthy the Head of a civilized nation. — He has constrained our fellow Citizens taken Captive on the high Seas to bear Arms against their Country, to become the executioners of their friends and Brethren, or to fall themselves by their Hands. — He has excited domestic insurrections amongst us, and has endeavoured to bring on the inhabitants of our frontiers, the merciless Indian Savages, whose known rule of warfare, is an undistinguished destruction of all ages, sexes and conditions. In every stage of these Oppressions We have Petitioned for Redress in the most humble terms: Our repeated Petitions have been answered /only\ by repeated injury. A Prince, whose character is thus marked by every act which may define a Tyrant, is unfit to be the ruler of a free people. Nor have We been wanting in attentions to our Brittish brethren. We have warned them from time to time of attempts by their legislature to extend an unwarrantable jurisdiction over us. We have reminded them of the circumstances of our emigration and settlement here. We have appealed to their native justice and magnanimity, and we have conjured them by the ties of our common kindred to disavow these usurpations, which, would inevitably interrupt our connections and correspondence. They too have been deaf to the voice of justice and of consanguinity. We must, therefore,* *acquiesce in the necessity, which denounces our Separation, and hold them, as we hold the rest of mankind, Enemies in War, in Peace Friends.—*

We, therefore, *the Representatives of the* **united States of America,** *in General Congress, Assembled, appealing to the Supreme Judge of the world for the rectitude of our intentions, do, in the Name, and by Authority of the good People of these Colonies, solemnly publish and declare, that these United Colonies are, and of Right ought to be* **Free and Independent States;** *that they are Absolved from all Allegiance to the British Crown, and that all political connection between them and the State of Great Britain, is and ought to be totally dissolved; and that as Free and Independent States, they have full Power to levy War, conclude Peace, contract Alliances, establish Commerce, and to do all other Acts and Things which Independent States may of right do.— And for the support of this Declaration with a firm reliance on the protection of divine Providence, we mutually pledge to each other our Lives, our Fortunes and our sacred Honor.*

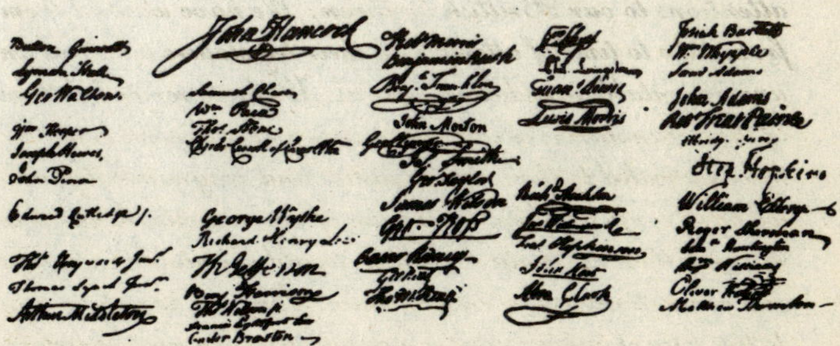

KANE & ABEL

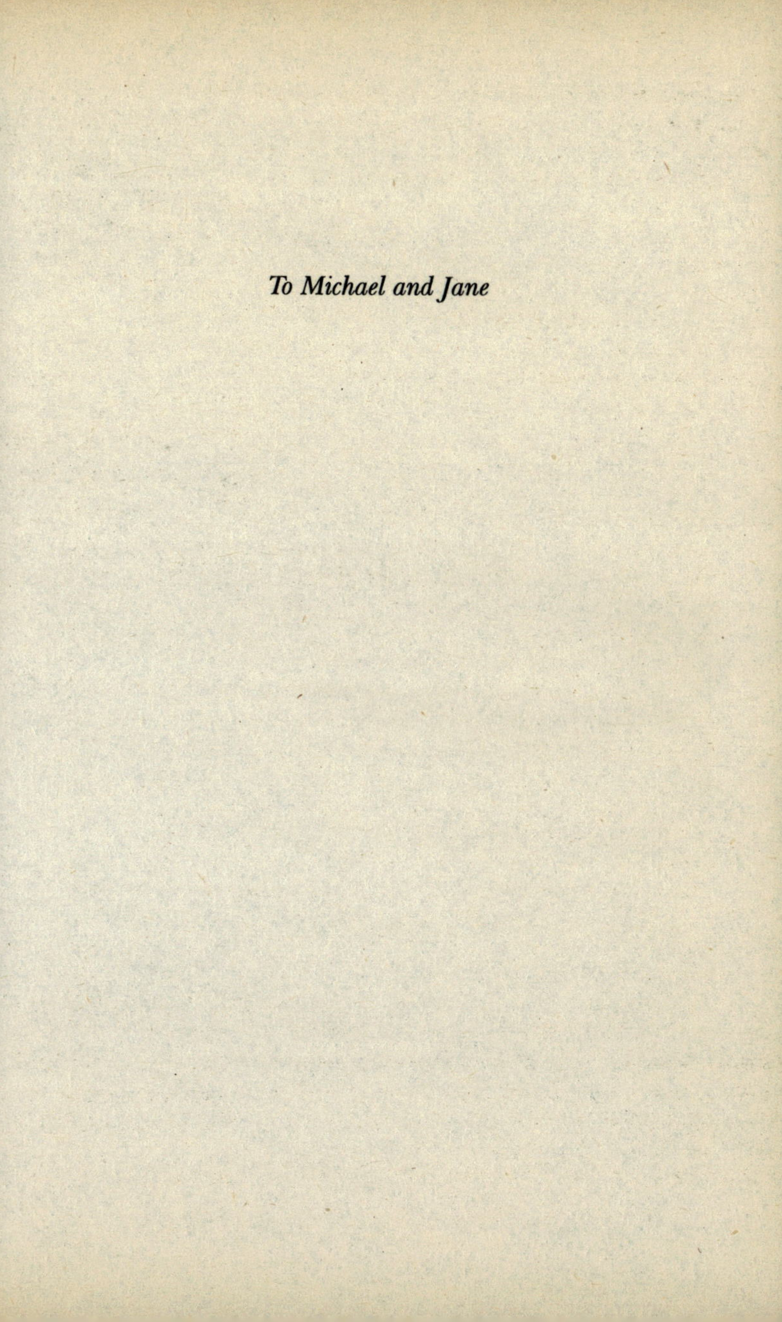

To Michael and Jane

Book One

I

April 18th, 1906 *Slonim, Poland*

She only stopped screaming when she died. It was then that he started to scream.

The young boy who was hunting rabbits in the forest was not sure whether it had been the woman's last cry or the child's first that alerted him. He turned suddenly, sensing the possible danger, his eyes searching for an animal that was so obviously in pain. He had never known any animal to scream in quite that way before. He edged towards the noise cautiously; the scream had now turned to a whine, but it still did not sound like any animal he knew. He hoped it would be small enough to kill; at least that would make a change from rabbit for dinner.

The young boy moved stealthily towards the river, where the strange noise came from, running from tree to tree, feeling the protection of the bark against his shoulder blades, something to touch. Never stay in the open, his father had taught him. When he reached the edge of the forest, he had a clear line of vision all the way down the valley to the river, and even then it took him some time to realise that the strange cry emanated from no ordinary animal. He continued to creep towards the whining, but he was out in the open on his own now. Then suddenly he saw the woman, with her dress above her waist, her bare legs splayed wide apart. He had never seen a woman like that before. He ran quickly to her side and stared down at her belly, quite frightened to touch. There, lying between the woman's legs, was the body of a small, damp, pink animal, attached by something that looked like rope. The young hunter dropped his freshly skinned rabbits and collapsed on his knees beside the little creature.

He gazed for a long, stunned moment and then turned his eyes towards the woman, immediately regretting the decision. She was already blue with cold; her tired twenty-three-year-old face looked middle-aged to the boy; he did not need to be told that she was dead. He picked up the slippery little body – had you asked him why, and no one ever did, he would have told you that the tiny fingernails clawing the crumpled face had worried him – and then he became aware that mother and child were inseparable because of the slimy rope.

He had watched the birth of a lamb a few days earlier and he tried to remember. Yes, that's what the shepherd had done, but dare he, with a child? The whining had stopped and he sensed that a decision was now urgent. He unsheathed his knife, the one he had skinned the rabbits with, wiped it on his sleeve and hesitating only for a moment, cut the rope close to the child's body. Blood flowed freely from the severed ends. Then what had the shepherd done when the lamb was born? He had tied a knot to stop the blood. Of course, of course; he pulled some grass out of the earth beside him and hastily tied a crude knot in the cord. Then he took the child in his arms. He rose slowly from his knees, leaving behind him three dead rabbits and the dead woman who had given birth to this child. Before finally turning his back on the mother, he put her legs together, and pulled her dress down over her knees. It seemed to be the right thing to do.

"Holy God," he said aloud, the first thing he always said when he had done something very good or very bad. He wasn't yet sure which this was.

The young hunter then ran towards the cottage where he knew his mother would be cooking supper, waiting only for his rabbits; all else would be prepared. She would be wondering how many he might have caught today; with a family of eight to feed, she needed at least three. Sometimes he managed a duck, a goose or even a pheasant that had strayed from the Baron's estate, on which his father worked.

Tonight he had caught a different animal, and when he reached the cottage the young hunter dared not let go of his prize even with one hand, so he kicked at the door with his bare foot until his mother opened it. Silently, he held out his offering to her. She made no immediate move to take the creature from him but stood, one hand on her breast, gazing at the wretched sight.

"Holy God," she said and crossed herself. The boy stared up at his mother's face for some sign of pleasure or anger. Her eyes were now showing a tenderness that the boy had never seen in them before. He knew then that the thing which he had done must be good.

"Is it a baby, Matka?"

"It's a little boy," said his mother, nodding her head sorrowfully. "Where did you find him?"

"Down by the river, Matka," he said.

"And the mother?"

"Dead."

She crossed herself again.

"Quickly, run and tell your father what has happened. He will find Urszula Wojnak on the estate and you must take them both to the mother, and then be sure they come back here."

The young hunter handed over the little boy to his mother, happy enough not to have dropped the slippery creature. Now, free of his quarry, he rubbed his hands on his trousers and ran off to look for his father.

The mother closed the door with her shoulder and called out for her eldest child, a girl, to put the pot on the stove. She sat down on a wooden stool, unbuttoned her bodice and pushed a tired nipple towards the little puckered mouth. Sophia, her younger daughter, only six months old, would have to go without her supper tonight; come to think of it, so would the whole family.

"And to what purpose?" the woman said out loud, tucking a shawl around her arm and the child together. "Poor little mite, you'll be dead by morning."

But she did not repeat those feelings to old Urszula Wojnak when the midwife washed the little body and tended to the twisted umbilical stump late that night. Her husband stood silently by, observing the scene.

"When a guest comes into the house, God comes into the house," declared the woman, quoting the old Polish proverb.

Her husband spat. "To the cholera with him. We have children enough of our own."

The woman pretended not to hear him as she stroked the dark, thin hairs on the baby's head.

"What shall we call him?" the woman asked, looking up at her husband.

He shrugged. "Who cares? Let him go to his grave nameless."

2

April 18th, 1906 ***Boston, Massachusetts***

The doctor picked up the newborn child by the ankles and slapped its bottom. The infant started to cry.

In Boston, Massachusetts, there is a hospital that caters mainly for those who suffer from the diseases of the rich, and on selected occasions allows itself to deliver the new rich. At the Massachusetts General Hospital the mothers don't scream, and certainly they don't give birth fully dressed. It is not the done thing.

A young man was pacing up and down outside the delivery room; inside, two obstetricians and the family doctor were on duty. This father did not believe in taking risks with his first-born. The two obstetricians would be paid a large fee merely to stand by and witness events. One of them, who wore evening clothes under his long white coat, had a dinner party to attend later, but he could not afford to absent himself from this particular birth. The three had earlier drawn straws to decide who should deliver the child, and Doctor MacKenzie, the family G.P., had won. A sound, secure name, the father considered, as he paced up and down the corridor. Not that he had any reason to be anxious. Roberts had driven his wife, Anne, to the hospital in the hansom carriage that morning, which she had calculated was the twenty-eighth day of her ninth month. She had started labour soon after breakfast, and he had been assured that delivery would not take place until his bank had closed for the day. The father was a disciplined man and saw no reason why a birth should interrupt his well-ordered life. Nevertheless, he continued to pace. Nurses and young doctors hurried past him, aware of his presence, their voices lowered when they were near him, and raised again only when they were out of his earshot. He didn't notice because everybody had always treated him that way. Most of them had never seen him in person; all of them knew who he was.

If it was a boy, a son, he would probably build the new children's wing that the hospital so badly needed. He had already built a library and a school. The expectant father tried to read the evening paper, looking over the words but not taking in their meaning. He was nervous, even worried. It would never do for them (he looked upon almost everyone as 'them') to realise that it had to be a boy, a boy who would one day take his place as president of the bank. He turned the pages of the *Evening Transcript*. The Boston Red Sox had beaten the New York Highlanders – others would be celebrating. Then he recalled the headline on the front page and returned to it. The worst-ever earthquake in the history of America. Devastation in San Francisco, at least four hundred people dead – others would be mourning. He hated that. That would take away from the birth of his son. People would remember something else had happened on that day. It never occurred to him, not even for a moment, that it might be a girl. He turned to the financial pages and checked the stock market, down sharply; that damned earthquake had taken one hundred thousand dollars off the value of his own holdings in the bank, but as his personal fortune remained comfortably over sixteen million dollars, it was going to take more than a Californian earthquake to move him. He could now live off the interest from his interest, so the sixteen million capital would always remain intact, ready for his son, still unborn. He continued to pace and pretend to read the *Transcript*.

The obstetrician in evening dress pushed through the swing doors of the delivery room to report the news. He felt he must do something for his large unearned fee and he was the most suitably dressed for the announcement. The two men stared at each other for a moment. The doctor also felt a little nervous, but he wasn't going to show it in front of the father.

"Congratulations, sir, you have a son, a fine-looking little boy."

What silly remarks people make when a child is born, the father thought; how could he be anything but little? The news hadn't yet dawned on him – a son. He almost thanked God. The obstetrician ventured a question to break the silence.

"Have you decided what you will call him?"

The father answered without hesitation. "William Lowell Kane."

3

Long after the excitement of the baby's arrival had passed and the rest of the family had gone to bed, the mother remained awake with the little child in her arms. Helena Koskiewicz believed in life, and she had borne nine children to prove it. Although she had lost three in infancy, she had not let any of them go easily.

Now at thirty-five she knew that her once lusty Jasio would give her no more sons or daughters. God had given her this one; surely he was destined to live. Helena's was a simple faith, which was good, for her destiny was never to afford her more than a simple life. She was grey and thin, not through choice but through little food, hard work, and no spare money. It never occurred to her to complain but the lines on her face would have been more in keeping with a grandmother than a mother in today's world. She had never worn new clothes even once in her life.

Helena squeezed her tired breasts so hard that dull red marks appeared around the nipples. Little drops of milk squirted out. At thirty-five, halfway through life's contract, we all have some useful piece of expertise to pass on and Helena Koskiewicz's was now at a premium.

"Matka's littlest one," she whispered tenderly to the child, and drew the milky teat across its pursed mouth. The blue eyes opened and tiny drops of sweat broke out on the baby's nose as he tried to suck. Finally the mother slumped unwillingly into a deep sleep.

Jasio Koskiewicz, a heavy, dull man with a full moustache, his only gesture of self-assertion in an otherwise servile existence, discovered his wife and the baby asleep in the rocking chair when he rose at five. He hadn't noticed her absence from their bed that night. He stared down at the bastard who had, thank God, at least stopped wailing. Was it dead? Jasio considered the easiest way out of the dilemma was to get himself to work and not interfere with the intruder; let the woman worry about life and death: his preoccupation was to be on the Baron's estate by first light. He took a few long swallows of goat's milk and wiped his luxuriant moustache on his sleeve. Then he grabbed a hunk of bread with one hand and his traps with the other, slipping noiselessly out of the cottage for fear of waking the woman and getting himself involved. He strode away towards the forest, giving no more thought to the little intruder other than to assume that he had seen him for the last time.

Florentyna, the elder daughter, was next to enter the kitchen, just before the old clock, which for many years had kept its own time, claimed that six a.m. had arrived. It was of no more than ancillary assistance to those who wished to know if it was the hour to get up or go to bed. Among Florentyna's daily duties was the preparation of the breakfast, in itself a minor task involving the simple division of a skin of goat's milk and a lump of rye bread among a family of eight. Nevertheless, it required the wisdom of Solomon to carry out the task in such a way that no one complained about another's portion.

Florentyna struck those who saw her for the first time as a pretty, frail, shabby little thing. It was unfair that for the last three years she had had only one dress to wear, but those who could separate their opinion of the child from that of her surroundings understood why Jasio had fallen in love with her mother. Florentyna's long fair hair shone while her hazel eyes sparkled in defiance of the influence of her birth and diet.

She tiptoed up to the rocking chair and stared down at her mother and the little boy whom she had adored at first sight. She had never in her eight years owned a doll. Actually she had only seen one once, when the family had been invited to a celebration of the feast of St. Nicholas at the Baron's castle. Even then she had not actually touched the beautiful object, but now she felt an inexplicable urge to hold this baby in her arms. She bent down and eased the child away from her mother and, staring down into the little blue eyes – such blue eyes – she began to hum. The change of temperature from the warmth of the mother's breast to the cold of the little girl's hands made the baby indignant. He immediately started crying which woke the mother, whose only reaction was of guilt for ever having fallen asleep.

"Holy God, he's still alive," she said to Florentyna. "You prepare breakfast for the boys while I try to feed him again."

Florentyna reluctantly handed the infant back and watched her mother once again pump her lank breasts. The little girl was mesmerised.

"Hurry up, Florcia," chided her mother, "the rest of the family must eat as well."

Florentyna obeyed, and as her brothers arrived from the loft where they all slept, they kissed their mother's hands in greeting and stared at the newcomer in awe. All they knew was that this one had not come from Matka's stomach. Florentyna was too excited to eat her breakfast that morning, so the boys divided her portion among them without a second thought and left their mother's share on the table. No one noticed, as they went about their daily tasks, that the mother had eaten nothing since the baby's arrival.

Helena Koskiewicz was pleased that her children had learned so early in life to fend for themselves. They could feed the animals, milk the goats and cows, tend the vegetable garden, and go about their daily tasks without her help or prodding. When Jasio returned home in the evening she suddenly realised that she had not prepared supper for him, but that Florentyna had taken the rabbits from Franck, her brother the hunter, and had already started to cook them. Florentyna was proud to be in charge of the evening meal, a responsibility she was entrusted with only when her mother was unwell, and Helena Koskiewicz rarely allowed herself that luxury. The young hunter had brought home four rabbits and the father six mushrooms and three potatoes: tonight would be a veritable feast.

After dinner, Jasio Koskiewicz sat in his chair by the fire

and studied the child properly for the first time. Holding the little baby under the armpits, with his two thumbs supporting the helpless neck, he cast a trapper's eye over the infant. Wrinkled and toothless, the face was redeemed only by the fine, blue, unfocusing eyes. Directing his gaze towards the thin body, something immediately attracted his attention. He scowled and rubbed the delicate chest with his thumbs.

"Have you noticed this, Helena?" said the trapper, prodding the baby's ribs. "The ugly little bastard has only one nipple."

His wife frowned as she in turn rubbed the skin with her thumb, as though the action would supply the missing organ. Her husband was right: the minute and colourless left nipple was there, but where its mirror image should have appeared on the right-hand side the shallow breast was completely smooth and uniformly pink.

The woman's superstitious tendencies were immediately aroused. "He has been given to me by God," she exclaimed. "See His mark upon him."

The man thrust the child angrily at her. "You're a fool, Helena. The child was given to its mother by a man with bad blood." He spat into the fire, the more precisely to express his opinion of the child's parentage. "Anyway, I wouldn't bet a potato on the little bastard's survival."

Jasio Koskiewicz cared even less than a potato that the child should survive. He was not by nature a callous man but the boy was not his, and one more mouth to feed could only compound his problems. But if it was so to be, it was not for him to question the Almighty, and with no more thought of the boy, he fell into a deep sleep by the fire.

As the days passed by, even Jasio Koskiewicz began to believe the child might survive and, had he been a betting man, he would have lost a potato. The eldest son, the hunter, with the help of his younger brothers, made the child a cot out of wood which they had collected from the Baron's forest. Florentyna made his clothes by cutting little pieces off her own dresses and then sewing them together. They would have called him Harlequin if they had known what it meant. In truth, naming him caused more disagreement in the household than any other single problem had done for months; only the father had no opinion to offer. Finally, they agreed on Wladek; the following Sunday, in the chapel on the Baron's great estate, the child was christened Wladek Koskiewicz, the mother thanking God for sparing his life, the father resigning himself to whatever must be.

That evening there was a small feast to celebrate the christening, augmented by the gift of a goose from the Baron's estate. They all ate heartily.

From that day on, Florentyna learned to divide by nine.

4

Anne Kane had slept peacefully through the night. When her son William returned after breakfast in the arms of one of the hospital's nurses, she could not wait to hold him again.

"Now then, Mrs. Kane," said the white-uniformed nurse briskly, "shall we give baby his breakfast too?"

She sat Anne, who was abruptly aware of her swollen breasts, up in bed and guided the two novices through the procedure. Anne, conscious that to appear embarrassed would be considered unmaternal, gazed fixedly into William's blue eyes, more blue even than his father's, and assimilated her new position, with which it would have been illogical to be other than pleased. At twenty-one, she was not conscious that she lacked anything. Born a Cabot, married into a branch of the Lowell family, and now had a first-born son to carry on the tradition summarised so succinctly in the card sent to her by an old school friend:

Here's to the city of Boston,
Land of the bean and the cod,
Where Cabots talk only to Lowells,
And Lowells talk only to God.

Anne spent half an hour talking to William but obtained little response. He was then retired for a sleep in the same manner in which he had arrived. Anne nobly resisted the fruit and candy piled by her bedside. She was determined to get back into all her dresses by the summer season and reassume her rightful place in all the fashionable magazines. Had not the Prince de Garonne said that she was the only beautiful object in Boston? Her long golden hair, fine delicate features, and slim figure had attracted excited admiration in cities she had never even visited. She checked in the mirror: no telltale lines on her face; people would hardly believe that she was the mother of a bouncing boy. Thank God it had been a bouncing boy, thought Anne.

She enjoyed a light lunch and prepared herself for the visitors who would appear during the afternoon, already screened by her private secretary. Those allowed to see her on the first days had to be family or from the very best families; others would be told she was not yet ready to receive them. But as Boston was the last city remaining in America where each knew his place to the finest degree of social prominence, there was unlikely to be any unexpected intruder.

The room which she alone occupied could have easily taken another five beds had it not already been smothered in flowers. A casual passer-by could have been forgiven for mistaking it for a minor horticultural show, if it had not been for the presence of the young mother sitting upright in bed. Anne switched on the electric light, still a novelty for her; Richard and she had waited for the Cabots to have them fitted, which all of Boston had interpreted as an oracular sign that electromagnetic induction was as of that moment socially acceptable.

The first visitor was Anne's mother-in-law, Mrs. Thomas Lowell Kane, the head of the family since her husband had died the previous year. In elegant late middle-age, she had perfected the technique of sweeping into a room to her own total satisfaction and to its occupants' undoubted discomfiture. She wore a long chemise dress, which made it impossible to view her ankles; the only man who had ever seen her ankles was now dead. She had always been lean. In her opinion, fat women meant bad food and even worse breeding. She was now the oldest Lowell alive; the oldest Kane, come to that. She therefore expected and was expected to be the first to arrive to view her new grandson. After all, had it not been she who had arranged the meeting between Anne and Richard? Love had seemed of little consequence to Mrs. Kane. Wealth, position and prestige she could always come to terms with. Love was all very well, but it rarely proved to be a lasting commodity; the other three were. She kissed her daughter-in-law approvingly on the forehead. Anne touched a button on the wall, and a quiet buzz could be heard. The noise took Mrs. Kane by surprise; she could not believe electricity would ever catch on. The nurse reappeared with the heir. Mrs. Kane inspected him, sniffed her satisfaction and waved him away.

"Well done, Anne," the old lady said, as if her daughter-in-law had won a minor gymkhana prize. "All of us are very proud of you."

Anne's own mother, Mrs. Edward Cabot, arrived a few minutes later. She, like Mrs. Kane, had been widowed in recent years and differed so little from her in appearance that those who observed them only from afar tended to get them muddled up. But to do Mrs. Cabot justice, she took considerably more interest in her new grandson and in her daughter. The inspection moved to the flowers.

"How kind of the Jacksons to remember," murmured Mrs. Cabot.

Mrs. Kane adopted a more cursory procedure. Her eyes skimmed over the delicate blooms, then settled on the donors' cards. She whispered the soothing names to herself: Adamses, Lawrences, Lodges, Higginsons. Neither grandmother commented on the names they didn't know; they were both past the age of wanting to learn of anything or anyone new. They left together, well pleased: an heir had been born and appeared, on first sight, to be adequate. They both considered that their final family obligation had been successfully, albeit vicariously, performed and that they themselves might now progress to the role of chorus.

They were both wrong.

Anne and Richard's close friends poured in during the afternoon with gifts and good wishes, the former of gold or silver, the latter in high-pitched Brahmin accents.

When her husband arrived after the close of business, Anne was somewhat overtired. Richard had drunk champagne at lunch for the first time in his life – old Amos Kerbes had insisted and, with the whole Somerset Club looking on, Richard could hardly have refused. He seemed to his wife to be a little less stiff than usual. Solid in his long black frock coat and pinstripe trousers, he stood fully six feet one; his dark hair with its centre parting gleamed in the light of the large electric bulb. Few would have guessed his age correctly as only thirty-three: youth had never been important to him; substance was the only thing that mattered. Once again William Lowell Kane was called for and inspected, as if the father were checking the balance at the end of the banking day. All seemed to be in order. The boy had two legs, two arms, ten fingers, ten toes and Richard could see nothing that might later embarrass him, so William was sent away.

"I wired the headmaster of St. Paul's last night. William has been admitted for September, 1918."

Anne said nothing. Richard had so obviously started planning William's career.

"Well, my dear, are you fully recovered today?" he went on to enquire, never having spent a day in hospital during his thirty-three years.

"Yes – no – I think so," responded his wife timidly, suppressing a rising tearfulness that she knew would only displease her husband. The answer was not of the sort that Richard could hope to understand. He kissed his wife on the cheek and returned in the hansom carriage to the Red House on Louisburg Square, their family home. With staff, servants, the new baby and his nurse, there would now be nine mouths to feed. Richard did not give the problem a second thought.

William Lowell Kane received the Church's blessing and the names his father had apportioned him before birth at the Protestant Episcopal Church of St. Paul's, in the presence of everybody in Boston who mattered and a few who didn't. Ancient Bishop Lawrence officiated, J. P. Morgan and Alan Lloyd, bankers of impeccable standing, along with Milly Preston, Anne's closest friend, were the chosen godparents. His Grace sprinkled the Holy Water on William's head; the boy didn't murmur. He was already learning the Brahmin approach to life. Anne thanked God for the safe birth of her son and Richard thanked God, whom he regarded as an external bookkeeper whose function was to record the deeds of the Kane family from generation to generation, that he had a son to whom he could leave his fortune. Still, he thought, perhaps he had better be certain and have a second boy. From his kneeling position he glanced sideways at his wife, well pleased with her.

Book Two

5

Wladek Koskiewicz grew slowly. It became apparent to his foster mother that the boy's health would always be a problem. He caught all the illnesses and diseases that growing children normally catch and many that they don't, and he passed them on indiscriminately to the rest of the Koskiewicz family. Helena treated him as any other of her brood and always vigorously defended him when Jasio began to blame the devil rather than God for Wladek's presence in their tiny cottage. Florentyna, on the other hand, took care of Wladek as if he were her own child. She loved him from the first moment she had set eyes on him with an intensity that grew from a fear that no one would ever want to marry her, the penniless daughter of a trapper. She must, therefore, be childless. Wladek was her child.

The eldest brother, the hunter, who had found Wladek, treated him like a plaything but was too afraid of his father to admit that he liked the frail infant who was growing into a sturdy toddler. In any case, next January the hunter was to leave school and start work on the Baron's estate, and children were a woman's problem, so his father had told him. The three younger brothers, Stefan, Josef and Jan, showed little interest in Wladek and the remaining member of the family, Sophia, was happy enough just to cuddle him.

What neither parent had been prepared for was a character and mind so different from those of their own children. No one could dismiss the physical or intellectual differences. The Koskiewiczes were all tall, large-boned with fair hair and grey eyes. Wladek was short and round, with dark hair and intensely blue eyes. The Koskiewiczes had minimal pretensions to scholarship and were removed from the village school as soon as age or discretion allowed. Wladek, on the other hand, though he was late in walking, spoke at eighteen months. Read at three, but was still unable to dress himself. Wrote at five, but continued to wet his bed. He became the despair of his father and the pride of his mother. His first four years on this earth were memorable only as a continual physical attempt through illness to try to depart from it, and for the sustained efforts of Helena and Florentyna to ensure that he did not succeed. He ran around the little wooden cottage barefoot, dressed in his harlequin outfit, a yard or so behind his mother. When Florentyna returned from school, he would transfer his allegiance, never leaving her side until she put him to bed. In her division of the food by nine, Florentyna often sacrificed half of her own share to Wladek, or if he were ill, the entire portion. Wladek wore the clothes she made for him, sang the songs she taught him and shared with her the few toys and presents she had been given.

Because Florentyna was away at school most of the day, Wladek wanted from a young age to go with her. As soon as he was allowed to (holding firmly on to Florentyna's hand until they reached the village school), he walked the eighteen wiorsta, some nine miles, through the woods of moss-covered birches and cypresses and the orchards of lime and cherry, to Slonim to begin his education.

Wladek liked school from the first day; it was an escape from the tiny cottage which had until then been his whole world. School also confronted him for the first time in life with the savage implications of the Russian occupation of eastern Poland. He learned that his native Polish was to be spoken only in the privacy of the cottage and that while at school, only Russian was to be used. He sensed in the other children around him a fierce pride in the oppressed mother tongue and culture. He, too, felt that same pride. To his surprise, Wladek found that he was not belittled by Mr. Kotowski, his schoolteacher, the way he was at home by his father. Although still the youngest, as at home, it was not long before he rose above all his classmates in everything except height. His tiny stature misled them into continual underestimation of his real abilities: children always imagine biggest is best. By the age of five, Wladek was first in every subject taken by his class except ironwork.

At night, back at the little wooden cottage, while the other children would tend the violets and poplars that bloomed so fragrantly in their spring-time garden, pick berries, chop wood, catch rabbits or make dresses, Wladek read and read, until he was reading the unopened books of his eldest brother and then those of his elder sister. It began to dawn slowly on Helena Koskiewicz that she had taken on more than she had bargained for when the young hunter had brought home the little animal in place of three rabbits; already Wladek was asking questions she could not answer. She knew soon that she would be quite unable to cope, and she wasn't sure what to do about it. She had an unswerving belief in destiny and so was not surprised when the decision was taken out of her hands.

One evening in the autumn of 1911 came the first turning point in Wladek's life. The family had all finished their plain supper of beetroot soup and meatballs, Jasio Koskiewicz was seated snoring by the fire, Helena was sewing, and the other children were playing. Wladek was sitting at the feet of his mother, reading, when above the noise of Stefan and Josef squabbling over the possession of some newly painted pine cones, they heard a loud knock on the door. All fell silent. A knock was always a surprise to the Koskiewicz family, for the little cottage was eighteen wiorsta from Slonim and over six from the Baron's estate. Visitors were almost unknown, and could be offered only a drink of berry juice and the company of noisy children. The whole family looked towards the door apprehensively. As if it had not happened, they waited for the knock to come again. It did, if anything a little louder. Jasio rose sleepily from his chair, walked to the door and opened it cautiously. When they saw the man standing there, everyone bowed their heads except Wladek, who stared up at the broad, handsome, aristocratic figure in the heavy bearskin coat, whose presence dominated the tiny room and brought fear into the father's eyes. A cordial smile allayed that fear, and the trapper invited the Baron Rosnovski into his home. Nobody spoke. The Baron had never visited them in the past and no one was sure what to say.

Wladek put down his book, rose, and walked towards the stranger, thrusting out his hand before his father could stop him.

"Good evening, sir," said Wladek.

The Baron took his hand and they stared into each other's eyes. As the Baron released him, Wladek's eyes fell on a magnificent silver band around his wrist with an inscription on it that he could not quite make out.

"You must be Wladek."

"Yes, sir," said the boy, neither sounding awed nor showing surprise that the Baron knew his name.

"It is about you that I have come to see your father," said the Baron.

Wladek remained before the Baron, staring up at him. The trapper signified to his children by a wave of the arm that they should leave him alone with his master, so two of them curtsied, four bowed and all six retreated silently into the loft. Wladek remained, and no one suggested he should do otherwise.

"Koskiewicz," began the Baron, still standing, as no one had invited him to sit. The trapper had not offered him a chair for two reasons: first, because he was too shy and second, because he assumed the Baron was there to issue a reprimand. "I have come to ask a favour."

"Anything, sir, anything," said the father, wondering what he could give the Baron that he did not already have a hundredfold.

The Baron continued. "My son, Leon, is now six and is being taught privately at the castle by two tutors, one from our native Poland and the other from Germany. They tell me he is a clever boy, but that he lacks competition as he has only himself to beat. Mr. Kotowski, the teacher of the village school at Slonim, tells me that Wladek is the only boy capable of providing the competition that Leon so badly needs. I wonder therefore if you would allow your son to leave the village school and to join Leon and his tutors at the castle."

Wladek continued to stand before the Baron, gazing, while before him there opened a wondrous vision of food and drink, books and teachers wiser by far than Mr. Kotowski. He glanced towards his mother. She, too, was gazing at the Baron, her face filled with wonder and sorrow. His father turned to his mother, and the instant of silent communication between them seemed an eternity to the child.

The trapper gruffly addressed the Baron's feet. "We would be honoured, sir."

The Baron looked interrogatively at Helena Koskiewicz.

"The Blessed Virgin forbid that I should ever stand in my child's way," she said softly, "though She alone knows how much it will cost me."

"But, Madam Koskiewicz, your son can return home regularly to see you."

"Yes, sir. I expect he will do so, at first." She was about to add some plea but decided against it.

The Baron smiled. "Good. It's settled then. Please bring the boy to the castle tomorrow morning by seven o'clock. During the school term Wladek will live with us, and when Christmas comes, he can return to you."

Wladek burst into tears.

"Quiet, boy," said the trapper.

"I will not go," said Wladek firmly, wanting to go.

"Quiet, boy," said the trapper, this time a little louder.

"Why not?" asked the Baron, with compassion in his voice.

"I will never leave Florcia – never."

"Florcia?" queried the Baron.

"My eldest daughter, sir," interjected the trapper. "Don't concern yourself with her, sir. The boy will do as he is told."

No one spoke. The Baron considered for a moment. Wladek continued to cry controlled tears.

"How old is the girl?" asked the Baron.

"Fourteen," replied the trapper.

"Could she work in the kitchens?" asked the Baron, relieved to observe that Helena Koskiewicz was not going to burst into tears, as well.

"Oh yes, Baron," she replied, "Florcia can cook and she can sew and she can . . ."

"Good, good, then she can come as well. I shall expect to see them both tomorrow morning at seven."

The Baron walked to the door and looked back and smiled at Wladek, who returned the smile. Wladek had won his first bargain, and accepted his mother's tight embrace while he stared at the closed door and heard her whisper, "Ah, Matka's littlest one, what will become of you now?"

Wladek couldn't wait to find out.

Helena Koskiewicz packed for Wladek and Florentyna during the night, not that it would have taken long to pack the entire family's possessions. In the morning, the remainder of the family stood in front of the door to watch them both depart for the castle, each holding a paper parcel under one arm. Florentyna, tall and graceful, kept looking back, crying and waving; but Wladek, short and ungainly, never once looked back. Florentyna held firmly to Wladek's hand for the entire journey to the Baron's castle. Their roles were now reversed; from that day on she was to depend on him.

They were clearly expected by the magnificent man in the embroidered suit of green livery who was summoned by their timid knock on the great oak door. Both children had gazed in admiration at the grey uniforms of the soldiers in the town who guarded the nearby Russian-Polish border, but they had never seen anything so resplendent as this liveried servant, towering above them and evidently of overwhelming importance. There was a thick carpet in the hall and Wladek stared at the green and red patterning, amazed by its beauty, wondering if he should take his shoes off and surprised when he walked across it, that his footsteps made no sound. The dazzling being conducted them to their bedrooms in the west wing. Separate bedrooms – would they ever get to sleep? At least there was a connecting door, so they needed never to be too far apart, and in fact for many nights they slept together in one bed.

When they had both unpacked, Florentyna was taken to the kitchen, and Wladek to a playroom in the south wing of the castle to meet the Baron's son, Leon. He was a tall, good-looking boy who was so immediately charming and welcoming to Wladek that he abandoned his prepared pugnacious posture with surprise and relief. Leon had been a lonely child, with no one to play with except his *niania*, the devoted Lithuanian woman who had breast-fed him and attended to his every need since the premature death of his mother. The stocky boy who had come out of the forest promised companionship. At least in one matter they both knew they had been deemed equals.

Leon immediately offered to show Wladek around the castle, and the tour took the rest of the morning. Wladek remained astounded by its size, the richness of the furniture and fabric, and those carpets in every room. To Leon he admitted only to being agreeably impressed: after all, he had won his place in the castle on merit. The main part of the building is early Gothic, explained the Baron's son, as if Wladek were sure to know what Gothic meant. Wladek nodded. Next Leon took his new friend down into the immense cellars, with line upon line of wine bottles covered in dust and cobwebs. Wladek's favourite room was the vast dining hall, with its massive pillared vaulting and stone-flagged floor. There were animals' heads all around the walls. Leon told him they were bison, bear, elk, boar and wolverine. At the end of the room, resplendent, was the Baron's coat of arms below stag's antlers. The Rosnovski family motto read 'Fortune favours the brave.' After a lunch, which Wladek ate little of because he couldn't master a knife and fork, he met his two tutors who did not give him the same warm welcome, and in the evening he climbed up on to the longest bed he had ever seen and told Florentyna about his adventures. Her excited eyes never once left his face, nor did she even close her mouth, agape with wonder, especially when she heard about the knife and fork, which Wladek described with the fingers of his right hand held out tight together, those of his left splayed wide apart.

The tutoring started at seven sharp, before breakfast, and continued throughout the day with only short breaks for meals. Initially, Leon was clearly ahead of Wladek, but Wladek wrestled determinedly with his books so that as the weeks passed the gap began to narrow, while friendship and rivalry between the two boys developed simultaneously. The German and Polish tutors found it hard to treat their two pupils, the son of a baron, and the son of a trapper, as equals, although they reluctantly conceded to the Baron when he enquired that Mr. Kotowski had made the right academic choice. The tutors' attitude towards Wladek never worried him because by Leon he was always treated as an equal.

The Baron let it be known that he was pleased with the progress the two boys were making and from time to time he would reward Wladek with clothes and toys. Wladek's initial distant and detached admiration for the Baron developed into respect and, when the time came for the boy to return to the little cottage in the forest to rejoin his father and mother for Christmas, he became distressed at the thought of leaving Leon.

His distress was well-founded. Despite the initial happiness he felt at seeing his mother, the short space of three months that he had spent in the Baron's castle had revealed to him deficiencies in his own home of which he had previously been quite unaware. The holiday dragged on. Wladek felt himself stifled by the little cottage with its one room and loft, and dissatisfied by the food dished out in such meagre amounts and then eaten by hand: no one had divided by nine at the castle. After two weeks Wladek longed to return to Leon and the Baron. Every afternoon he would walk the six wiorsta to the castle and sit and stare at the great walls that surrounded the estate. Florentyna, who had lived only among the kitchen servants, took to returning more easily and could not understand that the cottage would never be home again for Wladek. The trapper was not sure how to treat the boy, who was now well-dressed, well-spoken, and talked of things at six that the man did not begin to understand, nor did he want to. The boy seemed to do nothing but waste the entire day reading. Whatever would become of him, the trapper wondered. If he could not swing an axe or trap a hare, how could he ever hope to earn an honest living? He too prayed that the holiday would pass quickly.

Helena was proud of Wladek, and at first avoided admitting to herself that a wedge had been driven between him and the rest of the children. But in the end it could not be avoided. Playing at soldiers one evening, both Stefan and Franck, generals on opposing sides, refused to have Wladek in their armies.

"Why must I always be left out?" cried Wladek. "I want to learn to fight too."

"Because you are not one of us," declared Stefan. "You are not really our brother."

There was a long silence before Franck continued. "Ojciec never wanted you in the first place; only Matka was on your side."

Wladek stood motionless and cast his eye around the circle of children, searching for Florentyna.

"What does Franck mean, I am not your brother?" he demanded.

Thus Wladek came to hear of the manner of his birth and to understand why he had been always set apart from his brothers and sisters. Though his mother's distress at his now total self-containment became oppressive, Wladek was secretly pleased to discover that he came of unknown stock, untouched by the meanness of the trapper's blood, containing with it the germ of spirit that would now make all things seem possible.

When the unhappy holiday eventually came to an end, Wladek returned to the castle with joy. Leon welcomed him back with open arms; for him, as isolated by the wealth of his father as Wladek was by the poverty of the trapper, it had also been a Christmas with little to celebrate. From then on the two boys grew even closer and soon became inseparable. When the summer holidays came around, Leon begged his father to allow Wladek to remain at the castle. The Baron agreed, for he too had grown to love Wladek. Wladek was overjoyed and entered the trapper's cottage only once again in his life.

When Wladek and Leon had finished their classroom work, they would spend the remaining hours playing games. Their favourite was *chowanego*, a sort of hide and seek; as the castle had seventy-two rooms, the chance of repetition was small. Wladek's favourite hiding place was in the dungeons under the castle, in which the only light by which one could be discovered came through a small stone grille set high in the wall and even then one needed a candle to find one's way around. Wladek was not sure what purpose the dungeons served, and none of the servants ever made mention of them, as they had never been used in anyone's memory.

Wladek was conscious that he was Leon's equal only in the classroom, and was no competition for his friend when they played any game, other than chess. The river Strchara that bordered the estate became an extension to their playground. In spring they fished, in summer they swam, and in winter, when the river was frozen over, they would put on their wooden skates and chase each other across the ice, while Florentyna sat on the river bank anxiously warning them where the surface was thin. But Wladek never heeded her and was always the one who fell in. Leon grew quickly and strong; he ran well, swam well and never seemed to tire or be ill. Wladek became aware for the first time what good-looking and well-built meant, and he knew when he swam, ran, and skated he could never hope to keep up with Leon. Much worse, what Leon called the belly button was, on him, almost unnoticeable, while Wladek's was stumpy and ugly and protruded rudely from the middle of his plump body. Wladek would spend long hours in the quiet of his own room, studying his physique in a mirror, always asking why, and in particular why only one nipple for him when all the boys he had ever seen barechested had the two that the symmetry of the human body appeared to require. Sometimes as he lay in bed unable to sleep, he would finger his naked chest and tears of self-pity would flood on to the pillow. He would finally fall asleep praying that when he awoke in the morning, things would be different. His prayers were not answered.

Wladek put aside each night a time to do physical exercises that could not be witnessed by anyone, not even Florentyna. Through sheer determination he learned to hold himself so that he looked taller. He built up his arms and his legs and hung by the tips of his fingers from a beam in the bedroom in the hope that it would make him grow, but Leon grew taller even while he slept. Wladek was forced to accept the fact that he would always be a head shorter than the Baron's son, and that nothing, nothing was ever going to produce the missing nipple. Wladek's dislike of his own body was unprompted, for Leon never commented on his friend's appearance; his knowledge of other children stopped short at Wladek, whom he adored uncritically.

Baron Rosnovski became increasingly fond of the fierce dark-haired boy who had replaced the younger brother for Leon, so tragically lost when his wife had died in childbirth.

The two boys would dine with him in the great stone-walled hall each evening, while the flickering candles cast ominous shadows from the stuffed animal heads on the wall and the servants came and went noiselessly with the great silver trays and golden plates, bearing geese, hams, crayfish, fine wine and fruits, and sometimes the *mazureks* that had become Wladek's particular favourites. Afterwards, as the darkness fell ever more thickly around the table, the Baron dismissed the waiting servants and would tell the boys stories of Polish history and allowed them a sip of Danzig vodka, in which the tiny gold leaves sparkled bravely in the candlelight. Wladek begged as often as he dared for the story of Tadeusz Kosciuszko.

"A great patriot and hero," the Baron would reply. "The very symbol of our struggle for independence, trained in France . . ."

"Whose people we admire and love as we have learned to hate all Russians and Austrians," supplied Wladek, whose pleasure in the tale was enhanced by his word-perfect knowledge of it.

"Who is telling whom the story, Wladek?" The Baron laughed. ". . . And then fought with George Washington in America for liberty and democracy. In 1792 he led the Poles in battle at Dubienka. When our wretched king, Stanislas Augustus, deserted us to join the Russians, Kosciuszko returned to the homeland he loved to throw off the yoke of Tsardom. He won the battle of where, Leon?"

"Raclawice, sir, and then he freed Warsaw."

"Good, my child. Then, alas, the Russians mustered a great force at Maciejowice and he was finally defeated and taken prisoner. My great-great-great-grandfather fought with Kosciuszko on that day, and later with Dabrowski's legions for the mighty Emperor Napoleon Bonaparte."

"And for his service to Poland was created the Baron Rosnovski, a title your family will ever bear in remembrance of those great days," said Wladek, as stoutly as if the title would one day pass to him.

"Those great days will come again," said the Baron quietly. "I only pray that I may live to see them."

At Christmas time, the peasants on the estate would bring their families to the castle for the celebration of the blessed vigil. Throughout Christmas Eve they fasted and the children would look out of the windows for the first star, which was the sign the feast might begin. The Baron would say grace in his fine deep voice: "*Benedic nobis, Domine Deus, et his donis quae ex liberalitate tua sumpturi sumus,*" and once they had sat down Wladek would be embarrassed by the huge capacity of Jasio Koskiewicz, who addressed himself squarely to every one of the thirteen courses from the barsasz soup through to the cakes and plums, and would as in previous years be sick in the forest on the way home.

After the feast Wladek enjoyed distributing the gifts from the Christmas tree, laden with candles and fruit, to the awe-struck peasant children – a doll for Sophia, a forest knife for Josef, a new dress for Florentyna, the first gift Wladek had ever requested of the Baron.

"It's true," said Josef to his mother when he received his gift from Wladek, "he is not our brother, Matka."

"No," she replied, "but he will always be my son."

Through the winter and spring of 1914 Wladek grew in strength and learning. Then suddenly, in July, the German tutor left the castle without even saying farewell; neither boy was sure why. They never thought to connect his departure with the assassination in Sarajevo of the Archduke Francis

Ferdinand by a student anarchist, described to them by their other tutor in unaccountably solemn tones. The Baron became withdrawn; neither boy was sure why. The younger servants, the children's favourites, began to disappear one by one; neither boy was sure why. As the year passed Leon grew taller, Wladek grew stronger, and both boys became wiser.

One morning in the summer of 1915, a time of fine, lazy days, the Baron set off on the long journey to Warsaw to put, as he described it, his affairs in order. He was away for three and a half weeks, twenty-five days which Wladek marked off each morning on a calendar in his bedroom; it seemed to him a lifetime. On the day he was due to return, the two boys went down to the railway station at Slonim to await the weekly train with its one carriage and greet the Baron on his arrival. The three of them travelled home in silence.

Wladek thought the great man looked tired and older, another unaccountable circumstance, and during the following week the Baron often conducted with the chief servants a rapid and anxious dialogue, broken off whenever Leon or Wladek entered the room, an uncharacteristic surreptitiousness that made the two boys uneasy and fearful that they were the unwitting cause of it. Wladek despaired that the Baron might send him back to the trapper's cottage – always aware he was a stranger in a stranger's home.

One evening a few days after the Baron had returned he called for the two boys to join him in the great hall. They crept in, fearful of him. Without explanation he told them that they were about to make a long journey. The little conversation, insubstantial as it seemed to Wladek at the time, remained with him for the rest of his life.

"My dear children," began the Baron in a low, faltering tone, "the warmongers of Germany and the Austro-Hungarian empire are at the throat of Warsaw and will soon be upon us."

Wladek recalled an inexplicable phrase flung out by the Polish tutor at the German tutor during their last tense days together. "Does that mean that the hour of the submerged peoples of Europe is at last upon us?" he asked.

The Baron regarded Wladek's innocent face tenderly. "Our national spirit has not perished in one hundred and fifty years of attrition and repression," he replied. "It may be that the fate of Poland is as much at stake as that of Serbia, but we are powerless to influence history. We are at the mercy of the three mighty empires that surround us."

"We are strong, we can fight," said Leon. "We have wooden swords and shields. We are not afraid of Germans or Russians."

"My son, you have only played at war. This battle will not be between children. We will now find a quiet place to live until history has decided our fate and we must leave as soon as possible. I can only pray that this is not the end of your childhood."

Leon and Wladek were both mystified and irritated by the Baron's words. War sounded like an exciting adventure which they would be sure to miss if they had to leave the castle. The servants took several days to pack the Baron's possessions and Wladek and Leon were informed that they would be departing for their small summer home in the north of Grodno on the following Monday. The two boys continued, largely unsupervised, with their work and play but they could now find no one in the castle with the inclination or time to answer their myriad questions.

On Saturdays, lessons were held only in the morning. They were translating Adam Mickiewicz's *Pan Tadeusz* into Latin when they heard the guns. At first, Wladek thought the familiar sounds meant only that another trapper was out shooting on the estate; the boys returned to the poetry. A second volley of shots, much closer, made them look up and then they heard the screaming coming from downstairs. They stared at each other in bewilderment; they feared nothing as they had never experienced anything in their short lives that should have made them fearful. The tutor fled, leaving them alone, and then came another shot, this time in the corridor outside their room. The two boys sat motionless, terrified and unbreathing.

Suddenly the door crashed open and a man no older than their tutor, in a grey soldier's uniform and steel helmet, stood towering over them. Leon clung on to Wladek, while Wladek stared at the intruder. The soldier shouted at them in German, demanding to know who they were, but neither boy replied, despite the fact that they had mastered the language, and could speak it almost as well as their mother tongue. Another soldier appeared behind his compatriot as the first advanced on the two boys, grabbed them by the necks, not unlike chickens, and pulled them out into the corridor, down the hall to the front of the castle and then into the gardens, where they found Florentyna screaming hysterically as she stared at the grass in front of her. Leon could not bear to look, and buried his head in Wladek's shoulder. Wladek gazed as much in surprise as in horror at a row of dead bodies, mostly servants, being placed face downwards. He was mesmerised by the sight of a moustache in profile against a pool of blood. It was the trapper. Wladek felt nothing as Florentyna continued screaming.

"Is Papa there?" asked Leon. "Is Papa there?"

Wladek scanned the line of bodies once again. He thanked God that there was no sign of the Baron Rosnovski. He was about to tell Leon the good news when a soldier came up to them.

"*Wer hat gesprochen?*" he demanded fiercely.

"*Ich,*" said Wladek defiantly.

The soldier raised his rifle and brought the butt crashing down on Wladek's head. He sank to the ground, blood spurting over his face. Where was the Baron, what was happening, why were they being treated like this in their own home? Leon quickly jumped on top of Wladek, trying to protect him from the second blow which the soldier had intended for Wladek's stomach, but as the rifle came crashing down the full force caught the back of Leon's head.

Both boys lay motionless, Wladek because he was still dazed by the blow and the sudden weight of Leon's body on top of him, and Leon because he was dead.

Wladek could hear another soldier berating their tormentor for the action he had taken. They picked up Leon, but

Wladek clung on to him. It took two soldiers to prise his friend's body away and dump it unceremoniously with the others, face down on the grass. Wladek's eyes never left the motionless body of his dearest friend until he was finally marched back inside the castle, and, with a handful of dazed survivors, led to the dungeons. Nobody spoke for fear of joining the line of bodies on the grass, until the dungeon doors were bolted and the last murmur of the soldiers had vanished in the distance. Then Wladek said, "Holy God." For there in a corner, slumped against the wall, sat the Baron, uninjured but stunned, staring into space, alive only because the conquerors needed someone to be responsible for the prisoners. Wladek went over to him, while the others sat as far away from their master as possible. The two gazed at each other, as they had on the first day they had met. Wladek put his hand out, and as on the first day the Baron took it. Wladek watched the tears course down the Baron's proud face. Neither spoke. They had both lost the one person they had loved most in the world.

6

William Kane grew quickly, and was considered an adorable child by all who came in contact with him; in the early years of his life these were generally besotted relatives and doting servants.

The top floor of the Kanes' eighteenth-century house in Louisburg Square on Beacon Hill had been converted into nursery quarters, crammed with toys. A further bedroom and a sitting room were made available for the newly acquired nurse. The floor was far enough away from Richard Kane for him to be unaware of problems such as teething, wet nappies and the irregular and undisciplined cries for more food. First sound, first tooth, first step and first word were all recorded in a family book by William's mother along with the progress in his height and weight. Anne was surprised to find that these statistics differed very little from those of any other child with whom she came into contact on Beacon Hill.

The nurse, an import from England, brought the boy up on a regimen that would have gladdened the heart of a Prussian cavalry officer. William's father would visit him each evening at six o'clock. As he refused to address the child in baby language, he ended up not speaking to him at all; the two merely stared at each other. William would grip his father's index finger, the one with which balance sheets were checked, and hold on to it tightly. Richard would allow himself a smile. At the end of the first year the routine was slightly modified and the boy was allowed to come downstairs to see his father. Richard would sit in his high-backed, maroon leather chair watching his first-born weave his way on all fours in and out of the legs of the furniture, reappearing when least expected, which led Richard to observe that the child would undoubtedly become a senator. William took his first steps at thirteen months while clinging on to the tails of his father's topcoat. His first word was 'Dada', which pleased everyone, including Grandmother Kane and Grandmother Cabot, who were regular visitors. They did not actually push the vehicle in which William was perambulated around Boston, but they did deign to walk a pace behind the nurse in the park on Thursday afternoons, glaring at infants with a less disciplined retinue. While other children fed the ducks in the public gardens, William succeeded in charming the swans in the lagoon of Mr. Jack Gardner's extravagant Venetian Palace.

When two years had passed, the grandmothers intimated by hint and innuendo that it was high time for another prodigy, an appropriate sibling for William. Anne obliged them by becoming pregnant and was distressed to find herself feeling and looking progressively off-colour as she entered her fourth month.

Doctor MacKenzie ceased to smile as he checked the growing stomach and hopeful mother, and when Anne miscarried at sixteen weeks he was not altogether surprised, but did not allow her to indulge her grief. In his notes he wrote 'pre-eclampsia?' and then told her, "Anne, my dear, the reason you have not been feeling so well is that your blood pressure was too high, and would probably have become much higher as your pregnancy progressed. I fear doctors haven't found the answer to blood pressure yet, in fact we know very little other than it's a dangerous condition for anyone, particularly for a pregnant woman."

Anne held back her tears while considering the implications of a future without more children.

"Surely it won't happen in my next pregnancy?" she asked, phrasing her question to dispose the doctor to a favourable answer.

"I should be very surprised if it did not, my dear. I am sorry to have to say this to you, but I would strongly advise you against becoming pregnant again."

"But I don't mind feeling off-colour for a few months if it means . . ."

"I am not talking about feeling off-colour, Anne. I am talking about not taking any unnecessary risks with your life."

It was a terrible blow for Richard and Anne, who themselves had both been only children, largely as a result of their respective fathers' premature deaths. They had both assumed that they would produce a family appropriate to the commanding size of their house and their responsibilities to the next generation. "What else is there for a young woman to do?" enquired Grandmother Cabot of Grandmother Kane. No one cared to mention the subject again, and William became the centre of everyone's attention.

Richard, who had taken over as the president of Kane and Cabot Bank and Trust Company when his father had died in 1904, had always immersed himself in the work of the bank. The bank, which stood on State Street, a bastion of architectural and fiscal solidity, had offices in New York, London and San Francisco. The last had presented a problem to Richard soon after William's birth when, along with Crocker National Bank, Wells Fargo, and the California Bank, it collapsed to the ground, not financially, but literally, in the great earthquake of 1906. Richard, by nature a cautious man, was comprehensively insured with Lloyd's of London. Gentlemen all, they had paid up to the penny, enabling Richard to rebuild. Nevertheless, Richard spent an uncomfortable year jolting across America on the four-day train journey between Boston and San Francisco, supervising the rebuilding. He opened the new office in Union Square in October 1907, barely in time to turn his attention to other problems arising on the Eastern seaboard. There was a minor run on the New York banks, and many of the smaller establishments were unable to cope with large withdrawals and started going to the wall. J. P. Morgan, the legendary chairman of the mighty bank bearing his name, invited Richard to join a consortium to hold firm during the crisis. Richard agreed, the courageous stand worked, and the problem began to dissipate, but not before Richard had had a few sleepless nights.

William, on the other hand, slept soundly, unaware of earthquakes and collapsing banks. After all, there were swans that must be fed and endless trips to and from Milton, Brookline and Beverly to be shown to his distinguished relatives.

Early in the spring of the following year Richard acquired a new toy in return for a cautious investment of capital in a man called Henry Ford, who was claiming he could produce a motor car for the people. The bank entertained Mr. Ford at luncheon, and Richard was coaxed into the acquisition of a Model T for the princely sum of eight hundred and fifty dollars. Henry Ford assured Richard that if only the bank would back him, the cost could eventually fall to three hundred and fifty dollars within a few years and everyone would be buying his cars, thus ensuring a large profit for his backers. Richard did back him, and it was the first time he had placed good money behind someone who wished his product to halve in price.

Richard was initially apprehensive that his motor car, sombrely black though it was, might not be regarded as a serious mode of transport for the chairman of a bank, but he was reassured by the admiring glances from the pavements which the machine attracted. At ten miles an hour it was noisier than a horse but it did have the virtue of leaving no mess in the middle of Mount Vernon Street. His only quarrel with Mr. Ford was that the man would not listen to the suggestion that a Model T should be made available in a variety of colours. Mr. Ford insisted that every car should be black in order to keep the price down. Anne, more sensitive than her husband to the approbation of polite society, would not drive in the vehicle until the Cabots had acquired one.

William, on the other hand, adored the 'automobile', as the press called it, and immediately assumed that the vehicle had been bought for him to replace his now redundant and unmechanised pram. He also preferred the chauffeur – with his goggles and flat hat – to his nurse. Grandmother Kane and Grandmother Cabot claimed that they would never travel in the dreadful machine and never did, although it should be pointed out that Grandmother Kane travelled to her funeral in a motor car, but was never informed.

During the next two years the bank grew in strength and size, as did William. Americans were once again investing for expansion, and large sums of money found their way to Kane and Cabot's to be reinvested in such projects as the expanding Lowell leather factory in Lowell, Massachusetts. Richard watched the growth of his bank and his son with unsurprised satisfaction. On William's fifth birthday, he took the child out of women's hands by engaging at four hundred and fifty dollars per annum a private tutor, a Mr. Munro, personally selected by Richard from a list of eight applicants who had earlier been screened by his private secretary. Mr. Munro was charged to ensure that William was ready to enter St. Paul's by the age of twelve. William immediately took to Mr. Munro, whom he thought to be very old and very clever. He was, in fact, twenty-three and the possessor of a second-class honours degree in English from the University of Edinburgh.

William quickly learned to read and write with facility but saved his real enthusiasm for figures. His only complaint was that, of the eight lessons taught every weekday, only one was arithmetic. William was quick to point out to his father that one-eighth of the working day was a small investment of time for someone who would one day be the president of a bank.

To compensate for his tutor's lack of foresight, William dogged the footsteps of his accessible relatives with demands for sums to be executed in his head. Grandmother Cabot, who had never been persuaded that the division of an integer by four would necessarily produce the same answer as its multiplication by one quarter, and indeed in her hands the two operations often did result in two different numbers, found herself speedily outclassed by her grandson, but Grandmother Kane, with some small leanings to cleverness, grappled manfully with vulgar fractions, compound interest and the division of eight cakes among nine children.

"Grandmother," said William, kindly but firmly, when she had failed to find the answer to his latest conundrum, "you can buy me a slide-rule; then I won't have to bother you."

She was astonished at her grandson's precocity, but she bought him one just the same, wondering if he really knew how to use the gadget. It was the first time in her life that Grandmother Kane had been known to take the easy way out of any problem.

Richard's problems began to gravitate eastwards. The chairman of his London branch died at his desk and Richard felt himself required in Lombard Street. He suggested to Anne that she and William should accompany him to Europe, feeling that the education would not do the boy any harm: he could visit all the places about which Mr. Munro had so often talked. Anne, who had never been to Europe, was excited by the prospect, and filled three steamer trunks with elegant and expensive new clothes in which to confront the Old World. William considered it unfair of his mother not to allow him to take that equally essential aid to travel, his bicycle.

The Kanes travelled to New York by train to join the *Aquitania,* bound for her voyage to Southampton. Anne was appalled by the sight of the immigrant street pedlars pushing their wares, and she was glad to be safely on board and resting in her cabin. William, on the other hand, was amazed by the size of New York; he had, until that moment, always imagined that his father's bank was the biggest building in America, if not the world. He wanted to buy a pink and yellow ice-cream from a man all dressed in white and wearing a boater, but his father would not hear of it; in any case, Richard never carried small change.

William adored the great vessel on sight and quickly became friendly with the captain, who showed him all the secrets of the Cunard Steamships' prima donna. Richard and Anne, who naturally sat at the captain's table, felt it necessary, before the ship had long left America, to apologise for the amount of the crew's time that their son was occupying.

"Not at all," replied the white-bearded skipper. "William and I are already good friends. I only wish I could answer all his questions about time, speed and distance. I have to be coached each night by the first engineer in the hope of first anticipating and then surviving the next day."

The *Aquitania* sailed into the Solent to dock at Southampton after a six-day journey. William was reluctant to leave her, and tears would have been unavoidable had it not been for the magnificent sight of the Rolls-Royce Silver Ghost, waiting at the quayside complete with a chauffeur, ready to whisk them off to London. Richard decided on the spur of the moment that he would have the car transported back to New York at the end of the trip, which was the most out-of-character decision he made during the rest of his life. He informed Anne, rather unconvincingly, that he wanted to show the vehicle to Henry Ford.

The Kane family always stayed at the Ritz in Piccadilly when they were in London, which was convenient for Richard's office in the City. Anne used the time while Richard was occupied at the bank to show William the Tower of London, Buckingham Palace and the Changing of the Guard. William thought everything was 'great' except the English accent which he had difficulty in understanding.

"Why don't they talk like us, Mommy?" he demanded, and was surprised to be told that the question was more often put the other way around, as 'they' came first. William's favourite pastime was to watch the soldiers in their bright red uniforms with large shiny brass buttons who kept guard duty outside Buckingham Palace. He tried to engage them in conversation but they stared past him into space and never even blinked.

"Can we take one home?" he asked his mother.

"No, darling, they have to stay here and guard the King."

"But he's got so many of them, can't I have just one?"

As a 'special treat' – Anne's words – Richard allowed himself an afternoon off to take his wife and son to the West End to see a traditional English pantomime called *Jack and the Beanstalk* playing at the London Hippodrome. William loved Jack and immediately wanted to cut down every tree he laid his eyes on, imagining them all to be sheltering a monster. They had tea after the show at Fortnum and Mason in

Piccadilly, and Anne let William have two cream buns and a new-fangled thing called a doughnut. Daily thereafter William had to be escorted back to the tea-room at Fortnum's to consume another 'dough-bun', as he called them.

The holiday passed by all too quickly for William and his mother, whereas Richard, satisfied with his progress in Lombard Street and pleased with his newly appointed chairman, began to look forward to the day of their departure. Cables were daily arriving from Boston that made him anxious to be back in his own boardroom. Finally, when one such missive informed him that twenty-five thousand workers at a cotton mill with which his bank had a heavy investment in Lawrence, Massachusetts, had gone out on strike, he was relieved that his planned date of sailing was now only three days away.

William was looking forward to returning and telling Mr. Munro all the exciting things he had done in England and to being reunited with his two grandmothers again. He felt sure they had never done anything so exciting as visiting a real live theatre with the general public. Anne was also happy to be going home, although she had enjoyed the trip almost as much as William, for her clothes and beauty had been much admired by the normally undemonstrative North Sea Islanders. As a final treat for William the day before they were due to sail, Anne took him to a tea party in Eaton Square given by the wife of the newly appointed chairman of Richard's London branch. She, too, had a son, Stuart, who was eight – and William had, in the two weeks in which they had been playing together, grown to regard him as an indispensable grown-up friend. The party, however, was rather subdued because Stuart felt unwell and William, in sympathy with his new chum, announced to his mother that he was going to be ill too. Anne and William returned to the Ritz Hotel earlier than they had planned. She was not greatly put out as it gave her a little more time to supervise the packing of the large steamer trunks, although she was convinced William was only putting on an act to please Stuart. When she tucked William up in bed that night, she found that he had been as good as his word and was running a slight fever. She remarked on it to Richard over dinner.

"Probably all the excitement at the thought of going home," he offered, sounding unconcerned.

"I hope so," replied Anne. "I don't want him to be sick on a six-day sea voyage."

"He'll be just fine by tomorrow," said Richard, issuing an unheeded directive, but when Anne went to wake William the next morning, she found him covered in little red spots and running a temperature of one hundred and three. The hotel doctor diagnosed measles and was politely insistent that William should on no account be sent on a sea journey, not only for his own good but for the sake of the other passengers. There was nothing for it but to leave him in bed with his stone hot water bottle and wait for the departure of the next ship. Richard was unable to countenance the three-week delay and decided to sail as planned. Reluctantly, Anne allowed the hurried changes of booking to be made. William begged his father to let him accompany him: the twenty-one days before the *Aquitania* was due back in Southampton seemed like an eternity to the child. Richard was adamant, and hired a nurse to attend William and convince him of his poor state of health.

Anne travelled down to Southampton with Richard in the new Rolls-Royce.

"I shall be lonely in London without you, Richard," she ventured diffidently in their parting moment, risking his disapproval of emotional women.

"Well, my dear, I dare say that I shall be somewhat lonely in Boston without you," he said, his mind on the striking cotton workers.

Anne returned to London on the train, wondering how she would occupy herself for the next three weeks. William had a better night and in the morning the spots looked less ferocious. Doctor and nurse were unanimous, however, in their insistence that he should remain in bed. Anne used the extra time to write long letters to the family, while William remained in bed, protesting, but on Thursday morning he got himself up early and went into his mother's room, very much back to his normal self. He climbed into bed next to her and his cold hands immediately woke her up. Anne was relieved to see him so obviously fully recovered. She rang to order breakfast in bed for both of them, an indulgence William's father would never have countenanced.

There was a quiet knock on the door and a man in gold and red livery entered with a large, silver breakfast tray. Eggs, bacon, tomato, toast and marmalade – a veritable feast. William looked at the food ravenously as if he could not remember when he had last eaten a full meal. Anne casually glanced at the morning paper. Richard always read *The Times* when he stayed in London so the management assumed she would require it as well.

"Oh, look," said William, staring at the photograph on an inside page, "a picture of Daddy's ship. What's a CA-LA-MITY, Mommy?"

All across the width of the newspaper was a picture of the *Titanic*.

Anne, unmindful of behaving as should a Lowell or a Cabot, burst into frenzied tears, clinging on to her only son. They sat in bed for several minutes, holding on to each other, William wasn't sure why. Anne realised that they had both lost the one person whom they had loved most in the world.

Sir Piers Campbell, young Stuart's father, arrived almost immediately at Suite 107 of the Ritz Hotel. He waited in the lounge while the widow put on a suit, the only dark piece of clothing she possessed. William dressed himself, still not certain what a 'calamity' was. Anne asked Sir Piers to explain the full implications of the news to her son, who only said, "I wanted to be on the ship with him, but they wouldn't let me go." He didn't cry because he refused to believe anything could kill his father. He would be among the survivors.

In all Sir Piers' career as a politician, diplomat and now chairman of Kane and Cabot, London, he had never seen such self-containment in one so young. Presence is given to very few, he was heard to remark some years later. It had been given to Richard Kane and had been passed on to his only son.

The lists of survivors, arriving spasmodically from

America, were checked and double-checked by Anne. Each confirmed that Richard Lowell Kane was still missing at sea, presumed drowned. After a further week even William almost abandoned hope of his father's survival.

Anne found it hard to board the *Aquitania,* but William was strangely eager to put to sea. Hour after hour, he would sit on the observation deck, scanning the featureless water.

"Tomorrow I will find him," he promised his mother, at first confidently, and then in a voice that barely disclaimed his own disbelief.

"William, no one can survive for three weeks in the Atlantic."

"Not even my father?"

"Not even your father."

When Anne returned to Boston, both grandmothers were waiting for her at the Red House, mindful of the duty that had been thrust upon them.

The responsibility had been passed back to the grandmothers. Anne passively accepted their proprietary role. Life for her now had little purpose left other than William, whose destiny they now seemed determined to control. William was polite but uncooperative. During the day he sat silently in his lesson with Mr. Munro and at night wept into the lap of his mother.

"What he needs is the company of other children," declared the grandmothers briskly, and they dismissed Mr. Munro and the nurse and sent William off to Sayre Academy in the hope that an introduction to the real world and the constant company of other children might bring him back to his old self.

Richard had left the bulk of his estate to William, to remain in the family trust until his twenty-first birthday. There was a codicil added to the will. Richard expected his son to become chairman of Kane and Cabot on merit. It was the only part of his father's testament that inspired William, for the rest was his by birthright. Anne received a capital sum of five hundred thousand dollars and an income for life of one hundred thousand dollars a year after taxes, which would cease if she remarried. She also received the house on Beacon Hill, the summer mansion on the North Shore, the home in Maine, and a small island off Cape Cod, all of which were to pass to William on his mother's death. Both grandmothers received two hundred and fifty thousand dollars, and letters leaving them in no doubt about their responsibility if Richard died before them. The family trust was to be handled by the bank, with William's godparents acting as co-trustees. The income from the trust was to be reinvested each year in conservative enterprises.

It was a full year before the grandmothers came out of mourning, and although Anne was still only twenty-eight, she looked her age for the first time in her life.

The grandmothers, unlike Anne, concealed their grief from William until he finally reproached them for it.

"Don't you miss my father? " he asked, gazing at Grandmother Kane with the blue eyes that brought back memories of her own son.

"Yes, my child, but he would not have wished us to sit around and feel sorry for ourselves."

"But I want us to always remember him – always," said William, his voice cracking.

"William, I am going to speak to you for the first time as though you were quite grown up. We will always keep his memory hallowed between us, and you shall play your own part by living up to what your father would have expected of you. You are the head of the family now and the heir to a large fortune. You must, therefore, prepare yourself through work to be fit for that inheritance in the same spirit in which your father worked to increase the inheritance for you."

William made no reply. He was thus provided with the motive for life which he had lacked before, and he acted upon his grandmother's advice. He learned to live with his sorrow without complaining and from that moment on he threw himself steadfastly into his work at school, satisfied only if Grandmother Kane seemed impressed. At no subject did he fail to excel, and in mathematics he was not only top of his class but far ahead of his years. Anything his father had achieved, he was determined to better. He grew even closer to his mother and became suspicious of anyone who was not family, so that he was often thought of as a solitary child, a loner and, unfairly, as a snob.

The grandmothers decided on William's seventh birthday that the time had come to instruct the boy in the value of money. They therefore allowed him pocket money of one dollar a week, but insisted that he keep an inventory accounting for every cent he had spent. With this in mind, they presented him with a green leather-bound ledger book, at a cost of ninety-five cents, which they deducted from his first week's allowance of one dollar. From the second week the grandmothers divided the dollar every Saturday morning. William invested fifty cents, spent twenty cents, gave ten cents to any charity of his choice and kept twenty cents in reserve. At the end of each quarter the grandmothers would inspect the ledger and his written report on any transactions. When the first three months had passed, William was well ready to account for himself. He had given one dollar twenty cents to the newly founded Boy Scouts of America, and saved four dollars, which he had asked Grandmother Kane to invest in a savings account at the bank of his godfather, J. P. Morgan. He had spent a further three dollars eight cents for which he did not have to account and had kept a dollar in reserve. The ledger was a source of great satisfaction to the grandmothers: there was no doubt William was the son of Richard Kane.

At school, William made few friends, partly because he was shy of mixing with anyone other than Cabots, Lowells or children from families wealthier than his own. This restricted his choice severely, so he became a somewhat broody child, which worried his mother, who wanted William to lead a more normal existence, and did not in her heart approve of the ledgers or the investment programme. Anne would have preferred William to have a lot of young friends rather than old advisors, to get himself dirty and bruised rather than remain spotless, to collect toads and turtles rather than stocks and company reports; in short to be like any other little boy. But she never had the courage to tell the grandmothers about her misgivings and in any case the grandmothers were not interested in any other little boy.

On his ninth birthday William presented the ledger to his grandmothers for the second annual inspection. The green leather book showed a saving during the two years of more than fifty dollars. He was particularly proud to point out an entry marked B6 to the grandmothers, showing that he had taken his money out of J. P. Morgan's Bank immediately on hearing of the death of the great financier, because he had noted that his own father's bank shares had fallen in value after his death had been announced. He had reinvested the same amount three months later before the public realised the company was bigger than any one man.

The grandmothers were suitably impressed and allowed William to trade in his old bicycle and purchase a new one, after which he still had a capital sum of over one hundred dollars, which his grandmother had invested for him with the Standard Oil Company of New Jersey. Oil, said William knowingly, can only get more expensive. He kept the ledger meticulously up-to-date until his twenty-first birthday. Had the grandmothers still been alive then, they would have been proud of the final entry in the right hand column marked 'assets'.

7

Wladek was the only one of those left alive who knew the dungeons well. In his days of hide and seek with Leon he had spent many happy hours in the freedom of the small stone rooms, carefree in the knowledge that he could return to the castle whenever it suited him.

There were in all four dungeons, on two levels. Two of the rooms, a larger and a smaller one, were at ground level. The smaller one was adjacent to the castle wall, which afforded a thin filter of light through a grille set high in the stones. Down five steps there were two more stone rooms in perpetual darkness and with little air. Wladek led the Baron into the small upper dungeon where he remained sitting in a corner, silent and motionless, staring fixedly into space; he then appointed Florentyna to be his personal servant.

As Wladek was the only person who dared to remain in the same room as the Baron, the servants never questioned his authority. Thus, at the age of nine, he took charge of the day-to-day responsibility of his fellow prisoners. And in the dungeon he became their master. He split the remaining twenty-four servants into three groups of eight, trying to keep families together wherever possible. He moved them regularly in a shift system, the first eight hours in the upper dungeons for light, air, food and exercise; the second and most popular shift of eight hours working in the castle for their captors; and the final eight hours given to sleep in one of the lower dungeons. No one except the Baron and Florentyna could be quite sure when Wladek slept, as he was always there at the end of every shift to supervise the servants moving on. Food was distributed every twelve hours. The guards would hand over a skin of goat's milk, black bread, millet and occasionally some nuts which Wladek would divide by twenty-eight, always giving two portions to the Baron without ever letting him know. The new occupants of the dungeons, their placidity rendered into miserable stupefaction by incarceration, found nothing strange in a situation that had put a nine-year-old in control of their lives.

Once Wladek had each shift organised, he would return to the Baron in the smaller dungeon. Initially he expected guidance from him, but the fixed gaze of his master was as implacable and comfortless in its own way as were the eyes of the constant succession of German guards. The Baron had never once spoken from the moment he had been subjected to captivity in his own castle. His beard had grown long and matted on his chest and his strong frame was beginning to dwindle into frailty. The once proud look had been replaced with one of resignation. Wladek could scarcely remember the well-loved voice of his patron, and accustomed himself to the thought that he would never hear it again. After a while, he complied with the Baron's unspoken wishes by remaining silent in his presence.

When he had lived in the safety of the castle, Wladek had never thought of the previous day with so much occupying him from hour to hour. Now he was unable to remember even the previous hour, because nothing ever changed. Hopeless minutes turned into hours, hours into days, and then months that he soon lost track of. Only the arrival of food, darkness or light indicated that another twelve hours had passed, while the intensity of that light, and its eventual giving way to storms, and then ice forming on the dungeon walls, melting only when a new sun appeared, heralded each season in a manner that Wladek could never have learned from a nature study lesson. During the long nights Wladek became even more aware of the stench of death that permeated even the farthest corners of the four dungeons, alleviated occasionally by the morning sunshine, a cool breeze, or the most blessed relief of all, the return of rain.

At the end of one day of unremitting storms, Wladek and Florentyna took advantage of the rain by washing themselves in a puddle of water which formed on the stone floor of the upper dungeon. Neither of them noticed that the Baron's eyes were following Wladek with interest as he removed his tattered shirt and rolled over like a dog in the relatively clean water, continuing to rub himself until white streaks appeared on his body. Suddenly, the Baron spoke.

"Wladek" – the word was barely audible – "I cannot see you clearly," he said, the voice cracking. "Come here."

Wladek was stupefied by the sound of his patron's voice after so long a silence and didn't even look in his direction. He was immediately sure that it heralded the incipience of the madness which already held two of the older servants in its grip.

"Come here, boy."

Wladek obeyed fearfully, and stood before the Baron, who narrowed his enfeebled eyes in a gesture of intense concentration as he groped towards the boy. He ran his finger over Wladek's chest and then peered at him incredulously.

"Wladek, can you explain this small deformity?"

"No, sir," said Wladek, feeling embarrassed. "It has been with me since birth. My foster-mother used to say it was the mark of God the Father upon me."

"Stupid woman. It is the mark of your own father," the Baron said softly, and relapsed into silence for some minutes.

Wladek remained standing in front of him, not moving a muscle.

When at last the Baron spoke again, his voice was brisk. "Sit down, boy."

Wladek obeyed immediately. As he sat down, he noticed once again the heavy band of silver, now hanging loosely round the Baron's wrist. A shaft of light through a crack in the wall made the magnificent engraving of the Rosnovski coat of arms glitter in the darkness of the dungeon.

" I do not know how long the Germans intend to keep us locked up here. I thought at first that this war would be over in a matter of weeks. I was wrong, and we must now consider the possibility that it will continue for a very long time. With that thought in mind, we must use our time more constructively as I know my life is nearing an end."

"No, no," Wladek began to protest, but the Baron continued as if he had not heard him.

"Yours, my child, has yet to begin. I will, therefore, undertake the continuation of your education."

The Baron did not speak again that day. It was as if he were considering the implications of his pronouncement. Thus Wladek gained his new tutor, and as they possessed neither reading nor writing material he was made to repeat everything the Baron said. He was taught great tracts from the poems of Adam Mickiewicz and Jan Kochanowski and long passages from the *Aeneid*. In that austere classroom Wladek learned geography, mathematics and four languages: Russian, German, French and English. But his happiest moments were once again when he was taught history. The history of his nation through a hundred years of partition, the disappointed hopes for a united Poland, the further anguish of the Poles at Napoleon's crushing loss to Russia in 1812. He learnt of the brave tales of earlier and happier times, when King Jan Casimir had dedicated Poland to the Blessed Virgin after repulsing the Swedes at Czestochowa, and how the mighty Prince Radziwill, great landowner and lover of hunting, had held his court in the great castle near Warsaw. Wladek's final lesson each day was on the family history of the Rosnovskis. Again and again, he was told – never tiring of the tale – how the Baron's illustrious ancestor who had served in 1794 under General Dabrowski and then in 1809 under Napoleon himself had been rewarded by the great Emperor with land and a barony. He also learned how the Baron's grandfather had sat on the council of Warsaw and his father had played his own part in building the new Poland. Wladek found such happiness when the Baron turned his little dungeon into a classroom.

The guards at the dungeon door were changed every four hours and conversation between them and the prisoners was '*strengst verboten*'. In snatches and fragments Wladek learned of the progress of the war, of the actions of Hindenburg and Ludendorff, of the rise of revolution in Russia and of her subsequent withdrawal from the war by the Treaty of Brest-Litovsk.

Wladek began to believe that the only escape from the dungeons for the inmates was death. The doors opened nine times during the next two years and Wladek started to wonder if he was destined to spend the rest of his days in that filthy hell-hole, fighting a vain battle against despair, while equipping himself with a mind of useless knowledge that would never know freedom.

The Baron continued to tutor him despite his progressively failing sight and hearing. Wladek had to sit closer and closer to him each day.

Florentyna – his sister, mother and closest friend – engaged in a more physical struggle against the rankness of their prison. Occasionally the guards would provide her with a fresh bucket of sand or straw to cover the soiled floor, and the stench became a little less oppressive for the next few days. Vermin scuttled around in the darkness for any dropped scraps of bread or potato and brought with them disease and still more filth. The sour smell of decomposed human and animal urine and excrement assaulted their nostrils and regularly brought Wladek to a state of nausea. He longed above all to be clean again, and would sit for hours gazing at the dungeon ceiling, recalling the steaming tubs of hot water and the good, rough soap with which the *niania* had, so short a distance away and so long a time ago, washed the accretion of a mere day's fun from Leon and himself, with many a muttering and tut-tut for muddy knees or a dirty fingernail.

By the spring of 1918, only fifteen of the twenty-six captives who had been incarcerated with Wladek in the dungeons were still alive. The Baron was always treated by everyone as the master, while Wladek had become his acknowledged steward. Wladek felt saddest for his beloved Florentyna, now twenty. She had long since despaired of life and was convinced that she was going to spend her remaining days in the dungeons. Wladek never admitted in her presence to giving up hope, but although he was only twelve, he too was beginning to wonder if he dared believe in any future.

One evening, early in the autumn, Florentyna came to Wladek's side in the larger dungeon.

"The Baron is calling for you."

Wladek rose quickly, leaving the allocation of food to a senior servant, and went to the old man. The Baron was in severe pain, and Wladek saw with terrible clarity and – as though for the first time – how illness had eroded whole areas of the Baron's flesh, leaving the green-mottled skin covering a now skeletal face. The Baron asked for water and Florentyna brought it from the half-full mug that balanced from a stick outside the stone grille. When the great man had finished drinking, he spoke slowly and with considerable difficulty.

"You have seen so much of death, Wladek, that one more will make little difference to you. I confess that I no longer fear escaping this world."

"No, no, it can't be," cried Wladek, clinging on to the old man for the first time in his life. "We have so nearly triumphed. Don't give up, Baron. The guards have assured me that the war is coming to an end and then we will soon be released."

"They have been promising us that for months, Wladek. We cannot believe them any longer, and in any case I fear I have no desire to live in the new world they are creating." He paused as he listened to the boy crying. The Baron's only thought was to collect the tears as drinking water, and then he remembered that tears were saline and he laughed to himself.

"Call for my butler and first footman, Wladek."

Wladek obeyed immediately, not knowing why they should be required.

The two servants, woken from a deep sleep, came and stood in front of the Baron. After three years' captivity sleep was the easiest commodity to come by. They still wore their embroidered uniforms, but one could no longer tell that they had once been the proud Rosnovski colours of green and gold. They stood silently waiting for their master to speak.

"Are they there, Wladek?" asked the Baron.

"Yes, sir. Can you not see them?" Wladek realised for the first time that the Baron was now completely blind.

"Bring them forward so that I may touch them."

Wladek brought the two men to him and the Baron touched their faces.

"Sit down," he commanded. "Can you both hear me, Ludwik, Alfons?"

"Yes, sir."

"My name is Baron Rosnovski."

"We know, sir, " replied the butler innocently

"Do not interrupt me," said the Baron. "I am about to die."

Death had become so common that the two men made no protest.

"I am unable to make a new will as I have no paper, quill, or ink. Therefore I make my will in your presence and you can act as my two witnesses as recognised by the ancient law of Poland. Do you understand what I am saying?"

"Yes, sir," the two men replied in unison.

"My first born son, Leon, is dead." The Baron paused. "And so I leave my entire estate and possessions to the boy known as Wladek Koskiewicz."

Wladek had not heard his surname for many years and did not immediately comprehend the significance of the Baron's words.

"And as proof of my resolve," the Baron continued, "I give him the family band."

The old man slowly raised his right arm, removed from his wrist the silver band and held it forward to a speechless Wladek, whom he clasped on to firmly, running his fingers over the boy's chest as if to be sure that it was he. "My son," he said, as he placed the silver band on the boy's wrist.

Wladek wept, and lay in the arms of the Baron all night until he could no longer hear his heart, and could feel the fingers stiffening around him. In the morning the Baron's body was removed by the guards and they allowed Wladek to bury him by the side of his son, Leon, in the family churchyard, up against the chapel. As the body was lowered into its shallow grave, dug by Wladek's bare hands, the Baron's tattered shirt fell open. Wladek stared at the dead man's chest.

He had only one nipple.

* * *

Thus Wladek Koskiewicz, aged twelve, inherited sixty thousand acres of land, one castle, two manor houses, twenty-seven cottages, and a valuable collection of paintings, furniture and jewelry, while he lived in a small stone room under the earth. From that day on, the captives took him as their rightful master and his empire was four dungeons, his retinue thirteen broken servants and his only love Florentyna.

He returned to what he felt was now an endless routine until long into the winter of 1918. On a mild, dry day there burst upon the prisoners' ears a volley of shots and the sound of a brief struggle. Wladek was sure that the Polish army had come to rescue him and that he would now be able to lay claim to his rightful inheritance. When the German guards deserted the iron door of the dungeons, the inmates remained in terrified silence huddled in the lower rooms. Wladek stood alone at the entrance, twisting the silver band around his wrist, triumphant, waiting for his liberators. Eventually those who had defeated the Germans arrived and spoke in the coarse Slavic tongue, familiar from school days, which he had learned to fear even more than German. Wladek was dragged unceremoniously out into the passage with his retinue. The prisoners waited, then were cursorily inspected and thrown back into the dungeons. The new conquerors were unaware that this twelve-year-old boy was the master of all their eyes beheld. They did not speak his tongue. Their orders were clear and not to be questioned: kill the enemy if they resist the agreement of Brest-Litovsk, which made this section of Poland theirs and send those who do not resist to camp 201 for the rest of their days. The Germans had left meekly to retreat behind their new border while Wladek and his followers waited, hopeful of a new life, ignorant of their impending fate.

After spending two more nights in the dungeons, Wladek resigned himself to believing that they were to be incarcerated for another long spell. The new guards did not speak to him at all, a reminder to him of what life had been like three years before; he began to realise that discipline had at least become lax under the Germans but once again was tight.

On the morning of the third day, much to Wladek's

surprise, they were all dragged out on to the grass in front of the castle, fifteen thin filthy bodies. Two of the servants collapsed in the unaccustomed sunlight. Wladek himself found the intense brightness his biggest problem and kept having to shield his eyes from it. The prisoners stood in silence on the grass and waited for the soldiers' next move. The guards made them all strip and ordered them down to the river to wash. Wladek hid the silver band in his clothes and ran down to the water's edge, his legs feeling weak even before he reached the river. He jumped in, gasping for breath at the coldness of the water, although it felt glorious on his skin. The rest of the prisoners followed him, and tried vainly to remove three years of filth.

When Wladek came out of the river exhausted, he noticed that some of the guards were looking strangely at Florentyna as she washed herself in the water. They were laughing and pointing at her. The other women did not seem to arouse the same degree of interest. One of the guards, a large ugly man whose eyes had never left Florentyna for a moment, grabbed her arm as she passed him on her way back up the river bank, and threw her to the ground. He then started to take his clothes off quickly, hungrily, while at the same time folding them neatly on the grass. Wladek stared in disbelief at the man's swollen erect penis and flew at the soldier, who was now holding Florentyna down on the ground, and hit him in the middle of his stomach with his head with all the force he could muster. The man reeled back, and a second soldier jumped up and held Wladek helpless with his hands pinned behind his back. The commotion attracted the attention of the other guards, and they strolled over to watch. Wladek's captor was now laughing, a loud belly laugh with no humour in it. The other soldiers' words only added to Wladek's anguish.

"Enter the great protector," said the first.

"Come to defend his nation's honour." The second one.

"Let's at least allow him a ringside view." The one who was holding him.

More laughter interspersed the remarks that Wladek couldn't always comprehend. He watched the naked soldier advance his hard, well-fed body slowly towards Florentyna, who started screaming. Once again Wladek struggled, trying desperately to free himself from the vice-like grip, but he was helpless in the arms of his guard. The naked man fell clumsily on top of Florentyna and started kissing her and slapping her when she tried to fight or turn away; finally he lunged into her. She let out a scream such as Wladek had never heard before. The guards continued talking and laughing among themselves, some not even watching.

"Goddamn virgin," said the first soldier as he withdrew himself from her.

They all laughed.

"You've just made it a little easier for me," said the second guard.

More laughter. As Florentyna stared into Wladek's eyes, he began to retch. The soldier holding on to him showed little interest, other than to be sure that none of the boy's vomit soiled his uniform or boots. The first soldier, his penis now covered in blood, ran down to the stream, yelling as he hit the water. The second man undressed, while yet another held Florentyna down. The second guard took a little longer over his pleasure, and seemed to gain considerable satisfaction from hitting Florentyna; when he finally entered her, she screamed again but not quite as loud.

"Come on, Valdi, you've had long enough."

With that the man came out of her suddenly and joined his companion-at-arms in the stream. Wladek made himself look at Florentyna. She was bruised and bleeding between the legs. The soldier holding him spoke again.

"Come and hold the little bastard, Boris, it's my turn."

The first soldier came out of the river and took hold of Wladek firmly. Again he tried to hit out, and this made them laugh even louder.

"Now we know the full might of the Polish army."

The unbearable laughter continued as yet another guard started undressing to take his turn with Florentyna, who now lay indifferent to his charms. When he had finished, and had gone down to the river, the second soldier returned and started putting on his clothes.

"I think she's beginning to enjoy it," he said, as he sat in the sun watching his companion. The fourth soldier began to advance on Florentyna. When he reached her, he turned her over, forced her legs as wide apart as possible, his large hands moving rapidly over her frail body. The scream when he entered her had now turned into a groan. Wladek counted sixteen soldiers who raped his sister. When the last soldier had finished with her, he swore and then added, "I think I've made love to a dead woman," and left her motionless on the grass.

They all laughed even more loudly, as the disgruntled soldier walked down to the river. At last Wladek's guard released him. He ran to Florentyna's side, while the soldiers lay on the grass drinking wine and vodka taken from the Baron's cellar, and eating the bread from the kitchens.

With the help of two of the servants, Wladek carried Florentyna's light body to the edge of the river, weeping as he tried to wash away her blood and bruises. It was useless, for she was black and red all over, insensible to help and unable to speak. When Wladek had done the best he could, he covered her body with his jacket and held her in his arms. He kissed her gently on the mouth, the first woman he had ever kissed. She lay in his arms, but he knew she did not recognise him, and as the tears ran down his face on to her bruised body, he felt her go limp. He wept as he carried her dead body up the bank. The guards went silent as they watched him walk towards the chapel. He laid her down on the grass beside the Baron's grave and started digging with his bare hands. When the sinking sun had caused the castle to cast its long shadow over the graveyard, he had finished digging. He buried Florentyna next to Leon and made a little cross with two sticks which he placed at her head. Wladek collapsed on the ground between Leon and Florentyna, and fell asleep, caring not if he ever woke again.

8

William returned to Sayre Academy in September and immediately began to look for competition among those older than himself. Whatever he took up, he was never satisfied unless he excelled in it, and his contemporaries almost always proved too weak an opposition. William began to realise that most of those from backgrounds as privileged as his own lacked any incentive to compete, and that fiercer rivalry was to be found from boys who had, compared with himself, relatively little.

In 1915, a craze for collecting match-box labels hit Sayre Academy. William observed this frenzy for a week with great interest but did not join in. Within a few days, common labels were changing hands at a dime, while rarities commanded as much as fifty cents. William considered the situation and decided to become not a collector, but a dealer.

On the following Saturday, he went to Leavitt and Pearce, one of the largest tobacconists in Boston, and spent the afternoon taking down the names and addresses of all the major match-box manufacturers throughout the world, making a special note of those who were not at war. He invested five dollars in notepaper, envelopes and stamps, and wrote to the chairman or president of every company he had listed. His letter was simple despite having been rewritten seven times.

Dear Mr. Chairman or Mr. President,

I am a dedicated collector of match-box labels, but I cannot afford to buy all the matches. My pocket money is only one dollar a week, but I enclose a three-cent stamp for postage to prove that I am serious about my hobby. I am sorry to bother you personally, but yours was the only name I could find to write to.

Your friend,

William Kane (aged 9)

P.S. Yours are one of my favourites.

Within three weeks, William had a fifty-five per cent reply which yielded one hundred and seventy-eight different labels. Nearly all his correspondents also returned the three-cent stamp, as William had anticipated they would.

During the next seven days, William set up a market in labels within the school, always checking what he could sell on even before he had made a purchase. He noticed that some boys showed no interest in the rarity of the match-box label, only in its looks, and with them he made quick exchanges to obtain rare trophies for the more discerning collectors. After a further two weeks of buying and selling he sensed that the market was reaching its zenith and that if he were not careful, with the holidays fast approaching, interest might begin to die off. With much trumpeted advance publicity in the form of a printed handout which cost him a further half cent a sheet, placed on every boy's desk, William announced that he would be holding an auction of his match-box labels, all two hundred and eleven of them. The auction took place in the school washroom during the lunch hour and was better attended than most school hockey games.

The result was that William netted fifty-seven dollars thirty-two cents, a profit of fifty-two dollars thirty-two cents on his original investment. William put twenty-five dollars on deposit with the bank at two and a half per cent, bought himself a camera for eleven dollars, gave five dollars to the Young Men's Christian Association, who had broadened their activities to help the new flood of immigrants, bought his mother some flowers, and put the remaining few dollars into his pocket. The market in match-box labels collapsed even before the school term ended. It was to be the first of many occasions on which William got out at the top of the market. The grandmothers would have been proud of him;

it was not unlike the way their husbands had made their fortunes in the panic of 1873.

When the holidays came, William could not resist finding out if it was possible to obtain a better return on his invested capital than the two and a half per cent yielded by his savings account. For the next three months he invested – again through Grandmother Kane – in stocks highly recommended by the *Wall Street Journal*. During the next term at school he lost over half of the money he had made on the match-box labels. It was the only time in his life that he relied on the expertise of the *Wall Street Journal*, or on information available at any street corner.

Angry with his loss of over twenty dollars William decided that it must be recouped during the Easter holidays. On arriving home he worked out which parties and functions his mother would expect him to attend, and found he was left with only fourteen free days, just enough time for his new venture. He sold all his remaining *Wall Street Journal* shares, which netted him only twelve dollars. With this money he bought himself a flat piece of wood, two sets of wheels, axles and a piece of rope, at a cost, after some bargaining, of five dollars. He then put on a flat cloth cap and an old suit he had outgrown and went off to the local railroad station. He stood outside the exit, looking hungry and tired, informing selected travellers that the main hotels in Boston were near the railroad station, so that there was no need to take a taxi or the occasional surviving hansom carriage as he, William, could carry their luggage on his moving board for twenty per cent of what the taxis charged; he added that the walk would also do them good. By working six hours a day, he found he could make roughly four dollars.

Five days before the new school term was due to start, he had made back all his original losses and a further ten dollars profit. He then hit a problem. The taxi drivers were starting to get annoyed with him. William assured them that he would retire, aged nine, if each one of them would give him fifty cents to cover the cost of his home-made trolley – they agreed, and he made another eight dollars fifty cents. On the way home to Beacon Hill, William sold his trolley for five dollars to a school friend two years his senior, who was soon to discover that the market had passed its peak; moreover, it rained for every day of the following week.

On the last day of the holidays, William put his money back on deposit in the bank, at two and a half per cent. During the following term this decision caused him no anxiety as he watched his savings rise steadily. The sinking of the *Lusitania* and Wilson's declaration of war against Germany in April of 1917 didn't concern William. Nothing and no one could ever beat America, he assured his mother. William even invested ten dollars in Liberty Bonds to back his judgment.

By William's eleventh birthday the credit column of his ledger book showed a profit of four hundred and twelve dollars. He had given his mother a fountain pen and his two grandmothers brooches from a local jewelry shop. The fountain pen was a Parker and the jewelry arrived at his grandmothers' homes in Shreve, Crump and Low boxes, which he had found after much searching in the dustbins behind the famous store. To do the boy justice, he had not wanted to cheat his grandmothers, but he had already learned from his match-box label experience that good packaging sells products. The grandmothers, who noted the missing Shreve, Crump and Low hallmark, still wore their brooches with considerable pride.

The two old ladies continued to follow William's every move and had decided that when he reached the age of twelve, he should proceed as planned to St. Paul's School in Concord, New Hampshire. For good measure the boy rewarded them with the top mathematics scholarship, unnecessarily saving the family some three hundred dollars a year. William accepted the scholarship and the grandmothers returned the money for, as they expressed it, 'a less fortunate child'. Anne hated the thought of William leaving her to go away to boarding school, but the grandmothers insisted and, more importantly, she knew it was what Richard would have wanted. She sewed on William's name tapes, marked his boots, checked his clothes, and finally packed his trunk, refusing any help from the servants. When the time came for William to go, his mother asked him how much pocket money he would like for the new term ahead of him.

"None," he replied without further comment.

William kissed his mother on the cheek; he had no idea how much she was going to miss him. He marched off down the path, in his first pair of long trousers, his hair cut very short, carrying a small suitcase towards Roberts, the chauffeur. He climbed into the back of the Rolls-Royce and it drove him away. He didn't look back. His mother waved and waved, and later cried. William wanted to cry too, but he knew his father would not have approved.

The first thing that struck William Kane as strange about his new prep school was that the other boys did not care who he was. The looks of admiration, the silent acknowledgment of his presence were no longer there. One older boy actually asked his name, and what was worse, when told, was not manifestly impressed. Some even called him Bill which he soon corrected with the explanation that no one had ever referred to his father as Dick.

William's new domain was a small room with wooden bookshelves, two tables, two chairs, two beds and a comfortably shabby leather settee. The other chair, table and bed were occupied by a boy from New York called Matthew Lester, whose father was also in banking.

William soon became used to the school routine. Up at seven thirty, wash, breakfast in the main dining room, with the whole school – two hundred and twenty boys munching their way through eggs, bacon and porridge. After breakfast, chapel, three fifty-minute classes before lunch and two after it, followed by a music lesson which William detested because he could not sing a note in tune and he had even less desire to learn to play any musical instrument. Football in the autumn, hockey and squash in the winter, and rowing and tennis in the spring left him with very little free time. As a mathematics scholar, William had special tutorials in the subject three times a week from his housemaster, G. Raglan, Esquire, known to the boys as Grumpy.

During his first year, William proved to be well worthy

of his scholarship, among the top few boys in almost every subject, and in a class of his own in mathematics. Only his new friend, Matthew Lester, was any real competition for him, and that was almost certainly because they shared the same room. While establishing himself academically William also acquired a reputation as a financier. Although his first investment in the market had proved disastrous, he did not abandon his belief that to make a significant amount of money, sizeable capital gains on the stock market were essential. He kept a wary eye on the *Wall Street Journal*, company reports and, at the age of twelve, started to experiment with a ghost portfolio of investments. He recorded every one of his ghost purchases and sales, the good and the not-so-good in a newly acquired, different coloured ledger book, and compared his performance at the end of each month against the rest of the market. He did not bother with any of the leading listed stocks, concentrating instead on the more obscure companies, some of which traded only over the counter, so that it was impossible to buy more than a few shares in them at any one time. William expected four things from his investments: a low multiple of earnings, a high growth rate, strong asset backing and a favourable trading outlook. He found few shares which fulfilled all these rigorous criteria, but when he did, they almost invariably showed him a profit.

The moment he found that he was regularly beating the Dow-Jones Index with his ghost investment programme, William knew he was ready to invest his own money once again. He started with one hundred dollars and never stopped refining his method. He would always follow profits and cut losses. Once a stock had doubled, he would sell half his holding but keep the remaining half intact, trading the stock he still held as a bonus. Some of his early finds, such as Eastman Kodak and N.C.R., went on to become national leaders. He also backed the first mail order company, convinced it was a trend that would catch on.

By the end of his first year he was advising half the school staff and some of the parents. William Kane was happy at school.

* * *

Anne Kane had been unhappy and lonely at home with William away at St. Paul's and a family circle consisting only of the two grandmothers, now approaching old age. She was miserably conscious that she was past thirty, and that her smooth and youthful prettiness had disappeared without leaving much in its place. She started picking up the threads, severed by Richard's death, with some of her old friends. John Preston and his wife Milly, William's godmother, whom she had known all her life, began inviting her to dinners and the theatre, always including an extra man, trying to make a match for Anne. The Prestons' choices were almost always atrocious, and Anne used privately to laugh at Milly's attempts at match-making until one day in January 1919, just after William had returned to school for the winter term, Anne was invited to yet another dinner for four. Milly confessed she had never met her other guest, Henry Osborne, but that they thought he had been at Harvard at the same time as John.

"Actually," confessed Milly over the phone, "John doesn't know much about him, darling, except that he is rather good-looking."

On that score, John's opinion was verified by Anne and Milly. Henry Osborne was warming himself by the fire when Anne arrived and he rose immediately to allow Milly to introduce them. A shade over six feet, with dark eyes, almost black, and straight black hair, he was slim and athletic looking. Anne felt a quick flash of pleasure that she was paired for the evening with this energetic and youthful man, while Milly had to content herself with a husband who was showing signs of middle-age by comparison with his dashing college contemporary. Henry Osborne's arm was in a sling, almost completely covering his Harvard tie.

"A war wound?" asked Anne sympathetically.

"No, I fell down the stairs the week after I got back from the Western Front," he said, laughing.

It was one of those dinners, lately so rare for Anne, at which the time at the table slipped by happily and unaccountably. Henry Osborne answered all Anne's inquisitive questions. After leaving Harvard, he had worked for a real estate management firm in Chicago, his home town, but when the war came he couldn't resist having a go at the Germans. He had a fund of splendid stories about Europe and the life he had led there as a young lieutenant preserving the honour of America on the Marne. Milly and John had not seen Anne laugh so much since Richard's death and smiled at one another knowingly when Henry asked if he might drive her home.

"What are you going to do now that you've come back to a land fit for heroes?" asked Anne, as Henry Osborne eased his Stutz out on to Charles Street.

"Haven't really decided," he replied. "Luckily, I have a little money of my own, so I don't have to rush into anything. Might even start my own real estate firm right here in Boston. I've always felt at home in the city since my days at Harvard."

"You won't be returning to Chicago, then?"

"No, there's nothing to take me back there. My parents are both dead, and I was an only child, so I can start afresh anywhere I choose. Where do I turn?"

"Oh, first on the right," said Anne.

"You live on Beacon Hill?"

"Yes. About a hundred and fifty yards on the right-hand side up Chestnut and it's the red house on the corner of Louisburg Square."

Henry Osborne parked the car and accompanied Anne to the front door of her home. After saying goodnight, he was gone almost before she had time to thank him. She watched his car glide slowly back down Beacon Hill knowing that she wanted to see him again. She was delighted, though not entirely surprised, when he telephoned her the following morning.

"Boston Symphony Orchestra, Mozart, and that flamboyant new fellow, Mahler, next Monday – can I persuade you?"

Anne was a little taken aback by the extent to which she looked forward to Monday. It seemed so long since a man whom she found attractive had pursued her. Henry Osborne arrived punctually for the outing, they shook hands rather awkwardly, and he accepted a Scotch highball.

"It must be pleasant to live on Louisburg Square. You're a lucky girl."

"Yes, I suppose so, I've never really given it much thought. I was born and raised on Commonwealth Avenue. If anything, I find this slightly cramped."

"I think I might buy a house on the Hill myself if I do decide to settle in Boston."

"They don't come on the market all that often," said Anne, "but you may be lucky. Hadn't we better be going? I hate being late for a concert and having to tread on other people's toes to reach my seat."

Henry glanced at his watch. "Yes I agree, wouldn't do to miss the conductor's entrance, but you don't have to worry about anyone's feet except mine. We're on the aisle."

The cascades of sumptuous music made it natural for Henry to take Anne's arm as they walked to the Ritz. The only other person who had done that since Richard's death had been William, and only after considerable persuasion as he considered it sissy. Once again the hours slipped by for Anne: was it the excellent food, or was it Henry's company? This time he made her laugh with his stories of Harvard and cry with recollections of the war. Although she was well aware that he looked younger than herself, he had done so much with his life that she always felt deliciously youthful and inexperienced in his company. She told him about her husband's death, and cried a little more. He took her hand and she spoke of her son with glowing pride and affection. He said he had always wanted a son. Henry scarcely mentioned Chicago or his own home life but Anne felt sure that he must miss his family. When he took her home that night, he stayed for a quick drink and kissed her gently on the cheek as he left. Anne went back over the evening minute by minute before she fell asleep.

They went to the theatre on Tuesday, visited Anne's cottage on Cape Cod on Wednesday, gyrated to the Grizzly Bear and the Temptation Rag on Thursday, shopped for antiques on Friday, and made love on Saturday. After Sunday, they were rarely apart. Milly and John Preston were 'absolutely delighted' that their match-making had at last proved so successful. Milly went around Boston telling everyone that she had been responsible for putting the two of them together.

The announcement during that summer of the engagement came as no surprise to anyone except William. He had disliked Henry intensely from the day that Anne, with a well-founded sense of misgiving, introduced them to each other. Their first conversation took the form of long questions from Henry, trying to prove he wanted to be a friend, and monosyllabic answers from William, showing that he didn't. And he never changed his mind. Anne ascribed her son's resentment to an understandable feeling of jealousy; William had been the centre of her life since Richard's death. Moreover, it was perfectly proper that in William's estimation, no one could possibly take the place of his own father. Anne convinced Henry and herself that given time William would get over his sense of outrage.

Anne Kane became Mrs. Henry Osborne in October of that year at the Old North Church just as the golden and red leaves were beginning to fall, a little over ten months after they had met. William feigned illness in order not to attend the wedding and remained firmly at school. The grandmothers did attend, but were unable to hide their disapproval of Anne's re-marriage, particularly to someone who appeared to be so much younger than herself. "It can only end in disaster," said Grandmother Kane.

The newlyweds sailed for Greece the following day, and did not return to the Red House on the Hill till the second week of December, just in time to welcome William home for the Christmas holidays. William was shocked to find the house had been redecorated, leaving almost no trace of his father. Over Christmas, William's attitude to his step-father showed no sign of softening despite the present as Henry saw it – bribe as William construed it – of a new bicycle. Henry Osborne accepted this rebuff with surly resignation. It saddened Anne that her splendid new husband made so little effort to win over her son's affection.

William felt ill at ease in his invaded home and would often disappear for long periods during the day. Whenever Anne enquired where he was going, she received little or no response: it certainly was not to the grandmothers. When the Christmas holidays came to an end, William was only too happy to return to school and Henry was not sad to see him go. Only Anne was uneasy about both the men in her life.

9

"Up, boy. Up, boy."

One of the soldiers was digging his rifle butt into Wladek's ribs. He sat up with a start and looked at the grave of his sister and those of Leon and of the Baron, and he did not shed a single tear as he turned towards the soldier.

"I will live, you will not kill me," he said in Polish. "This is my home, and you are on my land."

The soldier spat on Wladek and pushed him back to the lawn where the servants were waiting, all dressed in what looked like grey pyjamas with numbers on their backs. Wladek was horrified at the sight of them, realising what was about to happen to him. He was taken by the soldier to the north side of the castle and made to kneel on the ground. He felt a knife scrape across his head as his thick black hair fell on to the grass. With ten bloody strokes, like the shearing of a sheep, the job was completed. Shaven-headed, he was ordered to put on his new uniform, a grey rubaskew shirt and trousers. Wladek managed to keep the silver band well hidden and rejoined his servants at the front of the castle.

While they all stood waiting on the grass – numbers now, not names – Wladek became conscious of a noise in the distance that he had never heard before. His eyes turned towards the menacing sound. Through the great iron gates came a vehicle moving on four wheels, but not drawn by horses or oxen. All the prisoners stared at the moving object in disbelief. When it had come to a halt, the soldiers dragged the reluctant prisoners towards it and made them climb aboard. Then the horseless wagon turned round, moved back down the path and through the iron gates. Nobody dared to speak. Wladek sat at the rear of the truck and stared at his castle until he could no longer see the Gothic turrets.

The horseless wagon somehow drove itself towards Slonim. Wladek would have worried about how the vehicle worked if he had not been even more worried about where it was taking them. He began to recognise the roads from his days at school, but his memory had been dulled by three years in the dungeons, and he could not recall where the road finally led. After only a few miles, the truck came to a stop and they were all pushed out. It was the local railway station. Wladek had only seen it once before in his life, when he and Leon had gone there to welcome the Baron home from his trip to Warsaw. He remembered the guard had saluted them when they first walked on to the platform; this time no guard saluted them. The prisoners were fed on goat's milk, cabbage soup and black bread, Wladek again taking charge, dividing the portions carefully among the remaining fourteen. He sat on a wooden bench, assuming that they were waiting for a train. That night they slept on the ground below the stars, paradise compared with the dungeons. He thanked God for the mild winter.

Morning came and still they waited. Wladek made the servants take some exercise but most collapsed after only a few minutes. He began to make a mental note of the names of those who had survived thus far. Eleven of the men and two of the women, spared from the original twenty-seven in the dungeons. Spared for what? he thought. They spent the rest of the day waiting for a train that never came. Once, a train did arrive, from which more soldiers disembarked, speaking their hateful tongue, but it departed without Wladek's pitiful army. They slept yet another night on the platform.

Wladek lay awake below the stars considering how he might escape, but during the night one of his thirteen made a run for it across the railway track and was shot down by a guard even before he had reached the other side. Wladek gazed at the spot where his compatriot had fallen, frightened to go to his aid for fear he would meet the same fate. The guards left the body on the track in the morning, as a warning to those who might consider a similar course of action.

No one spoke of the incident the next day, although Wladek's eyes rarely left the body of the dead man. It was the Baron's butler, Ludwik – one of the witnesses to the Baron's will, and his heritage – dead.

On the evening of the third day another train chugged into the station, a great steam locomotive pulling open freight cars, the floors strewn with straw and the word 'cattle' painted on the sides. Several cars were already full, full of humans, but from where Wladek could not judge, so hideously did their appearance resemble his own. He and his band were thrown together into one of the cars to begin the journey. After a wait of several more hours the train started to move out of the station, in a direction which Wladek judged, from the setting sun, to be eastward.

To every three carriages there was a guard sitting crosslegged on a roofed car. Throughout the interminable journey an occasional flurry of bullet shots from above demonstrated to Wladek the futility of any further thoughts of escape.

When the train stopped at Minsk, they were given their first proper meal: black bread, water, nuts, and more millet, and then the journey continued. Sometimes they went for three days without seeing another station. Many of the reluctant travellers died of starvation and were thrown overboard from the moving train. And when the train did stop they would often wait for two days to allow another train going west use of the track. These trains which delayed their progress were inevitably full of soldiers, and it became obvious to Wladek that the troop trains had priority over all other transport. Escape was always uppermost in Wladek's mind, but three things prevented him from advancing that ambition. First, no one had yet succeeded; second, there was nothing but miles of wilderness on both sides of the track; and third, those who had survived the dungeons were now totally dependent on him to protect them. It was Wladek who organised their food and drink, and tried to give them all the will to live. He was the youngest and the last one still to believe in life.

At night, it became bitterly cold, often thirty degrees below zero, and they would all lie up against each other in a line on the carriage floor so that each body would keep the person next to him warm. Wladek would recite the *Aeneid* to himself while he tried to snatch some sleep. It was impossible to turn over unless everyone agreed, so Wladek would lie at the end and each hour, as near as he could judge by the changing of the guards, he would slap the side of the carriage, and they would all roll over and face the other way. One after the other, the bodies would turn like falling dominoes. Sometimes a body did not move – because it no longer could – and Wladek would be informed. He in turn would inform the guard and four of them would pick up the body and throw it over the side of the moving train. The guards would pump bullets into the head to be sure it was not someone hoping to escape.

Two hundred miles beyond Minsk, they arrived in the small town of Smolensk, where they received warm cabbage soup and black bread. Wladek was joined in his car by some new prisoners who spoke the same tongue as the guards. Their leader seemed to be about the same age as Wladek. Wladek and his ten remaining companions, nine men and one woman, were immediately suspicious of the new arrivals, and they divided the carriage in half, with the two groups remaining apart for several days.

One night, while Wladek lay awake staring at the stars, trying to get warm, he watched the leader of the Smolenskis crawl towards the end man of his own line with a small piece of rope in his hand. He watched him slip it round the neck of Alfons, the Baron's first footman, who was sleeping. Wladek knew if he moved too quickly, the boy would hear him and escape back to his own half of the carriage and the protection of his comrades, so he crawled slowly on his belly down the line of Polish bodies. Eyes stared at him as he passed, but nobody spoke. When he reached the end of the line, he leaped forward upon the aggressor, immediately waking everyone in the truck. Each faction shrank back to its own end of the carriage, with the exception of Alfons, who lay motionless in front of them.

The Smolenski leader was taller and more agile than Wladek, but it made little difference while the two were fighting on the floor. The struggle lasted for several minutes, with the guards laughing and taking bets as they watched the two gladiators. One guard, who was getting bored by the lack of blood, threw a bayonet into the middle of the car. Both boys scrambled for the shining blade with the Smolenski leader grabbing it first. The Smolenski band cheered their hero as he thrust the bayonet into the side of Wladek's leg, pulled the blood-covered steel back out and lunged again. On the second thrust the blade lodged firmly in the wooden floor of the jolting car next to Wladek's ear. As the Smolenski leader tried to wrench it free, Wladek kicked him in the groin with every ounce of energy he had left, and in throwing his adversary backwards released the bayonet. With a leap, Wladek grabbed the handle and jumped on top of the Smolenski, running the blade right into his mouth. The man gave out a shriek of agony that awoke the entire train. Wladek pulled the blade out, twisting it as he did so, and thrust it back into the Smolenski again and again, long after he had ceased to move. Wladek knelt over him, breathing heavily, and then picked up the body and threw it out of the carriage. He heard the thud as it hit the bank and the shots that the guards pointlessly aimed after it.

Wladek limped towards Alfons, still lying motionless on the wooden boards, and knelt by his side shaking his lifeless body: his second witness dead. Who would now believe that he, Wladek, was the chosen heir to the Baron's fortune? Was there any purpose left in life? He collapsed to his knees. He picked up the bayonet with both hands, pointing the blade towards his stomach. Immediately a guard jumped down and wrested the weapon away from him.

"Oh no, you don't," he grunted. "We need the lively ones like you for the camps. You can't expect us to do all the work."

Wladek buried his head in his hands, aware for the first time of an aching pain in his bayoneted leg. He had lost his inheritance and traded it to become the leader of a band of penniless Smolenskis.

The whole truck once again became his domain and he now had twenty prisoners to care for. He immediately split them up so that a Pole would always sleep next to a Smolenski, making it impossible for there to be any further warfare between the two groups.

Wladek spent a considerable part of his time learning their strange tongue, not realising for several days that it was actually Russian, so greatly did it differ from the classical Russian language taught him by the Baron, and then the real significance of the discovery dawned on him for the first time when he realised where the train was heading.

During the day Wladek used to take on two Smolenskis at a time to tutor him, and as soon as they were tired, he would take on two more, and so on until they were all exhausted.

Gradually he became able to converse easily with his new dependents. Some of them were Russian soldiers, exiled after repatriation for the crime of having been captured by the Germans. The rest were White Russians, farmers, miners, labourers, all bitterly hostile to the Revolution.

The train jolted on past terrain more barren than Wladek had ever seen before, and through towns of which he had never heard – Omsk, Novo Sibirsk, Krasnoyarsk – the names rang ominously in his ears. Finally, after three months and more than three thousand miles, they reached Irkutsk, where the railway track came to an abrupt end.

They were hustled off the train, fed, and issued with felt boots, jackets and heavy coats and although fights broke out for the warmest clothing, they still provided little protection from the ever intensifying cold.

Horseless wagons appeared, not unlike the one which had borne Wladek away from his castle, and long chains were thrown out. Then, to Wladek's disbelief and horror, the prisoners were cuffed to the chain by one hand, twenty-five pairs side by side on each chain. The trucks pulled the mass of prisoners along while the guards rode on the back. They marched like that for twelve hours, before being given a two-hour rest, and then they marched again. After three days, Wladek thought he would die of cold and exhaustion, but once clear of populated areas they travelled only during the day and rested at night. A mobile field kitchen run by prisoners from the camp supplied turnip soup and bread at first light and then again at night. Wladek learned from these prisoners that conditions at the camp were even worse.

For the first week they were never unshackled from those chains, but later when there could be no thought of escape they were released at night to sleep, digging holes in the snow for warmth. Sometimes on good days they found a forest in which to bed down: luxury began to take strange forms. On and on they marched, past enormous lakes and across frozen rivers, ever northwards, into the face of viciously cold winds and deeper falls of snow. Wladek's injured leg gave him a constant dull pain, soon surpassed in intensity by the agony of frostbitten fingers and ears. There was no sign of life or food in all the expanse of whiteness, and Wladek knew that to attempt an escape at night could only mean slow death by starvation. The old and the sick were starting to die, quietly at night, if they were lucky. The unlucky ones, unable to keep up the pace, were uncuffed from the chains and cast off to be left alone in the endless snow. Those who survived walked on, on, on, always towards the north, until Wladek lost all sense of time and was simply conscious of the inexorable tug of the chain, not even sure when he dug his hole in the snow to sleep at night that he would wake the next morning: those that didn't had dug their own grave.

After a trek of nine hundred miles, those who had survived were met by Ostyaks, nomads of the Russian steppes, in reindeer-drawn sleds. The trucks discharged their cargo and turned back. The prisoners, now chained to the sleds, were led on. A great blizzard forced them to halt for the greater part of two days and Wladek seized the opportunity to communicate with the young Ostyak to whose sled he was chained. Using classical Russian, with a Polish accent, he was understood only very imperfectly but he did discover that the Ostyaks hated the Russians of the south, who treated them almost as badly as they treated their captives. The Ostyaks were not unsympathetic to the sad prisoners with no future, the 'unfortunates' as they called them.

Nine days later, in the half light of the early Arctic winter night, they reached Camp 201. Wladek would never have believed he could have been glad to see such a place: row upon row of wooden huts in the stark open space. The huts, like the prisoners, were numbered. Wladek's hut was 33. There was a small black stove in the middle of the room, and, projecting from the walls, tiered wooden bunks on which were hard straw mattresses and one thin blanket. Few of them managed to sleep at all that first night, and the groans and cries that came from hut 33 were often louder than the howls of the wolves outside.

The next morning before the sun rose, they were woken by the sound of a hammer against an iron triangle. There was thick frost on both sides of the window and Wladek thought that he must surely die of the cold. Breakfast in a freezing communal hall lasted for ten minutes and consisted of a bowl of lukewarm gruel, with pieces of rotten fish and a leaf of cabbage floating in it. The newcomers spat the fish bones out on the table while the more seasoned prisoners ate the bones and even the fishes' eyes.

After breakfast, they were allocated tasks. Wladek became a wood chopper. He was taken seven miles through the featureless steppes into a forest and ordered to cut a certain number of trees each day. The guard would leave him and his little group of six to themselves with their food ration, tasteless yellow magara porridge and bread. The guards had no fear of the prisoners attempting to escape, for it was over a thousand miles to the nearest town, even if you knew in which direction to head.

At the end of each day, the guard would return and count the number of logs of wood they had chopped; he informed the prisoners that if they failed to reach the required number, he would stop the group's food for the following day. But when he came back at seven in the evening to collect the reluctant woodsmen, it was already dark, and he could not always see exactly how many new logs they had cut. Wladek taught the others in his team to spend the last part of the afternoon clearing the snow off the wood cut the previous day and lining it up with what they had chopped that day. It was a plan that always worked, and Wladek's group never lost a day's food. Sometimes they managed to return to the camp with a small piece of wood, tied to the inside of their legs, to put in the coal stove at night. Caution was required, for at least one of them was searched every time they left and entered the camp, often having to remove one or both boots, and to stand there in the numbing snow. If they were caught with anything on them it meant three days without food.

As the weeks went by, Wladek's leg started to become very stiff and painful. He longed for the coldest days, when the temperature went down to forty below zero, and outside work was called off, even though the lost day would have to be made up on a free Sunday when they were normally allowed to lie on their bunks all day.

One evening when Wladek had been hauling logs across the waste, his leg began to throb unmercifully. When he looked at the scar caused by the Smolenski, he found that it had become puffy and shiny. That night, he showed the wound to a guard, who ordered him to report to the camp doctor before first light in the morning. Wladek sat up all night with his leg nearly touching the stove, surrounded by wet boots, but the heat was so feeble that it couldn't ease the pain.

The next morning Wladek rose an hour earlier than usual. If you had not seen the doctor before work was due to start, then you missed him until the next day. Wladek couldn't face another day of such intense pain. He reported to the doctor, giving his name and number. Pierre Dubien was a sympathetic old man, bald-headed, with a pronounced stoop, and Wladek thought he looked even older than the Baron. He inspected Wladek's leg without speaking.

"Will the wound be all right, doctor?" asked Wladek.

"You speak Russian?"

"Yes, sir."

"Although you will always limp, young man, your leg

will be good again. But good for what? A life here dragging wood."

"No, doctor, I intend to escape and get back to Poland," said Wladek.

The doctor looked sharply at him. "Keep your voice down, stupid boy. You must realise by now that escape is impossible. I have been in captivity fifteen years, and not a day has passed that I have not thought of escape. There is no way; no one has ever escaped and lived, and even to talk of it means ten days in the punishment cell, and there they feed you every third day and light the stove only to melt the ice off the walls. If you come out of that place alive, you can consider yourself lucky."

"I will escape, I will, I will," said Wladek, staring at the old man.

The doctor looked into Wladek's eyes and smiled. "My friend, never mention escape again or they may kill you. Go back to work, keep your leg exercised and report to me first thing every morning."

Wladek returned to the forest and to the chopping of wood, but found that he could not drag the logs more than a few feet, and that the pain was so intense he believed his leg might fall off. When he returned the next morning, the doctor examined the leg more carefully.

"Worse, if anything," he said. "How old are you, boy?"

"I think I am thirteen," said Wladek. "What year is it?"

"Nineteen hundred and nineteen," replied the doctor.

"Yes, thirteen. How old are you?" asked Wladek.

The old man looked down into the young boy's blue eyes, surprised by the question.

"Thirty-eight," he said quietly.

"God help me," said Wladek.

"You will look like this when you have been a prisoner for fifteen years, my boy," said the doctor matter of factly.

"Why are you here at all?" said Wladek. "Why haven't they let you go after all this time?"

"I was taken prisoner in Moscow in 1904, soon after I had qualified as a doctor and I was working in the French Embassy. They said I was a spy and put me in a Moscow jail. I thought that was bad until after the Revolution when they sent me to this hell-hole. Even the French have now forgotten that I exist. Few have been known to complete their sentence at Camp 201 so I must die here, like everyone else, and it can't be too soon."

"No, you must not give up hope, doctor."

"Hope? I gave up hope for myself a long time ago; perhaps I shall not give it up for you, but always remember never to mention that hope to anyone; there are prisoners here who trade in loose tongues, when their reward can be nothing more than an extra piece of bread or perhaps a blanket. Now Wladek, I am going to put you on kitchen duty for a month and you must continue to report to me every morning. It is the only chance that you have of not losing that leg, and I do not relish being the man who has to cut it off. We don't exactly have the latest surgical instruments here," he added, staring at a large carving knife.

Wladek shuddered.

Doctor Dubien wrote out Wladek's name on a slip of paper. Next morning, Wladek reported to the kitchens, where he cleaned the plates in freezing water and helped to prepare food that required no refrigeration. After carrying logs all day, he found it a welcome change: extra fish soup, thick black bread with shredded nettles, and the chance to stay inside and keep warm. On one occasion he even shared half an egg with the cook, although neither of them could be sure what fowl had laid it. Wladek's leg mended slowly, leaving him with a pronounced limp. There was little Doctor Dubien could do in the absence of any real medical supplies except keep an eye on his progress. As the days went by, the doctor began to befriend Wladek and even to believe in his youthful hope for the future. They would converse in a different language each morning, but the old man most enjoyed speaking in French, his native tongue.

"In seven days' time, Wladek, you will have to return to forest duty; the guards will inspect your leg and I will not be able to keep you in the kitchens any longer. So listen carefully, for I have decided upon a plan for your escape."

"Together, doctor," said Wladek. "Together."

"No, only you. I am too old for such a long journey, and although I have dreamed about escape for over fifteen years, I would only hold you up. It will be enough for me to know someone else has achieved it, and you are the first person I've ever met who has convinced me that he might succeed."

Wladek sat on the floor in silence listening to the doctor's plan.

"I have, over the last fifteen years, saved two hundred rubles – you don't exactly get overtime as a Russian prisoner." Wladek tried to laugh at the camp's oldest joke. "I keep the money hidden in a drug bottle, four fifty-ruble notes. When the time comes for you to leave, the money must be sewn into your clothes. I will have already done this for you."

"What clothes?" asked Wladek.

"I have a suit and a shirt I bribed from a guard twelve years ago when I still believed in escape. Not exactly the latest fashion, but they will serve your purpose."

Fifteen years to scrape together two hundred rubles, a shirt and a suit, and the doctor was willing to sacrifice them to Wladek in a moment. Wladek never again in his life experienced such an act of selflessness.

"Next Thursday will be your only chance," the doctor continued. "New prisoners arrive by train at Irkutsk, and the guards always take four people from the kitchen to organise the food truck for the new arrivals. I have already arranged with the senior cook" – he laughed at the word – "that in exchange for some drugs you will find yourself on the kitchen truck. It was not too hard. No one exactly wants to make the trip there and back – but you will only be making the journey there."

Wladek was still listening intently.

"When you reach the station, wait until the prisoners' train arrives. Once they are all on the platform, cross the line and get yourself on to the train going to Moscow, which cannot leave until the prisoners' train comes in, as there is only one track outside the station. You must pray that with hundreds of new prisoners milling around the guards will not notice you disappear. From then on you're on your own.

Remember if they do spot you, they will shoot you on sight without a second thought. There is only one last thing I can do for you. Fifteen years ago when I was brought here, I drew a map from memory of the route from Moscow to Turkey. It may not be totally accurate any longer, but it should be adequate for your purpose. Be sure to check that the Russians haven't taken over Turkey as well. God knows what they have been up to recently. They may even control France for all I know."

The doctor walked over to the drug cabinet and took out a large bottle which looked as if it was full of a brown substance. He unscrewed the top and took out an old piece of parchment. The black ink had faded over the years. It was marked October, 1904. It showed a route from Moscow to Odessa, and from Odessa to Turkey, seventeen hundred miles to freedom.

"Come to me every morning this week, and we will go over the plan again and again. If you fail, it must not be from lack of preparation."

Wladek stayed awake each night, gazing at the wolves' sun through the window, rehearsing what he would do in any given situation, preparing himself for every eventuality. In the morning he would go over the plan again and again with the doctor. On the Wednesday evening before Wladek was to try the escape, the doctor folded the map into eight, placed it with the four fifty-ruble notes in a small package and sewed the package into a sleeve of the suit. Wladek took off his clothes, put on the suit and then replaced the prison uniform on top of it. As he put on the uniform again, the doctor's eye caught the Baron's band of silver which Wladek, ever since he had been issued his prison uniform, had always kept above his elbow for fear the guards would spot his only treasure and steal it.

"What's that?" he asked. "It's quite magnificent."

"A gift from my father," said Wladek. "May I give it to you to show my thanks?" He slipped the band off his wrist and handed it to the doctor.

The doctor stared at the silver band for several moments and bowed his head. "Never," he said. "This can only belong to one person." He stared silently at the boy. "Your father must have been a great man."

The doctor placed the band back on Wladek's wrist and shook him warmly by the hand.

"Good luck, Wladek. I hope we never meet again."

They embraced and Wladek parted for what he prayed was his last night in the prison hut. He was unable to sleep at all that night for fear one of the guards would discover the suit under his prison clothes. When the morning bell sounded, he was already dressed and he made sure that he was not late reporting to the kitchen. The senior prisoner in the kitchen pushed Wladek forward when the guards came for the truck detail. The team chosen were four in all and Wladek was by far the youngest.

"Why this one?" asked the guard, pointing to Wladek. "He has been at the camp for less than a year."

Wladek's heart stopped and he went cold all over. The doctor's plan was going to fail; and there would not be another batch of prisoners coming to the camp for at least three months. By then he would no longer be in the kitchens.

"He's an excellent cook," said the senior prisoner. "Trained in the castle of a baron. Only the best for the guards."

"Ah," said the guard, greed overcoming suspicion. "Hurry up, then."

The four of them ran to the truck, and the convoy started. The journey was again slow and arduous, but at least he was not walking this time, nor, being summer, was it unbearably cold. Wladek worked hard on preparing the food and, as he had no desire to be noticed, hardly spoke to anyone for the entire journey other than Stanislaw, the chief cook.

When they eventually reached Irkutsk, the drive had taken nearly sixteen days. The train waiting to go to Moscow was already standing in the station. It had been there for several hours, but was unable to continue its journey until the train bringing the new prisoners had arrived. Wladek sat on the side of the platform with the others from the field kitchen, three of them with no interest or purpose in anything around them, dulled by the experience, but one of them intent on every move, studying the train on the other side of the platform carefully. There were several open entrances and Wladek quickly selected the one he would use when his moment came.

"Are you going to try an escape?" asked Stanislaw suddenly.

Wladek began to sweat but did not answer.

Stanislaw stared at him. "You *are?*"

Still Wladek said nothing.

The old cook stared at the thirteen-year-old boy. He nodded his head up and down in agreement. If he had had a tail, it would have wagged.

"Good luck. I'll make sure they don't realise you're missing for at least two days."

Stanislaw touched his arm and Wladek caught sight of the prisoners' train in the distance, slowly inching its way towards them. He tensed in anticipation, his heart pounding, his eyes following the movement of every soldier. He waited for the incoming train to come to a halt and watched the tired prisoners pile out on to the platform, hundreds of them, anonymous men with only a past. When the station was a chaos of people and the guards were fully occupied, Wladek ran under the carriage and jumped on to the other train. No one showed any interest as he went into a lavatory at the end of the carriage. He locked himself in and waited and prayed, every moment expecting someone to knock on the door. It seemed a lifetime to Wladek before the train began to move out of the station. It was, in fact, seventeen minutes.

"At last, at last," he said out loud. He looked through the little window and watched the station growing smaller and smaller in the distance, a mass of new prisoners being hitched up to the chains, ready for the journey to Camp 201, the guards laughing as they locked them in. How many would reach the camp alive? How many would be fed to the wolves? How long before they missed him?

Wladek sat in the lavatory for several more minutes, terrified to move, not sure what he ought to do next. Suddenly there was a banging on the door. Wladek thought quickly – the guard, the ticket collector, a soldier – a succession of images flashed through his mind, each one more frightening than the last. He needed to use the lavatory for the first time. The banging persisted.

"Come on, come on," said a man in coarse Russian.

Wladek had little choice. If it was a soldier, there was no way out, a dwarf could not have squeezed through the little window. If it wasn't a soldier, he would only draw attention to himself by staying there. He took off his prison clothes, made them into as small a bundle as possible, and threw them out of the window. Then he removed a soft hat from the pocket of his suit to cover his shaved head, and opened the door. An agitated man rushed in, pulling down his trousers even before Wladek had left.

Once in the corridor, Wladek felt isolated and terrifyingly conspicuous in his out-of-date suit, an apple placed on a pile of oranges. He immediately went in search of another lavatory. When he found one that was unoccupied, he locked himself in and quickly undid the stitches in his suit, extracting one of the four fifty-ruble notes. He replaced the other three and returned to the corridor. He looked for the most crowded carriage he could find and hid himself in a corner. Some men were playing pitch-and-toss in the middle of the carriage for a few rubles to while away the time. Wladek had always beaten Leon when they had played in the castle, and he would have liked to have joined the contestants, but he feared winning and drawing attention to himself. The game went on for a long time and Wladek began to remember the stratagems. The temptation to risk his two hundred rubles was almost irresistible.

One of the gamblers, who had parted with a considerable amount of his money, retired in disgust and sat down by Wladek, swearing.

"The luck wasn't with you," said Wladek, wanting to hear the sound of his own voice.

"Ah, it's not luck," the gambler replied. "Most days I could beat that lot of peasants, but I have run out of rubles."

"Do you want to sell your coat?" asked Wladek.

The gambler was one of the few passengers in the carriage

wearing a good, old, thick bearskin coat. He stared at the youth.

"Looking at that suit I'd say you couldn't afford it, boy." Wladek could tell from the man's voice that he hoped he could. "I would want seventy-five rubles."

"I'll give you forty," said Wladek.

"Sixty," said the gambler.

"Fifty," said Wladek.

"No. Sixty is the least I'd let it go for; it cost over a hundred," said the gambler.

"A long time ago," said Wladek, as he considered the implications of taking extra money from inside the lining of his coat in order to secure the full amount needed. He decided against doing so as it would only draw further attention to himself; he would have to wait for another opportunity. Wladek was not willing to show he could not afford the coat, and he touched the collar of the garment and said, with considerable disdain, "You paid too much for it, my friend; fifty rubles, not a kopeck more." Wladek rose as if to leave.

"Wait, wait," said the gambler. "I'll let you have it for fifty."

Wladek took the fifty rubles out of his pocket and the gambler took off the coat and exchanged it for the grimy red note. The coat was far too big for Wladek, nearly touching the ground, but it was exactly what he needed to cover his conspicuous suit. For a few moments, he watched the gambler, back in the game, once again losing. From his new tutor he had learned two things: never to gamble unless the odds are tipped in your favour by superior knowledge or skill, and always to be willing to walk away from a deal when you have reached your limit.

Wladek left the carriage, feeling a little safer under his new-old coat. He started to examine the layout of the train with a little more confidence. The carriages seemed to be in two classes: general ones where passengers stood or sat on the wooden boards and special ones where they could sit on upholstered seats. Wladek found that all the carriages were packed, with but one exception, a sitting carriage with a solitary woman in it. She was middle-aged, as far as Wladek could tell, and dressed a little more smartly with a little more flesh on her bones than most of the other passengers on the train. She wore a dark blue dress and a scarf over her head. She smiled at Wladek as he stood staring at her, and this gesture gave him the confidence to enter the carriage.

"May I sit down?"

"Please do," said the woman, looking at him carefully.

Wladek did not speak again, but studied the woman and the contents of the carriage. She had a sallow skin covered with tired lines, a little overweight – the little bit you could be on Russian food. Her short black hair and brown eyes suggested that she once might have been quite attractive. She had two large cloth bags on the rack and a small valise by her side. Despite the danger of his position Wladek was suddenly aware of feeling desperately tired. He was wondering if he dared to sleep when the woman spoke.

"Where are you travelling?"

The question took Wladek by surprise and he tried to think quickly. "Moscow," he said, holding his breath.

"So am I," she replied.

Wladek was already regretting the isolation of the carriage and the information he had given. Don't talk to anyone, the doctor had warned him; remember, trust nobody.

To his relief the woman asked no more questions. As he began to regain his lost confidence, the ticket collector arrived. Wladek started to sweat, despite the temperature being minus twenty degrees. The collector took the woman's ticket, tore it, gave it back to her, and then turned to Wladek.

"Ticket, comrade," was all he said in a slow, monotonous tone.

Wladek was speechless, and started thumbing around in his coat pocket.

"He's my son," said the woman firmly.

The ticket collector looked back at the woman, once more at Wladek, and then he bowed to the woman and left the carriage without another word.

Wladek stared at her. "Thank you," he breathed, not quite sure what else he could say.

"I watched you come from under the prisoners' train," the woman remarked quietly. Wladek felt sick. "But I shall not give you away. I have a young cousin in one of those terrible camps, and all of us fear that one day we might end up there. What do you have on under your coat?"

Wladek weighed the relative merits of dashing out of the carriage and unfastening his coat. If he dashed out of the carriage there was no escape. He unfastened his coat.

"Not as bad as I had feared," she said. "What did you do with your prison uniform?"

"Threw it out of the window."

"Let's hope they don't find it before you reach Moscow."

Wladek said nothing.

"Do you have anywhere to stay in Moscow?"

He thought again of the doctor's advice to trust nobody, but he had to trust her.

"I have nowhere to go."

"Then you can stay with me until you find somewhere to live. My husband," she explained, "is the station master in Moscow, and this carriage is for government officials only. If you ever make that mistake again, you will be taking the train back to Irkutsk."

Wladek swallowed. "Should I leave now?"

"No, not now that the ticket collector has seen you. You will be safe with me for the time being. Do you have any identity papers?"

"No. What are they?"

"Since the Revolution every Russian citizen must have identity papers to show who he is, where he lives and where he works, otherwise he ends up in jail until he can produce them, and as he can never produce them once in jail, he stays there for ever," she added matter of factly. "You will have to stick by me once we reach Moscow, and be sure you don't open your mouth."

"You are being very kind to me," said Wladek suspiciously.

"Now the Tsar is dead, none of us is safe. I was lucky to be married to the right man," she added, "but there is not a citizen in Russia, including government officials, who does not live in constant fear of arrest and the camps. What is your name?"

"Wladek."

"Good, now you sleep, Wladek, because you look exhausted, the journey is long and you are not safe yet."

Wladek slept.

When he woke, several hours had passed, and it was now dark outside. He stared at his protectress, and she smiled. Wladek returned her smile, praying that she could be trusted not to tell the officials who he was – or had she already done so? She produced some food from one of her bundles and Wladek ate the offering silently. When they reached the next station, nearly all the passengers got out, some of them permanently, but most to seek what little refreshment was available or to stretch their stiff limbs.

The middle-aged woman rose, looked at Wladek. "Follow me," she said.

He stood up and followed her on to the platform. Was he about to be given up? She put out her hand, and he took it as any thirteen-year-old child accompanying his mother would do. She walked towards a lavatory marked for women only. Wladek hesitated. She insisted, and once inside she told Wladek to take off his clothes. He obeyed her unquestioningly as he hadn't anyone since the death of the Baron. While he undressed she turned on the solitary tap, which with reluctance yielded a trickle of cold brownish water. She was disgusted. But to Wladek, it was a vast improvement on the camp water. The woman started to bathe his wounds with a wet rag and attempted hopelessly to wash him. She winced when she saw the scar on his leg. Wladek didn't murmur from the pain that came with each touch, gentle as she tried to be.

"When we get you home, I'll make a better job of those wounds," she said, "but that will have to do for now."

Then she saw the silver band, studied the inscription and looked carefully at Wladek. "Is that yours?" she asked. "Who did you steal it from?"

Wladek looked offended. "I didn't steal it. My father gave it to me before he died."

She stared at him again, and a different look came into her eyes. Was it fear or respect? She bowed her head. "Be careful, Wladek, men would kill for such a valuable prize."

He nodded his agreement and started to dress quickly. They returned to their carriage. A delay of an hour at a station was not unusual and when the train started lurching forward, Wladek was glad to feel the wheels clattering underneath him again. The train took twelve and a half days to reach Moscow. Whenever a new ticket collector appeared, they went through the same routine, Wladek unconvincingly trying to look innocent and young. The woman a convincing mother. The ticket collectors always bowed respectfully to the middle-aged lady, and Wladek began to think that station masters must be very important in Russia.

By the time they completed the one-thousand-mile journey to Moscow, Wladek had put his trust completely in the middle-aged lady and was looking forward to seeing her house. It was early afternoon when the train came to its final halt and despite everything Wladek had been through, he had never visited a big city, let alone the capital of all the Russias. He was terrified, once again tasting the fear of the unknown. So many people all rushing around in different directions. The middle-aged lady sensed his apprehension.

"Follow me, do not speak, and whatever you do don't take your cap off."

Wladek took her bags down from the rack, pulled his cap over his head – now covered in a black stubble – down to his ears and followed her out on to the platform. A throng of people at the barrier were waiting to go through a tiny exit, which caused a holdup as everyone had to show their identification papers to the guard. As they approached the barrier, Wladek could hear his heart beating like a soldier's drum, but when their turn came the fear was over in a moment. The guard only glanced at the woman's documents.

"Comrade," he said, and saluted. He looked at Wladek.

"My son," she explained.

"Of course, comrade." He saluted again.

Wladek was in Moscow.

Despite the trust he had placed in his new-found companion, his first instinct was to run but as one hundred and fifty rubles was hardly enough to live on, he decided for the time being to stay put. He could always run at some later time. A horse and cart was waiting at the station and took the woman and her new son home. The station master was not there when they arrived, so the woman immediately set about making up the spare bed for Wladek. Then she poured water, heated on a stove, into a large tin tub and told him to get in. It was the first bath he had had in over four years, unless he counted the dip in the stream. She heated some more water and reintroduced him to soap, scrubbing his back, the only part of his body with unbroken skin. The water began to change colour and after twenty minutes, it was black. Once Wladek was dry, the woman put some ointment on his arms and legs, and bandaged the parts of his body that looked particularly fierce. She stared at his one nipple. He dressed quickly and then joined her in the kitchen. She had already prepared a bowl of hot soup and some beans. Wladek ate the magnificent feast hungrily. Neither of them spoke.

When he had finished the meal, she suggested that it might be wise for him to go to bed and rest.

"I do not want my husband to see you before I have told him why you are here," she explained. "Would you like to stay with us, Wladek, if my husband agrees?"

Wladek nodded thankfully.

"Then off you go to bed," she said.

Wladek obeyed and prayed that her husband would allow him to live with them. He undressed slowly and climbed on to the bed. He was too clean, the sheets were too clean, the mattress was too soft, and he threw the pillow on the floor, but he was so tired that he slept despite the comfort of the bed. He was woken from his deep sleep some hours later by the sound of raised voices coming from the kitchen. He could not tell how long he had slept. It was already dark outside as he crept off the bed, walked to the door, eased it open and listened to the conversation taking place in the kitchen below.

"You stupid woman." Wladek heard a piping voice. "Do

you not understand what would have happened if you had been caught? It would have been you who would have been sent to the camps."

"But if you had seen him, Piotr, like a hunted animal."

"So you decided to turn us into hunted animals," said the male voice. "Has anyone else seen him?"

"No," said the woman, "I don't think so."

"Thank God for that. He must go immediately before anyone knows he's here, it's our only hope."

"But go where, Piotr? He is lost, and has no one," Wladek's protectress pleaded. "And I have always wanted a son."

"I do not care what you want or where he goes, he is not our responsibility and we must be quickly rid of him."

"But Piotr, I think he is royal, I think his father was a Baron. He wears a silver band around his wrist and inscribed on it are the words . . ."

"That only makes it worse. You know what our new leaders have decreed. No tsars, no royalty, no privileges. We would not even have to bother to go to the camp, the authorities would just shoot us."

"We have always wanted a son, Piotr. Can we not take this one risk in our lives?"

"With your life, perhaps, but not mine. I say he must go and go now."

Wladek did not need to listen to any more of their conversation. Deciding that the only way he could help his benefactress would be to disappear without trace into the night, he dressed quickly and stared at the slept-in bed, hoping it would not be four more years before he saw another one. He was unlatching the window when the door was flung open and into the room came the station master, a tiny man, no taller than Wladek, with a large stomach and an almost bald head covered in long strands of grey hair. He wore rimless spectacles, which had produced little red semicircles under each eye. The man carried a paraffin lamp. He stood, staring at Wladek. Wladek stared defiantly back.

"Come downstairs," he commanded.

Wladek followed him reluctantly to the kitchen. The woman was sitting at the table crying.

"Now listen, boy," he said.

"His name is Wladek," the woman interjected.

"Now listen, boy," he repeated."You are trouble, and I want you out of here and as far away as possible. I'll tell you what I am going to do to help you."

Help? Wladek gazed at him stonily.

"I am going to give you a train ticket. Where do you want to go?"

"Odessa," said Wladek, ignorant of where it was or how much it would cost, knowing only that it was the next city on the doctor's map to freedom.

"Odessa, the mother of crime – an appropriate destination," sneered the station master. "You can only be among your own kind and come to harm there."

"Then let him stay with us, Piotr. I will take care of him, I will . . ."

"No, never. I would rather pay the bastard."

"But how can he hope to get past the authorities?" the woman pleaded.

"I will have to issue him a working pass for Odessa." He turned his head towards Wladek. "Once you are on that train, boy, if I see or hear of you again in Moscow, I will have you arrested on sight and thrown into the nearest jail. You will then be back in that prison camp as fast as the train can get you there if they don't shoot you first."

He stared at the clock on the kitchen mantelpiece: five after eleven. He turned to his wife. "There is a train that leaves for Odessa at midnight. I will take him to the station myself. I want to be sure he leaves Moscow. Have you any baggage, boy?"

Wladek was about to say no, when the woman said, "Yes, I will go and fetch it."

Wladek and the station master stood, staring at each other with mutual contempt. The woman was away for a long time. The grandfather clock struck once in her absence. Still neither spoke, and the station master's eyes never left Wladek. When his wife returned, she was carrying a large brown paper parcel wrapped up with string. Wladek stared at it and began to protest, but as their eyes met, he saw such fear in hers that he only just got out the words, "Thank you."

"Eat this," she said, thrusting her bowl of cold soup towards him.

He obeyed, although his shrunken stomach was now overfull, gulping down the soup as quickly as possible, not wanting her to be in any more trouble.

"Animal," the man said.

Wladek looked at him, hatred in his eyes. He felt pity for the woman, bound to such a man for life.

"Come, boy, it's time to leave," the station master said. "We don't want you to miss your train, do we?"

Wladek followed the man out of the kitchen. He hesitated as he passed the woman and touched her hand, feeling the response. Nothing was said; no words would have been adequate. The station master and the refugee crept through the streets of Moscow, hiding in the shadows, until they reached the station. The station master obtained a one-way ticket to Odessa and gave the little red slip of paper to Wladek.

"My pass?" said Wladek defiantly. From his inside pocket the man drew out an official-looking form, signed it hurriedly, and handed it over furtively to Wladek. The station master's eyes kept looking all around him for any possible danger. Wladek had seen those eyes so many times during the past four years: the eyes of a coward.

"Never let me see or hear of you again," he said, the voice of a bully.

Wladek had also heard that voice many times before in the last four years. He looked up, wanting to say something, but the station master had already retreated into the shadows of the night where he belonged. He looked at the eyes of the people who hurried past him. The same eyes, the same fear; was anyone in the world free? Wladek gathered the brown paper parcel under his arm, checked his hat, and walked towards the barrier. This time he felt more confident, showing his pass to the guard; he was ushered through without comment. He climbed on board the train. It had been a short visit to Moscow, and he would never see the city again in his life, though he would always remember the kindness of the woman, the station master's wife, Comrade . . . He didn't even know her name.

Wladek stayed in the general class standing carriages for his journey. Odessa looked less distant from Moscow than Irkutsk, about a thumb's length on the doctor's sketch, eight hundred and fifty miles in reality. While Wladek was studying his rudimentary map, he became distracted by another game of pitch-and-toss which was taking place in the carriage. He folded the parchment, replaced it safely in the lining of his suit and began taking a closer interest in the game. He noticed that one of the gamblers was winning consistently, even when the odds were stacked against him. Wladek watched the man more carefully and soon realised that he was cheating.

He moved to the other side of the carriage to make sure he could still spot the man cheating when facing him, but he couldn't. He edged forward and made a place for himself in the circle of gamblers. Every time the cheat had lost twice in a row, Wladek backed him with one ruble, doubling his stake until he won. The cheat was either flattered or considered he would be wise to remain silent about Wladek's luck, because he never once even glanced in his direction. By the time they reached the next station, Wladek had won fourteen rubles, two of which he used to buy himself an apple and a cup of hot soup. He had won enough to last the entire journey to Odessa and, pleased with the thought that he could win even more rubles with his new safe system, he silently thanked the unknown gambler and climbed back on to the train ready to resume the strategy. As his foot touched the top step, he was knocked flying into a corner. His arm was jerked painfully behind his back and his face was pushed hard against the carriage wall. His nose began to bleed and he could feel the point of a knife touching the lobe of his ear.

"Do you hear me, boy?"

"Yes," said Wladek, petrified.

"If you go back to my carriage again, I take this ear right off, then you won't be able to hear me, will you?"

"No, sir," said Wladek.

Wladek felt the point of the knife breaking the surface of the skin behind his ear and blood began trickling down his neck.

"Let that be a warning to you, boy."

A knee suddenly came up into his kidneys with as much force as the gambler could muster. Wladek collapsed to the ground. A hand rummaged into his coat pockets and the recently acquired rubles were removed.

"Mine, I think," the voice said.

Blood was now coming out of Wladek's nose and from behind his ear. When he summoned up the courage to look up from the corner of the corridor, it was empty, and there was no sign of the gambler. Wladek tried to get to his feet, but his body refused to obey the order from his brain, so he remained slumped in the corner for several minutes. Eventually when he was able to rise, he walked slowly to the other end of the train, as far away from the gambler's carriage as possible, his limp grotesquely exaggerated. He hid in a carriage occupied mostly by women and children, and fell into a deep sleep.

At the next stop, Wladek didn't leave the train. He undid his little parcel and started to investigate. Apples, bread, nuts, two shirts, a pair of trousers and even shoes were contained in that brown-papered treasure trove. What a woman, what a husband.

He ate, he slept, he dreamed. And finally, after six nights and five days, the train chugged into the terminal at Odessa. The same check at the ticket barrier, but the guard hardly gave Wladek a second look. This time his papers were all in order, but now he was on his own. He still had one hundred and fifty rubles in the lining of his suit, and no intention of wasting any of them.

Wladek spent the rest of the day walking around the town trying to familiarise himself with its geography, but he found he was continually distracted by sights he had never seen before: big town houses, shops with windows, hawkers selling their colourful trinkets on the street, gaslights, and even a monkey on a stick. Wladek walked on until he reached the harbour and stopped to stare at the open sea beyond it. Yes, there it was – what the Baron had called an ocean. He gazed into the blue expanse longingly: that way was freedom and escape from Russia. The city must have seen its fair share of fighting: burnt-out houses and squalor were all too evident, grotesque in the mild, flower-scented sea air. Wladek wondered whether the city was still at war. There was no one he could ask. As the sun disappeared behind the high buildings, he began to look for somewhere to spend the night. Wladek took a side road and kept walking. He must have looked a strange sight with his skin coat dragging along the ground and the brown paper parcel under his arm. Nothing looked safe to him until he came across a railway siding in which a solitary old carriage stood in isolation. He stared into it cautiously; darkness and silence: no one was there. He threw his paper parcel into the carriage, raised his tired body up on to the boards, crawled into a corner and lay down to sleep. As his head touched the wooden floor, a body leaped on top of him and two hands were quickly around his throat. He could barely breathe.

"Who are you?" hissed a boy who, in the darkness, sounded no older than himself.

"Wladek Koskiewicz."

"Where do you come from?"

"Moscow." Slonim had been on the tip of Wladek's tongue.

"Well, you're not sleeping in my carriage, Muscovite," said the voice.

"Sorry," said Wladek. "I didn't know."

"Got any money?" His thumbs pressed into Wladek's throat.

"A little," said Wladek.

"How much?"

"Seven rubles."

"Hand it over."

Wladek rummaged in the pocket of his overcoat, while the boy also pushed one hand firmly into it, releasing the pressure on Wladek's throat.

In one movement, Wladek brought up his knee with every

ounce of force he could muster into the boy's crotch. His attacker flew back in agony, clutching his testicles. Wladek leaped on him, hitting him in places the boy would never have thought of. The rules had suddenly changed. He was no competition for Wladek; sleeping in a derelict carriage was five-star luxury compared to the dungeons and a Russian labour camp.

Wladek stopped only when his adversary was pinned to the carriage floor, helpless. The boy pleaded with Wladek.

"Go to the far end of the carriage and stay there," said Wladek. "If you so much as move a muscle, I'll kill you."

"Yes, yes," said the boy, scrambling away.

Wladek heard him hit the far end of the carriage. He sat still and listened for a few moments – no movement – then he lowered his head once more on to the floor, and in moments he was sleeping soundly.

When he woke, the sun was already shining through the slits between the boards of the carriage. He turned over slowly and studied his adversary of the previous night for the first time. He was lying in a foetal position, still asleep at the other end of the carriage.

"Come here," commanded Wladek.

The boy woke slowly.

"Come here," repeated Wladek, a little more loudly.

The boy obeyed immediately. It was the first chance Wladek had had to look at him properly. They were about the same age, but the boy was a clear foot taller with a younger-looking face and scruffy fair hair. His general appearance suggested that talk of soap and water would have been treated as an insult.

"First things first," said Wladek. "How does one get something to eat here?"

"Follow me," said the boy, leaping out of the carriage. Wladek limped after him and followed the boy up the hill into the town where the morning market was being set up. He had not seen so much wholesome food since those magnificent dinners with the Baron. Row upon row of stalls with fruit, vegetables, greens, and even his favourite nuts. The boy could see Wladek was overwhelmed by the sight.

"Now I'll tell you what we do," the boy said, sounding confident for the first time. "I will go over to the corner stall and steal an orange, and then make a run for it. You will shout at the top of your voice, 'Stop, thief.' The stallkeeper will chase me and when he does, you move in and fill your pockets. Don't be greedy; enough for one meal. Then you return here. Got it?"

"Yes, I think so," said Wladek.

"Let's see if you're up to it, Muscovite." The boy looked at him, snarled, and was gone. Wladek watched him in admiration as he swaggered to the corner of the first market stall, removed an orange from the top of a pyramid, made some short unheard remark to the stallkeeper and started to run slowly. He glanced back at Wladek, who had entirely forgotten to shout 'Stop, thief,' but the stall owner looked up and immediately began to chase the boy. While everyone's eyes were on Wladek's accomplice, he moved in quickly and managed to take three oranges, an apple and a potato, and put them in the large pockets of his overcoat. When the stallkeeper looked as if he were about to catch his accomplice, the boy lobbed the orange back at him. The man stopped to pick it up and swore at him, waving his fist, complaining vociferously to the other merchants as he returned to his stall.

Wladek was shaking with mirth as he took in the scene when a hand was placed firmly on his shoulder. He turned round in the horror of having been caught.

"Did you get anything, Muscovite, or are you only here as a sightseer?"

Wladek burst out laughing with relief and produced the three oranges, apple and potato. The boy joined in the laughter.

"What's your name?" said Wladek.

"Stefan."

"Let's do it again, Stefan."

"Hold on, Muscovite, don't you start getting too clever. If we do *my* scheme again, we'll have to go to the other end of the market and wait for at least an hour. You're working with a professional now, but don't imagine you won't get caught occasionally."

The two boys went quietly through to the other end of the market, Stefan walking with a swagger for which Wladek would have traded the three oranges, apple, potato and his one hundred and fifty rubles. They mingled with the morning shoppers and when Stefan decided the time was right, they repeated the trick twice. Satisfied with the results, they returned to the railway carriage to enjoy their captured spoils: six oranges, five apples, three potatoes, a pear, several varieties of nuts, and the special prize, a melon. In the past, Stefan had never had pockets big enough to hold one. Wladek's greatcoat took care of that.

"Not bad," said Wladek, as he dug his teeth into a potato.

"Do you eat the skins as well?" asked Stefan, horrified.

"I've been places where the skins are a luxury," replied Wladek.

Stefan looked at him with admiration.

"Next problem is how do we get some money?" said Wladek.

"You want everything in one day, don't you, O Master?" said Stefan. "Chain gang on the waterfront is the best bet, if you think you're up to some real work, Muscovite."

"Show me," said Wladek.

After they had eaten half the fruit and hidden the rest under the straw in the corner of the carriage, Stefan took Wladek down the steps to the harbour and showed him all the ships. Wladek couldn't believe his eyes. He had been told by the Baron of the great ships that crossed the high seas delivering their cargoes to foreign lands, but these were so much bigger than he had ever imagined, and they stood in a line as far as the eye could see.

Stefan interrupted his thoughts. "See that one over there, the big green one; well, what you have to do is pick up a basket at the bottom of the gangplank, fill it with grain, climb up the ladder and then drop your load in the hold. You get a ruble for every four trips you make. Be sure you can count, Muscovite, because the bastard in charge of the gang will swindle you as soon as look at you and pocket the money for himself."

Stefan and Wladek spent the rest of the afternoon carrying

grain up the ladder. They made twenty-six rubles between them. After a dinner of stolen nuts, bread, and an onion they hadn't intended to take, they slept happily in their carriage.

Wladek was the first to wake the next morning and Stefan found him studying his map.

"What's that?" asked Stefan.

"This is a route showing me how to get out of Russia."

"What do you want to leave Russia for when you can stay here and team up with me?" said Stefan. "We could be partners."

"No, I must get to Turkey; there I will be a free man for the first time. Why don't you come with me, Stefan?"

"I could never leave Odessa. This is my home, the railway is where I live and these are the people I have known all my life. It's not good, but it might be worse in the place you call Turkey. But if that's what you want, I will help you to escape because I know how to find out where every ship has come from."

"How do I discover which ship is going to Turkey?" asked Wladek.

"Easy. We'll get the information from One Tooth Joe at the end of the pier. You'll have to give him a ruble."

"I'll bet he splits the money with you."

"Fifty-fifty," said Stefan. "You're learning fast, Muscovite." And with that he leaped out of the carriage.

Wladek followed him as he ran swiftly between the carriages, again conscious of how easily other boys moved, and how he limped. When they reached the end of the pier, Stefan took him into a small room full of dust-covered books and old timetables. Wladek couldn't see anyone there, but then he heard a voice from behind a large pile of books saying, "What do you want, urchin? I don't have time to waste on you."

"Some information for my travelling companion, Joe. When is the next luxury cruise to Turkey?"

"Money up front," said an old man whose head appeared from behind the books, a lined weatherbeaten face wearing a seaman's cap. His black eyes were taking in Wladek.

"Used to be a great sea dog," said Stefan in a whisper loud enough for Joe to hear.

"None of your cheek, boy. Where is the ruble?"

"My friend carries my purse," said Stefan. "Show him the ruble, Wladek."

Wladek pulled out a coin. Joe bit it with his one remaining tooth, shuffled over to the bookcase and pulled out a large green timetable. Dust flew everywhere. He started coughing as he thumbed through the dirty pages, moving his short, stubby, rope-worn finger down the long columns of names.

"Next Thursday the *Renaska* is coming in to pick up coal, probably will leave on Saturday. If the ship can load quickly enough, she may sail on the Friday night and save the berthing tariffs. She'll dock on berth 17."

"Thanks, One Tooth," said Stefan. "I'll see if I can bring along any more of my wealthy associates in the future."

One Tooth Joe raised his fist cursing, as Stefan and Wladek ran out on to the wharf.

For the next three days the two boys stole food, loaded grain and slept. By the time the Turkish ship arrived on the following Thursday, Stefan had almost convinced Wladek that he should remain in Odessa. But Wladek's fear of the Russians outweighed the attraction of his new life with Stefan.

They stood on the quayside, staring at the new arrival docking at berth 17.

"How will I ever get on the ship?" asked Wladek.

"Simple," said Stefan. "We can join the chain gang tomorrow morning. I'll take the place behind you, and when the coal hold is nearly full, you can jump in and hide while I pick up your basket and walk on down the other side."

"And collect my share of the money, no doubt," said Wladek.

"Naturally," said Stefan. "There must be some financial reward for my superior intelligence or how could a man hope to sustain his belief in free enterprise?"

They joined the chain gang first thing the next morning and hauled coal up and down the gangplank until they were both ready to drop, but it still wasn't enough. The hold wasn't half full by nightfall. The two black boys slept soundly that night. The following morning, they started again and by mid-afternoon, when the hold was nearly full, Stefan kicked Wladek's ankle.

"Next time, Muscovite," he said.

When they reached the top of the gangway, Wladek threw his coal in, dropped the basket on the deck, jumped over the side of the hold and landed on the coal, while Stefan picked up his basket and continued down the other side of the gangplank whistling.

"Goodbye, my friend," he said, "and good luck with the infidel Turks."

Wladek pressed himself against a corner of the hold and watched the coal come pouring in beside him. The dust was everywhere, in his nose and mouth, in his lungs and eyes. With painful effort he avoided coughing for fear of being heard by one of the ship's crew. Just as he thought that he could no longer bear the air of the hold, and would have to return to Stefan and think of some other way of escape, he saw the doors slide shut above him. He coughed luxuriously.

After a few moments he felt something take a bite at his ankle. His blood went cold, realising what it had to be. He looked down, trying to work out where it had come from. No sooner had he thrown a piece of coal at the monster and sent him scurrying away than another one came at him, then another and another. The braver ones went for his legs. They seemed to appear from nowhere. Black, large, and hungry. It was the first time in his life that Wladek realised that rats had red eyes. He clambered to the top of the pile of coal and pulled open the hatch. The sunlight came flooding through and the rats disappeared back into their tunnels in the coal. He started to climb out, but the ship was already well clear of the quayside. He fell back into the hold, terrified. If the ship were forced to return and hand Wladek over, he knew it would mean a one-way journey back to Camp 201 and the White Russians. He chose to stay with the black rats. As soon as Wladek closed the hatch, they came at him again. As fast as he could throw lumps of coal at the verminous creatures, a new one would appear from another angle. Every few moments Wladek had to open the hatch to let some light in, for light seemed to be the only ally that would frighten the black rodents away.

For two days and three nights Wladek waged a running battle with the rats without ever catching a moment of quiet sleep. When the ship finally reached the port of Constantinople and a deck-hand opened the hold, Wladek was black from his head to his knees with dirt, and red from his knees to his toes with blood. The deck-hand dragged him out. Wladek tried to stand up but collapsed in a heap on the deck.

When Wladek came to – he knew not where or how much later – he found himself on a bed in a small room with three men in long white coats who were studying him carefully, speaking a tongue he did not know. How many languages were there in the world? He looked at himself, still red and black, and when he tried to sit up one of the white-coated men, the oldest of the three, with a thin, lined face and a goatee, pushed him back down. He addressed Wladek in the strange tongue. Wladek shook his head. He then tried Russian. Wladek again shook his head – that would be the quickest way back to where he had come. The next language the doctor tried was German, and Wladek realised that his command of that language was greater than his inquisitor's.

"You speak German?"

"Yes."

"Ah, so you're not Russian, then?"

"No."

"What were you doing in Russia?"

"Trying to escape."

"Ah." He then turned to his companions and seemed to report the conversation in his own tongue. They left the room.

A nurse came in and scrubbed him clean, taking little notice of his cries of anguish. She covered his legs in a thick, brown ointment and left him to sleep again. When Wladek awoke for the second time, he was quite alone. He lay staring at the white ceiling, considering his next move.

Still not sure of which country he was in, he climbed on to the window sill and stared out of the window. He could see a market place, not unlike the one in Odessa, except that the men wore long white robes and had darker skins. They also wore colourful hats that looked like small flower pots upside down, and sandals on their feet. The women were all in black and had even their faces covered except for their black eyes. Wladek watched the strange race in the market place bargaining for their daily food; that was one thing at least that seemed to be international.

He watched the scene for several minutes before he noticed that running down by the side of the building was a red iron ladder stretching all the way to the ground, not unlike the fire escape in his castle in Slonim. His castle. Who would believe him now? He climbed down from the window sill, walked cautiously to the door, opened it and peered into the corridor. Men and women were walking up and down, but none of them showed any interest in him. He closed the door gently, found his belongings in a cupboard in the corner of his room and dressed quickly. His clothes were still black with coal dust and felt gritty on his clean skin. Back to the window sill. The window opened easily. He gripped the fire escape, swung out of the window and started to climb down towards freedom. The first thing that hit him was the heat. He wished he was no longer wearing the heavy overcoat.

Once he touched the ground Wladek tried to run, but his legs were so weak and painful that he could only walk slowly. How he wished he could rid himself of that limp. He did not look back at the hospital until he was lost in the throng of the crowd in the market place.

Wladek stared at the tempting food on the stalls and decided to buy an orange and some nuts. He went to the lining in his suit; surely the money had been under his right arm? Yes it had, but it was no longer there, and far worse, the silver band had also gone. The men in the white coats had stolen his possessions. He considered going back to the hospital to retrieve the lost heirloom and decided against returning until he had had something to eat. Perhaps there was still some money in his pockets. He searched around in the large overcoat pocket and immediately found the three notes and some coins. They were all together with the doctor's map and the silver band. Wladek was overjoyed at the discovery. He slipped the silver band on, and pushed it above his elbow.

Wladek chose the largest orange he could see and a handful of nuts. The stallkeeper said something to him that he could not understand. Wladek felt the easiest way out of the language barrier was to hand over a fifty-ruble note. The stallkeeper looked at it, laughed, and threw his arms in the sky.

"Allah," he cried, snatching back the nuts and the orange from Wladek and waving him away with his forefinger. Wladek walked off in despair; a different language meant different money, he supposed. In Russia he had been poor; here he was penniless. He would have to steal an orange; if he were caught, he would throw it back to the stallkeeper. Wladek walked to the other end of the market place in the same way as Stefan had done, but he couldn't imitate the swagger, and he didn't feel the same confidence. He chose the end stall and when he was sure no one was watching, he picked up an orange and started to run. Suddenly there was uproar. It seemed as if half the city were chasing him.

A big man jumped on the limping Wladek and threw him to the ground. Six or seven people seized hold of different parts of his body while a larger group thronged around as he was dragged back to the stall. A policeman awaited them. Notes were taken, and there was a shouted exchange between the stall owner and the policeman, each man's voice rising with each new statement. The policeman then turned to Wladek and shouted at him too, but Wladek could not understand a word. The policeman shrugged his shoulders and marched Wladek off by the ear. People continued to bawl at him. Some of them spat on him. When Wladek reached the police station, he was taken underground and thrown into a tiny cell, already occupied by twenty or thirty criminals; thugs, thieves or he knew not what. Wladek did not speak to them, and they showed no desire to talk to him. He remained with his back to a wall, cowering, quiet, terrified. For at least a day and a night, he was left there with no food or light. The smell of excreta made him vomit until there was nothing left in him. He never thought the day would come when the dungeons in Slonim would seem uncrowded and peaceful.

The next morning Wladek was dragged from the basement by two guards and marched to a hall where he was lined up with several other prisoners. They were all roped to each other around the waist and led from the jail in a long line down into the street. Another large crowd had gathered outside and their loud cheer of welcome made Wladek feel that they had been waiting some time for the prisoners to appear. The crowd followed them all the way to the market place – screaming, clapping and shouting – for what reason Wladek feared even to contemplate. The line came to a halt when they reached the market square. The first prisoner was unleashed from his rope and taken into the centre of the square, which was already crammed with hundreds of people, all shouting at the top of their voices.

Wladek watched the scene in disbelief. When the first prisoner reached the middle of the square, he was knocked to his knees by the guard and then his right hand was strapped to a wooden block by a giant of a man who raised a large sword above his head and brought it down with terrible force, aiming at the prisoner's wrist. He only managed to catch the tips of the fingers. The prisoner screamed with pain as the sword was raised again. This time the sword hit the wrist but still did not finish the job properly and the wrist dangled from the prisoner's arm, blood pouring out on to the sand. The sword was raised for a third time, and for the third time it came down. The prisoner's hand at last fell to the ground. The crowd roared its approval. The prisoner was at last released, and he slumped in a heap, unconscious. He was dragged off by a disinterested guard and left on the edge of the crowd. A weeping woman, his wife, Wladek presumed, hurriedly tied a tourniquet of dirty cloth around the bloody stump. The second prisoner died of shock before the fourth blow was struck. The giant executioner was not interested in death so he continued his task; he was paid to remove hands.

Wladek looked around in terror and would have vomited

if there had been anything left in his stomach to bring up. He searched in every direction for help or some means of escape; no one had told him that under Islamic law the punishment for trying to escape would be the loss of a foot. His eyes darted around the mass of faces until he saw a man in the crowd dressed like a European, wearing a dark suit. The man was standing about twenty yards away from Wladek and was watching the spectacle with obvious disgust. But he did not once look in Wladek's direction, nor could he hear his shouts for help in the uproar arising from the crowd every time the sword was brought down. Was he French, German, English or even Polish? Wladek could not tell, but for some reason he was there to witness this macabre spectacle. Wladek stared at him, willing him to look his way. But he did not. Wladek waved his free arm but still could not gain the European's attention. They untied the man two in front of Wladek and dragged him along the ground towards the block. When the sword went up again and the crowd cheered, the man in the dark suit turned his eyes away in disgust and Wladek waved frantically at him again.

The man stared at Wladek and then turned to talk to a companion, whom Wladek had not noticed. The guard was now struggling with the prisoner immediately in front of Wladek. He placed the prisoner's hand under the strap; the sword went up and removed the hand in one blow. The crowd seemed disappointed. Wladek stared again at the Europeans. They were now both looking at him. He willed them to move, but they only continued to stare.

The guard came over, threw Wladek's fifty-ruble overcoat to the ground, undid his shirt and rolled up his sleeve. Wladek struggled futilely as he was dragged across the square. He was no match for the guard. When he reached the block, he was kicked in the back of his knees and collapsed to the ground. The strap was fastened over his right wrist, and there was nothing left for him to do but close his eyes as the sword was raised above the executioner's head. He waited in agony for the terrible blow, and then there was a sudden hush in the crowd as the Baron's silver band fell from Wladek's elbow down to his wrist and on to the block. An eerie silence came over the crowd as the heirloom shone brightly in the sunlight. The executioner stopped and put down his sword and studied the silver band. Wladek opened his eyes. He tried to pull it over Wladek's wrist, but he couldn't get it past the leather strap. A man in uniform ran quickly forward and joined the executioner. He, too, studied the band and the inscription and then ran to another man, who must have been of higher authority, because he walked more slowly towards Wladek. The sword was resting on the ground and the crowd were now beginning to jeer and hoot. The second officer also tried to pull the silver band off, but could not get it over the block either and he seemed unwilling to undo the strap. He shouted words at Wladek, who did not understand what he was saying and replied in Polish, "I do not speak your language."

The officer looked surprised and threw his hands in the air shouting, "Allah." That must be the same as "Holy God," thought Wladek. The officer walked slowly towards the two men in the crowd wearing western suits, arms going in every direction like a disorganised windmill. Wladek prayed to God; in such situations any man prays to any god, be it Allah or the Ave Maria. The Europeans were still staring at Wladek, and Wladek nodded his head up and down frantically. One of the men in the dark suits joined the Turkish officer as he walked back towards the block. The former knelt down by Wladek's side, studied the silver band and then looked carefully at him. Wladek waited. He could converse in five languages and prayed that the gentleman would speak one of them. His heart sank when the European turned to the officer and addressed him in his own tongue. The crowd was now hissing and throwing rotten fruit at the block. The officer was nodding his agreement, while the gentleman stared intently at Wladek.

"Do you speak English?"

Wladek heaved a sigh of relief. "Yes, sir, not bad. I am Polish citizen."

"How did you come into possession of that silver band?"

"It belong my father, sir. He die in prison by the Germans in Poland, and I captured and sent to a prison camp in

Russia. I escape and come here by ship. I have no eat for days. When stallkeeper no accept my rubles for orange, I take one because I much, much hungry."

The Englishman rose slowly from his knees, turned to the officer and spoke to him very firmly. The latter, in turn, addressed the executioner who looked doubtful, but when the officer repeated the order a little louder, he bent down and reluctantly undid the leather strap. This time Wladek did vomit.

"Come with me," said the Englishman. "And quickly, before they change their minds."

Still in a daze, Wladek grabbed his coat and followed him. The crowd booed and jeered, throwing things at him as he departed, and the swordsman quickly put the next prisoner's hand on the block and with his first blow only managed to remove a thumb. This seemed to pacify the mob.

The Englishman moved swiftly through the hustling crowd out of the square where he was joined by his companion.

"What's happening, Edward?"

"The boy says he is a Pole and that he escaped from Russia. I told the official in charge that he was English, so now he is our responsibility. Let's get him to the embassy and find out if the boy's story bears any resemblance to the truth."

Wladek ran between the two men as they hurried on through the bazaar and into the Street of Seven Kings. He could still faintly hear the mob behind him screaming their approval every time the executioner brought down his sword.

The two Englishmen walked over a pebbled courtyard towards a large grey building and beckoned Wladek to follow them. On the door were the welcoming words, British Embassy. Once inside the building Wladek began to feel safe for the first time. He walked a pace behind the two men down a long hall with walls filled with paintings of strangely clad soldiers and sailors. At the far end was a magnificent portrait of an old man in a blue naval uniform liberally adorned with medals. His fine beard reminded Wladek of the Baron. A soldier appeared from nowhere and saluted.

"Take this boy, Corporal Smithers, and see that he gets a bath. Then feed him in the kitchens. When he has eaten and smells a little less like a walking pigsty, bring him to my office."

"Yes, sir," said the corporal and saluted.

"Come with me, my lad." The soldier marched away. Wladek followed him obediently, having to run to keep up with his walking pace. He was taken to the basement of the embassy and left in a little room; this time it had a window. The corporal told him to get undressed and then left him on his own. He returned a few minutes later to find Wladek still sitting on the edge of the bed fully dressed, dazedly twisting the silver band around and around his wrist.

"Hurry up, lad; you're not on a rest cure."

"Sorry, sir," Wladek said.

"Don't call me sir, lad. I am Corporal Smithers. You call me corporal."

"I am Wladek Koskiewicz. You call me Wladek."

"Don't be funny with me, lad. We've got enough funny people in the British Army without you wishing to join their ranks."

Wladek did not understand what the soldier meant. He undressed quickly.

"Follow me at the double."

Another marvellous bath with hot water and soap. Wladek thought of his Russian protectress, and of the son he might have become to her but for her husband. A new set of clothes, strange but clean and fresh-smelling. Whose son had they belonged to? The soldier was back at the door.

Corporal Smithers took Wladek to the kitchen and left him with a fat, pink-faced cook, with the warmest face he had seen since leaving Poland. She reminded him of *niania*. Wladek could not help wondering what would happen to her waistline after a few weeks in Camp 201.

"Hello," she said with a beaming smile. "What's your name, then?"

Wladek told her.

"Well, laddie, it looks as though you could do with a good British meal inside of you – none of this Turkish muck will suffice. We'll start with some hot soup and beef. You'll need something substantial if you're to face Mr. Prendergast." She laughed. "Just remember, his bite's not as bad as his bark. Although he is an Englishman, his heart's in the right place."

"You are not an English, Mrs. Cook?" asked Wladek, surprised.

"Good Lord no, laddie, I'm Scottish. There's a world of difference. We hate the English more than the Germans do," she said, laughing. She set a dish of steaming soup, thick with meat and vegetables, in front of Wladek. He had entirely forgotten that food could smell and taste so appetising. He ate the meal slowly for fear it might not happen again for a very long time.

The corporal reappeared. "Have you had enough to eat, my lad?"

"Yes, thank you, Mr. Corporal."

The corporal gave Wladek a suspicious look, but he saw no trace of cheek in the boy's expression. "Good, then let's be moving. Can't be late on parade for Mr. Prendergast."

The corporal disappeared through the kitchen door, and Wladek stared at the cook. He hated always having to say goodbye to someone he'd just met, especially when they had been so kind.

"Off you go, laddie, if you know what's good for you."

"Thank you, Mrs. Cook," said Wladek. "Your food is best I can ever remember."

The cook smiled at him. He again had to limp hard to catch up with the corporal, whose marching pace still kept Wladek trotting. The soldier came to a brisk halt outside a door that Wladek nearly ran into.

"Look where you're going, my lad, look where you're going."

The corporal gave a short rap-rap on the door.

"Come," said a voice.

The corporal opened the door and saluted. "The Polish boy, sir, as you requested, scrubbed and fed."

"Thank you, Corporal. Perhaps you would be kind enough to ask Mr. Grant to join us."

Edward Prendergast looked up from his desk. He waved Wladek to a seat without speaking and continued to work at some papers. Wladek sat looking at him and then at the portraits on the wall. More generals and admirals and that old, bearded gentleman again, this time in khaki army uniform. A few minutes later the other Englishman he remembered from the market square came in.

"Thank you for joining us, Harry. Do have a seat, old boy."

Mr. Prendergast turned to Wladek. "Now, my lad, let's hear your story from the beginning, with no exaggerations, only the truth. Do you understand?"

"Yes, sir."

Wladek started his story with his days in Poland. It took him some time to find the right English words. It was apparent from the looks on the faces of the two Englishmen that they were at first incredulous. They occasionally stopped him and asked questions, nodding to each other at his answers. After an hour of talking Wladek's life history had reached the office of His Britannic Majesty's second consul to Turkey.

"I think, Harry," said the second consul, "it is our duty to inform the Polish Delegation immediately and then hand young Koskiewicz over to them as I feel in the circumstances he is undoubtedly their responsibility."

"Agreed," said the man called Harry. "You know, my boy, you had a narrow escape in the market today. The Sher – that is the old Islamic religious law – which provides for cutting off a hand for theft was officially abandoned years ago. In fact it is a crime under the Ottoman Penal Code to inflict such a punishment. Nevertheless, in practice the barbarians still continue to carry it out." He shrugged.

"Why not my hand?" asked Wladek, holding on to his wrist.

"I told them they could cut off all the Moslem hands they wanted, but not an Englishman's," Edward Prendergast interjected.

"Thank God," said Wladek faintly.

"Edward Prendergast, actually," he said, smiling for the first time. The second consul continued. "You can spend the night here, and we will take you to your own delegation tomorrow. The Poles do not actually have an embassy in Constantinople," he said, slightly disdainfully, "but my opposite number is a good fellow considering he's a foreigner." He pressed a button and the corporal reappeared immediately.

"Sir."

"Corporal, take young Koskiewicz to his room, and in the morning see he is given breakfast and is brought to me at nine sharp."

"Sir. This way, boy, at the double."

Wladek was led away by the corporal. He was not even given enough time to thank the two Englishmen who had saved his hand – and perhaps his life. Back in the clean little room, with its clean little bed neatly turned down as if he were an honoured guest, he undressed, threw his pillow on the floor and slept soundly until the morning light shone through the tiny window.

"Rise and shine, lad, sharpish."

It was the corporal, his uniform immaculately smart and knife-edge pressed, looking as though he had never been to bed. For an instant Wladek, surfacing from sleep, thought himself back in Camp 201, as the corporal's banging on the end of the bed frame with his cane resembled the noise he had grown so accustomed to. He fell out of bed and reached for his clothes.

"Wash first, my lad, wash first. We don't want your horrible smells worrying Mr. Prendergast so early in the morning, do we?"

Wladek was unsure which part of himself to wash, so unusually clean did he feel himself to be. The corporal was staring at him.

"What's wrong with your leg, lad?"

"Nothing, nothing," said Wladek, turning himself away from the staring eyes.

"Right. I'll be back in three minutes. Three minutes, do you hear, my lad, be sure you're ready."

Wladek washed his hands and face quickly and then dressed. He was waiting at the end of the bed in his long bearskin coat when the corporal returned to take him to the second consul. Mr. Prendergast welcomed him and seemed to have softened considerably since their first meeting.

"Good morning, Koskiewicz."

"Good morning, sir."

"Did you enjoy your breakfast?"

"I no had breakfast, sir."

"Why not?" said the second consul, looking towards the corporal.

"Overslept, I'm afraid, sir. He would have been late for you."

"Well, we must see what we can do about that. Corporal, will you ask Mrs. Henderson to try and rustle up an apple or something?"

"Yes, sir."

Wladek and the second consul walked slowly along the corridor towards the embassy front door, and across the pebbled courtyard to a waiting car, an Austin, one of the few engine driven vehicles in Turkey and Wladek's first journey in one. He was sorry to be leaving the British Embassy. It was the first place in which he had felt safe for years. He wondered if he was ever going to sleep more than one night in the same bed for the rest of his life. The corporal ran down the steps and took the driver's seat. He passed Wladek an apple and some fresh warm bread.

"See there are no crumbs left in the car, lad. The cook sends her compliments."

The drive through the hot busy streets was conducted at walking pace as the Turks did not believe anything could go faster than a camel, and made no attempt to clear a path for the little Austin. Even with all the windows open Wladek was sweating from the oppressive heat while Mr. Prendergast remained quite cool and unperturbed. Wladek hid himself in the back of the car for fear that someone who had witnessed the previous day's events might recognise him and stir the mob to anger again. When the little black Austin came to a halt outside a small decaying building marked 'Konsulat Polski', Wladek felt a twinge of excitement mingled with disappointment.

The three of them climbed out.

"Where's the apple core, boy?" demanded the corporal.

"I eat him."

The corporal laughed and knocked on the door. A friendly-looking little man with dark hair and firm jaw opened the door to them. He was in shirt sleeves and deeply tanned, obviously by the Turkish sun. He addressed them in Polish. His words were the first Wladek had heard in his native tongue since leaving the labour camp. Wladek answered quickly, explaining his presence. His fellow countryman turned to the British second consul.

"This way, Mr. Prendergast," he said in perfect English. "It was good of you to bring the boy over personally."

A few diplomatic niceties were exchanged before Prendergast and the corporal took their leave. Wladek gazed at them, fumbling for an English expression more adequate than 'Thank you.'

Prendergast patted Wladek on the head as he might a cocker spaniel. The corporal closed the door, and winked at Wladek. "Good luck, my lad; God knows you deserve it."

The Polish consul introduced himself to Wladek as Pawel Zaleski. Again Wladek was required to recount the story of his life, finding it easier in Polish than he had in English. Pawel Zaleski heard him out in silence, shaking his head sorrowfully.

"My poor child," he said heavily. "You have borne more than your share of our country's suffering for one so young. And now what are we to do with you?"

"I must return to Poland and reclaim my castle," said Wladek.

"Poland," said Pawel Zaleski. "Where's that? The area of land where you lived remains in dispute and there is still heavy fighting going on between the Poles and the Russians. General Piłsudski is doing all he can to protect the territorial integrity of our fatherland. But it would be foolish for any of us to be optimistic. There is little left for you now in Poland. No, your best plan would be to start a new life in England or America."

"But I don't want to go to England or America. I am Polish."

"You will always be Polish, Wladek, no one can take that away from you wherever you decide to settle, but you must be realistic about your life – which hasn't even begun."

Wladek lowered his head in despair. Had he gone through all this only to be told he could never return to his native land? He fought back the tears.

Pawel Zaleski put his arm round the boy's shoulders. "Never forget that you are one of the lucky ones who escaped and came out of the holocaust alive. You only have to remember your friend, Doctor Dubien, to be aware of what life might have been like."

Wladek didn't speak.

"Now, you must put all thoughts of the past behind you and think only for the future, Wladek, and perhaps in your lifetime you will see Poland rise again, which is more than I dare hope for."

Wladek remained silent.

"Well, there's no need to make an immediate decision," said the consul kindly. "You can stay here for as long as it takes you to decide on your future."

10

The future was something that was worrying Anne. The first few months of her marriage were happy, marred only by her anxiety over William's increasing dislike of Henry, and her new husband's seeming inability to start working. Henry was a little touchy on the point, explaining to Anne that he was still disorientated by the war and that he wasn't willing to rush into something he might well have to stick with for the rest of his life. She found this hard to swallow and finally it brought on their first row.

"I don't understand why you haven't opened that real estate business you used to be so keen on, Henry."

"I can't. The time isn't quite right. The real estate market's not looking that promising at the moment."

"You've been saying that now for nearly a year; I wonder if it will ever be promising enough for you."

"Sure it will; truth is, I need a little more capital to help myself set up. Now if you would loan me some of your money, I could get cracking tomorrow."

"That's impossible, Henry. You know the terms of Richard's will; my allowance was stopped the day we were married, and now I have only the capital left."

"A little of that would help me on my way, and don't forget that precious boy of yours has well over twenty million in the family trust."

"You seem to know a lot about William's trust," said Anne suspiciously.

"Oh, come on, Anne, give me a chance to be your husband. Don't make me feel like a guest in my own home."

"What's happened to your money, Henry? You always

led me to believe that you had enough to start your own business."

"You've always known I was not in Richard's class financially, and there was a time, Anne, when you claimed it didn't matter. I'd marry you, Henry, if you were penniless," he mocked.

Anne burst into tears, and Henry tried to console her. She spent the rest of the evening in his arms talking the problem over. Anne managed to convince herself she was being unwifely and ungenerous. She had more money than she could possibly need: couldn't she trust a little of it to the man to whom she was so willing to entrust the rest of her life?

Acting upon these thoughts, she agreed to let Henry have one hundred thousand dollars to set up his own real estate firm in Boston. Within a month Henry had found a smart new office in a fashionable part of town, appointed staff, and started work. Soon he was mixing with all the city politicians and real estate men of Boston. They talked of the boom in farm land, and they flattered Henry. Anne didn't care very much for them as social company, but Henry was happy and appeared to be successful at his work.

William, now fourteen, was in his third year at St. Paul's, sixth in his class overall and first in mathematics. He had also become a rising figure in the Debating Society. He wrote to his mother once a week, reporting his progress, always addressing his letters to Mrs. Richard Kane, refusing to acknowledge that Henry Osborne even existed. Anne wasn't sure whether she should talk to him about it, and each Monday she would carefully extract William's letter from the box to be certain that Henry never saw the envelope. She continued to hope that in time William would come around to liking Henry, but it became clear that that hope was unrealistic when, in one particular letter to his mother, he sought her permission to stay with his friend, Matthew Lester, for the summer holidays. The request came as a painful blow to Anne, but she took the easy way out and fell in with William's plans, which Henry also seemed to favour.

William hated Henry Osborne, and nursed the hatred passionately, not sure what he could actually do about it. He was relieved that Henry never visited him at school; he could not have tolerated the other boys seeing his mother with that man. It was bad enough that he had to live with him in Boston.

For the first time since his mother's marriage, William was anxious for the holidays to come.

The Lester's Packard chauffeured William and Matthew noiselessly to the summer camp in Vermont. On the journey, Matthew casually asked William what he intended to do when the time came for him to leave St. Paul's.

"When I leave I will be top of the class, Class President, and have won the Hamilton Memorial Mathematics Scholarship to Harvard," replied William without hesitation.

"Why is all that so important?" asked Matthew innocently.

"My father did all three."

"When you've finished beating your father, I will introduce you to mine."

William smiled.

The two boys had an energetic and enjoyable four weeks in Vermont playing every game from chess to American football. When the month came to an end they travelled to New York to spend the last part of the holiday with the Lester family. They were greeted at the door by a butler who addressed Matthew as sir and a twelve-year-old girl covered in freckles who called him Fatty. It made William laugh because his friend was so thin and it was she who was fat. The little girl smiled and revealed teeth almost totally hidden behind braces.

"You would never believe Susan was my sister, would you?" asked Matthew disdainfully.

"No, I suppose not," said William, smiling at Susan. "She's so much better looking than you."

She adored William from that moment on.

William adored Matthew's father the moment they met; he reminded him in so many ways of his own father and he begged Charles Lester to let him see the great bank of which he was chairman. Charles Lester thought carefully about the request. No child had been allowed to enter the orderly precincts of 17 Broad Street before, not even his own son. He compromised, as bankers often do, and showed the boy around the Wall Street building on a Sunday afternoon.

William was fascinated to see the different offices, the vaults, the foreign exchange dealing room, the board room and the chairman's office. Compared with Kane and Cabot, the Lester bank was considerably more extensive, and William knew from his own small personal investment account, which provided him with a copy of the annual general report, that they had a far larger capital base than Kane and Cabot. William was silent, pensive, as they were driven home in the car.

"Well, William, did you enjoy your visit to my bank?" asked Charles Lester genially.

"Oh, yes, sir," replied William. "I certainly did enjoy it." William paused for a moment and then added, "I intend to be chairman of your bank one day, Mr. Lester."

Charles Lester laughed, and dined out on the story of how young William Kane had reacted to Lester and Co., which in turn made those who heard it laugh too.

Only William had not meant the remark as a joke.

Anne was shocked when Henry came back to her for more money.

"It's as safe as a house," he assured her. "Ask Alan Lloyd. As chairman of the bank he can only have your best interests at heart."

"But two hundred and fifty thousand?" Anne queried.

"A superb opportunity, my dear. Look upon it as an investment that will be worth double that amount within two years."

After another more prolonged row, Anne gave in once again and life returned to the same smooth routine. When she checked her investment portfolio with the bank, Anne found she was down to one hundred and fifty thousand dollars, but Henry seemed to be seeing all the right people and clinching all the right deals. She considered discussing the whole problem with Alan Lloyd at Kane and Cabot, but in the end dismissed the idea; it would have meant displaying distrust in the husband whom she wished the world to respect, and surely Henry would not have made the suggestion at all had he not been sure that the loan would have met with Alan's approval.

Anne also started seeing Doctor MacKenzie again to find out if there was any hope of her having another baby, but he still advised against the idea. With the high blood pressure that had caused her earlier miscarriage, Andrew MacKenzie did not consider thirty-five a good age for Anne to start thinking about being a mother again. Anne raised the idea with the grandmothers, but they agreed wholeheartedly with the views of the good doctor. Neither of them cared for Henry very much, and they cared even less for the thought of an Osborne offspring making claims on the Kane family fortune after they were gone. Anne began to resign herself to the fact that William was going to be her only child. Henry became very angry about what he described as her betrayal, and told Anne that if Richard were still alive, she would have tried again. How different the two men were, she thought, and couldn't account for why she had loved them both. She tried to soothe Henry, praying that his business projects would work out well and keep him fully occupied. He certainly had taken to working very late at the office.

It was on a Monday in October, the weekend after they had celebrated their second wedding anniversary, that Anne started receiving the letters from an unsigned 'friend', informing her that Henry could be seen escorting other women around Boston, and one lady in particular whom the writer didn't care to name. To begin with Anne burned the letters immediately and although they worried her, she never discussed them with Henry, praying that each letter would be the last. She couldn't even summon up the courage to raise the matter with Henry when he asked her for the last hundred and fifty thousand dollars.

"I am going to lose the whole deal if I don't have that money right now, Anne."

"But it's all I have, Henry. If I give you that amount, I'll be left with nothing."

"This house alone must be worth over two hundred thousand. You could mortgage it tomorrow."

"The house belongs to William."

"William, William, William. It's always William who gets in the way of my success," shouted Henry as he stormed out.

He returned home after midnight, contrite, and told her he would rather she kept her money and that he went under, for at least they would still have each other. Anne was comforted by his words and later they made love. She signed a cheque for one hundred and fifty thousand dollars the next morning, trying to forget that it would leave her penniless until Henry pulled off the deal he was pursuing. She couldn't help wondering if it was more than a coincidence that Henry had asked for the exact amount that remained of her inheritance.

The next month Anne missed her period.

Doctor MacKenzie was anxious but tried not to show it; the grandmothers were horrified and did; while Henry was delighted and assured Anne that it was the most wonderful thing that had ever happened to him in his whole life, and even agreed to building a new children's wing for the hospital that Richard had planned before he died.

When William heard the news by letter from his mother, he sat deep in thought all evening unable to tell even Matthew what was preoccupying him. The following Saturday morning, having been granted special permission by his housemaster, Grumpy Raglan, he boarded a train to Boston and on arrival withdrew one hundred dollars from his savings account. He then proceeded to the law offices of Cohen, Cohen and Yablons in Jefferson Street. Mr. Thomas Cohen, the senior partner, a tall angular man with a dark jowl was somewhat surprised when William was ushered into his office.

"I have never been retained by a sixteen-year-old before," Mr. Cohen began. "It will be quite a novelty for me – " he hesitated " – Mr. Kane." He found Mr. Kane did not run easily off the tongue. "Especially as your father was not exactly – how shall I put it? – known for his sympathy for my co-religionists."

"My father," replied William, "was a great admirer of the achievements of the Hebrew race and in particular had considerable respect for your firm when you acted on behalf of rivals. I heard him mention your name on several occasions. That's why I have chosen you, Mr. Cohen, not you me. That should be reassurance enough."

Mr. Cohen quickly put aside the fact that William was only sixteen. "Indeed, indeed. I feel I can make an exception for the son of Richard Kane. Now, what can we do for you?"

"I wish you to answer three questions for me, Mr. Cohen. One, I want to know if my mother, Mrs. Henry Osborne, were to give birth to a child, son or daughter, whether that child would have any legal rights to the Kane family trust. Two, do I have any legal obligations to Mr. Henry Osborne because he is married to my mother, and three, at what age can I insist that Mr. Henry Osborne leave my house on Louisburg Square in Boston?"

Thomas Cohen's quill pen sped furiously across the paper in front of him, spattering little blue spots on an already ink-stained desk top.

William placed one hundred dollars on the desk. The lawyer looked taken aback but picked the notes up and counted them.

"Use the money prudently, Mr. Cohen. I will need a good lawyer when I leave Harvard."

"You have already been accepted at Harvard, Mr. Kane? My congratulations. I am hoping my son will go there too."

"No, I have not, but I shall have done so in two years' time. I will return to Boston to see you in one week, Mr. Cohen. If I ever hear in my lifetime from anyone other than yourself on this subject, you may consider our relationship at an end. Good day, sir."

Thomas Cohen would have also said good day, if he could have spluttered the words out before William closed the door behind him.

* * *

William returned to the offices of Cohen, Cohen and Yablons seven days later.

"Ah, Mr. Kane," said Thomas Cohen, "how nice to see you again. Would you care for some coffee?"

"No, thank you."

"Shall I send someone out for a Coca-Cola?"

William's face was expressionless.

"To business, to business," said Mr. Cohen, slightly embarrassed. "We have dug around a little on your behalf, Mr. Kane, with the help of a very respectable firm of private investigators to assist us with the questions you asked that were not purely academic. I think I can safely say we have the answers to all your questions. You asked if Mr. Osborne's offspring by your mother, were there to be any, would have a claim on the Kane estate, or in particular on the trust left to you by your father. No is the simple answer, but of course Mrs. Osborne can leave any part of the five hundred thousand dollars bequeathed to her by your father to whom she pleases."

Mr. Cohen looked up.

"However, it may interest you to know, Mr. Kane, that your mother has drawn out the entire five hundred thousand from her private account at Kane and Cabot during the last eighteen months, but we have been unable to trace how the money has been used. It is possible she may have decided to deposit the amount in another bank."

William looked shocked, the first sign of any lack of the self-control that Thomas Cohen had noted.

"There would be no reason for her to do that," William said. "The money can only have gone to one person."

The lawyer remained silent, expecting to hear more, but William steadied himself and added nothing, so Mr. Cohen continued.

"The answer to your second question is that you have no personal or legal obligations to Mr. Henry Osborne at all. Under the terms of your father's will, your mother is a trustee of the estate along with a Mr. Alan Lloyd and a Mrs. John Preston, your surviving godparents, until you come of age at twenty-one."

Thomas Cohen looked up again. William's face showed no expression at all. Cohen had already learned that that meant he should continue.

"And thirdly, Mr. Kane, you can never remove Mr. Osborne from Beacon Hill as long as he remains married to your mother and continues to reside with her. The property comes into your possession by natural right on her death. Were he still alive then, you could require him to leave. I think you will find that covers all your questions, Mr. Kane."

"Thank you, Mr. Cohen," said William. "I am obliged for your efficiency and discretion in this matter. Now perhaps you could let me know your professional charges?"

"One hundred dollars doesn't quite cover the work, Mr. Kane, but we have faith in your future and . . ."

"I do not wish to be beholden to anyone, Mr. Cohen. You must treat me as someone with whom you might never deal again. With that in mind, how much do I owe you?"

Mr. Cohen considered the matter for a moment. "In those circumstances we would have charged you two hundred and twenty dollars, Mr. Kane."

William took six twenty-dollar notes from his inside pocket and handed them over to Cohen. This time, the lawyer did not count them.

"I am grateful to you for your assistance, Mr. Cohen, I am sure we shall meet again. Good day, sir."

"Good day, Mr. Kane. May I be permitted to say that I never had the privilege of meeting your distinguished father but having dealt with you, I wish that I had."

William smiled and softened. "Thank you, sir."

Preparing for the baby kept Anne fully occupied; she found herself easily tired and resting a good deal. Whenever she enquired of Henry how business was going, he always had some plausible answer to hand, enough to reassure her that all was well without supplying her with any actual details.

Then one morning the anonymous letters started coming again. This time they gave more details, the names of the women involved and the places they could be seen with Henry. Anne burned them even before she could commit the names or places to memory. She didn't want to believe that her husband could be unfaithful while she was carrying his child. Someone was jealous and had it in for Henry, and he or she had to be lying.

The letters kept coming, sometimes with new names. Anne continued to destroy them, but now they were beginning to prey on her mind. She wanted to discuss the whole problem with someone, but couldn't think of anybody in whom she could confide. The grandmothers would have been appalled and were, in any case, already prejudiced against Henry. Alan Lloyd at the bank could not be expected to understand as he had never married, and William was far too young. No one seemed suitable. Anne considered consulting a psychiatrist after listening to a lecture given by Sigmund Freud, but a Lowell could never discuss a family problem with a complete stranger.

The matter finally came to a head in a way that even Anne had not been prepared for. One Monday morning, she received three letters, the usual one from William addressed to Mrs. Richard Kane, asking if he could once again spend his summer holidays with his friend Matthew Lester in New York. Another anonymous letter alleging that Henry was having an affair with, with . . . Milly Preston, and the third from Alan Lloyd, as chairman of the bank, asking if she would be kind enough to telephone and make an appointment to see him. Anne sat down heavily, feeling breathless and unwell, and forced herself to re-read all three letters. William's letter stung her by its detachment. She hated knowing that he preferred to spend his holidays with Matthew Lester. They had been growing continually further apart since her marriage to Henry. The anonymous letter suggesting that Henry was having an affair with her closest friend was impossible to ignore. Anne couldn't help remembering that it had been Milly who had introduced her to Henry in the first place, and that she was William's godmother. The third letter from Alan Lloyd somehow filled her with even more apprehension. The only other letter she had ever received from Alan was one of condolence on the death of Richard. She feared another could only mean more bad news.

She called the bank. The operator put her straight through.

"Alan, you wanted to see me?"

"Yes, my dear, I would like to have a chat sometime. When would suit you?"

"Is it bad news?" asked Anne.

"Not exactly, but I would rather not say anything over the phone, but there's nothing for you to worry about. Are you free for lunch, by any chance?"

"Yes, I am, Alan."

"Well, let's meet at the Ritz at one o'clock. I look forward to seeing you then, Anne."

One o'clock, only three hours away. Her mind switched from Alan to William to Henry, but settled on Milly Preston. Could it be true? Anne decided to take a long warm bath and put on a new dress. It didn't help. She felt, and was beginning to look, bloated. Her ankles and calves, which had always been so elegant and so slim, were becoming mottled and puffy. It was a little frightening to conjecture how much worse things might become before the baby was born. She sighed at herself in the mirror and did the best she could with her outward appearance.

"You look very smart, Anne. If I weren't an old bachelor considered well past it, I'd flirt with you shamelessly," said the silver haired banker, greeting her with a kiss on both cheeks as though he were a French general.

He guided her to his table. It was an unspoken tradition that the table in the corner was always occupied by the chairman of Kane and Cabot, if he were not lunching at the bank. Richard had done so and now it was the turn of Alan Lloyd. It was the first occasion that Anne had sat at that table with anyone. Waiters fluttered around them like starlings, seeming to know exactly when to disappear and reappear without interrupting a private conversation.

"When's the baby due, Anne?"

"Oh, not for another three months."

"No complications, I hope. I seem to remember . . ."

"Well," admitted Anne, "the doctor sees me once a week

and pulls long faces about my blood pressure, but I'm not too worried."

"I'm so glad, my dear," he said and touched her hand gently as an uncle might. "You do look rather tired, I hope you're not overdoing things."

Alan Lloyd raised his hand slightly. A waiter materialised at his side, and they both ordered.

"Anne, I want to seek some advice from you."

Anne was painfully aware of Alan Lloyd's gift for diplomacy. He wasn't having lunch with her for advice. There was no doubt in her mind that he had come to dispense it – kindly.

"Do you have any idea how well Henry's real estate projects are going?"

"No, I don't," said Anne. "I never involve myself with Henry's business activities. You'll remember I didn't with Richard's either. Why? Is there any cause for concern?"

"No, no, none of which we at the bank are aware. On the contrary, we know Henry is bidding for a large city contract to build the new hospital complex. I was only enquiring, because he has come to the bank for a loan of five hundred thousand dollars."

Anne was stunned.

"I see that surprises you," he said. "Now, we know from your stock account that you have a little under twenty thousand dollars in reserve, while running a small overdraft of seventeen thousand dollars on your personal account."

Anne put down her soup spoon, horrified. She had not realised that she was so badly overdrawn. Alan could see her distress.

"That's not what this lunch is about, Anne," he added quickly. "The bank is quite happy to lose money on the personal account for the rest of your life. William is making over a million dollars a year on the interest from his trust, so your overdraft is hardly significant, nor indeed is the five hundred thousand Henry is requesting, if it were to receive your backing as William's legal guardian."

"I didn't realise that I had any authority over William's trust money," said Anne.

"You don't on the capital sum, but legally the interest earned from his trust can be invested in any project thought to benefit William, and is under the guardianship of yourself, myself and Milly Preston as godparents until William is twenty-one. Now as chairman of William's trust I can put up that five hundred thousand with your backing. Milly has already informed me that she would be quite happy to give her approval so that would give you two votes and my opinion would therefore be invalid."

"Milly Preston has already given her approval, Alan?"

"Yes. Hasn't she mentioned the matter to you?"

Anne did not reply immediately. "What is *your* opinion?" she asked finally.

"Well, I haven't seen Henry's accounts, because he only started his company eighteen months ago and he doesn't bank with us, so I have no idea what expenditure is over income for the current year and what return he is predicting for 1923."

"You realise that during the last eighteen months I've given Henry five hundred thousand of my own money?" said Anne.

"My chief teller informs me any time a large amount of cash is withdrawn from any account. I didn't know that was what you were using the money for, and it was none of my business, Anne. That money was left to you by Richard and is yours to spend as you see fit.

"Now, in the case of the interest from the family trust, that is a different matter. If you did decide to withdraw five hundred thousand dollars to invest in Henry's firm, then the bank will have to inspect Henry's books, because the money would be considered as another investment for William's portfolio. Richard did not give the trustees the authority to make loans, only to invest on William's behalf. I have already explained this situation to Henry, and if we were to go ahead and make this investment, the trustees would have to decide what percentage of Henry's company would be an appropriate exchange for the five hundred thousand. William, of course, is always aware what we are doing with his trust income, because we saw no reason not to comply with his request that he receive a quarterly investment programme statement from the bank in the same way as all the trustees do. I have no doubt in my own mind that he will have his own ideas on the subject which he will be fully aware of after he receives the next quarterly report.

"It may amuse you to know, that since William's sixteenth birthday he has been sending me back his own opinions on every investment we make. To begin with I looked on them with the passing interest of a benevolent guardian. Of late, I have been studying them with considerable respect. When William takes his place on the board of Kane and Cabot, this bank may well turn out to be too small for him."

"I've never been asked for advice on William's trust before," said Anne forlornly.

"Well, my dear, you do see the reports that the bank sends you on the first day of every quarter, and it has always been in your power as a trustee to query any of the investments we make on William's behalf."

Alan Lloyd took a slip of paper from his pocket, and remained silent until the sommelier had finished pouring the Nuits Saint Georges. Once he was out of earshot, Alan continued.

"William has over twenty-one million invested in the bank at four and a half per cent until his twenty-first birthday. We reinvest the interest for him each quarter in stocks and shares. We have never in the past invested in a private company. It may surprise you to hear, Anne, that we now carry out this reinvestment on a fifty-fifty basis: fifty per cent following the bank's advice and fifty per cent following the suggestions put forward by William. At the moment we are a little ahead of him, much to the satisfaction of Tony Simmons, our investment director, whom William has promised a Rolls-Royce in any year that he can beat the boy by over ten per cent."

"But where would William get hold of the ten thousand dollars for a Rolls-Royce if he lost the bet – when he's not allowed to touch the money in his trust until he is twenty-one?"

"I do not know the answer to that, Anne. What I do know

is he would be far too proud to come to us direct and I am certain he would not have made the wager if he could not honour it. Have you by any chance seen his famous ledger book lately?"

"The one given to him by his grandmothers?"

Alan Lloyd nodded.

"No, I haven't seen it since he went away to school. I didn't know it still existed."

"It still exists and I would," said the banker, "give a month's wages to know what the credit column in that ledger book now stands at. I suppose you are aware that he banks that money with Lester's in New York, and not with us? They don't take on private accounts at under ten thousand dollars. I'm also fairly certain they wouldn't make an exception, even for the son of Richard Kane."

"The son of Richard Kane," said Anne.

"I'm sorry, I didn't mean to sound rude, Anne."

"No, no, there is no doubt he is the son of Richard Kane. Do you know he has never asked me for a penny since his twelfth birthday?" She paused. "I think I should warn you, Alan, that he won't take kindly to being told he has to invest five hundred thousand dollars of his trust money in Henry's company."

"They don't get on well?" enquired Alan, his eyebrows rising.

"I'm afraid not," said Anne.

"I'm sorry to hear that. It certainly would make the transaction more complicated if William really stood out against the whole scheme. Although he has no authority over the trust until he is twenty-one, we have already discovered through sources of our own that he is not beyond going to an independent lawyer to find out his legal position."

"Good God," said Anne, "you can't be serious."

"Oh, yes, quite serious, but there's nothing for you to worry about. To be frank, we at the bank were all rather impressed and once we realised where the enquiry was coming from, we released information we would normally have kept very much to ourselves. For some private reason he obviously didn't want to approach us directly."

"Good heavens," said Anne, "what will he be like when he's thirty?"

"That will depend," said Alan, "on whether he is lucky enough to fall in love with someone as lovely as you. That was always Richard's strength."

"You are an old flatterer, Alan. Can we leave the problem of the five hundred thousand until I have had a chance to discuss it with Henry?"

"Of course, my dear. I told you I had come to seek your advice."

Alan ordered coffee and took Anne's hand gently in his. "And do remember to take care of yourself, Anne. You're far more important than the fate of a few thousand dollars."

When Anne returned home from lunch she immediately started to worry about the other two letters she had received that morning. Of one thing she was now certain, after all she had learned about her own son from Alan Lloyd; she would be wise to give in gracefully and let William spend the forthcoming holidays with his friend, Matthew Lester.

Henry and Milly's relationship raised a problem to which she was unable to compose so simple a solution. She sat in the maroon leather chair, Richard's favourite, looking out through the bay window on to a beautiful bed of red and white roses, seeing nothing, only thinking. Anne always took a long time to make a decision, but once she had, she seldom went back on it.

Henry came home earlier than usual that evening, and she couldn't help wondering why. She soon found out.

"I hear you had lunch with Alan Lloyd today," he said as he entered the room.

"Who told you that, Henry?"

"I have spies everywhere," he said, laughing.

"Yes, Alan invited me to lunch. He wanted to know how I felt about the bank investing five hundred thousand dollars of William's trust money in your company."

"What did you say?" asked Henry, trying not to sound anxious.

"I told him I wanted to discuss the matter with you first,

but why in heaven's name didn't you let me know earlier that you had approached the bank, Henry? I felt such a fool hearing the whole thing from Alan for the first time."

"I didn't think you took any interest in business, my dear, and I only found out by sheer accident that you, Alan Lloyd and Milly Preston are all trustees, and each have a vote on William's investment income."

"How did you find out," asked Anne, "when I wasn't aware of the situation myself?"

"You don't read the small print, my darling. As a matter of fact, I didn't myself until just recently. Quite by chance Milly Preston told me the details of the trust and, as William's godmother, it seems she is also a trustee. It came as quite a surprise. Now let's see if we can turn the position to our advantage. Milly says she will back me, if you agree."

The mere sound of Milly's name made Anne feel uneasy. "I don't think we ought to touch William's money," she said. "I've never looked upon the trust as having anything to do with me. I would be much happier leaving well enough alone and just continue letting the bank reinvest the interest as it has always done in the past."

"Why be satisfied with the bank's investment programme when I am on to such a good thing with this city hospital contract? William would make a lot more money out of my company. Surely Alan went along with that?"

"I'm not certain how he felt. He was his usual discreet self though he certainly said the contract would be an excellent one to win and that you had a good chance of being awarded it."

"Exactly."

"But he did want to see your books before he came to any firm conclusions, and he also wondered what had happened to my five hundred thousand."

"Our five hundred thousand, my darling, is doing very well as you will soon discover. I'll send the books around to Alan tomorrow morning so that he can inspect them for himself. I can assure you that he will be very impressed."

"I hope so, Henry, for both our sakes," said Anne. "Now

let's wait and see what opinion he forms; you know how much I have always trusted Alan."

"But not me," said Henry.

"Oh, no, Henry, I didn't mean . . ."

"I was only teasing. I assumed you would trust your own husband."

Anne felt the tearfulness that she had always suppressed in front of Richard welling up. For Henry she didn't even try to hold it back.

"I hope I can. I've never had to worry about money before, and it's all too much to cope with just now. The baby always makes me feel so tired and depressed."

Henry's manner changed quickly to one of solicitude. "I know, my darling. I don't want you ever to have to bother your head with business matters; I can always handle that side of things. Look, why don't you go to bed early and I'll bring you up some supper on a tray? That will give me a chance to go back to the office and pick up those files I need to show Alan in the morning."

Anne complied, but once Henry had left, she made no attempt to sleep, tired as she was, but sat up in bed reading Sinclair Lewis. She knew it would take Henry about fifteen minutes to reach his office, so she waited a full twenty and then called his number. The ringing tone continued for almost a minute.

Anne tried a second time twenty minutes later; still no one answered the phone. She kept trying every twenty minutes, but no one ever came on the line. Henry's remark about trust began to echo bitterly in her head.

When Henry eventually returned home after midnight, he appeared apprehensive at finding Anne sitting up in bed. She was still reading Sinclair Lewis.

"You shouldn't have stayed awake for me."

He gave her a warm kiss. Anne thought she could smell perfume – or was she becoming overly suspicious?

"I had to stay on a little later than I had expected since I couldn't immediately find all the papers Alan would require. Damn silly secretary filed some of them under the wrong headings."

"It must be lonely sitting there in the office all on your own in the middle of the night," said Anne.

"Oh, it's not that bad if you have a worthwhile job to do," said Henry, climbing into bed and settling against Anne's back. "At least there's one thing to be said for it, you can get a lot more done when the phone isn't continually interrupting you."

He was asleep in minutes. Anne lay awake, now resolved to carry through the plan she had made that afternoon.

When Henry had left for work after breakfast the next morning – not that Anne was sure where Henry went to work any more – she studied the *Boston Globe* and did a little research among the small advertisements. Then she picked up the phone and made an appointment which took her to the south side of Boston, a few minutes before midday. Anne was shocked by the dinginess of the buildings. She had never previously visited the southern district of the city, and in normal circumstances she could have gone through her entire life without even knowing such places existed.

A small wooden staircase littered with matches, cigarette ends and rubbish created its own paper chase to a door with a frosted glass window on which appeared in large black letters, 'Glen Ricardo', and underneath 'Private Detective (Registered in the Commonwealth of Massachusetts)'. Anne knocked quietly.

"Come right in, the door's open," shouted a deep, hoarse voice.

Anne entered. The man seated behind the desk, his legs stretched over its surface, glanced up from what might have been a girly magazine. His cigar stub nearly fell out of his mouth when he caught sight of Anne. It was the first time a mink coat had ever walked into his office.

"Good morning," he said, rising quickly. "My name is Glen Ricardo." He leant across the desk and offered a hairy, nicotine-stained hand to Anne. She took it, glad that she was wearing gloves. "Do you have an appointment?" Ricardo asked, not that he cared whether she did or not. He was always available for a consultation with a mink coat.

"Yes, I do."

"Ah, then you must be Mrs. Osborne. Can I take your coat?"

"I prefer to keep it on," said Anne, unable to see anywhere Ricardo could hang it except on the floor.

"Of course, of course."

Anne eyed Ricardo covertly as he sat back in his seat and lit a new cigar. She did not care for his light green suit, the motley-coloured tie, or his thickly greased hair. It was only the fact that she doubted if it would be better anywhere else that kept her seated.

"Now, what's the problem?" said Ricardo, who was sharpening an already short pencil with a blunt knife. The wooden shavings dropped everywhere except into the wastepaper basket. "Have you lost your dog, your jewelry, or your husband?"

"First, Mr. Ricardo, I want to be assured of your complete discretion," Anne began.

"Of course, of course, it goes without saying," replied Ricardo, not looking up from his disappearing pencil.

"Nevertheless, I am saying it," said Anne.

"Of course, of course."

Anne thought that if the man said 'of course' once more, she would scream. She drew a deep breath. "I have been receiving anonymous letters which allege that my husband has been having an affair with a close friend. I want to know who is sending the letters, and if there is any truth in the accusations."

Anne felt an immense sense of relief at having voiced her fears out loud for the first time. Ricardo looked at her impassively, as if it were not the first time he had heard such fears expressed. He put his hand through his long black hair which, Anne noticed for the first time, matched his fingernails.

"Right," he began. "The husband will be easy. Who's responsible for sending the letters will be a lot harder. You've kept the letters, of course?"

"Only the last one," said Anne.

Glen Ricardo sighed and stretched his hand across the

table wearily. Anne reluctantly took the letter out of her bag and then hesitated for a moment.

"I know how you feel, Mrs. Osborne, but I can't do the job with one hand tied behind my back."

"Of course, Mr. Ricardo, I'm sorry."

Anne couldn't believe she had said 'of course'.

Ricardo read the letter through two or three times before speaking. "Have they all been typed on this sort of paper and sent in this sort of envelope?"

"Yes, I think so," said Anne. "As far as I can remember."

"Well, when the next one comes be sure to – "

"Can you be so certain there will be another one?" interrupted Anne.

"Of course, so be sure to keep it. Now give me all the details about your husband. Do you have a photograph?"

"Yes." Once again she hesitated.

"I only want to look at the face. Don't want to waste my time chasing the wrong man, do I?" said Ricardo.

Anne opened her bag again and passed him a worn-edged photograph of Henry in a lieutenant's uniform.

"Good-looking man, Mr. Osborne," said the detective. "When was this photograph taken?"

"About five years ago, I think," said Anne. "I didn't know him when he was in the army."

Ricardo questioned Anne for several minutes on Henry's daily movements. She was surprised to find how little she really knew of Henry's habits, or past.

"Not a lot to go on, Mrs. Osborne, but I'll do the best I can. Now, my charges are ten dollars a day plus expenses. I will make a written report for you once a week. Two weeks' payment in advance, please." His hand came across the desk again, this time more eagerly.

Anne opened her handbag once more and took out two crisp new one hundred-dollar notes and passed them over to Ricardo. He studied the notes carefully as if he wasn't certain which distinguished American should be engraved on them. Benjamin Franklin gazed imperturbably at Ricardo, who obviously had not seen him for some time. Ricardo handed Anne sixty dollars in grubby fives.

"I see you work on Sundays, Mr. Ricardo," said Anne, pleased with her mental arithmetic.

"Of course," he said. "Will the same time next week suit you, Mrs. Osborne?"

"Of course," said Anne and left quickly to avoid having to shake hands with the man behind the desk.

When William read in his quarterly trust report from Kane and Cabot that Henry Osborne – Henry Osborne, he repeated the name out loud to be sure he could believe it – was requesting five hundred thousand dollars for a personal investment, he had a bad day. For the first time in four years at St. Paul's he came second in a maths test. Matthew Lester, who beat him, asked if he was feeling well.

That evening, William rang Alan Lloyd at home. The chairman of Kane and Cabot was not altogether surprised to hear from him after Anne's disclosure of the unhappy relationship between her son and Henry.

"William, dear boy, how are you and how are things at St. Paul's?"

"All is well this end, thank you, sir, but that's not why I telephoned."

The tact of an advancing Mack truck, thought Alan. "No, I didn't imagine it was," he replied drily. "What can I do for you?"

"I'd like to see you tomorrow afternoon."

"On a Sunday, William?"

"Yes, as it's the only day I can get away from school, I'll come to you any time any place." William made the statement sound as though it were a concession on his part. "And under no condition is my mother to know of our meeting."

"Well, William . . ." Alan Lloyd began.

William's voice grew firmer. "I don't have to remind you, sir, that the investment of trust money in my stepfather's personal venture, while not actually illegal, could undoubtedly be considered as unethical."

Alan Lloyd was silent for a few moments, wondering if he should try and placate the boy over the telephone. The boy.

He also thought about remonstrating with him, but the time for that had now passed.

"Fine, William. Why don't you join me for a spot of lunch at the Hunt Club, say one o'clock?"

"I'll look forward to seeing you then, sir." The telephone clicked.

At least the confrontation is to be on my home ground, thought Alan Lloyd with some relief as he replaced the mouth-piece, cursing Mr. Bell for inventing the damn machine.

Alan had chosen the Hunt Club because he did not want the meeting to be too private. The first thing William asked when he arrived at the clubhouse was that he should be allowed a round of golf after lunch.

"Delighted, my boy," said Alan, and reserved the first tee for three o'clock.

He was surprised when William did not discuss Henry Osborne's proposal at all during lunch. Far from it, the boy talked knowledgeably about President Harding's views on tariff reform and the incompetence of Charles G. Dawes as the President's fiscal adviser. Alan began to wonder whether William, having slept on it, had now changed his mind about discussing Henry Osborne's loan, but was going through with the meeting not wishing to admit a change of heart. Well, if that's the way the boy wants to play it, thought Alan, that's fine by me. He looked forward to a quiet afternoon of golf. After an agreeable lunch, and the better part of a bottle of wine – William limited himself to one glass – they changed in the clubhouse and walked to the first tee.

"Do you still have a nine handicap, sir?" asked William.

"Thereabouts, my boy. Why?"

"Will ten dollars a hole suit you?"

Alan Lloyd hesitated, remembering that golf was the one game that William played competently. "Yes, fine."

Nothing was said at the first hole, which Alan managed in four while William took a five. Alan also won the second and the third quite comfortably, and began to relax a little, rather pleased with his game. By the time they reached the fourth, they were over half a mile from the clubhouse.

William waited for Alan to raise his club.

"There are no conditions under which you will loan five hundred thousand dollars of my trust money to any company or person associated with Henry Obsorne."

Alan hit a bad tee shot which went wildly into the rough. Its only virtue was that it put him far enough away from William, who had made a good drive, to give him a few minutes to think about how to address both William and the ball. After Alan Lloyd had played three more shots, they eventually met on the green. Alan conceded the hole.

"William, you know I only have one vote out of three as a trustee and you must also be aware that you have no authority over trust decisions, as you will not control the money in your own right until your twenty-first birthday. You must also realise that we ought not to be discussing this subject at all."

"I am fully aware of the legal implications, sir, but as both the other trustees are sleeping with Henry Osborne . . ."

Alan Lloyd looked shocked.

"Don't tell me you are the only person in Boston who doesn't know that Milly Preston is having an affair with my stepfather?"

Alan Lloyd said nothing.

William continued. "I want to be certain that I have your vote, and that you intend to do everything in your power to influence my mother against this loan, even if it means going to the extreme of telling her the truth about Milly Preston."

Alan hit an even worse tee shot. William's went right down the middle of the fairway. Alan chopped the next shot into a bush he had never even realised existed before and swore out loud for the first time in forty-three years. He had got a hiding on that occasion as well.

"That's asking a little too much," said Alan, as he joined up with William on the fifth green.

"It's nothing compared with what I'd do if I couldn't be sure of your support, sir."

"I don't think your father would have approved of threats, William," said Alan as he watched William's ball sink from fourteen feet.

"The only thing of which my father would not have approved is Osborne," retorted William. Alan Lloyd two-putted four feet from the hole.

"In any case, sir, you must be well aware that my father had a clause inserted in the deed that money invested by the trust was a private affair, and the benefactor should never know that the Kane family was personally involved. It was a rule he never broke in his life as a banker. That way he could always be certain there was no conflict of interest between the bank's investments and those of the family trust."

"Well, your mother obviously feels that the rule can be broken for a member of the family."

"Henry Osborne is not a member of my family, and when I control the trust it is a rule I, like my father, would never break."

"You may live to regret taking such a rigid stance, William."

"I think not, sir."

"Well, try and consider for a moment the effect such actions might have on your mother," added Alan.

"My mother has already lost five hundred thousand dollars of her own money, sir. Isn't that enough for one husband? Why do I have to lose five hundred thousand of mine as well?"

"We don't know that to be the case, William. The investment may still yield an excellent return; I haven't had a chance yet to look carefully into Henry's books."

William winced when Alan Lloyd called his stepfather Henry.

"I can assure you, sir, he's blown nearly every penny of my mother's money. To be exact, he has thirty-three thousand, four hundred and twelve dollars of the original sum left. I suggest you take very little notice of Osborne's books and check more thoroughly into his background, past business record and associates. Not to mention the fact that he gambles – heavily."

From the eighth tee Alan hit his ball into a lake directly in front of them, a lake even novice players managed to clear. He conceded the hole.

"How did you come by your information on Henry?" asked Alan, fairly certain it had been through Thomas Cohen's office.

"I prefer not to say, sir." Alan kept his own counsel; he thought he might need that particular ace up his sleeve to play a little later in William's life.

"If all you claim turned out to be accurate, William, naturally I would have to advise your mother against any investment in Henry's firm, and it would be my duty to have the whole thing out in the open with Henry as well."

"So be it, sir."

Alan hit a better shot, but felt he wasn't winning.

William continued. "It may also interest you to know that Osborne needs the five hundred thousand from my trust not for the hospital contract but to clear a long-standing debt in Chicago. I take it that you were not aware of that, sir?"

Alan said nothing; he certainly had not been aware. William won the hole.

When they reached the eighteenth, Alan was eight holes down and was about to complete the worst round he cared to remember. He had a five-foot putt that would at least enable him to halve the final hole with William.

"Do you have any more bombshells for me?" asked Alan.

"Before or after your putt, sir?"

Alan laughed and decided to call his bluff. "Before the putt, William," he said, leaning on his club.

"Osborne will not be awarded the hospital contract. It is thought by those who matter that he's been bribing junior officials in the city government. Nothing will be brought out into the open, but to be sure of no repercussions later his company has been removed from the final list. The contract will actually be awarded to Kirkbride and Carter. The last piece of information, sir, is confidential. Even Kirkbride and Carter will not be informed until a week from Thursday, so I'd be obliged if you would keep it to yourself."

Alan missed his putt. William holed his, walked over to the chairman and shook him warmly by the hand.

"Thank you for the game, sir. I think you'll find you owe me ninety dollars."

Alan took out his wallet and handed over a hundred-dollar note. "William, I think the time has come for you to stop calling me 'sir'. My name, as you well know, is Alan."

"Thank you, Alan." William handed him ten dollars.

Alan Lloyd arrived at the bank on Monday morning with a little more to do than he had originally anticipated before the weekend. He put five departmental managers to work immediately on checking out the accuracy of William's allegations. He feared that he already knew what their enquiries would reveal and, because of Anne's position at the bank, he made certain that no one department was aware of what the others were up to. His instructions to each manager were clear: all reports were to be strictly confidential and for the chairman's eyes only. By Wednesday of the same week he had five preliminary reports on his desk. They all seemed to be in agreement with William's judgment although each manager had asked for more time to verify some of the details. Alan decided against worrying Anne until he had some more concrete evidence to go on. The best he felt he could do for the time being was to take advantage of a buffet supper the Osbornes were giving that evening to advise Anne against any immediate decision on the loan.

When Alan arrived at the party, he was shocked to see how tired and drawn Anne looked, which predisposed him to soften his approach even more. When he managed to catch her alone, they only had a few moments together. If only she were not having a baby just at the time all this was happening, he thought.

Anne turned and smiled at him. "How kind of you to come Alan, when you must be so busy at the bank."

"I couldn't afford to miss out on one of your parties, my dear, they're still the toast of Boston."

She smiled. "I wonder if you ever say the wrong thing."

"All too frequently. Anne, have you had time to give any more thought to the loan?" He tried to sound casual.

"No, I am afraid I haven't. I've been up to my eyes with other things, Alan. How did Henry's accounts look?"

"Fine, but we only have one year's figures to go on, so I

think we ought to bring in our own accountants to check them over. It's normal banking policy to do that with anyone who has been operating for less than three years. I am sure Henry would understand our position and agree."

"Anne, darling, lovely party," said a loud voice over Alan's shoulder. He did not recognise the face; presumably one of Henry's politician friends. "How's the little mother-to-be?" continued the effusive voice.

Alan slipped away, hoping that he had bought some time for the bank. There were a lot of politicians at the party, from City Hall and even a couple from Congress, which made him wonder if William would turn out to be wrong about the big contract. Not that he needed the bank to investigate that: the official announcement from City Hall was due the following week. He said goodbye to his host and hostess, picked up his black overcoat from the cloakroom and left.

"This time next week," he said aloud, as if to reassure himself as he walked back down Chestnut Street to his own house.

During the party Anne found time to watch Henry whenever he was near Milly Preston. There was certainly no outward sign of anything between them; in fact, Henry spent more of his time with John Preston. Anne began to wonder if she had not misjudged her husband and thought about cancelling her appointment with Glen Ricardo the next day. The party came to an end two hours later than Anne had anticipated; she hoped it meant that everybody had enjoyed themselves.

"Great party, Anne, thanks for inviting us." It was the loud voice again, leaving last. Anne couldn't remember his name, something to do with City Hall. He disappeared down the drive.

Anne stumbled upstairs, undoing her dress even before she had reached the bedroom, promising herself that she would give no more parties before having the baby in ten weeks' time.

Henry was already undressing. "Did you get a chance to have a word with Alan, darling?"

"Yes, I did," replied Anne. "He said the books look fine,

but as the company can only show one year's figures, he must bring his own accountants in to double check; apparently that's normal banking policy."

"Normal banking policy be damned. Can't you sense William's presence behind all this? He's trying to hold up the loan, Anne."

"How can you say that? Alan said nothing about William."

"Didn't he?" said Henry, his voice rising. "He didn't bother to mention to you that William had lunch with him on Sunday at the golf club while we sat here at home alone?"

"What?" said Anne. "I don't believe it. William would never come to Boston without seeing me. You must be mistaken, Henry."

"My dear, half of the city was there, and I don't imagine that William travelled some fifty miles just for a round of golf with Alan Lloyd. Listen, Anne, I need that loan or I'm going to fail to qualify as a bidder for the city contract. Some time – and very soon now – you are going to have to decide whether you trust William or me. I must have the money by a week from tomorrow, only eight days from now, because if I can't show City Hall I'm good for that amount, I'll be disqualified. Disqualified because William didn't approve of your wanting to marry me. Please, Anne, will you call Alan tomorrow and tell him to transfer the money?"

His angry voice boomed in Anne's head, making her feel faint and dizzy.

"No, not tomorrow, Henry. Can it wait until Friday? I have a heavy day tomorrow."

Henry collected himself with an effort and came over to her as she stood naked looking at herself in the mirror. He ran his hand over her bulging stomach. "I want this little fellow to be given as good a chance as William."

The next day Anne told herself a hundred times that she would not go to see Glen Ricardo, but a little before noon she found herself hailing a cab. She climbed the creaky wooden stairs, apprehensive of what she might learn. She could still turn back. She hesitated, then knocked quietly on the door.

"Come in."

She opened the door.

"Ah, Mrs. Osborne, how nice to see you again. Do have a seat."

Anne sat and they stared at each other.

"The news, I am afraid, is not good," said Glen Ricardo, pushing his hand through his long dark hair.

Anne's heart sank. She felt sick.

"Mr. Osborne has not been seen with Mrs. Preston or any other woman during the past seven days."

"But you said the news wasn't good," said Anne.

"Of course, Mrs. Osborne, I assumed you were looking for grounds for divorce. Angry wives don't normally come to me hoping I'll prove their husbands are innocent."

"No, no," said Anne, suffused with relief. "It's the best piece of news I've had in weeks."

"Oh, good," said Mr. Ricardo, slightly taken aback. "Let us hope the second week reveals nothing as well."

"Oh, you can stop the investigation now, Mr. Ricardo. I am sure you'll not find anything of any consequence next week."

"I don't think that would be wise, Mrs. Osborne. To make a final judgment on only one week's observation would be, to say the least, premature."

"All right, if you believe it will prove the point, but I still feel confident that you won't uncover anything new next week."

"In any case," continued Glen Ricardo, puffing away at his cigar, which looked bigger and smelled better to Anne than it had the previous week, "you have already paid for the two weeks."

"What about the letters?" asked Anne, suddenly remembering them. "I suppose they must have come from someone jealous of my husband's achievements."

"Well, as I pointed out to you last week, Mrs. Osborne, tracing the sender of anonymous letters is never easy. However, we have been able to locate the shop where the stationery was bought, as the brand was fairly unusual, but for the moment I have nothing further to report on that front.

Again, I may have a lead by this time next week. Have you received any more letters in the past few days?"

"No, I haven't."

"Good, then it all seems to be working out for the best. Let us hope, for your sake, that next week's meeting will be our last."

"Yes," said Anne happily, "let us hope so. Can I settle your expenses next Thursday?"

"Of course, of course."

Anne had nearly forgotten the phrase, but this time it made her laugh. She decided as she was driven home that Henry must have the five hundred thousand loan and the chance to prove William and Alan wrong. She had still not recovered from the knowledge that William had come to Boston without letting her know; perhaps Henry had been right in his suggestion that William was trying to work behind their backs.

Henry was delighted when Anne told him that night of her decision on the loan, and he produced the legal documents the following morning for her signature. Anne couldn't help thinking that he must have had the papers prepared for some time, especially as Milly Preston's signature was already on them, or was she being overly suspicious again? She dismissed the thought and signed quickly.

She was fully prepared for Alan Lloyd when he telephoned the following Monday morning.

"Anne, let me at least hold things over until Thursday. Then we'll know who has been awarded the hospital contract."

"No, Alan, the decision can't wait. Henry needs the money now. He has to prove to City Hall that he's financially strong enough to fulfil the contract and you already have the signatures of two trustees so the responsibility is no longer yours."

"The bank could always guarantee Henry's position without actually passing over the money. I'm sure City Hall would find that acceptable. In any case, I haven't had enough time to check over his company's accounts."

"But you did find enough time to have lunch with William a week ago Sunday, without informing me."

There was a momentary silence from the other end of the line.

"Anne, I . . ."

"Don't say you didn't have the opportunity. You came to our party on Wednesday, and you could easily have mentioned it to me then. You chose not to, but you did find the time to advise me to postpone judgment on the loan to Henry."

"Anne, I am sorry. I can understand how that might look and why you are upset, but there really was a reason, believe me. May I come around and explain everything to you?"

"No, Alan, you can't. You're all ganging up against my husband. None of you wants to give him a chance to prove himself. Well, I am going to give him that chance."

Anne put the telephone down, pleased with herself, feeling she had been loyal to Henry in a way that fully atoned for her ever having doubted him in the first place.

Alan Lloyd rang back, but Anne instructed the maid to say she was out for the rest of the day. When Henry returned home that night, he was delighted to hear how Anne had dealt with Alan.

"It will all turn out for the best, my love, you'll see. On Thursday morning I will be awarded the contract, and you can kiss and make up with Alan; still, you had better keep out of his way until then. In fact, if you like we can have a celebration lunch on Thursday at the Ritz and wave at him from the other side of the room."

Anne smiled and agreed. She could not help remembering that she was meant to be seeing Ricardo for the last time at twelve o'clock that day. Still, that would be early enough for her to be at the Ritz by one and she could celebrate both triumphs at once.

Alan tried repeatedly to reach Anne, but the maid always had a ready excuse. Since the document had been signed by two trustees, he could not hold up the payment for more than twenty-four hours. The wording was typical of a legal agreement drawn up by Richard Kane; there were no loop-holes to crawl out of. When the cheque for five hundred thousand dollars left the bank by special messenger on Tuesday afternoon, Alan sat down and wrote a long letter to William setting out the events that had culminated in the transfer of the money, withholding only the unconfirmed findings of his departmental reports. He sent a copy of the letter to each director of the bank, conscious that although he had behaved with the utmost propriety, he had laid himself open to accusations of concealment.

William received Alan Lloyd's letter at St. Paul's on the Thursday morning while having breakfast with Matthew.

Breakfast on Thursday morning at Beacon Hill was the usual eggs and bacon, hot toast, cold oatmeal, and a pot of steaming coffee. Henry was simultaneously tense and jaunty, snapping at the maid, joking with a junior city official who telephoned to say the name of the company who had been awarded the hospital contract would be posted on the notice board at City Hall around ten o'clock. Anne was almost looking forward to her last meeting with Glen Ricardo. She flicked through *Vogue*, trying not to notice that Henry's hands, clutching the *Boston Globe*, were trembling.

"What are you going to do this morning?" Henry asked, trying to make conversation.

"Oh, nothing much before we have our celebration lunch. Will you be able to build the children's wing in memory of Richard?" Anne asked.

"Not in memory of Richard, my darling. This will be my achievement, so let it be in your honour – 'The Mrs. Henry Osborne Wing'," he added grandly.

"What a good idea," Anne said, as she put her magazine down and smiled at him. "But you mustn't let me drink too much champagne at lunch as I have a full check-up with Doctor MacKenzie this afternoon, and I don't think he would approve of me being drunk only nine weeks before the baby is due. When will you know for certain that the contract is yours?"

"I know now," Henry said. "The clerk I just spoke to was a hundred per cent confident, but it will be official at ten o'clock."

"The first thing you must do then, Henry, is to phone Alan and tell him the good news. I'm beginning to feel quite guilty about the way I treated him last week."

"No need for you to feel any guilt; he didn't bother to keep you informed of William's actions."

"No, but he tried to explain later, Henry, and I didn't give him a chance to tell me his side of the story."

"All right, all right, anything you say. If it'll make you happy, I'll phone him at five past ten, and then you can tell William I've made him another million."

He looked at his watch. "I'd better be going. Wish me luck."

"I thought you didn't need any luck," said Anne.

"I don't, I don't. It's only an expression. See you at the Ritz at one o'clock." He kissed her on the forehead. "By tonight, you'll be able to laugh about Alan, William, contracts, and treat them all as problems of the past, believe me. Goodbye, darling."

"I hope so, Henry."

An uneaten breakfast was laid out in front of Alan Lloyd. He was reading the financial pages of the *Boston Globe*, noting a small paragraph in the right hand column reporting that the city would be announcing at ten o'clock that morning which company had been awarded the five-million-dollar hospital contract.

Alan Lloyd had already decided what course of action he must take if Henry failed to secure the contract and everything that William had claimed turned out to be accurate. He would do exactly what Richard would have done faced with the same predicament, and act only in the best interests of the bank. The latest departmental reports on Henry's personal finances disturbed Alan Lloyd greatly. Osborne was indeed a heavy gambler and no trace could be found of the trust's five hundred thousand dollars having gone into Henry's company. Alan Lloyd sipped his orange juice and left the rest of his breakfast untouched, apologised to his housekeeper and walked to the bank. It was a pleasant day.

"William, are you up to a game of tennis this afternoon?"

Matthew Lester was standing over William as he read the letter from Alan Lloyd for a second time.

"What did you say?"

"Are you going deaf or just becoming a senile adolescent? Do you want me to beat you black and blue on the tennis court this afternoon?"

"No, I won't be here this afternoon, Matthew. I have more important things to attend to."

"Naturally, old buddy, I forgot that you're off on another of your mysterious trips to the White House. I know President Harding is looking for someone to be his new fiscal adviser, and you're exactly the right man to take the place of that posturing fool, Charles G. Dawes. Tell him you'll accept, subject to his inviting Matthew Lester to be the Administration's next Attorney General."

There was still no response from William.

"I know the joke was pretty weak, but I thought it worthy of some comment," said Matthew as he sat down beside William and looked more carefully at his friend. "It's the eggs, isn't it? Taste as though they've come out of a Russian prisoner-of-war camp."

"Matthew, I need your help," said William, as he put Alan's letter back into its envelope.

"You've had a letter from my sister and she thinks you'll do as a temporary replacement for Rudolf Valentino."

William stood up. "Quit kidding, Matthew. If your father's bank was being robbed, would you sit around making jokes about it?"

The expression on William's face was unmistakably serious. Matthew's tone changed. "No, I wouldn't."

"Right, then let's get out of here, and I'll explain everything."

Anne left Beacon Hill a little after ten to do some shopping before going on to her final meeting with Glen Ricardo. The telephone started to ring as she disappeared down Chestnut Street. The maid answered it, looked out the window and decided that her mistress was too far away to be pursued. If Anne had returned to take the call she would have been informed of City Hall's decision on the hospital contract, whereas instead she selected some silk stockings and tried out a new perfume. She arrived at Glen Ricardo's office a little after twelve, hoping her new perfume might counter the smell of cigar smoke.

"I hope I'm not late, Mr. Ricardo," she began briskly.

"Have a seat, Mrs. Osborne." Ricardo did not look particularly cheerful, but, thought Anne to herself, he never does. Then she noticed that he was not smoking his usual cigar.

Glen Ricardo opened a smart brown file, the only new thing Anne could see in the office, and unclipped some papers.

"Let's start with the anonymous letters, shall we, Mrs. Osborne?"

Anne did not like the tone of his voice at all or the word 'start'. "Yes, all right," she managed to get out.

"They are being sent by a Mrs. Ruby Flowers."

"Who? Why?" said Anne, impatient for an answer she did not want to hear.

"I suspect one of the reasons must be that Mrs. Flowers is at present suing your husband."

"Well, that explains the whole mystery," said Anne. "She must want revenge. How much does she claim Henry owes her?"

"She is not suggesting debt, Mrs. Osborne."

"Well, what is she suggesting then?"

Glen Ricardo pushed himself up from the chair, as if the movement required the full strength of both his arms to raise his tired frame. He walked to the window and looked out over the crowded Boston harbour.

"She is suing for a breach of promise, Mrs. Osborne."

"Oh, no," said Anne.

"It appears that they were engaged to be married at the time that Mr. Osborne met you, when the engagement was suddenly terminated for no apparent reason."

"Gold digger; she must have wanted Henry's money."

"No, I don't think so. You see, Mrs. Flowers is already well off. Not in your class, of course, but well off all the same. Her late husband owned a soft drink bottling company, and had left her financially secure."

"Her late husband – how old is she?"

The detective walked back to the table and flicked over a page or two of his file before his thumb started moving down the page. The black nail came to a halt.

"She'll be fifty-three on her next birthday."

"Oh, my God," said Anne. "The poor woman. She must hate me."

"I dare say she does, Mrs. Osborne, but that will not help us. Now I must turn to your husband's other activities."

The nicotine-stained finger turned over some more pages.

Anne began to feel sick. Why had she come, why hadn't she left well enough alone last week? She didn't have to know. She didn't want to know. Why didn't she get up and walk away? How she wished Richard was by her side. He would have known exactly how to deal with the whole situation. She found herself unable to move, transfixed by Glen Ricardo and the contents of his smart new file.

"On two occasions last week Mr. Osborne spent over three hours alone with Mrs. Preston."

"But that doesn't prove anything," began Anne desperately, "I know they were discussing a very important financial document."

"In a small hotel on La Salle Street."

Anne didn't interrupt the detective again.

"On both occasions they were seen walking into the hotel holding hands, whispering and laughing. It's not conclusive of course, but we have photographs of them together entering and leaving the hotel."

"Destroy them," said Anne quietly.

Glen Ricardo blinked. "As you wish, Mrs. Osborne. I'm afraid there is more. Further inquiries show that Mr. Osborne was never at Harvard nor was he an officer in the American armed forces. There was a Henry Osborne at Harvard who was five-foot-five, sandy-haired and came from Alabama. He was killed on the Marne in 1917. We also know that your husband is considerably younger than he claims to be and that his real name is Vittorio Togna, and he has served – "

"I don't want to hear any more," said Anne, tears flooding down her cheeks. "I don't want to hear any more."

"Of course, Mrs. Osborne, I understand. I am only sorry that my news is so distressing. In my job sometimes . . ."

Anne fought for a measure of self-control. "Thank you, Mr. Ricardo. I appreciate all you have done. How much do I owe you?"

"Well, you have already paid for the two weeks in advance, and my expenses came to seventy-three dollars."

Anne passed him a hundred-dollar note and rose from her chair.

"Don't forget your change, Mrs. Osborne."

She shook her head and waved a disinterested hand.

"Are you feeling all right, Mrs. Osborne? You look a little pale to me. Can I get you a glass of water or something?"

"I'm fine," lied Anne.

"Perhaps you would allow me to drive you home?"

"No, thank you, Mr. Ricardo, I'll be able to get myself home." She turned and smiled at him. "It was kind of you to offer."

Glen Ricardo closed the door quietly behind his client, walked slowly to the window, bit the end off his last big cigar, spat it out and cursed his job.

Anne paused at the top of the stairs, clinging to the banister, almost fainting. The baby kicked inside her, making her feel nauseous. She found a cab on the corner of the block and, huddled in the back, was unable to stop herself sobbing or to think what to do next. As soon as she was dropped at the Red House, she went to her bedroom before any of the staff could see her crying. The telephone was ringing as she entered the room, and she picked it up, more from habit than from any curiosity to know who it might be.

"Could I speak to Mrs. Kane, please?"

She recognised Alan's clipped tone at once. Another tired, unhappy voice.

"Hello, Alan. This *is* Anne."

"Anne, my dear, I was so sorry to learn about this morning's news."

"How do you know about it, Alan, how can you possibly know? Who told you?"

"City Hall phoned me and gave me the details soon after ten this morning. I tried to call you then, but your maid said that you had already left to do some shopping."

"Oh, my God," said Anne. "I had quite forgotten about the contract." She sat down heavily, unable to breathe freely.

"Are you all right, Anne?"

"Yes, I'm just fine," she said, trying unsuccessfully to hide the sobbing in her voice. "What did City Hall have to say?"

"The hospital contract was awarded to a firm called Kirkbride and Carter. Apparently Henry wasn't even placed in the top three. I've been trying to reach him all morning, but it seems he left his office soon after ten and he hasn't been back since. I don't suppose you know where he is, Anne?"

"No, I haven't any idea."

"Do you want me to come around, my dear?" he said. "I could be with you in a few minutes."

"No, thank you, Alan." Anne paused to draw a shaky breath. "Please forgive me for the way I have been treating you these past few days. If Richard were still alive, he would never have forgiven me."

"Don't be silly, Anne, our friendship has lasted for far too many years for a silly little incident like that to be of any significance."

The kindness of his voice triggered off a fresh burst of weeping. Anne staggered to her feet.

"I must go, Alan. I can hear someone at the front door; it might be Henry."

"Take care, Anne, and don't worry about today. As long as I'm chairman, the bank will always support you. Don't hesitate to call if you need me."

Anne put the telephone down, the noise thudding in her ears. The effort of breathing was stupendous. She sank to the floor and as she did so, the long-forgotten sensation of a vigorous contraction overwhelmed her.

A few moments later the maid knocked quietly on the door. She looked in; William was at her shoulder. He had not entered his mother's bedroom since her marriage to Henry Osborne. The two rushed to Anne's side. She was shaking convulsively, unaware of their presence. Little flecks of foam spattered her upper lip. In a few seconds the attack passed, and she lay moaning quietly.

"Mother," said William urgently. "What's the matter?"

Anne opened her eyes and stared wildly at her son. "Richard. Thank God you've come. I need you."

"It's William, Mother."

Her gaze faltered. "I have no more strength left, Richard. I must pay for my mistakes. Forgive . . ."

Her voice trailed off to a groan as another powerful contraction started.

"What's happening?" said William helplessly.

"I think it must be the baby coming," the maid said, "although it isn't due for several weeks."

"Get Doctor MacKenzie on the phone immediately," William said to the maid as he ran to the bedroom door. "Matthew," he shouted, "come up quickly."

Matthew bounded up the stairs and joined William in the bedroom.

"Help me get my mother down to the car," he said.

Matthew knelt down. The two boys picked Anne up and carried her gently downstairs and out to the car. She was panting and groaning, and obviously still in immense pain. William ran back to the house and grabbed the phone from the maid while Matthew waited in the car.

"Doctor MacKenzie."

"Yes, who's this?"

"My name is William Kane; you won't know me, sir."

"Don't know you, young man? I delivered you. What can I do for you now?"

"I think my mother is in labour. I'll bring her to the hospital immediately. I should be there in a few minutes' time."

Doctor MacKenzie's tone changed. "All right, William, don't worry. I'll be here waiting for you and everything will be under control by the time you arrive."

"Thank you, sir." William hesitated. "She seemed to have some sort of a fit. Is that normal?"

William's words chilled the doctor. He too hesitated.

"Well, not quite normal. But she'll be all right once she has had the baby. Get here as quickly as you can."

William put down the phone, ran out of the house and jumped into the Rolls-Royce.

He drove the car in fits and starts, never once getting out of first gear and never stopping for anything until they had reached the doctor at the hospital. The two boys carried Anne, and a nurse with a stretcher guided them through to the maternity section. Doctor MacKenzie was standing at the entrance of an operating room, waiting. He took over and asked them both to remain outside.

The two boys sat in silence on the small bench and waited. Frightening cries and screams, unlike any sound they had ever heard anyone make, came from the delivery room; to be succeeded by an even more frightening silence. For the first time in his life William felt totally helpless. The two of them sat there for over an hour, without a word passing between them. Eventually a tired Doctor MacKenzie emerged. The two boys rose, and the doctor looked at Matthew Lester.

"William?" he asked.

"No, sir, I am Matthew Lester; this is William."

The doctor turned to William and put a hand on his shoulder. "William, I'm so sorry, your mother died a few minutes ago . . . and the child, a little girl, was stillborn." William's legs gave way and he sank on to the bench. "We did everything in our power to save them, but it was hopeless." The doctor shook his head wearily. "She wouldn't listen to me, she insisted on having the baby. It should never have happened."

William sat silently, stunned by the whiplash sound of the doctor's words.

"How *could* she die?" he whispered. "How could you *let* her die?"

The doctor sat down on the bench between the boys. "She wouldn't listen," he repeated slowly. "I warned her repeatedly after her miscarriage not to have another child, but when she married again, she and your stepfather never took my warnings seriously. She had high blood pressure during her last pregnancy. It was worrying me during this one, although it was never near danger level. But when you brought her in today, for no apparent reason it had soared up to the level where eclampsia ensues."

"Eclampsia?"

"Convulsions. Sometimes patients can survive several attacks. Sometimes they simply – stop breathing."

William drew a shuddering breath and placed his head in his hands. Matthew Lester guided his friend gently along the corridor. The doctor followed them. When they reached the door, he looked at William.

"Her blood pressure went up so suddenly. It's very unusual, and she didn't put up a real fight, almost as if she didn't care. Strange, had something been troubling her lately?"

William raised his tear-streaked face. "Not some*thing*," he said with hatred. "Some*one*."

Alan Lloyd was sitting in a corner of the drawing room when the two boys arrived back at the Red House. He rose as they entered.

"William," he said immediately. "I blame myself for allowing the loan."

William stared at him, not taking in what he was saying.

Matthew Lester stepped into the silence. "I don't think that's important any longer, sir," he said quietly. "William's mother has just died in childbirth."

Alan Lloyd turned ashen, steadied himself by grasping the mantelpiece, and turned away. It was the first time that either of them had seen a grown man weep.

"It's my fault," said the banker. "I'll never forgive myself. I didn't tell her everything I knew. I loved her so much that I never wanted her to be distressed."

His anguish enabled William to be calm.

"It certainly was not your fault, Alan," he said firmly. "You did everything you could, I know that, and now it's I who am going to need your help."

Alan Lloyd braced himself. "Has Osborne been informed about your mother's death?"

"I neither know nor care."

"I've been trying to reach him all day about the investment. He left his office soon after ten this morning, and he hasn't been seen since."

"He'll turn up here sooner or later," said William grimly.

After Alan Lloyd left, William and Matthew sat alone in the front room most of the night, dozing off and on. At four o'clock in the morning, William counted the chimes of the grandfather clock and thought that he heard a noise in the street. Matthew was staring out of the window down the drive. William walked stiffly over to join him. They both watched Henry Osborne stagger across Louisburg Square with a half-full bottle in his hand. He fumbled with some keys for some time and finally appeared in the doorway, blinking dazedly at the two boys.

"I want Anne, not you. Why aren't you at school? I don't want you," he said, his voice thick and slurred, trying to push William aside. "Where's Anne?"

"My mother is dead," said William quietly.

Henry Osborne looked at him stupidly for a few seconds. The incomprehension of his gaze snapped William's self-control.

"Where were you when she needed a husband?" he shouted.

Still Osborne stood, swaying slightly. "What about the baby?"

"Stillborn, a little girl."

Henry Osborne slumped into a chair, drunken tears starting to run down his face. "She lost my little baby?"

William was nearly incoherent with rage and grief. "Your baby? Stop thinking about yourself for once," he shouted. "You know Doctor MacKenzie advised her against becoming pregnant again."

"Expert in that as well, are we, like everything else? If you had minded your own fucking business, I could have taken care of my own wife without your interference."

"And her money, it seems."

"Money. You tight-fisted little bastard, I bet losing that hurts you more than anything else."

"Get up," William said between his teeth.

Henry Osborne pushed himself up, and smashed the bottle across the corner of the chair. Whisky splashed all over the carpet. He swayed towards William with the broken bottle in his raised hand. William stood his ground while Matthew came between them and easily removed the bottle from the drunken man's grasp.

William pushed his friend aside and advanced until his face was only inches away from Henry Osborne's.

"Now, you listen to me and listen carefully. I want you out of this house in one hour. If I ever hear from you again in my life, I shall instigate a full legal investigation into what has happened to my mother's half million dollar investment in your firm, and I shall re-open my research into who you really are and your past life in Chicago. If, on the other hand, I do not hear from you again, ever, I shall consider the ledger balanced and the matter closed. Now get out before I kill you."

The two boys watched him leave, sobbing, incoherent and furious.

The next morning William paid a visit to the bank. He was immediately shown into the chairman's office. Alan Lloyd was packing some documents into a briefcase. He looked up, and handed a piece of paper to William without speaking. It was a short letter to all board members tendering his resignation as chairman of the bank.

"Could you ask your secretary to come in?" said William quietly.

"As you wish."

Alan Lloyd pressed a button on the side of his desk, and a middle-aged, conservatively dressed lady entered the room from a side door.

"Good morning, Mr. Kane," she said when she saw

William. "I was so sorry to learn about your mother."

"Thank you," said William. "Has anyone else seen this letter?"

"No, sir," said the secretary. "I was about to type twelve copies for Mr. Lloyd to sign."

"Well, don't type them, and please forget that this draft ever existed. Never mention its existence to anyone, do you understand?"

She stared into those blue eyes of the sixteen-year-old boy. So like his father, she thought. "Yes, Mr. Kane." She left, quietly closing the door. Alan Lloyd looked up.

"Kane and Cabot doesn't need a new chairman at the moment, Alan. You did nothing my father would not have done in the same circumstances."

"It's not as easy as that," Alan said.

"It's as easy as that," said William. "We can discuss this again when I am twenty-one and not before. Until then I would be obliged if you would run my bank in your usual diplomatic and conservative manner. I want nothing of what has happened to be discussed outside this office. You will destroy any information you have on Henry Osborne and consider the matter closed."

William tore up the letter of resignation and dropped the pieces of paper into the fire. He put his arm around Alan's shoulders.

"I have no family now, Alan, only you. For God's sake, don't desert me."

William was driven back to Beacon Hill. On his arrival the butler informed him that Mrs. Kane and Mrs. Cabot were waiting for him in the drawing room. They both rose as he entered the room. It was the first time that William realised that he was now the head of the Kane family.

The funeral took place quietly two days later at the Old North Church on Beacon Hill. None but the family and close friends were invited, and the only notable absentee was Henry Osborne. As the mourners departed, they paid their respects to William. The grandmothers stood one pace behind him, like sentinels, watching, approving the calm and dignified way in which he conducted himself. When everyone had left, William accompanied Alan Lloyd to his car.

The chairman was delighted by William's one request of him.

"As you know, Alan, my mother had always intended to build a children's wing to the new hospital, in memory of my father. I would like her wishes carried out."

11

Wladek stayed at the Polish Delegation in Constantinople for eighteen months, working day and night for Pawel Zaleski, becoming an indispensable aide and close friend. Nothing was too much trouble for him and Zaleski soon began to wonder how he had managed before Wladek arrived. He visited the British Embassy once a week to eat in the kitchen with Mrs. Henderson, the Scottish cook, and, on one occasion, with His Britannic Majesty's second consul himself.

Around them the old Islamic way of life was dissolving, and the Ottoman Empire was beginning to totter. Mustafa Kemal was the name on everyone's lips. The sense of impending change made Wladek restless. His mind returned incessantly to the Baron and all whom he had loved in the castle. The necessity to survive from day to day in Russia had kept them from his mind's eye, but in Turkey they rose up before him, a silent and slow procession. Sometimes, he could see them strong and happy, Leon swimming in the river, Florentyna playing cat's cradle in his bedroom, the Baron's face strong and proud in the evening candlelight, but always each well-remembered, well-loved face would waver and, try as Wladek did to hold them firm, they would change horribly to that last dreadful aspect, Leon dead on top of him, Florentyna bleeding in agony, and the Baron almost blind and broken.

Wladek began to face the fact that he could never return to a land peopled by such ghosts, until he had made something worthwhile of his life. With that single thought in mind he set his heart on going to America, as his countryman Tadeusz Kosciuszko, of whom the Baron had told so many enthralling tales, had done so long before him. The United States, described by Pawel Zaleski as the 'New World'. The very name inspired Wladek with a hope for the future and a chance to return to Poland in triumph. It was Pawel Zaleski who put up the money to purchase an immigrant passage for him to the United States. They were difficult to come by, for they were always booked at least a year in advance. It seemed to Wladek as though the whole of Eastern Europe was trying to escape and start afresh in the New World.

In the spring of 1921, Wladek Koskiewicz finally left Constantinople and boarded the S.S. *Black Arrow*, bound for Ellis Island, New York. He possessed one suitcase, containing all his belongings, and a set of papers issued by Pawel Zaleski.

The Polish consul accompanied him to the wharf, and embraced him affectionately. "Go with God, my boy."

The traditional Polish response came naturally from the depths of Wladek's early childhood. "Remain with God," he replied.

As he reached the top of the gangplank, Wladek recalled his terrifying journey from Odessa to Constantinople. This time there was no coal in sight, only people, people everywhere, Poles, Lithuanians, Estonians, Ukrainians and others of many racial types unfamiliar to Wladek. He clutched his few belongings and waited in the line, the first of many long waits with which he later associated his entry into the United States.

His papers were sternly scrutinised by a deck officer who was clearly predisposed to the suspicion that Wladek was trying to avoid military service in Turkey, but Pawel Zaleski's documents were impeccable; Wladek invoked a silent blessing on his fellow countryman's head as he watched others being turned back.

Next came a vaccination and a cursory medical examination which, had he not had eighteen months of good food and the chance to recover his health in Constantinople, Wladek would certainly have failed. At last with all the checks over he was allowed below deck into the steerage quarters. There were separate compartments for males, females and married couples. Wladek quickly made his way to the male quarters and found the Polish group occupying a large block of iron berths, each containing four two-tiered bunk beds. Each bunk had a thin straw mattress, a light blanket and no pillow. Having no pillow did not worry Wladek who had never been able to sleep on one since leaving Russia.

Wladek selected a bunk below a boy of roughly his own age and introduced himself.

"I'm Wladek Koskiewicz."

"I'm Jerzy Nowak from Warsaw," volunteered the boy in his native Polish, "and I'm going to make my fortune in America."

The boy thrust forward his hand.

Wladek and Jerzy spent the time before the ship sailed telling each other of their experiences, both pleased to have someone to share their loneliness with, neither willing to admit their total ignorance of America. Jerzy, it turned out, had lost both his parents in the war but had few other claims to attention. He was entranced by Wladek's stories: the son of a baron, brought up in a trapper's cottage, imprisoned by the Germans and the Russians, escaped from Siberia and then from a Turkish executioner thanks to the heavy silver band which Jerzy couldn't take his eyes off. Wladek had packed more into his fifteen years than Jerzy thought he would manage in a lifetime. Wladek talked all night of the past while Jerzy listened intently, neither wanting to sleep and neither wanting to admit their apprehension of the future.

The following morning the *Black Arrow* sailed. Wladek and Jerzy stood at the rail and watched Constantinople slip away in the blue distance of the Bosphorus. After the calm of the Sea of Marmara the choppiness of the Aegean afflicted them and most of the other passengers with a horrible abruptness. The two washrooms for steerage passengers, with ten basins apiece, six toilets and cold salt water taps were rapidly inundated. After a couple of days the stench of their quarters was nauseating.

Food was served in a large filthy dining hall on long tables: warm soup, potatoes, fish, boiled beef and cabbage, brown or black bread. Wladek had tasted worse food but not since Russia and was glad of the provisions he had brought along with him: sausages, nuts and a little brandy. He and Jerzy shared them huddled in the corner of their berth. It was an unspoken understanding. They ate together, explored the ship together and at night, slept one above the other.

On the third day at sea Jerzy brought a Polish girl to their table for supper. Her name, he informed Wladek casually, was Zaphia. It was the first time in his life that Wladek had ever looked at a woman twice, but he couldn't stop looking at Zaphia. She rekindled memories of Florentyna. The warm grey eyes, the long fair hair that fell on to her shoulders and the soft voice. Wladek found he wanted to touch her. The girl occasionally smiled across at Wladek, who was miserably aware how much better looking Jerzy was than he. He tagged along as Jerzy escorted Zaphia back to the women's quarters.

Jerzy turned to him afterwards, mildly irritated. "Can't you find a girl of your own? This one's mine."

Wladek was not prepared to admit that he had no idea how to set about finding a girl of his own.

"There will be enough time for girls when we reach America," he said scornfully.

"Why wait for America? I intend to have as many on this ship as possible."

"How will you go about that?" asked Wladek, intent on the acquisition of knowledge without admitting to his own ignorance.

"We have twelve more days in this awful tub, and I am going to have twelve women," boasted Jerzy.

"What can you do with twelve women?" asked Wladek.

"Fuck them, what else?"

Wladek looked perplexed.

"Good God," said Jerzy. "Don't tell me the man who survived the Germans and escaped from the Russians, killed a man at the age of twelve and narrowly missed having his hand chopped off by a bunch of savage Turks has never had a woman?"

He laughed, and a multilingual chorus from the surrounding bunks told him to 'shut up'.

"Well," Jerzy continued in a whisper, "the time has come to broaden your education, because at last I have found something I can teach you." He peered over the side of his bunk even though he could not see Wladek's face in the dark. "Zaphia's an understanding girl. I dare say she could be persuaded to expand your education a little. I shall arrange it."

Wladek didn't reply.

No more was said on the subject, but the next day Zaphia started to pay attention to Wladek. She sat next to him at meals, and they talked for hours of their experiences and hopes. She was an orphan from Poznan, on her way to join her cousins in Chicago. Wladek told Zaphia that he was going to New York and would probably live with Jerzy.

"I hope New York is very near Chicago," said Zaphia.

"Then you can come and see me when I am the mayor," said Jerzy expansively.

She sniffed disparagingly. "You're too Polish, Jerzy. You can't even speak nice English like Wladek."

"I'll learn," said Jerzy confidently, "and I'll start by making my name American. From today I shall be George Novak. Then I'll have no trouble at all. Everyone in the United States will think I'm American. What about you, Wladek Koskiewicz? Nothing much you can do with that name, is there?"

Wladek looked at the newly christened George in silent resentment of his own name. Unable to adopt the title to which he felt himself the rightful heir, he hated Koskiewicz and the continual reminder of his illegitimacy.

"I'll manage," he said. "I'll even help you with your English, if you like."

"And I'll help you find a girl."

Zaphia giggled. "You needn't bother, he's found one."

Jerzy, or George, as he now insisted they should call him, retreated after supper each night into one of the tarpaulin-covered lifeboats with a different girl. Wladek longed to know what he did there, even though some of the ladies of George's choice were not merely filthy, as they all were, but would clearly have been unattractive even when scrubbed clean.

One night after supper, when George had disappeared again, Wladek and Zaphia sat out on deck, she put her arms around him and asked him to kiss her. He pressed his mouth stiffly against hers until their teeth touched; he felt horribly unfamiliar with what he was meant to be doing. To his surprise and embarrassment, her tongue parted his lips. After a few moments of apprehension, Wladek found her open mouth intensely exciting and was alarmed to find his penis stiffening. He tried to draw away from her, ashamed, but she did not seem to mind in the least. On the contrary, she began to press her body gently and rhythmically against him and drew his hands down to her buttocks. His swollen penis throbbed against her, giving him almost unbearable pleasure. She disengaged her mouth and whispered in his ear.

"Do you want me to take my clothes off, Wladek?"

He could not bring himself to reply.

She detached herself from him, laughing. "Well, maybe tomorrow," she said, getting up from the deck and leaving him.

He stumbled back to his bunk in a daze, determined that the next day he would finish the job Zaphia had started. No sooner had he settled in his berth thinking of how he would go about the task than a large hand grabbed him by the hair and pulled him down from his bunk on to the floor. In an instant his sexual excitement vanished. Two men whom he had never seen before were towering above him. They dragged him to a far corner and threw him up against the wall. A large hand was now clamped firmly on Wladek's mouth while a knife touched his throat.

"Don't breathe," whispered the man holding the knife, pushing the blade against the skin. "All we want is the silver band around your wrist."

The sudden realisation that his treasure might be stolen from him was almost as horrifying to Wladek as had been the thought of losing his hand. Before he could think of anything to do, one of the men jerked the band off his wrist. He couldn't see their faces in the dark, and he feared he must have lost the band for ever, when someone leaped on to the back of the man holding the knife. This action gave Wladek the chance to punch the one who was holding him pinned to the ground. The sleepy immigrants around them began to wake and take an interest in what was happening. The two men escaped as quickly as they could, but not before George had managed to stick the knife in the side of one of the assailants.

"Go to the cholera," shouted Wladek at his retreating back.

"It looks as if I got here just in time," said George. "I don't think they'll be back in a hurry." He stared down at the silver band, lying in the trampled sawdust on the floor. "It's magnificent," he said, almost solemnly. "There will always be men who want to steal such a prize from you."

Wladek picked the band up and slipped it back on to his wrist.

"Well, you nearly lost the damn thing for good that time," said George. "Lucky for you I was a little late getting back tonight."

"Why were you a little late getting back?" asked Wladek.

"My reputation," said George boastfully, "now goes before me. In fact, I found some other idiot in my lifeboat tonight, already with his pants down. I soon got rid of him, though, when I told him he was with a girl I would have had last week but I couldn't be sure she hadn't got the pox. I've never seen anyone get dressed so quickly."

"What do you do in the boat?" asked Wladek.

"Fuck them silly, you ass, what do you think?" and with that he rolled over and went to sleep.

Wladek stared at the ceiling and, touching the silver band, thought about what George had said, wondering what it would be like to 'fuck' Zaphia.

The next morning they hit a storm, and all the passengers were confined below decks. The stench, intensified by the ship's steam heating system, seemed to permeate Wladek's very marrow.

"And the worst of it is," groaned George, "I won't make a round dozen now."

When the storm abated, nearly all the passengers escaped to the deck. Wladek and George fought their way around the crowded gangways, thankful for the fresh air. Many of the girls smiled at George, but it seemed to Wladek that they didn't notice him at all. He would have thought they couldn't miss him in his fifty-ruble coat. A dark-haired girl, her cheeks made pink by the wind, passed George and smiled at him. He turned to Wladek.

"I'll have her tonight."

Wladek stared at the girl and studied the way she looked at George.

"Tonight," said George, as she passed within earshot. She pretended not to hear him and walked away, a little too quickly.

"Turn round, Wladek, and see if she is looking back at me."

Wladek turned around. "Yes, she is," he said, surprised.

"She's mine tonight," said George. "Have you had Zaphia yet?"

"No," said Wladek. "Tonight."

"About time, isn't it? You'll never see the girl again once we've reached New York."

Sure enough, George arrived at supper that night with the dark-haired girl. Without a word being said, Wladek and Zaphia left them, arms round each other's waists, and went on to the deck and strolled around the ship several times. Wladek looked sideways at her pretty young profile. It was going to be now or never, he decided. He led her to a shadowy corner and started to kiss her as she had kissed him, open-mouthed. She moved backwards a little until her shoulders were resting against a bulwark, and Wladek moved with her. She drew his hands slowly down to her breasts. He touched them tentatively, surprised by their softness. She undid a couple of buttons on her blouse and slipped his hand inside. The first feel of the naked flesh was delicious.

"Christ, your hand is cold," Zaphia said.

Wladek crushed himself against her, his mouth dry, his breath heavy. She parted her legs a little and Wladek thrust clumsily against her through several intervening layers of cloth. She moved in sympathy with him for a couple of minutes and then pushed him away.

"Not here on the deck," she said. "Let's find a boat."

The first three they looked into were occupied, but they finally found an empty one and wriggled under the tarpaulin. In the constricted darkness Zaphia made some adjustments to her clothing that Wladek could not figure out, and pulled him gently on top of her. It took her very little time to bring Wladek to his earlier pitch of excitement through the few remaining layers of cloth between them. He thrust his penis into the yielding softness between her legs and was on the point of orgasm when she again drew her mouth away.

"Undo your trousers," she whispered.

He felt an idiot but hurriedly undid them, and thrust again, coming immediately, feeling the sticky wetness running down the inside of her thigh. He lay dazed, amazed by the abruptness of the act, suddenly aware that the wooden notches of the boat were digging uncomfortably into his elbows and knees.

"Was that the first time you've made love to a girl?" asked Zaphia, wishing he would move over.

"No, of course not," said Wladek.

"Do you love me, Wladek?"

"Yes, I do," he said, "and as soon as I've settled in New York, I'll come and find you in Chicago."

"I'd like that, Wladek," she said as she buttoned up her dress. "I love you, too."

"Did you fuck her?" was George's immediate question on Wladek's return.

"Yes."

"Was it good?"

"Yes," said Wladek, uncertainly, and then fell asleep.

In the morning, they were woken by a room full of excited passengers, happy in the knowledge that this was their last day on board the *Black Arrow*. Some of them had been up on deck before sunrise, hoping to catch the first sign of land. Wladek packed his few belongings in his new suitcase, put on his only suit, and his cap and then joined Zaphia and George on deck. The three of them stared into the mist that hung over the sea, waiting in silence for their first sight of the United States of America.

"There it is," shouted a passenger on a deck above them, and cheering went up at the sight of the grey strip of Long Island approaching through the spring morning.

Little tugs bustled up to the side of the *Black Arrow* and guided her between Brooklyn and Staten Island into New York Harbor. The colossal Statue of Liberty regarded them austerely as they gazed in awe at the emerging skyline of Manhattan, great long arms stretching high into the sky.

Finally they moored near the turreted and spired red brick buildings of Ellis Island. The passengers who had private cabins left the ship first. Wladek hadn't noticed them until that day. They must have been on a separate deck with their own dining hall. Their bags were carried for them by porters, and they were greeted by smiling faces at the quayside. Wladek knew that wasn't going to happen to him.

After the favoured few had disembarked, the captain announced over the loudspeaker to the rest of the passengers that they would not be leaving the ship for several hours. A groan of disappointment went up, and Zaphia sat on the deck and burst into tears. Wladek tried to comfort her. Eventually an official came around with coffee, a second with numbered labels which were hung around their necks. Wladek's was B.127; it reminded him of the last time he was a number. What had he let himself in for? Was America like the Russian camps?

In the middle of the afternoon, having been given no food or further information, they were ferried by slow moving barges from the dockside to Ellis Island. There the men were separated from the women and sent off to different sheds. Wladek kissed Zaphia and wouldn't let her go, which held up the line. A nearby official parted them.

"All right, let's get moving," he said. "Keep that up and we'll have you two married in no time."

Wladek lost sight of Zaphia as he was pushed forwards with George. They spent the night in an old, damp shed, unable to sleep as interpreters moved among the crowded rows of bunks, offering curt, but not unkind, assistance to the bewildered immigrants.

In the morning they were sent for medical examinations. The first hurdle was the hardest: Wladek was told to climb a steep flight of stairs. The blue-uniformed doctor made him do it twice, watching his gait carefully. Wladek tried very hard to minimise his limp, and finally the doctor was satisfied. Wladek was made to remove his hat and stiff collar so that his face, eyes, hair, hands and neck could be examined carefully. The man directly behind Wladek had a hare lip; the doctor stopped him immediately, put a chalk cross on his shoulder and sent him to the other end of the shed. After the physical was over, Wladek joined up with George again in another long line outside the Public Examination room where each person seemed to be taking about five minutes. Three hours later when George was ushered into the room Wladek began to wonder what they would ask him.

When George came out, he grinned at Wladek and said, "Easy, you'll walk right through it." Wladek could feel the palms of his hands sweating as he stepped forward.

He followed the official into a small, undecorated room. There were two examiners seated and writing furiously on what looked like official papers.

"Do you speak English?" asked the first.

"Yes, sir, I do quite good," replied Wladek, wishing he had spoken more English on the voyage.

"What is your name?"

"Wladek Koskiewicz, sir."

The men passed him a big black book. "Do you know what that is?"

"Yes, sir, the Bible."

"Do you believe in God?"

"Yes, sir, I do."

"Put your hand on the Bible, and swear that you will answer our questions truthfully."

Wladek took the Bible in his left hand, placed his right hand on it and said, "I promise I tell the truth."

"What is your nationality?"

"Polish."

"Who paid for your passage here?"

"I paid from my money that I earn in Polish Consulate in Constantinople."

One of the officials studied Wladek's papers, nodded and then asked, "Do you have a home to go to?"

"Yes, sir. I go stay at Mister Peter Novak. He my friend's uncle. He live in New York."

"Good. Do you have work to go to?"

"Yes, sir. I go work in bakery of Mister Novak."

"Have you ever been arrested?"

Russia flashed through Wladek's mind. It couldn't count. Turkey – he wasn't going to mention that.

"No, sir, never."

"Are you an anarchist?"

"No, sir. I hate Communists, they kill my sister."

"Are you willing to abide by the laws of the United States of America?"

"Yes, sir."

"Have you any money?"

"Yes, sir."

"May we see it?"

"Yes, sir." Wladek placed on the table a bundle of notes and a few coins.

"Thank you," said the examiner, "you may put the money back in your pocket."

The second examiner looked at him. "What is twenty-one plus twenty-four?"

"Forty-five," said Wladek, without hesitation.

"How many legs does a cow have?"

Wladek could not believe his ears. "Four, sir," he said, wondering if the question was a trick.

"And a horse?"

"Four, sir," said Wladek, still in disbelief.

"Which would you throw overboard if you were out at sea in a small boat which needed to be lightened, bread or money?"

"The money, sir," said Wladek.

"Good." The examiner picked up a card marked 'Admitted' and handed it over to Wladek. "After you have changed your money, show this card to the immigration officer. Tell him your full name and he will give you a registration card. You will then be given an entry certificate. If you do not commit a crime for five years and pass a simple reading and writing examination at the end of that time, you will be permitted to apply for full United States citizenship. Good luck, Wladek."

"Thank you, sir."

At the money exchange counter Wladek handed in eighteen months of Turkish savings and the three fifty-ruble notes. He was handed forty-seven dollars twenty cents in exchange for the Turkish money but was told the rubles were worthless. He could only think of Doctor Dubien and his fifteen years of diligent saving.

The final stop was the immigration officer, who was seated behind a counter at the exit barrier directly under a picture of President Harding. Wladek and George went over to him.

"Full name?" the officer said to George.

"George Novak," replied Jerzy firmly. The officer wrote the name on a card.

"And your address?" he asked.

"286 Broome Street, New York, New York."

The officer passed George the card. "This is your Immigration Certificate, 21871-George Novak. Welcome to the United States, George. I'm Polish too. You'll like it here. Many congratulations and good luck."

George smiled and shook hands with the officer, stood to one side and waited for Wladek. The officer stared at Wladek in his long bearskin coat. Wladek passed him the card marked 'Admitted'.

"Full name?" asked the officer.

Wladek hesitated.

"What's your name?" repeated the man, a little louder, slightly impatient, wondering if he couldn't speak English. Wladek couldn't get the words out. How he hated that peasant name.

"For the last time, what's your name?"

George was staring at Wladek. So were others who had joined the queue for the immigration officer. Wladek still didn't speak. The officer suddenly grabbed his wrist, stared closely at the inscription on the silver band, wrote on a card and passed it to Wladek.

"21872-Baron Abel Rosnovski. Welcome to the United States. Many congratulations and good luck, Abel."

12

William returned to start his last year at St. Paul's in September, 1923, and was elected president of the Senior Class, exactly thirty-three years after his father had held the same office. William did not win the election in the usual fashion, by virtue of being the finest athlete or the most popular boy in the school. Matthew Lester, his closest friend, would undoubtedly have won any contest based on those criteria. It was simply that William was the most impressive boy in the school, and for that reason Matthew Lester could not be prevailed upon to run against him. St. Paul's entered William's name as their candidate for the Hamilton Memorial Mathematics Scholarship at Harvard, and William worked single-mindedly towards that goal during the autumn term.

When William returned to Beacon Hill for Christmas, he was looking forward to an uninterrupted period in which to get to grips with *Principia Mathematica*. But it was not to be, for there were several invitations to parties and balls awaiting his arrival. To most of them he felt able to return a tactful regret, but one was absolutely inescapable. The grandmothers had arranged a ball, to be held at the Red House on Louisburg Square. William wondered at what age he would find it possible to defend his home against invasion by the two great ladies and decided the time had not yet come. He had few close friends in Boston, but this did not inhibit the grandmothers in their compilation of a formidable guest list.

To mark the occasion they presented William with his first dinner jacket in the latest double-breasted style; he received the gift with some pretence at indifference but later swaggered around his bedroom in the suit, often stopping to stare at himself in the mirror. The next day he put through a long distance call to New York and asked Matthew Lester to join him for the fateful weekend. Matthew's sister wanted to come as well but her mother didn't think it would be suitable.

William was there to meet him off the train.

"Come to think of it," said Matthew, as the chauffeur drove them back to Beacon Hill, "isn't it time you got yourself laid, William? There must be some girls in Boston with absolutely no taste."

"Why, have you had a girl, Matthew?"

"Sure, last winter in New York."

"What was I doing at the time?"

"Probably touching up on Bertrand Russell."

"You never told me about it."

"Nothing much to tell. In any case, you seemed more involved in my father's bank than my budding love life. It all happened at a staff party my father gave to celebrate Washington's birthday. Another first for old wooden teeth. Actually, to put the incident in its proper perspective, I was raped by one of the director's secretaries, a large lady called Cynthia with even larger breasts that wobbled when . . ."

"Did you enjoy it?"

"Yes, but I can't believe for one moment that Cynthia did. She was far too drunk to realise I was there at the time. Still, you have to begin somewhere and she was willing to give the boss's son a helping hand."

The vision of Alan Lloyd's prim, middle-aged secretary flashed across William's mind.

"I don't think my chances of initiation by the chairman's secretary are very good," he mused.

"You'd be surprised," said Matthew knowingly. "The ones that go around with their legs so firmly together are often the ones who can't wait to get them apart. I now accept most invitations, formal or informal, not that dress matters much on these occasions."

The chauffeur put the car in the garage while the two young men ran up the steps into William's house.

"You've certainly made some changes since I was last here," said Matthew, admiring the modern cane furniture and new paisley wallpapers. Only the crimson leather chair remained firmly rooted in its usual spot.

"The place needed brightening up a little," William offered. "It was like living in the Stone Age. Besides, I didn't want to be reminded of . . . Come on, this is no time to hang around discussing interior decoration."

"When is everybody arriving for this party?"

"Ball, Matthew, the grandmothers insist on calling the event a ball."

"There is only one thing that can be described as a ball on these occasions."

"Matthew, one director's secretary does not entitle you to consider yourself a national authority on sex education."

"Oh, such jealousy, and from one's dearest friend," Matthew sighed mockingly.

William laughed and looked at his watch. "The first guest should arrive in a couple of hours. Time for a shower and to change. Did you remember to bring a dinner jacket?"

"Yes, but if I didn't I can always wear my pyjamas. I usually leave one or the other behind, but I've never yet managed to forget both. In fact, it might start a whole new craze if I arrived at the ball in my pyjamas."

"I can't see my grandmothers enjoying the joke," said William.

The caterers arrived at six o'clock, twenty-three of them in all, and the grandmothers at seven, regal in long black lace that swept along the floor. William and Matthew joined them in the front room a few minutes before eight.

William was about to remove an inviting red cherry from the top of a magnificent iced cake when he heard Grandmother Kane's voice from behind him.

"Don't touch the food, William, it's not for you."

He swung round. "Then who is it for?" he asked, as he kissed her on the cheek.

"Don't be fresh, William, just because you're over six feet doesn't mean I wouldn't spank you."

Matthew Lester laughed.

"Grandmother, may I introduce my closest friend, Matthew Lester?"

Grandmother Kane subjected him to a careful appraisal through her pince-nez before venturing: "How do you do, young man?"

"It's an honour to meet you, Mrs. Kane. I believe you knew my grandfather."

"Knew your grandfather? Caleb Longworth Lester? He proposed marriage to me once, over fifty years ago. I turned him down. I told him he drank too much, and that it would lead him to an early grave. I was right, so don't you drink, either of you; remember, alcohol dulls the brain."

"We hardly get much chance with Prohibition," remarked Matthew innocently.

"That will end soon enough, I'm afraid," said Grandmother Kane, sniffing. "President Coolidge is forgetting his upbringing. He would never have become President if that idiot Harding hadn't foolishly died."

William laughed. "Really, Grandmother, your memory is getting selective. You wouldn't hear a word against him during the police strike."

Mrs. Kane did not reply.

The guests began to appear, many of them complete strangers to their host, who was delighted to see Alan Lloyd among the early arrivals.

"You're looking well, my boy," he said, finding himself looking up at William for the first time in his life.

"You too, Alan. It was kind of you to come."

"Kind? Have you forgotten that the invitation came from your grandmothers? I am possibly brave enough to refuse one of them, but both . . ."

"You too, Alan?" William laughed. "Can you spare a moment for a private word?" He guided his guest towards a quiet corner. "I want to change my investment plans slightly and start buying Lester's bank stock whenever it comes on to the market. I'd like to be holding about five per cent of their stock by the time I'm twenty-one."

"It's not that easy," said Alan. "Lester's shares don't come on the market all that often as they are all in private hands, but I'll see what can be done. What is going on in that mind of yours, William?"

"Well, my real aim is . . ."

"William." Grandmother Cabot was bearing down on them at speed. "Here you are conspiring in a corner with Mr. Lloyd and I haven't seen you dance with one young lady yet. What do you imagine we organised this ball for?"

"Quite right," said Alan Lloyd, rising. "You come and sit down with me, Mrs. Cabot, and I'll kick the boy out into the world. We can rest, watch him dance, and listen to the music."

"Music? That's not music, Alan. It's nothing more than a loud cacophony of sound with no suggestion of melody."

"My dear grandmother," said William, "that is 'Yes, We Have No Bananas', the latest hit song."

"Then the time has come for me to depart this world," said Grandmother Cabot, wincing.

"Never," Alan Lloyd said gallantly.

William danced with a couple of girls whom he had a vague recollection of knowing, but he had to be reminded of their names, and when he spotted Matthew sitting in a corner, he was glad of the excuse to escape the dance floor. He had not noticed the girl sitting next to Matthew until he was right on top of them. When she looked up into William's eyes, he felt his knees give way.

"Do you know Abby Blount?" asked Matthew casually.

"No," said William, barely restraining himself from straightening his tie.

"This is your host, Mr. William Lowell Kane."

The young lady cast her eyes demurely downwards as he took the seat on the other side of her. Matthew had noted the look William gave Abby and went off in search of some punch.

"How is it I've lived in Boston all my life, and we've never met?" William said.

"We did meet once before. On that occasion, you pushed

me into the pond on the Common; we were both three at the time. It's taken me fourteen years to recover."

"I am sorry," said William, after a pause during which he searched in vain for more telling repartee.

"What a lovely house you have, William."

There was a second busy pause. "Thank you," said William weakly. He glanced sideways at Abby, trying to look as though he were not studying her. She was slim – oh, so slim – with huge brown eyes, long eyelashes and a profile that captivated William. Abby had bobbed her auburn hair in the style William had hated until that moment.

"Matthew tells me you are going to Harvard next year," she tried again.

"Yes, I am. I mean, would you like to dance?"

"Thank you," she said.

The steps that had come to him so easily a few minutes before seemed now to forsake him. He trod on her toes and continually propelled her into other dancers. He apologised, she smiled. He held her a little more closely, and they danced on.

"Do we know that young lady who seems to have been monopolising William for the last hour?" said Grandmother Cabot suspiciously.

Grandmother Kane picked up her pince-nez and studied the girl accompanying William as he strolled through the open bay windows out on to the lawn.

"Abby Blount," Grandmother Kane declared.

"Admiral Blount's daughter?" enquired Grandmother Cabot.

"Yes."

Grandmother Cabot nodded a degree of approval.

William guided Abby Blount towards the far end of the garden and stopped by a large chestnut tree which he had used in the past only for climbing.

"Do you always try to kiss a girl the first time you meet her?" asked Abby.

"To be honest," said William, "I've never kissed a girl before."

Abby laughed. "I'm very flattered."

She offered first her pink cheek and then her rosy, pursed lips and then insisted upon returning indoors. The grandmothers observed their early re-entry with some relief.

Later, in William's bedroom, the two boys discussed the evening.

"Not a bad party," said Matthew. "Almost worth the trip from New York out here to the provinces, despite your stealing my girl."

"Do you think she'll help me lose my virginity?" asked William, ignoring Matthew's mock accusation.

"Well, you have three weeks to find out, but I fear you'll discover she hasn't lost hers yet," said Matthew. "Such is my expertise in these matters that I'm willing to bet you five dollars she doesn't succumb even to the charms of William Lowell Kane."

William planned a careful stratagem. Virginity was one thing, but losing five dollars to Matthew was quite another. He saw Abby Blount nearly every day after that, taking advantage for the first time of owning his own house and car at seventeen. He began to feel he would do better without the discreet but persistent chaperonage of Abby's parents who seemed always to be in the middle distance and he was not perceptibly nearer his goal when the last day of the holidays dawned.

Determined to win his five dollars, William sent Abby a dozen roses early in the day, took her out to an expensive dinner at Joseph's that evening and finally succeeded in coaxing her back into his front room.

"How did you get hold of a bottle of whisky while Prohibition is on?" asked Abby.

"Oh, it's not so hard," William boasted.

The truth was that he had hidden a bottle of Henry Osborne's bourbon in his bedroom soon after he had left, and was now glad he had not poured it down the drain as had been his original intention.

William poured drinks that made him gasp and brought tears to Abby's eyes.

He sat down beside her and put his arm confidently around her shoulder. She settled into it.

"Abby, I think you're terribly pretty," he murmured in a preliminary way at her auburn curls.

She gazed at him earnestly, her brown eyes wide. "Oh, William," she breathed. "And I think you're just wonderful."

Her doll-like face was irresistible. She allowed herself to be kissed. Thus emboldened, William slipped a tentative hand from her wrist on to her breast, and left it there like a traffic cop halting an advancing stream of automobiles. She became pinkly indignant and pushed his arm down to allow the traffic to move on.

"William, you mustn't do that."

"Why not?" said William, struggling vainly to retain his grasp of her.

"Because you can't tell where it might end."

"I've got a fair idea."

Before he could renew his advances, Abby pushed him away and rose hastily, smoothing her dress.

"I think I ought to be getting home now, William."

"But you've only just arrived."

"Mother will want to know what I've been doing."

"You'll be able to tell her – nothing."

"And I think it's best it stays that way," she added.

"But I'm going back tomorrow." He avoided saying, "to school".

"Well, you can write to me, William."

Unlike Valentino, William knew when he was beaten. He rose, straightened his tie, took Abby by the hand and drove her home.

The following day, back at school, Matthew Lester accepted the proffered five-dollar note with eyebrows raised in mock astonishment.

"Just say one word, Matthew, and I'll chase you right around St. Paul's with a baseball bat."

"I can't think of any words that would truly express my deep feeling of sympathy."

"Matthew, right around St. Paul's."

* * *

William began to be aware of his housemaster's wife during his last two terms at St. Paul's. She was a good-looking woman, a little slack around the stomach and hips perhaps, but she carried her splendid bosom well and the luxuriant dark hair piled on top of her head was no more streaked with grey than was becoming. One Saturday when William had sprained his wrist on the hockey rink, Mrs. Raglan bandaged it for him in a cool compress, standing a little closer than was necessary, allowing William's arm to brush against her breast. He enjoyed the sensation. Then on another occasion when he had a fever and was confined to the infirmary for a few days, she brought him all his meals herself and sat on his bed, her body touching his legs through the thin covering, while he ate. He enjoyed that too.

She was rumoured to be Grumpy Raglan's second wife. No one in the house could imagine how Grumpy had managed to secure even one spouse. Mrs. Raglan occasionally indicated by the subtlest of sighs and silences that she shared something of their incredulity at her fate.

As part of his duties as house captain, William was required to report to Grumpy Raglan every night at ten thirty when he had completed the lights-out round and was about to go to bed himself. One Monday evening, when he knocked on Grumpy's door as usual, he was surprised to hear Mrs. Raglan's voice bidding him to enter. She was lying on the chaise-longue dressed in a loose silk robe of faintly Japanese appearance.

William kept a firm grasp on the cold door knob. "All the lights are out and I've locked the front door, Mrs. Raglan. Good night."

She swung her legs on to the ground, a pale flash of thigh appearing momentarily from under the draped silk.

"You're always in such a hurry, William. You can't wait for your life to start, can you?" She walked over to a side table. "Why don't you stay and have some hot chocolate? Silly me, I made enough for two, I quite forgot that Mr. Raglan won't be back until Saturday."

There was a definite emphasis on the word 'Saturday'. She carried a steaming cup over to William and looked up at him to see whether the significance of her remarks had registered on him. Satisfied, she passed him the cup, letting her hand touch his. He stirred the hot chocolate assiduously.

"Gerald has gone to a conference," she continued explaining. It was the first time he had ever heard Grumpy Raglan's first name. "Do shut the door, William, and come and sit down."

William hesitated; he shut the door, but he did not want to take Grumpy's chair nor did he want to sit next to Mrs. Raglan. He decided Grumpy's chair was the lesser of two evils and moved towards it.

"No, no," she said, as she patted the seat next to her.

William shuffled over and sat down nervously by her side, staring into his cup for inspiration. Finding none, he gulped the contents down, burning his tongue. He was relieved to see Mrs. Raglan getting up. She refilled his cup, ignoring his murmured refusal, and then moved silently across the room, wound up the Victrola and placed the needle on the record.

"Nice and easy does it," were the first words that William heard. He was still looking at the floor, when she returned.

"You wouldn't let a lady dance by herself, would you, William?"

He looked up. Mrs. Raglan was swaying slightly in time to the music. "We're on the road to romance, that's clear to say," crooned Rudy Vallee. William stood up and put his arm formally round Mrs. Raglan. Grumpy could have fitted in between them without any trouble. After a few bars she moved closer to William, and he stared over her right shoulder fixedly to indicate to her that he had not noticed that her left hand had slipped from his shoulder to the small of his back. When the record stopped, William thought it would give him a chance to return to the safety of his hot chocolate, but she had turned the record over and was back in his arms before he could move.

"Mrs. Raglan, I think I ought to . . ."

"Relax a little, William."

At last he found the courage to look her in the eyes. He tried to reply, but he couldn't speak. Her hand was now exploring his back, and he felt her thigh move gently into his groin. He tightened his hold around her waist.

"That's better," she said.

They circled slowly around the room, closely entwined, slower and slower, keeping time with the music as the record gently ran down. When she slipped away and turned out the light, William wanted her to return quickly. He stood there in the dark, not moving, hearing the rustle of silk, and able only to see a silhouette discarding clothes.

The crooner had completed his song, and the needle was scratching at the end of the record by the time she had helped William out of all his clothes and led him back to the chaise-longue. He groped for her in the dark, and his shy novice's fingers encountered several parts of her body that did not feel at all as he had imagined they would. He withdrew them hastily to the comparatively familiar territory of her breast. Her fingers exhibited no such reticence, and he began to feel sensations he would never have dreamed possible. He wanted to moan out loud, but stopped himself, fearing it would sound stupid. Her hands were on his back, pulling him gently on top of her.

William moved around wondering how he would ever enter her without showing his total lack of experience. It was not as easy as he had expected, and he began to get more desperate by the second. Then, once again, her fingers moved across his stomach and guided him expertly. With her help he entered her easily and had an immediate orgasm.

"I'm sorry," said William, not sure what to do next. He lay silently on top of her for some time before she spoke.

"It will be better tomorrow."

The sound of the scratching record returned to his ears.

Mrs. Raglan remained in William's mind all that endless Tuesday. That night, she sighed. On Wednesday, she panted. On Thursday, she moaned. On Friday she cried out.

On Saturday Grumpy Raglan returned from his conference, by which time William's education was complete.

During the Easter holidays, on Ascension Day to be exact, Abby Blount finally succumbed to William's charms. It cost Matthew five dollars and Abby her virginity. She was, after Mrs. Raglan, something of an anticlimax. It was the only event of note that happened during the entire holiday, because Abby went off to Palm Beach with her parents, and William spent most of his time shut away indoors with his books, at home to no one other than the grandmothers and Alan Lloyd. His final examinations were now only a matter of weeks away, and as Grumpy Raglan went to no further conferences, William had no other outside activities.

During their last term, he and Matthew would sit in their study at St. Paul's for hours, never speaking unless Matthew had some mathematical problem he was quite unable to solve. When the long awaited examinations finally came, they lasted for only one brutal week. The moment they were over, both boys were sanguine about their results, but as the days went by, and they waited and waited, their confidence began to diminish. The Hamilton Memorial Scholarship to Harvard for mathematics was awarded on a strictly competitive basis and it was open to every schoolboy in America. William had no way of judging how tough his opposition might be. As more time went by and still he heard nothing, William began to assume the worst.

When the telegram arrived, he was out playing baseball with some other sixth formers, killing the last few days of the term before leaving school, those warm summer days when boys are most likely to be expelled for drunkenness, breaking windows or trying to get into bed with one of the master's daughters, if not their wives.

William was declaring in a loud voice to those who cared to listen that he was about to hit his first home run ever. The Babe Ruth of St. Paul's, declared Matthew. Much laughter greeted this exaggerated claim. When the telegram was handed to him, home runs were suddenly forgotten. He dropped his bat and tore open the little yellow envelope. The pitcher waited, impatient, ball in hand, and so did the outfielders as he read the communication slowly.

"They want you to turn professional," someone shouted from first base, the arrival of a telegram being an uncommon occurrence during a baseball game. Matthew walked in from the outfield to join William, trying to make out from his friend's face if the news were good or bad. Without changing his expression, William passed the telegram to Matthew, who read it, leaped high into the air with delight, and dropped the piece of paper to the ground to accompany William, racing around the bases on the way to the first home run ever scored without anyone actually hitting the ball. The pitcher watched them, picked the telegram up and read the missive himself and then he threw his ball into the bleachers with gusto. The little piece of yellow paper was then passed eagerly from player to player around the field. The last person to read the message was the second former who, having caused so much happiness but received no thanks, decided the least he deserved was to know the cause of so much excitement.

The telegram was addressed to Mr. William Lowell Kane, whom the boy assumed to be the incompetent hitter. It read: "Congratulations on winning the Hamilton Memorial Mathematics Scholarship to Harvard, full details to follow. Abbot Lawrence Lowell, President." William never did get his home run as he was sat heavily upon by several fielders before he reached home plate.

Matthew looked on with delight at the success of his closest friend, but he was sad to think that it meant they might now be parted. William felt it too, but said nothing; the two boys had to wait another nine days to learn that Matthew had also been accepted at Harvard.

Yet another telegram arrived, this one from Charles Lester, congratulating his son and inviting the boys to tea at the Plaza Hotel in New York. Both grandmothers sent congratulations to William, but as Grandmother Kane informed Alan Lloyd, somewhat testily, "The boy has done no less than was expected of him and no more than his father did before him."

The two young men sauntered down Fifth Avenue on the appointed day with considerable pride. Girls' eyes were drawn to the handsome pair, who affected not to notice. They removed their straw boaters as they entered the front door of the Plaza at three fifty-nine, strolled nonchalantly through the lounge and observed the family group awaiting them in the Palm Court. There, upright in the comfortable chairs sat both grandmothers, Kane and Cabot, flanking another old lady who, William assumed, was the Lester family's equivalent of Grandmother Kane. Mr. and Mrs. Charles Lester, their daughter Susan (whose eyes never left William), and Alan Lloyd completed the circle leaving two vacant chairs for William and Matthew.

Grandmother Kane summoned the nearest waiter with an imperious eyebrow. "A fresh pot of tea and some more cakes, please."

The waiter made haste to the kitchens. "Pot of tea and some more cakes for table twenty-three," he shouted above the clatter.

"Coming up," said a voice from the steamy obscurity.

"A pot of tea and some cream cakes, madam," the waiter said on his return.

"Your father would have been proud of you today, William," the older man was saying to the taller of the two youths.

The waiter wondered what it was that the good-looking young man had achieved to elicit such a comment.

William would not have noticed the waiter at all but for the silver band around his wrist. The piece so easily might have come from Tiffany's; the incongruity of it puzzled him.

"William," said Grandmother Kane. "Two cakes are quite sufficient; this is not your last meal before you go to Harvard."

He looked at the old lady with affection and quite forgot the silver band.

13

That night as Abel lay awake in his small room at the Plaza Hotel, thinking about the boy, William, whose father would have been proud of him, he realised for the first time in his life exactly what he wanted to achieve. He wanted to be thought of as an equal by the Williams of this world.

Abel had had quite a struggle on his arrival in New York. He occupied a room that contained only two beds which he was obliged to share with George and two of his cousins. As a result, Abel slept only when one of the beds was free. George's uncle was unable to offer him a job, and after a few anxious weeks during which most of his savings had to be spent on staying alive, Abel searched from Brooklyn to Queens before finding work in a butcher's shop which paid nine dollars for a six and a half day week, and allowed him to sleep above the premises. The shop was in the heart of an almost self-sufficient little Polish community on the lower East Side, and Abel rapidly became impatient with the insularity of his fellow countrymen, many of whom made no effort to learn to speak English.

Abel still saw George and his constant succession of girlfriends regularly at weekends, but he spent most of his free evenings during the week at night school learning how to read and write English. He was not ashamed of his slow progress, for he had had very little opportunity to write at all since the age of eight, but within two years he had made himself fluent in his new tongue, showing only the slightest trace of an accent. He now felt ready to move out of the butcher's shop – but to what, and how? Then, while dressing a leg of lamb one morning, he overheard one of the shop's biggest customers, the catering manager of the Plaza Hotel, grumbling to the butcher that he had had to fire a junior waiter for petty theft.

"How can I find a replacement at such short notice?" the manager remonstrated.

The butcher had no solution to offer. Abel did. He put on his only suit, walked forty-seven blocks, and got the job.

Once he had settled in at the Plaza, he enrolled for a night course in English at Columbia University. He worked steadily every night, dictionary open in one hand, pen scratching away in the other; during the mornings, between serving breakfast and setting up the tables for lunch, he would copy out the editorial from the *New York Times,* looking up any word he was uncertain of in his second-hand Webster's.

For the next three years, Abel worked his way through the ranks of the Plaza until he was promoted and became a waiter in the Oak Room, making about twenty-five dollars a week with tips. In his own world, he lacked for nothing.

Abel's instructor at Columbia was so impressed by his diligent progress in English that he advised Abel to enrol in a further night course, which was to be his first step towards a Bachelor of Arts degree. He switched his spare-time reading from English to economics and started copying out the editorials in the *Wall Street Journal* instead of those in the *New York Times.* His new world totally absorbed him, and with the exception of George he lost touch with his Polish friends of the early days.

When Abel served at table in the Oak Room, he would always study the famous among the guests carefully – the Bakers, Loebs, Whitneys, Morgans and Phelps – and try to work out why it was that the rich were different. He read H. L. Mencken, *The American Mercury,* Scott Fitzgerald, Sinclair Lewis and Theodore Dreiser in an endless quest for knowledge. He studied the *New York Times* while the other waiters flipped through the *Mirror,* and he read the *Wall Street Journal* in his hour's break while they dozed. He was not sure where his newly acquired knowledge would lead him, but he never doubted the Baron's maxim that there was no true substitute for a good education.

One Thursday in August, 1926 – he remembered the occasion well, because it was the day that Rudolph Valentino died, and many of the ladies shopping on Fifth Avenue wore black – Abel was serving as usual at one of the corner tables. The corner tables were always reserved for top business men who wished to eat in privacy without fear of being overheard by prying ears. He enjoyed serving at that particular table, for it was the era of expanding business, and he often picked up some inside information from the titbits of conversation. After the meal was over, if the host had been from a bank or large holding company, Abel would look up the financial record of the company of the guests at the lunch, and if he felt the meeting had gone particularly well, he would invest one hundred dollars in the smaller company, hoping it would be in line for a takeover or expansion with the help of the larger company. If the host had ordered cigars at the end of the meal, Abel would increase his investment to two hundred dollars. Seven times out of ten, the value of the stock he had selected in this way doubled within six months, the period Abel would allow himself to hold on to the shares. Using this system he lost money only three times during the four years he worked at the Plaza.

What made waiting on the corner table unusual on that particular day was that the guests had ordered cigars even before the meal had started. Later they were joined by more guests who ordered more cigars. Abel looked up the name of the host in the *maître d'*s reservation book. Woolworth. He had seen the name in the financial columns quite recently but he could not immediately place it. The other guest was Charles Lester, a regular patron of the Plaza, whom Abel knew to be a distinguished New York banker. He listened to as much of the conversation as he could while serving the meal. The guests showed absolutely no interest in the attentive waiter. Abel could not discover any specific details of importance, but he gathered that some sort of deal had been closed that morning and would be announced to an unsuspecting public later in the day. Then he remembered. He had seen the name in the *Wall Street Journal*. Woolworth was the man who was going to start the first American five-and-ten-cent stores. Abel was determined to get his five cents' worth. While the guests were enjoying their dessert course – most of them chose the strawberry cheese cake (Abel's recommendation) – he took the opportunity to leave the dining room for a few moments to call his broker in Wall Street.

"What are Woolworth's trading at?" he asked.

There was a pause from the other end of the line. "Two and one-eighth. Quite a lot of movement lately; don't know why though," came the reply.

"Buy up to the limit of my account until you hear an announcement from the company later today."

"What will the announcement say?" asked the puzzled broker.

"I am not at liberty to reveal that sort of information over the telephone," said Abel.

The broker was suitably impressed; Abel's record in the past had led him not to enquire too closely into the source of his client's information.

Abel hurried back to the Oak Room in time to serve the guests coffee. They lingered over it for some time, and Abel returned to the table only as they were preparing to leave. The man who picked up the bill thanked Abel for his attentive service, and turning so that his friends could hear him, said "Do you want a tip, young man?"

"Thank you, sir," said Abel.

"Buy Woolworth's shares."

The guests all laughed. Abel laughed as well, took five dollars from the man and thanked him. He took a further two thousand four hundred and twelve dollars' profit on Woolworth's shares during the next six months.

When Abel was granted full citizenship of the United States, a few days after his twenty-first birthday, he decided the occasion ought to be celebrated. He invited George and Monika, George's latest love, and a girl called Clara, an ex-love of George's, to the cinema to see John Barrymore in

Don Juan and then on to Bigo's for dinner. George was still an apprentice in his uncle's bakery at eight dollars a week, and although Abel still looked upon him as his closest friend, he was aware of the growing difference between the penniless George and himself, who now had over eight thousand dollars in the bank and was in his last year at Columbia University studying for his B.A. in economics. Abel knew where he was going, whereas George had stopped telling everyone he would be the mayor of New York.

The four of them had a memorable evening mainly because Abel knew exactly what to expect from a good restaurant. His three guests all had a great deal too much to eat, and when the bill was presented, George was aghast to see that it came to more than he earned in a month. Abel paid the bill without a second glance. If you have to pay a bill, make it look as if the amount is of no consequence. If it is, don't go to the restaurant again, but whatever you do, don't comment or look surprised – something else the rich had taught him.

When the party broke up at about two in the morning, George and Monika returned to the lower East Side, while Abel felt he had earned Clara. He smuggled her through the service entrance of the Plaza and up to his room in a laundry lift. She did not require much enticement to end up in bed, and Abel set about her with haste, mindful that he had some serious sleeping to do before reporting for breakfast duty. To his satisfaction, he had completed his task by two thirty and sank into an uninterrupted sleep until his alarm rang at six a.m. It left him just time enough to have Clara once again before he had to get dressed.

Clara sat up in his bed and regarded Abel sullenly as he tied his white bow tie, and kissed her a perfunctory goodbye.

"Be sure you leave the way you came, or you'll get me into a load of trouble," said Abel. "When will I see you again?"

"You won't," said Clara stonily.

"Why not?" asked Abel, surprised. "Something I did?"

"No, something you didn't do." She jumped out of bed and started to dress hastily.

"What didn't I do?" said Abel, aggrieved. "You wanted to go to bed with me, didn't you?"

She turned around and faced him. "I thought I did until I realised you have only one thing in common with Valentino – you're both dead. You may be the greatest thing the Plaza has seen in a bad year, but in bed, I can tell you, you are nothing." Fully dressed now, she paused with her hand on the door handle, composing her parting thrust. "Tell me, have you ever persuaded any girl to go to bed with you more than once?"

Stunned, Abel stared at the slammed door and spent the rest of the day worrying about Clara's words. He could think of no one with whom he could discuss the problem. George would only laugh at him, and the staff at the Plaza all thought he knew everything. He decided that this problem, like all the others he had encountered in his life, must be one he could surmount with knowledge or experience.

After lunch, on his half day, he went to Scribner's bookshop on Fifth Avenue. They had solved all his economic and linguistic problems, but he couldn't find anything there that looked as if it might even begin to help his sexual ones. Their special book on etiquette was useless and *The Nature of Morals* by W. F. Colbert turned out to be utterly inappropriate.

Abel left the bookshop without making a purchase and spent the rest of the afternoon in a dingy Broadway cinema, not watching the film, but thinking only about what Clara had said. The film, a love story with Greta Garbo that did not reach the kissing stage until the last reel, provided no more assistance than Scribner's had.

When Abel left the cinema, the sky was already dark and there was a cool breeze blowing down Broadway. It still surprised Abel that any city could be as noisy and light by night as it was by day. He started walking uptown towards Fifty-ninth Street, hoping the fresh air would clear his mind. He stopped on the corner of Fifty-second to buy an evening paper.

"Looking for a girl?" said a voice from behind the newsstand.

Abel stared at the voice. She was about thirty-five and heavily made up, wearing the new, fashionable lipstick. Her white silk blouse had a button undone, and she wore a long black skirt with black stockings and black shoes.

"Only five dollars, worth every penny," she said, pushing her hip out at an angle, allowing the slit in her skirt to part and reveal the top of her stockings.

"Where?" said Abel.

"I have a little place of my own in the next block."

She turned her head, indicating to Abel which direction she meant, and he could, for the first time, see her face clearly under the streetlight. She was not unattractive. Abel nodded his agreement, and she took his arm and started walking.

"If the police stop us," she said, "you're an old friend and my name's Joyce."

They walked to the next block and into a squalid little apartment building. Abel was horrified by the dingy room she lived in, with its single bare light bulb, one chair, a wash basin and a crumpled double bed, which had obviously already been used several times that day.

"You live here?" he said incredulously.

"Good God, no, I only use this place for my work."

"Why do you do this?" asked Abel, wondering if he now wanted to go through with his plan.

"I have two children to bring up and no husband. Can you think of a better reason? Now, do you want me or not?"

"Yes, but not the way you think," said Abel.

She eyed him warily. "Not another of those whacky ones, a follower of the Marquis de Sade, are you?"

"Certainly not," said Abel.

"You're not gonna burn me with cigarettes, then?"

"No, nothing like that," said Abel, startled. "I want to be taught properly. I want lessons."

"Lessons, are you joking? What do you think this is, darling, a fucking night school?"

"Something like that," said Abel and he sat down on the corner of the bed and explained to her how Clara had reacted the night before. "Do you think you can help?"

The lady of the night studied Abel carefully, wondering if it was April the First.

"Sure," she said finally, "but it's going to cost you five dollars a time for a thirty-minute session."

"More expensive than a B.A. from Columbia," said Abel. "How many lessons will I need?"

"Depends how quick a learner you are, doesn't it?" she said.

"Well, let's start right now," said Abel, taking five dollars out of his inside pocket and handing the money over to her. She put the note in the top of her stocking, a sure sign she never took them off.

"Clothes off, darling," she said. "You won't learn much fully dressed."

When he was stripped, she looked at him critically. "You're not exactly Douglas Fairbanks, are you? Don't worry about it, it doesn't matter what you look like once the lights are out; it only matters what you can do."

Abel sat on the edge of the bed while she started telling him about how to treat a lady. She was surprised that Abel really did not want her and was even more surprised when he continued to turn up every day for the next two weeks.

"When will I know I've made it?" Abel enquired.

"You'll know, baby," replied Joyce. "If you can make me come, you can make an Egyptian mummy come."

She taught him first where the sensitive parts of a woman's body were, and then to be patient in his love-making and the signs by which he might know that what he was doing was pleasing. How to use his tongue and lips on every place other than a woman's mouth.

Abel listened carefully to all she said and followed her instructions scrupulously and to begin with, a little bit too mechanically. Despite her assurance that he was improving out of all recognition, he had no real idea if she was telling the truth, until about three weeks and one hundred and ten dollars later, when to his surprise and delight, Joyce suddenly came alive in his arms for the first time. She held his head close to her as he gently licked her nipples. As he stroked her gently between the legs, he found she was wet – for the first time – and after he had entered her she moaned, a sound Abel had never heard before, and found intensely pleasing. She clawed at his back, commanding him not to stop. The moaning continued, sometimes loud, sometimes soft. Finally she cried out sharply, and the hands that had clutched him to her so fiercely relaxed.

When she had caught her breath, she said: "Baby, you just graduated top of the class."

Abel hadn't even come.

Abel celebrated the awarding of both his degrees by paying scalpers' price for ringside seats and taking George, Monika and a reluctant Clara to watch Gene Tunney fight Jack Dempsey for the heavyweight championship of the world. That night after the fight, Clara felt it was nothing less than her duty to go to bed with Abel as he had spent so much money on her. By the morning, she was begging him not to leave her.

Abel never asked her out again.

After he had graduated from Columbia, Abel became dissatisfied with his life at the Plaza Hotel, but could not figure out how to secure further advancement. Although he was surrounded by some of the most wealthy and successful men in America, he was unable to approach any of the customers directly, knowing that if he did so, it might well cost him his job and in any case, the customers could not take seriously the aspirations of a waiter. Abel had long ago decided that he wanted to be a head waiter.

One day, Mr. and Mrs. Ellsworth Statler came to lunch at the Plaza's Edwardian Room, where Abel had been on relief duty for a week. He thought his chance had come. He did everything he could think of to impress the famous hotelier, and the meal went splendidly. As he left, Statler thanked Abel warmly and gave him ten dollars, but that was the end of their association. Abel watched him disappear through the revolving doors of the Plaza, wondering if he was ever going to get a break.

Sammy, the head waiter, tapped him on the shoulder: "What did you get from Mr. Statler?"

"Nothing," said Abel.

"He didn't tip you?" asked Sammy in a disbelieving tone.

"Oh, yes, sure," said Abel. "Ten dollars." He handed the money over to Sammy.

"That's more like it," said Sammy. "I was beginning to think you was double-dealing me, Abel. Ten dollars, that's good even for Mr. Statler. You must have impressed him."

"No, I didn't."

"What do you mean?" asked Sammy.

"It doesn't matter," said Abel, as he started walking away.

"Wait a moment, Abel, I have a note here for you. The gentleman at table seventeen, a Mr. Leroy, wants to speak to you personally."

"What about, Sammy?"

"How should I know? Probably liked your blue eyes."

Abel glanced over to number seventeen, strictly for the meek and the unknown, because the table was so badly placed near a swing door into the kitchen. Abel usually tried to avoid serving any of the tables at that end of the room.

"Who is he?" asked Abel. "What does he want?"

"I don't know," said Sammy, not bothering to look up. "I'm not in touch with the life history of every customer the way you are. Give them a good meal, make sure you get yourself a big tip and hope they come again. You may feel it's a simple philosophy but it's sure good enough for me. Maybe they forgot to teach you the basics at Columbia. Now get your butt over there, Abel, and if it's a tip be certain you bring the money straight back to me."

Abel smiled at Sammy's bald head and went over to seventeen. There were two people seated at the table, a man in a colourful checked jacket, of which Abel did not approve, and an attractive young woman with a mop of blonde, curly hair, which momentarily distracted Abel, who uncharitably assumed she was the checked jacket's New York girlfriend. Abel put on his 'sorry smile', betting himself a silver dollar that the man was going to make a big fuss about the swing doors and try to get his table changed to impress the stunning blonde. No one liked being near the smell of the kitchens and the continual banging of waiters through the doors, but it was impossible to avoid using the table, when the hotel was already packed with residents and many New Yorkers who used the restaurant as their local eating place, and looked upon visitors as little less than intruders. Why did Sammy always leave the tricky customers for him to deal with? Abel approached the checked jacket cautiously.

"You asked to speak to me, sir?"

"Sure did," said a Southern accent. "My name is Davis Leroy, and this is my daughter Melanie."

Abel's eyes left Mr. Leroy momentarily and encountered a pair of eyes as green as any he had ever seen.

"I have been watching you, Abel, for the last five days," Mr. Leroy was saying in his Southern drawl.

If pushed, Abel would have had to admit that he had not noticed Mr. Leroy until the last five minutes.

"I have been very impressed by what I have seen, Abel, because you got class, real class, and I am always on the look-out for that. Ellsworth Statler was a fool not to pick you up right away."

Abel began to take a closer look at Mr. Leroy. His purple cheeks and double chin left Abel in no doubt that he had not been told about Prohibition, and the empty plates in front of him accounted for his basketball belly, but neither the name nor the face meant anything to him. At a normal lunchtime, Abel was familiar with the background of anyone sitting at thirty-seven of the thirty-nine tables in the Edwardian Room. That day Mr. Leroy was one of the unknown two.

The Southerner was still talking. "Now, I'm not one of those multi-millionaires who have to sit at your corner table when they stay at the Plaza."

Abel was impressed. The average customer wasn't supposed to appreciate the relative merits of the various tables.

"But I'm not doing so badly for myself. In fact, my best hotel may well grow to be as impressive as this one some day, Abel."

"I am sure it will be, sir," said Abel, playing for time.

Leroy, Leroy, Leroy. The name didn't mean a thing.

"Lemme git to the point, son. The number one hotel in my group needs a new assistant manager, in charge of the restaurants. If you're interested, join me in my room when you come off duty."

He handed Abel a large embossed card.

"Thank you, sir," said Abel, looking at it: Davis Leroy. The Richmond Group of Hotels, Dallas. Underneath was inscribed the motto: 'One day a hotel in every state.' The name still meant nothing to Abel.

"I look forward to seeing you," said the friendly, check-jacketed Texan.

"Thank you, sir," said Abel. He smiled at Melanie, whose eyes were as coolly green as before and returned to Sammy, still head down, counting his takings.

"Ever heard of the Richmond Group of Hotels, Sammy?"

"Yes, sure, my brother was a junior waiter in one once. Must be about eight or nine of them, all over the South, run by a mad Texan, but I can't remember the guy's name. Why you asking?" said Sammy, looking up suspiciously.

"No particular reason," said Abel.

"There's always a reason with you. Now what did table seventeen want?" said Sammy.

"Grumbling about the noise from the kitchen. Can't say I blame him."

"What does he expect me to do, put him out on the veranda? Who does the guy think he is, John D. Rockefeller?"

Abel left Sammy to his counting and grumbling and cleared his own tables as quickly as possible. Then he went to his room and started to check out the Richmond Group. A few calls and he'd learned enough to satisfy his curiosity. The group turned out to be a private company, with eleven hotels in all, the most impressive one a three hundred and forty-two bedroom de luxe establishment, in Chicago, the Richmond Continental. Abel decided he had nothing to lose by paying a call on Mr. Leroy and Melanie. He checked Mr. Leroy's room number – 85 – one of the better smaller rooms. He arrived a little before four o'clock and was disappointed to discover Melanie was no longer with her father.

"Glad you could drop by, Abel. Take a seat."

It was the first time Abel had sat down as a guest in the more than four years he had worked at the Plaza.

"What are you paid?" said Mr. Leroy.

The suddenness of the question took Abel by surprise. "I take in around twenty-five dollars a week with tips."

"I'll start you at thirty-five a week."

"Which hotel are you referring to?" asked Abel.

"If I'm a judge of character, Abel, you got off table duty about three-thirty and took the next thirty minutes finding out which hotel. Am I right?"

Abel was beginning to like the man. "The Richmond Continental in Chicago?" he ventured.

Davis Leroy laughed. "I was right, and right about you."

Abel's mind was working fast. "How many people are there over the assistant manager on the hotel staff?"

"Only the manager and me. The manager is slow, gentle, and near retirement, and as I have ten other hotels to worry about, I don't think you'll have too much trouble – although I must confess Chicago is my favourite, my first hotel in the North, and with Melanie at school there, I find I spend more time in the Windy City than I ought to. Don't ever make the mistake New Yorkers do of underestimating Chicago. They think Chicago is only a postage stamp on a very large envelope, and they are the envelope."

Abel smiled.

"The hotel is a little run down at the moment," Mr. Leroy continued, "and the last assistant manager walked out on me suddenly without an explanation, so I need a good man to take his place and to realise its full potential. Now listen, Abel, I've watched you carefully for the last five days and I know you're that man. Do you think you would be interested in coming to Chicago?"

"Forty dollars and ten per cent of any increased profits, and I'll take the job."

"What?" said Davis Leroy, flabbergasted. "None of my managers are paid on a profit basis. The others would raise hell if they ever found out."

"I'm not going to tell them if you don't," said Abel.

"Now I know I chose the right man, even if he bargains a damn sight better than a Yankee with six daughters." He slapped the side of his chair. "I agree to your terms, Abel."

"Will you be requiring references, Mr. Leroy?"

"References! I know your background and history since you left Europe right through to you getting a degree in economics at Columbia. What do you think I've been doing the last few days? I wouldn't put someone who needed references in as number two in my best hotel. When can you start?"

"A month from today."

"Good. I look forward to seeing you then, Abel."

Abel rose from the hotel chair; he felt happier standing. He shook hands with Mr. Davis Leroy, the man from table seventeen – the one that was strictly for unknowns.

Leaving New York and the Plaza Hotel, his first real home since the castle near Slonim, turned out to be more of a wrench than Abel had anticipated. Goodbyes to George, Monika, and his few Columbia friends were unexpectedly hard. Sammy and the waiters threw a farewell party for him.

"We haven't heard the last of you, Abel Rosnovski," Sammy said, and they all agreed.

The Richmond Continental in Chicago was well-placed on Michigan Avenue, in the heart of the fastest growing city in America. That pleased Abel, who was only too familiar with Ellsworth Statler's maxim that just three things about a hotel really mattered: position, position and position. Abel soon discovered that position was about the only good thing that the Richmond had. Davis Leroy had understated the case when he had said that the hotel was a little run down. Desmond Pacey, the manager, wasn't slow and gentle as Davis Leroy had described him; he was plain lazy and didn't endear himself to Abel by allocating him a tiny room in the staff annex across the road and leaving him out of the main hotel. A quick check on the Richmond's books revealed that the daily occupancy rate was running at less than forty per cent, and that the restaurant was never more than half full, not least because the food was so appalling. The staff spoke three or four languages among them, none of which seemed to be English, and there were certainly not any signs of welcome for the stupid Polack from New York. It was not hard to see why the last assistant manager had left in such a hurry. If the Richmond was Davis Leroy's favourite hotel, Abel feared for the other ten in the group, even though his new employer seemed to have a bottomless pot of gold at the end of his Texas rainbow.

The best news that Abel learned during his first days in Chicago was that Melanie Leroy was an only child.

14

William and Matthew started their freshmen year at Harvard in the fall of 1924. Despite his grandmothers' disapproval William accepted the Hamilton Memorial Scholarship and at a cost of two hundred and ninety dollars, treated himself to 'Daisy', the latest Model T Ford, and first real love of his life. He painted Daisy bright yellow, which halved her value and doubled the number of his girlfriends. Calvin Coolidge won a landslide election to return to the White House and the volume on the New York Stock Exchange reached a five-year record of two million, three hundred and thirty-six thousand, one hundred and sixty shares.

Both young men ('We can no longer refer to them as children,' pronounced Grandmother Cabot) had been looking forward to college. After an energetic summer of tennis and golf, they were ready to get down to more serious pursuits. William started work on the day he arrived in their new room on the 'Gold Coast', a considerable improvement on their small study at St. Paul's, while Matthew went in search of the university rowing club. Matthew was elected to captain the freshmen crew, and William left his books every Sunday afternoon to watch his friend from the banks of the Charles River. He covertly enjoyed Matthew's success but was outwardly scathing.

"Life is not about eight big men pulling unwieldy pieces of misshapen wood through choppy water while one smaller man shouts at them," declared William haughtily.

"Tell Yale that," said Matthew.

William, meanwhile, quickly demonstrated to his mathematics professors that he was in his studies what Matthew was in sport – a mile ahead of the field. He also became chairman of the Freshmen Debating Society and talked his great-uncle, President Lowell, into the first university insurance plan, whereby students leaving Harvard would take out a life policy for one thousand dollars each, naming the university as the beneficiary. William estimated that the cost to each participant would be less than a dollar per week and that if forty per cent of the alumni joined the scheme, Harvard would have a guaranteed income of about three million dollars a year from 1950 onwards. The president was impressed and gave the scheme his full support, and a year later he invited William to join the board of the University Fund Raising Committee. William accepted with pride without realising the appointment was for life. President Lowell informed Grandmother Kane that he had captured one of the best financial brains of his generation, free of charge. Grandmother Kane testily replied to her cousin that, "Everything has its purpose and this will teach William to read the fine print."

Almost as soon as the sophomore year began, it became time to choose (or to be chosen for) one of the Finals Clubs that dominated the social landscape of the well-to-do at Harvard. William was 'punched' for the Porcellian, the oldest, richest, most exclusive and least ostentatious of such clubs. In the clubhouse on Massachusetts Avenue, which was incongruously situated over a cheap Hayes-Bickford cafeteria, he would sit in a comfortable armchair, considering the four-colour map problem, discussing the repercussions of the Loeb-Leopold trial, and idly watching the street below through the conveniently angled mirror while listening to the large new-fangled radio.

During the Christmas holidays, he was persuaded to ski with Matthew in Vermont, and spent a week panting uphill in the footsteps of his fitter friend.

"Tell me, Matthew, what is the point of spending one hour climbing up a hill only to come back down the same hill in a few seconds at considerable risk to life and limb?"

Matthew grunted. "Sure gives me a bigger kick than graph

theory, William. Why don't you admit you're not very good either at the going up or the coming down?"

They both did enough work in their sophomore year to get by, although their interpretations of 'getting by' were wildly different. For the first two months of the summer holidays, they worked as junior management assistants in Charles Lester's bank in New York, Matthew's father having long since given up the battle of trying to keep William away. When the dog days of August arrived, they spent most of their time dashing about the New England countryside in 'Daisy', sailing on the Charles River with as many different girls as possible and attending any house party to which they could get themselves invited. In no time, they were among the accredited personalities of the university, known to the *cognoscenti* as the Scholar and the Sweat. It was perfectly understood in Boston society that the girl who married William Kane or Matthew Lester would have no fears for her future, but as fast as hopeful mothers appeared with their fresh-faced daughters, Grandmother Kane and Grandmother Cabot dispatched them unceremoniously.

On April 18th, 1927, William celebrated his twenty-first birthday by attending the final meeting of the trustees to his estate. Alan Lloyd and Tony Simmons had prepared all the documents for signature.

"Well, William dear," said Milly Preston as if a great responsibility had been lifted from her shoulders, "I'm sure you'll be able to do every bit as well as we did."

"I hope so, Mrs. Preston, but if ever I need to lose half a million overnight, I'll know just who to call."

Milly Preston went bright red but made no attempt to reply.

The trust now stood at over twenty-eight million dollars, and William had definite plans for the nurture of that money, but he had also set himself the task of making a million dollars in his own right before he left Harvard. It was not a large sum compared with the amount in his trust, but his inherited wealth meant far less to him than the balance in his account at Lester's.

That summer, the grandmothers, fearing a fresh outbreak of predatory girls, dispatched William and Matthew on the grand tour of Europe, which turned out to be a great success for both of them. Matthew, surmounting all language barriers, found a beautiful girl in every major European capital – love, he assured William, was an international commodity. William secured introductions to a director of most of the major European banks – money, he assured Matthew, was also an international commodity. From London to Berlin to Rome, the two young men left a trail of broken hearts and suitably impressed bankers. When they returned to Harvard in September, they were both ready to hit the books for their final year.

In the bitter winter of 1927, Grandmother Kane died, aged eighty-five, and William wept for the first time since his mother's death.

"Come on," said Matthew, after bearing with William's depression for several days. "She had a good run and waited a long time to find out whether God was a Cabot or a Lowell."

William missed the shrewd words he had so little appreciated in his grandmother's lifetime, and he arranged a funeral which she would have been proud to attend. Although the great lady arrived at the cemetery in a black Packard hearse ("One of those new-fangled contraptions – over my dead body," but, as it turned out, under it), this unsound mode of transport would have been her only criticism of William's orchestration of her departure. Her death drove William to work with even more purpose during that final year at Harvard. He dedicated himself to winning the top mathematics prize in her memory. Grandmother Cabot died some six months later, probably, said William, because there was no one left for her to talk to.

In February 1928, William received a visit from the captain of the Debating Team. There was to be a full-dress debate the following month on the motion 'Socialism or Capitalism for America's Future', and William was naturally asked to represent capitalism.

"And what if I told you I was only willing to speak on behalf of the downtrodden masses?" William enquired of the surprised captain, slightly nettled by the thought that his intellectual views were simply assumed by outsiders because he had inherited a famous name and a prosperous bank.

"Well, I must say, William, we did imagine your own preference would be for, er . . ."

"It is. I accept your invitation. I take it that I am at liberty to select my partner?"

"Naturally."

"Good, then I choose Matthew Lester. May I know who our opponents will be?"

"You will not be informed until the day before, when the posters go up in the Yard."

For the next month Matthew and William turned their breakfast critiques of the newspapers of the left and right, and their nightly discussions about the meaning of life, into strategy sessions for what the campus was beginning to call 'The Great Debate'. William decided that Matthew should lead off.

As the fateful day approached, it became clear that most of the politically aware students, professors, and even some Boston and Cambridge notables would be attending. On the morning before the debate they walked over to the Yard to discover who their opposition would be.

"Leland Crosby and Thaddeus Cohen. Either name ring a bell with you, William? Crosby must be one of the Philadelphia Crosbys, I suppose."

"Of course he is. 'The Red Maniac of Rittenhouse Square', as his own aunt once described him so accurately. He's the most convincing revolutionary on campus. He's loaded, and he spends all his money on the popular radical causes. I can hear his opening now."

William parodied Crosby's grating tone. " 'I know at first hand the rapacity and the utter lack of social conscience of the American monied class.' If everyone in the audience hasn't heard that fifty times already, I'd say he'll make a formidable opponent."

"And Thaddeus Cohen?"

"Never heard of him."

The following evening, refusing to admit to stage fright, they made their way through the snow and cold wind, heavy overcoats flapping behind them, past the gleaming columns of the recently completed Widener Libra.y – like William's father, the donor's son had gone down on the *Titanic* – to Boylston Hall.

"With weather like this, at least if we take a beating there won't be many to tell the tale," said Matthew hopefully.

But as they rounded the side of the library, they could see a steady stream of stamping, huffing figures ascending the stairs and filing into the hall. Inside, they were shown to chairs on the podium. William sat still but his eyes picked out the people he knew in the audience: President Lowell, sitting discreetly in the middle row; ancient old Newbury St. John, Professor of Botany; a pair of Brattle Street bluestockings he recognised from Red House parties; and to his right, a group of Bohemian-looking young men and women, some not even wearing ties, who turned and started to clap as their spokesmen – Crosby and Cohen – walked on to the stage.

Crosby was the more striking of the two, tall and thin almost to the point of caricature, dressed absent-mindedly – or very carefully – in a shaggy tweed suit, but with a stiffly pressed shirt, and dangling a pipe with no apparent connection to his body except at his lower lip. Thaddeus Cohen was shorter and wore rimless glasses and an almost too perfectly cut, dark worsted suit.

The four speakers shook hands cautiously as the last-minute arrangements were made. The bells of Memorial Church, only a hundred feet away, sounded vague and distant as they rang out seven times.

"Mr. Leland Crosby, Junior," said the captain.

Crosby's speech gave William cause for self-congratulation. He had anticipated everything, the strident tone Crosby would take, the overstressed, nearly hysterical points he would make. He recited the incantations of American radicalism – Haymarket, Money Trust, Standard Oil, even Cross of Gold. William didn't think he had made more than an exhibition of himself although he garnered the expected applause from his claque on William's right. When Crosby sat down, he had clearly won no new supporters, and it looked as though he might have lost a few old ones. The comparison with William and Matthew – equally rich, equally socially distinguished, but selfishly refusing martyrdom for the cause of the advancement of social justice – just might be devastating.

Matthew spoke well and to the point, soothing his listeners, the incarnation of liberal toleration. William pumped his friend's hand warmly when he returned to his chair to loud applause.

"It's all over bar the shouting, I think," he whispered.

But Thaddeus Cohen surprised virtually everyone. He had a pleasant, diffident manner and a sympathetic style. His references and quotations were catholic, pointed and illuminating. Without conveying to the audience the feeling that it was being deliberately impressed, he exuded a moral earnestness which made anything less seem a failure to a rational human being. He was willing to admit the excesses of his own side and the inadequacy of its leaders, but he left the impression that, in spite of its dangers, there was no alternative to socialism if the lot of mankind were ever to be improved.

William was flustered. A surgically logical attack on the political platform of his adversaries would be useless against Cohen's gentle and persuasive presentation. Yet to outdo him as a spokesman of hope and faith in the human spirit would be impossible. William concentrated first on refuting some of Crosby's charges and then countered Cohen's arguments with a declaration of his own faith in the ability of the American system to produce the best results through competition, intellectual and economic. He felt he had played a good defensive game, but no more, and sat down supposing that he had been well beaten by Cohen.

Crosby was his opponents' rebuttal speaker. He began ferociously, sounding as if he now needed to beat Cohen as much as William and Matthew, asking the audience if they could identify an 'enemy of the people' amongst themselves that night. He glared around the room for several long seconds, as members of the audience squirmed in embarrassed silence and his dedicated supporters studied their shoes. Then he leaned forward and roared.

"He stands before you. He has just spoken in your midst. His name is William Lowell Kane." Gesturing with one hand towards where William sat without looking at him, he thundered: "His bank owns mines in which the workers die to give its owners an extra million a year in dividends. His bank supports the bloody, corrupt dictatorships of Latin America. Through his bank, the American Congress is bribed into crushing the small farmer. His bank . . ."

The tirade went on for several minutes. William sat in stony silence, occasionally jotting down a comment on his yellow legal pad. A few members of the audience had begun shouting "No." Crosby's supporters shouted loyally back. The officials began to look nervous.

Crosby's allotted time was nearly up. He raised his fist and said, "Gentlemen, I submit that not more than two hundred yards from this very room we have the answer to the plight of America. There stands the Widener Library, the greatest private library in the world. Here poor and immigrant scholars come, along with the best educated Americans, to increase the knowledge and prosperity of the world. Why does it exist? Because one rich playboy had the misfortune to set sail sixteen years ago on a pleasure boat called the *Titanic*. I suggest, ladies and gentlemen, that not until the people of America hand each and every member of the ruling class a ticket for his own private cabin on the *Titanic* of capitalism, will the hoarded wealth of this great continent be freed and devoted to the service of liberty, equality and progress."

As Matthew listened to Crosby's speech, his sentiments changed from exultation that, by this blunder, the victory had been secured for his side, through embarrassment at the behaviour of his adversary, to rage at the reference to the *Titanic*. He had no idea how William would respond to such provocation.

When some measure of silence had been restored, the

captain walked to the lectern and said: "Mr. William Lowell Kane."

William strode to the platform and looked out over the audience. An expectant hush filled the room.

"It is my opinion that the views expressed by Mr. Crosby do not merit a response."

He sat down. There was a moment of surprised silence – and then loud applause.

The captain returned to the platform, but appeared uncertain what to do. A voice from behind him broke the tension.

"If I may, Mr. Chairman, I would like to ask Mr. Kane if I might use his rebuttal time." It was Thaddeus Cohen.

William nodded his agreement to the captain.

Cohen walked to the lectern and blinked at the audience disarmingly. "It has long been true," he began, "that the greatest obstacle to the success of democratic socialism in the United States has been the extremism of some of its allies. Nothing could have exemplified this unfortunate fact more clearly than my colleague's speech tonight. The propensity to damage the progressive cause by calling for the physical extermination of those who oppose it might be understandable in a battle-hardened immigrant, a veteran of foreign struggles fiercer than our own. In America it is pathetic and inexcusable. Speaking for myself, I extend my sincere apologies to Mr. Kane."

This time the applause was instantaneous. Virtually the entire audience rose to its feet and clapped continuously.

William walked over to shake hands with Thaddeus Cohen. It was no surprise to either of them that William and Matthew won the vote by a margin of more than one hundred and fifty votes. The evening was over, and the audiences filed out into the silent, snow-covered paths, walking in the middle of the street, talking animatedly at the tops of their voices.

William insisted that Thaddeus Cohen should join him and Matthew for a drink. They set off together across Massachusetts Avenue, barely able to see where they going in the drifting snow, and came to a halt outside a big black door almost directly opposite Boylston Hall.

William opened it with his key and the three entered the vestibule.

Before the door shut behind him, Thaddeus Cohen spoke. "I'm afraid I won't be welcome here."

William looked startled for a second. "Nonsense. You're with me."

Matthew gave his friend a cautionary glance but saw that William was determined.

They went up the stairs and into a large room, comfortably but not luxuriously furnished, in which there were about a dozen young men sitting in armchairs or standing in small knots of two and three. As soon as William appeared in the doorway, the congratulations started.

"You were marvellous, William. That's exactly the way to treat those sort of people."

"Enter in triumph, 'Bolshi' slayer."

Thaddeus Cohen hung back, still half-shadowed by the doorway, but William had not forgotten him.

"And, gentlemen, may I present my worthy adversary, Mr. Thaddeus Cohen."

Cohen stepped forward hesitantly.

All noise ceased. A number of heads were averted, as if they were looking at the elm trees in the yard, their branches weighed down with new snow.

Finally, there was the crack of a floorboard as one young man left the room by another door. Then there was another departure. Without haste, without apparent agreement, the entire group filed out. The last to leave gave William a long look before he, too, turned on his heel and disappeared.

Matthew gazed at his companions in dismay. Thaddeus Cohen had turned a dull red and stood with his head bowed. William's lips were drawn together in the same tight cold fury that had been apparent when Crosby had made his reference to the *Titanic*.

Matthew touched his friend's arm. "We'd better go."

The three trudged off to William's rooms and silently drank some indifferent brandy.

When William woke in the morning, there was an envelope under his door. Inside there was a short note, from the chairman of the Porcellian Club informing him that "he hoped there would never be a recurrence of last night's, best forgotten, incident."

By lunchtime the chairman had received two letters of resignation.

After months of long, studious days, William and Matthew were almost ready – no one ever thinks he is quite ready – for their final examinations. For six days they answered questions and filled up sheets and sheets of the little books, and then they waited, not in vain for they both graduated as expected from Harvard in June of 1928.

A week later it was announced that William was the winner of the President's Mathematics Prize. He wished his father had been alive to witness the presentation ceremony. Matthew managed an honest 'C', which came as a relief to him and no great surprise to anyone else. Neither had any interest in further education, both having elected to join the real world as quickly as possible.

William's bank account in New York edged over the million dollar mark eight days before he left Harvard. It was then that he discussed in greater detail with Matthew his long-term plan to gain control of Lester's Bank by merging it with Kane and Cabot.

Matthew was enthusiastic about the idea and confessed, "That's about the only way I'll ever improve on what my old man will undoubtedly leave me when he dies."

On graduation day, Alan Lloyd, now in his sixtieth year, came to Harvard. After the graduation ceremony, William took his guest for tea on the square. Alan eyed the tall young man affectionately.

"And what do you intend to do now that you have put Harvard behind you?"

"I'm going to join Charles Lester's bank in New York and gain some experience before I come to Kane and Cabot in a few years' time."

"But you've been living in Lester's bank since you were twelve years old, William. Why don't you come straight to us now? We would appoint you as a director immediately."

William said nothing. Alan Lloyd's offer came as a total surprise. With all his ambition, it had never occurred to him, even for a moment, that he might be invited to be a director of the bank before he was twenty-five, the age at which his father had achieved that distinction.

Alan Lloyd waited for his reply. It was not forthcoming.

"Well, I must say, William, it's most unlike you to be rendered speechless by anything."

"But I never imagined you would invite me to join the board before my twenty-fifth birthday, when my father . . ."

"It's true your father was elected when he was twenty-five. However, that's no reason to prohibit you from joining the board before then if the other directors support the idea, and I know that they do. In any case, there are personal reasons why I should like to see you a director as soon as possible. When I retire from the bank in five years' time, we must be sure of electing the right chairman. You will be in a stronger position to influence that decision if you have been working for Kane and Cabot during those five years rather than as a grand functionary at Lester's. Well, my boy, will you join the board?"

It was the second time that day that William wished his father were still alive.

"I should be delighted to accept, sir," he said.

Alan looked up at William. "That's the first time you've called me 'sir' since we played golf together. I shall have to watch you very carefully."

William smiled.

"Good," said Alan Lloyd, "that's settled then. You'll be a junior director in charge of investments, working directly under Tony Simmons."

"Can I appoint my own assistant?" asked William.

Alan Lloyd looked at him quizzically. "Matthew Lester, no doubt?"

"Yes."

"No. I don't want him doing in our bank what you intended to do in theirs. Thomas Cohen should have taught you that."

William said nothing but never underestimated Alan again.

Charles Lester laughed when William repeated the conversation word for word to him.

"I'm sorry to hear you won't be coming to us, even as a spy," he said genially, "but I have no doubt you'll end up here some day – in one capacity or another."

Book Three

When William started work at [illegible]
[illegible] in September [illegible] he felt for the first time in his life
that he was doing something really [illegible]
[illegible]
[illegible]. From the [illegible] that William
arrived, [illegible]

[illegible]
responsibility [illegible]
of his work, in particular, private investments in small businesses [illegible] and any [illegible] he recommended a division
[illegible] William's official
duties was to make a monthly report on the investments to
[illegible] at a [illegible] meeting of the board. The
[illegible]

[illegible]
[illegible] he must have been a hell of a man to have married [illegible]
[illegible]. There was ample room left on the walls for
his own portrait.

William conducted himself during those early months at
the bank with caution, and his fellow board members soon
came to [illegible] his judgement and follow his recommendations
with few exceptions, as it turned out [illegible]
[illegible] among the first that William ever gave. On the
first occasion, a Mr [illegible] sought a loan from the bank to
invest in [illegible] pictures, but the board refused to see that

15

When William started work as a junior director of Kane and Cabot in September, 1928, he felt for the first time in his life that he was doing something really worthwhile. He began his career in a small oak-panelled office next to Tony Simmons, the bank's director of finance. From the week that William arrived, he knew without a word being spoken that Tony Simmons was hoping to succeed Alan Lloyd as chairman of the bank.

The bank's entire investment programme was Simmons' responsibility. He quickly delegated to William some aspects of his work; in particular, private investment in small businesses, land, and any other outside entrepreneurial activities in which the bank became involved. Among William's official duties was to make a monthly report on the investments he wished to recommend, at a full meeting of the board. The fourteen board members met once a month in a larger oak-panelled room, dominated at both ends by portraits, one of William's father, the other of his grandfather. William had never known his grandfather, but had always considered he must have been a 'hell of a man' to have married Grandmother Kane. There was ample room left on the walls for his own portrait.

William conducted himself during those early months at the bank with caution, and his fellow board members soon came to respect his judgment and follow his recommendations with rare exceptions. As it turned out, the advice they rejected was among the best that William ever gave. On the first occasion, a Mr. Mayer sought a loan from thé bank to invest in 'talking pictures' but the board refused to see that the notion had any merit or future. Another time, a Mr. Paley came to William with an ambitious plan for United, the radio network. Alan Lloyd, who had about as much respect for telegraphy as for telepathy, would have nothing to do with the scheme. The board supported Alan's views, and Louis B. Mayer later headed M.G.M. and William Paley the company that was to become C.B.S. William believed in his own judgment and backed both men with money from his trust and, like his father, never informed the recipients of his support.

One of the more unpleasant aspects of William's day-to-day work was the handling of the liquidations and bankruptcies of clients who had borrowed large sums from the bank and had subsequently found themselves unable to repay their loans. William was not by nature a soft person, as Henry Osborne had learned to his cost, but insisting that old and respected clients liquidate their stocks and even sell their homes did not make for easy sleeping at nights. William soon learned that these clients fell into two distinct categories: those who looked upon bankruptcy as a part of everyday business and those who were appalled by the very word and who would spend the rest of their lives trying to repay every penny they had borrowed. William found it natural to be tough with the first category but was almost always far more lenient with the second, with the grudging approval of Tony Simmons.

It was during such a case that William broke one of the bank's golden rules and became personally involved with a client. Her name was Katherine Brookes, and her husband, Max Brookes, had borrowed over a million dollars from Kane and Cabot to invest in the Florida land boom of 1925, an investment William would never have backed had he then been working at the bank. Max Brookes had, however, been something of a hero in Massachusetts as one of the new intrepid breed of balloonists and flyers, and a close friend of Charles Lindbergh into the bargain. Brookes' tragic death when the small plane he was piloting, at a height of all of ten feet above the ground, hit a tree only a hundred yards after take-off was reported in the press across the length and breadth of America as a national loss.

William, acting for the bank, immediately took over the Brookes estate, which was already insolvent, dissolved it and tried to cut the bank's losses by selling all the land held in Florida except for two acres on which the family home stood. The bank's loss was still over three hundred thousand dollars. Some directors were slightly critical of William's snap decision to sell off the land, a decision with which Tony Simmons had not agreed. William had Simmons' disapproval of his actions entered on the minutes and was in a position to point out some months later, that if they had held on to the land, the bank would have lost most of its original investment of one million. This demonstration of foresight did not endear him to Tony Simmons although it made the rest of the board conscious of William's uncommon perspicacity

When William had liquidated everything the bank held in Max Brookes' name, he turned his attention to Mrs. Brookes, who was under a personal guarantee for her late husband's debts. Although William always tried to secure such a guarantee on any loans granted by the bank, the undertaking of such an obligation was not a course that he ever recommended to friends, however confident they might feel about the venture on which they were about to embark, as failure almost invariably caused great distress to the guarantor.

William wrote a formal letter to Mrs. Brookes, suggesting that she make an appointment to discuss the position. He had read the Brookes file conscientiously and knew that she was only twenty-two years old, a daughter of Andrew Higginson, the head of an old and distinguished Boston family, and that she had substantial assets of her own. He did not relish the thought of requiring her to make them over to the bank, but he and Tony Simmons were, for once, in agreement on the line to be taken, so he steeled himself for an unpleasant encounter.

What William had not bargained for was Katherine Brookes herself. In later life, he could always recall in great detail the events of that morning. He had had some harsh words with Tony Simmons about a substantial investment in copper and tin, which he wished to recommend to the board. Industrial demand for the two metals was rising steadily, and William was confident that a world shortage was certain to follow. Tony Simmons could not agree with him, insisting they should invest more cash in the stock market, and the matter was still uppermost in William's mind when his secretary ushered Mrs. Brookes into his office. With one tentative smile, she removed copper, tin and all other world shortages from his mind. Before she could sit down, he was around on the other side of his desk, settling her into a chair, simply to assure himself that she would not vanish, like a mirage, on closer inspection. Never had William encountered a woman he considered half as lovely as Katherine Brookes. Her long fair hair fell in loose and wayward curls to her shoulders, and little wisps escaped enchantingly from her hat and clung around her temples. The fact that she was in mourning in no way detracted from the beauty of her slim figure. The fine bone structure ensured that she was a woman who was going to look lovely at every age. Her brown eyes were enormous. They were also, unmistakably, apprehensive of him and what he was about to say.

William strove for his business tone of voice. "Mrs. Brookes, may I say how sorry I was to learn of your husband's death and how much I regret the necessity of asking you to come here today."

Two lies in a single sentence that would have been the truth five minutes before. He waited to hear her speak.

"Thank you, Mr. Kane." Her voice was soft and had a gentle, low pitch. "I am aware of my obligations to your bank and I assure you that I will do everything in my power to meet them."

William said nothing, hoping she would go on speaking. She did not, so he outlined how he had disposed of Max Brookes' estate. She listened with downcast eyes.

"Now, Mrs. Brookes, you acted as guarantor for your husband's loan and that brings us to the question of your personal assets." He consulted his file. "You have some eighty thousand dollars in investments – your own family money, I believe – and seventeen thousand four hundred and fifty-six dollars in your personal account."

She looked up. "Your grasp of my financial position is commendable, Mr. Kane. You should add, however, Buckhurst Park, our house in Florida, which was in Max's name, and some quite valuable jewelry of my own. I estimate that all together I am worth the three hundred thousand dollars you still require, and I have made arrangements to realise the full amount as soon as possible."

There was only the slightest tremor in her voice; William gazed at her in admiration.

"Mrs. Brookes, the bank has no intention of relieving you of your every last possession. With your agreement we would like to sell your stocks and bonds. Everything else you mentioned, including the house, we consider should remain in your possession."

She hesitated. "I appreciate your generosity, Mr. Kane. However, I have no wish to remain under any obligation to your bank or to leave my husband's name under a cloud." The little tremor again, but quickly suppressed. "Anyway, I have decided to sell the house in Florida and return to my parents' home as soon as possible."

William's pulse quickened to hear that she would be coming back to Boston. "In that case, perhaps we can reach some agreement about the proceeds of the sale," he said.

"We can do that now," she said flatly. "You must have the entire amount."

William played for another meeting. "Don't let's make too hasty a decision. I think it might be wise to consult my colleagues and discuss this with you again at a later date."

She shrugged slightly. "As you wish. I don't really care about the money either way, and I wouldn't want to put you to any inconvenience."

William blinked. "Mrs. Brookes, I must confess to have been surprised by your magnanimous attitude. At least allow me the pleasure of taking you to lunch."

She smiled for the first time, revealing an unsuspected dimple in her right cheek. William gazed at it in delight and did his utmost to provoke its reappearance over a long lunch at the Ritz. By the time he returned to his desk, it was well past three o'clock.

"Long lunch, William," commented Tony Simmons.

"Yes, the Brookes problem turned out to be trickier than I had expected."

"It looked fairly straightforward to me when I went over the papers," said Simmons. "She isn't complaining about our offer, is she? I thought we were being rather generous in the circumstances."

"Yes, she thought so too. I had to talk her out of divesting herself of her last dollar to swell our reserves."

Tony Simmons stared. "That doesn't sound like the William Kane we all know and love so well. Still, there has never been a better time for the bank to be magnanimous."

William grimaced. Since the day of his arrival, he and Tony Simmons had been in growing disagreement about where the stock market was heading. The Dow-Jones had been moving steadily upward since Herbert Hoover's election to the White House in November 1928. In fact, only ten days later, the New York Stock Exchange had a record of over six million shares volume in one day. But William was convinced that the upward trend, fuelled by the large influx of money from the automobile industry, would result in prices inflating to the point of instability. Tony Simmons, on the other hand, was confident that the boom would continue so that when William advocated caution at board meetings he was invariably overruled. However, with his trust money, he was free to follow his own intuition, and started investing heavily in land, gold, commodities and even in some carefully selected Impressionist paintings, leaving only fifty per cent of his cash in stocks.

When the Federal Reserve Bank of New York put out an edict declaring that they would not re-discount loans to those banks which were releasing money to their customers for the sole purpose of speculation, William considered that the first nail had been driven into the speculator's coffin. He immediately reviewed the bank's lending programme and estimated that Kane and Cabot had over twenty-six million dollars out on such loans. He begged Tony Simmons to call in these amounts, certain that, with such a government regulation in operation, stock prices would inevitably fall in the long term. They nearly had a stand-up fight at the monthly board meeting, and William was voted down by twelve to two.

On March 21st, 1929, Blair and Company announced its consolidation with the Bank of America, the third in a series of bank mergers which seemed to point to a brighter tomorrow, and on March 25th, Tony Simmons sent William a note pointing out to him that the market had broken through to yet another all time record, and proceeded to put more of the bank's money into stocks. By then, William had rearranged his capital so that only twenty-five per cent was in the stock market, a move that had already cost him over two million dollars – and a troubled reprimand from Alan Lloyd.

"I hope to goodness you know what you're doing, William."

"Alan, I've been beating the stock market since I was fourteen, and I've always done it by bucking the trend."

But as the market continued to climb through the summer of 1929, even William stopped selling, wondering if Tony Simmons' judgment was, in fact, correct.

As the time for Alan Lloyd's retirement drew nearer, Tony Simmons' clear intent to succeed him as chairman began to take on the look of a *fait accompli.* The prospect troubled William, who considered Simmons' thinking was far too conventional. He was always a yard behind the rest of the market, which is fine during boom years when things are going well, but can be dangerous for a bank in leaner, more competitive times. A shrewd investor, in William's eyes, did not invariably run with the herd, thundering or otherwise, but worked out in advance in which direction the herd would be turning next. William had already decided that future investment in the stock market still looked risky while Tony Simmons was convinced that America was entering a golden era.

William's other problem was simply that Tony Simmons was only thirty-nine years old and that meant that William could not hope to become chairman of Kane and Cabot for at least another twenty-six years. That hardly fitted into what they had called at Harvard 'one's career pattern'.

Meanwhile, the image of Katherine Brookes remained clearly in his mind. He wrote to her as often as he could about the sale of her stocks and bonds: formal, typewritten letters which elicited no more than formal handwritten responses. She must have thought he was the most conscientious banker in the world. Had she realised her file was becoming as large as any under William's control she might have thought about it – or at least him – more carefully. Early in the autumn she wrote to say she had found a firm buyer for the Florida estate. William wrote to request that she allow him to negotiate the terms of the sale on the bank's behalf, and she agreed.

He travelled down to Florida in early September 1929. Mrs. Brookes met him at the station and he was overwhelmed by how much more beautiful she appeared in person than in his memory. The slight wind blew her black dress against her body as she stood waiting on the platform, leaving a profile that ensured that every man except William would look at her a second time. William's eyes never left her.

She was still in mourning and her manner towards him was so reserved and correct that William initially despaired of making any impression on her. He spun out the negotiations with the farmer who was purchasing Buckhurst Park for as long as he could and persuaded Katherine Brookes to accept one-third of the agreed sale price while the bank took two-thirds. Finally, after the legal papers were signed, he could find no more excuses for not returning to Boston. He invited her to dinner at his hotel, resolved to reveal something of his feelings for her. Not for the first time, she took him by surprise. Before he had broached the subject, she asked him, twirling her glass to avoid looking at him, if he would like to stay over at Buckhurst Park for a few days.

"A sort of holiday for us both." She blushed; William remained silent.

As Abel walked down Michigan Avenue on his way back to the Stevens it started to drizzle. He found himself humming 'Singing in the Rain'. He took the lift up to his room and called William Kane to ask for an extension until the following Monday, telling him he hoped to have found a buyer. Kane seemed reluctant but eventually agreed.

"Bastard," Abel repeated several times as he put the phone back on the hook. "Just give me a little time, Kane. You'll live to regret killing Davis Leroy."

Abel sat on the end of his bed, his fingers tapping on the rail, wondering how he could pass the time waiting for Monday. He wandered down into the hotel lobby. There she was again, the waitress who had served him at lunch, now on tea duty in the Tropical Garden. Abel's curiosity got the better of him, and he went over and took a seat at the far side of the room. She came up.

"Good afternoon, sir," she said. "Would you like some tea?" The same familiar smile again.

"We know each other, don't we?" said Abel.

"Yes, we do, Wladek."

Abel cringed at the sound of the name and reddened slightly, remembering how the short fair hair had been long and smooth and the veiled eyes had been so inviting. "Zaphia, we came to America on the same ship. Of course, you went to Chicago. What are you doing here?"

"I work here, as you can see. Would you like some tea, sir?" Her Polish accent warmed Abel.

"Have dinner with me tonight," he said.

"I can't, Wladek. We're not allowed to go out with the customers. If we do, we automatically lose our jobs."

"I'm not a customer," said Abel. "I'm an old friend."

"Who was going to come and visit me in Chicago as soon as he had settled down, and when you did come you didn't even remember I was here," said Zaphia.

"I know, I know. Forgive me. Zaphia, have dinner with me tonight. Just this once," said Abel.

"Just this once," she repeated.

"Meet me at Brundage's at seven o'clock. Would that suit you?"

Zaphia flushed at the name. It was probably the most expensive restaurant in Chicago, and she would have been nervous to be there as a waitress, let alone as a customer.

"No, let's go somewhere less grand, Wladek."

"Where?" said Abel.

"Do you know The Sausage on the corner of Forty-third?"

"No, I don't," he admitted, "but I'll find it. Seven o'clock."

"Seven o'clock, Wladek. That will be lovely. By the way, do you want any tea?"

"No, I think I'll skip it," said Abel.

She smiled and walked away. He sat watching her serve tea for several minutes. She was much prettier than he had remembered her being. Perhaps killing time until Monday wasn't going to be so bad after all.

The Sausage brought back all of Abel's worst memories of his first days in America. He sipped a cold ginger beer while he waited for Zaphia and watched with professional disapproval as the waiters slapped the food around. He was unable to decide which looked worse: the service or the food. Zaphia was nearly twenty minutes late by the time she appeared in the doorway, as smart as a band-box in a crisp yellow dress that looked as if it had been recently taken up a few inches to conform with the latest fashion, but still revealed how appealing her formerly slight body had become. Her grey eyes searched the tables for Wladek, and her pink cheeks reddened as she became conscious of other men's eyes upon her.

"Good evening, Wladek," she said in Polish.

Abel rose and offered her his chair near the fire. "I am so glad you could make it," he replied in English.

She looked perplexed for a moment, then, in English, she said, "I'm sorry I'm late."

"Oh, I hadn't noticed. Would you like something to drink, Zaphia?"

"No, thank you."

Neither of them spoke for a moment, and then they both tried to talk at once.

"I'd forgotten how pretty . . . " said Abel.

"How have you . . . " said Zaphia.

She smiled shyly, and Abel wanted to touch her. He remembered so well experiencing the same reaction the first time he had ever seen her, over eight years before.

"How's George?" she asked.

"I haven't seen him for over two years," replied Abel, suddenly feeling guilty. "I've been stuck working in a hotel here in Chicago, and then . . . "

"I know," said Zaphia. "Somebody burnt the place down."

"Why didn't you ever come over and say hello?" asked Abel.

"I didn't think you'd remember, Wladek, and I was right."

"Then how did you ever recognise me?" said Abel. "I've put on so much weight."

"The silver band," she said simply.

Abel looked down at his wrist and laughed. "I have a lot to thank my band for, and now I can add that it has brought us back together."

She avoided his eyes. "What are you doing now that you no longer have a hotel to run?"

"I'm looking for a job," said Abel, not wanting to intimidate her with the fact that he'd been offered the chance to manage the Stevens.

"There's a big job coming up at the Stevens. My boyfriend told me."

"Your boyfriend told you?" said Abel, repeating each painful word.

"Yes," she said, "the hotel will soon be looking for a new assistant manager. Why don't you apply for the job? I'm sure you'd have a good chance of getting it, Wladek. I always knew you would be a success in America."

"I might well apply," Abel said. "It was kind of you to think of me. Why doesn't your boyfriend apply?"

"Oh, no, he's far too junior to be considered; he's only a waiter in the dining room with me."

Suddenly Abel wanted to change places with him.

"Shall we have dinner?" he said.

"I'm not used to eating out," Zaphia said. She gazed at the menu in indecision. Abel, suddenly aware she still could not read English, ordered for them both.

She ate with relish and was full of praise for the indifferent food. Abel found her uncritical enthusiasm a tonic after the bored sophistication of Melanie. They exchanged the history of their lives in America. Zaphia had started in domestic service and progressed to being a waitress at the Stevens where she had stayed put for six years. Abel told her of all his experiences until finally she glanced at his watch.

"Look at the time, Wladek," she said, "it's past eleven and I'm on first breakfast call at six tomorrow."

Abel had not noticed the four hours pass. He would have happily sat there talking to her for the rest of the night, soothed by the admiration which she confessed so artlessly.

"May I see you again, Zaphia?" he asked, as they walked back to the Stevens arm-in-arm.

"If you want to, Wladek."

They stopped at the servants' entrance at the back of the hotel.

"This is where I go in," she said. "If you were to become the assistant manager, Wladek, you'd be allowed to go in by the front entrance."

"Would you mind calling me Abel?" he asked her.

"Abel?" she said, as if she were trying the name on like a new glove. "But your name is Wladek."

"It was, but it isn't any longer. My name is Abel Rosnovski."

"Abel's a funny name, but it suits you," she said. "Thank you for dinner, Abel. It was lovely to see you again. Good night."

"Good night, Zaphia," he said, and she was gone.

He watched her disappear through the servants' entrance, then he walked slowly around the block and into the hotel by the front entrance. Suddenly – and not for the first time in his life – he felt very lonely.

Abel spent the weekend thinking about Zaphia and the images associated with her – the stench of the steerage quarters, the confused queues of immigrants on Ellis Island

and, above all, their brief but passionate encounter in the lifeboat. He took all his meals in the hotel restaurant to be near her and to study the boyfriend. He came to the conclusion that he must be the young, pimply one. He thought he had pimples, he hoped he had pimples, yes, he did have pimples. He was, regrettably, the best-looking boy among the waiters, pimples notwithstanding.

Abel wanted to take Zaphia out on Saturday, but she was working all day. Nevertheless, he managed to accompany her to church on Sunday morning and listened with mingled nostalgia and exasperation to the Polish priest intoning the unforgotten words of the Mass. It was the first time Abel had been in a church since his days at the castle in Poland. At that time he had yet to see or endure the cruelty which now made it impossible for him to believe in any benevolent deity. His reward for attending church came when Zaphia allowed him to hold her hand as they walked back to the hotel together.

"Have you thought any more about the position at the Stevens?" she enquired.

"I'll know first thing tomorrow morning what their final decision is."

"Oh, I'm so glad, Abel. I'm sure you would make a very good assistant manager."

"Thank you," said Abel, realising they had been talking at cross purposes.

"Would you like to have supper with my cousins tonight?" Zaphia asked. "I always spend Sunday evening with them."

"Yes, I'd like that very much."

Zaphia's cousins lived right near The Sausage itself, in the heart of the city. They were very impressed when she arrived with a Polish friend who drove a new Buick. The family, as Zaphia called them, consisted of two sisters, Katya and Janina, and Katya's husband, Janek. Abel presented the sisters with a bunch of roses and then sat down and answered, in fluent Polish, all their questions about his future prospects. Zaphia was obviously embarrassed, but Abel knew the same would be required of any new boyfriend in any Polish-American household. He made an effort to play down his progress since his early days in the butcher shop as he was conscious of Janek's envious eyes never leaving him. Katya served a simple Polish meal of *pierogi* and *bigos* which Abel would have eaten with a good deal more relish fifteen years earlier. He gave Janek up as a bad job and concentrated on making the sisters approve of him. It looked as though they did. Perhaps they also approved of the pimply youth. No, they couldn't; he wasn't even Polish – or maybe he was – Abel didn't even know his name and had never heard him speak.

On the way back to the Stevens, Zaphia asked, with a flash of the coquettishness he remembered, if it was considered safe to drive a motor car and hold a lady's hand at the same time. Abel laughed and put his hand back on the steering wheel for the rest of the drive back to the hotel.

"Will you have time to see me tomorrow?" he asked.

"I hope so, Abel," she said. "Perhaps by then you'll be my boss. Good luck anyway."

He smiled to himself as he watched her go through the back door, wondering how she would feel if she knew the real consequences of tomorrow's decision. He did not move until she disappeared through the service entrance.

"Assistant manager," he said, laughing out loud as he climbed into bed, wondering what Curtis Fenton's news would bring in the morning, trying to put Zaphia out of his mind as he threw his pillow on the floor. He woke a few minutes before five the next day. The room was still dark when he called for the early edition of the *Tribune*, and went through the motions of reading the financial section. He was dressed and ready for breakfast when the restaurant opened at seven o'clock. Zaphia was not serving in the main dining room that morning, but the pimply boyfriend was, which Abel took to be a bad omen. After breakfast he returned to his room; had he but known, only five minutes before Zaphia came on duty. He checked his tie in the mirror for the twentieth time and once again looked at his watch. He estimated that if he walked very slowly, he would arrive at the bank as the doors were opening. In fact, he arrived five minutes early and walked once around the block, staring aimlessly into store windows at expensive jewelry and new radios and hand-tailored suits. Would he ever be able to afford clothes like that? he wondered. He arrived back at the bank at four minutes past nine.

"Mr. Fenton is not free at the moment. Can you come back in half an hour or would you prefer to wait?" the secretary asked.

"I'll come back," said Abel, not wishing to appear overanxious.

It was the longest thirty minutes he could remember since he'd been in Chicago. He had studied every shop window on La Salle Street, even the women's clothes, which made him think happily of Zaphia.

On his return to Continental Trust the secretary informed him, "Mr. Fenton will see you now."

Abel walked into the bank manager's office, feeling his hands sweating.

"Good morning, Mr. Rosnovski. Do have a seat."

Curtis Fenton took a file out of his desk which Abel could see had 'Confidential' written across the cover.

"Now," he began, "I hope you will find my news is to your liking. The principal concerned is willing to go ahead with the purchase of the hotels on what I can only describe as favourable terms."

"God Almighty," said Abel.

Curtis Fenton pretended not to hear him and continued. "In fact, most favourable terms. He will be responsible for putting up the full two million required to clear Mr. Leroy's debt while at the same time he will form a new company with you in which the shares will be split sixty per cent to him and forty per cent to you. Your forty per cent is therefore valued at eight hundred thousand dollars, which will be treated as a loan to you by the new company, a loan which will be made for a term not to exceed ten years, at four per cent, which can be paid off from the company profits at the same rate. That is to say, if the company were to make in any one year a profit of one hundred thousand dollars, forty thousand of that profit would be set against your eight hundred thousand debt, plus the four per cent interest. If you clear the loan of eight hundred thousand in under ten years you will be given the one-time option to buy the remaining sixty per cent of the company for a further three million dollars. This would give my client a first-class return on his investment and you the opportunity to own the Richmond Group outright.

"In addition to this, you will receive a salary of three thousand dollars per annum, and your position as president of the group will give you complete day-to-day control of the hotels. You will be asked to refer back to me only on matters concerning finance. I have been entrusted with the task of reporting direct to your principal, and he has asked me to represent his interests on the board of the new Richmond Group. I have been happy to comply with this stipulation. My client does not wish to be involved personally. As I have said before, there might be a conflict of professional interests for him in this transaction, which I am sure you will thoroughly understand. He also insists that you will at no time make any attempt to discover his identity. He will give you fourteen days to consider his terms, on which there can be no negotiation, as he considers, and I must agree with him, that he is striking a more than fair bargain."

Abel could not speak.

"Pray do say something, Mr. Rosnovski."

"I don't need fourteen days to make a decision," said Abel finally. "I accept your client's terms. Please thank him and tell him I will certainly respect his request for anonymity."

"That's splendid," said Curtis Fenton, permitting himself a wry smile. "Now, a few small points. The accounts for all the hotels in the group will be placed with Continental Trust affiliates, and the main account will be here in this office under my direct control. I will, in turn, receive one thousand dollars a year as a director of the new company."

"I'm glad you're going to get something out of the deal," said Abel.

"I beg your pardon?" said the banker.

"I'll be pleased to be working with you, Mr. Fenton."

"Your principal has also placed two hundred and fifty thousand dollars on deposit with the bank to be used as the day-to-day finance for the running of the hotels during the next few months. This will also be regarded as a loan at four per cent. You are to advise me if this amount turns out to be insufficient for your needs. I consider it would enhance your reputation with my client if you found the two hundred and fifty thousand to be sufficient."

"I shall bear that in mind," said Abel, solemnly trying to imitate the banker's locution.

Curtis Fenton opened a desk drawer and produced a large Cuban cigar.

"Do you smoke?"

"Yes," said Abel, who had never smoked a cigar before in his life.

He coughed himself down La Salle Street all the way back to the Stevens. David Maxton was standing proprietorially in the foyer of the hotel as Abel arrived. Abel stubbed out his half-finished cigar with some relief and walked over to him.

"Mr. Rosnovski, you look a happy man this morning."

"I am, sir, and I am only sorry that I will not be working for you as the manager of this hotel."

"Then so am I, Mr. Rosnovski, but frankly the news doesn't surprise me."

"Thank you for everything," said Abel, injecting as much feeling as he could into the little phrase and the look with which he accompanied it.

He left David Maxton and went into the dining room in search of Zaphia, but she had already gone off duty. Abel took the lift to his room, re-lit the cigar, took a cautious puff, and called Kane and Cabot. A secretary put him through to William Kane.

"Mr. Kane, I have found it possible to raise the money required for me to take over ownership of the Richmond Group. A Mr. Curtis Fenton of Continental Trust will be in touch with you later today to provide you with the details. There will therefore be no necessity to place the hotels for sale on the open market."

There was a short pause. Abel thought with satisfaction how galling his news must be to William Kane.

"Thank you for keeping me informed, Mr. Rosnovski.

May I say how delighted I am that you found someone to back you? I wish you every success for the future."

"Which is more than I wish you, Mr. Kane."

Abel put the phone down, lay on his bed and thought about that future.

"One day," he promised the ceiling, "I am going to buy your goddamn bank and make you want to jump out of a hotel bedroom on the twelfth floor." He picked up the phone again and asked the girl on the switchboard to get him Mr. Henry Osborne at Great Western Casualty.

19

William put the telephone back on the hook, more amused than annoyed by Abel Rosnovski's pugnacious approach. He was sorry that he had been unable to persuade the bank to support the little Pole who believed so strongly that he could pull the Richmond Group through. He fulfilled his remaining responsibilities by informing the financial committee that Abel Rosnovski had found a backer, preparing the legal documents for the take-over of the hotels, and then finally closing the bank's file on the Richmond Group.

William was delighted when Matthew arrived in Boston a few days later to take up his position as manager of the bank's investment department. Charles Lester made no secret of the fact that any professional expertise gained in a rival establishment could do the boy no harm in his long-term preparation to be chairman of Lester's. William's work load was instantly halved but his time became even more fully occupied. He found himself dragged, protesting in mock horror, on to tennis courts and into swimming pools at every available free moment; only Matthew's suggestion of a ski trip to Vermont brought a determined "No" from William, but the sudden activity at least served to somewhat alleviate his loneliness and impatience to be with Kate.

Matthew was frankly incredulous. "I must meet the woman who can make William Kane daydream at a board meeting which is discussing whether the bank should buy more gold."

"Wait till you see her, Matthew. I think you'll agree she's a better investment than gold."

"I believe you. I just don't want to be the one to tell Susan. She still thinks you're the only man in the world."

William laughed. It had never crossed his mind.

The little pile of letters from Kate, which had been growing weekly, lay in the locked drawer of William's bureau in the Red House. He read them over again and again and soon knew them all virtually by heart. At last the one he had been waiting for came, appropriately dated.

Buckhurst Park
14 February 1930

Dearest William,

Finally I have packed up, sold off, given away or otherwise disposed of everything left here and I shall be coming up to Boston in a tea chest on the nineteenth. I am almost frightened at the thought of seeing you again. What if this whole marvellous enchantment bursts like a bubble in the cold of a winter on the Eastern seaboard? Dear God, I hope not. I can't be sure how I would have gotten through these lonely months but for you.

With love,
Kate

The night before Kate was due to arrive, William promised himself that he would not rush her into anything that either of them might later regret. It was impossible for him to assess to what extent her feelings had developed in a transient state of mind engendered by her husband's death, as he told Matthew.

"Stop being so pathetic," said Matthew. "You're in love, and you may as well face the fact."

When he first spotted Kate at the station, William almost abandoned his cautious intentions there and then in the joy of watching that simple smile light up her face. He pushed towards her through the throng of travellers and clasped her so firmly in his arms that she could barely breathe.

"Welcome home, Kate."

William was about to kiss her when she drew away. He was a little surprised.

"William, I don't think you've met my parents."

That night William dined with Kate's family and then saw her every day that he could escape from the bank's problems and Matthew's tennis racquet, even if only for a couple of hours. After Matthew had met Kate for the first time, he offered William all his gold shares in exchange for one Kate.

"I never undersell," replied William.

"Then I insist you tell me," demanded Matthew, "where you find someone as valuable as Kate?"

"In the liquidation department, where else?" replied William.

"Turn her into an asset, William, quickly, because if you don't, you can be sure I will."

Kane and Cabot's net loss from the 1929 crash came out at over seven million dollars, which turned out to be about average for a bank their size. Many not much smaller banks had gone under, and William found himself conducting a sustained holding operation through 1930 which kept him under constant pressure.

When Franklin D. Roosevelt was elected President of the United States on a ticket of relief, recovery and reform, William feared that the New Deal would have little to offer Kane and Cabot. Business picked up very slowly, and William found himself planning only tentatively for expansion.

Meanwhile Tony Simmons, still running the London office, had broadened the scope of its activities and made a respectable profit for Kane and Cabot during his first two years. His results looked all the better against those of William, who had barely been able to break even during the same period.

Late in 1932, Alan Lloyd recalled Tony Simmons to Boston to make a full report to the board on the bank's activities in London. No sooner had Simmons reappeared than he announced his intention of running for the chairmanship when Alan Lloyd retired in fifteen months' time. William was completely taken by surprise, for he had dismissed Simmons' chances when he had disappeared to London under a small cloud. It seemed to William unfair that that cloud had been dispelled, not by Simmons' acuity, but simply by dint of the fact that the English economy had some bright spots and was a little less paralysed than American business during the same period.

Tony Simmons returned to London for a further successful year and addressed the first board meeting, after his return, in a blaze of glory, with the announcement that the final third year's figures for the London office would show a profit of over a million dollars, a new record. William had to announce a considerably smaller profit for the same period. The abruptness of Tony Simmons' return to favour left William with only a few months in which to persuade the board that they should support him before his opponent's momentum became unstoppable.

Kate listened for hours to William's problems, occasionally offering an understanding comment, a sympathetic reply or chastising him for being over dramatic. Matthew, acting as William's eyes and ears, reported that the voting would fall, as far as was ascertainable, fifty-fifty, split between those who considered that William was too young to hold such a responsible post and those who still held Tony Simmons to blame for the extent of the bank's losses in 1929. It seemed that most of the non-executive members of the board, who had not worked directly with William, would be more influenced by the age difference between the two contenders than any of the single factors. Again and again Matthew heard: "William's time will come." Once, tentatively, he played the role of Satan the tempter to William: "With your holdings in the bank, William, you could remove the entire board, replace them with men of your own choosing and get yourself elected chairman."

William was only too aware of that route to the top, but he had already dismissed such tactics without needing seriously to consider them; he wished to become chairman solely on his own merits. That was, after all, the way his father had achieved the position and it was nothing less than Kate would expect of him.

On January 2nd, 1934, Alan Lloyd circulated to every member the notice of a board meeting that would be held on his sixty-fifth birthday, its sole purpose being to elect his successor. As the day for the crucial vote drew nearer, Matthew found himself carrying the investment department almost single-handed, and Kate found herself feeding them both while they went over the latest state of his campaign again and again. Matthew did not complain once about the extra work load that was placed on him while William spent hours planning his bid to capture the chair. William, conscious that Matthew had nothing to gain by his success, as he would one day take over his father's bank in New York – a far bigger proposition than Kane and Cabot – hoped a time might come when he could offer Matthew the same unselfish support.

It was to come sooner than he imagined.

When Alan Lloyd's sixty-fifth birthday was celebrated, all seventeen members of the board were present. The meeting was opened by the chairman, who made a farewell speech of only fourteen minutes, which William thought would never come to an end. Tony Simmons was nervously tapping the yellow legal pad in front of him with his pen, occasionally looking up at William. Neither was listening to Alan's speech. At last Alan sat down, to loud applause, or as loud as is appropriate to sixteen Boston bankers. When the clapping had died away, Alan Lloyd rose for the last time as chairman of Kane and Cabot.

"And now, gentlemen, we must elect my successor. The board is presented with two outstanding candidates, the director of our overseas division, Mr. Anthony Simmons, and the director of the American investment department, Mr. William Kane. They are both well known to you, gentlemen, and I have no intention of speaking in detail on their respective merits. Instead I have asked each candidate to address the board on how he would see the future of Kane and Cabot were he to be elected chairman."

William rose first, as had been agreed between the two contestants the night before on the toss of a coin, and addressed the board for twenty minutes, explaining in detail that it would be his ambition to move into new fields where the bank had not previously ventured. In particular he wanted to broaden the bank's base and to get out of a depressed New England, moving close to the centre of banking which he believed was now in New York. He even mentioned the possibility of opening a holding company which might specialise in commercial banking, at which the heads of some of the older board members shook in disbelief. He wanted the bank to consider more expansion, to challenge the new generation of financiers now leading America, and to see Kane and Cabot enter the second half of the twentieth century as one of the largest financial institutions in the United States. When he sat down, he was satisfied by the murmurs of approbation; his speech had, on the whole, been well received by the board.

When Tony Simmons rose he took a far more conservative line: the bank should consolidate its position for the next few years, moving only into carefully selected areas and sticking to the traditional modes of banking that had given Kane and Cabot the reputation they currently enjoyed. He had learnt his lesson during the crash and his main concern, he added – to laughter – was to be certain that Kane and Cabot did enter the second half of the twentieth century at all. Tony spoke prudently and with an authority that William was aware he was too young to match. When Tony sat down, William had no way of knowing in whose favour the board might swing, though he still believed that the majority would be more inclined to opt for expansion rather than standing still.

Alan Lloyd informed the other directors that neither he nor the two contestants intended to vote. The fourteen voting members received their little ballots, which they duly filled in and passed back to Alan who, acting as teller, began to count slowly. William found he could not look up from his doodle-covered pad which also bore the imprint of his sweating hand firmly upon it. When Alan had completed the task of counting, a hush came over the room and he announced six votes for Kane, six votes for Simmons, with two abstentions. Whispered conversation broke out among the board members, and Alan called for order. William took a deep and audible breath in the silence that followed.

Alan Lloyd paused and then said, "I feel that the appropriate course of action in the circumstances is to have a second vote. If any member who abstained on the first ballot finds himself able to support a candidate on this occasion, that might give one of the contestants an overall majority."

The little slips were passed out again. William could not bear even to watch the process this time. While members wrote their choices, he listened to the steel-nibbed pens scratching across the voting papers. Once again the ballots were returned to Alan Lloyd. Once again he opened them slowly one by one, and this time he called out the names as he read them.

William Kane.

Anthony Simmons, Anthony Simmons, Anthony Simmons.

Three votes to one for Tony Simmons.

William Kane, William Kane.

Anthony Simmons.

William Kane, William Kane, William Kane. Six to four for William.

Anthony Simmons, Anthony Simmons.

William Kane.

Seven votes to six in favour of William.

It seemed to William, holding his breath, to take Alan Lloyd a lifetime to open the final voting slip.

"Anthony Simmons," he declared. "The vote is seven all, gentlemen."

William knew that Alan Lloyd would now be obliged to cast the deciding vote, and although he had never told anyone whom he supported for the chair, William had always assumed that if the vote came to a deadlock, Alan would back him against Tony Simmons.

"As the voting has twice resulted in a dead heat, and since I assume that no member of the board is likely to change his mind, I must cast my vote for the candidate whom I feel should succeed me as chairman of Kane and Cabot. I know none of you will envy my position, but I have no alternative except to stand by my own judgment and back the man I feel should be the next chairman of the bank.

"That man is Tony Simmons."

William could not believe the words he heard and Tony Simmons looked almost as shocked. He rose from his seat opposite William to a round of applause, changed places with Alan Lloyd at the head of the table and addressed Kane and Cabot for the first time as the bank's new chairman. He thanked the board for its support and praised William for never having used his strong financial and familial position to try and influence the vote. He invited William to be vice-chairman of the board and suggested that Matthew Lester should replace Alan Lloyd as a director; both suggestions received unanimous support.

William sat staring at the portrait of his father, acutely conscious of having failed him.

20

Abel stubbed out the Corona for a second time and swore that he would not light another cigar until he had cleared the two million dollars that he needed for complete control of the Richmond Group. This was no time for big cigars, with the Dow-Jones Index at its lowest point in history and long soup lines in every major city in America. He gazed at the ceiling and considered his priorities. First, he needed to salvage the best of the staff from the Richmond Chicago.

He climbed off the bed, put on his jacket and went over to the hotel annex, where most of those who had not found employment since the fire were still living. Abel re-employed everyone whom he trusted, giving all those who were willing to leave Chicago work in one of the remaining ten hotels. He made it very clear that in a period of record unemployment their jobs were secure only as long as the hotels started to show a profit. He believed all the other hotels in the group were being run as dishonestly as the old Chicago Richmond had been; he wanted that changed – and changed quickly. His three assistant managers were each put in charge of one hotel, the Dallas Richmond, the Cincinnati Richmond and the St. Louis Richmond. He appointed new assistant managers for the remaining seven hotels in Houston, Mobile, Charleston, Atlanta, Memphis, New Orleans and Louisville. The original Leroy hotels had all been situated in the South and Mid-West including the Chicago Richmond, the only one Davis Leroy had been responsible for building himself. It took Abel another three weeks to get the old Chicago staff settled into their new hotels.

Abel decided to set up his own headquarters in the

Richmond annex and to open a small restaurant on the ground floor. It made sense to be near his backer and his banker rather than to settle in one of the hotels in the South. Moreover, Zaphia was in Chicago, and Abel felt with certainty that given a little time she would drop the pimply youth and fall in love with him. She was the only woman he had ever known with whom he felt self-assured. When Abel was about to leave for New York to recruit more specialised staff, he exacted a promise from her that she would no longer see the pimply boyfriend.

"Still pimply," said Abel to himself, "but no longer the boyfriend."

The night before his departure they slept together for the first time. She was soft, plump, giggly and delicious.

Abel's attentive care and gentle expertise took Zaphia by surprise.

"How many girls have there been since the *Black Arrow?*" she teased.

"None that I really cared about," he replied.

"Enough of them to forget *me,*" she accused.

"I never forgot you," he said untruthfully, leaning over to kiss her, convinced it was the only way to stop the conversation.

When Abel arrived in New York, the first thing he did was to look up George, whom he found out of work in a garret on East Third Street. He had forgotten what those houses could be like when shared by twenty families. The smell of stale food in every room, toilets that didn't flush and beds that were slept in by three different people every twenty-four hours. The bakery, it seemed, had been closed down, and George's uncle had had to find employment at a large mill on the outskirts of New York which could not take on George as well. George leaped at the chance to join Abel and the Richmond Group – in any capacity.

Abel recruited three new employees: a pastry chef, a comptroller and a head waiter before he and George travelled back to Chicago to set up base in the Richmond annex. Abel was pleased with the outcome of his trip. Most hotels on the East coast had cut their staff to a bare minimum which had made it easy to pick up experienced people, one of them from the Plaza itself.

In early March Abel and George set out for a tour of the remaining hotels in the group. Abel asked Zaphia to join them on the trip, even offering her the chance to work in any of the hotels she chose, but she would not budge from Chicago, the only American territory familiar to her. As a compromise she went to live in Abel's rooms at the Richmond annex while he was away. George, who had acquired middle-class morals along with his American citizenship, urged the advantages of matrimony on Abel, who, lonely in one impersonal hotel room after another, was a ready listener.

It came as no surprise to Abel to find that the other hotels were still being badly and, in some cases, dishonestly run, but high national unemployment encouraged most of the staff to welcome his arrival as the saviour of the group's fortunes. Abel did not find it necessary to fire staff in the grand manner he adopted when he had first arrived in Chicago. Most of those who knew of his reputation and feared his methods had already left. Some heads had to fall and they inevitably were attached to the necks of those people who had worked with the Richmond Group for a considerable time and were unable to change their unorthodox ways merely because Davis Leroy was dead. In several cases, Abel found a move of personnel from one hotel to another engendered a new attitude. By the end of his first year as chairman, the Richmond Group was operating with only half the staff they had employed in the past and showed a net loss of only a little over one hundred thousand dollars. The turnover among the senior staff was very low; Abel's confidence in the future of the group was infectious.

Abel set himself the target of breaking even in 1932. He felt the only way he could achieve such a rapid improvement in profitability was to let every manager in the group take the responsibility for his own hotel with a share in the profits, much in the way that Davis Leroy had treated him when he had first come to the Chicago Richmond.

Abel moved from hotel to hotel, never letting up, and never staying in one particular place for more than three weeks at a time. He did not allow anyone, other than the faithful George, his surrogate eyes and ears in Chicago, to know at which hotel he might arrive next. For months he broke this exhausting routine only to visit Zaphia or Curtis Fenton.

After a full assessment of the group's financial position Abel had to make some more unpleasant decisions. The most drastic was to close temporarily the two hotels, in Mobile and Charleston, which were losing so much money that he felt they would become a hopeless drain on the rest of the group's finances. The staff at the other hotels watched the axe fall and worked even harder. Every time he arrived back at his little office in the Richmond annex in Chicago there would be a clutch of memos demanding immediate attention – burst pipes in washrooms, cockroaches in kitchens, flashes of temperament in dining rooms, and the inevitable dissatisfied customer who was threatening a law suit.

Henry Osborne re-entered Abel's life with a welcome offer of a settlement of $750,000 from Great Western Casualty, who could find no evidence to implicate Abel with Desmond Pacey in the fire at the Chicago Richmond. Lieutenant O'Malley's evidence had proved very helpful on that point. Abel realised he owed him more than a milk shake. Abel was happy to settle at what he considered was a fair price but Osborne suggested to him that he should hold out for a larger amount and give him a percentage of the difference. Abel, whose shortcomings had never included peculation, regarded him somewhat warily after that: if Osborne could so readily be disloyal to his own company, there was little doubt that he would have no qualms about ditching Abel when it suited him.

In the spring of 1932 Abel was somewhat surprised to receive a friendly letter from Melanie Leroy, more welcoming in tone than she had ever been in person. He was flattered, even excited, and called her to make a date for dinner at the Stevens, a decision he regretted the moment they entered the dining room for there, looking unsophisticated, tired and vulnerable, was Zaphia. Melanie, in contrast, looked ravishing in a long mint green dress which indicated quite clearly what her body would be like if the mint were removed. Her eyes, perhaps taking courage from the dress, seemed greener and more captivating than ever.

"It's wonderful to see you looking so well, Abel," she remarked as she took her seat in the centre of the dining room, "and of course, everybody knows how well you are doing with the Richmond Group."

"The Baron Group," said Abel.

She flushed slightly. "I didn't realise you had changed the name."

"Yes, I changed it last year," lied Abel. He had in fact decided at that very moment that every hotel in the group would be known as a Baron hotel. He wondered why he had never thought of it before.

"An appropriate name," said Melanie, smiling.

Zaphia set the mushroom soup in front of Melanie with a little thud that spoke volumes to Abel. Some of the soup nearly ended up on the mint green dress.

"You're not working?" asked Abel, scribbling the words 'Baron Group' on the back of his menu.

"No, not at the moment, but things are looking up a little. A woman with a liberal arts degree in this city has to sit around and wait for every man to be employed before she can hope to find a job."

"If you ever want to work for the Baron Group," said Abel, emphasising the name slightly, "you only have to let me know."

"No, no," said Melanie. "I'm just fine."

She quickly changed the subject to music and the theatre. Talking to her was an unaccustomed and pleasant challenge for Abel; she teased him, but with intelligence. She made him feel more confident in her company than he had ever been in the past. The dinner went on until well after eleven, and when everyone had left the dining room, including Zaphia, ominously red-eyed, he drove Melanie home to her flat, and this time she did invite him in for a drink. He sat on the end of a sofa while she poured him a prohibited whisky and put a record on the phonograph.

"I can't stay long," Abel said. "Busy day tomorrow."

"That's what *I'm* supposed to say, Abel. Don't rush away, this evening has been such fun, just like old times."

She sat down beside him, her dress rising above her knees. Not quite like old times, he thought. Incredible legs. He made no attempt to resist when she edged towards him. In moments he found he was kissing her – or was she kissing him? His hands wandered on to those legs and then to her breasts, and this time she seemed to respond willingly. It was she who eventually led him by the hand to her bedroom, folded back the coverlet neatly, turned around and asked him to unzip her. Abel obliged in nervous disbelief and switched out the light before he undressed. After that it was easy for him to put Joyce's careful tuition into practice. Melanie certainly was not lacking in experience herself; Abel had never enjoyed the act of making love more and fell into a deep contented sleep.

In the morning Melanie made him breakfast and attended to his every need, right up to the moment he had to leave.

"I shall watch the Baron Group with renewed interest," she told him, "not that anyone doubts that it's going to be a huge success."

"Thank you," said Abel "for breakfast and a memorable night."

"I was hoping we'd be seeing each other again sometime soon," Melanie added.

"I'd like that," said Abel.

She kissed him on the cheek as a wife might who was seeing her husband off to work.

"I wonder what kind of woman you'll end up marrying," she asked innocently as she helped Abel on with his overcoat.

He looked at her and smiled sweetly. "When I make that decision, Melanie, you can be certain I shall only be influenced by your views."

"What do you mean?" asked Melanie, coyly.

"Simply that I shall heed your advice," replied Abel, as he reached the front door, "and be sure to find myself a nice Polish girl who will marry me."

Abel and Zaphia were married a month later. Zaphia's cousin Janek gave her away and George was the best man. The reception was held at the Stevens and the drinking and dancing went on far into the night. By tradition, each man paid a token sum to dance with Zaphia, and George perspired as he battled round the room, photographing the guests in every possible permutation and combination. After a midnight supper of *barszcz*, *pierogi* and *bigos* downed with wine, brandy and Danzig vodka, Abel and Zaphia were allowed to retire to the bridal suite, with many a wink from the men and tears from the women.

Abel was pleasantly surprised to be told by Curtis Fenton the next morning that the bill for his reception at the Stevens had been covered by Mr. Maxton and was to be treated as a wedding gift. He used the money he had saved for the reception as a down payment on a little house on Rigg Street.

For the first time in his life he possessed a home of his own.

21

In February of 1934 William decided to take a month's holiday in England before making any firm decision about his future; he even considered resigning from the board, but Matthew convinced him that that was not the course of action his father would have taken in the same circumstances. Matthew appeared to take his friend's defeat even harder than William himself. Twice in the following week he came into the bank with the obvious signs of a hangover and left important work unfinished. William decided to let these incidents pass without comment and invited Matthew to join him and Kate for dinner that night. Matthew declined, claiming that he had a backload of work on which to catch up. William would not have given the refusal a second thought if Matthew had not been dining at the Ritz Carlton that night with an attractive woman whom William could have sworn was married to one of Kane and Cabot's departmental managers. Kate said nothing, except that Matthew did not look very well.

William, preoccupied with his impending departure for Europe, took less notice of his friend's strange behaviour than he might otherwise have done. At the last moment William couldn't face a month in England alone and asked Kate to accompany him. To his surprise and delight she agreed.

William and Kate sailed to England on the *Mauretania* in separate cabins. Once they had settled into the Ritz, in separate rooms, even on separate floors, William reported to the London branch of Kane and Cabot in Lombard Street and fulfilled the ostensible purpose of his trip to England by reviewing the bank's European activities. Morale was high and Tony Simmons had evidently been a well-liked manager; there was little for William to do but murmur his approval.

He and Kate spent a glorious two weeks together in London, Hampshire and Lincolnshire, looking at some land William had acquired a few months previously, over twelve thousand acres in all. The financial return from farming land is never high but, as William explained to Kate, "It will always be there if things ever go sour again in America."

A few days before they were due to travel back to the United States, Kate decided she wanted to see Oxford, and William agreed to drive her down early the next morning. He hired a new Morris, a car he had never driven before. In the university city, they spent the day wandering around the colleges: Magdalen, superb against the river; Christchurch, grandiose but cloisterless; and Merton where they just sat on the grass and dreamed.

"Can't sit on the grass, sir," said the voice of a college porter.

They laughed and walked hand-in-hand like undergraduates by the side of the Cherwell watching eight Matthews straining to push a boat along as fast as possible. William could no longer imagine a life separated in any part from Kate.

They started back for London in mid-afternoon, and when they reached Henley-on-Thames, they stopped to have tea at the Bell Inn overlooking the river. After scones and a large pot of strong English tea (Kate was venturesome and drank it with only milk, but William added hot water to dilute it), Kate suggested that they should start back before it was too dark to see the countryside, but when William had re-inserted the crank into the Morris, despite strenuous effort he could not get the engine to turn over. Finally he gave up, and since it was getting late, decided that they would have to spend the night in Henley. He returned to the front desk of the Bell Inn and requested two rooms.

"Sorry, sir, I have only one double room left," said the receptionist.

William hesitated for a moment and then said, "We'll take it."

Kate looked somewhat surprised but said nothing; the receptionist looked suspiciously at her.

"Mr. and Mrs. . . . er . . . ?"

"Mr. and Mrs. William Kane," said William firmly. "We'll be back later."

"Shall I put your cases in the room, sir?" the hall porter asked.

"We don't have any," William replied, smiling.

"I see, sir."

A bewildered Kate followed William up Henley High Street until he came to a halt in front of the parish church.

"May I ask what we're doing, William?" she asked.

"Something I should have done a long time ago, my darling."

Kate asked no more questions. When they entered the vestry, William found a church-warden piling up some hymn books.

"Where can I find the vicar?" demanded William.

The church-warden straightened himself to his full height and regarded him pityingly.

"In the vicarage, I dare say."

"Where's the vicarage?" asked William, trying again.

"You're an American gentleman, aren't you, sir?"

"Yes," said William, becoming impatient.

"The vicarage will be next door to the church, won't it?" said the church-warden.

"I suppose it will," said William. "Can you stay here for the next ten minutes?"

"Why should I want to do that, sir?"

William extracted a large, white, five-pound note from his inside pocket and unfolded it. "Make it fifteen minutes to be on the safe side, please."

The church-warden studied the five pounds carefully and said: "Americans. Yes, sir."

William left the man with his five-pound note and hurried Kate out of the church. As they passed the main notice board in the porch, he read: "The Vicar of this Parish is The Very Reverend Simon Tukesbury, M.A. (Cantab)," and next to that pronouncement, hanging by one nail, was an appeal notice concerning a new roof for the church. Every penny towards the necessary five hundred pounds will help, declared the notice, not very boldly. William hastened up the path to the vicarage with Kate a few yards behind, and a smiling, pink-cheeked, plump lady answered his sharp knock on the door.

"Mrs. Tukesbury?" enquired William.

"Yes." She smiled.

"May I speak to your husband?"

"He's having his tea at the moment. Would it be possible for you to come back a little later?"

"I'm afraid it's rather urgent," William insisted.

Kate had caught up with him but said nothing.

"Well, in that case I suppose you'd better come in."

The vicarage was early sixteenth century and the small stone front room was warmed by a welcoming log fire. The vicar, a tall spare man who was eating wafer-thin cucumber sandwiches, rose to greet them.

"Good afternoon, Mr. . . .?"

"Kane, sir, William Kane."

"What can I do for you, Mr. Kane?"

"Kate and I," said William, "want to get married."

"Oh, how nice," said Mrs. Tukesbury.

"Yes indeed," said the vicar. "Are you a member of this parish? I don't seem to remember . . ."

"No, sir, I'm an American. I worship at St. Paul's in Boston."

"Massachusetts, I presume, not Lincolnshire," said The Very Reverend Tukesbury.

"Yes," said William, forgetting for a moment that there was a Boston in England.

"Splendid," said the vicar, his hands raised as if he were about to give a blessing. "And what date did you have in mind for this union of souls?"

"Now, sir."

"Now, sir?" said the startled vicar. "I am not aware of the traditions in the United States that surround the solemn, holy and binding institution of marriage, Mr. Kane, though one reads of some very strange incidents involving some of your compatriots from California. I do, however, consider it nothing less than my duty to inform you that those customs have not yet become acceptable in Henley-on-Thames. In England, sir, you must reside for a full calendar month in any parish before you can be married and the banns must be posted on three separate occasions, unless there are very special and extenuating circumstances. Even did such circumstances exist, I would have to seek the bishop's dispensation, and I couldn't do that in under three days," Mr. Tukesbury added, his hands now firmly at his side.

Kate spoke for the first time. "How much do you still need for the church's new roof?"

"Ah, the roof. Now there is a sad story, but I won't embark upon its history at this moment, early eleventh century, you know . . ."

"How much do you need?" asked William, tightening his grasp on Kate's hand.

"We are hoping to raise five hundred pounds. We've done commendably well so far; we've reached twenty-seven pounds four shillings and four pence in only seven weeks."

"No, no dear," said Mrs. Tukesbury. "You haven't counted the one pound eleven shillings and two pence I made from my 'Bring and Buy' sale last week."

"Indeed I haven't, my dear. How inconsiderate of me to overlook your personal contribution. That will make altogether . . . " began the Reverend Tukesbury as he tried to add the figures in his head, raising his eyes towards heaven for inspiration.

William took his wallet from his inside pocket, wrote out a cheque for five hundred pounds and silently proffered it to The Very Reverend Tukesbury.

"I . . . ah, I see there are special circumstances, Mr. Kane," said the surprised vicar. The tone changed. "Has either of you ever been married before?"

"Yes," said Kate. "My husband was killed in a plane crash over four years ago."

"Oh, how terrible," said Mrs. Tukesbury. "I am so sorry, I didn't . . ."

"Shush, my dear," said the man of God, now more interested in the church roof than in his wife's sentiments. "And you, sir?"

"I have never been married before," said William.

"I shall have to telephone the bishop." Clutching William's cheque, The Very Reverend disappeared into the next room.

Mrs. Tukesbury invited them to sit down and offered them the plate of cucumber sandwiches. She chatted on, but William and Kate did not hear her words as they sat gazing at each other.

The vicar returned three cucumber sandwiches later.

"It's highly irregular, highly irregular, but the bishop has agreed, on the condition, Mr. Kane, that you will confirm everything at the American Embassy tomorrow morning and then with your own bishop at St. Paul's in Boston . . . Massachusetts immediately you return home."

He was still clutching the five-hundred-pound cheque.

"All we need now is two witnesses," he continued. "My wife can act as one, and we must hope that the church-warden is still around, so that he can be the other."

"He is still around, I assure you," said William.

"How can you be so certain, Mr. Kane?"

"He cost me one per cent."

"One per cent?" said The Very Reverend Tukesbury, baffled.

"One per cent of your church roof," said William.

The vicar ushered William, Kate and his wife down the little path back to the church and blinked at the waiting church-warden.

"Indeed, I perceive that Mr. Sprogget has remained on duty . . . He has never done so for me; you obviously have a way with you, Mr. Kane."

Simon Tukesbury put on his vestments and a surplice while the church-warden stared at the scene in disbelief.

William turned to Kate and kissed her gently. "I know it's a damn silly question in the circumstances, but will you marry me?"

"Good God," said The Very Reverend Tukesbury, who

had never blasphemed in the fifty-seven years of his mortal existence. "You mean you haven't even asked her?"

Fifteen minutes later, Mr. and Mrs. William Kane left the parish church of Henley-on-Thames, Oxfordshire. Mrs. Tukesbury had had to supply the ring at the last moment, which she twitched from a curtain in the vestry. It was a perfect fit. The Very Reverend Tukesbury had a new roof, and Mr. Sprogget a yarn to tell them down at The Green Man where he spent most of his five pounds.

Outside the church the vicar handed William a piece of paper. "Two shillings and sixpence, please."

"What for?" asked William.

"Your marriage certificate, Mr. Kane."

"You should have taken up banking, sir," said William, handing Mr. Tukesbury half a crown.

He walked his bride in blissful silence back down the High Street to the Bell Inn. They had a quiet dinner in the fifteenth-century oak-beamed dining room, and went to bed at a few minutes past nine. As they disappeared up the old wooden staircase to their room, the chief receptionist turned to the hall porter and winked. "If they're married, I'm the King of England."

William started to hum 'God Save the King'.

The next morning Mr. and Mrs. Kane had a leisurely breakfast while the car was fixed. (His father would have told him all it needed was a new fan belt.) A young waiter poured them both coffee.

"Do you like it black or shall I add some milk?" asked William innocently.

An elderly couple smiled benignly at them.

"With milk, please," said Kate as she reached across and touched William's hand gently.

He smiled back at her, suddenly aware the whole room was now staring at them.

They returned to London in the cool early spring air, travelling through Henley, over the Thames, and then on up through Berkshire and Middlesex into London.

"Did you notice the look the porter gave you this morning, darling?" asked William.

"Yes, I think perhaps we should have shown him our marriage certificate."

"No, no, you'd have spoilt his whole image of the wanton American woman. The last thing he wants to tell his wife when he returns home tonight is that we were really married."

When they arrived back at the Ritz in time for lunch, the desk manager was surprised to find William cancelling Kate's room. He was heard to comment later: "Young Mr. Kane appeared to be such a gentleman. His late and distinguished father would never have behaved in such a way."

William and Kate took the *Aquitania* back to New York, having first called at the American Embassy in Grosvenor Gardens to inform a consul of their new marital status. The consul gave them a long official form to fill out, charged them one pound, and kept them waiting for well over an hour. The American Embassy, it seemed, was not in need of a new roof. William wanted to go to Cartier's in Bond Street and buy a gold wedding ring, but Kate would not hear of it – nothing was going to part her from the precious curtain ring.

William found it difficult to settle down in Boston under his new chairman. The precepts of the New Deal were passing into law with unprecedented rapidity, and William and Tony Simmons found it impossible to agree on whether the implications for investment would be good or bad. Expansion – on one front at least – became unstoppable when Kate announced soon after their return from England that she was pregnant, news which gave her parents and husband great joy. William tried to modify his working hours to suit his new role as a married man but found himself at his desk increasingly often throughout the hot summer evenings. Kate, cool and happy in her flowered maternity smock, methodically supervised the decoration of the nursery of the Red House. William found for the first time in his life that he could leave his work desk and look forward to going home. If he had work left over he just picked up the papers and took them back to the Red House, a pattern to which he adhered throughout their married life.

While Kate and the baby that was due about Christmas time brought William great happiness at home, Matthew was making him increasingly uneasy at work. He had taken to drinking and coming to the office late with no explanations. As the months passed, William found he could no longer rely on his friend's judgment. At first, he said nothing, hoping it was little more than an odd out-of-character reaction – which might quickly pass – to the repeal of Prohibition. But it wasn't, and the problem went from bad to worse. The last straw came one November morning when Matthew arrived two hours late, obviously suffering from a hangover, and made a simple, unnecessary mistake, selling off an important investment which resulted in a small loss for a client who should have made a handsome profit. William knew the time had come for an unpleasant but necessary head-on confrontation. Matthew admitted his error and apologised regretfully. William was thankful to have the row out of the way and was about to suggest they go to lunch together when his secretary uncharacteristically rushed into his office.

"It's your wife, sir, she's been taken to the hospital."

"Why?" asked William, puzzled.

"The baby," said his secretary.

"But it's not due for at least another six weeks," said William incredulously.

"I know, sir, but Doctor MacKenzie sounded rather anxious, and wanted you to come to the hospital as quickly as possible."

Matthew, who a moment before had seemed a broken reed, took over and drove William to the hospital. Memories of William's mother's death and her still-born daughter came flooding back to both of them.

"Pray God not Kate," said Matthew as he drew into the hospital car park.

William did not need to be guided to the Richard Kane Maternity Wing which Kate had officially opened only six months before. He found a nurse standing outside the delivery room who informed him that Doctor MacKenzie was with his wife, and that she had lost a lot of blood. William paced up and down the corridor helplessly, numbly waiting, exactly as he had done years before. The scene was all too familiar. How unimportant being chairman of the bank was compared with losing Kate. When had he last said to her "I love you"? Matthew sat with William, paced with William, stood with William, but said nothing. There was nothing to be said. William checked his watch each time a nurse ran in or out of the delivery room. Seconds turned into minutes and minutes into hours. Finally Doctor MacKenzie appeared, his forehead shining with little beads of sweat, a surgical mask covering his nose and mouth. William could see no expression on the doctor's face until he removed the white mask, revealing a large smile.

"Congratulations, William, you have a boy, and Kate is just fine."

"Thank God," breathed William, clinging on to Matthew.

"Much as I respect the Almighty," said Doctor MacKenzie, "I feel I had a little to do with this birth myself."

William laughed. "Can I see Kate?"

"No, not right now. I've given her a sedative and she's fallen asleep. She lost rather more blood than was good for her, but she'll be fine by morning. A little weak, perhaps, but well ready to see you. But there's nothing to stop you seeing your son. But don't be surprised by his size; remember he's quite premature."

The doctor guided William and Matthew down the corridor to a room in which they stared through a pane of glass at a row of six little pink heads in cribs.

"That one," said Doctor MacKenzie, pointing to the infant that had just arrived.

William stared dubiously at the ugly little face, his vision of a fine, upstanding son receding rapidly.

"Well, I'll say one thing for the little devil," said Doctor MacKenzie cheerfully, "he's better looking than you were at that age, and you haven't turned out too badly."

William laughed out of relief.

"What are you going to call him?"

"Richard Higginson Kane."

The doctor patted the new father affectionately on the

shoulder. "I hope I live long enough to deliver Richard's first-born."

William immediately wired the rector of St. Paul's, who put the boy down for a place in 1943, and then the new father and Matthew got thoroughly drunk and were both late arriving at the hospital the next morning to see Kate. William took Matthew for another look at young Richard.

"Ugly little bastard," said Matthew, "not at all like his beautiful mother."

"That's what I thought," said William.

"Spitting image of you, though."

William returned to Kate's flower-filled room.

"Do you like your son?" Kate asked her husband. "He's so like you."

"I'll hit the next person who says that," William said. "He's the ugliest little thing I've ever seen."

"Oh, no," said Kate in mock indignation, "he's beautiful."

"A face only a mother could love," said William and hugged his wife.

She clung to him, happy in his happiness.

"What would Grandmother Kane have said about our first-born entering the world after less than eight months of marriage? 'I don't wish to appear uncharitable, but anyone born in under fifteen months must be considered of dubious parentage; under nine months definitely unacceptable,'" William mimicked. "By the way, Kate, I forgot to tell you something before they rushed you into the hospital."

"What was that?"

"I love you."

Kate and young Richard had to stay in the hospital for nearly three weeks. Not until after Christmas did Kate fully recover her vitality. Richard, on the other hand, grew like an uncontrolled weed, no one having informed him that he was a Kane, and one was not supposed to do that sort of thing. William became the first male Kane to change a nappy and push a perambulator. Kate was very proud of him, and somewhat surprised. William told Matthew that it was high time he found himself a good woman and settled down.

Matthew laughed defensively. "You're getting positively middle-aged. I shall be looking for grey hairs next."

One or two had already appeared during the chairmanship battle. Matthew hadn't noticed.

William was not able to put a finger on exactly when his relationship with Tony Simmons began to deteriorate badly. Tony would continually veto one policy suggestion after another, and his negative attitude made William seriously consider resignation again. Matthew was not helping matters by returning to his old drinking habits. The period of reform had not lasted more than a few months, and, if anything, he was now drinking more heavily than before and arriving at the bank a few minutes later each morning. William was not quite sure how to handle the new situation and found himself continually covering Matthew's work. At the end of each day, William would double-check Matthew's mail and return his unanswered calls.

By the spring of 1936, as investors gained more confidence and depositors returned, William decided the time had come to go tentatively back into the stock market, but Tony vetoed the suggestion in an offhand, inter-office memorandum to the financial committee. William stormed into Tony's office to ask if his resignation would be welcome.

"Certainly not, William. I merely want you to recognise that it has always been my policy to run this bank in a conservative manner, and that I am not willing to charge headlong back into the market with our investors' money."

"But we're losing business hand-over-fist to other banks while we sit on the sidelines watching them take advantage of the present situation. Banks which we wouldn't even have considered as rivals ten years ago will soon be overtaking us."

"Overtaking us in what, William? Not in reputation. Quick profits perhaps, but not reputation."

"But I'm interested in profits," said William. "I consider it a bank's duty to make good returns for its investors, not to mark time in a gentlemanly fashion."

"I would rather stand still than lose the reputation that

this bank built up under your grandfather and father over the better part of half a century."

"Yes, but both of them were always looking for new opportunities to expand the bank's activities."

"In good times," said Tony.

"And in bad," said William.

"Why are you so upset, William? You still have a free hand in the running of your own department."

"Like hell I do. You block anything that even suggests enterprise."

"Let's start being honest with each other, William. One of the reasons I have had to be particularly cautious lately is that Matthew's judgment is no longer reliable."

"Leave Matthew out of this. It's me you're blocking; I am head of the department."

"I can't leave Matthew out of it. I wish I could. The final overall responsibility to the board for anyone's actions is mine, and he is the number two man in the bank's most important department."

"Yes, and therefore my responsibility, because I am the number one man in that department."

"No, William, it cannot remain your responsibility alone when Matthew comes into the office drunk at eleven o'clock in the morning, no matter how long and close your friendship has been."

"Don't exaggerate."

"I am not exaggerating, William. For over a year now this bank has been carrying Matthew Lester, and the only thing that has stopped me mentioning my worries to you before is your close personal relationship with him and his family. I wouldn't be sorry to see him hand in his resignation. A bigger man would have done so long ago, and his friends would have told him so."

"Never," said William. "If he goes, I go."

"So be it, William," said Tony. "My first responsibility is to our investors, not to your old school chums."

"You'll live to regret that statement, Tony," said William, as he stormed out of the chairman's office and returned to his own room in a furious temper.

"Where is Mr. Lester?" William demanded as he passed his secretary.

"He's not in yet, sir."

William looked at his watch, exasperated.

"Tell him I'd like to see him the moment he arrives."

"Yes, sir."

William paced up and down his office, cursing. Everything Tony Simmons had said about Matthew was accurate, which only made matters worse. He began to think back to when it had all begun, searching for a simple explanation. His thoughts were interrupted by his secretary.

"Mr. Lester has just arrived, sir."

Matthew entered the room looking rather sheepish, displaying all the signs of another hangover. He had aged badly in the past year, and his skin had lost its fine, athletic glow. William hardly recognised him as the man who had been his closest friend for nearly twenty years.

"Matthew, where the hell have you been?"

"I overslept," Matthew replied, uncharacteristically scratching at his face. "Rather a late night, I'm afraid."

"You mean you drank too much."

"No, I didn't have that much. It was a new girlfriend who kept me awake all night. She was insatiable."

"When will you stop, Matthew? You've slept with nearly every single woman in Boston."

"Don't exaggerate, William. There must be one or two left; at least I hope so. And then don't forget all the thousands of married ones."

"It's not funny, Matthew."

"Oh, come on, William. Give me a break."

"Give you a break? I've just had Tony Simmons on my back because of you, and what's more I know he's right. You'll jump into bed with anything wearing a skirt, and worse, you're drinking yourself to death. Your judgment has gone to pieces. Why, Matthew? Tell me why. There must be some simple explanation. Up until a year ago you were one of the most reliable men I have ever met in my life. What is it, Matthew? What am I supposed to say to Tony Simmons?"

"Tell Simmons to go to hell and mind his own business."

"Matthew, be fair, it *is* his business. We are running a bank, not a bordello, and you came here as a director on my personal recommendation."

"And now I'm not measuring up to your standards, is that what you're saying?"

"No, I'm not saying that."

"Then what the hell are you saying?"

"Buckle down and do some work for a few weeks. In no time everyone will have forgotten all about it."

"Is that all you want?"

"Yes," said William.

"I shall do as you command, O Master," said Matthew, and he clicked his heels and walked out of the door.

"Oh, hell," said William.

That afternoon William wanted to go over a client's portfolio with Matthew but nobody seemed to be able to find him. He had not returned to the office after lunch and was not seen again that day. Even the pleasure of putting young Richard to bed in the evening could not distract William from his worries about Matthew. Richard could already say two and William was trying to make him say three, but he insisted on saying 'tree'.

"If you can't say three, Richard, how can you ever hope to be a banker?" William demanded of his son as Kate entered the nursery.

"Perhaps he'll end up doing something worthwhile," said Kate.

"What's more worthwhile than banking?" William enquired.

"Well, he might be a musician, or a baseball player, or even President of the United States."

"Of those three I'd prefer him to be a ball player – it's the only one of your suggestions that pays a decent salary," said William as he tucked Richard into bed.

Richard's last words before sleeping were, "Tree, Daddy." William gave in. It wasn't his day.

"You look exhausted, darling. I hope you haven't forgotten that we're having drinks later with Andrew MacKenzie."

"Hell, Andrew's party had totally slipped my mind. What time is he expecting us?"

"In about an hour."

"Well, first I'm going to take a long, hot bath."

"I thought that was a woman's privilege," said Kate.

"Tonight I need a little pampering. I've had a nerve-racking day."

"Tony bothering you again?"

"Yes, but I am afraid this time he's in the right. He's been complaining about Matthew's drinking habits. I was only thankful he didn't mention the womanising. It's become impossible to take Matthew to any party nowadays without the eldest daughter, not to mention the occasional wife, having to be locked away for their own safety. Will you run my bath?"

William sat in the tub for more than half an hour, and Kate had to drag him out before he fell asleep. Despite her prompting they arrived at the MacKenzies' twenty-five minutes late, only to find that Matthew, already well on the way to being inebriated, was trying to pick up a congressman's wife. William wanted to intervene, but Kate prevented him from doing so.

"Don't say anything," she whispered.

"I can't stand here and watch him going to pieces in front of my eyes," said William. "He's my closest friend. I have to do something."

But in the end he took Kate's advice and spent an unhappy evening watching Matthew become progressively drunk. Tony Simmons, from the other side of the room, was glancing pointedly at William, who was relieved at Matthew's early departure, even though it was in the company of the only unattached woman left at the party. Once Matthew had gone William started to relax for the first time that day.

"How is little Richard?" Andrew MacKenzie asked.

"He can't say 'three'," said William.

"Might turn out to do something civilised after all," said Doctor MacKenzie.

"Exactly what I thought," said Kate. "What a good idea, William: he can be a doctor."

"Pretty safe," said Andrew. "Don't know many doctors who can count past two."

"Except when they send their bills," said William.

Andrew laughed. "Will you have another drink, Kate?"

"No thank you, Andrew. It's high time we went home. If we stay any longer, only Tony Simmons and William will be left, and they can both count past two so we would all have to talk banking the rest of the night."

"Agreed," said William. "Thank you for a lovely party, Andrew. By the way, I must apologise for Matthew's behaviour."

"Why?" said Doctor MacKenzie.

"Oh, come on, Andrew. Not only was he drunk, but there wasn't a woman in the room who felt safe left alone with him."

"I might well do the same if I were in his predicament," said Andrew MacKenzie.

"What makes you say that?" said William. "You can't approve of his habits just because he's single."

"No, I don't, but I try to understand them and realise I might be a little irresponsible faced with the same problem."

"What do you mean?" asked Kate.

"My God," said Doctor MacKenzie. "He's your closest friend, and he hasn't told you?"

"Told us what?" they said together.

Doctor MacKenzie stared at them both, a look of disbelief on his face.

"Come into my study."

William and Kate followed the doctor into a small room, lined almost wall-to-wall with medical books, interspersed only with occasional, sometimes unframed, photographs of student days at Cornell.

"Please have a seat, Kate," he said. "William, I make no apology for what I am about to say, because I assumed you knew that Matthew was gravely ill, dying, in fact, of Hodgkin's disease. He has known about his condition for over a year."

William fell back in his chair, for a moment unable to speak.

"Hodgkin's disease?"

"An almost invariably fatal inflammation and enlargement of the lymph nodes," said the doctor rather formally.

William shook his head incredulously. "Why didn't he tell me?"

"You've known each other since you were at school together. My guess is he's far too proud to burden anyone else with his problems. He'd rather die in his own way than let anyone realise what he's going through. I have begged him for the last six months to tell his father, and I have certainly broken my professional promise to him by letting you know, but I can't let you go on blaming him for something over which he has absolutely no control."

"Thank you, Andrew," said William. "How can I have been so blind and so stupid?"

"Don't blame yourself," said Doctor MacKenzie. "There's no way you could have known."

"Is there really no hope?" asked William. "Are there no clinics, no specialists? Money would be no problem . . ."

"Money can't buy everything, William, and I have consulted the three best men in America, and one in Switzerland. I am afraid they are all in agreement with my diagnosis, and medical science hasn't yet discovered a cure for Hodgkin's disease."

"How long has he got to live?" asked Kate in a whisper.

"Six months at the outside, more likely three."

"And I thought I had problems," said William. He held tightly on to Kate's hand as if it were a lifeline. "We must be going, Andrew. Thank you for telling us."

"Help him in any way you can," said the doctor, "but for God's sake, be understanding. Let him do what he wants to do. It's Matthew's last few months, not yours. And don't ever let him know I told you."

William drove Kate home in silence. As soon as they reached the Red House, William called the girl Matthew had left the party with.

"Would it be possible to speak to Matthew Lester?"

"He's not here," said a rather irritable voice. "He dragged me off to the In and Out Club, but he was already drunk by the time we got there, and I refused to go in that place with him." Then she hung up.

The In and Out Club. William had a hazy recollection of having seen the sign swinging from an iron bar but he couldn't remember exactly where the place was. He looked it up in the phone book, drove over to the north side of town and eventually, after questioning a passer-by, he found the club. William knocked on the door. A hatch slid back.

"Are you a member?"

"No," said William firmly, and passed a ten-dollar note through the grille.

The hatch slid closed, and the door opened. William walked on to the middle of the dance floor, looking slightly incongruous in his three-piece banker's suit. The dancers, twined around each other, swayed incuriously away from him. William's eyes searched the smoke-filled room for Matthew, but he wasn't there. Finally he thought he recognised one of Matthew's many recent casual girlfriends, whom he felt certain he'd seen coming out of his friend's apartment early one morning. She was sitting cross-legged in a corner with a sailor. William went over to her.

"Excuse me, miss," he said. She looked up but obviously didn't recognise William.

"The lady's with me, so beat it," said the sailor.

"Have you seen Matthew Lester?"

"Matthew?" said the girl. "Matthew who?"

"I told you to get lost," said the sailor, rising to his feet.

"One more word out of you, and I'll knock your block off," said William.

The sailor had seen anger like that in a man's eyes once before in his life and had nearly lost an eye for his trouble. He sat back down.

"Where is Matthew?"

"I don't know a Matthew, darling." Now she, too, was frightened.

"Six-feet-two, blond hair, dressed like me, and probably drunk."

"Oh, you mean Martin. He calls himself Martin here, darling, not Matthew." She began to relax. "Now let me see, who did he go off with tonight?" She turned her head towards the bar and shouted at the bartender. "Terry, who did Martin go out with?"

The bartender removed a dead cigarette butt from the corner of his mouth. "Jenny," he said, and put the unlit cigarette back in place.

"Jenny, that's right," said the girl. "Now let me see, she's short sessions. Never lets a man stay for more than half an hour, so they should be back soon."

"Thank you," said William.

He waited for almost an hour at the bar sipping a scotch with a lot of water, feeling more and more out of place by the minute. Finally, the bartender, the unlit cigarette still in his mouth, gestured to a girl who was coming through the door.

"That's Jenny," he said. Matthew was not with her. The bartender waved for Jenny to join them. A slim, short, dark, not unattractive girl, she winked at William and walked towards him swinging her hips.

"Looking for me, darling? Well, I am available, but I charge ten dollars for half an hour."

"No, I don't want you," said William.

"Charming," said Jenny.

"I'm looking for the man who's been with you, Matthew – I mean Martin."

"Martin, he was too drunk even to get it up with the help of a crane, darling, but he paid his ten dollars, he always does. A real gentleman."

"Where is he now?" asked William impatiently.

"I don't know, he gave it up as a bad job and started walking home."

William ran into the street. The cold air hit him, not that he needed to be awakened. He drove his car slowly away from the club, following the route towards Matthew's flat, looking carefully at each person he passed. Some hurried on when they saw his watchful eyes; others tried to engage him in conversation. When he was passing an all-night café, he caught sight of Matthew through the steamy window, weaving his way through the tables with a cup in his hand. William parked the car, went in and sat down beside him.

Matthew had slumped on to the table next to a cup of untouched spilt coffee. He was so drunk that he didn't even recognise William.

"Matthew, it's me," said William, looking at the crumpled man. The tears started to run down his cheeks.

Matthew looked up and spilled some more of his coffee. "You're crying, old fellow. Lost your girl, have you?"

"No, my closest friend," said William.

"Ah, they're much harder to come by."

"I know," said William.

"I have a good friend," said Matthew, slurring his words. "He's always stood by me until we quarrelled for the first time today. My fault though. You see I've let him down rather badly."

"No, you haven't," said William.

"How can you know?" said Matthew angrily. "You're not even fit to know him."

"Let's go home, Matthew."

"My name is Martin," said Matthew.

"I'm sorry, Martin, let's go home."

"No, I want to stay here. There's this girl who may come by later. I think I'm ready for her now."

"I have some fine old malt whisky at my house," said William. "Why don't you join me?"

"Any women at your place?"

"Yes, plenty of them."

"You're on, I'll come."

William hoisted Matthew up and put his arm under his shoulder, guiding him slowly through the café towards the door. It was the first time he'd ever realised how heavy Matthew was. As they passed two policemen sitting at the corner of the counter, William heard one say to the other, "Goddamn fairies."

He helped Matthew into the car and drove him back to Beacon Hill. Kate was waiting up for them.

"You should have gone to bed, darling."

"I couldn't sleep," she replied.

"I'm afraid he's nearly incoherent."

"Is this the girl you promised me?" said Matthew.

"Yes, she'll take care of you," said William, and he and Kate helped him up to the guest room and put him on the bed. Kate started to undress him.

"You must undress as well, darling," he said. "I've already paid my ten dollars."

"When you're in bed," said Kate lightly.

"Why are you looking so sad, beautiful lady?" said Matthew.

"Because I love you," said Kate, tears beginning to form in her eyes.

"Don't cry," said Matthew, "there's nothing to cry about. I'll manage it this time, you'll see."

When they had undressed Matthew, William covered him with a sheet and a blanket. Kate turned the light out.

"You promised you'd come to bed with me," said Matthew, drowsily.

She closed the door quietly.

William slept on a chair outside Matthew's room for fear he might wake up in the night and try to leave. Kate woke him in the morning before taking some breakfast in to Matthew.

"What am I doing here, Kate?" were Matthew's first words.

"You came back with us after Andrew MacKenzie's party last night," replied Kate rather feebly.

"No, I didn't. I went to the In and Out with that awful girl, Patricia something or other, who refused to come in with me. God, I feel lousy. Can I have a tomato juice? I don't want to be unsociable, but the last thing I need is breakfast."

"Of course, Matthew."

William came in. Matthew looked up at him. They stared at each other in silence.

"You know, don't you?" said Matthew finally.

"Yes," said William, "and I've been a fool and I hope you'll forgive me."

"Don't cry, William. I haven't seen you do that since you were twelve, when Covington was beating you up and I had to drag him off you. Remember? I wonder what Covington is up to now? Probably running a brothel in Tijuana; it's about all he was fit for. Mind you, if Covington is running it, the place will be damned efficient, so lead me to it. Don't cry, William. Grown men don't cry. Nothing can be done. I've seen all the specialists from New York to Los Angeles to Zurich, and there is nothing they can do. Do you mind if I skip the office this morning? I still feel awful. Wake me if I stay too long or if I'm any more trouble, and I'll find my own way home."

"This is your home," said William.

Matthew's face changed. "Will you tell my father, William? I can't face him. You're an only son, too; you understand the problem."

"Yes, I will," said William. "I'll go down to New York tomorrow and tell him if you'll promise to stay with Kate and me. I won't stop you from getting drunk if that's what you wish to do, or from having as many women as you want, but you must stay here."

"Best offer I've had in weeks, William. Now I think I'll sleep some more. I get so tired nowadays."

William watched Matthew fall into a deep sleep and removed the half-empty glass from his hand. A tomato stain was forming on the sheets.

"Don't die," he said quietly. "Please don't die, Matthew. Have you forgotten that you and I are going to run the biggest bank in America?"

William went to New York the following morning to see Charles Lester. The great man aged visibly at William's news and seemed to shrink into his seat.

"Thank you for coming, William, and telling me personally. I knew something must be wrong when Matthew stopped his monthly visits to see me. I'll come up every weekend. He will want to be with you and Kate, and I'll try not to make it too obvious how hard I took the news. God knows what he's done to deserve this. Since my wife died, I built everything for Matthew, and now there is no one to leave it to. Susan has no interest in the bank."

"Come to Boston whenever you want to, sir. You'll always be most welcome."

"Thank you, William, for everything you're doing for Matthew."

The old man looked up at him. "I wish your father were alive to see how worthy his son is of the name Kane. If only I could change places with Matthew, and let him live . . ."

"I ought to be getting back to him soon, sir."

"Yes, of course. Tell him I love him and I took the news stoically. Don't tell him anything different."

"Yes, sir."

William travelled back to Boston that night to find that Matthew had stayed at home with Kate and started reading America's latest best seller, *Gone With The Wind*, as he sat out on the veranda. He looked up as William came through the French windows.

"How did the old man take it?"

"He cried," said William.

"The chairman of Lester's bank cried?" said Matthew. "Never let the shareholders know that."

Matthew stopped drinking and worked as hard as he could until the last few days. William was amazed by his determination and had continually to make him slow down. He was always on top of his work and would tease William by checking his mail at the end of each day. In the evenings before a large dinner, Matthew would play tennis with William or row against him on the river. "I'll know I'm dead when I can't beat you," he mocked. Although Matthew slowed down he never entered the hospital, preferring to stay on at the Red House. The weeks went so slowly and yet so quickly for William, waking each morning wondering if Matthew would still be alive.

Matthew died on a Thursday, forty pages still to read of *Gone With The Wind*.

The funeral was held in New York, and William and Kate stayed with Charles Lester. In six months, he had become an old man, and as he stood by the graves of his wife and only son, he told William that he no longer saw any purpose in this life. William said nothing; no words of his could help the grieving father. William and Kate returned to Boston the next day. The Red House seemed strangely empty without Matthew. The past few months had been at once the happiest and unhappiest period in William's life. Death had brought him a closeness, both to Matthew and to Kate, that normal life would never have allowed.

When William returned to the bank after Matthew's death, he found it hard to get back into any sort of normal routine. He would get up and start to head towards Matthew's office for advice or a laugh, or merely to be assured of his existence, but he was no longer there. It was weeks before William could prevent himself from doing this.

Tony Simmons was very understanding, but it didn't help. William lost all interest in banking, even in Kane and Cabot itself, as he went through months of remorse over Matthew's death. He had always taken it for granted that he and Matthew would grow old together and share a common destiny. No one commented that William's work was not up to its usual high standard. Even Kate grew worried by the hours William would spend alone.

Then one morning she awoke to find him sitting on the edge of the bed staring down at her. She blinked up at him. "Is something wrong, darling?"

"No, I'm just looking at my greatest asset and making sure I don't take it for granted."

22

By the end of 1932, with America still in the grip of a depression, Abel was becoming a little apprehensive about the future of the Baron Group. Two thousand banks had been closed during the past two years, and more were shutting their doors every week. Nine million people were still unemployed, which had as its only virtue the assurance that Abel could maintain a highly professional staff in his hotels. Still, the Baron Group lost seventy-two thousand dollars during a year in which he had predicted that they would break even, and he began to wonder whether his backer's purse and patience would hold out long enough to allow him the chance to turn things around.

Abel had begun to take an active interest in American politics during Anton Cermak's successful campaign to become mayor of Chicago. Cermak talked Abel into joining the Democratic Party, which had launched a virulent campaign against Prohibition; Abel threw himself wholeheartedly behind Cermak, as Prohibition had proved very damaging to the hotel trade. The fact that Cermak was himself an immigrant, from Czechoslovakia, created an immediate bond between the two men, and Abel was delighted to be chosen as a delegate representative at the Democratic Convention held in Chicago that year where Cermak brought a packed audience to its feet with the words: "It's true I didn't come over on the *Mayflower*, but I came as soon as I could."

At the convention Cermak introduced Abel to Franklin D. Roosevelt, who made a lasting impression on him. F.D.R. went on to win the Presidential election easily and he swept

Democratic candidates into office all over the country. One of the newly elected aldermen at Chicago City Hall was Henry Osborne. When Anton Cermak was killed a few weeks later in Miami by an assassin's bullet intended for F.D.R., Abel decided to contribute a considerable amount of time and money to the cause of the Polish Democrats in Chicago.

During 1933 the group lost only twenty-three thousand dollars, and one of the hotels, the St. Louis Baron, actually showed a profit. When President Roosevelt had delivered his first fireside chat on March 12th, exhorting his countrymen 'to once again believe in America', Abel's confidence soared and he decided to re-open the two hotels that he had closed the previous year.

Zaphia grew querulous at his long absences in Charleston and Mobile, while he took the two hotels out of mothballs. She had never wanted Abel to be more than the deputy manager of the Stevens, a level at which she felt she could keep pace. The pace was quickening as every month passed, and she became conscious of falling behind Abel's ambitions and feared he was beginning to lose interest in her.

She was also becoming anxious about her childlessness, and started to see doctors who reassured her that there was nothing to prevent her from becoming pregnant. One offered the suggestion that Abel should also be examined, but Zaphia demurred, knowing he would regard the very mention of the subject as a slur on his manhood. Finally, after the subject had become so charged that it was difficult for them to discuss it at all, Zaphia missed her period. She waited hopefully for another month before saying anything to Abel or even seeing the doctor again. He confirmed that she was at last pregnant. To Abel's delight, Zaphia gave birth to a daughter, on New Year's Day, 1934. They named her Florentyna, after Abel's sister. Abel was besotted the moment he set eyes on the child and Zaphia knew from that moment she could no longer be the first love of his life. George and Zaphia's cousin were the child's Kums, and Abel gave a traditional ten-course Polish dinner on the evening of the christening. Many gifts were presented to the child, including a beautiful antique ring from Abel's backer. He returned the gift in kind when the Baron Group made a profit of sixty-three thousand dollars at the end of the year. Only the Mobile Baron was still losing money.

After Florentyna's birth Abel found he was spending much more of his time in Chicago which prompted him to decide that the time had come to build a Baron there. Hotels in the city were booming in the aftermath of the World's Fair. Abel intended to make his new hotel the flagship of the group in memory of Davis Leroy. The company still owned the site of the old Richmond Hotel on Michigan Avenue, and although Abel had had several offers for the land, he had always held out, hoping that one day he would be in a strong enough financial position to rebuild the hotel. The project required capital and Abel decided to use the seven hundred and fifty thousand dollars he had eventually received from Great Western Casualty for the old Chicago Richmond to start construction. As soon as his plans were formulated, he told Curtis Fenton of his intention, with the sole reservation that if David Maxton did not want a rival to the Stevens, Abel was willing to drop the whole project; he felt it was the least he could do in the circumstances. A few days later, Curtis Fenton advised him that his backer was delighted by the idea of 'The Chicago Baron'.

It took Abel twelve months to build the new Baron with a large helping hand from Alderman Henry Osborne, who hurried through the permits required from City Hall in the shortest possible time. The building was opened in 1936 by the mayor of the city, Edward J. Kelly, who, after the death of Anton Cermak, had become the prime organiser of the Democratic machine. In memory of Davis Leroy, the hotel had no twelfth floor – a tradition Abel continued in every new Baron he built.

Both Illinois senators were also in attendance to address the two thousand assembled guests. The Chicago Baron was superb both in design and construction. Abel had wound up spending well over a million dollars on the hotel, and it looked as though every penny had been put to good use. The public rooms were large and sumptuous with high stucco ceilings and decorations in pastel shades of green, pleasant and relaxing; the carpets were thick. The dark green embossed 'B' was discreet but ubiquitous, adorning everything from the flag that fluttered on the top of the forty-two storey building to the neat lapel of the most junior bellhop.

"This hotel already bears the hallmark of success," said J. Hamilton Lewis, the senior senator from Illinois, "because, my friends, it is the man, not the building, who will always be known as 'The Chicago Baron'." Abel beamed with undisguised pleasure as the two thousand guests roared their approval.

Abel's reply of acknowledgment was well turned and confidently delivered, and it earned him a standing ovation. He was beginning to feel very much at home among big business men and senior politicians. Zaphia hovered uncertainly in the background during the lavish celebration: the occasion was a little too much for her. She neither understood nor cared for success on Abel's scale; and even though she could now afford the most expensive clothes, she still looked unfashionable and out-of-place, and she was only too aware that it annoyed Abel. She stood by while Abel chatted with Henry Osborne.

"This must be the high point of your life," Henry was saying, slapping Abel on the back.

"High point – I've just turned thirty," said Abel. A camera flashed as he placed an arm round Henry's shoulder. Abel beamed, realising for the first time how pleasant it was to be treated as a public figure. "I'm going to put Baron hotels right across the globe," he said, just loud enough for the reporter to hear. "I intend to be to America what César Ritz was to Europe. Stick with me, Henry, and you'll enjoy the ride."

23

At breakfast the next morning, Kate pointed to a small item on page seventeen of the *Globe*, reporting the opening of the Chicago Baron.

William smiled as he read the article. Kane and Cabot had been foolish not to listen when he had advised them to support the Richmond Group. It pleased him that his own judgment on Rosnovski had turned out to be right even though the bank had lost out on the deal. His smile broadened as he read the nickname 'The Chicago Baron'. Then, suddenly, he felt sick. He examined the accompanying photograph more closely, but there was no mistake, and the caption confirmed his first impression: 'Abel Rosnovski, the chairman of the Baron Group talking with Mieczyslaw Szymczak, a governor of the Federal Reserve Board, and Alderman Henry Osborne.'

William dropped the paper on to the breakfast table and thought for a moment. As soon as he arrived at his office, he called Thomas Cohen at Cohen, Cohen and Yablons.

"It's been a long time, Mr. Kane," were Thomas Cohen's first words. "I was very sorry to learn of the death of your friend, Matthew Lester. How are your wife and your son – Richard – isn't that his name?"

William always admired Thomas Cohen's instant recall of names and relationships.

"Yes, it is. They're both well, thank you, Mr. Cohen."

"Well, what can I do for you this time, Mr. Kane?" Thomas Cohen also remembered that William could only manage about one sentence of small talk.

"I want to employ, through you, the services of a reliable

investigator. I do not wish my name to be associated with this inquiry, but I need another run-down on Henry Osborne. Everything he's done since he left Boston, and in particular whether there is any connection between him and Abel Rosnovski of the Baron Group."

There was a pause before the lawyer said, "Yes."

"Can you report to me in one week?"

"Two please, Mr. Kane, two," said Mr. Cohen.

"Full report on my desk at the bank in two weeks, Mr. Cohen?"

"Two weeks, Mr. Kane."

Thomas Cohen was as reliable as ever, and a full report was on William's desk on the fifteenth morning. William read the dossier with care. There appeared to be no formal business connections between Abel Rosnovski and Henry Osborne. Rosnovski, it seemed, found Osborne useful as a political contact, but nothing more. Osborne himself had bounced from job to job since leaving Boston, ending up in the main office of the Great Western Casualty Insurance Company. In all probability, that was how Osborne had come in contact with Abel Rosnovski, as the old Chicago Richmond had always been insured by Great Western. When the hotel burned down, the insurance company had originally refused to pay the claim. A certain Desmond Pacey, the manager, had been sent to prison for ten years, after pleading guilty to arson, and there was some suspicion that Abel Rosnovski might himself have been involved. Nothing was proved, and the insurance company settled later for three-quarters of a million dollars. Osborne, the report went on, is now an alderman and full-time politician at City Hall, and it is common knowledge that he hopes to become a congressman for Chicago. He has recently married a Miss Marie Axton, the daughter of a wealthy drug manufacturer, and as yet they have no children.

William went over the report again to be sure that he had not missed anything, however inconsequential. Although there did not seem to be a great deal to connect the two men, he couldn't help feeling that the association between Abel Rosnovski and Henry Osborne, both of whom hated him, for totally disparate reasons, was potentially dangerous to him. He mailed a cheque to Thomas Cohen and requested that he update the file every quarter, but as the months passed, and the quarterly reports revealed nothing new, he began to stop worrying, thinking perhaps he had over-reacted to the photograph in the *Boston Globe*.

Kate presented her husband with a daughter in the spring of 1937, whom they christened Virginia. William started changing nappies again, and such was his fascination with 'the little lady' that Kate had to rescue the child each night for fear she would never get any sleep. Richard, now two and a half, didn't care too much for the new arrival to begin with, but time and a new wooden soldier on a horse, combined to allay his jealousy.

By the end of the year, William's department at Kane and Cabot had made a handsome profit for the bank. He had emerged from the lethargy that had overcome him on Matthew's death and was fast regaining his reputation as a shrewd investor in the stock market, not least when 'sell 'em short' Smith admitted he had only perfected a technique developed by William Kane of Boston. Even Tony Simmons' direction had become less irksome. Nevertheless, William was secretly worried by the prospect that he could not become chairman of Kane and Cabot until Simmons retired in seventeen years' time, and he began to consider looking around for employment in another bank.

William and Kate had taken to visiting Charles Lester in New York about once a month at weekends. The great man had grown very old over the three years since Matthew's death, and rumours in financial circles were that he had lost all interest in his work and was rarely seen at the bank. William was beginning to wonder how much longer the old man would live, and then a few weeks later he died. William travelled down to the funeral in New York. Everyone seemed to be there including the Vice-President of the United States, John Nance Garner. After the funeral, William and Kate took the train back to Boston, numbly conscious that they had lost their last close link with the Lester family.

It was some six months later that William received a communication from Sullivan and Cromwell, the distinguished New York lawyers, asking him if he would be kind enough to attend the reading of the will of the late Charles Lester at their offices in Wall Street. William went to the reading, more from loyalty to the Lester family than from any curiosity to know what Charles Lester had left him. He hoped for a small memento that would remind him of Matthew and join the 'Harvard Oar' that still hung on the wall of the main guest room of the Red House. He also looked forward to the opportunity of renewing his acquaintance with many members of the Lester family whom he had come to know in school and college holidays spent with Matthew.

William drove down to New York in his newly acquired Daimler the night before the reading and stayed at the Harvard Club. The will was to be read at ten o'clock the following morning, and William was surprised to find on his arrival in the offices of Sullivan and Cromwell that over fifty people were already present. Many of them glanced up at William as he entered the room, and he greeted several of Matthew's cousins and aunts, looking rather older than he remembered them; he could only conclude that they must be thinking the same about him. His eyes searched for Matthew's sister Susan, but he couldn't see her. At ten o'clock precisely Mr. Arthur Cromwell entered the room, accompanied by an assistant carrying a brown leather folder. Everyone fell silent in hopeful expectation. The lawyer began by explaining to the assembled would-be beneficiaries that the contents of the will had not been disclosed until six months after Charles Lester's death at Mr. Lester's specific instruction: having no son to whom to leave his fortune he had wanted the dust to settle after his death before his final intentions were made clear.

William looked around the room at the intent faces which were hanging on every syllable issuing from the lawyer's mouth. Arthur Cromwell took nearly an hour to read the will. After reciting the expected bequests to family retainers, charities and Harvard University, Cromwell went on to reveal that Charles Lester had divided his personal fortune among all his relatives, treating them more or less according to their degree of kinship. His daughter, Susan, received the largest share of the estate while the five nephews and three nieces each received an equal portion of the rest. All their money and shares were to be held in trust by the bank until they were thirty. Several other cousins, aunts and distant relations were given immediate cash payments.

William was surprised when Mr. Cromwell announced: "That disposes of all the known assets of the late Charles Lester."

People began to shuffle around in their seats, as a murmur of nervous conversation broke out. No one wanted to admit that the unfortunate death had made them fortunate.

"That is not, however, the end of Mr. Charles Lester's last will and testament," said the imperturbable lawyer, and everyone sat still again, fearful of some late and unwelcome thunderbolt.

Mr. Cromwell went on. "I shall now continue in Mr. Charles Lester's own words: 'I have always considered that a bank and its reputation are only as good as the people who serve it. It was well known that I had hoped my son Matthew would succeed me as chairman of Lester's, but his tragic and untimely death has intervened. Until now, I have never divulged my choice of successor for Lester's bank. I therefore wish it to be known that I desire William Lowell Kane, son of one of my dearest friends, the late Richard Lowell Kane, and at present the vice-chairman of Kane and Cabot, be appointed chairman of Lester's Bank and Trust Company following the next full board meeting.' "

There was an immediate uproar. Everyone looked around the room for the mysterious Mr. William Lowell Kane of whom few but the immediate Lester family had ever heard.

"I have not yet finished," said Arthur Cromwell quietly.

Silence fell once more, as the members of the audience, anticipating another bombshell, exchanged fearful glances.

The lawyer continued. "All the above grants and division of shares in Lester's and Company are expressly conditional upon the beneficiaries voting for Mr. Kane at the next annual board meeting, and continuing to do so for at least the following five years, unless Mr. Kane himself indicates that he does not wish to accept the chairmanship."

Uproar broke out again. William wished he was a million miles away, not sure whether to be deliriously happy or to concede that he must be the most detested person in that room.

"That concludes the last will and testament of the late Charles Lester," said Mr. Cromwell, but only the front row heard him.

William looked up. Susan Lester was walking towards him. The puppy fat had disappeared while the attractive freckles had remained. He smiled, but she walked straight past him without even acknowledging his presence. William frowned.

Ignoring the babble, a tall, grey-haired man wearing a pin-striped suit and a silver tie moved quickly towards William.

"You are William Kane, are you not, sir?"

"Yes, I am," said William nervously.

"My name is Peter Parfitt," said the stranger.

"The bank's vice-chairman," said William.

"Correct, sir," he said. "I do not know you, but I do know something of your reputation, and I count myself lucky to have been acquainted with your distinguished father. If Charles Lester thought you were the right man to be chairman of his bank, that's good enough for me."

William had never been so relieved in his life.

"Where are you staying in New York?" continued Peter Parfitt before William could reply.

"At the Harvard Club."

"Splendid. May I ask if you are free for dinner tonight by any chance?"

"I had intended to return to Boston this evening," said William, "but I expect I shall now have to stay in New York for a few days."

"Good. Why don't you come to my house for dinner, say about eight o'clock?"

The banker handed William his card with an address embossed in copperplate script. "I shall enjoy the opportunity of chatting with you in more convivial surroundings."

"Thank you, sir," said William, pocketing the card as others began crowding around him. Some stared at him in hostility; others waited to express their congratulations. When William eventually managed to make his escape and returned to the Harvard Club, the first thing he did was to call Kate and tell her the news.

She said very quietly, "How happy Matthew would be for you, darling."

"I know," said William.

"When are you coming home?"

"God knows. I'm dining tonight with a Mr. Peter Parfitt who is a vice-chairman of Lester's. He's being most helpful over the whole affair, which is making life much easier. I'll spend the night here at the club, and then call you sometime tomorrow to let you know how things are working out."

"All right, darling."

"All quiet on the Eastern seaboard?"

"Well, Virginia has cut a tooth and seems to think she deserves special attention, Richard was sent to bed early for being rude to Nanny, and we all miss you."

William laughed. "I'll call you tomorrow."

"Yes, please do. By the way, many congratulations. I approve of Charles Lester's judgment even if I'm going to hate living in New York."

It was the first time William had thought about living in New York.

William arrived at Peter Parfitt's home on East Sixty-fourth Street at eight o'clock that night and was taken by surprise to find his host had dressed for dinner. William felt slightly embarrassed and ill at ease in his dark banker's suit. He quickly explained to his hostess that he had originally anticipated returning to Boston that evening. Diana Parfitt, who turned out to be Peter's second wife, could not have been more charming to her guest, and she seemed delighted that William was to be the next chairman of Lester's. During an excellent dinner William could not resist asking Peter Parfitt how he thought the rest of the board would react to Charles Lester's wishes.

"They'll all fall in line," said Parfitt. "I've spoken to most of them already. There's a full board meeting on Monday morning to confirm your appointment and I can only see one small cloud on the horizon."

"What's that?" said William, trying not to sound anxious.

"Well, between you and me, the other vice-chairman, Ted Leach, was rather expecting to be appointed chairman himself. In fact, I think I would go as far as saying that he anticipated it. We had all been informed that no nomination could be made until after the will had been read, but Charles Lester's wishes must have come as rather a shock to Ted."

"Will he put up a fight?" asked William.

"I'm afraid he might, but there's nothing for you to worry about."

"I don't mind admitting," said Diana Parfitt, as she studied the rather flat soufflé in front of her, "that he has never been my favourite man."

"Now, dear," said Parfitt reprovingly, "we mustn't say anything behind Ted's back before Mr. Kane has had a chance to judge for himself. There is no doubt in my mind that the board will confirm Mr. Kane's appointment at the meeting on Monday, and there's even the possibility that Ted Leach will resign."

"I don't want anyone to feel they have to resign because of me," said William.

"A very creditable sentiment," said Parfitt. "But don't bother yourself about a puff of wind. I'm confident that the whole matter is well under control. You go quietly back to Boston tomorrow, and I'll keep you informed on the lay of the land."

"Perhaps it might be wise if I dropped in at the bank in the morning. Won't your fellow officers find it a little curious if I make no attempt to meet any of them?"

"No, I don't think that would be advisable given the circumstances. In fact, I feel it might be wiser for you to stay out of their way until the Monday board meeting is over. They won't want to seem any less independent than necessary, and they may already feel like glorified rubber stamps. Take my advice, Bill, you go back to Boston, and I'll call you with the good news before noon on Monday."

William reluctantly agreed to Peter Parfitt's suggestion and went on to spend a pleasant evening discussing with both of them where he and Kate might stay in New York while they were looking for a permanent home. William was somewhat surprised to find that Peter Parfitt seemed to have no desire to discuss his own views on banking, and he assumed the reason was because of Diana Parfitt's presence. An excellent evening ended with a little too much brandy, and William did not arrive back at the Harvard Club until after one o'clock.

Once William had returned to Boston he made an immediate report to Tony Simmons of what had transpired in New York as he did not want him to hear about the appointment from anyone else. Tony turned out to be surprisingly sanguine about the news.

"I'm sorry to learn that you will be leaving us, William. Lester's may well be two or three times the size of Kane and Cabot, but I shall be unable to replace you, and I hope you'll consider very carefully before accepting the appointment."

William was surprised and couldn't help showing it. "Frankly, Tony, I would have thought you'd have been only too glad to see the back of me."

"William, when will you ever believe that my first interest has always been the bank, and there has never been any doubt in my mind that you are one of the shrewdest investment advisers in America today? If you leave Kane and Cabot now, many of the bank's most important clients will naturally want to follow you."

"I would never transfer my own money to Lester's," said William, "any more than I would expect any of the bank's clients to move with me."

"Of course you wouldn't solicit them to join you, William, but some of them will want you to continue managing their portfolios. Like your father and Charles Lester, they believe quite rightly that banking is about people and reputations."

William and Kate spent a tense weekend waiting for Monday and the result of the board meeting in New York.

William sat nervously in his office the whole of Monday morning, answering every telephone call personally, but he heard nothing as the morning dragged into the afternoon. He didn't even leave the office for lunch, and Peter Parfitt finally called a little after six.

"I'm afraid there's been some unexpected trouble, Bill," were his opening words.

William's heart sank.

"Nothing for you to worry about since I still feel I have the situation well under control, but the board wants the right to oppose your nomination with their own candidate. Some of them have produced legal opinions that go as far as saying the relevant clause of the will has no real validity. I've been given the unpleasant task of asking if you would be willing to fight an election against the board's candidate."

"Who would be the board's candidate?" asked William.

"No names have been mentioned by anyone yet, but I imagine their choice will be Ted Leach. No one else has shown the slightest interest in running against you."

"I'd like a little time to think about it," William replied. "When will the next board meeting be?"

"A week from today," said Parfitt. "But don't you go and get yourself all worked up about Ted Leach; I'm still confident that you will win easily, and I'll keep you informed of any further developments as the week goes by."

"Do you want me to come down to New York, Peter?"

"No, not for the moment. I don't think that would help matters."

William thanked him and put the phone down. He packed his old leather briefcase and left the office, feeling more than a little depressed. Tony Simmons, carrying a suitcase, caught up with him in the private parking lot.

"I didn't know you were going out of town, Tony."

"It's only the monthly bankers' dinner in New York. I'll be back by tomorrow afternoon. I think I can safely leave Kane and Cabot for twenty-four hours in the capable hands of the next chairman of Lester's."

William laughed. "I may already be the ex-chairman,"

he said and explained the latest development. Once again, William was surprised by Tony Simmons' reaction.

"It's true that Ted Leach has always expected to be the next chairman of Lester's," he mused. "That's common knowledge in financial circles. But he's a loyal servant of the bank, and I can't believe he would oppose Charles Lester's express wishes."

"I didn't realise you even knew him," said William.

"I don't know him all that well," said Tony. "He was a class ahead of me at Yale, and now I see him from time to time at these damned bankers' dinners that you'll have to attend when you're a chairman. He's bound to be there tonight. I'll have a word with him if you like."

"Yes, please do, but be very careful, won't you?" said William.

"My dear William, you've spent nearly ten years of your life telling me I'm far too careful."

"I'm sorry, Tony. Funny how one's judgment is impaired when one is worrying about one's own problems, however sound the same judgment might be considered when dealing with other people's. I'll put myself in your hands and do whatever you advise."

"Good then, you leave it to me. I'll see what Leach has to say for himself and call you first thing in the morning."

Tony called from New York a few minutes after midnight and woke William from a deep sleep.

"Have I woken you, William?"

"Yes, who is it?"

"Tony Simmons."

William switched on the light by his side of the bed and looked at his alarm clock. Ten minutes past twelve.

"Well, you did say you would call first thing in the morning."

Tony laughed. "I'm afraid what I have to tell you won't seem quite so funny. The man who is opposing you for chairman of Lester's Bank is Peter Parfitt."

"*What?*" said William, suddenly awake.

"He's been trying to push the board into supporting him behind your back. Ted Leach, as I expected, is in favour of your appointment as chairman, but the board is now split down the middle."

"Hell. First, thank you, Tony, and second, what do I do now?"

"If you want to be the next chairman of Lester's, you'd better get down here fast before the members of the board wonder why you're hiding away in Boston."

"Hiding away?"

"That's what Parfitt has been telling the directors for the past few days."

"The bastard."

"Now that you mention the subject, I am unable to vouch for his parentage," said Tony.

William laughed.

"Come and stay at the Yale Club. Then we can talk the whole thing out first thing in the morning."

"I'll be there as quickly as I can," said William.

"I may be asleep when you arrive. It'll be your turn to wake me."

William put the phone down and looked over at Kate, blissfully oblivious to his new problems. She had slept right through the entire conversation. How he wished he could manage that. A curtain had only to flutter in the breeze, and he was awake. She would probably sleep right through the Second Coming. He scribbled a few lines of explanation to her and put the note on her bedside table, dressed, packed – this time including a dinner jacket – and set off for New York.

The roads were clear and the run in the new Daimler took him only five hours. He drove into New York with cleaners, mailmen, newsboys, and the morning sun, and checked in at the Yale Club as the hall clock chimed once. It was six-fifteen. He unpacked and decided to rest for an hour before waking Tony. The next thing he heard was an insistent tapping on his door. Sleepily, he got up to open it only to find Tony Simmons standing outside.

"Nice dressing gown, William," said Tony, grinning. He was fully dressed.

"I must have fallen asleep. If you wait a minute, I'll be right with you," said William.

"No, no, I have to catch a train back to Boston. You take a shower and get yourself dressed while we talk."

William went into the bathroom and left the door open.

"Now your main problem . . ." started Tony.

William put his head around the bathroom door. "I can't hear you while the water's running."

Tony waited for it to stop. "Peter Parfitt is your main problem. He assumed he was going to be the next chairman, and that his would be the name that was read out in Charles Lester's will. He's been manoeuvring the directors against you and playing board-room politics ever since. Ted Leach can fill you in on the finer details and would like you to join him for lunch today at the Metropolitan Club. He may bring two or three other board members with him on whom you can rely. The board, by the way, still seems to be split right down the middle."

William nicked himself with his razor. "Damn. Which club?"

"Metropolitan, just off Fifth Avenue on East Sixtieth Street."

"Why there and not somewhere down in Wall Street?"

"William, when you're dealing with the Peter Parfitts of this world, you don't telegraph your intentions. Keep your wits about you, and play the whole thing very coolly. From what Leach tells me, I believe you can still win."

William came back into the bedroom with a towel round his waist. "I'll try," he said, "to be cool, that is."

Tony smiled. "Now, I must get back to Boston. My train leaves Penn Station in ten minutes." He looked at his watch. "Damn, six minutes."

Tony paused at the bedroom door. "You know, your father never trusted Peter Parfitt. Too smooth, he always used to say. Never anything more, just a little too smooth." He picked up his suitcase. "Good luck, William."

"How can I begin to thank you, Tony?"

"You can't. Just put it down to my trying to atone for the lousy way I treated Matthew."

William watched the door close as he put in his collar stud and then straightened his tie, reflecting on how curious it was that he had spent years working closely with Tony Simmons without ever really getting to know him but that now, in only a few days of personal crisis, he found himself instantly liking and trusting a man he had never before really seen. He went down to the dining room and had a typical club breakfast: a cold boiled egg, one piece of hard toast, butter and English marmalade from someone else's table. The porter handed him a copy of the *Wall Street Journal*, which hinted on an inside page that everything was not running smoothly at Lester's following the nomination of William Kane as their next chairman. At least the *Journal* did not seem to have any inside information.

William returned to his room and asked the operator for a number in Boston. He was kept waiting for a few minutes before he was put through.

"I do apologise, Mr. Kane. I had no idea that you were on the line. May I congratulate you on your appointment as chairman of Lester's. I hope this means that our New York office will be seeing a lot more of you in the future."

"That may well depend on you, Mr. Cohen."

"I don't think I quite understand," the lawyer replied.

William explained what had happened over the past few days and read out the relevant section of Charles Lester's will.

Thomas Cohen spent some time taking down each word and then going over his notes carefully.

"Do you think his wishes would stand up in court?" asked William.

"Who knows? I can't think of a precedent for such a situation. A nineteenth-century Member of Parliament once bequeathed his constituency in a will, and no one objected, and the beneficiary went on to become Prime Minister. But that was over a hundred years ago – and in England. Now in this case, if the board decided to contest Mr. Lester's will, and you took their decision to court, I wouldn't care to predict which way the judge might jump. Lord Melbourne didn't have to contend with a surrogate of New York County. Nevertheless, a nice legal conundrum, Mr. Kane."

"What do you advise?" said William.

"I am a Jew, Mr. Kane. I came to this country on a ship from Germany at the turn of the century, and I have always had to fight hard for anything I've wanted. Do you want to be chairman of Lester's that badly?"

"Yes, Mr. Cohen, I do."

"Then you must listen to an old man who has, over the years, come to view you with great respect, and if I may say so, with some affection, and I'll tell you exactly what I'd do if I were faced with your predicament."

An hour later William put the phone down, and having some time to kill, he strolled up Park Avenue. Along the way, he passed a site on which a huge building was well into construction. A large, neat billboard announced 'The next Baron Hotel will be in New York. When the Baron has been your host, you'll never want to stay anywhere else.' William smiled for the first time that morning and walked with a lighter step towards the Metropolitan Club.

Ted Leach, a short dapper man with dark brown hair and a lighter moustache, was standing in the foyer of the club, waiting for him. He ushered William into the bar. William admired the Renaissance style of the club, built by Otto Kuhn and Standford White in 1894. J. P. Morgan had founded the club when one of his closest friends was blackballed at the Union League.

"A fairly extravagant gesture even for a very close friend," Ted Leach suggested, trying to make conversation. "What will you have to drink, Mr. Kane?"

"A dry sherry, please," said William.

A boy in a smart blue uniform returned a few moments later with a dry sherry and a scotch and water; he hadn't needed to ask Mr. Leach for his order.

"To the next chairman of Lester's," said Ted Leach, raising his glass.

William hesitated.

"Don't drink, Mr. Kane. As you know, you should never drink to yourself."

William laughed, unsure how to reply.

A few minutes later two older men were walking towards

them, both tall and confident in the bankers' uniform of grey three-piece suits, stiff collars and dark unpatterned ties. Had they been strolling down Wall Street, William would not have given them a second glance. In the Metropolitan Club he studied them carefully.

"Mr. Alfred Rodgers and Mr. Winthrop Davies," said Ted Leach as he introduced them.

William smiled reservedly, still unsure whose side anyone was on. The two newcomers were studying him equally carefully. No one spoke for a moment.

"Where do we start?" said the one called Rodgers, a monocle falling from his eye as he spoke.

"By going on up to lunch," said Ted Leach.

The three of them turned around, obviously knowing exactly where they were going. William followed. The dining room on the second floor was vast, with another magnificent high ceiling. The *maître d'* placed them in the window seat, overlooking Central Park, where no one could overhear their conversation.

"Let's order and then talk," said Ted Leach.

Through the window William could see the Plaza Hotel. Memories of his graduation celebration with the grandmothers and Matthew came flooding back to him – and there was something else he was trying to recall about that tea at the Plaza . . .

"Mr. Kane, let's put our cards on the table," said Ted Leach.

"Charles Lester's decision to appoint you as chairman of the bank came as a surprise, not to put too fine a point on it. But if the board ignores his wishes, the bank could be plunged into chaos and that is an outcome none of us needs. He was a shrewd old man, and he will have had his reasons for wanting you as the bank's next chairman, and that's good enough for me."

William had heard those words before – from Peter Parfitt.

"All three of us," said Winthrop Davies, taking over, "owe everything we have to Charles Lester, and we will carry out his wishes if it's the last thing we do as members of the board."

"It may turn out to be just that," said Ted Leach, "if Peter Parfitt does succeed in becoming chairman."

"I'm sorry, gentlemen," said William, "to have caused so much consternation. If my appointment as chairman came as a surprise to you, I can assure you it was nothing less than a bolt from the blue for me. I imagined I would receive some minor personal memento of Matthew's from Charles Lester's will, not the responsibility of running the entire bank."

"We understand the position you've been placed in, Mr. Kane," said Ted Leach, "and you must trust us when we say we are here to help you. We are aware that you will find that difficult to believe after the treatment that has been meted out to you by Peter Parfitt and the tactics he has been using behind your back to try and secure the chair for himself."

"I have to believe you, Mr. Leach, because I have no choice but to place myself in your hands and seek your advice as to how you view the current situation."

"Thank you," said Leach. "That situation is clear to me. Peter Parfitt's campaign is well organised, and he now feels he is acting from a position of strength. We, therefore, Mr. Kane, must be entirely open with each other if we are to have any chance of beating him. I am assuming, of course, that you have the stomach for such a fight."

"I wouldn't be here if I didn't, Mr. Leach. And now that you have put the position so succinctly, perhaps you will allow me to suggest how we should go about defeating Mr. Parfitt."

"Certainly," said Ted Leach.

All three men listened intently.

"You are undoubtedly right in saying that Parfitt feels he is now in a strong position because to date he has always been the one on the attack, always knowing what is going to happen next. Might I suggest that the time has come for us to reverse that trend and take up the attack ourselves where and when he least expects it – in his own board room."

"How do you propose we go about that, Mr. Kane?" enquired Winthrop Davies, looking somewhat surprised.

"I'll tell you if you will first permit me to ask you some

questions. How many full-time executive directors are there with a vote on the board?"

"Sixteen," said Ted Leach instantly.

"And with whom does their allegiance lie at this moment?" William asked.

"Not the easiest question to answer, Mr. Kane," Winthrop Davies chipped in. He took a crumpled envelope from his inside pocket and studied the back of it before he continued. "I think we can count on six sure votes, and Peter Parfitt can be certain of five. It came as a shock for me to discover this morning that Rupert Cork-Smith, who was Charles Lester's closest friend, is unwilling to support you, Mr. Kane. Really strange, because I know he doesn't care for Parfitt. I think that may make the voting six apiece."

"That gives us until Thursday," added Ted Leach, "to find out how the other four board members are likely to react to your appointment."

"Why Thursday?" asked William.

"Day of the next board meeting," answered Leach, stroking his moustache, which William had noticed he always did when he started to speak. "And more important, Item One on the agenda is the election of a new chairman."

"I was told the next meeting would not take place until Monday," said William in astonishment.

"By whom?" Davies asked.

"Peter Parfitt," said William.

"His tactics," Ted Leach commented, "have not been altogether those of a gentleman."

"I've learned enough about that gentleman," William said, placing an ironic stress on the word, "to make me realise that I shall have to take the battle to him."

"Easier said than done, Mr. Kane. He is very much in the driver's seat at this moment," said Winthrop Davies, "and I'm not sure how we go about removing him from it."

"Switch the traffic lights to red," replied William. "Who has the authority to call a board meeting?"

"While the board is without a chairman, either vice-chairman," said Ted Leach. "Which in reality means Peter Parfitt or myself."

"How many board members form a quorum?"

"Nine," said Davies.

"And if you are one of the two vice-chairmen, Mr. Leach, who is the company secretary?"

"I am," said Alfred Rodgers, who until then had hardly opened his mouth, the exact quality William always looked for in a company secretary.

"How much notice do you have to give to call an emergency board meeting, Mr. Rodgers?"

"Every director must be informed at least twenty-four hours beforehand although that has never actually happened except during the crash of twenty-nine. Charles Lester always tried to give at least three days' notice."

"But the bank's rules do allow for an emergency meeting to be held on twenty-four hours' notice?" asked William.

"They do, Mr. Kane," Alfred Rodgers affirmed, his monocle now firmly in place and focused on William.

"Excellent, then let's call our own board meeting."

The three bankers stared at William as if they had not quite heard him clearly.

"Think about it, gentlemen," William continued. "Mr. Leach, as vice-chairman, calls the board meeting and Mr. Rodgers, as company secretary, informs all the directors."

"When would you want this board meeting to take place?" asked Ted Leach.

"Tomorrow afternoon." William looked at his watch. "Three o'clock."

"Good God, that's cutting it a bit fine," said Alfred Rodgers.

"I'm not sure . . ."

"Cutting it very fine for Peter Parfitt, wouldn't you say?" said William.

"That's true," said Ted Leach, "if you know precisely what you have planned for the meeting?"

"You leave the meeting to me. Just be sure that it's correctly convened and that every director is properly informed."

"I wonder how Peter Parfitt is going to react," said Ted Leach.

"Don't worry about Parfitt," said William. "That's the mistake we've made all along. Let him start to worry about us for a change. As long as he is given the full twenty-four hours' notice and he's the last director informed, we have nothing to fear. We don't want him to have any more time than necessary to stage a counter-attack. And, gentlemen, do not be surprised by anything I do or say tomorrow. Trust my judgment, and be there to support me."

"You don't feel we ought to know exactly what you have in mind?"

"No, Mr Leach, you must appear at the meeting as disinterested directors doing no more than carrying out your duty."

It was beginning to dawn on Ted Leach and his two colleagues why Charles Lester had chosen William Kane to be their next chairman. They left the Metropolitan Club a good deal more confident than when they had arrived, despite their being totally in the dark as to what would actually happen at the board meeting they were about to instigate. William, on the other hand, having carried out the first part of Thomas Cohen's instructions, was now looking forward to pulling off the harder second part.

He spent most of the afternoon and evening in his room at the Yale Club, meticulously considering his tactics for the next day's meeting and taking only a short break to call Kate.

"Where are you, darling?" she said. "Stealing away in the middle of the night to I know not where."

"To my mistress in New York," said William.

"Poor girl," said Kate. "She probably doesn't know the half of it. What's her advice on the devious Mr. Parfitt?"

"Haven't had time to ask her, we've been so busy doing other things. While I have you on the phone, what's your advice?"

"Do nothing Charles Lester or your father wouldn't have done in the same circumstances," said Kate, suddenly serious.

"They're probably playing golf together on the eighteenth cloud and taking a side bet watching us the whole time."

"Whatever you do, William, you won't go far wrong if you do remember they are watching you."

When dawn broke, William was already awake, having only managed to sleep for short, fitful intervals. He rose a little after six, had a cold shower, went for a long walk through Central Park to clear his head, and returned to the Yale Club for a light breakfast. There was a message waiting for him in the front hall – from his wife. William laughed when he read it for a second time at the line, 'If you're not too busy could you remember to buy Richard a baseball glove.' William picked up the *Wall Street Journal* which was still running the story of trouble in the Lester's board room over the selection of a new chairman. It now had Peter Parfitt's version of the story, hinting that his appointment as chairman would probably be confirmed at Thursday's meeting. William wondered whose version would be reported in tomorrow's paper. Oh, for a look at tomorrow's *Journal* now. He spent the morning double checking the articles of incorporation and by-laws of Lester's Bank. He had no lunch but did find time to visit Schwalts and buy a baseball glove for his son.

At two-thirty William took a cab to the bank on Wall Street and arrived a few minutes before three. The young doorman asked him if he had an appointment to see anyone.

"I'm William Kane."

"Yes, sir; you'll want the board room."

Good God, thought William, I can't even remember where it is.

The doorman observed his embarrassment. "You take the corridor on the left, sir, and then it's the second door on the right."

"Thank you," said William, and walked as confidently as he could down the corridor. He had always thought the expression a stomach full of butterflies a stupid one until that moment. He felt his heartbeat was louder than the clock in the front hall; he would not have been surprised to hear himself chiming three o'clock.

Ted Leach was standing alone at the entrance to the board room. "There's going to be trouble," were his opening words.

"Good," said William. "That's the way Charles Lester would have liked it, and he would have faced the trouble head on."

William strode into the impressive oak-panelled room and did not need to count heads to be sure that every director was present. This was not going to be one of those board meetings a director could occasionally afford to skip. The conversation stopped the moment William entered the room, and there was an awkward silence as they all stood around and stared at him. William quickly took the chairman's seat at the head of the long mahogany table before Peter Parfitt could realise what was happening.

"Gentlemen, please be seated," said William, hoping his voice sounded firm.

Ted Leach and some of the other directors took their seats immediately; others were more reluctant. Murmuring started.

William could see that two directors whom he didn't know were about to rise and interrupt him.

"Before anyone else says anything I would, if you will allow me, like to make an opening statement, and then you can decide how you wish to proceed from there. I feel that is the least we can do to comply with the wishes of the late Charles Lester."

The two men sat down.

"Thank you, gentlemen. To start with, I would like to make it clear to all those present that I have absolutely no desire to be the chairman of this bank – " William paused for effect " – unless it be the wish of the majority of its directors."

Every eye in the room was now fixed on William.

"I am, gentlemen, at present vice-chairman of Kane and Cabot, and I own fifty-one per cent of their stock. Kane and Cabot was founded by my grandfather, and I think it compares favourably in reputation, though not in size, with Lester's. Were I required to leave Boston and move to New York to become the next chairman of Lester's, in compliance with Charles Lester's wishes, I cannot pretend the move would be an easy one for myself or for my family.

However, as it was Charles Lester's wish that I should do just that – and he was not a man to make such a proposition lightly – I am, gentlemen, bound to take his wishes seriously myself. I would also like to add that his son, Matthew Lester, was my closest friend for over fifteen years, and I consider it a tragedy that it is I, and not he, who is addressing you today as your nominated chairman."

Some of the directors were nodding their approval.

"Gentlemen, if I am fortunate enough to secure your support today, I will sacrifice everything I have in Boston in order to serve you. I hope it is unnecessary for me to give you a detailed account of my banking experience. I shall assume that any director present who has read Charles Lester's will must have taken the trouble to find out why he considered that I was the right man to succeed him. My own chairman, Anthony Simmons, whom many of you will know, has asked me to stay on at Kane and Cabot.

"I had intended to inform Mr. Parfitt yesterday of my final decision, had he taken the trouble to call me and seek out that information. I had the pleasure of dining with Mr. and Mrs. Parfitt last Friday evening at their home, and on that occasion Mr. Parfitt informed me that he had no interest in becoming the next chairman of this bank. My only rival, in his opinion, was Mr. Edward Leach, your other vice-chairman. I have since consulted with Mr. Leach himself, and he informs me that I have always had his support for the chair. I assumed, therefore, that both vice-chairmen were backing me. After reading the *Wall Street Journal* this morning, not that I have ever trusted their forecasting since the age of eight" – a little laughter – "I felt I should attend today's meeting to assure myself that I had not lost the support of the two vice-chairmen, and that the *Journal*'s account was inaccurate. Mr. Leach called this board meeting, and I must ask him at this juncture if he still supports me to succeed Charles Lester as the bank's next chairman."

William looked towards Ted Leach, whose head was bowed. The wait for his verdict was palpable. A thumbs-down from him would mean the Parfittlians could eat the Christian.

Ted Leach raised his head slowly and said, "I support Mr. Kane unreservedly."

William looked directly at Peter Parfitt for the first time that day. He was sweating profusely, and when he spoke, he did not take his eyes off the yellow pad in front of him.

"Well, some members of the board," he began, "felt I should throw my hat in the ring . . ."

"So you have changed your mind about supporting me and complying with Charles Lester's wishes?" interrupted William, allowing a small note of surprise to enter his voice.

Peter Parfitt raised his head a little. "The problem is not quite that easy, Mr. Kane."

"Yes or no, Mr. Parfitt?"

"Yes, I shall stand against you," said Peter Parfitt suddenly, forcefully.

"Despite telling me last Friday you had no interest in being chairman yourself?"

"I would like to be able to state my own position," said Parfitt, "before you assume too much. This is not your board room yet, Mr. Kane."

"Certainly, Mr. Parfitt."

So far, the meeting had gone exactly as William had planned. His own speech had been carefully prepared and delivered, and Peter Parfitt now laboured under the disadvantage of having lost the initiative, to say nothing of having been publicly called a liar.

"Gentlemen," he began, as if searching for words. "Well," he said.

The eyes had turned their gaze from William and now fixed on Parfitt. It gave William the chance to relax and study the faces of the other directors.

"Several members of the board approached me privately after I had dinner with Mr. Kane, and I felt that it was no more than my duty to consider their wishes and offer myself for election. I have never at any time wanted to oppose the wishes of Mr. Charles Lester, whom I always admired and respected. Naturally, I would have informed Mr. Kane of my intention before tomorrow's scheduled board meeting, but I confess to have been taken somewhat by surprise by today's events."

He drew a deep breath and started again. "I have served Lester's for twenty-two years, six of them as your vice-chairman. I feel, therefore, that I have the right to be considered for the chair. I would be delighted if Mr. Kane were to join the board, but I now find myself unable to back his appointment as chairman. I hope my fellow directors will find it possible to support someone who has worked for this bank for over twenty years rather than elect an unknown outsider on the whim of a man distraught by the death of his only son. Thank you, gentlemen."

He sat down.

In the circumstances, William was rather impressed by the speech, but Parfitt did not have the benefit of Mr. Cohen's advice on the power of the last word in a close contest. William rose again.

"Gentlemen, Mr. Parfitt has pointed out that I am personally unknown to you. I, therefore, want none of you to be in any doubt as to the type of man I am. I am, as I said, the grandson and the son of bankers. I've been a banker all my life and it would be less than honest of me to pretend I would not be delighted to serve as the next chairman of Lester's. If, on the other hand, after all you have heard today, you decide to back Mr. Parfitt as chairman, so be it. I shall return to Boston and serve my own bank quite happily. I will, moreover, announce publicly that I have no wish to be the chairman of Lester's, and that will insure you against any claims that you have been derelict in fulfilling the provisions of Charles Lester's will.

"There are, however, no conditions on which I would be willing to serve on your board under Mr. Parfitt. I have no intention of being less than frank with you on that point. I come before you, gentlemen, at the grave disadvantage of being, in Mr. Parfitt's words, 'an unknown outsider'. I have, however, the advantage of being supported by a man who cannot be present today. A man whom all of you respected and admired, a man not known for yielding to whims or making hasty decisions. I therefore suggest this board wastes no more of its valuable time in deciding whom they wish to serve as the next chairman of Lester's. If any of you have any doubts in your mind about my ability to run this bank, then I can only suggest you vote for Mr. Parfitt. I shall not vote in this election myself, gentlemen, and I assume Mr. Parfitt will not do so either."

"You *cannot* vote," said Peter Parfitt, angrily. "You are not a member of this board yet. I am, and I shall vote."

"So be it, Mr. Parfitt. No one will ever be able to say you did not have the opportunity to gain every possible vote."

William waited for the effect of his words to sink in, and as a director who was a stranger to William was about to interrupt, he continued, "I will ask Mr. Rodgers as company secretary to carry out the electoral procedure, and when you have completed your vote, gentlemen, perhaps you could pass the ballot papers back to him."

Alfred Rodgers' monocle had been popping out periodically during the entire meeting. Nervously, he passed voting slips around to each director. When each had written down the name of the candidate whom he supported, the slips were returned to him.

"Perhaps it might be prudent under the circumstances, Mr. Rodgers, if the votes were counted aloud, thus making sure no inadvertent error is made that might lead the directors to require a second ballot."

"Certainly, Mr. Kane."

"Does that meet with your approval, Mr. Parfitt?"

Peter Parfitt nodded his agreement without looking up.

"Thank you. Perhaps you would be kind enough to read the votes out to the board, Mr. Rodgers."

The company secretary opened the first voting slip.

"Parfitt."

And then the second.

"Parfitt," he repeated.

The game was now out of William's hands. All the years of waiting for the prize he had told Charles Lester so long ago would be his would be over in the next few seconds.

"Kane. Parfitt. Kane."

Three votes to two against him; was he going to meet the same fate as he had in his contest with Tony Simmons?

"Kane. Kane. Parfitt."

Four votes all. He could see that Parfitt was sweating profusely at the other side of the table and he didn't exactly feel relaxed himself.

"Parfitt."

No expression crossed William's face. Parfitt allowed himself a smile.

Five votes to four.

"Kane. Kane. Kane."

The smile disappeared.

Just two more, two more, pleaded William, nearly out loud.

"Parfitt. Parfitt."

The company secretary took a long time opening a voting slip which someone had folded and refolded several times.

"Kane." Eight votes to seven in William's favour.

The last piece of paper was now being opened. William watched Alfred Rodgers' lips. The company secretary looked up; for that one moment he was the most important man in the room.

"Kane." Parfitt's head sank into his hands.

"Gentlemen, the tally is nine votes for Mr. William Kane, seven votes for Mr. Peter Parfitt. I therefore declare Mr. William Kane to be the duly elected chairman of Lester's Bank."

A respectful silence fell over the room and every head except Peter Parfitt's turned towards William and waited for the new chairman's first move.

William exhaled a great rush of air and stood once again, this time to face his board.

"Thank you, gentlemen, for the confidence you have placed in me. It was Charles Lester's wish that I should be your next chairman and I am delighted you have confirmed that wish with your vote. I now intend to serve this bank to the best of my ability, which I shall be unable to do without the whole-hearted support of the board. If Mr. Parfitt would be kind enough . . ."

Peter Parfitt looked up hopefully.

". . . to join me in the chairman's office in a few minutes' time, I would be much obliged. After I have seen Mr. Parfitt, I would like to see Mr. Leach. I hope, gentlemen, that tomorrow I shall have the opportunity of meeting all of you individually. The next board meeting will be the monthly one. This meeting is now adjourned."

The directors began to rise and talk among themselves. William walked quickly into the corridor, avoiding Peter Parfitt's stare. Ted Leach caught up with him and directed him to the chairman's office.

"That was a great risk you took," said Ted Leach, "and you only just pulled it off. What would you have done if you'd lost the vote?"

"Gone back to Boston," said William, sounding unperturbed.

Ted Leach opened the door to the chairman's office for William. The room was almost exactly as he remembered it; perhaps it had seemed a little larger when, as a prep-school boy, he had told Charles Lester that he would one day run the bank. He stared at the portrait of the great man behind his desk and winked at the late chairman. Then he sat down in the big red leather chair, and put his elbows on the mahogany desk. As he took a small, leather-bound book out of his jacket pocket and placed it on the desk in front of him, there was a knock on the door. An old man entered, leaning heavily on a black stick with a silver handle. Ted Leach left them alone.

"My name is Rupert Cork-Smith," he said, with a hint of an English accent.

William rose to greet him. He was the oldest member of the board. His grey hair, long sideburns and heavy gold watch all came from a past era, but his reputation for probity was legendary in banking circles. No man needed to sign a contract with Rupert Cork-Smith: his word had always been his bond. He looked William firmly in the eye.

"I voted against you, sir, and naturally you can expect my resignation to be on your desk within the hour."

"Will you have a seat, sir?" said William gently.

"Thank you, sir," he replied.

"I think you knew my father and grandfather."

"I had that privilege. Your grandfather and I were at

Harvard together, and I still remember with regret your father's tragic death."

"And Charles Lester?" said William.

"Was my closest friend. The provisions in his will have preyed upon my conscience. It was no secret that my choice would not have been Peter Parfitt. I would have had Ted Leach for chairman, but as I have never abstained from anything in my life, I felt I had to support the candidate who stood against you, as I found myself unable to vote for a man I had never even met."

"I admire your honesty, Mr. Cork-Smith, but now I have a bank to run. I need you at this moment far more than you need me so I, as a younger man, beg you not to resign."

The old man raised his head and stared into William's eyes. "I'm not sure it would work, young man. I can't change my attitudes overnight," said Cork-Smith, both hands resting on his stick.

"Give me six months, sir, and if you still feel the same way I won't put up a fight."

They both sat in silence before Cork-Smith spoke again. "Charles Lester was right: you are the son of Richard Kane."

"Will you continue to serve this bank, sir?"

"I will, young man. There's no fool like an old fool, don't you know."

Rupert Cork-Smith rose slowly with the aid of his stick. William moved to help him but was waved away.

"Good luck, my boy. You can rely on my total support."

"Thank you, sir," said William.

When he opened the door, William saw Peter Parfitt waiting in the corridor. As Rupert Cork-Smith left, the two men did not speak.

Peter Parfitt blustered in. "Well, I tried and I lost. A man can't do more," he said laughing. "No hard feelings, Bill?" He extended his hand.

"There are no hard feelings, Mr. Parfitt. As you so rightly say, you tried and you lost, and now you will resign from your post at this bank."

"I'll do what?" said Parfitt.

"Resign," said William.

"That's a bit rough, isn't it, Bill? My action wasn't at all personal, I simply felt . . ."

"I don't want you in my bank, Mr. Parfitt. You'll leave by tonight and never return."

"And if I say I won't go? I own a good many shares in the bank, and I still have a lot of support on the board, you know, and what's more I could take you to court."

"Then I would recommend that you read the bank's by-laws, Mr. Parfitt, which I spent some considerable time studying only this morning."

William picked up the small, leather-bound book which was still lying on the desk in front of him and turned a few pages over. Having found a paragraph he had marked that morning, he read aloud: "The chairman has the right to remove any office holder in whom he has lost confidence." He looked up. "I have lost confidence in you, Mr. Parfitt, and you will therefore resign, receiving two years' pay. If, on the other hand, you force me to remove you, I shall see that you leave the bank with nothing other than your stock. The choice is yours."

"Won't you give me a chance?"

"I gave you a chance last Friday night, and you lied and cheated. Not traits I am looking for in my next vice-chairman. Will it be resignation or do I throw you out, Mr. Parfitt?"

"Damn you, Kane, I'll resign."

"Good. Sit down and write the letter now."

"No, I'll let you have it in the morning in my own good time." He started walking towards the door.

"Now – or I fire you," said William.

Peter Parfitt hesitated and then came back and sank heavily into a chair by the side of William's desk. William handed him a piece of the bank's stationery and proffered him a pen. Parfitt took out his own pen and started writing. When he had finished, William picked up the letter and read it through carefully.

"Good day, Mr. Parfitt."

Peter Parfitt left without speaking. Ted Leach came in a few moments later.

"You wanted to see me, Mr. Chairman?"

"Yes," said William. "I want to appoint you as the bank's overall vice-chairman. Mr. Parfitt felt he had to resign."

"Oh, I'm surprised to hear that, I would have thought . . ."

William passed him the letter. Ted Leach read it and then looked at William.

"I shall be delighted to be overall vice-chairman. Thank you for your confidence in me."

"Good. I will be obliged if you will arrange for me to meet every director during the next two days. I shall start work at eight o'clock tomorrow morning."

"Yes, Mr. Kane."

"Perhaps you will also be kind enough to give Mr. Parfitt's letter of resignation to the company secretary?"

"As you wish, Mr. Chairman."

"My name is William, another mistake Mr. Parfitt made."

Ted Leach smiled tentatively. "I'll see you tomorrow morning – " he hesitated " – William."

When he had left, William sat in Charles Lester's chair and whirled himself around in an uncharacteristic burst of sheer glee till he was dizzy. Then he looked out of the window on to Wall Street, elated by the bustling crowds, enjoying the view of the other great banks and brokerage houses of America. He was part of all that now.

"And who, pray, are you?" said a female voice from behind him.

William swivelled round, and there standing in front of him was a middle-aged woman, primly dressed, looking very irate.

"Perhaps I may ask you the same question," said William.

"I am the chairman's secretary," said the woman stiffly.

"And I," said William, "am the chairman."

During the next few weeks William moved his family to New York where they found a house on East Sixty-eighth Street. Settling in took longer than they had originally anticipated possible. For the first three months William wished, as he tried to extricate himself from Boston in order to carry out his job in New York, that every day had forty-eight hours in it, and he found the umbilical cord was hard to sever completely. Tony Simmons was most helpful, and William began to appreciate why Alan Lloyd had backed him to be chairman of Kane and Cabot, and for the first time was willing to admit Alan had been right.

Kate's life in New York was soon fully occupied. Virginia could already crawl across a room and get into William's study before Kate could turn her head, and Richard wanted a new windbreaker, like every other boy in New York. As the wife of the chairman of a New York bank Kate regularly had to give cocktail parties and dinners, subtly making sure certain directors and major clients were always given the chance to catch the private ear of William to seek his advice or voice their own opinions. Kate handled all situations with great charm, and William was eternally grateful to the liquidation department of Kane and Cabot for supplying his greatest asset. When she informed William that she was going to have another baby, all he could ask was "When did I find the time?" Virginia was thrilled by the news, not fully understanding why Mummy was getting so fat, and Richard refused to discuss it.

Within six months the clash with Peter Parfitt was a thing of the past, and William had become the undisputed chairman of Lester's Bank and a figure to be reckoned with in New York financial circles. Not many more months had passed before he began to wonder in which direction he should start to set himself a new goal. He had achieved his life's ambition by becoming chairman of Lester's at the age of thirty-three although, unlike Alexander, he felt there were more worlds still to conquer, and he had neither the time nor the inclination to sit down and weep.

Kate gave birth to their third child at the end of William's first year as chairman of Lester's, a second girl, whom they named Lucy. William taught Virginia, who was now walking, how to rock Lucy's cradle; while Richard, now almost five years old and due to enter kindergarten at The Buckley School, used the new arrival as the opportunity to talk his father into buying a bigger baseball bat.

In William's first year as chairman of Lester's the bank's profits were slightly up and he was forecasting a considerable improvement in his second year.

Then on September 1st, 1939, Hitler marched into Poland.

One of William's first reactions was to think of Abel Rosnovski and his new Baron on Park Avenue, already becoming the toast of New York. Quarterly reports from Thomas Cohen showed that Rosnovski went from strength to strength although his latest ideas for expansion to Europe looked as if they might be in for a slight delay. Cohen continued to find no direct association between Henry Osborne and Abel Rosnovski, but he admitted that it was becoming increasingly difficult to ascertain all the facts he required.

William never thought that America would involve herself in a European war, but nevertheless he kept the London branch of Lester's open to show clearly which side he was on and not for one moment did he consider selling his twelve thousand acres in Hampshire and Lincolnshire. Tony Simmons in Boston, on the other hand, informed William that he intended to close Kane and Cabot's London branch. William used the problems created in London by the war as an excuse to visit his beloved Boston and have a meeting with Tony.

The two chairmen now met on extremely easy and friendly terms since they no longer had any reason to see themselves as rivals. In fact, each had come to use the other as a springboard for new ideas. As Tony had predicted, Kane and Cabot had lost some of its more important clients when William became the chairman of Lester's, but William always kept Tony fully informed whenever an old client expressed a desire to move his account and he never solicited a single one. When they sat down at the corner table of Locke-Ober's for lunch, Tony Simmons lost little time in repeating his intent to close the London branch of Kane and Cabot.

"My first reason is simple," he said as he sipped the imported burgundy, apparently not giving a moment's thought to the strong likelihood that German boots were about to trample on the grapes in most of the vineyards in

France. "I think the bank will lose money if we don't cut our losses and get out of England."

"Of course, you will lose a little money," said William, "but we must support the British."

"Why?" asked Tony. "We're a bank, not a supporters' club."

"Britain's not a baseball team, Tony; it's a nation of people to whom we owe our entire heritage . . ."

"You should take up politics," said Tony. "I'm beginning to think your talents are wasted in banking. Nevertheless, I feel there's a far more important reason why we should close the branch. If Hitler marches into Britain the way he has into Poland and France – and I'm sure that is exactly what he intends to do – the bank will be taken over, and we would lose every penny we have in London."

"Over my dead body," said William. "If Hitler puts so much as a foot on British soil, America will enter the war the same day."

"Never," said Tony. "F.D.R. has said, 'all aid short of war'. And the America Firsters would raise an almighty hue and cry."

"Never listen to a politician," said William. "Especially Roosevelt. When he says 'never', that only means not today, or at least not this morning. You only have to remember what Wilson told us in 1916."

Tony laughed. "When are you going to run for the Senate, William?"

"Now there is a question to which I can safely answer never."

"I respect your feelings, William, but I want out."

"You're the chairman," replied William. "If the board backs you, you can close the London branch tomorrow, and I would never use my position to act against a majority decision."

"Until you join the two banks together, and it becomes your decision."

"I told you once, Tony, that I would never attempt to do that while you were chairman. It's a promise I intend to honour."

"But I think we *ought* to merge."

"What?" said William, spilling his burgundy on the tablecloth, unable to believe what he had just heard. "Good heavens, Tony, I'll say one thing for you, you're never predictable."

"I have the best interests of the bank at heart, as always, William. Think about the present situation for a moment. New York is now, more than ever, the centre of U.S. finance, and when England goes under to Hitler, it will be the centre of world finance, so that's where Kane and Cabot needs to be. Moreover, if we merged, we would create a more comprehensive institution because our specialities are complementary. Kane and Cabot has always done a great deal of ship and heavy industry financing while Lester's does very little. Conversely, you do a lot of underwriting, and we hardly touch it. Not to mention the fact that in many cities we have unnecessary duplicating offices."

"Tony, I agree with everything you've said, but I would still want to stay in Britain."

"Exactly proving my point, William. Kane and Cabot's London branch would be closed, but we would still keep Lester's. Then, if London goes through a rough passage, it won't matter as much because we would be consolidated and therefore stronger."

"But how would you feel if I said that while Roosevelt's restrictions on merchant banks will only allow us to work out of one state, a merger could succeed only if we ran the entire operation from New York, treating Boston as nothing more than a holding office?"

"I'd back you," said Tony and added, "you might even consider going into commercial banking and dropping the straight investment work."

"No, Tony. F.D.R. has made it impossible for an honest man to do both, and in any case my father believed that you could either serve a small group of rich people or a large group of poor people so Lester's will always remain in traditional merchant banking as long as I'm chairman. But if we did decide to merge the two banks don't you foresee major problems?"

"Very few we couldn't surmount given goodwill on both sides. However, you will have to consider the implications carefully, William, as you would undoubtedly lose overall control of the new bank as a minority shareholder which would always make you vulnerable to a takeover bid."

"I'd risk that to be chairman of one of the largest financial institutions in America."

William returned to New York that evening, elated by his discussion and called a board meeting of Lester's to outline Tony Simmons' proposal. When he found that the board approved of a merger in principle, he instructed each manager in the bank to consider the whole plan in greater detail.

The departmental heads took three months before they reported back to the board, and to a man they came to the same conclusion: a merger was no more than common sense, as the two banks were complementary in so many ways. With different offices all over America and branches in Europe, they had a great deal to offer each other. Moreover, the chairman of Lester's had continued to own fifty-one per cent of Kane and Cabot, making the merger simply a marriage of convenience. Some of the directors on Lester's board could not understand why William hadn't thought of the idea before. Ted Leach was of the opinion that Charles Lester must have had it in his mind when he nominated William as his successor.

The details of the merger took nearly a year to negotiate and lawyers were kept at work into the small hours to complete the necessary paperwork. In the exchange of shares, William ended up as the largest stockholder with eight per cent of the new company and was appointed the new bank's president and chairman. Tony Simmons remained in Boston as one vice-chairman and Ted Leach in New York as the other. The new merchant bank was renamed Lester, Kane and Company, but was still to be referred to as Lester's.

William decided to hold a press conference in New York to announce the successful merger of the two banks and he chose Monday, December 8th, 1941, to inform the financial business world at large. The press conference had to be cancelled, because the morning before the Japanese had launched an attack on Pearl Harbor.

The prepared press release had already been mailed to the newspapers some days before, but the Tuesday morning financial pages understandably allocated the announcement of the merger only a small amount of space. This lack of coverage was no longer foremost in William's mind.

He couldn't quite work out how or when he was going to tell Kate that he intended to enlist. When Kate heard the news she was horrified and immediately tried to talk him out of the decision.

"What do you imagine you can do that a million others can't?" she demanded.

"I'm not sure," William replied, "but all I can be certain of is that I must do what my father or grandfather would have done given the same circumstances."

"They would have undoubtedly done what was in the best interest of the bank."

"No," replied William quickly. "They would have done what was in the best interest of America."

Book Four

[illegible]

[illegible]

[illegible] the news [illegible] Wilf and [illegible] ... elevated to the implications of [illegible] Carrian, he would have missed the [illegible] accompanied by a small [illegible] photograph of W[illegible] [illegible]

[illegible] and Gracie of [illegible] ... the most important [illegible] [illegible] As far as the [illegible]

[illegible] realising [illegible] the news [illegible] again. William [illegible] and he [illegible]

So [illegible] had the [illegible] over the [illegible] that [illegible] ... of the [illegible]

By [illegible]

24

Abel studied the news item on Lester, Kane and Company in the financial section of the *Chicago Tribune*. With all the space devoted to the implications of the Japanese attack on Pearl Harbor, he would have missed the brief article had it not been accompanied by a small out-of-date photograph of William Kane, so out-of-date that Kane looked much as he had when Abel had visited him in Boston over ten years before. Certainly Kane appeared too young in that photograph to live up to the journal's description of him as the brilliant chairman of the newly formed Lester, Kane and Company. The article went on to predict: "The new bank, a joining of Lester's of New York and Kane and Cabot of Boston, could well become one of the most important financial institutions in America after Mr. Kane's decision to merge the two distinguished family banks. As far as the *Trib* could ascertain the shares would be in the hands of about twenty people related to, or closely associated with the two families."

Abel was delighted by that particular piece of information, realising that Kane must have lost overall control. He read the news item again. William Kane had obviously risen in the world since they had crossed swords, but then so had he, and he still had an old score to settle with the newly appointed chairman of Lester's.

So handsomely had the Baron Group's fortunes prospered over the decade that Abel had paid back all the loans to his backer and honoured to the letter the original agreement with his backer and had secured one hundred per cent ownership of the company within the required ten-year period.

By the last quarter of 1939, not only had Abel paid off the

loan, but the profits for 1940 passed the half million mark. This milestone coincided with the opening of two new Barons, one in Washington, the other in San Francisco.

Though Abel had become a less devoted husband during this period, he could not have been a more doting father. Zaphia, longing for a second child, finally goaded him into seeing his doctor. When he learned that, because of a low sperm count, probably caused by sickness and malnutrition in his days under the Germans and Russians, Florentyna would almost certainly be his only child, he gave up all hope for a son and proceeded to lavish everything on her.

Abel's fame was now spreading across America and even the press had taken to referring to him as 'The Chicago Baron'. He no longer cared about the jokes behind his back. Wladek Koskiewicz had arrived and, more importantly, he was here to stay. By 1941 the profits from his thirteen hotels were just short of one million and, with his new surplus of capital, he decided the time had come for even further expansion.

Then the Japanese attacked Pearl Harbor.

Abel had already been sending considerable sums of money to the British Red Cross for the relief of his countrymen since that dreadful day in September 1939 on which the Nazis had marched into Poland, later to meet the Russians at Brest Litovsk and once again divide his homeland between them. He had waged a fierce battle, both within the Democratic Party and in the press, to push an unwilling America into the war even if now it had to be on the side of the Russians. His efforts so far had been fruitless, but on that December Sunday, with every radio station across the country blaring out the details to an incredulous nation, Abel knew that America must now be committed to the war. On December 11th he listened to President Roosevelt tell the nation that Germany and Italy had officially declared war on the United States. Abel had every intention of joining in, but first he had a private declaration of war he wished to make, and to that end he placed a call to Curtis Fenton at the Continental Trust Bank. Over the years Abel had grown to trust Fenton's judgment and had kept him on the board of the Baron Group when he gained overall control in order to keep a close link between the group and Continental Trust.

Curtis Fenton came on the line, his usual formal and always polite self.

"How much spare cash am I holding in the group's reserve account?" asked Abel.

Curtis Fenton picked out the file marked 'Number 6 Account', remembering the days when he could put all Mr. Rosnovski's affairs into one file. He scanned some figures.

"A little under two million dollars," he said.

"Good," said Abel. "I want you to look into a newly formed bank called Lester, Kane and Company. Find out the name of every shareholder, what percentage they control and if there are any conditions under which they would be willing to sell. All this must be done without the knowledge of the bank's chairman, Mr. William Kane and without my name ever being mentioned."

Curtis Fenton held his breath and said nothing. He was glad that Abel Rosnovski could not see his surprised face. Why did Abel Rosnovski want to put money into anything to do with William Kane? Fenton had also read in the *Wall Street Journal* about the merging of the two famous family banks. What with Pearl Harbor and his wife's headache, he too had nearly missed the item. Rosnovski's request jogged his memory – he must send a congratulatory wire to William Kane. He pencilled a note on the bottom of the Baron Group file while listening to Abel's instructions.

"When you have a full rundown. I want to be briefed in person, nothing on paper."

"Yes, Mr. Rosnovski."

I suppose someone knows what's going on between those two, Curtis Fenton added silently to himself, but I'm damned if I do.

Abel continued. "I'd also like to know in your quarterly reports the details of every official statement issued by Lester's and which companies they are involved with."

"Certainly, Mr. Rosnovski."

"Thank you, Mr. Fenton. By the way, my market research team is advising me to open a new Baron in Montreal."

"The war doesn't worry you, Mr. Rosnovski?"

"Good God, no. If the Germans reach Montreal we can all close down, Continental Trust included. In any case, we beat the bastards last time, and we'll beat them again. The only difference is that this time I'll be able to join the action. Good day, Mr. Fenton."

Will I ever understand what goes on in the mind of Abel Rosnovski, Curtis Fenton wondered, as he hung up the phone. His thoughts switched back to Abel's other request, for the details of Lester's shares. That worried him even more. Although William Kane no longer had any connection with Rosnovski, he feared where this might all end if his client obtained a substantial holding in Lester's. He decided against giving his views to Rosnovski for the time being, supposing the day would come when one of them would explain what they were both up to.

Abel also wondered if he should tell Curtis Fenton why he wanted to buy stock in Lester's but came to the conclusion that the fewer the number of people who knew of his plan, the better.

He put William Kane temporarily out of his mind and asked his secretary to find George, who was now a vice-president of the Baron Group. He had grown along with Abel and was now his most trusted lieutenant. Sitting in his office on the forty-second floor of the Chicago Baron, Abel looked down at Lake Michigan, on what was known as the Gold Coast, but his own thoughts returned to Poland. He wondered if he would ever live to see his castle again, now well inside the Russian borders under Stalin's control. Abel knew he would never settle in Poland, but he still wanted his castle restored to him. The idea of the Germans or Russians occupying his magnificent home once again made him want to . . . His thoughts were interrupted by George.

"You wanted to see me, Abel?"

George was the only member of the group who still called the Chicago Baron by his first name.

"Yes, George. Do you think you could keep the hotels ticking along for a few months if I were to take a leave of absence?"

"Sure I can," said George. "Why, are you finally going to take that vacation you promised yourself?"

"No," replied Abel. "I'm going to war."

"What?" said George. "What?" he repeated.

"I'm going to New York tomorrow morning to enlist in the army."

"You're crazy, you could get yourself killed."

"That isn't what I had in mind," replied Abel. "Killing some Germans is what I plan to do. The bastards didn't get me the first time around and I have no intention of letting them get me now."

George continued to protest that America could win the war without Abel. Zaphia protested too; she hated the very thought of war and little Florentyna, just turned eight years old, burst into tears. She did not quite know what war meant, but she did understand that Daddy would have to go away for a very long time.

Despite their protests, Abel took his first plane flight to New York the next day. All of America seemed to be going in different directions and he found the city full of young men in khaki saying their farewells to parents, sweethearts and wives, all assuring each other that the war would be over in a few weeks but none of them believing it.

Abel arrived at the New York Baron in time for dinner. The dining room was packed with young people, girls clinging desperately to soldiers, sailors and airmen, while Frank Sinatra crooned to the rhythms of Tommy Dorsey's big band. As Abel watched the young people on the dance floor, he wondered how many of them would ever have a chance to enjoy an evening like this again. He couldn't help remembering Sammy explaining how he had become *maître d'* at the Plaza. The three men senior to him had returned from the Western Front with one leg between them. None of the young people dancing could begin to know what war was really like. He didn't join in the celebration – if that's what it was. He went to his room instead.

In the morning, he dressed in a plain dark suit and went down to the recruiting office in Times Square. He had chosen to enlist in New York because he feared someone might recognise him in Chicago and all he could hope to end up with would be a swivel chair. The office was even more crowded than the dance floor had been the night before, but here no one was clinging on to anyone else. Abel hung around the entire morning in order to fill out one form that would have taken him three minutes in his own office. He couldn't help noticing that all the other recruits looked fitter than him. He then stood in line for two more hours waiting to be interviewed by a recruiting sergeant who asked him what he did for a living.

"Hotel management," said Abel, and went on to tell the officer of his experiences in the first war. The sergeant stared silently at the five foot seven, one hundred and ninety pound man with an expression of incredulity. If Abel had told him he was the Chicago Baron, the officer would not have doubted his stories of imprisonment and escape, but he chose to keep this information to himself and be treated like any of his fellow countrymen.

"You'll have to take a full physical tomorrow morning," was all the recruiting sergeant said at the end of Abel's monologue, adding, as though he felt the comment was no less than his duty, "Thank you for volunteering."

The next day Abel had to wait several more hours for his physical examination. The doctor in charge was fairly blunt about Abel's general condition. He had been protected from such comments for several years by his position and success. It came as a rude awakening when the doctor classified him 4F.

"You're overweight, your eyes are not too good, your heart is weak, and you limp. Frankly, Rosnovski, you're plain unfit. We can't take soldiers into battle who are likely to have a heart attack even before they find the enemy. That doesn't mean we can't use your talents; there's a lot of paperwork to be done in this war if you are interested."

Abel wanted to hit him, but he knew that wouldn't help get him into uniform.

"No, thank you . . . sir," he said. "I want to fight the Germans, not send letters to them."

He returned to the hotel that evening despondent, but

determined, decided that he wasn't licked yet. The next day he tried again, going to another recruiting office, but he came back to the Baron with the same result. Admittedly, the second doctor had been a little more polite, but he was every bit as firm about his condition, and once again Abel had ended up with a 4F. It was obvious to Abel that he was not going to be allowed to fight anybody in his present state of health.

The next morning, he found a gymnasium on West Fifty-seventh Street and paid a private instructor to do something about his physical condition. For three months he worked every day on his weight and general fitness. He boxed, wrestled, ran, jumped, skipped, pressed weights and starved. When he was down to one hundred and fifty-five pounds, the instructor assured him he was never going to be much fitter or thinner. Abel returned to the first recruiting office and filled in the same form under the name of Wladek Koskiewicz. Another recruiting sergeant was a lot more hopeful this time, and the medical officer who gave him several tests finally accepted him as a reserve, waiting to be called up.

"But I want to go to war now," said Abel. "I want to fight the bastards."

"We'll be in touch with you, Mr. Koskiewicz," said the sergeant. "Please keep yourself fit and prepared. You can never be sure when we will need you."

Abel left, furious as he watched younger, leaner Americans being readily accepted for active service, and as he barged through the door, not sure what his next ploy should be, he walked straight into a tall, gangling man wearing a uniform adorned with stars on the shoulders.

"I'm sorry, sir," said Abel, looking up and backing away.

"Young man," said the general.

Abel walked on, not thinking that the officer was addressing him, as no one had called him young man for . . . he didn't want to think for how long, despite the fact he was still only thirty-five.

The general tried again. "Young man," he said a little more loudly.

This time Abel turned around. "Me, sir?" he asked.

"Yes, you, sir."

Abel walked over to the general.

"Will you come to my office please, Mr. Rosnovski?"

Damn, thought Abel, this man knows who I am, and now nobody's going to let me fight in this war. The general's temporary office turned out to be at the back of the building, a small room with a desk, two wooden chairs, peeling green paint and an open door. Abel would not have allowed a junior member of his staff at a Baron to work in such surroundings.

"Mr. Rosnovski," the general began, exuding energy, "my name is Mark Clark and I command the U.S. Fifth Army. I'm over from Governors Island for the day on an inspection tour, so literally bumping into you is a pleasant surprise. I have for a long time been an admirer. Your story is one to gladden the heart of any American. Now tell me what you are doing in this recruiting office."

"What do you think?" said Abel, not thinking. "I'm sorry, sir," he corrected himself quickly. "I didn't mean to be rude, it's only that no one will let me get into this damn war."

"What do you want to do in this damn war?" asked the general.

"Sign up," said Abel, "and fight the Germans."

"As a foot soldier?" enquired the incredulous general.

"Yes," said Abel, "don't you need every man you can get?"

"Naturally," said the general, "but I can put your particular talents to a far better use than as a foot soldier."

"I'll do anything," said Abel, "anything."

"Will you now?" said the general, "and if I asked you to place your New York hotel at my disposal as army headquarters here, how would you react to that? Because frankly, Mr. Rosnovski, that would be of far more use to me than if you managed to kill a dozen Germans personally."

"The Baron is yours," said Abel. "Now will you let me go to war?"

"You know you're mad, don't you?" said General Clark.

"I'm Polish," said Abel. They both laughed. "You must understand," he continued in a more serious tone. "I was born near Slonim. I saw my home taken over by the Germans, my sister raped by the Russians. I later escaped from a Russian labour camp and was lucky enough to reach America. I'm not mad. This is the only country in the world where you can arrive with nothing and become a millionaire through damned hard work regardless of your background. Now those same bastards want another war. I'm not mad, General. I'm human."

"Well, if you're so eager to join up, Mr. Rosnovski, I could use you, but not in the way you imagine. General Denvers needs someone to take over responsibility as quartermaster for the Fifth Army while they are fighting in the front lines. If you believe Napoleon was right when he said an army marches on its stomach, you could play a vital role. The job carries the rank of major. That is one way in which you could unquestionably help America to win this war. What do you say?"

"I'll do it, General."

"Thank you, Mr. Rosnovski."

The general pressed a buzzer on his desk and a very young lieutenant came in and saluted smartly.

"Lieutenant, will you take Major Rosnovski to personnel and then bring him back to me?"

"Yes, sir." The lieutenant turned to Abel. "Will you come this way, please, Major?"

Abel followed him, turning as he reached the door. "Thank you, General," he said.

He spent the weekend in Chicago with Zaphia and Florentyna. Zaphia asked him what he wanted her to do with his fifteen suits.

"Hold on to them," he replied, wondering what she meant. "I'm not going to get myself killed in this war."

"I'm sure you're not, Abel," she replied. "That wasn't what was worrying me. It's just that now they're all three sizes too large for you."

Abel laughed and took the suits to the Polish refugee centre. He then returned to New York, went to the Baron, cancelled the advance guest list, and twelve days later handed the building over to the American Fifth Army. The press hailed Abel's decision as a 'selfless gesture', worthy of a man who had been a refugee of the First World War.

It was another three months before Abel was called to active duty, during which time he organised the smooth running of the New York Baron for General Clark and then reported to Fort Benning, to complete an officers' training programme. When he finally did receive his orders to join General Denvers and the Fifth Army, his destination turned out to be somewhere in North Africa. He began to wonder if he would ever get to Germany.

The day before Abel left, he drew up a will, instructing his executors to offer the Baron Group to David Maxton on favourable terms, and dividing the rest of his estate between Zaphia and Florentyna. It was the first time in nearly twenty years that he had contemplated death, not that he was sure how he could get himself killed in the regimental canteen.

As his troop ship sailed out of New York Harbor, Abel stared back at the Statue of Liberty. He could well remember how he had felt on seeing the statue for the first time nearly twenty years before. Once the ship had passed the Lady, he did not look at her again, but said out loud, "Next time I look at you, you French bitch, America will have won this war."

Abel crossed the Atlantic, taking with him two of his top chefs and five kitchen staff. The ship docked at Algiers on February 17th, 1943. He spent almost a year in the heat and the dust and the sand of the desert, making sure that every member of the division was as well fed as possible.

"We eat badly, but we eat a damn sight better than anyone else," was General Clark's comment.

Abel commandeered the only good hotel in Algiers and turned the building into a headquarters for General Clark. Although Abel could see he was playing a valuable role in the war, he itched to get into a real fight, but majors in charge of catering are rarely sent into the front line.

He wrote to Zaphia and George and watched his beloved daughter Florentyna grow up by photograph. He even received an occasional letter from Curtis Fenton, reporting that the Baron Group was making an even larger profit because every hotel in America was packed because of the continual movement of troops and civilians. Abel was sad not to have been at the opening of the new hotel in Montreal, where George had represented him. It was the first time that he had not been present at the opening of a Baron, but George wrote at reassuring length of the new hotel's great success. Abel began to realise how much he had built up in America and how much he wanted to return to the land he now felt was his home.

He soon became bored with Africa and its mess kits, baked beans, blankets and fly swatters. There had been one or two spirited skirmishes out there in the western desert, or so the men returning from the front assured him, but he never saw any real action, although often when he took the food to the front he would hear the firing, and it made him even angrier. One day to his excitement, General Clark's Fifth Army was ordered to invade Southern Europe.

The Fifth Army landed on the Italian coast in amphibious craft while American aircraft gave them tactical cover. They met considerable resistance, first at Anzio and then at Monte Cassino but the action never involved Abel and he dreaded the end of a war in which he had seen no combat. But he could never devise a plan which would get him into the front lines. His chances were not improved when he was promoted to Lieutenant Colonel and sent to London to await further orders.

With D-Day, the great thrust into Europe began. The Allies marched into France and liberated Paris on August 25th, 1944. As Abel paraded with the American and Free French soldiers down the Champs Elysées behind General de Gaulle to a hero's welcome, he studied the still magnificent city and decided exactly where he was going to build his first Baron hotel in France.

The Allies moved on through northern France and across the German border in a final drive towards Berlin. Abel was posted to the First Army under General Bradley. Food was coming mainly from England: local supplies were almost non-existent, as each succeeding town at which they arrived had already been ravaged by the retreating German Army. When Abel arrived in a new city, it would take him only a few hours to commandeer the entire remaining food supply before other American quartermasters had worked out exactly where to look. British and American officers were always happy to dine with the Ninth Armoured Division and would leave wondering how they had managed to requisition such excellent supplies. On one occasion when General George S. Patton joined General Bradley for dinner, Abel was introduced to the famous general who always led his troops into battle brandishing an ivory-handled revolver.

"The best meal I've had in the whole damn war," said Patton.

By February 1945, Abel had been in uniform for nearly three years and he knew the war would be over in a matter of months. General Bradley kept sending him congratulatory notes and meaningless decorations to adorn his ever-expanding uniform, but they didn't help. Abel begged the general to let him fight in just one battle, but Bradley wouldn't hear of it. Although it was the duty of a junior officer to drive the food trucks up to the front lines and then supervise the meals for the troops, Abel often carried out the responsibility himself. And, as in the running of his hotels, he would never let any of his staff know when or where he next intended to pounce.

It was the continual flow of blanket-covered stretchers into the camp that damp St. Patrick's Day that made Abel want to go up to the Front and take a look for himself. When it reached a point where he could no longer bear a one-way traffic of bodies, Abel rounded up his men and personally organised the fourteen food trucks. He took with him one lieutenant, one sergeant, two corporals, and twenty-eight privates.

The drive to the Front, although only twenty miles, was tiresomely slow that morning. Abel took the wheel of the first truck – it made him feel a little like General Patton – through heavy rain and thick mud; he had to pull off the road several times to allow ambulance details the right of way in their return from the Front. Wounded bodies took precedence over empty stomachs. Abel wished that most of them were no more than wounded, but only the occasional nod or wave suggested any sign of life. It became obvious to Abel with each mud-tracked mile that something big was going on near Remagen, and he could feel the beat of his heart quicken. Somehow, he knew this time he was going to be involved.

When he finally reached the command post he could hear the enemy fire in the distance, and he started pounding his leg in anger as he watched stretchers bringing back yet more dead and wounded comrades from he knew not where. Abel was sick of learning nothing about the real war until it was part of history. He suspected that any reader of the *New York Times* was better informed than he was.

Abel brought his convoy to a halt by the side of the field kitchen and jumped out of the truck shielding himself from the heavy rain, feeling ashamed that others only a few miles away were shielding themselves from bullets. He began to supervise the unloading of one hundred gallons of soup, a ton of corned beef, two hundred chickens, half a ton of butter, three tons of potatoes and one hundred and ten pound cans of baked beans – plus the inevitable K rations – in readiness for those going to, or returning from, the Front. When Abel arrived in the mess tent he found it full of long tables and empty benches. He left his two chefs to prepare the meal and the orderlies to start peeling one thousand potatoes while he went off in search of the duty officer.

Abel headed straight for Brigadier-General John Leonard's tent to find out what was going on, continually passing stretchers of dead and – worse – nearly dead soldiers, the sight of whom would have made any ordinary man sick but at Remagen had the air of being commonplace. As Abel was about to enter the tent, General Leonard, accompanied by his aide, was rushing out. He conducted a conversation with Abel while continuing to walk.

"What can I do for you, Colonel?"

"I have started preparing the food for your battalion as requested in overnight orders, sir. What . . . ?"

"You needn't bother with the food for now, Colonel. At first light this morning Lieutenant Burrows of the Ninth discovered an undamaged railroad bridge north of Remagen, and I gave orders that it should be crossed immediately and every effort made to establish a bridge head on the east bank of the river. Up to now, the Germans have been successful in blowing up every bridge across the Rhine long before we reached it so we can't hang around waiting for lunch before they demolish this one."

"Did the Ninth succeed in getting across?" asked a puffing Abel.

"Sure did," replied the general, "but they encountered heavy resistance when they reached the forest on the far side of the river. The first platoons were ambushed and God knows how many men we lost. So you had better eat the food yourself, Colonel, because my only interest is getting as many of my men back alive as possible."

"Is there anything I can do?" asked Abel.

The fighting commander stopped running for a moment and studied the fat colonel. "How many men have you under your direct command?"

"One lieutenant, one sergeant, two corporals, and twenty-eight privates; thirty-three in all including myself, sir."

"Good. Report to the field hospital with your men and make yourself useful out there by bringing back as many dead and wounded as you can find."

"Yes, sir," said Abel and ran all the way back to the field kitchen where he found his own men sitting in a corner smoking. None of them noticed when he entered the tent.

"Get up, you bunch of lazy bastards. We've got real work to do for a change."

Thirty-two men snapped to attention.

"Follow me," shouted Abel, "on the double."

He turned and started running again, this time towards the field hospital. A young doctor was briefing sixteen medical corpsmen when Abel and his out-of-breath, unfit men appeared at the entrance to the tent.

"Can I help you, sir?" asked the doctor.

"No, I hope I can help you," replied Abel. "I have thirty-two men here who have been detailed by General Leonard to join your group" – it was the first time they had heard of it.

The doctor stared in amazement at the colonel. "Yes, sir."

"Don't call me sir," said Abel. "We're here to find out how we can assist you."

"Yes, sir," the doctor said again.

He handed Abel a carton of Red Cross armbands which the chefs, kitchen orderlies and potato peelers proceeded to put on as they listened to the doctor continue his briefing, giving details of the action in the forest on the far side of the Ludendorff bridge.

"The Ninth has sustained heavy casualties," he continued. "Those soldiers with medical expertise will remain in the battle zone, while the rest of you will bring back as many of the wounded as possible to this field hospital."

Abel was delighted at the opportunity to do something positive for a change. The doctor, now in command of a team of forty-nine men, passed out eighteen stretchers, and each soldier received a full medical pack. He then led his motley band towards the Ludendorff bridge. Abel was only a yard behind him. They started singing as they marched through the mud and rain; they stopped singing when they reached the bridge and were greeted by stretcher after stretcher showing clearly the outline of a body covered only in blankets. They marched silently across the bridge in single file by the side of the railroad track where they could see the results of the German explosion that had failed to destroy its foundations. On up towards the forest and the sound of fire, Abel found he was excited by the thought of being so near the enemy, and horrified by the realisation of what that enemy was capable of inflicting on his fellow countrymen. Everywhere he turned he saw pain, or worse, heard cries of anguish coming from his comrades. Comrades who until that day had wistfully thought the end of the war was near – but not that near.

He watched the young doctor stop again and again and do the best he could for each man. Sometimes he would mercifully kill a man quickly when there was not the slightest hope of trying to patch him up. Abel ran from soldier to soldier organising the stretchers of those unable to help themselves and guiding the wounded who could still walk back towards the Ludendorff bridge. By the time their group reached the edge of the forest only the doctor, one of the potato peelers and himself were left of the original party; all the others were carrying the dead and wounded back to the camp.

As the three of them marched into the forest they could hear the enemy guns close by. Abel could see the outline of a big gun, hidden in undergrowth and still pointing towards the bridge, but now damaged beyond repair. Then he heard a volley of bullets that sounded so loud that he realised for the first time that the enemy were only a few hundred yards ahead of him. He quickly crouched down on one knee, expectant, his senses heightened to screaming pitch. Suddenly there was another burst of fire in front of him. He jumped up and ran forward, reluctantly followed by the doctor and the potato peeler. They ran on for another hundred yards, when they came across a beautiful stretch of lush green grass in a hollow covered in a bed of white crocuses, littered with the bodies of American soldiers. Abel and the doctor ran from corpse to corpse. "It must have been a massacre," screamed Abel in anger, as he heard the retreating fire. The doctor made no comment: he had screamed three years before.

"Don't worry about the dead," was all he said. "Just see if you can find anyone who is still alive."

"Over here," shouted Abel as he kneeled down beside a sergeant lying in the German mud. Both his eyes were missing.

"He's dead, Colonel," said the doctor, not giving the man a second glance. Abel ran to the next body and then the next but it was always the same and only the sight of a severed head placed upright in the mud stopped Abel in his tracks. He kept having to look back at it, like the bust of some Greek god that could no longer move. Abel recited like a child words he had learned at the feet of the Baron: "'Blood and destruction shall be so in use and dreadful objects so familiar that mothers shall but smile when they behold their infants quarter'd with the hands of war.' Does nothing change?" cried Abel outraged.

"Only the battlefield," replied the doctor.

When Abel had checked thirty – or was it forty? – men, he once again returned to the doctor who was trying to save the life of a captain who but for a closed eye and his mouth was already swathed in blood-soaked bandages. Abel stood over the doctor watching helplessly, studying the captain's shoulder patch – the Ninth Armoured – and remembered General Leonard's words, "God knows how many men we lost today."

"Fucking Germans," said Abel.

"Yes, sir," said the doctor.

"Is he dead?" asked Abel.

"Might as well be," replied the doctor mechanically. "He's losing so much blood it can only be a matter of time." He looked up. "There's nothing left for you to do here, Colonel, so why don't you try and get the one survivor back to the field hospital before he dies and let the base commander know that I intend to go forward and need every man he can spare."

"Right," said Abel as he helped the doctor carefully lift the captain on to a stretcher. Abel and the potato peeler tramped slowly back towards the camp, the doctor having warned him that any sudden movement to the stretcher could only result in an even greater loss of blood. Abel didn't let the potato peeler rest for one moment during the entire two-mile trek to the base camp. He wanted to give the man a chance to live and then return to the doctor in the forest.

For over an hour they trudged through the mud and the rain, and Abel felt certain the captain had died. When they finally reached the field hospital both men were exhausted, and Abel handed the stretcher over to a medical team.

As the captain was wheeled slowly away he opened his unbandaged eye which focused on Abel. He tried to raise his arm. Abel saluted and could have leapt with joy at the sight of the open eye and the moving hand. How he prayed that man would live.

He ran out of the hospital, eager to return to the forest with his little band of men when he was stopped by the duty officer.

"Colonel," he said, "I have been looking for you everywhere. There are over three hundred men who need feeding. Christ, man, where have you been?"

"Doing something worthwhile for a change."

Abel thought about the young captain as he headed slowly back to the field kitchen.

For both men the war was over.

25

The stretcher bearers took the captain into a tent and laid him gently on an operating table. Captain William Kane could see a nurse looking sadly down at him, but he was unable to hear anything she was saying. He wasn't sure if it was because his head was swathed in bandages or because he was now deaf. He watched her lips move, but learned nothing. He shut his eye and thought. He thought a lot about the past; he thought a little about the future; he thought quickly in case he died. He knew if he lived, there would be a long time for thinking. His mind turned to Kate in New York. She had refused to accept his determination to enlist. He knew she would never understand, and that he would not be able to justify his reasons to her so he had stopped trying. The memory of her desperate face now haunted him. He never really considered death – no man does – and now he wanted only to live and return to his old life.

William had left Lester's under the joint control of Ted Leach and Tony Simmons until he returned . . . until he returned. He had given no instructions for them to follow if he did not return. Both of them had begged him not to go. Two more men who couldn't understand. When he signed up a few days later, he couldn't face the children. Richard, aged ten, had found his own way to the station; he had held back the tears until his father told him he could not go along with him to fight the Germans.

They sent him first to an Officers' Candidate School in Vermont. Last time he had seen Vermont, he had been skiing with Matthew, slowly up the hills and quickly down.

Now the journey was slow both ways. The course lasted for three months and made him fit again for the first time since he had left Harvard.

His first assignment was in a London full of Yanks, where he acted as a liaison officer between the Americans and the British. He was billeted at the Dorchester, which the British War Office had taken over and seconded for use by the American Army. William had read somewhere that Abel Rosnovski had done the same thing with the Baron in New York and he had thoroughly approved at the time. The blackouts, the doodle-bugs, and the air raid warnings all made him believe that he was involved in a war, but he felt strangely detached from what was going on only a few hundred miles from Hyde Park Corner. Throughout his life he had taken the initiative, and had never been an onlooker. Moving between Eisenhower's staff headquarters in St. James and Churchill's War Operations room in Storey's Gate wasn't William's idea of initiative. It didn't look as if he was going to meet a German face-to-face for the entire duration of the war unless Hitler invaded Trafalgar Square.

When part of the First Army was posted to Scotland for training exercises with the Black Watch, William was sent along as an observer and told to report back with his findings. The long, slow journey to Scotland and back in a train that never stopped stopping made him realise that he was fast becoming a glorified messenger boy and he was beginning to wonder why he had ever signed up. Scotland, William found, was different. There at least they had the air of preparing for war and when he returned to London, he put in a request for an immediate transfer to join the First Army. His colonel, who never believed in keeping a man who wanted to see action behind a desk, released him.

Three days later William returned to Scotland to join his new regiment and begin his training with the American troops at Inveraray for the invasion they all knew had to come soon. Training was hard and intense. Nights spent in the Scottish hills fighting mock battles with the Black Watch made more than a slight contrast to evenings at the Dorchester writing reports.

Three months later they were parachuted into northern France to join Omar N. Bradley's army, moving across Europe. The scent of victory was in the air and William wanted to be the first soldier in Berlin.

The First Army advanced towards the Rhine, determined to cross any bridge they could find. Captain Kane received orders that morning that his division was to advance over the Ludendorff bridge and engage the enemy a mile north-east of Remagen in a forest on the far side of the river. He stood on the crest of a hill and watched the Ninth Division cross the bridge, expecting it to be blown sky high at any moment.

His colonel led his own division in behind them. He followed with the hundred and twenty men under his command, most of them, like William, going into action for the first time. No more exercises with wily Scots pretending to kill him, with blank cartridges and then a meal together afterwards. Germans, with real bullets, death – and perhaps no afterwards.

When William reached the edge of the forest, he and his men met with no resistance, so they decided to press further on into the woods. The going was slow and dull and William was beginning to think the Ninth must have done such a thorough job that his division would only have to follow them through, when from nowhere they were suddenly ambushed by a hail of bullets and mortars. Everything seemed to be coming at them at once. William's men went down, trying to protect themselves among the trees, but he lost over half of the platoon in a matter of seconds. The battle, if that's what it could be called, had lasted for less than a minute, and he hadn't even seen a German. William crouched in the wet undergrowth for a few more seconds and then saw, to his horror, the next division coming through the forest. He ran from his shelter behind a tree to warn them of the ambush. The first bullet hit him in the head and, as he sank to his knees in the German mud and continued to wave a frantic warning to his advancing comrades, the second hit him in the neck and a third in the chest. He lay still in the mud and waited to die, not having even seen the enemy – a dirty, unheroic death.

The next thing William knew, he was being carried on a stretcher, but he couldn't hear or see anything and he wondered if it was night or whether he was blind.

It seemed a long journey. When his eye opened, it focused on a short fat colonel limping out of a tent. There was something familiar about him, but he couldn't think what. The stretcher bearers took him into the operating tent and placed him on the table. He tried to fight off sleep for fear it might be death. He slept.

William woke. He was conscious of two people trying to move him. They were turning him over as gently as they could, and then they stuck a needle into him. William dreamed of seeing Kate, and then his mother, and then Matthew playing with his son Richard. He slept.

He woke. He knew they had moved him to another bed; slight hope replaced the thought of inevitable death. He lay motionless, his one eye fixed on the canvas roof of the tent, unable to move his head. A nurse came over to study a chart and then him. He slept.

He woke. How much time had passed? Another nurse. This time he could see a little more and – joy, oh joy – he could move his head, if only with great pain. He lay awake as long as he possibly could; he wanted to live. He slept.

He woke. Four doctors were studying him, deciding what? He could not hear them and so learnt nothing.

They moved him once again. This time he was able to watch them put him in an army ambulance. The doors closed behind him, the engine started, and the ambulance began to move over rough ground while a new nurse sat by his side holding him steady. The journey felt like an hour, but he no longer could be sure of time. The ambulance reached smoother ground and then came to a halt. Once again they moved him. This time they were walking on a flat surface and then up some stairs into a dark room. They waited again and then the room began to move, another car perhaps. The room took off. The nurse stuck another needle into him, and he remembered nothing until he felt a plane landing and taxiing to a halt. They moved him yet again. Another ambulance, another nurse, another smell, another city. New York, or at least America, he thought, no other smell like that in the world. The new ambulance took him over another smooth surface, continually stopping and starting, until it finally arrived at where it wanted to be. They carried him out once again and up some more steps into a small white-walled room. They placed him in a comfortable bed. He felt his head touch the pillow, and when next he woke, thought he was totally alone. Then his eye focused and he saw Kate standing in front of him. He tried to lift his hand and touch her, to speak, but no words came. She smiled, but he knew she could not see his smile, and when he woke again Kate was still there but wearing a different dress. Or had she come and gone many times? She smiled again. How long had it been? He tried to move his head a little, and saw his son Richard, so tall, so good-looking. He wanted to see his daughters, but couldn't move his head any further. They moved into his line of vision, Virginia – she couldn't be that old, and Lucy, it wasn't possible. Where had the years gone? He slept.

He woke. No one was there, but now he could move his head. Some bandages had been removed and he could see more clearly; he tried to say something, but no words came. He slept.

He woke. Less bandages than before. Kate was there again, her fair hair longer, now falling to her shoulders, her soft brown eyes and unforgettable smile, looking beautiful, so beautiful. He said her name. She smiled. He slept.

He woke. Even fewer bandages than before. This time his son spoke.

Richard said, "Hello, Daddy."

He heard him and replied, "Hello, Richard," but didn't recognise the sound of his own voice. The nurse helped him to sit up ready to greet his family. He thanked her. A doctor touched his shoulder.

"The worst is over, Mr. Kane. You'll soon be well, and then you can return home."

He smiled as Kate came into the room, followed by Virginia and Lucy. So many questions to ask them. Where should he begin? There were gaps in his memory that demanded satisfaction. Kate told him that he had nearly died. He knew that but had not realised that over a year had passed since his division had been ambushed in the forest at Remagen.

Where had the months of being unaware gone, life lost resembling death? Richard was almost twelve, already hoping to go to Harvard, Virginia was nine, and Lucy nearly seven. Their dresses seemed rather short. He would have to get to know them all over again.

Kate was somehow more beautiful than William ever remembered her. She told William how she never learned to face the fact that he might have died, how well Richard was doing at Buckley and how Virginia and Lucy needed a father. She braced herself to tell him of the scars on his face and chest that would never heal and thanked God that the doctors felt certain there would be nothing wrong with his mind and his sight would be restored. Now all she wanted to do was help him recover. Kate slowly, William quickly.

Each member of the family played their part in the process. First sound, then sight, then speech. Richard helped his father to walk, until he no longer needed the crutches. Lucy helped him with his food, until he could feed himself once more and Virginia read Mark Twain to him. William was not sure if the reading was for her benefit or his, they both enjoyed it so much. And then at last, after Christmas had passed, they allowed him to return to his own home.

Once William was back in East Sixty-eighth Street, he recovered more quickly, and his doctors were predicting that he would be able to return to work at the bank within six months. A little scarred, but very much alive, he was allowed to see visitors.

The first was Ted Leach, somewhat taken aback at

William's appearance. Something else he would have to learn to live with for the time being. From Ted Leach, William learned news that brought him satisfaction. Lester's had progressed in his absence and his colleagues looked forward to welcoming him back as their chairman. A visit from Tony Simmons brought him news that made him sad. Alan Lloyd and Rupert Cork-Smith had both died. He would miss their prudent wisdom. And then Thomas Cohen called to say how glad he was to learn of his recovery and to prove, as if it were still necessary, that time had moved on by informing William he was now semi-retired and had turned over many of his clients to his son Thaddeus who had opened an office in New York. William remarked on both of them being named after apostles. Thomas Cohen laughed and expressed the hope that Mr. Kane would continue to use the firm. William assured him he would.

"By the way, I do have one piece of information you ought to know about."

William listened to the old lawyer in silence and became angry, very angry.

Book Five

Book Five

General Alfred Jodl signed the unconditional surrender at Rheims on May 7th, 1945, [illegible] New York [illegible] celebrations [illegible] put an end to the war [illegible]. The streets were filled with young people [illegible]

When [illegible] months [illegible]. Why [illegible] had [illegible] clothes [illegible] before. There were [illegible] The first they now saw was [illegible]

"It's [illegible]," [illegible] replied.

"We'll go [illegible] on the phone," said Abel.

"Who shall [illegible] is calling?"

"[illegible] Rosnovski."

The guard [illegible] quickly.

George's [illegible] down [illegible] sixth [illegible] reached [illegible] to the [illegible]. He [illegible] in New York [illegible] hundred miles [illegible] Chicago. He took with him George's [illegible] reports [illegible] the plane. He read every [illegible] of the Baron Group's progress during the

26

General Alfred Jodl signed the unconditional surrender at Rheims on May 7th, 1945, as Abel arrived back into a New York preparing for victory celebrations and an end to the war. Once again, the streets were filled with young people in uniform, but this time their faces showed elation, not fear. Abel was saddened by the sight of so many men with one leg, one arm, blind or badly scarred. For them the war would never be over, whatever piece of paper had been signed four thousand miles away.

When Abel walked into the Baron in his colonel's uniform, no one recognised him. Why should they? When they had last seen him in civilian clothes two years before, there were no lines on his still youthful face. The face they now saw was older than its thirty-nine years and the deep, worn ridges on his forehead showed that the war had left its mark on him. He took the lift to his forty-second floor office, and a security guard told him firmly he was on the wrong floor.

"Where's George Novak?" asked Abel.

"He's in Chicago, Colonel," the guard replied.

"Well, get him on the phone," said Abel.

"Who shall I say is calling him?"

"Abel Rosnovski."

The guard moved quickly.

George's familiar voice crackled down the line with welcome. At once Abel realised just how good it felt to be back home. He decided not to stay in New York that night but to fly the eight hundred miles on to Chicago. He took with him George's up-to-date reports to study on the plane. He read every detail of the Baron Group's progress during the war, and it became obvious that George had done well in keeping the group on an even keel during Abel's absence. His cautious stewardship left Abel with no complaints; the profits were still high because so many staff had been called up to fight in the war, while the hotels had remained full because of the continual movement of personnel across America. Abel decided that he would have to start employing new staff immediately, before other hotels picked up the best of those returning from the Front.

When he arrived at Midway Airport, Terminal 11C, George was standing by the gate waiting to greet him. He'd hardly changed, a little more weight, a little less hair perhaps, and within an hour of swapping stories and bringing each other up to date on the past three years, it was almost as though Abel had never been away. Abel would always be thankful to the *Black Arrow* for the introduction to his senior vice-president.

George, however, was uncharitable about Abel's limp which seemed more pronounced since he'd gone off to the war.

"The Hopalong Cassidy of the hotel business," he said mockingly. "Now you don't have a leg to stand on."

"Only a Pole would make such a dumb crack," replied Abel.

George stared at Abel, looking slightly hurt, as a puppy does when scolded by its master.

"Thank God I had a dumb Polack to take care of everything while I was away looking for Germans," Abel added reassuringly.

Abel couldn't resist checking once around the Chicago Baron before he drove home. The veneer of luxury had worn rather thin during the wartime shortages. He could see several things that needed renovation, but they would have to wait, because now all he wanted to do was see his wife and daughter. That was when the first shock came. In George he had seen little change in three years, but Florentyna was now eleven and had blossomed into a beautiful young girl, while Zaphia, although only thirty-eight, had become plump, dowdy and distinctly middle-aged.

To begin with, the two of them were not sure quite how to treat one another, and after only a few weeks Abel began to realise that their relationship was never going to be the same again. Zaphia made little effort to excite Abel or take any pride in his achievements. It saddened Abel to observe her lack of interest and he tried to get her involved in his life once again but she did not respond to any of his suggestions. She only seemed contented when staying at home and having as little to do with the Baron Group as possible. He resigned himself to the fact that she could never change and wondered how long he could remain faithful to her. While he was enchanted with Florentyna, Zaphia, without her looks and with her figure gone, left him cold. When they slept together he avoided making love, and, on the rare occasions when they did, he thought of other women. Soon he began to find any excuse to be away from Chicago and Zaphia's despondent and silently accusing face.

He began by making long trips to his other hotels, taking Florentyna along with him during her school holidays. He spent the first six months after his return to America visiting every hotel in the Baron Group in the same way he had done when he had taken over the company after Davis Leroy's death. Within the year, they were all back to the high standard he expected of them, but Abel wanted to move forward again. He informed Curtis Fenton at the group's next quarterly meeting that his market research team was now advising him to build a hotel in Mexico and another in Brazil, and they were also searching for new lands on which to erect a Baron.

"The Mexico City Baron and the Rio de Janeiro Baron," said Abel. He liked the ring of those names.

"Well, you have adequate funds to cover the building costs," said Curtis Fenton. "The cash has certainly been accumulating in your absence. You could build a Baron almost anywhere you choose. Heaven knows where you'll stop, Mr. Rosnovski."

"One day, Mr. Fenton, I'll put a Baron in Warsaw, and then I'll think about stopping," replied Abel. "I may have licked the Germans, but I still have a little score to settle with the Russians."

Curtis Fenton laughed. Only later that evening when he repeated the story to his wife did he decide that Abel Rosnovski had meant exactly what he had said . . . a Baron in Warsaw.

"Now where do I stand with Kane's bank?"

The sudden change in Abel's tone bothered Curtis Fenton. It worried him that Abel Rosnovski still clearly held Kane responsible for Davis Leroy's premature death. He opened the special file and started reading.

"Lester, Kane and Company's shares are divided among fourteen members of the Lester family and six past and present employees while Mr. Kane himself is the largest stockholder, holding eight per cent."

"Are any of the Lester family willing to sell their shares?" enquired Abel.

"Perhaps if we can offer the right price. Miss Susan Lester, the late Charles Lester's daughter, has given us reason to believe she might consider parting with her shares, and Mr. Peter Parfitt, a former vice-chairman of Lester's, has also showed some interest in our approaches."

"What percentage do they both hold?"

"Susan Lester holds six per cent. While Peter Parfitt has only two per cent."

"How much do they want for their shares?"

Curtis Fenton looked down at his file again while Abel glanced at Lester's latest annual report. His eyes came to a halt on Article Seven.

"Miss Susan Lester wants two million dollars for her six per cent and Mr. Parfitt one million dollars for his two per cent."

"Mr. Parfitt is greedy," said Abel. "We will therefore wait until he is hungry. Buy Miss Susan Lester's shares immediately without revealing whom you represent and keep me briefed on any change of heart by Mr. Parfitt."

Curtis Fenton coughed.

"Is something bothering you, Mr. Fenton?" asked Abel.

Curtis Fenton hesitated. "No, nothing," he said unconvincingly.

"From now on I am putting someone in overall charge of the account whom you will know or certainly know of – Henry Osborne."

"Congressman Osborne?" asked Curtis Fenton.

"Yes – are you acquainted with him?"

"Only by reputation," said Fenton, with a faint note of disapproval, his head bowed.

Abel ignored the implied comment. He was only too aware of his reputation, but while Henry had the ability to cut out all the middle men of bureaucracy and could ensure quick political decisions, Abel considered the risk was worthwhile. Not to mention the bond of common loathing of Kane. "I'm also inviting Mr. Osborne to be a director of the Baron Group with special responsibility for the Kane account. This information must, as always, be treated in the strictest confidence."

"As you wish," said Fenton unhappily, wondering if he should express his personal misgivings to Abel Rosnovski.

"Brief me as soon as you have closed the deal with Miss Susan Lester."

"Yes, Mr. Rosnovski," said Curtis Fenton without raising his head.

Abel returned to the Baron for lunch, where Henry Osborne was waiting to join him.

"Congressman," said Abel as they met in the foyer.

"Baron," said Henry, and they laughed and went arm-in-arm into the dining room and sat at the corner table.

Abel chastised a waiter for serving at table when a button was missing from his tunic.

"How's your wife, Abel?"

"Swell. And yours, Henry?"

"Just great."

They were both lying.

"Any news to report?"

"Yes. That concession you needed in Atlanta has been taken care of," said Henry in a conspiratorial voice. "The necessary documents will be pushed through some time in the next few days. You'll be able to start building the Atlanta Baron round the first of the month."

"We're not doing anything too illegal, are we?"

"Nothing your competitors aren't up to – that I can promise you, Abel." Henry Osborne laughed.

"I'm glad to hear that, Henry. I don't want any trouble with the law."

"No, no," said Henry. "Only you and I know all the facts."

"Good," said Abel. "You've made yourself very useful to me over the years, Henry, and I have a little reward for your past services. How would you like to become a director of the Baron Group?"

"I'd be flattered, Abel."

"Don't give me that. You know you've been invaluable with these state and city permits. I'd never have had the time to deal with all those politicians and bureaucrats. In any case, Henry, they prefer to deal with a Harvard man even if he doesn't so much open doors, as simply kick them down."

"You've been very generous in return, Abel."

"It's no more than you have earned. Now, I want you to take on an even bigger job which is close to my heart. This exercise will also require complete secrecy, but it shouldn't take too much of your time and it will give us a little revenge on our mutual friend from Boston, Mr. William Kane."

The *maître d'hôtel* arrived with two large rump steaks, medium rare. Henry listened intently as Abel unfolded his plans for William Kane.

A few days later on May 8th, 1946, Abel travelled to New York to celebrate the first anniversary of VE day. He had laid on a dinner for over a thousand Polish veterans at the Baron Hotel and had invited General Kazimierz Sosnkowski, commander-in-chief of the Polish Forces in France after 1943, to be the guest of honour. Abel had looked forward impatiently to the event for weeks and took Florentyna with him to New York while leaving Zaphia behind in Chicago.

On the night of the celebration, the banqueting room of the New York Baron looked magnificent, each of the one hundred and twenty tables decorated with the stars and stripes of America and the white and red of the Polish national flag. Huge photographs of Eisenhower, Patton,

Bradley, Hodges, Paderewski and Sikorski festooned the walls. Abel sat at the centre of the head table with the general on his right and Florentyna on his left.

When General Sosnkowski rose to address the gathering, he announced that Lieutenant Colonel Rosnovski had been made a life president of the Polish Veterans' Society, in acknowledgment of the personal sacrifices he had made for the Polish-American cause, and in particular for his generous gift of the New York Baron throughout the entire duration of the war. Someone who had drunk a little too much shouted from the back of the room.

"Those of us who survived the Germans had to survive Abel's food as well."

The thousand veterans laughed and cheered, toasted Abel in Danzig vodka and then fell silent as the general talked of the plight of post-war Poland, in the grip of Stalinist Russia, urging his fellow expatriates to be tireless in their campaign to secure the ultimate sovereignty of their native land. Abel wanted to believe that Poland would one day be free again and that he might even live to see his castle restored to him, but doubted if that was realistic after Stalin's success at the Yalta agreement.

The general went on to remind the guests that Polish-Americans had, per capita, sacrificed more lives and given more money for the war than any other single ethnic group in the United States. ". . . How many Americans would believe that Poland lost six million of her countrymen while Czechoslovakia only lost one hundred thousand? Some observers declare we were stupid not to surrender when we must have known we were beaten. How could a nation that staged a cavalry charge against the might of the Nazi tanks ever believe they were beaten, and, my friends, I tell you we are not beaten now." Every Pole in the room applauded the general loudly.

Abel felt sad to think that most Americans would still laugh at the thought of the Polish war effort – or, funnier still, a Polish war hero. The general then waited for complete silence to tell an intent audience the story of how Abel had led a band of men to recover troops who had been killed or wounded at the battle of Remagen. When the general had finished his speech and sat down, the veterans stood and cheered the two men resoundingly. Florentyna felt very proud of her father.

Abel was surprised when the story hit the papers the next morning, as Polish achievements were rarely reported in any medium other than *Dziennik Zwiazkiwy*. He doubted that the press would have bothered on this occasion had he not been the Chicago Baron. Abel basked in his new-found glory as an unsung American hero and spent most of the day having his photograph taken and giving interviews to newsmen.

By the evening Abel felt a sense of anti-climax. The general had flown on to Los Angeles and another function, Florentyna had returned to school in Lake Forest, George was in Chicago, and Henry Osborne in Washington. The hotel seemed rather large and empty, and he felt no desire to return to Zaphia in Chicago.

He decided to have an early dinner and go over the weekly reports from the other hotels in the group before returning to the penthouse adjoining his office. He seldom ate alone in his private suite as he welcomed the opportunity of being served in one of the dining rooms whenever possible; it was one of the sure ways to keep in constant touch with hotel life. The more hotels he acquired and built, the more he feared losing touch with his staff on the ground.

He took the lift downstairs and stopped at the reception desk to ask how many people were booked into the hotel that night, but he was distracted by a striking woman signing a registration form. He could have sworn he recognised the profile, but it was difficult to be certain from the side. Mid-thirties, he thought. When she had finished writing, she turned and looked at him.

"Abel," she said. "How marvellous to see you."

"Good God, Melanie. I hardly recognised you."

"No one could fail to recognise you, Abel."

"I didn't know you were in New York."

"Only overnight. I'm here on some business for my magazine."

"You're a journalist?" asked Abel with a hint of disbelief.

"No, I'm the economic adviser to a group of magazines whose headquarters are in Dallas, and they've sent me to New York on a market research project."

"Sounds very impressive."

"I can assure you it isn't," said Melanie, "but it keeps me out of mischief."

"Are you free for dinner, by any chance?"

"What a nice idea, Abel, but I need a bath and a change of clothes if you don't mind waiting?"

"Sure, I can wait. I'll meet you in the main dining room whenever you're ready. Come to my table, say in about an hour."

She smiled in agreement and followed a bellhop to the lift. He noticed her perfume as she passed him.

Abel spent the hour checking the dining room to be sure that his table had fresh flowers, and the kitchen to select the dishes he would order for Melanie. Finally, for lack of anything better to do, he was compelled to sit down. He found himself glancing at his watch and looking at the dining room door every few moments to see if Melanie would walk in. She took a little over an hour but it turned out to be worth the wait. When at last she appeared at the doorway, in a long clinging dress that shimmered and sparkled in the dining room lights in an unmistakably expensive way, she looked ravishing. The *maître d'* ushered her to Abel's table. He rose to greet her as a waiter opened a bottle of vintage Krug and poured them both a glass.

"Welcome, Melanie," said Abel as he raised his goblet. "It's good to see you in the Baron."

"It's good to see the Baron," she replied, "especially on his day of celebration."

"What do you mean?" asked Abel.

"I read all about your big dinner in the *New York Post* tonight, how you risked your own life to save those who had been wounded at Remagen. It kept me glued to the page all the way over here from the station. They made you sound like a cross between Audie Murphy and the Unknown Soldier."

"It's all exaggerated," said Abel.

"I've never known you to be modest about anything

before, Abel, so I can only believe every word must be true."

He poured her a second glass of champagne.

"The truth is, I've always been a little frightened of you, Melanie."

"The Baron is frightened of someone? I don't believe it."

"Well, I'm no Southern gentleman, as you once made very clear, my dear."

"And you have never stopped reminding me." She smiled, teasingly. "Did you marry your nice Polish girl?"

"Yes, I did."

"How did that work out?"

"Not so well. She's now fat and forty and no longer has any appeal for me."

"You'll be telling me next that she doesn't understand you," said Melanie, the tone of her voice betraying her pleasure at his reply.

"And did you find yourself a husband?" asked Abel.

"Oh, yes," replied Melanie. "I married a real Southern gentleman with all the right credentials."

"Many congratulations," said Abel.

"I divorced him last year . . . with a large settlement."

"Oh, I'm sorry," said Abel, sounding pleased. "More champagne?"

"Are you by any chance trying to seduce me, Abel?"

"Not before you've finished your soup, Melanie. Even first-generation Polish immigrants have some standards, although I must admit it's my turn to do the seducing."

"Then I must warn you, Abel, I haven't slept with another man since my divorce came through. No lack of offers, but no one's been quite right. Too many groping hands and not enough affection."

After smoked salmon, young lamb, crême brulée and a pre-war Mouton Rothschild, they had both thoroughly reviewed their lives since their last meeting.

"Coffee in the penthouse, Melanie?"

"Do I have any choice, after such an excellent meal?" she enquired.

Abel laughed and escorted her out of the dining room and

into the lift. She was teetering very slightly on her high heels as she entered. Abel touched the button marked 'forty-two'. Melanie looked up at the numbers as they ticked by.

"Why no twelfth floor?" she asked innocently. Abel could not find the words to reply.

"The last time I had coffee in your room . . . " Melanie tried again.

"Don't remind me," said Abel, remembering his own vulnerability. As they stepped out of the lift on the forty-second floor, the bellhop opened the door of his suite.

"Good God," said Melanie, as her eyes swept round the inside of the penthouse for the first time. "I must say, Abel, you've learned how to adjust to the style of a multi-millionaire. I've never seen anything more extravagant in my life."

A knock at the door stopped Abel as he was about to reach out for her. A young waiter appeared with a pot of coffee and a bottle of Rémy Martin.

"Thank you, Mike," said Abel. "That will be all for tonight."

"Will it?" She smiled.

The waiter would have turned red if he hadn't been black, and he left quickly.

Abel poured Melanie coffee and brandy. She sipped slowly, sitting cross-legged on the floor. Abel would have sat cross-legged as well, but he couldn't quite manage the position, so instead he lay down beside her. She stroked his hair, and tentatively he began to move his hand up her leg. God, how well he remembered those legs. As they kissed for the first time, Melanie kicked a shoe off and knocked her coffee all over the Persian carpet.

"Oh, hell," she said. "I've ruined your beautiful carpet."

"Forget it," said Abel, as he pulled her back into his arms and started to unzip her dress. Melanie unbuttoned his shirt, and Abel tried to get it off while he was still kissing her, but his cufflinks stopped him, so he helped her out of her dress instead. Her figure had lost none of its beauty and was exactly as he remembered it, except that it was enticingly fuller. Those firm breasts and long graceful legs. He gave up the one-handed battle with the cufflinks and released her from his grasp to undress himself, aware what an abrupt physical contrast he must have appeared compared to her beautiful body. He hoped all he had read about women being fascinated by powerful men was true. She didn't seem to grimace as she once had at the sight of him. Gently, he caressed her breasts and began to part her legs. The Persian carpet was proving better than any bed. It was her turn to try to undress completely while they were kissing. She too gave up and finally took off everything except for – at Abel's request – her garter belt and nylon stockings.

When he heard her moan, he was aware how long it had been since he had experienced such ecstasy – and then – how quickly the sensation was past. Neither of them spoke for several moments, both breathing heavily.

Then Abel chuckled.

"What are you laughing at?" Melanie enquired.

"Nothing," said Abel, recalling Dr. Johnson's observation about the position being ridiculous and the pleasure momentary.

Abel rolled over, and Melanie rested her head on his shoulder. Abel was surprised to find that he no longer wanted to be near Melanie, and as he lay there wondering how to get rid of her without actually being rude, she said, "I'm afraid I can't stay all night, Abel, I have an early appointment tomorrow and I must get *some* sleep. I don't want to look as if I spent the night on your Persian carpet."

"Must you go?" said Abel, sounding desperate, but not too desperate.

"I'm sorry, darling, yes." She stood up and walked to the bathroom.

Abel watched her dress, and helped her with her zipper. How much easier the garment was to fasten at leisure than it had been to unfasten in haste. He kissed her gallantly on the hand as she left.

"I hope we'll see each other again soon," he said, lying.

"I hope so, too," she said, aware that he did not mean it.

He closed the door behind her and walked over to the phone by his bed.

"Which room was Miss Melanie Leroy booked into?" he asked.

There was a moment's pause; he could hear the flicking of the registration cards.

Abel tapped impatiently on the table.

"There's no one registered under that name, sir," came the eventual reply. "We have a Mrs. Melanie Seaton from Dallas, Texas, who arrived this evening, sir, and checks out tomorrow morning."

"Yes, that will be the lady," said Abel. "See that her bill is charged to me."

"Yes, sir."

Abel replaced the phone and took a long cold shower before preparing for bed. He felt relaxed as he walked over to the fire to turn out the lamp that had illuminated his first adulterous act and noticed that the large coffee stain had now dried on his Persian carpet.

"Silly bitch," he said out loud and switched off the light.

After that night, Abel found that several more coffee stains appeared on the Persian carpet during the next few months, some caused by waitresses, some by other nocturnal visitors, as he and Zaphia grew further apart. What he hadn't anticipated was that she would hire a private detective to check on him and then sue for a divorce. Divorce was almost unknown in Abel's circle of Polish friends, separation or desertion being far more common. Abel even tried to talk Zaphia out of her desired course, only too aware it would do nothing to enhance his standing in the Polish community, and certain it would not advance any social or political ambitions he had started to hanker after. But Zaphia was determined to carry the divorce proceedings to their bitter conclusion. Abel was surprised to find that the woman who had been so unsophisticated in his triumph was, to use George's words, a little demon in her revenge.

When Abel consulted his own lawyer, he found out for the second time just how many waitresses and non-paying guests there had been during the last year. He gave in and the only thing he fought for was the custody of Florentyna, now thirteen, and the first true love of his life. Zaphia agreed after a long struggle, accepting a settlement of five hundred thousand dollars, the deed to the house in Chicago, and the right to see Florentyna on the last weekend in every month.

Abel moved his headquarters and permanent home to New York and George dubbed him the Chicago Baron-in-exile, as he roamed America north and south building new hotels, only returning to Chicago when he had to see Curtis Fenton.

27

The letter lay open on a table by William's chair in the living room. He sat in his dressing gown reading it for the third time, trying to figure out why Abel Rosnovski would want to buy so heavily into Lester's Bank, and why he had appointed Henry Osborne as a director of the Baron Group. William felt he could no longer take the risk of guessing and picked up the phone.

The new Mr. Cohen turned out to be a younger version of his father. When he arrived at East Sixty-eighth Street, he had no need to introduce himself; the hair was beginning to go grey and thin in exactly the same places and the round body was encased in an exactly similar suit. Perhaps, it was in fact the same suit. William stared at him, but not simply because he looked so like his father.

"You don't remember me, Mr. Kane," said the lawyer.

"Good God," said William. "The great debate at Harvard. Nineteen twenty . . ."

"Twenty-eight. You won the debate and sacrificed your membership of the Porcellian."

William burst out laughing. "Maybe we'll do better on the same team, if your brand of socialism will allow you to act for an unabashed capitalist."

He rose to shake hands with Thaddeus Cohen. For a moment, they both might have been undergraduates again.

William smiled. "You never did get that drink at the Porcellian. What would you like?"

Thaddeus Cohen declined the offer. "I don't drink," he said, blinking in the same disarming way that William recalled so well. "... And I'm afraid I'm now an unabashed capitalist, too."

He turned out to have his father's head on his shoulders mentally as well as physically, and had clearly briefed himself on the Rosnovski-Osborne file to the finest detail before he faced William. William explained exactly what he now required.

"An immediate report and a further updated one every three months as in the past. Secrecy is still of paramount importance," he said, "but I want every fact you can lay your hands on. Why is Abel Rosnovski buying the bank's shares? Does he still feel I am responsible for Davis Leroy's death? Is he continuing his battle with Kane and Cabot even now that they are part of Lester's? What role does Henry Osborne play in all of this? Would a meeting between myself and Rosnovski help, especially if I tell him that it was the bank, not I, who refused to support the Richmond Group?"

Thaddeus Cohen's pen was scratching away as furiously as his father's had before him.

"All these questions must be answered as quickly as possible so that I can decide if it's necessary to brief my board."

Thaddeus Cohen gave his father's shy smile as he shut his briefcase. "I'm sorry that you should be troubled in this way while you are still convalescing. I'll be back to you as soon as I can ascertain the facts." He paused at the door. "I admire greatly what you did at Remagen."

William recovered his sense of well-being and vigour rapidly in the following months, and the scars on his face and chest faded into relative insignificance. At night Kate would sit up with him until he fell asleep and whisper, "Thank God you were spared." The terrible headaches and periods of amnesia grew to be things of the past, and the strength returned to his right arm. Kate would not allow him to return to work until they had taken a long and relaxing cruise in the West Indies. William relaxed with Kate more than at any time since their two weeks together in London. She revelled in the fact that there were no banks on the ship for him to do business with, although she feared if they stayed on board another week William would have acquired the floating vessel as one of Lester's latest assets, reorganising the crew, routes, timings and even the way they sailed 'the boat', as William insisted on calling the great liner. He was tanned and restless once the ship docked in New York Harbor, and Kate could not dissuade him from returning immediately to the bank.

He soon became deeply involved again in Lester's problems. A new breed of men, toughened by war, enterprising and fast-moving, seemed to be running America's modern banks, under the watchful eye of President Truman, the man who had won a surprise victory for a second term in the White House after the world had been informed that Dewey was certain to win the election. As if not satisfied with their prediction, the *Chicago Tribune* went on to announce that Dewey had actually won the election, but it was Harry S. Truman who remained in the White House. William knew very little about the diminutive ex-senator from Missouri, except what he read in the newspapers, and as a staunch Republican, he hoped that his party would find the right man to lead them into the 1952 campaign.

The first report came in from Thaddeus Cohen: Abel Rosnovski was still looking for shares in Lester's Bank and had approached all the other benefactors of the will but only one agreement had been concluded. Susan Lester had refused to see William's lawyer when he approached her, so he was unable to discover why she had sold her six per cent. All he could ascertain was that she had no financial reason for doing so. "Hell hath no fury," murmured William.

The document was admirably comprehensive.

Henry Osborne, it seemed, had been appointed a director of the Baron Group in May of 1947, with special responsibility for the Lester's account. More importantly, Abel Rosnovski secured Susan Lester's shares without it being possible directly to trace the acquisition back to either him or to Osborne. Rosnovski now owned six per cent of Lester's Bank and appeared to be willing to pay at least another $750,000 to obtain Peter Parfitt's two per cent. William was only too aware of the actions Abel Rosnovski could carry out once he was in possession of eight per cent. Even more worrying to William was the fact that the growth rate of Lester's compared unfavourably with that of the Baron Group, which was already catching up its main rivals, the Hilton and the Sheraton Groups. William began to wonder if it would now be wise to brief his board of directors on this newly obtained information, and even whether he ought not to contact Abel Rosnovski direct. After some sleepless nights, he turned to Kate for advice.

"Do nothing," was Kate's reaction, "until you can be absolutely certain that his intentions are as disruptive as you fear. The whole affair may turn out to be a tempest in a teapot."

"With Henry Osborne as his hatchet man you can be sure that the tempest will pour far beyond the teacup: nothing can be totally innocent. I don't have to sit around and wait to find out what he is planning for me."

"He might have changed, William. It must be twenty years since you've had any personal dealings with him."

"Al Capone might have changed, if he had been allowed to complete his jail sentence. We'll never know for certain, but I would not be willing to put a bet on it."

Kate added nothing more, but William let himself be persuaded by her and did little except to keep a close eye on Thaddeus Cohen's quarterly reports and hope that Kate's intuition would turn out to be right.

28

The Baron Group profited greatly from the post-war explosion in the American economy. Not since the twenties had it been so easy to make so much money so quickly – and by the early fifties, people were beginning to believe that this time it was going to last. But Abel was not content with financial success alone; as he grew older, he began to worry about Poland's place in the post-war world and to feel that his success did not allow him to be a bystander four thousand miles away. What had Pawel Zaleski, the Polish consul in Turkey, said? 'Perhaps in your lifetime you will see Poland rise again.' Abel did everything he could to influence and persuade the United States Congress to take a more militant attitude towards Russian control of its Eastern European satellites. It seemed to Abel, as he watched one puppet socialist government after another come into being, that he had risked his life for nothing. He began to lobby Washington politicians, brief journalists and organise dinners in Chicago and New York and other centres of the Polish-American community, until the Polish cause itself became synonymous with the Chicago Baron.

Dr. Teodor Szymanowski, formerly professor of history at the university of Cracow, wrote a glowing editorial about Abel's 'Fight To Be Recognised' in the journal *Freedom*, which prompted Abel to contact him and see what else he could do to help. The professor was now an old man, and when Abel was ushered into his study, he was surprised by the frailty of his appearance, knowing the vigour of his opinions. He greeted Abel warmly and poured him a Danzig vodka. "Baron Rosnovski," he said handing him the glass,

"I have long admired the way you work on and on for our cause and although we make such little headway, you never seem to lose faith."

"Why should I? I have always believed anything is possible in America."

"But I fear, Baron, the very men you are now trying to influence are the same ones who have allowed these things to take place. They will never do anything positive to free our people."

"I do not understand what you mean, Professor," said Abel. "Why will they not help us?"

The professor leaned his back in his chair. "You are surely aware, Baron, that the American armies were given specific orders to slow down their advance east to allow the Russians to take as much of central Europe as they could lay their hands on. Patton could have been in Berlin long before the Russians but Eisenhower told him to hold back. It was our leaders in Washington – the same men you are trying to persuade to put American guns and troops back into Europe – who gave those orders to Eisenhower."

"But they couldn't have known then what the U.S.S.R. would eventually become. The Russians were then our allies. I accept that we were too weak and conciliatory with them in 1945, but it was not the Americans who directly betrayed the Polish people."

Before Szymanowski spoke, he leaned back again and closed his eyes wearily.

"I wish you could have known my brother, Baron Rosnovski. I had word only last week that he died six months ago, in a Soviet camp not unlike the one from which you escaped."

Abel moved forward as if to offer sympathy, but Szymanowski raised his hand.

"No, don't say anything. You have known the camps yourself. You would be the first to realise that sympathy is no longer important. We must change the world, Baron, while others sleep." Szymanowski paused. "My brother was sent to Russia by the Americans."

Abel looked at him in astonishment.

"By the Americans? How is that possible? If your brother was captured in Poland by Russian troops . . ."

"My brother was never taken prisoner in Poland. He was liberated from a German war camp near Frankfurt. The Americans kept him in a D.P. camp for a month and then they handed him over to the Russians."

"It can't be true. Why would they do that?"

"The Russians wanted all Slavs repatriated. Repatriated so that they could then be exterminated or enslaved. The ones that Hitler didn't get, Stalin did. And I can prove my brother was in the American Sector for over a month."

"But," Abel began, "was he an exception or were there many others like him?"

"He was no exception: there were many others," said Szymanowski without apparent emotion. "Hundreds of thousands. Perhaps as many as a million. I don't think we will ever know the true figures. It's most unlikely the American authorities ever kept careful records of Operation Kee Chanl."

"Operation Kee Chanl? Why don't people ever mention this? Surely if others realised that we, the Americans, had been sending liberated prisoners back to die in Russia, they would be horrified."

"There is no proof, no known documentation of Operation Kee Chanl. Mark Clark, God bless him, disobeyed his orders and a few of the prisoners were warned in advance by some kindly disposed G.I.s, and they managed to escape before the Americans could send them to the camps. But they are now lying low and would never admit as much. One of the unlucky ones was with my brother. Anyway, it's too late now."

"But the American people must be told. I'll form a committee, print pamphlets, make speeches. Surely Congress will listen to us if we tell them the truth."

"Baron Rosnovski, I think this one is too big even for you."

Abel rose from his seat.

"No, no, I do not underestimate you, my friend. But you do not yet understand the mentality of world leaders. America agreed to hand over those poor devils because Stalin demanded as much. I am sure they never thought that there would be trials, labour camps and executions to follow. But now, as we approach the fifties, no one is going to admit they were indirectly responsible? No, they will never do that. Not for a hundred years. And then, all but a few historians will have forgotten that Poland lost more lives in the war than any other single nation on earth, including Germany.

"I had hoped the one conclusion you might come to was that you must play a more direct role in politics."

"I have already been considering the idea but cannot decide what form it should take."

"I have my own views on that subject, Baron, so keep in touch."

The old man raised himself slowly to his feet and embraced Abel. "In the meantime do what you can for our cause, but don't be surprised when you meet closed doors."

The moment Abel returned to The Baron, he picked up the phone and told the hotel operator to get him Senator Douglas' office. Paul Douglas was Illinois' liberal Democratic senator, elected with the help of the Chicago machine, and he had always been helpful and responsive to any of Abel's past requests, mindful of the fact that his constituency contained the largest Polish community in the country. His assistant Adam Tomaszewicz always dealt with his Polish constituents.

"Hello, Adam. It's Abel Rosnovski. I have something very disturbing to discuss with the senator. Could you arrange an early meeting with him?"

"I'm afraid he's out of town today, Mr. Rosnovski. I know he'll be glad to speak with you as soon as he returns on Thursday. I'll ask him to call you direct. Can I tell him what it's all about?"

"Yes. As a Pole you will be interested. I've heard reports from reliable sources that the U.S. authorities in Germany assisted in the return of displaced Polish citizens to territories occupied by the Soviet Union, and that many of these Polish citizens were then sent on to Russian labour camps and have never been heard of since."

There was a moment's silence from the other end of the line.

"I'll brief the senator on his return, Mr. Rosnovski," said Adam Tomaszewicz. "Thank you for calling."

The senator did not get in touch with Abel on Thursday. Nor did he try on Friday or over the weekend. On Monday morning, Abel put through another call to his office. Again, Adam Tomaszewicz answered the telephone.

"Oh, yes, Mr. Rosnovski." Abel could almost hear him blushing. "The senator did leave a message for you. He's been very busy, you know, what with all the emergency bills that have to be acted on before Congress recesses. He asked me to let you know that he'll call back just as soon as he has a spare moment."

"Did you give him my message?"

"Yes, of course. He asked me to assure you that he felt certain the rumour you heard was nothing more than a piece of anti-American propaganda. He added that he'd been told personally by one of the Joint Chiefs that American troops had orders not to release any of the D.P.s under their supervision."

Tomaszewicz sounded as if he was reading a carefully prepared statement, and Abel sensed that he had encountered the first of those closed doors. Senator Douglas had never evaded him in the past.

Abel put down the phone and dialled the number of another senator who did make news and didn't evade sitting in judgment on anybody.

Senator Joseph McCarthy's office came on the line asking who was calling. "I'll try and find the senator," said a young voice when she heard who it was and his reason for wanting to speak to her boss. McCarthy was approaching the peak of his power, and Abel realised he would be lucky to have more than a few moments on the phone with him.

"Mr. Rosenevski," were McCarthy's first words.

Abel wondered if he had mangled his name on purpose, or if it was a bad connection. "What is it you wanted to discuss with me and no one else, this matter of grave urgency?" the senator asked. Abel hesitated; actually speaking to McCarthy directly had slightly taken him aback.

"Your secrets are safe with me," he heard the senator say, sensing his hesitation.

"If you say so," said Abel and paused for a moment to collect his thoughts. "You, Senator, have been a forthright spokesman for those of us who would like to see the Eastern European nations freed from the yoke of communism."

"So I have. So I have. And I'm glad to see you appreciate the fact, Mr. Rosenevski."

This time Abel was sure he had mispronounced his name on purpose, but resolved not to comment on it.

"As for Eastern Europe," the senator continued, "you must realise that only after the traitors have been driven from within our own government can any real action be taken to free your captive country."

"That is exactly what I want to speak to you about, Senator. You have had a brilliant success in exposing treachery within our own government. But to date, one of the communists' greatest crimes has as yet gone unpublicised."

"Just what great crime did you have in mind, Mr. Rosenevski? I have found so many since I came to Washington."

"I am referring" – Abel drew himself up a little straighter in his chair – "to the forced repatriation of thousands of displaced Polish citizens by the American authorities after the war ended. Innocent enemies of communism who were sent back to Poland, and then on to the U.S.S.R., to be enslaved and sometimes murdered."

Abel waited for a response, but none was forthcoming. He heard a click and wondered if someone else was listening to the conversation.

"Now, Rosenevski, listen to me, you simpleton. You dare to phone me to say that Americans – loyal United States soldiers – sent thousands of Poles back to Russia and nobody heard a word about it? Are you asking me to believe that? Even a Polack couldn't be that stupid. And I wonder what kind of person accepts a lie like that without any proof? Do you want me also to believe that American soldiers are disloyal? Is that what you want? Tell me, Rosenevski, tell me what it is with you people? Are you too stupid to recognise communist propaganda even when it hits you right in the face? Do you have to waste the time of an overworked United States senator because of a rumour cooked up by the *Pravda* slime to create unrest in America's immigrant communities?"

Abel sat motionless, stunned by the outburst. Before half of his tirade was over, Abel felt that any counter-argument was going to be pointless. He waited for the histrionic speech to come to an end, and was glad the senator couldn't see his startled face.

"Senator, I'm sure you're right and I'm sorry to have wasted your time," Abel said quietly. "I hadn't thought of it in quite that light before."

"Well, it just goes to show how tricky those commie bastards can be," said McCarthy, his tone softening. "You have to keep an eye on them all the time. Anyway, I hope you're more alert now to the continual danger the American people face."

"I am indeed, Senator. Thank you once again for taking the trouble to speak to me personally. Goodbye, Senator."

"Goodbye, Rosenovski."

Abel heard the phone click and realised it was the same sound as a closing door.

29

William became aware of feeling older when Kate teased him about his greying hair, hairs which he used to be able to count and now no longer could, and Richard started to bring girls home whom he found attractive. William almost always approved of Richard's choice of young ladies, as he called them, perhaps because they were all rather like Kate who, he considered, was more beautiful in middle-age than she had ever been. His daughters, Virginia and Lucy, now also becoming young ladies, brought him great happiness as they grew in the image of their mother. Virginia was becoming quite an artist and the kitchen and children's bedrooms were always covered in her latest works of genius, as Richard described them mockingly. Virginia's revenge came the day Richard started cello lessons when even the servants were heard to murmur unsavoury comments whenever the bow came in contact with the strings. Lucy adored them both and considered Virginia with uncritical prejudice the new Picasso and Richard the new Casals. William began to wonder what the future would hold for all three of them when he was no longer around. In Kate's eyes all three children advanced satisfactorily. Richard, now at St. Paul's, had improved enough at the cello to be chosen to play in a school concert, while Virginia was painting well enough for one of her pictures to be hung in the front room. But it became obvious to all the family that Lucy was going to be the beauty when, aged only eleven, she started receiving little love notes from boys who until then had only shown an interest in baseball.

In 1951, Richard was accepted at Harvard and although

he did not win the top mathematics scholarship, Kate was quick to point out to William that he had played baseball and the cello for St. Paul's, two accomplishments William had never so much as attempted to master. William was secretly proud of Richard's achievements but grumbled to Kate something about not knowing many bankers who played baseball or the cello.

Banking was moving into an expansionist period as Americans began to believe in a lasting peace. William soon found himself overworked and, for a short time, the threat of Abel Rosnovski and the problems associated with him had to be pushed into the background.

The flow of quarterly reports from Thaddeus Cohen indicated that Rosnovski had embarked on a course which he had no intention of abandoning – through a third party he had let every stockholder other than William know of his interest in Lester's shares. William wondered if that course was heading towards a direct confrontation between himself and the Pole. He began to feel that the time was fast approaching when he would have to inform the Lester's board of Rosnovski's actions and perhaps even to offer his resignation if the bank looked to be under siege, a move that would result in a complete victory for Abel Rosnovski, which was the one reason William did not seriously contemplate such a move. He decided that if he had to fight for his life, fight he would, and if one of the two had to go under, he would do everything in his power to ensure that it wasn't William Kane.

The problem of what to do about Abel Rosnovski's investment programme was finally taken out of William's hands.

Early in 1951, the bank had been invited to represent one of America's new airline companies, Interstate Airways, when the Federal Aviation Agency granted them a franchise for flights between the East and West coasts. The airline approached Lester's Bank when they needed to raise the thirty million dollars to provide them with the financial backing required by governmental regulations.

William considered the airline and the whole project to be well worth supporting, and he spent virtually his entire time setting up a public offering to raise the necessary thirty million. The bank, acting as the sponsor for the project, put all their resources behind the new venture. The project became William's biggest since he had returned to Lester's, and he realised that his personal reputation was at stake when he went to the market for the thirty million dollars. In July, when the details of the offering were announced the stock was snapped up in a matter of days. William received lavish praise from all quarters for the way he had handled the project and carried it through to such a successful conclusion. He could not have been happier about the outcome himself, until he read in Thaddeus Cohen's next report that ten per cent of the airline's stock had been obtained by one of Abel Rosnovski's dummy corporations.

William knew then that the time had come to acquaint Ted Leach and Tony Simmons with his worst fears. He asked Tony to come to New York where he called both of the vice-chairmen to his office and related to them the saga of Abel Rosnovski and Henry Osborne.

"Why didn't you let us know about all this before?" was Tony Simmons' first reaction.

"I dealt with a hundred companies like the Richmond Group when I was at Kane and Cabot, Tony, and I couldn't know at the time that he was that serious about revenge. I was only finally convinced of his obsession when Rosnovski purchased ten per cent of Interstate Airways."

"I suppose it's possible you may be over-reacting," said Ted Leach. "Of one thing I am certain: it would be unwise to inform the rest of the board of this information. The last thing we want a few days after launching a new company is a panic on our hands."

"That's for sure," said Tony Simmons. "Why don't you see this fellow Rosnovski and have it out with him?"

"I expect that's exactly what he'd like me to do," replied William. "It would leave him in no doubt that the bank feels it's under siege."

"Don't you think his attitude might change if you told him how hard you tried to talk the bank into backing the Richmond Group, but they wouldn't support you and . . ."

"I've no reason to believe he doesn't know that already," said William. "He seems to know everything else."

"Well, what do you feel the bank should do about Rosnovski?" asked Ted Leach. "We certainly can't stop him from purchasing our stock if he can find a willing seller. If we went in for buying our own stock, far from stopping him, we would play right into his hands by raising the value of his holding and jeopardising our own financial position. I think you can be certain he would enjoy watching us sweat that one out. We are about the perfect size to be taken on by Harry Truman, and there's nothing the Democrats would enjoy more than a banking scandal with an election in the offing."

"I realise there's little I can do about it," said William, "but had to let you know what Rosnovski was up to in case he springs another surprise on us."

"I suppose there's still an outside chance," said Tony Simmons, "that the whole thing is innocent, and he simply respects your talent as an investor."

"How can you say that, Tony, when you know my stepfather is involved? Do you think Rosnovski employed Henry Osborne to further my career in banking? You obviously don't understand Rosnovski as I do. I've watched him operating now for over twenty years. He's not used to losing; he simply goes on throwing the dice until he wins. I couldn't know him much better if he was one of my own family. He will . . ."

"Now don't become paranoid, William. I expect . . ."

"Don't become paranoid you say, Tony. Remember the power our Articles of Incorporation give to anyone who gets his hands on eight per cent of the bank's stock. An article I had originally inserted to protect myself from being removed. The man already has six per cent and if that's not a bad enough prospect for the future, remember that Rosnovski could wipe out Interstate Airways overnight just by placing his entire stock on the market at once."

"But he would gain nothing from that," said Ted Leach. "On the contrary, he would stand to lose a great deal of money."

"Believe me, you don't understand how Abel Rosnovski's

mind works," said William. "He has the courage of a lion, and the loss would mean nothing to him. I'm fast becoming convinced his only interest is in getting even with me. Yes, of course he'd lose money on those shares if he dumped them, but he always has his hotels to fall back on. There are twenty-one of them now, you know, and he must realise that if Interstate stock collapses overnight, we will also be knocked backwards. As bankers, our credibility depends on the fickle confidence of the public, confidence Abel Rosnovski can now shatter as and when it suits him."

"Calm down, William," said Tony Simmons. "It hasn't come to that yet. Now we know what Rosnovski is up to, we can keep a closer watch on his activities and counter them as and when we need to. The first thing we must be sure of is that no one else sells their shares in Lester's before first offering them to you. The bank is always going to support any action you take. My own feeling is still that you should speak to Rosnovski personally and have it out in the open with him. At least that way we will know how serious his intentions are, and we can prepare ourselves accordingly."

"Is that also your opinion, Ted?" asked William.

"Yes, it is. I agree with Tony. I think you should contact the man directly. It can only be in the bank's interests to discover how innocent or otherwise his intentions really are."

William sat silently for a few moments. "If you both feel that way, I'll give it a try," he eventually said. "I must add that I don't agree with you, but I may be too personally involved to make a dispassionate judgment. Give me a few days to think about how I should best approach him, and I'll let you know the outcome."

After the two vice-chairmen had left his office, William sat alone, thinking about the action he had agreed to take, certain there could be little hope of success with Abel Rosnovski if Henry Osborne was involved.

Four days later, William sat alone in his office, having given instructions that he was not to be interrupted under any circumstances. He knew that Abel Rosnovski was also sitting in his office in the New York Baron: he had had a man posted at the hotel all morning whose only task had been to report the moment Rosnovski showed up. The waiting man had phoned; Abel Rosnovski had arrived that morning at eight twenty-seven, had gone straight up to his office on the forty-second floor and had not been seen since. William picked up his telephone and asked the operator to get him the Baron Hotel.

"New York Baron."

"Mr. Rosnovski, please," said William nervously. He was put through to a secretary.

"Mr. Rosnovski, please," he repeated. This time his voice was a little steadier.

"May I ask who is calling?" she said.

"My name is William Kane."

There was a long silence – or did it simply seem long to William?

"I'm not sure if he's in, Mr. Kane. I'll find out for you."

Another long silence.

"Mr. Kane?"

"Mr. Rosnovski?"

"What can I do for you, Mr. Kane?" asked a very calm, lightly accented voice.

Although William had prepared his opening remarks carefully, he was aware that he sounded anxious.

"I'm a little worried about your holdings in Lester's Bank, Mr. Rosnovski," he said, "and indeed about the strong position you have built up in one of the companies we represent. I thought perhaps the time had come for us to meet and discuss your full intentions. There is also a private matter I should like to make known to you."

Another long silence. Had he been cut off?

"There are no conditions which would ever make a meeting with you possible, Kane. I know enough about you already without wanting to hear your excuses about the past. You keep your eyes open all the time, and you'll find out only too clearly what my intentions are, and they differ greatly from those you will find in the Book of Genesis, Mr. Kane. One day you're going to want to jump out of the twelfth floor window of one of my hotels, because you'll be in deep trouble with Lester's Bank over your own holdings. I only need two more per cent to invoke Article Seven, and we both know what that means, don't we? Then perhaps you'll appreciate for the first time what it felt like for Davis Leroy, wondering for months what the bank might do with his life. Now you can sit and wonder for years what I am going to do with yours once I obtain that eight per cent."

Abel Rosnovski's words chilled William, but somehow he forced himself to carry on calmly, while at the same time banging his fist angrily on the table. "I can understand how you feel, Mr. Rosnovski, but I still think it would be wise for us to get together and talk this whole thing out. There are one or two aspects of the affair I know you can't be aware of."

"Like the way you swindled Henry Osborne out of five hundred thousand dollars, Mr. Kane?"

William was momentarily speechless and wanted to explode, but once again managed to control his temper.

"No, Mr. Rosnovski, what I wanted to talk to you about has nothing to do with Mr. Osborne. It's a personal matter and it involves only you. However, I most emphatically assure you that I have never swindled Henry Osborne out of one red cent."

"That's not Henry's version. He says you were responsible for the death of your own mother, to make sure that you didn't have to honour a debt to him. After your treatment of Davis Leroy, I find that only too easy to believe."

William had never had to fight harder to control his emotions, and it took him several seconds to muster a reply.

"May I suggest we clear this whole misunderstanding up once and for all by meeting at a neutral place of your choice where no one would recognise us?"

"There's only one place left where no one would recognise you, Mr. Kane."

"Where's that?" asked William.

"Heaven," said Abel, and placed the phone back on the hook.

"Get me Henry Osborne at once," he said to his secretary.

He drummed his fingers on the desk while the girl took

nearly fifteen minutes to find Congressman Osborne who, it turned out, had been showing some of his constituents around the Capitol building.

"Abel, is that you?"

"Yes, Henry, I thought you'd want to be the first to hear that Kane knows everything, so now the battle is out in the open."

"What do you mean, he knows everything? Do you think he knows I'm involved?" asked Henry anxiously.

"He sure does, and he also seems to be aware of the special company accounts, my holdings in Lester's Bank and Interstate Airways."

"How could he possibly know everything in such detail? Only you and I know about the special accounts."

"And Curtis Fenton," said Abel, interrupting him.

"Right. But he would never inform Kane."

"He must have. There's no one else. Don't forget that Kane dealt directly with Curtis Fenton when I bought the Richmond Group from his bank. I suppose they must have maintained some sort of contact all along."

"Jesus."

"You sound worried, Henry."

"If William Kane knows everything, it's a different ball game. I'm warning you, Abel, he's not in the habit of losing."

"Nor am I," replied Abel. "And William Kane doesn't frighten me; not while I'm holding all the aces in my hand. What is our latest holding in Kane's stock?"

"Off the top of my head, you own six per cent of Lester's Bank, and ten per cent of Interstate Airways, and odd bits of other companies they're involved with. You only need another two per cent of Lester's to invoke Article Seven and Peter Parfitt is still biting."

"Excellent," said Abel. "I don't see how the situation could be better. Continue talking to Parfitt, remembering that I'm in no hurry while Kane can't even approach him. For the time being we'll let Kane wonder what we're up to. And be sure you do nothing until I return from Europe. After my phone conversation with Mr. Kane this morning, I can assure you that, to use a gentleman's expression, he's perspiring but I'll let you into a secret, Henry. I'm not sweating. He can go on that way because I have no intention of making a move until I'm good and ready."

"Fine," said Henry. "I'll keep you informed if anything comes up at this end that we should worry about."

"You must get it through your head, Henry, there's nothing for *us* to worry about. We have your friend, Mr. Kane, by the balls, and I now intend to squeeze them very slowly."

"I shall enjoy watching that," said Henry, sounding a little happier.

"Sometimes I think you hate Kane more than I do."

Henry laughed nervously. "Have a good trip to Europe."

Abel put the phone back on the hook and sat staring into space as he considered his next move, his fingers still tapping noisily on the desk. His secretary came in.

"Get Mr. Curtis Fenton at the Continental Trust Bank," he said, without looking at her. His fingers continued to tap. His eyes continued to stare. A few moments later the phone rang.

"Fenton?"

"Good morning, Mr. Rosnovski, how are you?"

"I want you to close all my accounts with your bank."

There was no reply from the other end.

"Did you hear me, Fenton?"

"Yes," said the stupefied banker. "May I ask why, Mr. Rosnovski?"

"Because Judas never was my favourite apostle, Fenton, that's why. As of this moment, you are no longer on the board of the Baron Group. You will shortly receive written instructions confirming this conversation and telling you to which bank the accounts should be transferred."

"But I don't understand why, Mr. Rosnovski. What have I done . . .?"

Abel hung up as his daughter walked into the office.

"That didn't sound very pleasant, Daddy."

"It wasn't meant to be pleasant, but it's nothing to concern yourself with, darling," said Abel, his tone changing immediately. "Did you manage to find all the clothes you need for Europe?"

"Yes, thank you, Daddy, but I'm not absolutely sure what they're wearing in London and Paris. I can only hope that I've got it right. I don't want to stick out like a sore thumb."

"You'll stick out all right, my darling, by being the most beautiful thing the British have seen in years. They'll know your clothes didn't come out of a ration book with your natural flair and sense of colour. Those young Europeans will be falling all over themselves to get alongside you, but I'll be there to stop them. Now let's go and have some lunch and discuss what we are going to do while we're in London."

Ten days later, after Florentyna had spent a long weekend with her mother – Abel never enquired after her – the two of them flew from New York's Idlewild Airport to London's Heathrow. The flight in a Boeing 377 took nearly fourteen hours, and although they had private berths, when they arrived at Claridge's in Brook Street, the only thing they both wanted to do was have another long sleep.

Abel was making the trip to Europe for three reasons: first, to confirm building contracts for new Baron hotels in London, Paris and possibly Rome; second, to give Florentyna her first view of Europe before she went to Radcliffe to study modern languages; and third, and most important to him, to revisit his castle in Poland to see if there was even an outside chance of proving his ownership.

London turned out to be a success for both of them. Abel's advisers had found a site on Hyde Park Corner, and he instructed solicitors to proceed immediately with all the negotiations for the land and the permits that would be needed before England's capital could boast a Baron. Florentyna found the austerity of post-war London forbidding after the excess of her own home, but the Londoners seemed to be undaunted by their war-damaged city, still believing themselves to be a world power. She was invited to lunches, dinners and balls, and her father was proved right about her taste in clothes and the reaction of young European men. She returned each night with sparkling eyes and stories of new conquests made – and forgotten by the following morning. She couldn't make up her mind whether she wanted to marry an Etonian from the Grenadier Guards who saluted her all the time or a member of the House of Lords who was in waiting to the King. She wasn't quite sure what 'in waiting' meant, but he certainly knew exactly how to treat a lady.

In Paris, the pace never slackened and because they both spoke good French, they both managed as well with the Parisians as they had with the English. Abel was normally bored by the end of the second week of any holiday, and would start counting the days until he could return home to work. But not while he had Florentyna as his companion. She had, since his separation from Zaphia, become the centre of his life and the sole heir to his fortune.

When the time came for Abel to leave Paris, neither of them wanted to go, so they stayed on a few more days claiming as an excuse that Abel was still negotiating to buy a famous but now run-down hotel on the Boulevard Raspail. He did not inform the owner, a Monsieur Neuffe, who looked, if it were possible, even more run-down than the hotel, that he planned to demolish the building and start again from scratch. When Monsieur Neuffe signed the papers a few days later, Abel ordered the building to be razed to the ground while he and Florentyna, with no more excuses left for remaining in Paris, departed reluctantly for Rome.

After the friendliness of the British and the gaiety of the French capital, the sullen and dilapidated Eternal City immediately dampened their spirits, for the Romans felt they had nothing to celebrate. The life of London and Paris seemed infinitely behind them. In London, they had strolled through the magnificent Royal parks together, admired historic buildings, and Florentyna had danced until the small hours. In Paris, they had been to the Opéra, lunched on the banks of the Seine, and taken a boat down the river past Notre Dame and on to supper in the Latin Quarter. In Rome, Abel found only an overpowering sense of financial instability and decided that he would have to shelve his plans to build a Baron in the Italian capital. Florentyna sensed her father's anxiety to once again see his castle in Poland, so she suggested they leave Italy a day early.

Abel had found bureaucracy more reluctant to grant a visa for Florentyna and himself to enter an Iron Curtain country than it had been to issue a permit to build a new five-hundred-room hotel in London. A less persistent visitor would probably have given up, but with the appropriate visas firmly stamped in their passports, Abel and Florentyna set off in a hired car for Slonim. The two travellers were kept waiting for hours at the Polish border, helped along only by the fact that Abel was fluent in the language. Had the border guards known why his Polish was so good, they would doubtless have taken an entirely different attitude to allowing him to return. Abel changed five hundred dollars into zlotys – that at least seemed to please the Poles – and motored on. The nearer they came to Slonim, the more Florentyna was aware of how much the journey meant to her father.

"Daddy, I can never remember you being so excited about anything."

"This is where I was born," Abel explained. "After such a long time in America, where things change every day, it's almost unreal to be back where it looks as if nothing has changed since I left."

They drove on towards Slonim, Abel's senses heightened in anticipation, while horrified and angry at the devastation of the once trim countryside and small, neat cottages. Across a time span of nearly forty years he heard his childish voice ask the Baron whether the hour of the submerged peoples of Europe had arrived and would he be able to play his part, and tears came to his eyes to think how short that hour had been, and what a little part he had played.

When they rounded the final corner before approaching the Baron's estate and saw the great iron gates that led to the castle, Abel laughed aloud in excitement as he brought the car to a halt.

"It's all just as I remember it. Nothing's changed. Come on, let's start by visiting the cottage where I spent the first five years of my life – I don't expect anyone is living there now – and then we'll go and see my castle."

Florentyna followed her father as he marched confidently down a small track into the forest of moss-covered birches and oaks, which was not going to change in a hundred years. After they had walked for about twenty minutes, the two of them came out into a small clearing, and there in front of them was the trapper's cottage. Abel stood and stared. He had forgotten how tiny his first home was: could nine people really have lived there? The thatched roof was now in disrepair, and the building left the impression of being uninhabited with its eroded stone and broken windows. The once tidy vegetable garden was indistinguishable in the matted undergrowth.

Had the cottage been deserted? Florentyna took her father by the arm and led him slowly to the front door. Abel stood there, motionless, so Florentyna knocked gently. They waited in silence. Florentyna knocked again, this time a little more loudly, and they heard someone moving within.

"All right, all right," said a querulous voice in Polish, and a few moments later, the door inched open. They were being studied by an old woman, bent and thin, dressed entirely in black. Wisps of untidy snow-white hair escaped from her handkerchief and her grey eyes looked vacantly at the visitors.

"It's not possible," said Abel softly in English.

"What do you want?" asked the old woman suspiciously.

She had no teeth and the line of her nose, mouth and chin formed a perfect concave arc.

Abel answered in Polish, "May we come in and talk to you?"

Her eyes looked from one to the other fearfully. "Old Helena hasn't done anything wrong," she said in a whine.

"I know," said Abel gently. "I have brought good news for you."

With some reluctance, she allowed them to enter the bare, cold room but she didn't offer them a seat. The room hadn't changed: two chairs, one table and the memory that until he had left the cottage, he hadn't known what a carpet was. Florentyna shuddered.

"I can't get the fire going," wheezed the old woman, prodding the grate with her stick. The faintly glowing log refused to rekindle, and she scrabbled ineffectually in her pocket. "I need paper." She looked at Abel, showing a spark of interest for the first time. "Do you have any paper?"

Abel looked at her steadily. "Don't you remember me?" he said.

"No, I don't know you."

"You do, Helena. My name is . . . Wladek."

"You knew my little Wladek?"

"I am Wladek."

"Oh, no," she said with sad and distant finality. "He was too good for me, the mark of God was upon him. The Baron took him away to be an angel, yes, he took away Matka's littlest one . . ."

Her old voice cracked and died away. She sat down, but the ancient, lined hands were busy in her lap.

"I have returned," said Abel, more insistently, but the old woman paid him no attention, and her old voice quavered on as though she were quite alone in the room.

"They killed my husband, my Jasio, and all my lovely children were taken to the camps, except little Sophia. I hid her, and they went away." Her voice was even and resigned.

"What happened to little Sophia?" asked Abel.

"The Russians took her away in the other war," she said dully.

Abel shuddered.

The old woman roused herself from her memories. "What do you want? Why are you asking me these questions?" she demanded.

"I wanted you to meet my daughter, Florentyna."

"I had a daughter called Florentyna once, but now there's only me."

"But I . . ." began Abel, starting to unbutton his shirt.

Florentyna stopped him. "We know," she said, smiling at the old lady.

"How can you possibly know? It was all so long before you were even born."

"They told us in the village," said Florentyna.

"Have you any paper with you?" the old lady asked. "I need paper for the fire."

Abel looked at Florentyna helplessly. "No," he replied, "I'm sorry, we didn't bring any with us."

"What do you want?" reiterated the old woman, once again hostile.

"Nothing," said Abel, now resigned to the fact that she would not remember him. "We just wanted to say hello." He took out his wallet, removed all the new zloty notes he had acquired at the border and handed them over to her.

"Thank you, thank you," she said as she took each note, her old eyes watering with pleasure.

Abel bent over to kiss his foster-mother, but she backed away.

Florentyna took her father's arm and led Abel out of the cottage and back down the forest track in the direction of their car.

The old woman watched from her window until she was sure they were out of sight. Then she took the new bank notes, crumpled each one into a little ball and placed them all carefully in the grate. They kindled immediately. She placed twigs and small logs on top of the blazing zlotys and sat slowly down by her fire, the best in weeks, rubbing her hands together at the comfort of the warmth.

Abel did not speak on the walk back to the car until the iron gates were once again in sight. Then he promised Florentyna, trying his best to forget the little cottage, "You are about to see the most beautiful castle in the world."

"You must stop exaggerating, Daddy."

"In the world," Abel repeated quietly.

Florentyna laughed. "I'll let you know how it compares with Versailles."

They climbed back into the car and Abel drove through the gates, remembering the vehicles he had been in when he last passed through them, and up the mile-long drive to the castle. Memories came flooding back to him. Happy days as a child with the Baron and Leon, unhappy days of his life when he was taken away from his beloved castle by the Russians, imagining he would never see the building again. But now he, Wladek Koskiewicz, was returning, returning in triumph to reclaim what was his.

The car bumped up the winding road and both remained silent in anticipation as they rounded the final bend to the first sight of Baron Rosnovski's home. Abel brought the car to a halt and gazed at his castle. Neither of them spoke, but simply stared in disbelief at the devastation of the bombed-out remains of his dream.

He and Florentyna climbed slowly out of the car. Still neither spoke. Florentyna held her father's hand very, very tightly as the tears rolled down his cheeks. Only one wall remained precariously standing in a semblance of its former glory; the rest was nothing more than a neglected pile of rubble and red stone. He could not bear to tell her of the great halls, the wings, the kitchens, the bedrooms. Abel walked over to the three mounds, now smooth with thick green grass, that were the graves of the Baron and his son Leon and of the other beloved Florentyna. He paused at each one and could not help but think that Leon and Florentyna could still be alive today. He knelt at their heads, the dreadful visions of their final moments returning to him vividly. His daughter stood by his side, her hand resting on his shoulder, saying nothing. A long time passed before Abel rose slowly and then they tramped over the ruins together. Stone slabs marked the places where once magnificent rooms had been filled with laughter. Abel still said nothing. Holding hands, they reached the dungeons. There Abel sat down on the floor of the damp little room near the grille, or the half of the grille that was still left. He twisted the silver band round and round.

"This is where your father spent four years of his life."

"It can't be possible," said Florentyna, who did not sit down.

"It's better now than it was then," said Abel. "At least now there is fresh air, birds, the sun and a feeling of freedom. Then there was nothing, only darkness, death, the stench of death, and worst of all, the hope of death."

"Come on, Daddy, let's leave. Staying here can only make you feel worse."

Florentyna led her reluctant father to the car and drove him slowly down the long avenue. Abel didn't look back towards the ruined castle as they passed for the last time through its iron gates.

On the journey back to Warsaw he hardly spoke and Florentyna abandoned her attempts at vivacity. When her father said, "There is now only one thing left that I must achieve in this life," Florentyna wondered what he could mean but did not press him to explain. She did, however, manage to coax him into spending another weekend in London on the return journey, which she convinced herself would cheer her father up a little and perhaps even help him to forget the memory of his demented old foster-mother and the remains of his castle in Poland.

They flew to London the next day. Abel was glad to be back in a country where he could communicate quickly with America. Once they had booked into Claridge's, Florentyna went off to reunite with old friends and make new ones. Abel spent his time reading all the papers he could lay his hands on, in the hope of bringing himself up to date with what had happened in America while he had been abroad. He didn't like to feel things *could* happen while he was away; it reminded him only too clearly that the world could get along very well without him.

A little item on an inside page of Saturday's *Times* caught his eye. Things had happened while he was away. A Vickers Viscount of Interstate Airways had crashed immediately after take-off at the Mexico City airport the previous morning. The seventeen passengers and crew had all been killed. The Mexican authorities had been quick to place the blame on Interstate's bad servicing of their aircraft. Abel picked up the phone and asked the girl for the overseas operator.

Saturday, he's probably back in Chicago, thought Abel. He thumbed through his little phone book to find the home number.

"There'll be a delay of about thirty minutes," said a precise, not unattractive, English voice.

"Thank you," said Abel, and he lay down on the bed with the phone by his side, thinking. It rang twenty minutes later.

"Your overseas call is on the line, sir," said the same precise voice.

"Abel, is that you? Where are you?"

"Sure is, Henry. I'm in London."

"Are you through?" said the girl, who was back on the line.

"I haven't even started," said Abel.

"I'm sorry, sir, I mean are you speaking to America?"

"Oh yes, sure. Thank you. Jesus, Henry, they speak a different language over here."

Henry Osborne laughed.

"Now listen. Did you read that item in the press about an Interstate Airways' Vickers Viscount crashing at the Mexico City airport?"

"Yes, I did," said Henry, "but there's nothing for you to worry about. The plane was properly insured and the company is completely covered, so they incurred no loss and the stock has remained steady."

"The insurance is the last thing I'm interested in," said Abel. "This could be our best chance yet for a little trial run to discover just how strong Mr. Kane's constitution is."

"I don't think I understand, Abel. What do you mean?"

"Listen carefully, and I'll explain exactly what I want you to do when the Stock Exchange opens on Monday morning. I'll be back in New York by Tuesday to orchestrate the final crescendo myself."

Henry Osborne listened attentively to Abel Rosnovski's instructions. Twenty minutes later, Abel replaced the phone on the hook.

He was through.

30

William realised he could expect more trouble from Abel Rosnovski the morning that Curtis Fenton phoned to let him know that the Chicago Baron was closing all the group's bank accounts with Continental Trust and was accusing Fenton himself of disloyalty and unethical conduct.

"I thought I did the correct thing in writing to you about Mr. Rosnovski's acquisitions in Lester's," said the banker unhappily, "and it has ended with me losing one of my biggest customers. I don't know what my board of directors will say."

William formulated an inadequate apology, and calmed Fenton down a little by promising him he would speak to his superiors. He was, however, more preoccupied with wondering what Abel Rosnovski's next move would be.

Nearly a month later, he found out. He was going through the bank's Monday morning mail when a call came through from his broker, telling him that someone had placed a million dollars' worth of Interstate Airways' stock on the market. William had to make the instant decision that his personal trust should pick up the shares, and he issued an immediate buy order for them. At two o'clock that afternoon, another million dollars' worth was put on the market. Before William had a chance to pick them up, the price had started falling. By the time the New York Stock Exchange closed at three o'clock, the price of Interstate Airways had fallen by a third.

At ten minutes past ten the next morning, William received a call from his now agitated broker. Another million dollars' worth of shares had been placed on the market at the opening bell. The broker reported that the latest dumping had had an avalanche effect: Interstate sell orders were coming on to the floor from every quarter, the bottom had fallen out, and the stock was now trading at only a few cents a share. Only twenty-four hours previously, Interstate had been quoted at four and a half.

William instructed Alfred Rodgers, the company secretary, to call a board meeting for the following Monday. He needed the time to confirm who was responsible for the dumping. By Wednesday, he had abandoned any attempt at shoring up Interstate by buying all the shares that came on the market himself. At the close of business that day, the Securities and Exchange Commission announced that they would be conducting an inquiry into all Interstate transactions. William knew that Lester's board would now have to decide whether to support the airline for the three to six months it would take the S.E.C. to complete their investigation or whether to let the company go under. The alternatives looked extremely damaging, both to William's pocket and to the bank's reputation.

It came as no surprise to William to discover from Thaddeus Cohen the next day that the company that had dumped the original three million dollars' worth of Interstate shares was one of those fronting for Abel Rosnovski, Guaranty Investment Corporation by name. A corporation spokesman had issued a plausible little press release explaining their reasons for selling: they had been concerned for the future of the company after the Mexican government's responsible statement about Interstate Airways' inadequate servicing facilities.

"Responsible statement," said William, outraged. "The Mexican government hasn't made a responsible statement since they claimed Speedy Gonzales would win the one hundred metres at the Helsinki Olympics."

The media made the most of Guaranty Investment's press release, and on Friday, the Federal Aviation Agency grounded the airline until it could conduct an in-depth investigation of its servicing facilities.

William was confident Interstate had nothing to fear from

such an inspection, but the action proved disastrous for the short-term passenger bookings. No aviation company can afford to leave aircraft on the ground; they can only make money when they are in the air.

To compound William's problems, other major companies represented by Lester's were reconsidering future commitments. The press had been quick to point out that Lester's was Interstate Airways' underwriters. Surprisingly, Interstate's shares began to pick up again late Friday afternoon, and it did not take William long to guess why, a guess that was later confirmed by Thaddeus Cohen: the buyer was Abel Rosnovski. He had sold his Interstate shares at the top and was now buying them back in small amounts while they were at the bottom. William shook his head in grudging admiration. Rosnovski was making a small fortune for himself while bankrupting William both in reputation and financial terms.

William worked out that although the Baron Group must have risked over three million dollars, they might well end up making a huge profit. Moreover, it was evident that Rosnovski was unconcerned about a temporary loss, which he could in any case use as a tax write-off; his only interest was in the total destruction of Lester's reputation.

When the board met on Monday, William explained the entire history of his clash with Rosnovski and offered his resignation. It was not accepted, nor was a vote taken, but there were murmurings, and William knew that if Rosnovski attacked again, his colleagues might not take the same tolerant attitude a second time.

The board went on to consider whether they should continue the support for Interstate Airways. Tony Simmons convinced them that the F.A.A.'s inquiry would come out in the bank's favour, and that Interstate would in time recover all their money. Tony had to admit to William after the meeting that their decision could only help Rosnovski in the long run, but the bank had no choice if it wished to protect its reputation.

He proved right on both counts. When the S.E.C. finally published its findings, they declared Lester's 'reproach-proof' although they had some stern words for Guaranty

Investment Corporation. When the market started trading in Interstate shares that morning, William was surprised to find the stock rising steadily. It was soon back up to its original four and a half.

Thaddeus Cohen informed William that the principal purchaser was once again Abel Rosnovski.

"That's all I need at the moment," said William. "Not only does he make a large profit on the whole transaction, but now he can repeat the same exercise again whenever the time suits him."

"In fact," said Thaddeus Cohen, "that is exactly what you do need."

"Whatever do you mean, Thaddeus?" said William. "I've never known you speak in riddles."

"Mr. Abel Rosnovski has made his first error in judgment, because he's breaking the law and now it's your turn to go after him. He probably doesn't even realise that what he was involved in was illegal, because he was doing it for all the wrong reasons."

"What are you talking about?" asked William.

"Simple," said Thaddeus Cohen. "Because of your obsession with Rosnovski – and his with you – it seems that both of you have overlooked the obvious: if you sell shares with the sole intention of causing the market to drop in order to pick up those same shares at the bottom and therefore be certain of a profit, you're breaking Rule 10b-5 of the Securities and Exchange Commission and you are committing the crime of fraud. There's no doubt in my mind that making a quick profit was not Mr. Rosnovski's original intention; in fact, we know very well he only wanted to embarrass you personally. But who is going to believe Rosnovski if he gives as an explanation that he dumped the stock because he thought the company was unreliable, when he has bought all the same shares back when they reached rock bottom? Answer: nobody – and certainly not the S.E.C. I'll have a full written report sent around to you by tomorrow, William, explaining the legal implications."

"Thank you," said William, jubilant over the news.

Thaddeus Cohen's report was on William's desk at nine

the next morning and after William had read over the contents very carefully, he called another board meeting. The directors agreed with the course of action William wanted to take. Thaddeus Cohen was instructed to draft a carefully written press release to be issued that evening. The *Wall Street Journal* ran a piece on their front page the following morning.

> Mr. William Kane, the chairman of Lester's Bank, has reason to believe that the sell orders placed by Guaranty Investment Corporation in November 1952 on Interstate Airways shares, a company underwritten by Lester's Bank, were issued for the sole purpose of making an illegal profit.
>
> It has been established that Guaranty Investment Corporation was responsible for placing a million dollars' worth of Interstate stock on the market when the exchange opened on Monday, May 12th, 1952. A further million dollars' worth was on the market six hours later. A third million dollars worth was placed on a sell order by Guaranty Investment Corporation when the exchange reopened on Tuesday, May 13th, 1952. This caused the stock to fall to a record low. After an S.E.C. inquiry showed there had been no illegal dealing within either Lester's Bank or Interstate Airways, the market picked up again with the stock trading at the depressed price. Guaranty Investment was quickly back in the market to purchase the shares at as low a price as possible. They continued to buy until they had replaced the three million dollars' worth of stock they had originally released on to the market.
>
> The chairman and directors of Lester's Bank have sent a copy of all the relevant documents to the Fraud Division of the Securities and Exchange Commission, and have asked them to proceed with a full inquiry.

The story below the statement gave S.E.C. Rule 10b-5 in full and commented that this was exactly the sort of test case that President Truman had been looking for; a cartoon below the article showed Harry S. Truman catching a businessman with his hands in the cookie jar.

William smiled as he read through the item, confident that that would be the last he would hear of Abel Rosnovski.

Abel Rosnovski frowned and said nothing as Henry Osborne read the statement over to him. Abel looked up, his fingers tapping in irritation on the desk.

"The boys in Washington," said Osborne, "are determined to get to the bottom of this one."

"But Henry, you know very well I didn't sell Interstate shares to make a quick killing on the stock market," said Abel. "The profit I made was of no interest to me at all."

"I know that," said Henry, "but you try and convince the Senate Finance Committee that the Chicago Baron had no interest in financial gain, that all he really wanted to do was settle a personal grudge against one William Kane, and they'll laugh you right out of court – or out of the Senate, to be more exact."

"Damn," said Abel. "Now what the hell do I do?"

"Well, first you'll have to lie very low until this has had time to blow over. Start praying that some bigger scandal comes along for Truman to get himself worked up about, or that the politicians become so involved in the election that they haven't time to press for an inquiry. With luck, a new administration may even drop the whole thing. Whatever you do, Abel, don't buy any more shares that are connected with Lester's Bank, or the least you're going to end up with is a very large fine. Leave me to swing what I can with the Democrats in Washington."

"Remind Harry Truman's office that I gave fifty thousand dollars to his campaign fund during the last election and I intend to do the same for Adlai."

"I've already done that," said Henry. "In fact I would advise you to give fifty thousand to the Republicans as well."

"They're making a mountain out of a molehill," said Abel.

"A molehill that Kane will turn into a mountain if we give him the chance." His fingers continued to tap on the table.

31

Thaddeus Cohen's next quarterly report revealed that Abel Rosnovski had stopped buying or selling stock in any of Lester's companies. It seemed he was now concentrating all his energy on building more hotels in Europe. Cohen's opinion was that Rosnovski was lying low, until a decision had been made by the S.E.C. on the Interstate affair.

Representatives of the S.E.C. had visited William at the bank on several occasions. He had spoken to them with complete frankness, but they never revealed how their inquiries were progressing. The S.E.C. finally finished their investigation and thanked William for his co-operation. He heard nothing more from them.

As the Presidential election grew nearer and Truman seemed to be concentrating his own efforts on the dissolution of the Du Pont industrial combine, William began to fear that Abel Rosnovski might have been let off the hook. He couldn't help feeling that Henry Osborne must have been able to pull a few strings in Congress. He remembered that Cohen had once underlined a note about a fifty thousand dollar donation from the Baron Group to Harry Truman's campaign fund and was surprised to read in Cohen's latest report that Rosnovski had repeated the donation for Adlai Stevenson, the Democrats' choice for President, along with another fifty thousand for the Eisenhower campaign fund.

William, who had never considered supporting anyone for public office who was not a Republican, wanted General Eisenhower, the candidate who had emerged on the first ballot at the convention in Chicago, to defeat Adlai Stevenson, although he was aware that a Republican administration was less likely to press for a share manipulation inquiry than the Democrats.

When General Dwight D. Eisenhower – it appeared that the nation did like Ike – was elected as the thirty-fourth President of the United States on November 4th, 1952, William assumed that Abel Rosnovski had escaped any charge and could only hope that the experience would persuade him to leave Lester's affairs well enough alone in the future. The one small compensation to come out of the election for William was that Congressman Henry Osborne lost his Congressional seat to a Republican candidate. The Eisenhower jacket had turned out to have coat-tails, and Osborne's rival had clung to them. Thaddeus Cohen was inclined to think that Henry Osborne no longer exerted quite the same influence over Abel Rosnovski that he had in the past. The rumour in Chicago was that, since divorcing his rich wife, Osborne owed large sums of money to Rosnovski and was gambling heavily again.

William was happier and more relaxed than he had been for some time and looked forward to joining the prosperous and peaceful era that Eisenhower had promised in his Inauguration speech.

As the first years of the new President's administration went by, William began to put Rosnovski's threats at the back of his mind and to think of them as a thing of the past. He informed Thaddeus Cohen that he believed they had heard the last of Abel Rosnovski. The lawyer made no comment. He wasn't asked to.

William put all his efforts into building Lester's, both in size and reputation, increasingly aware that he was now doing it as much for his son as for himself. Some of his staff at the bank had already started referring to him as the 'old man'.

"It had to happen," said Kate.

"Then why hasn't it happened to you?" replied William.

Kate looked up at William and smiled. "Now I know the secret of how you have closed so many deals with vain men."

William laughed. "And one beautiful woman," he added.

With Richard's twenty-first birthday only a year away,

William revised the provisions of his will. He set aside five million dollars for Kate and two million for each of the girls, and left the rest of the family fortune to Richard, noting ruefully the bite that would go in estate tax. He also left one million dollars to Harvard.

Richard had been making good use of his four years at Harvard. At the start of his senior year, not only did he look set for a *Summa Cum Laude*, but he was also playing the cello in the university orchestra, and was a pitcher with the varsity baseball team, which even William had to admire. As Kate liked rhetorically to ask, how many students spent Saturday afternoon playing baseball for Harvard against Yale and Sunday evening playing the cello in the Lowell concert hall for the university string quartet?

The final year passed quickly and when Richard left Harvard, armed with a Bachelor of Arts degree in mathematics, a cello and a baseball bat, all he required before reporting to the business school on the other side of the Charles River was a good holiday. He flew to Barbados with a girl called Mary Bigelow of whose existence his parents were blissfully unaware. Miss Bigelow had studied music, among other things, at Vasser, and when they returned two months later almost the same colour as the natives, Richard took her home to meet his parents. William approved of Miss Bigelow; after all, she was Alan Lloyd's great-niece.

Richard returned to the Harvard Business School on October 1st, 1955, to start his graduate work. He took up residence in the Red House, threw out all William's cane furniture, removed the paisley wallpaper that Matthew Lester had once found so modern, and installed a wall-to-wall carpet in the living room, an oak table in the dining room, a dishwasher in the kitchen and, more than occasionally, Miss Bigelow in the bedroom.

32

Abel returned from a trip to Istanbul in October 1952, immediately upon hearing the news of David Maxton's fatal heart attack. He attended the funeral in Chicago with George and Florentyna and later told Mrs. Maxton that she could be a guest at any Baron in the world whenever she so pleased for the rest of her life. She could not understand why Abel had made such a generous gesture.

When Abel returned to New York the next day, he was delighted to find on the desk of his forty-second floor office a report from Henry Osborne indicating that the heat was now off. In Henry's opinion, the new Eisenhower administration was unlikely to pursue an inquiry into the Interstate Airways fiasco, especially as the stock had now held steady for nearly a year. There had, therefore, been no further incidents to renew any interest in the scandal. Eisenhower's Vice-President, Richard M. Nixon, seemed more involved in chasing the spectral communists whom Joe McCarthy had missed.

Abel spent the next two years concentrating on building his hotels in Europe. He opened the Paris Baron in 1953 and the London Baron at the end of 1954. Barons were also in various stages of development for Brussels, Rome, Amsterdam, Geneva, Bonn, Edinburgh, Cannes and Stockholm in a ten-year expansion programme.

Abel became so overworked that he had little time to consider William Kane's continued prosperity. He had not made any attempt to buy shares in Lester's Bank or its subsidiary companies, although he held on to those he already possessed in the hope that another opportunity might be forthcoming to deal a blow against William Kane from which he would not recover so easily. The next time, Abel promised himself, he'd make sure he didn't unwittingly break the law.

During Abel's increasingly frequent absences abroad George ran the Baron Group and Abel was hoping that Florentyna would join the board as soon as she left Radcliffe in June of 1955. He had already decided that she should take over responsibility for all the shops in the hotels and consolidate their buying, as they were fast becoming an empire in themselves.

Florentyna was very excited by the prospect but was insistent that she wanted some outside experience before joining her father's group. She did not consider her natural gifts for design, colour, and organisation were any substitute for experience. Abel suggested that she train in Switzerland under Monsieur Maurice at the famed *Ecole Hôtelière* in Lausanne. Florentyna baulked at the idea, explaining that she wanted to work for two years in a New York store before she would consider taking over the shops. She was determined to be worth employing, ". . . and not just as my father's daughter," she informed him. Abel thoroughly approved.

"A New York store, that's done easily enough," he said. "I'll ring up Walter Hoving at Tiffany's and you can start at the top."

"No," said Florentyna, revealing that she'd inherited her father's streak of stubbornness. "What's the equivalent of a junior waiter at the Plaza Hotel?"

"A sales girl at a department store," said Abel, laughing.

"Then that's exactly what I'm going to be," she said.

Abel stopped laughing. "Are you serious? With a degree from Radcliffe and all the experience and knowledge you've gained from your European trips, you want to be an anonymous sales girl?"

"Being an anonymous waiter at the Plaza didn't do you any harm when the time came to set up one of the most successful hotel groups in the world," replied Florentyna.

Abel knew when he was beaten. He had only to look into the steel grey eyes of his beautiful daughter to realise she had made up her mind, and that no amount of persuasion, gentle or otherwise, was going to change her views.

After Florentyna had graduated from Radcliffe, she spent a month in Europe with her father, watching the progress of the latest Baron hotels. She officially opened the Brussels Baron where she made a conquest of the handsome young French-speaking managing director, whom Abel accused of smelling of garlic. She had to give him up three days later when it reached the kissing stage, but she never admitted to her father that garlic had been the reason.

Florentyna returned to New York with her father and immediately applied for the vacant position (the words used in the classified advertisement) of 'junior sales assistant' at Bloomingdale's. When she filled in the application form, she gave her name as Jessie Kovats, well aware that no one would leave her in peace if they ever thought she was the daughter of the Chicago Baron.

Despite protests from her father, she also left her suite in the Baron Hotel and started looking for her own place to live. Once again Abel gave in and presented Florentyna with a small but elegant co-operative flat on Fifty-seventh Street near the East River as a twenty-second birthday present.

Florentyna already knew her way around New York and enjoyed a full social life, but she had long ago resolved not to let her friends know that she was going to work at Bloomingdale's. She feared that they would want to come and visit her and, in days, her cleverly constructed cover would be blown, making it impossible to be treated as a normal trainee.

When her friends did enquire, she merely told them that she was helping to run the shops in her father's hotels. None of them gave her reply a second thought.

Jessie Kovats – it took her some time to get used to the name – started in cosmetics. After six months, she was ready to run her own beauty shop. The girls in Bloomingdale's worked in pairs, which Florentyna immediately turned to her advantage by choosing to work with the laziest girl in the department. This arrangement suited both girls as Florentyna's choice was a gorgeous, unenlightened blonde called Maisie who had only two interests in life: the clock pointing to the hour of six p.m. and men. The former happened once a day, the latter all the time.

The two girls soon became comrades without exactly being friends. Florentyna learned a lot from her partner about how to avoid work without being spotted by the floor manager, and also how to get picked up by a man.

The cosmetic counter's profits were well up after their first six months together, despite the fact that Maisie spent most of her time trying out the products rather than selling them. She could take two hours repainting her fingernails alone. Florentyna, in contrast, had a natural gift for selling that could not have been picked up at night school. That combined with an ability to learn quickly made it seem to her employers, after only a few weeks, as if she had been around for years.

The partnership with Maisie suited Florentyna ideally, and when they moved her to Better Dresses, by mutual agreement Maisie went along and passed her time by trying on new dresses all day while Florentyna sold them. Maisie could attract men – in tow with their wives or sweethearts – irrespective of the merchandise, simply by looking at them. Once they were ensnared, Florentyna could move in and sell something to them. It seemed hardly possible that the combination could work in Better Dresses, but Florentyna made Maisie's victims buy something, few escaping with untouched wallets.

The profits for that six months were up again, and the floor supervisor decided that the two girls obviously worked well together. Florentyna said nothing to contradict that impression. While other assistants in the shop were always complaining about how little work their partners did, Florentyna continually praised Maisie as the ideal workmate, who had taught her so much about how a big store operated. She didn't mention the useful advice that Maisie also imparted on how to deal with over-amorous men.

The greatest compliment an assistant can receive at Bloomingdale's is to be put on one of the counters facing the Lexington Avenue entrance, the first person to be seen by customers coming in through the main doors. To work on that counter was considered as a small promotion and it was rare for a girl to be invited to sell there until she had been with the store at least five years. Maisie had been with Bloomingdale's since she was seventeen, a full five years, while Florentyna had only just completed her first twelve months. But as their results had been so impressive, the manager decided to try the two girls out on the ground floor in the stationery department. Maisie was unable to derive any personal advantage from the stationery department, as she didn't care too much for reading and even less for writing. Florentyna wasn't sure after a year with her that she could read or write. Nevertheless, her new position pleased Maisie greatly because she adored being the centre of attention. So the girls continued their perfect partnership.

Abel admitted to George that he had once sneaked into Bloomingdale's to watch Florentyna at work, and he had to confess that she was damned good. He assured his vice-president that he was looking forward to her finishing the two years' training, so that he could employ the girl himself. They had both agreed that when Florentyna left Bloomingdale's, she would be made a vice-president of the group, with special responsibility for the hotel stores. As Bloomingdale's was finding out, she was a chip off a formidable old block, and Abel had no doubt that Florentyna would have few problems taking on the responsibilities he was planning for her.

Florentyna spent her last six months at Bloomingdale's on the ground floor in charge of six counters with the new title of junior supervisor. Her duties now included stock checking, the cash desks and overall supervision of eighteen sales clerks. Bloomingdale's had already decided that Jessie Kovats was the ideal candidate to be a future buyer.

Florentyna had not yet informed her employers that she would be leaving shortly to join her father as a vice-president of the Baron Group. As the six months was drawing to its conclusion, she began to wonder what would happen to poor Maisie after she had left. Maisie assumed Jessie was at Bloomingdale's for life – wasn't everybody? – and never gave the question a second thought. Florentyna thought she might even offer her a job in one of the shops in the New York Baron. As long as it was behind a counter at which men spent money, Maisie was a valuable asset.

One afternoon when Maisie was waiting on a customer – she was now in gloves, scarves and woolly hats – she pulled Florentyna aside and pointed to a young man who was loitering over the mittens.

"What do you think of him?" she asked, giggling.

Florentyna glanced up at Maisie's latest desire with her customary disinterest, but on this occasion she had to admit to herself that he was rather attractive, and for once she was almost envious of Maisie.

"They only want one thing, Maisie."

"I know," said Maisie, "and he can have it."

"I'm sure he'll be pleased to hear that," said Florentyna, laughing as she turned to wait on a customer who was becoming impatient at Maisie's indifference to her presence. Maisie took advantage of Florentyna's move and rushed off to serve the gloveless young man. Florentyna watched them both out of the corner of her eye. She was amused that he kept glancing nervously towards her, checking that Maisie wasn't being spied on by her supervisor. Maisie giggled away and the young man departed with a pair of dark blue leather gloves.

"Well, how did he measure up to your hopes?" asked Florentyna, conscious that she felt a little jealous of Maisie's new conquest.

"He didn't," replied Maisie. "But I'm sure he'll be back again," she added, grinning.

Maisie's prediction turned out to be correct, for the next day there he was, thumbing among the gloves and looking even more embarrassed.

"I suppose you had better go and wait on him," said Florentyna.

Maisie hurried obediently away. Florentyna nearly laughed out loud when, a few minutes later, the young man departed with another pair of dark blue gloves.

"Two pairs," declared Florentyna. "I think I can say on behalf of Bloomingdale's, he deserves you."

"But he still didn't ask me out," said Maisie.

"What?" said Florentyna in mock disbelief. "He must have a glove fetish."

"It's very disappointing," said Maisie, "because I think he's neat."

"Yes, he's not bad," said Florentyna.

The next day when the young man arrived in the shop Maisie leapt forward, leaving an old lady in mid-sentence. Florentyna quickly took her place, once again watching Maisie out of the corner of her eye. This time the two of them appeared to be in deep conversation and the young man finally departed with yet another pair of dark blue leather gloves.

"It must be the real thing," ventured Florentyna.

"Yes, I think it is,' replied Maisie, "but he still hasn't suggested a date."

Florentyna was flabbergasted.

"Listen," said Maisie desperately, "if he comes in tomorrow could you serve him? I think he is scared to ask me directly. He might find it easier to make a date through you."

Florentyna laughed. "A Viola to your Orsino."

"What?" said Maisie.

"It doesn't matter," said Florentyna. "I wonder if I will be able to sell him a pair of gloves?"

If the man was anything he was consistent, thought Florentyna, as he pushed his way through the doors at exactly the same time the next day and immediately headed towards the glove counter. Maisie dug Florentyna in the ribs, and Florentyna decided the time had come to enjoy herself.

"Good afternoon, sir."

"Oh, good afternoon," said the young man looking surprised – or was it disappointment?

"Can I help you?" offered Florentyna.

"No – I mean, yes, I would like a pair of gloves," he added unconvincingly.

"Yes, sir. Have you considered a dark blue pair? In leather? I'm sure we have your size – unless we're all sold out."

The young man looked at her suspiciously as she handed him the gloves. He tried them on. They were a little too big.

Florentyna offered him another pair but they were slightly too tight. He looked towards Maisie for inspiration but she was surrounded by a sea of male customers but she wasn't sinking because she even found the time to glance towards the young man and grin. He grinned back nervously. Florentyna handed him another pair of gloves. They fitted perfectly.

"I think that's what you're looking for," said Florentyna.

"No, it's not really," replied the embarrassed customer.

Florentyna decided the time had come to let the poor man off the hook and, lowering her voice, she said, "I'll go and rescue Maisie. Why don't you ask her out? I'm sure she will say yes."

"Oh no," said the young man. "You don't understand. It's not her I want to take out – it's you."

Florentyna was speechless. The young man seemed to muster courage.

"Will you have dinner with me tonight?"

She heard herself saying, "Yes."

"Shall I pick you up at your home?"

"No," said Florentyna a little too firmly. The last thing she wanted was to be met at her apartment where it would be obvious to anyone that she was not a salesgirl. "Let's meet at a restaurant," she added quickly.

"Where would you like to go? . . ."

Florentyna tried to think quickly of a place that would not be too ostentatious.

"Allen's at Seventy-third and Third?" he ventured.

"Yes, fine," said Florentyna, thinking how much better Maisie would have been at handling the whole situation.

"Around eight o'clock suit you?"

"Around eight," replied Florentyna. The young man left with a smile on his face. Florentyna watched him disappear on to the street, and suddenly realised that he had left without buying a pair of gloves.

Florentyna took a long time choosing which dress she should wear for her evening out. She wanted to be certain that the outfit didn't scream of Bergdorf Goodman. She had acquired a small wardrobe especially for Bloomingdale's, but the clothes were strictly for daytime use, and she had never worn anything from that selection in the evening. If her date – heavens, she didn't even know his name – thought she was a salesgirl she mustn't disillusion him. She couldn't help feeling that she was actually looking forward to the evening more than she ought to be.

She left her flat on East Fifty-seventh Street a little before eight and had to wait for several minutes before she managed to hail an empty taxi.

"Allen's, please," she said to the taxi driver.

"On Third Avenue?"

"Yes."

"Sure thing, miss," he replied.

When Florentyna arrived at the restaurant, she was a few minutes late. Her eyes began to search for the young man. He was standing at the bar, waving. He had changed into a pair of grey flannel slacks and a blue blazer. Very Ivy League, thought Florentyna, but very good looking.

"I'm sorry to be late," she began.

"It's not important. What's important is that you came."

"You thought I wouldn't?" said Florentyna.

"I wasn't sure." He smiled. "I'm sorry, I don't know your name."

"Jessie Kovats," said Florentyna, determined not to give away her alias. "And yours?"

"Richard Kane," said the young man, thrusting out his hand.

She took it and he held on to hers a little longer than she had expected.

"And what do you do when you're not buying gloves at Bloomingdale's?" she teased.

"I'm at Harvard Business School."

"I'm surprised they didn't teach you that most people only have two hands."

He laughed and smiled in such a relaxed and friendly way that she wished she could start again and tell him they might have met in Cambridge when she was at Radcliffe.

"Shall we order?" he said, taking her arm and leading her to a table.

Florentyna looked up at the menu on the blackboard.

"Salisbury steak?" she queried.

"A hamburger by any other name," said Richard.

They both laughed, in the way two people do when they don't know each other, but want to. She could see he was surprised that she might have known his out-of-context quotation.

Florentyna had rarely enjoyed anyone's company more. Richard chatted about New York, the theatre and music – so obviously his first love – with such grace and charm that she was fully at ease. He may have thought she was a salesgirl but he was treating her as if she'd come from one of the oldest Brahmin families. She hoped he wasn't too surprised by her passion for the same things because, when he enquired, she told him nothing more than that she was Polish and lived in New York with her parents. As the evening progressed the deception became increasingly intolerable. Still, she thought, we may never see each other again after tonight, and then it will all be irrelevant.

When the evening did come to an end and neither of them could drink any more coffee, they left Allen's and Richard looked for a taxi; the only ones they saw were all full.

"Where do you live?" he asked.

"Fifty-seventh Street," she said, not thinking about her reply.

"Then let's walk," said Richard, taking Florentyna's hand.

She smiled her agreement. They started walking, stopping and looking at shop windows, laughing and smiling. Neither of them noticed the empty taxis that now rushed past them. It took them almost an hour to cover the sixteen blocks and Florentyna nearly told him the truth. When they reached Fifty-seventh Street she stopped outside a small old apartment house, some hundred yards from her own home.

"This is where my parents live," she said.

He seemed to hesitate and then let go of her hand.

"I hope you will see me again," said Richard.

"I'd like that," replied Florentyna in a polite, dismissive way.

"Tomorrow?" asked Richard diffidently.

"Tomorrow?"

"Yes, why don't we go to the Blue Angel and see Bobby Short?" He took her hand again. "It's a little more romantic than Allen's."

Florentyna was momentarily taken aback.

"Not if you don't want to," he added before she could recover.

"I'd love to," she said quietly.

"I'm having dinner with my father, so why don't I pick you up at ten o'clock?"

"No, no," said Florentyna, "I'll meet you there. It's only two blocks away."

"Ten o'clock then," he bent forward and kissed her gently on the cheek. "Good night, Jessie," he said, and disappeared into the night.

Florentyna walked slowly back to her apartment, wishing she hadn't told so many lies about herself. Still, it might be over in a few days. She couldn't help feeling that she hoped it wouldn't.

Maisie, who hadn't yet forgiven her, spent a considerable part of the next day asking all about Richard. Florentyna kept trying unsuccessfully to change the subject.

Florentyna left Bloomingdale's the moment the store closed, the first time in nearly two years that she had left before Maisie. She had a long bath, put on the prettiest dress she thought she could get away with, and walked to the Blue Angel. When she arrived, Richard was already waiting for her outside the cloak-room. He held her hand as they walked into the lounge where the words of Bobby Short came floating through the air.

Are you telling me the truth, or am I just another lie?

As Florentyna walked in, Short raised his arm in acknowledgment. Florentyna pretended not to notice. Mr. Short had been a guest performer at The Baron on two or three occasions and it never occurred to Florentyna that he would remember her. Richard looked puzzled and then assumed the singer had been greeting someone else. When they took a table in the dimly-lit room, Florentyna sat with her back to the piano to be certain it wouldn't happen again.

Richard ordered a bottle of wine without letting go of her hand and then asked about her day. She didn't want to tell him; she wanted to tell him the truth – "Richard, there is something I must . . ."

"Hi, Richard." A tall, handsome man stood at Richard's side.

"Hi, Steve. Can I introduce Jessie Kovats – Steve Mellon. Steve and I were at Harvard together."

Florentyna listened to them chat about the New York Yankees, Eisenhower's handicap – his golf – and why Yale was going from bad to worse. Steve eventually left with a gracious, "Nice to have met you, Jessie."

The moment had passed.

Richard began to tell her of his plans once he had left business school, how he hoped to come to New York and join his father's bank, Lester's. She had heard the name before but couldn't remember in what connection. For some reason it worried her. They spent a long evening together, laughing, eating, talking, and just sitting, holding hands, listening to Bobby Short. When they walked home, Richard stopped on the corner of Fifty-seventh and kissed her for the first time. She couldn't recall any other occasion when she was so aware of a first kiss. When he returned her to the shadows of Fifty-seventh Street, she left him and her white lies, aware that this time he had not mentioned tomorrow. She felt slightly wistful about the whole non-affair.

She was taken aback by how pleased she felt when Richard phoned her at Bloomingdale's on Monday, asking if she would go out with him on Friday evening.

They wound up spending most of that weekend together: a concert, a film – even the New York Knicks did not escape them. When the weekend was over Florentyna found she had told so many innocent lies about her background that she became inconsistent in her fabrication and puzzled Richard more than once by contradicting herself. It seemed to make it all the more impossible to tell him another entirely different, albeit true, story. When Richard returned to Harvard on the Sunday night, she persuaded herself that the deception would seem unimportant once the relationship had ended. But Richard phoned every day during the week and spent the next few weekends in her company: she began to realise it wasn't going to end that easily. She was falling in love with him. Once she had admitted that to herself, she realised that she had to tell him the truth the following weekend.

33

Richard sat through his morning lecture, daydreaming. He was so much in love with that girl, he could not even concentrate on the 'Twenty-nine crash'. He wished he could work out how to tell his father that he intended to marry a Polish girl who worked behind the scarf, glove and woolly hats counter at Bloomingdale's. Richard was unable to fathom why she was so unambitious for herself when she was obviously very bright: he was certain that if she had had the chances he had been given, she would not have ended up in Bloomingdale's. Richard decided that his parents would have to learn to live with his choice, because that weekend he was going to ask Jessie to be his wife.

Whenever Richard returned to his parents' home in New York on a Friday evening, he would always leave the house on East Sixty-eighth Street to go and pick up something from Bloomingdale's, normally a useless and unwanted item, simply so that he could let Jessie know that he was back in town; he had already given a pair of gloves to every relation he possessed. That Friday, he told his mother that he was going out to buy some razor blades.

"Don't bother, darling, you can use your father's," she said.

"No, no, it's all right," he said. "I'll go and get some of my own. We don't use the same brand in any case," he added feebly. "I'll only be a few minutes."

He almost ran the eight blocks to Bloomingdale's and managed to rush in just as they were closing the doors. He knew he would be seeing Jessie at seven thirty, but he could never resist a chance to chat with her. Steve had told him once that love was for suckers. He had written on his steamed-up shaving mirror that morning 'I am a sucker'. But when he reached Jessie's counter, she was nowhere to be seen. Maisie was standing in a corner filing her finger nails, and he asked her if Jessie was still around. Maisie looked up as if she had been interrupted from her one important task of the day.

"No, she's already gone home, Richard. Left a few seconds ago. She can't have gone far. I thought you were meeting her later."

Richard ran out on to Lexington Avenue without replying. He searched for Jessie among the faces hurrying home, then spotted her on the other side of the street, heading towards Fifth Avenue. Since she obviously wasn't going home, he somewhat guiltily decided to follow her. As she reached Scribner's at Forty-eighth Street, he stopped and watched her go into the bookshop. If she wanted something to read, surely she could find what she wanted from Bloomingdale's. He was puzzled. He peered through the window as Jessie talked to a sales clerk who left her for a few moments and then returned with two books. He could just make out their titles: *The Affluent Society* by John Kenneth Galbraith and *Inside Russia Today* by John Gunther. Jessie signed for them – that surprised Richard – and left as he ducked around the corner.

"Who *is* she?" said Richard out loud as he watched her enter Bendel's. The doorman saluted respectfully, leaving a distinct impression of recognition. Once again Richard peered through the window as assistants fluttered around Florentyna with more than casual respect. An older lady appeared with a package which she had obviously been expecting. She opened it to reveal a simple, stunning, evening dress. Florentyna smiled and nodded as the assistant placed the dress in a brown and white box. Florentyna mouthed the words 'Thank you' and turned towards the door without even signing for her purchase. Richard was mesmerised by the scene and barely managed to avoid colliding with her as she ran out of the shop and jumped into a cab. He grabbed one himself, telling the driver to follow her. When the cab passed the small building outside of which they normally parted, he began to feel queasy. No wonder she had never asked him in. The cab in front continued for another hundred yards and stopped outside a spanking new block of flats complete with a uniformed hall porter who opened the door for her. With mingled anger and astonishment, he jumped out of the cab and started to march up to the door through which she had disappeared.

"That'll be ninety-five cents, fella," said a voice behind him.

"Oh, sorry," said Richard and thrust five dollars at him, showing no interest in his change.

"Thank you," said the driver. "Someone sure is happy today."

Richard ran to the door of the building and managed to catch Florentyna at the lift. Florentyna watched the door slide open and stared at him speechlessly.

"Who are you?" demanded Richard.

"Richard," she stammered. "I was going to tell you everything this evening. I never seemed to find the right opportunity."

"Like hell you were going to tell me," he said, following Florentyna into her apartment. "Stringing me along with a pack of lies for nearly three months. Now the time has come for the truth."

Florentyna had never seen Richard angry before and suspected that it was very rare. He pushed his way past her brusquely and inspected the flat. At the end of the entrance hall, there was a large living room with a fine oriental rug. A superb grandfather clock stood opposite a side table on which there was a bowl of fresh flowers. The room was beautiful, even by the standards of Richard's own home.

"Nice place you've got yourself for a sales girl," said Richard. "I wonder which of your lovers pays for this."

Florentyna slapped him so hard that her own palm stung.

"How dare you?" she said. "Get out of my home."

As she heard herself saying the words, she started to cry. She didn't want him to leave – ever. Richard took her in his arms.

"Oh, God, I'm sorry," he said. "That was a terrible thing

to say. Please forgive me. It's just that I love you so much and thought I knew you so well, and now I find I don't know anything about you."

"Richard, I love you too, and I'm sorry I slapped you. I didn't want to deceive you, but there's no one else – I promise you that." Her voice cracked.

"I deserved it," he said as he kissed her.

Clasped tightly in one another's arms, they sank on to the couch and remained almost motionless for some moments. Gently, he stroked her hair until her tears subsided. Help me to take my clothes off, she wanted to say, but remained silent, slipping her fingers through the gap between his two top shirt buttons. Richard seemed unwilling to make the next move.

"Do you want to sleep with me?" she asked quietly.

"No," he replied. "I want to stay awake with you all night."

Without speaking, they undressed and made love, gently and shyly, frightened to hurt each other, desperately trying to please. Finally, with her head on his shoulder, they talked.

"I love you," said Richard. "I have since the first moment we met. Will you marry me? Because I don't give a damn who you are, Jessie, or what you do, but I know I must spend the rest of my life with you."

"I want to marry you too, Richard, but first I have to tell you the truth."

Florentyna pulled Richard's jacket over their naked bodies and told him all about herself, ending by explaining how she had come to be working at Bloomingdale's. When she had completed her story, Richard did not speak.

"Have you stopped loving me already?" she said. "Now you know who I really am?"

"Darling," said Richard, very quietly, "my father hates your father."

"What do you mean?"

"Just that, the only time I ever heard your father's name mentioned in his presence, he flew completely off the handle saying your father's sole purpose in life seemed to be a desire to ruin the Kane family."

"What? Why?" said Florentyna, shocked. "I've never heard of your father. How do they even know each other?"

It was Richard's turn to tell Florentyna everything his mother had told him about the quarrel with her father.

"Oh, my God," she said. "That must have been the 'disloyalty' my father referred to when he changed banks after twenty-five years. What shall we do?"

"Tell them the truth," said Richard, "that we met innocently, fell in love and now we're going to be married, and nothing they can do will stop us."

"Let's wait a few weeks," said Florentyna.

"Why?" asked Richard. "Do you think your father can talk you out of marrying me?"

"No, Richard," she said, touching him gently as she placed her head back on his shoulder. "Never, my darling, but let's find out if we can do anything to break it gently, before we present them both with a *fait accompli*. Anyway, maybe they won't feel as strongly as you imagine. After all, you said the affair with the airlines company was nearly five years ago."

"They still feel strongly, I promise you that. My father would be outraged if he saw us together, let alone thought we were considering marriage."

"All the more reason to leave it for a little before we break the news to them. That will give us time to think about the best way to go about it."

He kissed her again. "I love you, Jessie."

"Florentyna."

"That's something else I'm going to have to get used to," he said. "I love you, Florentyna."

During the next four weeks, Florentyna and Richard found out as much as they could about their parents' feud, Florentyna by asking her mother and George Novak a set of carefully worded questions, Richard from his father's filing cabinet. The extent of the mutual hatred appalled them. It became more obvious with each discovery that there was no gentle way to break the news of their love. During the next four weeks they spent every free moment they could find together. Richard was always attentive and kind, and nothing was too much trouble. He went to extremes to take her mind off the problem that they knew they would eventually have to face. They went to the theatre, skating, and on Sundays took long walks through Central Park, always ending up in bed long before it was dark. Florentyna even accompanied Richard to watch the New York Yankees which she 'couldn't understand' and the New York Philharmonic which she 'adored'. She refused to believe Richard could play the cello until he gave her a private recital. She applauded enthusiastically when he had finished his favourite Brahms sonata without noticing that he was staring into her grey eyes.

"We have got to tell them," he said, placing his bow on the stand and taking her into his arms.

"I know we must. I just don't want to hurt my father."

It was his turn to say, "I know."

She avoided his eyes. "Next Friday Daddy will be back from Washington."

"Then it's next Friday," said Richard, holding her so close she could hardly breathe.

Richard returned to Harvard on Monday morning and they spoke to each other on the phone every night, never weakening, determined that nothing would stop them.

On Friday Richard arrived in New York earlier than usual and spent an hour alone with Florentyna who had asked for a half-day off. As they walked to the corner of Fifty-seventh and Park, they stopped at the flashing red 'Don't Walk' sign, and Richard turned to Florentyna and asked her once again to marry him. He took a small red leather box out of his pocket, opened it and placed a ring on the third finger of her left hand, a sapphire set in diamonds, so beautiful that tears came to Florentyna's eyes; it was a perfect fit. Passers-by looked at them strangely as they stood on the corner, clinging to each other, ignoring the green light flashing 'Walk'. When eventually they did obey its command, they kissed before parting and walked in opposite directions to confront their parents. They had agreed to meet again at Florentyna's flat as soon as the ordeal was over. She tried to smile through her tears.

Florentyna walked towards the Baron Hotel, occasionally looking at her ring. It felt new and strange on her finger and she imagined that the eyes of all who passed by would be drawn to the magnificent sapphire and to her, it looked so beautiful next to the antique ring, her favourite of the past. She had been astonished when Richard had placed it on her finger. The problem of their parents' rivalry had made her forget rings or any of the other trappings that attend a happy engagement. She touched the diamond-encircled sapphire and found that it gave her courage, although she was aware that she was walking more and more slowly as the hotel drew nearer and nearer.

When she reached the reception desk, the clerk told her that her father was in the penthouse with George Novak. He called to say that Florentyna was on her way up. The lift reached the forty-second floor far too quickly for Florentyna, and she hesitated before leaving its safety. She stepped out on to the green carpet and heard the lift door slide closed behind her. She stood alone in the corridor for a moment before knocking quietly at her father's door. Abel opened it immediately.

"Florentyna, what a pleasant surprise. Come on in, my darling. I wasn't expecting to see you today."

George Novak was standing by the window, looking down at Park Avenue. He turned to greet his god-daughter. Florentyna's eyes pleaded with him to leave. If he stayed, she knew she would lose her nerve. Go, go, go, she said inside her brain. George sensed her anxiety immediately.

"I must get back to work, Abel. There's a goddamn maharajah checking in tonight."

"Tell him to park his elephants at the Plaza," said Abel genially. "Now Florentyna's here, stay and have another drink."

George looked at Florentyna. "No, Abel, I have to go. The man's taken the whole of the thirty-third floor. The least he'll expect is the vice-president to greet him. Good night, Florentyna," he said, kissing her on the cheek and briefly clasping her arm, almost as though he knew that she needed strength. He left them alone and suddenly Florentyna wished he had not gone.

"How's Bloomingdale's?" said Abel, ruffling his daughter's hair affectionately. "Have you told them yet they're going to lose the best floor manager they've had in years? They're sure going to be surprised when they hear that Jessie Kovats' next job will be to open the Cannes Baron." He laughed out loud.

"I'm going to be married," said Florentyna, shyly extending her left hand. She could think of nothing to add so she simply waited for his reaction.

"This is a bit sudden, isn't it?" said Abel, more than a little taken aback.

"Not really, Daddy. I've known him for some time."

"Do I know the boy? Have I ever met him?"

"No, Daddy, you haven't."

"Where does he come from? What's his background? Is he Polish? Why have you been so secretive about him, Florentyna?"

"He's not Polish, Daddy. He's the son of a banker."

Abel went white and picked up his drink, swallowing the liquor in one gulp. Florentyna knew exactly what must be going through his mind as he poured himself another drink, so she got the truth out quickly.

"His name is Richard Kane, Daddy."

Abel swung round to face her. "Is he William Kane's son?" he demanded.

"Yes, he is," said Florentyna.

"You could consider marrying William Kane's son? Do you know what that man did to me? He's the man who was responsible for the death of my closest friend. Yes, he's the man who made Davis Leroy commit suicide and, not satisfied with that, he tried to bankrupt me. If David Maxton hadn't rescued me in time, Kane would have taken away my hotels and sold them without a second thought. And where would I be now if William Kane had had his way? You'd have been lucky to have ended up as a shop girl at Bloomingdale's. Have you thought about that, Florentyna?"

"Yes, Daddy, I've thought of little else these past few

weeks. Richard and I are horrified about the hatred that exists between you and his father. He's facing him now."

"Well, I can tell you how he'll react," said Abel. "He'll go berserk. That man would never allow that precious WASP son of his to marry you so you might as well forget the whole crazy idea, young lady."

His voice had risen to a shout.

"I can't forget it, Father," she said evenly. "We love each other, and we both need your blessing, not your anger."

"Now you listen to me, Florentyna," said Abel, his face now red with fury. "I forbid you to see the Kane boy ever again. Do you hear me?"

"Yes, I hear you. But I will see him. I'll not be parted from Richard because you hate his father."

She found herself clutching her ring finger and trembling slightly.

"It will not happen," said Abel. "I will never allow the marriage. My own daughter deserting me for the son of that bastard Kane. I say you will not marry him."

"I am not deserting you. I would have run away with him if that was true, but I couldn't do that behind your back. I'm over twenty-one, and I will marry Richard. I intend to spend the rest of my life with him. Please help us, Daddy. Won't you meet him, and then you'll begin to understand why I feel the way I do about him?"

"He will never be allowed to enter my home. I do not want to meet any child of William Kane. Never, do you hear me?"

"Then I must leave you."

"Florentyna, if you leave me, to marry the Kane boy, I'll cut you off without a penny. Without a penny, do you hear me?" Abel's voice softened. "Now use your common sense, girl, you'll get over him. You're still young, and there are lots of other men who'd give their right arms to marry you."

"I don't want lots of other men," said Florentyna. "I've met the man I'm going to marry, and it's not his fault that he is his father's son. Neither of us chose our fathers."

"If my family isn't good enough for you, then get out," said Abel. "And I swear I won't have your name mentioned in my presence again." He turned away and stared out of the window. "For the last time, I warn you, Florentyna – do not marry that boy."

"Daddy, we are going to be married. Although we're both past the stage of needing your consent, we do ask for your approval."

Abel looked away from the window and walked towards her. "Are you pregnant? Is that the reason? Do you have to get married?"

"No, Father."

"Have you ever slept with him?" Abel demanded.

The question shook Florentyna but she didn't hesitate. "Yes," she replied. "Many times."

Abel raised his arm and hit her full across the face. The silver band caught the corner of her lip and she nearly fell. Blood started to trickle down her chin. She turned, ran out of the room crying, and leaned on the lift button, holding her bloody face. The door slid open and George stepped out. She had a fleeting glimpse of his shocked expression as she stepped quickly in to the car and jabbed at the button continuously. As George stood and watched her crying, the lift doors closed slowly.

Once Florentyna had reached the street, she took a cab straight to her own apartment. On the way, she dabbed at her cut lip with a Kleenex. Richard was already there, standing under the marquee, head bowed and looking miserable.

She jumped out of the cab and ran to him. Once they were upstairs, she opened the door and quickly closed it behind them, feeling blessedly safe.

"I love you, Richard."

"I love you, too," said Richard, as he threw his arms around her.

"I don't have to ask how your father reacted," said Florentyna, clinging to him desperately.

"I've never seen him so angry," said Richard. "Called your father a liar and a crook, nothing more than a jumped-up Polish immigrant. He asked me why I didn't marry somebody from my own background."

"What did you say to that?"

"I told him someone as wonderful as you couldn't be

replaced by a suitably Brahmin family friend, and he completely lost his temper."

Florentyna didn't let go of Richard as he spoke.

"Then he threatened to cut me off without a penny if I married you," he continued. "When will they understand we don't care a damn about their money? I tried appealing to my mother for support, but even she could not control his temper. He insisted that she leave the room. I have never seen him treat my mother that way before. She was weeping, which only made my resolve stronger. I left him in mid-sentence. God knows, I hope he doesn't take it out on Virginia and Lucy. What happened when you left?"

"My father hit me," said Florentyna very quietly. "For the first time in my life. I think he'll kill you if he finds us together. Richard darling, we must get out of here, before he finds out where you are, and he's bound to try here first. I'm so frightened."

"No need for you to be frightened, Florentyna. We'll leave tonight and go as far away as possible and to hell with them both."

"How quickly can you pack?" asked Florentyna.

"I can't," said Richard. "I can never return home now. You pack your things and then we'll go. I've got about a hundred dollars on me. How do you feel about marrying a hundred-dollar man?"

"As much as a shop girl can hope for, I suppose – and to think I'd dreamed of being a kept woman. Next you'll be wanting a dowry," Florentyna added while rummaging in her bag. "Well, I've got two hundred and twelve dollars and an American Express card, so you owe me fifty-six dollars, Richard Kane, but I'll consider repayment at a dollar a year."

In thirty minutes Florentyna was packed. Then she sat down at her desk, scrawled a note and left the envelope on the table by the side of her bed.

Richard hailed a cab. Florentyna was delighted to find how capable Richard was in a crisis and it made her feel more relaxed. "Idlewild," he said, placing Florentyna's three cases in the boot.

At the airport he booked a flight to San Francisco; they chose the Golden Gate City simply because it seemed the most distant point on the map of America.

At seven thirty, the American Airlines Super Constellation 1049 taxied out on to the runway to start its seven-hour flight.

Richard helped Florentyna with her seat belt. She smiled at him.

"Do you know how much I love you, Mr. Kane?"

"Yes, I think so – Mrs. Kane," he replied.

34

Abel and George arrived at Florentyna's flat on East Fifty-seventh Street a few minutes after she and Richard had left for the airport. Abel was already remorseful and regretting the blow he had struck his daughter. He did not care to conjecture about what his life would be like without his only child. He thought if he could only reach her before it was too late, he might, with gentle persuasion, still talk her out of marrying the Kane boy. He was willing to offer her anything to stop the marriage.

George rang the door bell as he and Abel stood outside her door. No one answered. George pressed the bell again, and they waited for some time before Abel used the key Florentyna had always left with him for emergencies. They searched the place, neither really expecting to find her.

"She must have left already," said George, as he joined Abel in the bedroom.

"Yes, but where?" said Abel, and then he saw an envelope addressed to him on the table. He remembered the last letter left for him by the side of a bed that had not been slept in. He ripped it open.

Dear Daddy,

Please forgive me for running away but I do love Richard and will not give him up because of your hatred for his father. We will be married right away and nothing you can do will prevent it. If you ever try to harm him in any way, you will be harming me. Neither of us intend to return to New York until you have ended the senseless feud between our family and the Kanes. I love you more than you will ever realise and I shall always be thankful for everything you have done for me. I pray that this is not the end of our relationship but until you can change your mind, 'Never seek the wind in the field – it is useless to try and find what is gone.'

Your loving daughter,
Florentyna

Abel collapsed on to the bed, and passed the letter to George, who read the handwritten note and asked helplessly, "Is there anything I can do?"

"Yes, George. I want my daughter back, even if it means dealing direct with that bastard Kane. There's only one thing I feel certain of: he will want this marriage stopped whatever sacrifice he has to make. Get him on the phone."

It took George some time to locate William Kane's unlisted number. The night security officer at Lester's Bank finally gave it to him when George insisted that it was a family emergency. Abel sat silently on the bed, Florentyna's letter in his hand, remembering how when she was a little girl, he had taught her the old Polish proverb that she had now quoted back to him.

When George was put through to the Kane residence, a male voice answered the phone.

"May I speak to Mr. William Kane?" asked George.

"Whom shall I say is calling?" asked the imperturbable voice.

"Mr. Abel Rosnovski," said George.

"I'll see if he is in, sir."

"I think that was Kane's butler. He's gone to look for him," said George, as he passed the receiver over to Abel. Abel waited, his fingers tapping on the bedside table.

"William Kane speaking."

"This is Abel Rosnovski."

"Indeed?" William's tone was icy. "And when exactly did you think of setting up your daughter with my son? At the time, no doubt, when you failed so conspicuously to cause the downfall of my bank?"

"Don't be such a damn . . . " Abel checked himself. "I

want this marriage stopped every bit as much as you do. I never tried to take away your son. I only learned of his existence today. I love my daughter even more than I hate you, and I don't want to lose her. Can't we get together and work something out between us?"

"No," said William. "I asked you that same question once in the past, Mr. Rosnovski, and you made it very clear when and where you would meet me. I can wait until then, because I am confident you will find it is you who are there, not me."

"What's the good of raking over the past now, Kane? If you know where they are, perhaps we can stop them. That's what you want, too. Or are you so goddamn proud that you'll stand by and watch your son marry my girl rather than help . . . ?"

The telephone clicked as he spoke the word 'help'. Abel buried his face in his hands and wept. George took him back to the Baron.

Through that night and the following day, Abel tried every way he could think of to find Florentyna. He even rang her mother, who admitted that their daughter had told her all about Richard Kane.

"He sounded rather nice," she added spitefully.

"Do you know where they are right now?" asked Abel impatiently.

"Yes."

"Where?"

"Find out for yourself." Another telephone click.

Abel placed advertisements in newspapers and even bought radio time. He tried to get the police involved, but they could only put out a general call since she was over twenty-one. No word came from her. Finally, he had to admit to himself that by the time he found her she would undoubtedly be married to the Kane boy.

He re-read her letter many times, and resolved that he would never attempt to harm the boy in any way. But the father, that was a different matter. He, Abel Rosnovski, had gone down on his knees and pleaded, and the bastard hadn't even listened. Abel vowed that when the chance presented itself, he would finish William Kane off once and for all.

George became fearful at the intensity of his old friend's passion.

"Shall I cancel your European trip?" he asked.

Abel had completely forgotten that he was meant to accompany Florentyna to Europe after she had finished her two years with Bloomingdale's at the end of the month. She was going to open the Edinburgh Baron and the Cannes Baron. Now he didn't care who opened what, or whether the hotels were opened at all.

"I can't cancel," replied Abel. "I'll have to go and open the hotels myself, but while I'm away, George, you find out exactly where Florentyna is without letting her know. She mustn't think I'm spying on her; she would never forgive me if she found out. Your best bet may well be Zaphia, but be careful because you can be sure she will want to take every advantage of what has happened. It was obvious she had already briefed Florentyna on everything she knew about Kane."

"Do you want Osborne to do anything about the Kane shares?"

"No, nothing for the moment. Now is not the appropriate time for finishing Kane off. When I do, I want to be certain that it's once and for all. Leave Kane alone for the time being. I can always come back to him. For now, concentrate on finding Florentyna."

George promised that he would have found her by the time Abel returned.

Abel opened the Edinburgh Baron three weeks later. The hotel looked quite magnificent as it stood on the hill dominating the Athens of the north. It was always little things that annoyed Abel most when he opened a new hotel and he would always check them on arrival. A small electric shock when you touched a light switch caused by nylon carpets. Room service that took forty minutes to materialise or a bed that was too small for anyone who was either fat or tall. The press was quick to point out that it had been expected that Florentyna Rosnovski, daughter of the Chicago Baron, would perform the opening ceremony.

One of the gossip columnists, from the *Sunday Express,* hinted at a family rift and reported that Abel had not been his usual exuberant, bouncy self. Abel denied the suggestion unconvincingly, retorting that he was over fifty – not an age for bouncing, his public relations man had told him to say. The press remained unconvinced and the following day the *Daily Mail* printed a photograph of a discarded engraved bronze plaque, discovered on a rubbish heap, which read:

The Edinburgh Baron
opened by
Florentyna Rosnovski
October 17, 1957

Abel flew on to Cannes. Another splendid hotel, this time overlooking the Mediterranean but it didn't help him to get Florentyna out of his mind. Another discarded plaque, this one in French. The openings were ashes without her.

Abel was beginning to dread that he might spend the rest of his life without seeing his daughter again. To kill the loneliness, he slept with some very expensive and some rather cheap women. None of them helped. William Kane's son now possessed the one person he truly loved. France no longer held any excitement for him, and once he had finished his business there, Abel flew on to Bonn where he completed negotiations for the site on which he would build the first Baron in Germany. He kept in constant touch with George by phone, but Florentyna had not been found, and there was some very disturbing news concerning Henry Osborne.

"He's got himself in heavy debt with the bookmakers again," said George.

"I warned him last time that I was through bailing him out," said Abel. "He's been no damn use to anyone since he lost his seat in Congress. I suppose I'll have to deal with the problem when I get back."

"He's making threats," said George.

"There's nothing new about that. I've never let them worry me in the past," said Abel. "Tell him whatever it is he wants, it will have to wait until my return."

"When do you expect to be back?" asked George.

"Three weeks, four at the most. I want to look at some sites in Turkey and Egypt. Hilton's already started building there, so I'm going to find out why. Which reminds me, George, the experts tell me you'll never be able to reach me once the plane has landed in the Middle East. Those damned Arabs haven't worked out how to find each other, let alone visitors from foreign countries, so I'll leave you to run everything as usual until you hear from me."

Abel spent over three weeks looking at sites for new hotels all over the Arab states. His advisers were legion, most of them claiming the title of Prince, each assuring Abel that they had the real influence as a very close personal friend of the key minister, a distant cousin in fact. However, it always turned out to be the wrong minister or too distant a cousin. The only solid conclusion Abel reached, after twenty-three days in the dust, sand, and heat with soda but no whisky, was that if his advisers' forecasts on the Middle East oil reserves were accurate, the Gulf States were going to need a lot of hotels in the long term and the Baron Group had to start planning carefully if they were not to be left behind.

Abel managed to find several sites on which to build hotels, through his several princes, but he did not have the time to discover which of them had the real power to fix the officials. He objected to bribery only when the money reached the wrong hands. At least in America, Henry Osborne had always known which officials needed to be taken care of. Abel set up a small office in Bahrain, leaving his local representative in no doubt that the Baron Group was looking for sites throughout the Arab world, but not for princes or the cousins of ministers.

He flew on to Istanbul, where he almost immediately found the perfect place to build a hotel, overlooking the Bosphorus, only a hundred yards from the old British Embassy. He mused as he stood on the barren ground of his latest acquisition, recalling when he had last been there. He clenched his fist and held the wrist of his right hand. He could hear again the cries of the mob – it still made him feel frightened and sick although more than thirty years had passed.

Exhausted from his travels, Abel flew home to New York. During the interminable journey he thought of little but Florentyna, and whether George had found her. As always, George was standing, waiting outside the customs gate to meet him. His expression indicated nothing.

"What news?" asked Abel as he climbed into the back of the Cadillac while the chauffeur put his bags in the trunk.

"Some good, some bad," said George, as he pressed a button by the side window. A sheet of glass glided up between the front and rear sections of the car. "Florentyna has been in touch with her mother. She's living in a small apartment in San Francisco."

"Married?" said Abel.

"Yes," said George.

Neither spoke for some moments.

"And the Kane boy?" asked Abel.

"He's found a job in a bank. It seems a lot of people turned him down because word got around that he didn't finish at the Harvard Business School, and his father wouldn't supply a reference. Not many people will consider employing him if as a consequence they might lose his father's business. He finally was hired as a teller with the Bank of America. Way below what he might have expected with his qualifications."

"And Florentyna?"

"She's working as the assistant manager in a fashion shop called 'Wayout Columbus' near Golden Gate Park. She's also been trying to borrow money from several banks."

"Why? Is she in any sort of trouble?" asked Abel anxiously.

"No, she's looking for capital to open her own shop."

"How much is she looking for?"

"Only thirty-four thousand dollars which she needs for the lease on a small building on Nob Hill."

Abel sat back thinking about what George had said, his short fingers tapping on the car window. "See that she gets the money, George. Make it look as if the transaction is an ordinary bank loan and be sure that it's not traceable back to me." He continued tapping. "This must always remain simply between the two of us, George."

"Anything you say, Abel."

"And keep me informed of every move she makes, however trivial."

"What about him?"

"I'm not interested in him," said Abel. "Now what's the bad news?"

"Trouble with Henry Osborne again. It seems he owes money everywhere. I'm also fairly certain his only source of income is now you. He's started making veiled threats about you condoning bribes in the early days when we were setting up the group. Says he's kept all the papers from the first day he met you when he claims he fixed an extra payment after the fire at the old Richmond in Chicago, and he now has a file three inches thick."

"I'll deal with Henry in the morning," said Abel.

George spent the remainder of the drive into Manhattan bringing Abel up to date on the rest of the group's affairs which were all satisfactory, except for a takeover of the Baron in Lagos after yet another coup. That never worried Abel.

The next morning Abel saw Henry Osborne. He looked old and tired, and the once smooth handsome face was now heavily lined. He made no mention of the three-inch thick file.

"I need a little money to get me through a tricky period," said Henry. "I've been a bit unlucky."

"Again, Henry? You should know better at your age. You're a born loser with horses and women. How much do you need this time?"

"Ten thousand would see me through," said Henry.

"Ten thousand," said Abel spitting out the words. "What do you think I am, a gold mine? It was only five thousand last time."

"Inflation," said Henry, trying to laugh.

"This is the last time, do you understand me?" said Abel as he took out his cheque book. "Come begging once more, Henry, and I'll remove you from the board as a director and turn you out without a penny."

"You're a real friend, Abel. I swear I'll never come back again, I promise you that, never again." Henry plucked a

Romeo y Julieta from the humidor on the table in front of Abel and lit it. "Thanks, Abel, you'll never regret your decision."

Henry left, puffing away at the cigar, as George came in. George waited for the door to be closed.

"What happened with Henry?"

"I gave in for the last time," said Abel. "I don't know why – it cost me ten thousand."

"Jesus, I feel like the brother of the prodigal son," said George. "Because he'll be back again. I'd be willing to put money on that."

"He'd better not," said Abel, "because I'm through with him. Whatever he has done for me in the past, it's now quits. What's the latest news on Florentyna?"

"Florentyna's fine, but you were right about Zaphia: she's been making regular monthly trips to the coast to see them both."

"Bloody woman," said Abel.

"Mrs. Kane has been out a couple of times as well," added George.

"And Kane?"

"No sign of him relenting."

"That's one thing we have in common," said Abel.

"I've set up a facility for her with the Crocker National Bank of San Francisco," continued George. "She made an approach to the loan officer there less than a week ago. The agreement will appear to her as if it's one of the bank's ordinary loan transactions, with no special favours. In fact, they're charging her half a per cent more than usual so there can be no reason for her to be suspicious. What she will never know is that the loan is covered by your guarantee."

"Thanks, George, that's perfect. I'll bet you ten dollars she pays off the loan within two years and never needs to go back for another."

"I'd want odds of five to one on that," said George. "Why don't you try Henry; he's more of a sucker."

Abel laughed. "Keep me briefed, George, on everything she's up to, everything."

35

William felt he had been briefed on everything as he studied Thaddeus Cohen's quarterly report, and only one thing now worried him. Why was Abel Rosnovski still doing nothing with his vast shareholding in Lester's? William couldn't help remembering that he still owned six per cent of the bank and with two more per cent he could invoke Article Seven of Lester's by-laws. It was hard to believe that Rosnovski still feared S.E.C. regulations, especially as the Eisenhower administration was settled into its second term in the White House and had never shown any interest in pursuing the original inquiry.

William was fascinated to read that Henry Osborne was once again in financial trouble, and that Rosnovski still kept bailing him out. William wondered for how much longer that would go on, and what Henry had on Rosnovski. Was it possible that Rosnovski had enough problems of his own without adding William Kane to them? Cohen's report reviewed progress on the eight new hotels Rosnovski was building across the world. The London Baron was losing money and the Lagos Baron was out of commission; otherwise he continued to grow in strength. William re-read the attached clipping from the *Sunday Express*, reporting that Florentyna Rosnovski had not opened the Edinburgh Baron, and he thought about his son. Then he closed the report and locked the file in his safe, convinced there was nothing in it of importance to concern himself with. His chauffeur drove him home.

William regretted his early loss of temper with Richard. Although he did not want the Rosnovski girl in his life, he wished he had not turned his back so irrevocably on his only son. Kate had pleaded on Richard's behalf, and she and William had had a long and bitter argument – so rare in their married life – which they had been unable to resolve. Kate tried every tactic from gentle persuasion to tears, but nothing seemed to move William. Virginia and Lucy also missed their brother.

"There's no one who will be critical of my paintings," said Virginia.

"Don't you mean rude?" asked Kate.

Virginia tried to smile.

Lucy used to lock herself in the bathroom, turn on the water, and write secret letters to Richard, who could never figure out why they always seemed damp. No one dared to mention Richard's name in the house in front of William, but it was causing a sad rift within the family.

William had tried spending more time at the bank, even working round the clock in the hope that it might help. It didn't. The bank was once again making heavy demands on his energy at the very time when he most felt like a rest. He had appointed six new vice-presidents over the previous two years, hoping they would take some of the load off his shoulders. The reverse had turned out to be the case. They had created more work and more decisions for him to make and the brightest of them, Jake Thomas, already looked the most likely candidate to take William's place as chairman if Richard did not give up the Rosnovski girl. Although the profits of the bank continued to rise each year, William found he was no longer interested in making money for money's sake. Perhaps he now faced the same problem that Charles Lester had encountered: he had no son to leave his fortune and the chairmanship to now that he had cut Richard out of his life, rewritten his will and reorganised his trust in favour of his daughters.

In the year of their silver wedding anniversary, William decided to take Kate and the girls for a long holiday to Europe in the hope that it might help to put Richard out of their minds. They flew to London on a Boeing 707 and stayed at the Ritz. The hotel brought back many happy memories of William's first trip to Europe with Kate. They made a sentimental journey to Oxford and showed Virginia and Lucy the university city, and then went on to Stratford-on-Avon to see some Shakespeare: *Richard III* with Laurence Olivier. They could have wished for a king with another name.

On the return journey from Stratford they stopped at the church in Henley-on-Thames where William and Kate had been married. They would have stayed at the Bell Inn again, but they still had only one vacant room. An argument started between William and Kate in the car on the way back to London as to whether it had been the Reverend Tukesbury or the Reverend Dukesbury who had married them. They came to no satisfactory conclusion before reaching the Ritz. On one thing they were able to agree; the new roof on the parish church had worn well.

William kissed Kate gently when he climbed into bed that night. "Best five hundred pounds I ever invested," he said.

They flew on to Italy a week later, having seen every English sight any self-respecting American tourist is meant to visit and many they usually miss. In Rome, the girls drank too much bad Italian wine and made themselves ill on the night of Virginia's birthday, while William ate too much good pasta and put on seven pounds. All of them would have been so much happier if they could have talked of the forbidden topic of Richard. Virginia cried that night and Kate tried to comfort her.

"Why doesn't someone tell Daddy that some things are more important than pride?" Virginia kept asking.

Kate had no reply.

When they returned to New York, William was refreshed and eager once again to plunge back into his work at the bank. He lost the seven pounds in seven days.

As the months passed by, he felt things were becoming quite routine again. Routine disappeared from his mind when Virginia, just out of Sweetbriar, announced she was going to marry a student from the University of Virginia Law School. The news shook William.

"She's not old enough," he said.

"Virginia's twenty-two," said Kate. "She's not a child any longer, William. How do you feel about becoming a grandfather?" she added, regretting the sequence of her words immediately she had spoken them.

"What do you mean?" said William, horrified. "Virginia isn't pregnant, is she?"

"Good gracious, no," said Kate, and then she spoke more softly as if she had been found out. "Richard and Florentyna have had a baby."

"How do you know?"

"Richard wrote to tell me the good news," replied Kate. "Hasn't the time come for you to forgive him, William?"

"Never," said William and marched out of the room in anger.

Kate sighed wearily: he had not even asked if his grandchild was a boy or a girl.

Virginia's wedding took place in Trinity Church, Boston, on a beautiful spring afternoon in late March of the following year. William thoroughly approved of David Telford, the young lawyer with whom Virginia had chosen to spend the rest of her life.

Virginia had wanted Richard to be an usher and Kate had begged William to invite him to the wedding, but he had steadfastly refused. He had wanted to say yes, but he knew that Richard would never agree to coming without the Rosnovski girl. On the day of the wedding, Richard sent a present and a telegram to his sister. William would not allow the telegram to be read at the reception afterwards.

Book Six

36

Abel was sitting alone in his office on the forty-second floor of the New York Baron waiting to see a fund raiser from the Kennedy campaign. The man was already twenty minutes late. Abel was tapping his fingers impatiently on his desk when his secretary came in.

"Mr. Vincent Hogan to see you, sir."

Abel sprang out of his chair. "Come in, Mr. Hogan," he said, slapping the good-looking young man on the back. "How are you?"

"I'm fine, Mr. Rosnovski. I'm sorry I'm a little late," said the unmistakably Bostonian voice.

"I didn't notice," said Abel. "Would you care for a drink, Mr. Hogan?"

"No, thank you, Mr. Rosnovski. I try not to drink when I have to see so many people in one day."

"Absolutely right. I hope you won't mind if I have one," said Abel. "I'm not planning on seeing many people today."

Hogan laughed like a man who knew he was in for a day of other people's jokes. Abel poured a whisky.

"Now, what can I do for you, Mr. Hogan?"

"Well, Mr. Rosnovski, we were hoping the party could once again count on your support."

"I've always been a Democrat, as you know, Mr. Hogan. I supported Franklin D. Roosevelt, Harry Truman, and Adlai Stevenson, although I couldn't understand what Adlai was talking about half the time."

Both men laughed falsely.

"I also helped my old friend, Dick Daley, in Chicago and I've been backing young Ed Muskie – the son of a Polish immigrant, you know – since his campaign for governor of Maine back in '54."

"You've been a loyal supporter of the party in the past, there's no denying that, Mr. Rosnovski," said Vincent Hogan, in a tone that indicated that the statutory time for small talk had run out. "We also know the Democrats, not least of all former Congressman Osborne, have done the odd favour for you in return. I don't think it's necessary for me to go into any details of that unpleasant little incident."

"That's long since past," said Abel, "and well behind me."

"I agree," said Mr. Hogan, "and although most self-made multi-millionaires couldn't face having their affairs looked into too closely, you will be the first to appreciate that we have to be especially careful. The candidate, as you will understand, cannot afford to take any personal risks so near the election. Nixon would love a scandal at this stage of the race."

"We understand each other clearly, Mr. Hogan. Now that's out of the way, how much were you expecting from me for the election campaign?"

"I need every penny I can lay my hands on." Hogan's words came across clipped and slow. "Nixon is gathering a lot of support across the country, and it's going to be a very close thing getting our man into the White House."

"Well, I'll support Kennedy," said Abel, "if he supports me. It's as simple as that."

"He's delighted to support you, Mr. Rosnovski. We all realise that you're now a pillar of the Polish community, and Senator Kennedy is personally aware of the brave stand you took on behalf of your countrymen who are still in slave labour camps behind the Iron Curtain, not to mention the service you gave in the war. I have been authorised to let you know that the candidate has already agreed to open your new hotel in Los Angeles during his campaign trip."

"That's good news," said Abel.

"The candidate is also fully aware of your desire to grant Poland most favoured nation status in foreign trade with the United States."

"No more than we deserve after our service in the last

war," said Abel, and paused briefly. "What about the other little matter?" he asked.

"Senator Kennedy is canvassing Polish-American opinion at the moment, and we haven't met with any objections. He naturally cannot come to a final decision until after he is elected

"Naturally. Would two hundred and fifty thousand dollars help him make that decision?" asked Abel.

Vincent Hogan didn't speak.

"Two hundred and fifty thousand dollars it is then," said Abel. "The money will be in your campaign fund headquarters by the end of the week, Mr. Hogan. You have my word on it."

The business was over, the bargain struck. Abel rose. "Please give Senator Kennedy my best wishes, and add that of course I hope he'll be the next President of the United States. I always loathed Richard Nixon after his despicable treatment of Helen Gahagan Douglas, and in any case, there are personal reasons why I don't want Henry Cabot Lodge as Vice-President."

"I shall be delighted to pass on your message," said Mr. Hogan, "and thank you for your continued support of the Democratic party, and in particular, of the candidate." The Bostonian thrust out his hand. Abel grasped it.

"Keep in touch, Mr. Hogan. I don't part with that sort of money without expecting a return on my investment."

"I fully understand," replied Vincent Hogan. Abel showed his guest to the lift and returned smiling to his office. His fingers started to tap on the desk again. His secretary reappeared.

"Ask Mr. Novak to come in," said Abel.

George came through from his office a few moments later.

"I think I've pulled it off, George."

"Congratulations, Abel, I'm delighted. If Kennedy becomes the next President, then one of your biggest dreams will be fulfilled. How proud Florentyna will be of you."

Abel smiled when he heard her name. "Do you know what that little minx has been up to?" he said, laughing. "Did you see the *Los Angeles Times* last week, George?"

George shook his head, and Abel passed him a copy of the paper. One of the items was circled in red ink. George read the article aloud: "Florentyna Kane opens her third shop in Los Angeles. She already owns two in San Francisco and is hoping to open another in San Diego before the end of the year. 'Florentyna's', as they are known, are fast becoming to California what Balenciaga is to Paris."

George laughed as he put the paper down.

"She must have written the piece herself," said Abel. "I can't wait for her to open a Florentyna's in New York. I'll bet she achieves that within five years, ten at the most. Do you want to take another bet on that, George?"

"I didn't take the first one, if you remember, Abel, otherwise I would already have been out ten dollars."

Abel looked up, his voice quieter. "Do you think she'd come and see Senator Kennedy open the new Baron in Los Angeles, George? Do you think she might?"

"Not unless the Kane boy is invited along as well."

"Never," said Abel. "That Kane boy is nothing. I read all the facts in your last report, George. He's left the Bank of America to work with Florentyna; couldn't even hold down a good job, had to fall back on her success."

"You're becoming a selective reader, Abel. You know very well that's not the way it was. I made the circumstances very clear. The Kane boy is in charge of the finances while Florentyna runs the shops, and it's proving to be an ideal partnership. Don't ever forget that a major bank offered Kane the chance to head up its European department but Florentyna begged him to join her when she no longer found it possible to control the finances herself. Abel, you'll have to face the fact that their marriage is a success. I know it's hard for you to stomach, but why don't you climb down off your high horse and meet the boy?"

"You're my closest friend, George. No one else in the world would dare to speak to me like that. So no one knows better than you why I can't climb down, not until that bastard Kane shows he is willing to meet me halfway, but until then, I won't crawl again while he's still alive to watch me."

"What if you were to die first, Abel? You're exactly the same age."

"Then I'd lose and Florentyna inherits everything."

"You told me she wouldn't get a thing. You were going to change your will in favour of your grandson."

"I couldn't do it, George. When the time came to sign the documents, I just couldn't do it. What the hell, that damned grandson is going to end up with both our fortunes in the end."

Abel removed a wallet from his inside pocket, shuffled through several old pictures of Florentyna and took out a new one of his grandson, which he proffered to George.

"Good-looking little boy," said George.

"Sure is," said Abel. "The spitting image of his mother."

George laughed. "You never give up, do you, Abel?"

"What do you think they call him?"

"What do you mean?" said George. "You know very well what his name is."

"I mean what do you think they actually call him?"

"How should I know?" said George.

"Find out," said Abel. "I care."

"How am I meant to do that?" said George. "Have someone follow them while they're pushing the pram around Golden Gate Park? You left clear instructions that Florentyna must never find out that you're still taking an interest in her or the Kane boy."

"That reminds me, I still have a little matter to settle with his father," said Abel.

"What are you going to do about the Lester shares?" asked George. "Because Peter Parfitt has been showing more interest in selling his two per cent lately, and I wouldn't trust Henry with the negotiations. With those two working on the sale, everybody will be in on the deal except you."

"I'm doing nothing. Much as I hate Kane, I don't want any trouble with him until we know if Kennedy has won the election. So I'm leaving the whole situation dormant for the moment. If Kennedy fails, I'll buy Parfitt's two per cent and go ahead with the plan that we've already discussed. And don't worry yourself about Henry; I've already taken him off the Kane file. From now on I'm handling that myself."

"I do worry, Abel. I know he's in debt again to half the bookmakers in Chicago, and I wouldn't be surprised if he arrived in New York on the scrounge any minute now."

"Henry won't be coming here. I made the situation very clear last time I saw him that he wouldn't get another dime out of me. If he does come begging, he'll only lose his seat on the board and with it his only source of income."

"That worries me even more," said George. "Let's say he took it on himself to go to Kane direct for the money."

"Not possible, George. Henry is the one man alive who hates Kane even more than I do, and not without reason."

"How can you be so sure of that?"

"William Kane's mother was Henry's second wife," said Abel, "and young William, aged only sixteen, threw him out of his own home."

"Good God, how did you come across that piece of information?"

"There's nothing I don't know about William Kane," said Abel. "Or Henry, for that matter. Absolutely nothing – from the fact that we started life on the same day, and I'd be willing to bet my good leg there's nothing he doesn't know about me so we have to be circumspect for the time being, but you need have no fear of Henry turning stool pigeon. He'd die before he had to admit his real name was Vittorio Togna and he once served a jail sentence."

"Good God – does Henry realise you know all this?"

"No, he doesn't. I've kept it to myself for years, always believing, George, that if you think a man might threaten you at some time then you should keep a little more up your sleeve than your arm. I've never trusted Henry since the days he suggested swindling Great Western Casualty while he was still actually working for them, although I'd be the first to admit he's been very useful to me in the past and I am confident he isn't going to cause me any trouble in the future, because without his director's salary, he becomes penniless overnight. So forget Henry and let's be a little more positive. What's the latest date for the completion of the Los Angeles Baron?"

"Middle of September," replied George.

"Perfect. That will be six weeks before the election. When Kennedy opens that hotel, the news will hit every front page in America."

37

When William returned to New York, after a bankers' conference in Washington, he found a message awaiting him, requesting that he contact Thaddeus Cohen immediately. He hadn't spoken to Cohen for a considerable time, as Abel Rosnovski had caused no direct trouble since the abortive telephone conversation on the eve of Richard and Florentyna's marriage, nearly three years before. The successive quarterly reports had merely confirmed that Rosnovski was neither trying to buy or sell any of the bank's shares. Nevertheless, William called Thaddeus Cohen immediately and somewhat apprehensively. The lawyer told William that he had stumbled across some information which he did not wish to divulge over the phone. William asked him to come over to the bank as soon as it was convenient.

Thaddeus Cohen arrived forty minutes later. William heard him out in attentive silence.

When Cohen had finished his revelation, William said, "Your father would never have approved of such underhand methods."

"Neither would yours," replied Thaddeus Cohen, "but they didn't have to deal with the likes of Abel Rosnovski."

"What makes you think your plan will work?"

"Look at the Bernard Goldfine and Sherman Adams case, only one thousand six hundred and forty-two dollars involved in hotel bills and a vicuna coat, but it sure embarrassed the hell out of the President when Adams was accused of preferred treatment because he was a Presidential assistant. We know Mr. Rosnovski is aiming a lot higher than that. It should, therefore, be easier to bring him down."

"Game, set and match. How much is it going to cost me?"

"Twenty-five thousand at the outside, but I may be able to pull the whole deal off for less."

"How can you be sure that Rosnovski doesn't realise that I am personally involved?"

"I'd use a third person who won't even know your name to act as an intermediary."

"And if you pull it off, what would you recommend we do then?"

"You send all the details to Senator John Kennedy's office, and I guarantee that will finish off Abel Rosnovski's ambitious plans once and for all because the moment his credibility has been shattered he will be a spent force and find it quite impossible to invoke Article Seven of the bank's by-laws – even if he did get hold of eight per cent of Lester's."

"Maybe – if Kennedy becomes the President," said William. "But what happens if Nixon wins the election? He's way ahead in the opinion polls and I'd certainly back his chances against Kennedy. Can you really imagine that America would ever send a Roman Catholic to the White House? I can't, but then on the other hand I admit that an investment of twenty-five thousand is small enough if there's better than an outside chance the move will finish Abel Rosnovski off once and for all and leave me secure at the bank."

"If Kennedy becomes President . . ."

William opened the drawer of his desk, took out a large cheque book marked 'private account' and wrote out the figures. Two, five, zero, zero, zero.

38

Abel's prediction that Kennedy's opening of the Baron would hit every front page did not turn out to be wholly accurate. Although the candidate did indeed open the hotel, he had to appear at dozens of other events in Los Angeles that day and face Nixon for a televised debate the following evening. Nevertheless, the opening of the newest Baron gained fairly wide coverage in the national press, and Vincent Hogan assured Abel privately that Kennedy had not forgotten the other little matter. Florentyna's shop was only a few hundred yards away, but father and daughter never did meet.

After the Illinois returns came in, and John F. Kennedy looked certain to be the thirty-fifth President of the United States, Abel drank Mayor Daley's health and celebrated at the Democratic National Headquarters on Times Square. He did not return home to his bed until nearly five the next morning.

"Hell, I have a lot to celebrate," he told George. "I'm going to be the next . . ." He fell asleep before he finished the sentence. George smiled and put him to bed.

William watched the results of the election in the peace of his study on East Sixty-eighth Street. After the Illinois returns which were not confirmed until ten o'clock the next morning (William never had trusted Mayor Daley), Walter Cronkite declared it was all over bar the shouting, and William picked up his phone and dialled Thaddeus Cohen's home number.

All he said was, "The twenty-five thousand dollars has turned out to be a wise investment, Thaddeus. Now let us be sure that there is no honeymoon period for Mr. Rosnovski. But don't do anything until he makes his trip to Turkey."

William placed the phone back on the hook and went to bed. He was disappointed that Richard Nixon had failed to beat Kennedy and that his distant cousin Henry Cabot Lodge would not be the Vice-President but it is an ill wind...

When Abel received his invitation to be a guest at one of President Kennedy's inauguration balls in Washington, D.C., there was only one person he wanted to share the honour with. He talked the idea over with George and had to agree that Florentyna would never be willing to accompany him unless she was convinced that the feud with Richard's father could be finally resolved. So he knew he would have to go alone.

In order to be in Washington to attend the celebrations, Abel had had to postpone his latest trip to Europe and the Middle East for a few days. He could not afford to miss the inauguration, whereas he could always put back the date for the opening of the Istanbul Baron.

Abel had a new, rather conservative dark blue suit made specially for the occasion, and took over the Presidential Suite at the Washington Baron for the day of the inauguration. He enjoyed watching the vital young President deliver his inaugural speech, full of hope and promise for the future.

"A new generation of Americans, born in this century" – Abel only just qualified – "tempered by war" – Abel certainly qualified – "disciplined by a hard and bitter peace" – Abel made it again. "Ask not what your country can do for you. Ask what you can do for your country."

The crowd rose to a man and everyone ignored the snow that had failed to dampen the impact of John F. Kennedy's brilliant oration.

Abel returned to the Washington Baron exhilarated. He showered before changing for dinner into white tie and tails, also made especially for the occasion. When he studied his ample frame in the mirror, Abel had to admit to himself that he was not the last word in sartorial elegance. His tailor had done the best he could in the circumstances and did not complain that he had had to make three new and ever larger evening suits for Abel in the past three years. Florentyna would have chastised him for those unnecessary inches, as she used to call them, and for her he would have done something about it. Why did his thoughts always return to Florentyna? He checked his medals. First The Polish Veterans' Medal, next the decorations for his service in the desert and in Europe, and then his cutlery medals, as Abel called them, for distinguished service with knives and forks.

In all, seven inaugural balls were held in Washington that evening, and Abel's invitation directed him to the D.C. Armory. He was placed at a table of Polish Democrats from New York and Chicago. They had a lot to celebrate. Edmund Muskie was in the Senate and ten more Polish Democrats had been elected to Congress. No one mentioned the two newly elected Polish Republicans. Abel spent a happy evening with two old friends, who along with him were founding members of the Polish-American Congress. They both asked after Florentyna.

The dinner was interrupted by the entrance of John F. Kennedy and his beautiful wife, Jacqueline. They stayed about fifteen minutes, chatted with a few carefully selected people and then moved on. Although Abel didn't actually speak to the President, despite leaving his table and placing himself strategically in his path, he did manage to have a word with Vincent Hogan as he was leaving with the Kennedy entourage.

"Mr. Rosnovski, what a fortuitous meeting."

Abel would like to have explained to the boy that with him nothing was fortuitous, but now was neither the time nor the place. Hogan took Abel's arm and guided him quickly behind a large marble pillar.

"I can't say too much at the moment, Mr. Rosnovski, as I must stick with the President, but I think you can expect a call from us in the near future. Naturally, the President has rather a lot of appointments to deal with at the moment."

"Naturally," said Abel.

"But I am hoping," continued Vincent Hogan, "that in

your case everything will be confirmed by late March or early April. May I be the first to offer my congratulations, Mr. Rosnovski? I am confident you will serve the President well."

Abel watched Vincent Hogan literally run off to be sure he caught up with the Kennedy party, who were already climbing into a fleet of open-doored limousines.

"You look pleased with yourself," said one of his Polish friends as Abel returned to his table and sat down to attack a tough steak, which would not have been allowed inside a Baron. "Did Kennedy invite you to be his new Secretary of State?"

They all laughed.

"Not yet," said Abel. "But he did tell me the accommodation in the White House was not in the same class as the Baron."

Abel flew back to New York the next morning after first visiting the Polish Chapel of Our Lady of Czestochowa in the National Shrine. It made him think of both Florentynas. Washington National airport was chaos and Abel eventually arrived at the New York Baron three hours later than planned. George joined him for dinner, and knew that all had gone well when Abel ordered a magnum of Dom Perignon.

"Tonight we celebrate," said Abel. "I saw Hogan at the ball and my appointment will be confirmed in the next few weeks. The official announcement will be made soon after I return from the Middle East."

"Congratulations, Abel. I know of no one who deserves the honour more."

"Thank you, George. I can assure you that your reward will not be in heaven, because when it's all official, I'm going to appoint you acting president of the Baron Group in my absence."

George drank another glass of champagne. They were already halfway through the bottle.

"How long do you think you'll be away this time, Abel?"

"Only three weeks. I want to check that those Arabs aren't robbing me blind and then go on to Turkey to open the Istanbul Baron. I think I'll take in London and Paris on the way."

George poured some more champagne.

Abel had to spend three more days in London than he had originally anticipated, trying to sort out the hotel's problems, with a manager who kept blaming everything on the British unions. The London Baron had turned out to be one of Abel's few failures, although he never could put his finger on why the hotel continually lost money. He would have considered closing it, but the Baron Group had to have a presence in England's capital city, so once again he fired the manager and made a new appointment.

Paris presented a striking contrast. The hotel was one of his most successful in Europe, and he'd once admitted to Florentyna, as reluctantly as a parent admits to having a favourite child, that the Paris Baron was his favourite hotel. Abel found everything on the Boulevard Raspail well organised and spent only two days in Paris before flying on to the Middle East.

Abel now had sites in five of the Persian Gulf States, but only the Riyadh Baron had actually started construction. If he'd been a younger man, Abel would have stayed in the Middle East for a couple of years himself and sorted the Arabs out. But he couldn't abide the sand, the heat, and never being certain when he could order a whisky. He thought he must be getting older, because he couldn't stand the natives either. He left them to one of his young assistant vice-presidents, who had been told that he would only be allowed to return and manage the infidels in America once Abel was sure he had proved a success with the holy and blessed ones from the Middle East.

He left the poor assistant vice-president in the richest private hell in the world and flew on to Turkey.

Abel had visited Turkey several times during the past few years to watch the progress of the Istanbul Baron. For Abel, there would always be something special about Constantinople, as he remembered the city. He was looking forward to opening a Baron in the country he had left to start a new life in America.

While he was unpacking his suitcase in yet another Presidential Suite, Abel found fifteen invitations awaiting his reply. There were always several invitations about the time of a hotel opening; a galaxy of freeloaders who wanted to be invited to any opening night party appeared on the scene as if by magic. On this occasion, however, two of the dinner invitations came as an agreeable surprise to Abel from men who certainly could not be classified as freeloaders: namely the ambassadors of America and Britain. The invitation to the old British Embassy was particularly irresistible as he had not been inside the building for nearly forty years.

That evening, Abel dined as the guest of Sir Bernard Burrows, Her Majesty's Ambassador to Turkey. To his surprise he found that he had been placed at the right of the ambassador's wife, a privilege Abel had never been afforded in any other embassy in the past. When the dinner was over, he observed the quaint English tradition of the ladies leaving the room while the gentlemen sat alone to smoke cigars and drink port or brandy. Abel was invited to join the American ambassador, Fletcher Warren, for port in Sir Bernard's study. Sir Bernard was taking the American ambassador to task for allowing him to have the Chicago Baron to dinner before he had.

"The British have always been a presumptuous race," said the American ambassador, lighting a large Cuban cigar.

"I'll say one thing for the Americans," said Sir Bernard. "They don't know when they're fairly beaten."

Abel listened to the two diplomats' banter, wondering why he had been included in such a private gathering. Sir Bernard offered Abel some vintage port, and the American ambassador raised his glass.

"To Abel Rosnovski," he said.

Sir Bernard also raised his glass. "I understand that congratulations are in order," he said.

Abel reddened and looked hastily towards Fletcher Warren, hoping he would help him out.

"Oh, have I let the cat out of the bag, Fletcher?" said Sir Bernard, turning to the American ambassador. "You told me the appointment was common knowledge, old chap."

"Fairly common," said Fletcher Warren. "Not that the British could ever keep a secret for very long."

"Is that why your lot took such a devil of a time to discover we were at war with Germany?" replied Sir Bernard.

"And then moved in to make sure of the victory?"

"And the glory," said Sir Bernard.

The American ambassador laughed. "I'm told the official announcement will be made in the next few days."

Both men looked at Abel, who remained silent.

"Well, then may I be the first to congratulate you, Your Excellency," said Sir Bernard. "I wish you every happiness in your new appointment."

Abel flushed to hear aloud the appellation he had whispered so often to his shaving mirror during the past few months.

"You'll have to get used to being called Your Excellency, you know," continued the British ambassador, "and a whole lot of worse things than that, particularly all these damned functions you'll be made to attend one after another. If you have a weight problem now, it will be nothing compared to the one you'll have when you finish your term of office. You may yet live to be grateful for the Cold War. It's the one thing that might keep your social life within bounds."

The American ambassador smiled. "Well done, Abel, and may I add my best wishes for your continued success. When were you last in Poland?" he enquired.

"I've only been back home once for a short visit a few years ago," said Abel. "I've wanted to return ever since."

"Well, you will be returning in triumph," said Fletcher Warren. "Are you familiar with our embassy in Warsaw?"

"No, I'm not," admitted Abel.

"Not a bad building," said Sir Bernard. "Remembering you colonials couldn't get a foothold in Europe until after the Second World War. But the food is appalling. I shall expect you to do something about that, Mr. Rosnovski. I'm afraid the only thing for it is that you'll have to build a Baron Hotel in Warsaw. As ambassador, that's the least they'll expect from an old Pole."

Abel sat in a state of euphoria, laughing and enjoying Sir Bernard's feeble jokes. He found he was drinking a little more port than usual and felt at ease with himself and the world. He couldn't wait to return to America and tell Florentyna his news, now that the appointment seemed to be official. She would be so proud of him. He decided then and there that the moment he arrived back in New York he would go straight on to San Francisco and make everything up with her. It was what he had wanted to do all along and now he had an excuse. Somehow he'd force himself to like the Kane boy. He must stop referring to him as 'the Kane boy'. What was his name – Richard? Yes, Richard. Abel felt a sudden rush of relief at having made the decision.

After the three men had returned to the main reception room and the ladies, Abel reached up and touched the British ambassador on the shoulder. "I should be getting back, Your Excellency."

"Back to the Baron," said Sir Bernard. "Allow me to accompany you to your car, my dear fellow."

The ambassador's wife bade him goodnight at the door.

"Goodnight, Lady Burrows, and thank you for a memorable evening."

She smiled. "I know I'm not meant to know, Mr. Rosnovski, but many congratulations on your appointment. You must be so proud to be returning to the land of your birth as your country's senior representative."

"I am," replied Abel simply.

Sir Bernard accompanied him down the marble steps of the British Embassy to the waiting car. The chauffeur opened the door.

"Goodnight, Rosnovski," said Sir Bernard, "and good luck in Warsaw. By the way, I hope you enjoyed your first meal in the British Embassy."

"My second, actually, Sir Bernard."

"You've been before, old boy? When we checked through the guest book we couldn't find your name."

"No," said Abel. "Last time I had dinner in the British

Embassy, I ate in the kitchen. I don't think they keep a guest book down there, but the meal was the best I'd had in years."

Abel smiled as he climbed into the back of the car. He could see that Sir Bernard wasn't sure whether to believe him or not. As Abel was driven back to the Baron, his fingers tapped on the side windows, and he hummed to himself. He would have liked to have returned to America the next morning, but he couldn't cancel the invitation to dine with Fletcher Warren at the American Embassy the following evening. Hardly the sort of thing a future ambassador does, old fellow, he could hear Sir Bernard saying.

Dinner with the American ambassador turned out to be another pleasant occasion. Abel was made to explain to the assembled guests how he had come to eat in the kitchens of the British Embassy. When he told them the truth, they looked on in surprised admiration. He wasn't sure if many of them believed the story of how he nearly lost his hand, but they all admired the silver band, and that night, everyone called him "Your Excellency".

The next day, Abel was up early, ready for his flight to America. The D.C. 8 flew into Belgrade, where he was grounded for sixteen hours, waiting for the plane to be serviced. Something wrong with the landing gear, they told him. He sat in the airport lounge, sipping undrinkable Yugoslavian coffee. The contrast between the British Embassy and the snack bar in a communist-controlled country was not entirely lost on Abel. At last the plane took off, only to be delayed again in Amsterdam. This time they made him change planes.

When he finally arrived at Idlewild, Abel had been travelling for nearly thirty-six hours. He was so tired he could hardly walk. As he left the customs area he suddenly found himself surrounded by newsmen, and the cameras started flashing and clicking. Immediately he smiled. The announcement must have been made, he thought. Now it's official. He stood as straight as he could and walked slowly and with dignity, disguising his limp. There was no sign of George, as the cameramen jostled each other unceremoniously to be sure of a picture.

Then he saw George standing at the edge of the crowd, looking like death. Abel's heart lurched as he passed the barrier and a journalist, far from asking him what it felt like to be the first Polish-American to be appointed ambassador to Warsaw, shouted: "Do you have any answers to the charges?"

The cameras went on flashing and so did the questions.

"Are the accusations true, Mr. Rosnovski?"

"How much did you actually pay Congressman Osborne?"

"Do you deny the charges?"

"Have you returned to America to face trial?"

They wrote down Abel's replies although he never spoke.

"Get me out of here," shouted Abel above the crowd.

George squeezed forward and managed to reach Abel and then pushed his way back through the crowd and bundled him into the waiting Cadillac. Abel bent down and hid his head in his hands, as the cameras' flashbulbs kept popping, and George shouted at the chauffeur to get moving.

"To the Baron, sir?" he asked.

"No, to Miss Rosnovski's flat on Fifty-seventh Street."

"Why?" said Abel.

"Because the press is crawling all over the Baron."

"I don't understand," said Abel. "In Istanbul they treat me as if I was the ambassador elect, and I return home to find I'm a criminal. What the hell is going on, George?"

"Do you want to hear it all from me, or wait until you've seen your lawyer?" asked George.

"Who have you got to represent me?" asked Abel.

"H. Trafford Jilks, the best defence attorney in America."

"And the most expensive."

"I didn't think you would be worrying about money at a time like this, Abel."

"You're right, George. I'm sorry. Where is he now?"

"I left him at the courthouse, but he said he'd come to the flat as soon as he was through."

"I can't wait that long, George. For God's sake put me in the picture. Tell me the worst."

George drew a deep breath. "There's a warrant out for your arrest," he said.

"What the hell's the charge?"

"Bribery of government officials."

"I've never been directly involved with a government official in my whole life," protested Abel.

"I know, but it turns out that Henry Osborne has been all along, and everything he did seems to have been in your name or on your behalf."

"Oh, my God," said Abel. "I should never have employed the man. I let the fact that we both hated Kane cloud my judgment. But I still find it hard to believe Henry has given anyone the dirt, because he would only end up implicating himself."

"But Henry has disappeared," said George, "and suddenly, mysteriously, all his debts have been cleared up."

"William Kane," said Abel, hissing the words out.

"We've found nothing that points in that direction," said George. "There's no proof he's involved in this at all."

"Who needs proof? You tell me how the authorities got hold of all the details."

"We do know that much," said George. "It seems an anonymous package containing a file was sent direct to the Justice Department in Washington."

"Postmarked New York, no doubt," said Abel.

"No. Chicago."

Abel was silent for a few moments. "It couldn't have been Henry who sent the evidence to them," he said finally. "That doesn't make any sense."

"How can you be so sure?" asked George.

"Because you said all his debts have been cleared up, and the Justice Department wouldn't pay out that sort of money unless they thought they were going to catch Al Capone. Henry must have sold his file to someone else. But who? The one thing we can be certain of is that he would never have released any information directly to Kane."

"Directly?" said George.

"Directly," repeated Abel. "Perhaps he didn't sell it directly. Kane could have arranged for an intermediary to deal with the whole thing if he already knew that Henry was heavily in debt, and the bookmakers were threatening him."

"That might be right, Abel, and it certainly wouldn't have taken an ace detective to discover the extent of Henry's financial problems. They were common knowledge to anyone sitting on a bar stool in Chicago, but don't jump to hasty conclusions just yet. Let's find out what your lawyer has to say."

The Cadillac came to a halt outside Florentyna's former home, which Abel had retained and kept spotless in the hope that his daughter would one day return. George opened the door, and they walked through to join H. Trafford Jilks. Once they had settled down, George poured Abel a large whisky. He drank the malt in one gulp, and gave the empty glass back to George who re-filled it.

"Tell me the worst, Mr. Jilks. Let's get it over with."

"I am sorry, Mr. Rosnovski," he began. "Mr. Novak told me about Warsaw."

"That's all over now, so we may as well forget 'Your Excellency'. You can be sure if Vincent Hogan were asked, he wouldn't even remember my name. Come on, Mr. Jilks, what am I facing?"

"You've been indicted on seventeen charges of bribery and corruption of officials in fourteen different states. I've made provisional arrangements with the Justice Department for you to be arrested here at the flat tomorrow morning, and they will make no objection to bail being granted."

"Very cosy," said Abel, "but what if they can prove the charges?"

"Oh, they should be able to prove some of the charges," said H. Trafford Jilks matter of factly, "but as long as Henry Osborne stays tucked away, they're going to find it very difficult to nail you on most of them. But you're going to have to live with the fact, Mr. Rosnovski, that most of the real damage has already been done whether you're convicted or not."

"I can see that only too well," said Abel, glancing across at a picture of himself on the front page of the *Daily News*.

"So you find out, Mr. Jilks, who the hell bought that file from Henry Osborne. Put as many people to work on the case as you need. I don't care about the cost. But you find out and find out quickly, because if it turns out to be William Kane, I'm going to finish that man off once and for all."

"Don't get yourself into any more trouble than you are already," said H. Trafford Jilks. "You're knee deep in as it is."

"Don't worry," said Abel. "When I finish Kane, it'll be legal and way above board."

"Now listen carefully, Mr. Rosnovski. You forget about William Kane for the time being and start worrying about your impending trial, because it will be the most important event ever to take place in your life unless you don't mind spending the next ten years in jail. Now there's not much more we can do tonight, so go to bed and catch some sleep. In the meantime, I'll issue a short press statement denying the charges and saying that we have a full explanation which will exonerate you completely."

"Do we?" asked George hopefully.

"No," said Jilks, "but it will give me some much needed time to think. When Mr. Rosnovski has had a chance to check through that file of names, it wouldn't surprise me to discover that he's never had direct contact with any of them. It's possible that Henry Osborne always acted as an intermediary without ever putting Mr. Rosnovski fully in the picture. Then my job will be to prove that Osborne exceeded his authority as a director of the group. Mind you, Mr. Rosnovski, if you did meet any of the people mentioned in that file, for God's sake let me know, because you can be sure the Justice Department will put them on the stand as witnesses to testify against us. But we'll start worrying about that tomorrow. You go to bed and get some sleep. You must be exhausted after your trip. I will see you first thing in the morning."

Abel was arrested quietly in his daughter's apartment at eight thirty a.m. and driven away by a U.S. marshal to the Federal District Court for the Southern District of New

York. The brightly coloured St. Valentine's Day decorations in store windows heightened Abel's sense of loneliness. Jilks had hoped that his arrangements had been so discreet that the press would not have picked them up, but when Abel reached the courthouse, he was once again surrounded by photographers and reporters. He ran the gauntlet into the courtroom with George in front of him and Mr. Jilks behind. They sat silently in an anteroom waiting for their case to be called.

When they were called, the indictment hearing lasted only a few minutes and was a strange anti-climax. The clerk read the charges, H. Trafford Jilks answered "Not Guilty" to each one on behalf of his client and requested bail. The government, as agreed, made no objection. Jilks asked Judge Prescott for at least three months to prepare his defence. The judge set a trial date of May 17th and, seemingly uninterested, moved on to the next case.

Abel was free again, free to face the press and more flashing bulbs of their cameras. George had the car waiting for him at the bottom of the steps with the doors open. The engine was already running and Abel's chauffeur had to do some very skilful driving to free himself from the determined reporters who were still pursuing their story. He did not head back to the flat on East Fifty-seventh Street until he was certain he had shaken them all off. Abel said nothing during the entire chase. When they reached their destination, he turned to George and put his arm on his shoulder.

"Now listen, George, you're going to have to run the group for at least three months while I get my defence sorted out with Mr. Jilks. Let's hope you don't have to run it alone after that," said Abel, trying to laugh.

"Of course I won't have to, Abel. Mr. Jilks will get you off, you'll see." George picked up his briefcase and touched Abel on the arm. "Keep smiling," he said and left.

"I don't know what I'd do without George," Abel told his lawyer as they settled down in the front room. "We came over on the boat together nearly forty years ago, and we've been through a hell of a lot since then. Now it looks as if there's a whole lot more ahead of us, so let's get on with it, Mr. Jilks. Any sign of Henry Osborne yet?"

"No, but I have six men working on it, and I understand the Justice Department have at least another six so we can be pretty sure he'll turn up, not that we want them to find him first."

"What about the man Osborne sold the file to?" asked Abel.

"I have some people I trust in Chicago detailed to run that down."

"Good," said Abel. "Now the time has come to go over that file of names you left with me last night."

Trafford Jilks began by reading the indictment and then he went over each of the charges in detail with Abel.

After nearly three weeks of constant meetings, when Jilks was finally convinced there was nothing else Abel could tell him, he left his client to rest. The three weeks had failed to turn up any leads as to the whereabouts of Henry Osborne, either from Trafford Jilks' men or the Justice Department. Jilks' men had also had no breakthrough on finding the person to whom Henry had sold his information and were beginning to wonder if Abel had guessed right.

As the trial date drew nearer, Abel started to face the possibility of actually going to jail. He was now fifty-five and afraid and ashamed at the prospect of spending the last few years of his life the same way as he had spent the first few. As H. Trafford Jilks had pointed out, if the government could prove they had a case, there was enough in Osborne's file to send him to the pen for a very long time. The injustice – as it seemed to him – of his predicament angered Abel. The malfeasances that Henry Osborne had committed in his name had been substantial but not exceptional; Abel doubted that any new business could have grown or any new money have been made without the sort of handouts and bribes documented with sickening accuracy in Trafford Jilks' file. He thought bitterly of the smooth, impassive face of the young William Kane, sitting in his Boston office all those years ago on a pile of inherited money whose probably disreputable origins were safely buried under generations of respectability. Then Florentyna wrote, a touching letter enclosing some photographs of her son, saying that she still loved and respected Abel, and believed in his innocence.

Three days before the trial was due to open, the Justice Department found Henry Osborne in New Orleans. They undoubtedly would have missed him completely if he hadn't ended up in a local hospital with two broken legs. A zealous policeman discovered Henry had received his injuries for welching on gambling debts. They don't like that in New Orleans. The policeman put two and two together and later that night, after the hospital had put plaster casts on both Osborne's legs, the Justice Department wheeled him onto an Eastern Airlines flight to New York.

Henry Osborne was charged the next day with conspiracy to defraud, and he was denied bail. H. Trafford Jilks asked the court's permission to be allowed to question him. The court granted his request, but Jilks gained very little satisfaction from the interview. It became obvious that Osborne had already made his deal with the government, promising to turn state's evidence against Abel in return for lesser charges against him.

"No doubt Mr. Osborne will find the charges against him are surprisingly minor," commented the lawyer drily.

"So that's his game," said Abel. "I take the rap while he escapes. Now we'll never find out who he sold that goddamn file to."

"No, there you are wrong, Mr. Rosnovski. That was the one thing he was willing to talk about," said Jilks. "He said it wasn't William Kane. He would never have sold the file to Kane under any circumstances. A man from Chicago called Harry Smith paid Mr. Osborne cash for the evidence, and, would you believe it, Harry Smith turns out to be an alias because there are dozens of Harry Smiths in the Chicago area and not a single one of them fits the description."

"Find him," said Abel. "And find him before the trial starts."

"We're already working on that," said Jilks. "If the man is still in Chicago we'll pin him down within the week. Osborne also added that this so-called Smith assured him he only wanted the file for private purposes. He had no intention of revealing the contents to anyone in authority."

"Then why did 'Smith' want the details in the first place?" asked Abel.

"The inference was blackmail. That's why Henry Osborne disappeared, to avoid you. If you think about that, Mr. Rosnovski, he could be telling the truth. After all, the disclosures are extremely damaging to him, and he must have been as distressed as you when he heard the file was in the hands of the Justice Department. It's no wonder he decided to stay out of sight and turned state's evidence when he was eventually caught."

"Do you know," said Abel, "the only reason I ever employed that man was because he hated William Kane as much as I did, and now Kane has done us both."

"There's no proof that Mr. Kane was in any way involved," said Jilks.

"I don't need proof."

The trial was delayed at the request of the government. They claimed they needed more time to question Henry Osborne before presenting their case, as he was now their principal witness. Trafford Jilks objected strongly and informed the court that the health of his client, who was no longer a young man, was failing under the strain of false accusations. The plea did not move Judge Prescott, who agreed to the government's request and postponed the trial for a further four weeks.

The month dragged on for Abel and two days before the trial was due to open, he resigned himself to being found guilty and facing a long jail sentence. Then H. Trafford Jilks' investigator in Chicago found the man called Harry Smith, who turned out to be a local private detective, who had used an alias under strict instructions from his client, a firm of lawyers in New York. It cost Jilks one thousand dollars and another twenty-four hours before Harry Smith revealed that the firm concerned had been Cohen, Cohen and Yablons.

"Kane's lawyer," said Abel immediately on being told.

"Are you sure?" asked Jilks. "I would have thought from

all we know about William Kane that he would be the last person to use a Jewish firm."

"Way back, when I bought the hotels from Kane's bank, some of the paperwork was covered by a man called Thomas Cohen. For some reason, the bank used two lawyers for the transaction."

"What do you want me to do about it?" George asked Abel.

"Nothing," said Trafford Jilks. "I don't want any more trouble before the trial. Do you understand me, Mr. Rosnovski?"

"Yes, sir," said Abel. "I'll deal with Kane when the trial's over. Now, Mr. Jilks, listen and listen carefully. You must go back to Osborne immediately and tell him the file was sold by Harry Smith to William Kane, and that Kane used the contents to gain revenge on both of us, and stress the 'both of us'. I promise you when Osborne hears that, he's not going to open his mouth in the witness box, no matter what promises he's made to the Justice Department. Henry Osborne's the one man alive who may hate Kane more than I do."

"Anything you say," said Jilks, who clearly wasn't convinced, "but I feel I must warn you, Mr. Rosnovski, he's still putting the blame firmly on your shoulders, and to date he's been no help to our side at all."

"You take my word for this, Mr. Jilks. His attitude will change the moment he knows about Kane's involvement."

H. Trafford Jilks obtained permission to spend ten minutes that night with Henry Osborne in his cell before going on home. Osborne listened but said nothing. Jilks was sure that his news had made no impression on the government's star witness and he decided he would wait until the next morning before telling Abel Rosnovski. He preferred that his client try to get a good night's sleep before the trial opened the next morning.

Four hours before the trial was due to start, Henry Osborne was found hanging in his cell by the guard bringing in his breakfast. He'd used a Harvard tie.

* * *

The trial opened for the government without their star witness and they appealed for a further extension. After hearing another impassioned plea by H. Trafford Jilks on the state of his client's health, Judge Prescott refused their request. The public followed every word of the 'Chicago Baron Trial' on television and in the newspapers and, to Abel's horror, Zaphia sat in the public gallery seeming to enjoy every moment of his discomfort. After nine days in court, the prosecution knew that their case was not standing up too well and offered to make a deal with H. Trafford Jilks. During an adjournment, Jilks briefed Abel on their offer.

"They will drop all the main indictments of bribery if you will plead guilty to the misdemeanours on two of the minor counts of attempting to improperly influence a public official."

"What do you estimate are my chances of getting off completely if I turn them down?"

"Fifty-fifty, I would say," said Jilks.

"And if I don't get off?"

"Judge Prescott is tough. The sentence wouldn't be a day under six years."

"And if I agree to the deal and plead guilty to the two minor charges, what then?"

"A heavy fine. I would be surprised if it came to anything more than that," said Jilks.

Abel sat and considered the alternatives for a few moments.

"I'll plead guilty. Let's get the damn thing over with."

The government lawyers informed the judge that they were dropping fifteen of the charges against Abel Rosnovski. H. Trafford Jilks rose from his place and told the court that his client wished to change his plea to guilty on the two remaining misdemeanour charges. The jury was dismissed and Judge Prescott was very hard on Abel in his summing-up, reminding him that the right to do business did not include the right to suborn public officials. Bribery was a crime and a worse crime when condoned by an intelligent and competent man, who should not need to stoop to such levels. In other countries, the judge added pointedly, making

Abel feel like a raw immigrant once again, bribery might be an accepted way of going about one's daily life, but that was not the case in the United States of America. Judge Prescott gave Abel a six months' suspended sentence and a twenty-five thousand dollar fine plus costs.

George took Abel back to the Baron and they sat in the penthouse drinking whisky for over an hour before Abel spoke.

"George, I want you to contact Peter Parfitt and pay him the one million dollars he asked for his two per cent of Lester's, because once I have my hands on eight per cent of that bank I am going to invoke Article Seven of their by-laws and kill William Kane in his own board room."

George nodded sadly in agreement.

A few days later the State Department announced that Poland had been granted most favoured nation status in foreign trade with the United States, and that the next American ambassador to Warsaw would be John Moors Cabot.

39

On a bitter February evening, William sat back and re-read Thaddeus Cohen's report. Henry Osborne had released all the information he had needed to finish Abel Rosnovski and had taken his twenty-five thousand dollars and disappeared. Very much in character, thought William as he replaced the well-worn copy of the Rosnovski file back in his safe. The original had been sent to the Justice Department in Washington, D.C., some days before by Thaddeus Cohen.

When Abel Rosnovski had returned from Turkey and was subsequently arrested, William had waited for him to retaliate, expecting him to dump all his Interstate stock on the market immediately. This time, William was prepared. He had already warned his broker that Interstate might come on to the open market in large amounts with little warning. His instructions were clear. They were to be bought immediately so that the price did not drop. He was prepared to put up the money from his trust as a short-term measure, to avoid any unpleasantness at the bank. William had also circulated a memo among all the stockholders of Lester's asking them not to sell any Interstate stock without consulting him.

As the weeks passed and Abel Rosnovski made no move, William began to believe that Thaddeus Cohen had been correct in assuming that nothing had been traceable back to him. Rosnovski must surely be placing the blame firmly on Henry Osborne's shoulders.

Thaddeus Cohen was certain that with Osborne's evidence, Abel Rosnovski would end up behind bars for a very long time, which would prevent him from ever finding it possible to invoke Article Seven and be a threat to the bank or William Kane. William hoped that the verdict might also make Richard come to his senses and return home. Surely these latest revelations about that family could only make him detest the Rosnovski girl and realise that his father had been right all along.

William would have welcomed Richard back. There was now a gap on the board of Lester's created by the retirement of Tony Simmons and the death of Ted Leach. Richard would have to return to New York before William's sixty-fifth birthday in ten years, or it would be the first time in over a century that a Kane had not sat in a bank's board room. Cohen had reported that Richard had made a series of brilliant takeover bids for shops that Florentyna needed: but surely the opportunity to become the next chairman of Lester's Bank would mean more to Richard than living with that Rosnovski girl.

Another factor that worried William was that he did not care too much for the new breed of directors now working at the bank. Jake Thomas, the new vice-chairman was the firm favourite to succeed him as chairman. He might have been educated at Princeton and graduated Phi Beta Kappa, but he was flashy – too flashy – thought William and far too ambitious, not at all the right sort to be the next chairman of Lester's. He would have to hang on until his sixty-fifth birthday and try to convince Richard that he should join Lester's before then. William was only too aware that Kate would have had Richard back on any terms, but as the years passed, he had found it harder to give way to his better judgment. Thank heaven Virginia's marriage was going well, and now she was pregnant. If Richard refused to return home and give up that Rosnovski girl, he could still leave everything to Virginia – if only she produced a grandson.

William was at his desk in the bank when he had his first heart attack. Not a very serious one. The doctors told him he should rest a little and he would still live another twenty years. He told his doctor, another bright young man – how he missed Andrew MacKenzie – that he only wanted to survive for ten years to see out his term of office as chairman of the bank.

For the few weeks that he had to convalesce at home, William reluctantly allowed Jake Thomas the overall responsibility for the bank's decisions, but as soon as he returned, he quickly re-established his position as chairman for fear that Thomas might have taken on too much authority in his absence. From time to time, Kate plucked up the courage to beg him to let her make some direct approach to Richard, but William remained obstinate, saying, "The boy knows he can come home whenever he wants to. All he has to do is end his relationship with that scheming girl."

The day Henry Osborne killed himself, William had a second heart attack. Kate sat by his bedside all through the night, fearing he would die, but Abel Rosnovski's trial kept him alive. William followed the trial devoutly every day, and he knew Osborne's suicide could only put Rosnovski in a far stronger position. When Rosnovski was finally released with nothing more than a six months' suspended sentence and a twenty-five thousand dollar fine, the lightness of the penalty did not come as a surprise to William. It wasn't hard to figure out that the government must have agreed to a deal with Rosnovski's brilliant lawyer.

William was, however, surprised to find himself feeling slightly guilty and somewhat relieved that Abel Rosnovski had not been sent to prison.

Once the trial was over William didn't care if Rosnovski dumped his Interstate Airways stock or not. He was still ready for him. But nothing happened, and as the weeks passed, William began to lose interest in the Chicago Baron and could only think of Richard, whom he now desperately wanted to see again. 'Old age and fear of death allows for sudden changes of the heart,' he had once read. One morning in September, he informed Kate of his wish. She didn't ask why he had changed his mind; it was enough for her that William wanted to see his only son.

"I'll call Richard in San Francisco immediately and invite them both," she told him, and was pleasantly surprised that the word 'both' didn't seem to shock her husband.

"That will be fine," said William quietly. "Please tell Richard that I want to see him again before I die."

"Don't be silly, darling. The doctor said that if you take it easy you'll live for another twenty years."

"I only want to complete my term as chairman at the bank and see Richard take my place on the board. That will be enough. Why don't you fly to the coast again and tell Richard of my request, Kate?"

"What do you mean, 'again'?" asked Kate nervously.

William smiled. "I know you've been to San Francisco several times already, my darling. For the last few years whenever I go away on a business trip, you've always used the excuse to visit your mother, but when she died last year, your excuses became increasingly improbable. We've been married for twenty-eight years and by now I think I'm aware of all your habits. You're still as lovely as the day I met you, my darling, but I do believe that at fifty-four you're unlikely to have a lover. So it wasn't all that hard for me to work out that you had been visiting Richard."

"Yes, I have been seeing him," said Kate. "Why didn't you mention that you knew before?"

"In my heart I was glad," said William. "I hated the thought of his losing contact with us both. How is he?"

"Both of them are well, and you have a granddaughter now as well as a grandson."

"A granddaughter as well as a grandson," William repeated.

"Yes, she's called Annabel," said Kate.

"And my grandson?" said William, enquiring for the first time.

When Kate told him his name he had to smile. It was only half a lie.

"Good," said William. "Well, you fly to San Francisco and see what can be done. Tell him I love him." He had once heard another old man who was going to lose his son say that.

Kate was more content that night than she had been in years. She called Richard to say she would be flying out to stay with them the following week, bringing good news with her.

When Kate returned to New York three weeks later,

William was pleased to learn that Richard and Florentyna could visit them at the end of November, which was the first opportunity for them to get away from San Francisco together. Kate was full of stories of how successful they both were, how young William Kane was the image of his grandfather and how they were all so much looking forward to coming back to New York for a visit.

William listened intently and found he was happy too, and at peace with himself. He had begun to fear that if Richard did not return home soon, he never would, and then the chairmanship of the bank would fall into Jake Thomas's lap. William did not care to think about that.

William returned to work the following Monday in high spirits after his lengthy absence, having made a good recovery from his second heart attack and now feeling he had something worth living for.

"You must pace yourself a little more carefully," the clever young doctor had told him, but he was determined to re-establish himself as chairman and president of the bank so he could make way for his only son. On his arrival at the bank he was greeted by the doorman, who told him that Jake Thomas was looking for him and had tried to reach him at home earlier. William thanked the senior member of the bank, the only person who had served Lester's more years than the chairman himself.

"Nothing's so important that it can't wait," he said.

"No, sir."

William walked slowly to the chairman's office. When he opened his door, he found three of his directors already in conference and Jake Thomas sitting firmly in William's chair.

"Have I been away that long," said William, laughing. "Am I no longer chairman of the board?"

"Yes, of course you are. Welcome back, William," said Jake Thomas, moving quickly out of the Chairman's seat.

William had found it impossible to get used to Jake Thomas calling him by his first name. The new generation were all too familiar. They had only known each other a few years, and the man couldn't have been a day over forty.

"What's the problem?" he asked.

"Abel Rosnovski," said Jake Thomas without expression.

William felt a sick feeling in the pit of his stomach and sat down in the nearest leather seat.

"What does he want this time?" he said wearily. "Won't he let me finish my days in peace?"

Jake Thomas stood up and walked towards William.

"He intends to invoke Article Seven and hold a proxy meeting with the sole purpose of removing you from the chair."

"He can't. He doesn't have the necessary eight per cent and the bank's by-laws state clearly that the chairman must be informed immediately if any outside person comes into possession of eight per cent of the stock."

"He says he'll have the eight per cent by tomorrow morning."

"No, no," said William. "I've kept a careful check on all the stock. No one would sell to Rosnovski. No one."

"Peter Parfitt," said Jake Thomas.

"No," said William smiling triumphantly. "I bought his shares a year ago through a third party."

Jake Thomas looked shocked, and no one spoke for some time. William realised for the first time just how much Thomas wanted to be the next chairman of Lester's.

"Well," said Jake Thomas. "We must face the fact that he claims he'll have eight per cent by tomorrow which would entitle him to elect three directors to the board and hold up any major policy decision for three months. The very provisions you put into the articles of incorporation to protect your long-term position. He also intends to announce his decision in advertisements placed all across the country. For good measure, he's threatening to make a reverse takeover bid for Lester's using the Baron Group as the vehicle if he receives any opposition to his plans. He has made it clear that there is only one way he will drop the whole plan."

"What's that?" said William.

"If you submit your resignation as chairman of the bank," replied Jake Thomas.

"That's blackmail," said William, nearly shouting.

"Maybe, but if you do not resign by noon next Monday, he intends to make his announcement to all shareholders. He has already booked space in forty newspapers and magazines."

"The man's gone mad," said William. He took his handkerchief from his breast pocket and mopped his brow.

"That's not all he said," Jake Thomas added. "He has also demanded that no Kane replace you on the board during the next ten years and that your resignation should not give ill health or, indeed, any reason for your sudden departure."

He held out a lengthy document bearing 'The Baron Group's' letterhead.

"Mad," repeated William, when he had scanned the letter rapidly.

"Nevertheless, I've called a board meeting for tomorrow," said Jake Thomas. "At ten o'clock. I think we should discuss his demands in detail then, William."

The three directors left William alone in his office and no one visited him during the day. He sat at his desk trying to contact some of the other directors, but he only managed to have a word with one or two of them and couldn't feel certain of their support. He realised the meeting was going to be a close-run thing but as long as no one else had eight per cent he was safe, and he began to prepare his strategy to retain control of his own board room. He checked the list of stockholders: as far as he could tell, not one of them intended to release his stock. He laughed to himself. Abel Rosnovski had failed with his coup. He went home early that night, only telling Kate to cancel Richard's proposed visit, and then retired to his study to consider his tactics for defeating Abel Rosnovski for the last time. He didn't go to bed until three a.m., but by then he had decided what had to be done. Jake Thomas must be removed from the board so that Richard could take his place.

William arrived early for the board meeting the next morning and sat waiting in his office looking over his notes, confident of victory. He felt his plan had taken everything into account. At five to ten his secretary buzzed. "A Mr. Rosnovski is on the phone for you," she said.

"What?" said William.

"Mr. Rosnovski."

"Mr. Rosnovski." William repeated the name in disbelief.

"Put him through," he said, his voice quavering.

"Yes, sir."

"Mr. Kane?"

The slight accent that William could never forget. "Yes, what do you want this time?"

"Under the by-laws of the bank I have to inform you that I now own eight per cent of Lester's shares and intend to invoke Article Seven unless my earlier demands are met by noon on Monday."

"How did you get the final two per cent?" stammered William. The phone clicked. He quickly studied the list of shareholders trying to work out who had betrayed him. He was still trembling when it rang again.

"The board meeting is just about to begin, sir."

As ten o'clock struck William entered the board room. Looking round the table, he suddenly realised how few of the younger directors he knew well. Last time he'd had a fight in this same room, he hadn't known any of the directors and he'd won. He smiled to himself, reasonably confident he could still beat Abel Rosnovski, and rose to address the board.

"Gentlemen, this meeting has been called because the bank has received a demand from Mr. Abel Rosnovski of the Baron Group; a convicted criminal who has had the effrontery to issue a direct threat to me, namely that he will use his eight per cent holding in my bank to embarrass us and if this tactic fails he will attempt a reverse takeover bid, unless I resign from the presidency and chairmanship of this board without explanation. You all know that I have only nine years left to serve this bank until my retirement and, if I were to leave before then, my resignation would be totally misinterpreted in the financial world."

William looked down at his notes, deciding to lead with his ace.

"I am willing, gentlemen, to pledge my entire shareholding and a further ten million dollars from my private trust to be placed at the disposal of the bank in order that you can counter any move Mr. Rosnovski makes while still insuring Lester's against any financial loss. I hope, gentlemen, in those circumstances, I can expect your full support in my battle against Abel Rosnovski. I am sure you are not men to give in to vulgar blackmail."

The room went silent. William felt certain he had won, but then Jake Thomas asked if the board might question him about his relationship with Abel Rosnovski. The request took William by surprise, but he agreed without hesitation. Jake Thomas didn't frighten him.

"This vendetta between you and Abel Rosnovski," said Jake Thomas, "has been going on for over thirty years. Do you believe if we followed your plan that would be the end of the matter?"

"What else can the man do? What else can he do?" stuttered William, looking around the room for support.

"We can't be sure until he does it, but with an eight per cent holding in the bank he has powers every bit as great as yours," said the new company secretary – not William's choice, he talked too much. "And all we know is that neither of you seems able to give up this personal feud. Although you have offered ten million to protect our financial position, if Rosnovski were continually to hold up policy decisions, call proxy meetings, arrange takeover bids with no interest in the goodwill of the bank, it would undoubtedly cause panic. The bank and its subsidiary companies, to whom we have a duty as directors, would, at best, be highly embarrassed and, at worst, might eventually collapse."

"No, no," said William. "With my personal backing we could meet him head on."

"The decision we have to make today," continued the company secretary, "is whether there are any circumstances in which this board wants to meet Mr. Rosnovski head on. Perhaps we are bound to be the losers in the long run."

"Not if I cover the cost from my private trust," said William.

"That you could do," said Jake Thomas, "but it's not just money we're discussing; much bigger problems arise for the bank. If Rosnovski has enough shares to invoke Article Seven, he can play with us when and as he pleases. The bank could be spending its entire time doing nothing but trying to anticipate Abel Rosnovski's every move."

Jake Thomas waited for the effect of what he had said to sink in. William remained silent. Then Thomas looked at William and continued: "Now I must ask you a very serious personal question, Mr. Chairman, which worries every one of us around this table, and I hope you'll be nothing less than frank with us when answering it, however unpleasant that may be for you."

William looked up, wondering what the question could be. What had they been discussing behind his back? Who the hell did Jake Thomas think he was? William felt he was losing the initiative.

"I will answer anything that the board requires," said William. "I have nothing and no one to fear," he said, looking pointedly at Jake Thomas.

"Thank you," said Jake Thomas. "Mr. Chairman, were you in any way involved with sending a file to the Justice Department in Washington which caused Abel Rosnovski to be arrested and charged with fraud when at the same time you knew he was a major shareholder of the bank's?"

"Did he tell you that?" demanded William.

"Yes, he claims you were the sole reason for his arrest."

William stayed silent for a few moments, considering his reply, while he looked down at his notes. They didn't help. He had not thought that question would arise but he had never lied to the board in over twenty-three years. He couldn't start now.

"Yes, I did," he said, breaking the silence. "The information came into my hands, and I considered that it was nothing less than my duty to pass it on to the Justice Department."

"How did the information come into your hands?"

William did not reply.

"I think we all know the answer to that question, Mr. Chairman," said Jake Thomas. "Moreover, you let the authorities know without briefing the board of your action and by so doing you put all of us in jeopardy. Our reputations, our careers, everything this bank stands for over a personal vendetta."

"But Rosnovski was trying to ruin me," said William, aware he was now shouting.

"So in order to ruin him you risked the bank's stability and reputation."

"It's my bank," said William.

"It is not," said Jake Thomas. "You own eight per cent of the stock, as does Mr. Rosnovski, and at the moment you are president and chairman of Lester's, but the bank is not yours to use for your own personal whim without consulting the other directors."

"Then I will have to ask the board for a vote of confidence," said William. "I'll ask you to support me against Abel Rosnovski."

"That is not what a vote of confidence would be about," said the company secretary. "The vote would be about whether you are the right man to run this bank in the present circumstances. Can't you see that, Mr. Chairman?"

"So be it," said William, turning his eyes away. "This board must decide whether it wishes to end my career in disgrace now, after nearly a quarter of a century's service, or fight the threats of a convicted criminal."

Jake Thomas nodded to the company secretary and voting slips were passed around to every board member. It looked to William as if everything had been decided before the meeting. He glanced around the crowded table at the twenty-nine men. Many of them he had chosen himself, but some of them he didn't know at all well. He had once heard that a small group of young directors openly supported the Democratic party and John Kennedy. Some of them were looking at him; some were not. Surely they'd back him; they wouldn't let Rosnovski beat him. Not now. Please let me finish my term as chairman, he said to himself, then I'll go quietly and without any fuss – but not this way.

He watched the members of the board as they passed their voting slips back to the secretary. He was opening them slowly. The room was silent and all eyes were turned towards the secretary as he began opening the last few slips, noting down each aye and nay meticulously on a piece of paper placed in front of him that revealed two columns. William could see that one list of names was considerably longer than the other, but his failing eyesight did not permit him to decipher which was which. He could not accept that the day could have come when there would be a vote in his own board room between himself and Abel Rosnovski.

The secretary was saying something. William couldn't believe what he heard. By seventeen votes to twelve he had lost the confidence of the board. He managed to stand up. Abel Rosnovski had beaten him in the final battle. No one spoke as William left the board room. He returned to the Chairman's office and picked up his coat, stopping only to look at the portrait of Charles Lester for the last time, and then walked slowly down the long corridor and out of the front entrance.

The doorman said, "Nice to have you back again, Mr. Chairman. See you tomorrow, sir."

William realised he would never see him again. He turned around and shook hands with the man who had directed him to the board room twenty-three years before.

The rather surprised doorman said, "Goodnight, sir," as he watched William climb into the back of his car for the last time.

His chauffeur took him home and when he reached East Sixty-eighth Street, William collapsed on his front door step. The chauffeur and Kate helped him into the house. Kate could see he was crying, and she put her arms round him.

"What is it, William? What's happened?"

"I've been thrown out of my own bank," he wept. "My own board no longer have confidence in me. When it mattered, they supported Abel Rosnovski."

Kate managed to get him up to bed and sat with him through the night. He never spoke. Nor did he sleep.

* * *

The announcement in the *Wall Street Journal* the following Monday morning said simply: "William Lowell Kane, the president and chairman of Lester's Bank, resigned after yesterday's board meeting."

No mention of illness or any explanation was given for his sudden departure, and there was no suggestion that his son would take his place on the board. William knew that rumour would sweep through Wall Street and that the worst would be assumed. He sat in bed alone, caring no longer for this world.

Abel read the announcement of William Kane's resignation in the *Wall Street Journal* the same day. He picked up the phone, dialled Lester's Bank and asked to speak to the new chairman. A few seconds later Jake Thomas came on the line. "Good morning, Mr. Rosnovski."

"Good morning, Mr. Thomas. I'm just phoning to confirm that I shall release all my Interstate Airways shares to the bank at the market price this morning and my eight per cent holding in Lester's to you personally for two million dollars."

"Thank you, Mr. Rosnovski, that's most generous of you."

"No need to thank me, Mr. Chairman, it's no more than we agreed on when you sold me your two per cent of Lester's," said Abel Rosnovski.

Book Seven

40

Abel was surprised to find how little satisfaction his final triumph had given him.

George tried to persuade him that he should go to Warsaw to look over sites for the new Baron but Abel didn't want to. As he grew older Abel became fearful of dying abroad and never seeing Florentyna again, and for months he showed no interest in the group's activities. When John F. Kennedy was assassinated on November 22nd, 1963, Abel became even more depressed and feared for America. Eventually George did convince him that a trip abroad could do no harm, and that things would perhaps seem a little easier for him when he returned.

Abel travelled to Warsaw where he obtained a highly confidential agreement to build the first Baron in the communist world. His command of the language impressed Warsawians, and he was proud to beat Holiday Inns and Intercontinental behind the Iron Curtain. He couldn't help thinking . . . and it didn't help when Lyndon Johnson appointed John Gronowski to be the first Polish-American ambassador to Warsaw. But now nothing seemed to give any satisfaction. He had defeated Kane and lost his own daughter, and he wondered if the man felt the same way about his son. After Warsaw, he travelled the world, staying in his hotels, watching the construction of new ones. He opened the first Baron in Cape Town, South Africa, and flew back to Germany to open one in Düsseldorf.

Abel then spent six months in his favourite Baron in Paris, roaming the streets by day, and attending the opera at night, hoping it might revive happy memories of Florentyna.

He eventually left Paris and returned to America, after his long exile. As he descended the metal steps of an Air France 707 at Kennedy International Airport, his back hunched and his bald head covered with a black hat, nobody recognised him. George was there to greet him, loyal, honest George, looking quite a bit older. On the ride to the New York Baron, George, as always, brought him up to date on group news. The profits, it seemed, were even higher as his keen young executives thrust forward in every major country in the world. Seventy-two hotels run by twenty-two thousand staff. Abel didn't seem to be listening. He only wanted news of Florentyna.

"She's well," said George, "and coming to New York early next year."

"Why?" said Abel, suddenly excited.

"She's opening one of her shops on Fifth Avenue."

"Fifth Avenue?"

"The eleventh Florentyna," said George.

"Have you seen her?"

"Yes," he admitted.

"Is she well, is she happy?"

"Both of them are very well and happy, and so successful. Abel, you should be very proud of them. Your grandson is quite a boy, and your granddaughter's beautiful. The image of Florentyna when she was that age."

"Will she see me?" said Abel.

"Will you see her husband?"

"No, George. I can never meet that boy, not while his father is still alive."

"What if you die first?"

"You mustn't believe everything you read in the Bible."

Abel and George drove in silence back to the hotel, and Abel dined alone in his room that night.

For the next six months, he never left the penthouse.

41

When Florentyna Kane opened her new boutique on Fifth Avenue in March 1967, everyone in New York seemed to be there, except William Kane and Abel Rosnovski.

Kate and Lucy had left William in bed muttering to himself while they went off to the opening of 'Florentyna's'.

George left Abel alone in his suite so that he could attend the celebrations. He had tried to talk Abel into going along with him. Abel grunted that his daughter had opened ten shops without him, and one more wouldn't make any difference. George told him he was a stubborn old fool and left for Fifth Avenue on his own. When he arrived at the shop, a magnificent modern boutique with thick carpets and the latest Swedish furniture – it reminded him of the way Abel used to do things – he found Florentyna, wearing a long blue gown with the now famous F on the high collar. She gave George a glass of champagne and introduced him to Kate and Lucy Kane who were chatting with Zaphia. Kate and Lucy were clearly happy and they surprised George by enquiring after Abel Rosnovski.

"I told him he was a stubborn old fool to miss such a good party. Is Mr. Kane here?" he asked.

George was delighted by Kate Kane's happy reply.

William was still muttering angrily at the *New York Times*, something about Johnson's pulling his punches in Vietnam, when he folded the newspaper and got himself out of bed. He started to dress slowly, staring at himself in the mirror when he had finished. He looked like a banker. He scowled. How else should he look? He put on a heavy black overcoat and his old Homburg hat, picked up his black walking stick with the silver handle, the one Rupert Cork-Smith had left him, and somehow got himself out on to the street. The first time he had been out on his own, he thought, for the best part of three years, since that last serious heart attack. The maid was surprised to see him leaving the house unaccompanied.

It was an unusually warm spring evening, but William felt the cold after being in the house so long. It took him a considerable time to reach Fifth Avenue and Fifty-sixth Street, and when he eventually did arrive, the crowd was so large outside Florentyna's that he felt he didn't have the strength to fight his way through it. He stood at the kerb, watching the people enjoying themselves. Young people, happy and excited, thrusting their way into Florentyna's beautiful shop. Some of the girls were wearing the new mini skirts from London. What next? thought William, and then he saw his son talking to Kate. He had grown into such a fine-looking man – tall, confident, and relaxed, he had an air of authority about him that reminded William of his own father. But in the bustle and continual movement, he couldn't quite work out which one was Florentyna. He stood there for nearly an hour enjoying the comings and goings, regretting the stubborn years he had thrown away.

The wind was beginning to race down Fifth Avenue. He'd forgotten how cold that March wind could be. He turned his collar up. He must get home, because they were all coming to dinner that night, and he was going to meet Florentyna and the grandchildren for the first time. His grandson and little Annabel and their father, his beloved son. He had told Kate what a fool he'd been and begged her forgiveness. All he remembered her saying was "I'll always love you." Florentyna had written to him. Such a generous letter. She had been so understanding and kind about the past. She had ended with "I can't wait to meet you."

He must get home. Kate would be cross with him if she ever discovered he'd been out on his own in that cold wind. But he had to see the opening of the shop and in any case tonight he would be with them all. He must leave now and let them enjoy their celebrations. They could tell him all about the opening over dinner. He wouldn't tell them he'd been there, that would always be his secret.

He turned to go home and saw an old man standing a few yards away in a black coat, with a hat pulled way down on his head, and a scarf around his neck. He, too, was cold. Not a night for old men, thought William, as he walked towards him. And then he saw the silver band on his wrist, just below his sleeve. In a flash it all came back to him, fitting into place for the first time. First the Plaza, then Boston, then Germany, and now Fifth Avenue. The man turned and started to walk towards him. He must have been standing there for a long time because his face was red from the wind. He stared at William out of those unmistakable blue eyes. They were now only a few yards apart. As they passed, William raised his hat to the old man. He returned the compliment, and they continued on their separate ways without a word.

I must get home, thought William, before they do. The joy of seeing Richard and his two grandchildren would make everything worthwhile again. He must come to know Florentyna, ask for her forgiveness, and trust that she would understand what he could scarcely understand himself now. Such a fine girl, they all told him.

When he reached East Sixty-eighth Street, he fumbled for his key and opened the front door. Must turn on all the lights, he told the maid, and build the fire up to make them feel welcome. He was very contented and very, very tired.

"Draw the curtains," he said, "and light the candles on the dining room table. There's so much to celebrate."

William couldn't wait for them all to return. He sat in the old crimson leather chair by a blazing fire and thought happily of the evening that lay ahead of him. Grandchildren around him, the years he had missed. When had his little grandson first said three? A chance to bury the past and earn forgiveness in the future. The room was so nice and warm after that cold wind, but the journey had been well worthwhile.

A few minutes later there was an excited bustle downstairs and the maid came in to tell William that his son had arrived. Richard Kane was in the hall with his mother, and his wife and two of the loveliest children the maid had ever seen. And then she ran off to be sure that dinner would be ready for Mr. Kane on time. He would want everything to be perfect for them that night.

When Richard came into the room, Florentyna was by his side. She looked quite radiant.

"Father," he said, "I would like you to meet my wife."

William Lowell Kane would have turned to greet them but he could not. He was dead.

42

Abel placed the envelope on the table by the side of his bed. He hadn't dressed yet. Nowadays he rarely rose before noon. He tried to remove his breakfast tray from his knees on to the floor. A bending movement that demanded too much dexterity for his stiff body to accomplish. He inevitably ended by dropping the tray with a bang. It was no different today. He no longer cared. He picked up the envelope once more, and read the covering note for a second time.

"We were instructed by the late Mr. Curtis Fenton, sometime manager of the Continental Trust Bank, La Salle Street, Chicago, to send you the enclosed letter, when certain circumstances have come about. Please acknowledge receipt of this letter by signing the enclosed copy, returning it to us in the stamped addressed envelope supplied herewith."

"Goddamn lawyers," said Abel, and tore open the letter.

Dear Mr. Rosnovski:

This letter has been in the keeping of my lawyers until today for reasons which will become apparent to you as you read on.

When in 1951 you closed your accounts at the Continental Trust after over twenty years with the bank, I was naturally very unhappy and very concerned. My concern was engendered not by losing one of the bank's most valued customers, sad though that was, but because I know you felt that I had acted in a dishonourable fashion. What you were not aware of at the time was that I had specific instructions from your backer not to reveal certain facts to you.

When you first visited me at the bank in 1929, you requested financial help to clear the debt incurred by Mr. Davis Leroy, in order that you might take possession of the hotels which then formed the Richmond Group. I was unable to find a backer, despite approaching several leading financiers myself. I took a personal interest, as I believed that you had an exceptional flair for your chosen career. It has given me a great deal of satisfaction to observe in old age that my confidence was not misplaced. I might add at this point that I also felt some responsibility, having advised you to buy twenty-five per cent of the Richmond Group from my client, Miss Amy Leroy, when I did not know the financial predicament that was facing Mr. Leroy at that time. I digress.

I did not succeed in finding a backer for you and had given up all hope when you came to visit me on that Monday morning. I wonder if you remember that day. Only thirty minutes before your appointment I had a call from a financier who was willing to put up the necessary money, who, like me, had a great confidence in you personally. His only stipulation was, as I advised you at the time, that he insisted on remaining anonymous because of a potential conflict between his professional and private interests. The terms he offered, allowing you to gain eventual control of the Richmond Group, I considered at the time to be extremely generous, and you rightly took full advantage of them. Indeed, your backer was delighted when you found it possible, through your own diligence, to repay his original investment.

I lost contact with you both after 1951, but after I retired from the bank, I read a distressing story in the newspapers concerning your backer, which prompted me to write this letter, in case I died before either of you.

I write not to prove my good intentions in this whole affair, but so that you should not continue to live under the illusion that your backer and benefactor was Mr. David Maxton of the Stevens Hotel. Mr. Maxton was a great admirer of yours, but he never approached the bank in that capacity. The gentleman who made the Baron

Group possible, by his foresight and personal generosity, was William Lowell Kane, the chairman of Lester's Bank, New York.

I begged Mr. Kane to inform you of his personal involvement, but he refused to break the clause in his trust deed that stipulated that no beneficiary should be privy to the investments of the family trust. After you had paid off the loan and he later learned of Henry Osborne's personal involvement with the Baron Group he became even more adamant that you should never be informed.

I have left instructions that this letter is to be destroyed if you die before Mr. Kane. In those circumstances, he will receive a letter, explaining your total lack of knowledge of his personal generosity.

Whichever one of you receives a letter from me, it was a privilege to have served you both.

As ever,
your faithful servant,
Curtis Fenton

Abel picked up the phone by the side of his bed. "Find George for me," he said. "I need to get dressed."

43

William Lowell Kane's funeral was well attended. Richard and Florentyna stood on one side of Kate; Virginia and Lucy were on the other. Grandmother Kane would have approved of the turn-out. Three senators, five congressmen, two bishops, most of the leading banks' chairmen, and the publisher of the *Wall Street Journal* were all there. Jake Thomas and every director of the Lester's board were also present, their heads bowed in prayer to the God in whom William had never really believed.

No one noticed two old men, standing at the back of the gathering, their heads also bowed, looking as if they were not attached to the main party. They had arrived a few minutes late and left quickly at the end of the service. Florentyna thought she recognised the limp as the shorter old man hurried away. She told Richard. They didn't mention their suspicion to Kate Kane.

A few days later, the taller of the two old men went to see Florentyna in her shop on Fifth Avenue. He had heard she was returning to San Francisco and needed to seek her help before she left. She listened carefully to what he had to say and agreed to his request with joy.

Richard and Florentyna Kane arrived at the Baron Hotel the next afternoon. George Novak was there to meet and escort them to the forty-second floor. After ten years, Florentyna hardly recognised her father, now propped up in bed, half-moon glasses on the end of his nose, still no pillows, but smiling defiantly. They talked of happier days and both laughed a little and cried a lot.

"You must forgive us, Richard," said Abel. "The Polish are a sentimental race."

"I know, my children are half Polish," said Richard.

Later that evening they dined together, magnificent roast veal, appropriate for the return of the prodigal daughter, said Abel.

He talked of the future and how he saw the progress of his group.

"We ought to have a Florentyna's in every hotel," he said.

She laughed and agreed.

He told Richard of his sadness concerning his father, revealing in detail the mistakes he had made for so many years, and how it had never crossed his mind even for a moment that William Kane could have been his benefactor, and how he would have liked one chance to thank him personally.

"He would have understood," said Richard.

"We met, you know, the day he died," said Abel.

Florentyna and Richard stared at him in surprise.

"Oh yes," said Abel. "We passed each other on Fifth Avenue; he had come to watch the opening of your shop. He raised his hat to me. It was enough, quite enough."

Abel had only one request of Florentyna. That she and Richard would accompany him on his journey to Warsaw in nine months' time for the opening of the latest Baron.

"Can you imagine," he said, again excited, his fingers tapping the side table. "The Warsaw Baron. Now there is a hotel that could only be opened by the president of the Baron Group."

During the following months the Kanes visited Abel regularly and Florentyna grew very close to her father again. Abel came to admire Richard and the common sense that tempered all his daughter's ambitions. He adored his grandson. And little Annabel was – what was that awful modern expression? – she was something else. Abel had rarely been happier in his life and began elaborate plans for his triumphant return to Poland to open the Warsaw Baron.

The president of the Baron Group opened the Warsaw Baron six months later than had been originally scheduled.

Building contracts run late in Warsaw just as they do in every other part of the world.

In her first speech, as president of the group, she told her guests that her pride in the magnificent hotel was mingled with a feeling of sadness that her late father could not have been present to open the Warsaw Baron himself.

In his will, Abel left everything to Florentyna, with the single exception of a small bequest. The testament described the gift as a heavy engraved silver bracelet, rare, but of unknown value, and bearing the legend 'Baron Abel Rosnovski'.

The beneficiary was his grandson, William Abel Kane.